The Black Knight

For the Good and Prosperity of our Realm, the ennobling of Men's Passions by most wholesome Literature, and a humble contribution to the cultivation of Culture, the Novel that follows,

The Black Knight

Authored by an esteemed and well-Reputed Gentleman of our lands, a one

Michael P. Halloran

Is hereby Solemnly Published and Promulgated under the Authority and Crest of his Majesty,

Mundo Luporum

Shenanigans

The King of Blendon

First Edition 2025

Edited by Eric Postma of *Gingerman Editorial*
Cover Art by Wade Gugino of *GooGenius*
Royal Crest by Wade Gugino of *GooGenius*

ISBN 979-8-9928383-0-5

Dear Kathryn,

Thank you for giving me the inspiration to start this book and the motivation to see it through to the end. I hope you and your siblings enjoy your father's story about what it means to be a knight.

Contents

Author's Preface, by Sir Asinus the Scholar *1*

Volume I: Knights and Robbers **3**

    Chapter 1: Ambush 4

    Chapter 2: Prayers for the Dead 15

    Chapter 3: The Glade of Jove 28

    Chapter 4: Miracles and Dreams 48

    Chapter 5: The Indictment 56

Interlude *66*

Volume II: Stranger in a Strange Land **75**

    Chapter 1: Where Civilization Ends 76

    Chapter 2: An Unholy Ruckus 85

    Chapter 3: Shopping at Curly's 93

    Chapter 4: A Swift and Speedy Trial 101

Interlude *113*

Volume III: Dewford **131**

    Chapter 1: The Knife Edge of History 132

    Chapter 2: Thirst 136

    Chapter 3: An Almost Thorough Interrogation 156

    Chapter 4: The Duke of Nouen 173

    Chapter 5: Slow Drinks Between Fast Friends 183

    Chapter 6: The Morning Dew 202

    Chapter 7: Silence 214

Interlude *231*

Volume IV: Temptation in the Desert **245**

    Chapter 1: The First Temptation 246

    Chapter 2: Veritas and Caritas 255

    Chapter 3: The First Temptation Revealed 269

    Chapter 4: The Second Temptation 280

    Chapter 5: The Grand Empire's Final Hour 294

    Chapter 6: The Third and Greatest Temptation 300

    Chapter 7: Walking in the Moonlight 317

    Chapter 8: Winthrop's Trial 335

Interlude *346*

Volume V: Winthrop Reborn **361**

    Chapter 1: The Duchess of Nouen 362

    Chapter 2: An Honest Prayer 366

    Chapter 3: All Roads Lead to Dewford 370

    Chapter 4: More Silence 384

    Chapter 5: The Bloody Baron 387

    Chapter 6: The Baron Returns 393

    Chapter 7: A Trick of the Light 415

    Chapter 8: Fallout 430

Interlude *436*

Prelude to Volume VI: Ballad of the Black Knight *446*

Volume VI: A Hidden Title **451**

    Chapter 1: In the Shadow of Darkness 452

    Chapter 2: Winthrop's Words 459

    Chapter 3: Sunset Thursday 471

    Chapter 4: Dark Night of the Senses 475

    Chapter 5: The Scar 481

    Chapter 6: The Triumph of Sir Judas 486

    Chapter 7: Judas and Goliath 495

    Chapter 8: Reflections 504

Postlude to Volume VI: A Very Odd Wedding Toast *508*

Interlude *510*

Volume VII: Unto the End, to Him That Shall Overcome **513**

    Chapter 1: Lords and Killers 514

    Chapter 2: Last Ride of the Lessguard 529

    Chapter 3: Dark Night of the Soul 533

    Chapter 4: Some Thoughts Concerning Natural Evil 540

    Chapter 5: The Return of the King 544

    Chapter 6: The Day that Dawned in the Afternoon 552

Epilogue: The Final Test *560*

Author's Preface, by Sir Asinus the Scholar

When I first told my wife I wanted to write a history of the Day that Dawned in the Afternoon, she said what I imagine most people will say when they first see this history in a bookstore window; "Oh, come now, Asinus! Everybody already knows that story!" Indeed, they do. I have an associate at university who is considered one of the foremost experts in the world on that Day, and he estimates that by the end of the decade there will be over one thousand books in circulation that claim to be histories of those events. "What possible value would it have," my wife asked me, "if instead of one thousand histories, you labored to bring us to one thousand and one?"

I understand the objection, which is why before I begin my history, I must persuade you, the reader, why my book is worth the time it will take to read. The answer I offer you is the same I gave my wife; there are one thousand books that *claim* to be histories of that Day, but there are only two that are actually worthy of the title 'history.' Instead nearly every book veers either to the right or to the left, distorting what happened in its own peculiar way.

First, there are those books that exaggerate the events beyond all recognition, to the point where it is more of a daydream than a true chronicle. Consider this excerpt from one of the popular accounts that has sold more than a million copies; "...and then Sir David smote the giant Goliath into a thousand glittering pieces using the unblockable WORDS OF POWER that could be heard throughout the world, a spell he cast from his magic dagger." It pains me to even put those words on a page...Sir David was a twelve-year-old boy when these events happened, and never cast a magic spell in his entire life. Besides which, it is widely suspected that Goliath was totally immune to any sort of magical attack. How then did Sir David kill him with magic?

Then there is the other kind of book, which is so skeptical and unbelieving that these events are reduced to totally mundane occurrences exaggerated by rumors of the uneducated masses. If those who are unfamiliar with what passes for 'scholarship' in academia think I go too far, consider this quote from one of the most widely used textbooks in university courses; "The story of 'words heard around the world,' was most likely a large earthquake that the more primitive peoples of that age attached great spiritual meaning to. Because people back then still needed to believe that man was at the center of the universe and that nature revolved around his actions, the earthquake was turned into a mythological event of apocalyptic proportions with a full cast of guilty 'sinners' who caused the disaster, and an accompanying cast of 'saviors' who averted it." Oh, God have mercy. 'More primitive peoples of that age…' 'People back then.' These events happened less than a century ago! Sir David is still *alive*! I don't know who makes me more despairing of man's intellect; the author who wrote that book, or the students who actually believe it?

Yes, out of the one thousand books written on this subject, I would say four hundred and ninety-nine sway too far into mythology, an equal number into academic insanity, and there are only two books that I could recommend without a guilty conscience. And for the sake of those two books, I might have considered myself excused from writing this history, and simply told my potential readers to go read those instead. But there was something that bothered me. One singular quote that I couldn't get out of my head that sparked my whole grand adventure.

These are the words Sir Patrick said about the hero of that great and dreadful Day; "It seemed to me it was the saddest death ever died, at the end of the saddest life ever lived. On that Day, the taste of victory was far more bitter than any defeat." That brought me to tears. That was something magnificently *human*. Stuck in my head was a little piece of history I couldn't allow to slip away, yet neither of the good scholarly works I would recommend captured what was (to me) the entire essence of the tale. Neither of those histories captured the tragic story of human triumph as it must have seemed to the people who lived through it.

I wrestled with that quote for a long time, until eventually I could wrestle with it no longer. I told my wife I wanted to write this history, we made our arrangements, and then we set off to travel the world, tracking down all of the surviving witnesses who might be able to help our cause. We labored for ten years to conduct all the interviews, and then another two years to organize them into a single coherent narrative. The result of our labors is the seven volume tome you now hold in your hands. While we chose to arrange it in an easy-to-read style and filled in some gaps with reasonable speculations, you may be sure that we cleaved as closely as we could to the eyewitness testimony we had available. Without further ado, I present to you,

The Black Knight

Volume I

Knights and Robbers

Chapter 1: Ambush

The summer sun was just beginning to rise on August 9 (Monday in the Week of the Day) when David spied their first mark. These hills were well known for favoring bandit ambushes, with broken clefts and thick branches crowding the path to such an extent that a man could come within one foot of an enemy and never know it. Moreover, the many forking trails provided plenty of avenues to approach and flee the main road by routes no law-abiding man would dare to travel. Lastly, and most importantly, the hills were on an essential trade route between Reswick, 'the gate to the East,' and Chelles, the capital city of this land. The potential profits of working this route were too great for most merchants to resist, and so there was always a steady flow of valuable goods along the uncivilized roads despite the risks. Yes, these roads were well-known for favoring bandit ambushes. That was why they were such a terrible place for bandit ambushes.

For two days now the little bandit camp had watched the road from dawn until mid-afternoon, and they had not seen so much as a single opportunity. The merchants all formed caravans with hired guards and even the occasional knight. Time after time the lookout would come down to camp, tell the other three that a huge caravan was approaching, and then they would lay low and hide until a fortune in untouchable goods rolled slowly by. Their food stock was starting to run low, and the patience of Rowan and Garrett was running even lower. Winthrop, the captain of this band of four, was beginning to fear he would have a mutiny on his hands. Then David came down the hill to announce his glad tidings.

"We've got a mark! About a mile away on horseback, traveling all alone!"

"What are ya whisperin' for, boy?" Garrett asked without looking up from his game of cards. "No one can hear us from a mile away." The heavyset man scratched his black stubble in a vigorous and agitated fashion before throwing down a random card. "Besides, he won't be comin' our way."

"Why not?" David asked.

"Because no one travels a two-day journey alone," Winthrop answered. "If he was destined for Chelles he would have at least one or two companions. The fact that he is alone means that he is a local, and he'll be turning off the main road in a couple minutes to take the trail to Pawnshire."

"Trail to Pawnshire is where we ought've setup," Rowan said, slamming his cards down on the empty chest between him and Garrett. "Tha's what I told ya. We already saw half-a-dozen marks go that way, and now it'll be half-a-dozen an' one. Everyone's too stinkin' careful on this road. We would already have a chest full-a loot if you had just listened to me an' Garrett!" As he mentioned the 'chest full-a loot' he knocked on the empty wooden trunk repeatedly, letting the hollow sound intensify his already angry glare. Rowan had numerous scars and old injuries crisscrossing his face–the intimidating legacy of life in the Bloody Baron's manor back before he fell in with Winthrop…

"Do you know what else would be full if I had listened to you?" Winthrop asked. "The prison cart taking us to the gallows. No good trails to retreat, the only town we could flee to is a small one where everybody knows each other…and then you have the problem that they would probably recognize the loot we're trying to fence. Unless we hiked across the mountains just to drag our half-starved butts back *here*, we would surely be caught."

"Bah!" Rowan yelled, upending the chest and the card game. "All I'm hearin' is cowardice and 'scuses. Most bandits don't blink at 'dem risks. It's part-a the job."

"Do you want to be like most bandits?" Winthrop asked. "Then please observe that most bandits don't have one of *these*!" he yelled while grabbing and shaking his gray-haired beard. "…and if you lot ever want to make the ripe old age of fifty-six, you'll need to learn to start thinking about your next move before you make the current one! What are you going to do after the robbery? How long do you have until the law is looking for you? How will you get away? Where will you sell the goods? If you don't start looking ahead, you're going to end up where you never thought you'd go."

At this point the two rebellious members of the bandit crew fell silent, still stewing with the frustrations of long days and light pockets. Winthrop returned his gaze to David and said, "Alright, David, take a break. I'll watch the road for a little while."

Not wanting to be around Rowan and Garrett while they were in such a mood, David asked, "Could I perhaps take my break with you, and you could teach me a little more about fighting?"

Winthrop gave a soft smile and said, "Sure. Bring your spear and your waterskin and I'll put you through the paces."

At the mention of his new weapon, David's copper eyes lit up, and he ran over to his effects to grab the spear. The two of them then ascended the lookout hill, Winthrop taking the lead. At first he casually followed the easiest available path, but as he neared the summit he lowered himself to all fours and proceeded very slowly, careful not to disturb any bushes or trees that might be visible from the lowlands. David paid careful attention to how Winthrop was ascending, and did his best to imitate his every move. Finding a thick burning bush (thorny, not flaming) at the crest of the hill, Winthrop eased himself up to it and peered down towards Reswick.

The rider David had spotted was now approaching the bottom of the hill. As soon as he espied him, Winthrop had misgivings, an intuition that this rider was trouble. He wore a long, black cloak, pulled tight around him on a warm summer morning. Moreover, the horse he rode was no pack animal; it was a warhorse, tall and proud. Now that he saw the loaded saddle bags himself, Winthrop was also doubting his first assessment. This man was on a journey, a traveler with a long way to go and enough food and daring to get there. Such a one turning off to Pawnshire was absurd; he was coming to the hills alone, and he intended to pass. Only one sort of man would venture such hazards all by himself.

"Black knight," Winthrop muttered under his breath. A sword without a lord. Such a discovery would normally be cause for celebration. After all, even a black knight was no match for three armed men, if only they could get him off his horse. The loot was likely to be good between his armor and arms, and there was even a chance of taking the horse alive. Best of all, black knights were drifters, and troublesome ones at that. The guards in Reswick probably breathed a sigh of relief when the black knight departed that morning, and no one would be waiting for him in Chelles. Yet for all these boons, there was a nagging sense that this knight wasn't to be trifled with, even if Winthrop had three times as many men. He stared at the knight, hoping for some unknown reason that he was destined for Pawnshire after all.

He was approaching the juncture where he would either turn off to the left or begin the switch-back ascent up into the hills. David saw the intensity of Winthrop's gaze and crouched there silently, not sure what he should do. The older robber was clenching his fists. He began to mutter repeatedly under his breath, "Turn left...turn left...turn left already!"

The rider came to the crossroads.

The horse stopped.

Winthrop's heart leapt into his throat.

The rider produced a black helm, pulled it down over his head, and resumed his journey into the hills.

Winthrop's stomach dropped.

At first he thought of not saying anything, of just letting the knight pass without notifying Rowan and Garrett. But as he heard the faint sounds of them bickering at the bottom of the hill, Winthrop knew that would never work. He would have to tell Rowan and Garrett to keep quiet until the knight was gone. With their hunger for gold already aching, that seemed like an impossible sell. Taking a deep breath, Winthrop said, "Back down the hill now, David. We need to have a chat with the others." Taking one last look at the knight, he turned and muttered, "This is going to be a black day."

Rowan shoved the elder member of the crew, "Whaddaya mean 'Let him go?' A lone traveler with more valuables than the tinkers we usually shake down, and you wanna 'Let him go'?"

"Yes," Winthrop replied, "Don't forget a black knight fights better than those tinkers too."

"Oh, don't give us that dung!" Garrett interjected, "...we've taken knights before. Jump outta the woods, one man grabs the horse, one grabs the knight, and after he falls a third finishes him off. Easy pickins."

"You aren't *listening*," Winthrop growled. "I have a bad feeling on this one. If you want to get to my age, you don't just need good instincts, but also the sense to follow them. Let this one go."

"Oh forget getting to your age!" Rowan sneered. "Why would I wanna be fifty-six and poor when I can be thirty-five and rich? This ain't about the sense of an old man. It's about that injury of yours! You can't take the hand-to-hand throwin' down anymore, and you're a'scared of tryin' to take a mark with some fight left in him. You ain't the kinda man fit to be leadin' a robbin' operation, right, Garrett?" With that Rowan hefted his maul, looking at Winthrop with murderous intent. Garrett fingered his crossbow, but did not go so far as to raise it yet.

Winthrop's initial reaction was to rise to their challenge, to defend his reputation, and to assert his rights over the crew. Discretion prevailed, however, for one of Winthrop's greatest assets was the ability to always keep his head in the midst of conflict. Garrett would surely side with Rowan, and two on one would be a difficult scrum to survive. And even if he did, what crew would he then command? With half the members dead on the ground, he would have no profit but cold comfort for his pride.

Instead, Winthrop called to mind one of his favorite adages; 'Youth and vigor are no match for old age and treachery.' He softened his expression, hung his head, and said, "You're right, I'm getting too old for this. It's time one of you two stepped up to lead this little band, and I can take a job more suited for me."

Rowan and Garrett both looked at each other in surprise, not expecting their mutiny to proceed so easily. "So you're givin' up the double share for the captain?" Rowan asked. "Which one of us is takin' over?" He paused for a moment before remembering to add, "...boss."

Winthrop shrugged. "Whoever earns it I suppose." Then he snapped his fingers and said, "Hey! I've got a fine idea! How about whoever lands the final blow on the knight gets the captain's share? You two can duke it out on the front lines, while the old man cuts off any attempt by the knight to race right past us. What do you say?"

Now the dangerous looks the two men had aimed at their captain were turned upon each other. "Fine by me," Garrett said, trusting in his crossbow to end things swiftly.

"Aye, an' me too," said Rowan, planning on dismounting the knight so there was no good shot at him.

Winthrop clapped his hands. "It's settled then! We don't have any time to lose. Let's get into position, and make ourselves a score. The last score of my tenure as boss, and the first score for our new captain, whoever that might be. Are you with me?"

"Aye!" Rowan and Garrett replied at once, turning to make their way to the road. Winthrop headed to his tent to grab his crossbow, chuckling to himself over how well this went. If only one of Rowan and Garrett lived through this fight, he could easily pick off the survivor and go into retirement with a little nest egg. Perhaps he would even have enough to get David out of this life of crime. If both survived, they would quickly fall to blows with one another, and he would be in the same spot. Finish the winner off, run away with the treasure. And lastly, if this knight was indeed as much trouble as Winthrop feared he was, he and David would be safely out of harm's way when the battle went sour.

Such was his intention, but Winthrop had overlooked one very important possibility. While Winthrop was in his tent, Rowan separated from Garrett and came back to grab David. Ruffling the boy's mess of brown hair and putting an arm around his slender frame, Rowan said, "This is it, kid, your first crack at a real score. You excited to put that ole spear to good use?"

David looked at him inquisitively. "But Winthrop told me I'm not allowed to help yet. I'm supposed to watch from the northern overlook and study how you three do it."

"You ain't been *listenin'* kid!" Rowan said while roughly sticking his finger in David's ear. "Winthrop ain't in charge anymore! He's over the hill! Said so himself! By tonight, I'm gonna be runnin' things. Now don't it seem like a good idea to get on your new captain's good side?"

"How can I do that?"

"Easy. By helpin' me get that knight off his horse. You take that spear of yours, hide in the bush I point ya towards, and when I yell, you jump out and stab the horse right in his heart. Down goes the knight, and ole' Rowan will take it from there."

David waffled on this proposal, torn between the excitement of finally joining the raids and the apprehension of knowing his own inexperience. Rowan gave one final nudge, saying, "If you don't think you're ready for the real men's work yet, I understand. That hill Winthrop pointed out is perfect for a kid to watch from."

David now steeled his gaze and tightened his jaw. "I'm ready! Just show me where to go."

Rowan smiled.

Winthrop picked his spot forty yards down the road, west from Rowan, while Garrett was twenty yards to the east of him. Garrett was visible from Winthrop's location, but shielded from view in the direction the knight would be coming from. The knight would ride right past him, unobserved, and come into Garrett's line of fire near the thicket Rowan was hiding in. Rowan was not visible to Winthrop, but his location was easy to discern. The road narrowed to just eight feet at that point, with two oppressing juniper bushes crowding the path. He did not know which bush hid Rowan, but it was clearly one of them. What Winthrop did not suspect was that David was hidden in the opposing bush, spear in hand, and far closer to the bloodbath than Winthrop would have ever let him get.

Winthrop hid behind a tree with a bush immediately to his left. He and his crossbow were totally hidden from view, while a small pocket in the bush allowed him to see the road. Taking a deep breath, Winthrop put the stock of the crossbow in his hip and slowly pulled back on the goat's foot lever with his right hand. In the decade since he injured his left (and dominant) arm, he had learned to do many tasks right-handed. His left arm had even healed to the point where he could use it to shoot a crossbow, but he needed his right hand to support its weight and span it. He placed his goat foot against the tree, and stuck a single bolt into the ground. Long ago he had learned that two shots are the most a crossbowman can hope to loose. Any more than that was impossible, as the battle would close to melee first. Thinking through his role in battle, he could feel his spirit rising to match the intensity of what that lay before him.

But as the minutes passed by, Winthrop began to grow nervous. His palms were clammy, his breathing tremorous, and despite his very best efforts, his hands were shaking. Something was wrong. He was *never* nervous. After three decades in this line of work, robbery had become second nature to him, and there had been far more dangerous fights than this. Yet he was nervous. Winthrop could not get the black knight off his mind. As he waited in the safety of his hiding place, his misgivings continued to gnaw at him. There was something familiar about the knight. Something about the way he rode the horse, or perhaps the way he held his head. Winthrop had only seen him at a great distance. What could have possibly lodged itself in his brain? He couldn't put his finger on it, but he had this terrible sense that a long-forgotten nightmare was at hand.

Why am I afraid of one black knight? Aren't Rowan and Garrett the ones in harm's way? And isn't the most likely outcome that one of them kills him anyway? I should be more afraid of them than of the knight! Calm down, Winthrop! he thought, but to no avail. Irrational fear continued to consume him as the battle drew ever closer.

After about a quarter hour of hiding, the sound of approaching hooves could be heard. The clopping grew gradually louder, until at last the rider appeared around the bend in the road. Now that he was closer, it was apparent the knight was very old. From beneath his helm came long white hair and a beard falling to his breast. Instead of feeling relief, Winthrop felt a great weight come upon him, as if his very soul was being dragged to the ground. Just to raise his head and keep looking through the bush required a herculean effort. The rider had passed Garrett; Winthrop's knees began to knock. He was ten feet from the junipers; the crossbow was too heavy to hold any longer. The horse was within arm's reach of Rowan; Winthrop closed his eyes and buried his head in his arms. With a sudden flash everything came back to him, as tears flowed freely down his face.

He *remembered.*

He remembered a childhood spent in the duchy of Nouen, taking frequent trips to the royal city. He remembered the knights on parade and everyone gathered to applaud. There was crying and hugging and throwing of flowers, and everyone's soul soared just to look upon the men in white.

He remembered a vast multitude, thronged around an altar thirty feet high at noon. And as the bells rang and the golden chalice was raised, seven men drew their holy weapons and thrust them skywards. Seven beams of light shot forth, dancing with each other and meeting at the sun, where they cracked the sky and the glory of heaven shone forth.

He remembered the military campaign his father left for and his own dream of following when he came of age. City after city was freed from tyrants, and the people cheered their liberators. And whenever an army marshaled to oppose them, one of the seven riders would lead the forces to battle, work great wonders, and bring victory without loss.

He remembered how it ended. Like lightning the empire had swept across the land, and as lightning flashes and is gone, so too the empire was soon nothing but the rumbles of thunder. Day after day, the heralds brought tidings of new rebellions, new disasters, new conquests by the fearsome giant, until only the royal city remained. As the dark army drew near to the gates, six riders sallied forth to avenge their fallen comrade. Horses charging, weapons glowing, and many hopeful eyes watching the last ride of those mighty champions. The giant strode forth, ten feet tall, breathing fire from his mouth and wielding a sword of magma in his black scaled hands. And as the battle was joined, the flaming sword flashed forth, arcs of fire cutting knights down with every swing.

As each of the six glowing weapons went dark, it was like watching the death of all things good.

Here dies justice!
Here dies courage!
Temperance, prudence, faith!
All are slain!
Hope lives on!
See him ride now!
The winged horse is flying to the rear to strike his blow!

It seemed the rider with the holy lance was about to smite the giant, but at the last moment something went wrong. The flaming sword found and slew him, and as he fell so too fell the ancient world. Never was there one like it, and never would one rise again.

The rest of that day was forgotten, lost to the black of endless night. Fear and fleeing, death of brethren, city after city sacked and filled with horrors. A few years later Winthrop was a bandit, not really knowing how it happened. He had the skills and the willingness to use them. In this fallen world, every man was a criminal; what separated Winthrop from the rest was that he was honest about it. There was no integrity, no valor, no mercy for a man in need. Those were the virtues of the prior age. Those virtues were for men who were dead and buried.

Yet still he lived, this single knight, riding right out of the ancient world. He had traded his white cloak for a black one, but there was no mistaking what he was.

"Paladin," Winthrop whispered, sobs shaking his body with every breath. The fear was gone, the weight lifted, and he felt both the pain and joy of seeing–for a moment–his life as it really was. That joy died an instant later, as Winthrop heard Rowan yell, "Now, David!" The paladin turned to face the bush that Rowan was in, not realizing his horse's flank was exposed. Without leaving his hiding place, David drove his spear through the horse's lungs, right behind the front shoulder. The great beast rasped a scream, twisted, and came crashing down.

As his horse gave out from under him, the paladin tried to make a flying dismount. He almost succeeded too, but his right foot caught on the stirrup, tripping him up and causing him to land hard on his back beside the dying steed. Rowan now leapt from the bush with a heavy hammer raised high. The paladin rolled over, got one knee under him, seemed to reach for his sword–but it was too late! Rowan wheeled the hammer back, down, and up in a devastating upward swing. Winthrop was certain that would be the end of the paladin, but at the last moment he managed to roll his left shoulder back, causing the hammer to only land a glancing blow on his chest. Even so, that would have been his death, but a metallic rattle revealed the paladin was wearing chain mail beneath his cloak, and the armor did its job. He was driven sideways, rolled with the momentum of the strike, and got his feet under him to stand. Looking at the knight's white hairs, Winthrop shook his head and wondered, *How does he move like that?*

Rowan pursued his prey with a ferocious side swipe. The knight surprised him by leaping *towards* Rowan, pulling close and rendering the hammer swing harmless. Rowan dropped the hammer and made to strangle the knight, but was stopped cold by a sudden pain in his ribs. As he looked down he saw the paladin's hand gripping a jeweled cross, the bottom of which was touching Rowan's side, and a red stain was blossoming on his shirt from the place where the cross touched it. With a shove the paladin pulled his dagger free. Rowan fell backwards to the ground, still not understanding what had happened.

The paladin then had a look of alarm on his face. Before he even saw his assailant, he drew his sword, tucked his chin against his shoulder to protect his neck, and turned so that his side was towards Garrett. A short moment later, Garrett's bolt was loosed, missing wide of the narrower target the paladin had given him.

Sense of deadly intent… Winthrop knew they were over matched and could only watch as Garrett hastily reloaded his crossbow. The paladin charged in a rapid side step, keeping his sword held high and his armored arms in front of his face. When the paladin was ten yards away, Garrett loosed another bolt. It hit the knight's armor near his chest, drew a pained groan, but failed to penetrate and do any real damage. Garrett reached for another bolt. As he struggled to pull the goat's foot back, the knight slashed downwards and cut him right across the chest. The goat's foot flopped forward and flung itself into the dirt. Garrett fell.

Winthrop's heart was hammering. Now was the decisive moment. Did the knight know David was hidden in the bush? Winthrop had barely seen it, and the knight hadn't been looking in his direction when it happened. Maybe he would think Rowan had wielded the spear. Or maybe he would think Garrett shot the horse with his crossbow. *Come on, come on…stop and loot the bodies!*

Give David a chance to escape! With bloody sword still drawn, the paladin stalked to where David was hidden.

"Out of that bush! Throw your weapon out before you!" Winthrop felt as if ice water was running through his veins. The knight was pointing his sword at the bush now. "I see you in there! Throw out your weapon and you'll be taken alive!" David did not respond. "If you don't come out on your own, I will have no choice but to run you through and drag you out!" Still no response.

The paladin crouched in an aggressive stance. "On the count of three you die unless you surrender! One!" Still no response. "Two!" Nothing. "Three!" As the knight drove his sword towards the bush, Winthrop loosed his bolt. It passed three inches in front of the knight's face, causing him to jump backwards in surprise. As he turned to face Winthrop, Winthrop came out from behind the tree. He placed his crossbow on the ground and raised his hands.

"He's just a boy! He won't hurt you! He's probably so frightened he can't move, if he's even conscious."

The paladin warily shifted between pointing his sword at Winthrop, then the bush, then back again. "What black witchery is this, you sorcerer? Why didn't I sense your attack?"

"Because I wasn't attacking you." Winthrop answered. "If I was, I wouldn't have missed. I just needed to get your attention before you killed a witless youth." Turning to the bush, Winthrop yelled "David! Come out of there!" As he stumbled out of the bush, David was visibly shaking. "Drop the spear! And what were you doing there in the first place?"

With a pale face, he looked at Rowan's body and stammered, "R-R-Rowan told me to kill the horse. He-e said that…that…" Unable to look away from the open, unseeing eyes of Rowan, David dropped to his knees crying.

The paladin then turned to Winthrop. "Are you the leader of this band of robbers? Are you the one who led this boy into a life of blood?"

"I am."

"Then by the power vested in me by the king, God rest his soul, I am placing you under arrest. You have serious crimes to answer for, especially given your position of authority here."

Winthrop made a face halfway between a grimace and a smile. "You don't know how right you are."

Chapter 2: Prayers for the Dead

The paladin looked Winthrop up and down for some time, debating what to do with his new prisoner. The obvious option would be to restrain him. He was a killer, and there was little reason to think he would come quietly all the way to Chelles. But he had also just surrendered willingly, and an ally with a weapon in his hands would be priceless at a time like this. After all, these hills *were* known for having bandits.

Something else was troubling the paladin, a series of oddities that didn't add up. Winthrop's beard was well-trimmed and neatly managed, and his salt and pepper hair that came down to his shoulders was nicely parted and combed. Even though his clothes were rather ordinary, they were neat, clean, and in a much better state than the fraying rags Garrett and Rowan were wearing–more typical of bandits in the wilds. It was a small thing, but it gave the paladin the impression that this man could be reasoned with. This robber had foresight. Even though he *was* a bandit in the wilderness, he didn't wallow in the usual muck of one. He maintained a comely appearance, so that he could fit in in civilized lands whenever he returned to them. This was a man who would come along with the paladin so long as he thought it was to his advantage. Of course, he was also the kind of man who would kill the paladin if he ever thought it was to his advantage, and that was something to which the black knight was not blind.

The key would be the boy. This robber clearly had some connection to him that would make him willing to surrender and stay with the boy rather than save his own skin and abandon him. It would be hard to persuade the adult robber that going to trial would be to his own advantage, but perhaps he could show both him and the boy that a lawful life would be better for the child than a life of crime.

Seeing David weeping over Rowan's body, the knight knew what their first order of business had to be. He went to the saddlebags of his dead horse and produced a shovel, then walking over to Winthrop he said quietly, "We'd better set to work burying these two young men. How many shovels does your company have?"

"None," Winthrop answered.

"No shovel in the wilds? What a sorry state of preparation…thankfully I have one. Why don't you begin digging, my good man? Just over yonder, beyond the brambles looks like a promising spot." As he held the shovel out to Winthrop, the paladin smiled and said, "Lest I loan my tools to a total stranger, would you care to introduce yourself?"

Winthrop laid a hand on the shovel offered to him. "Winthrop. The boy over there is David, obviously. And just who are you?" After the briefest pause, manners long-forgotten reminded him to add, "...Sir?"

The knight covered his chest with his hand and bowed his head. "I am Sir Judas, Last of the Kingsguard."

Winthrop's knuckles went white clenching the shovel, but he gave no other outward sign of his excitement. Instead he raised his eyebrows, and casually asked, "The Kingsguard? But that would make you a paladin. They say all the paladins died on the plains of Nouen."

A sadness came to Sir Judas's eyes, but still he smiled a painful smile that made Winthrop regret his words. "So they say…yet here I am."

Winthrop nodded slowly. "Yet here you are…" He took the shovel to the spot indicated by Sir Judas and began to dig the graves of his partners in crime.

Sir Judas called after him, "Remember that you're under arrest. Please stay where I can see you the whole time."

Winthrop nodded and said, "Of course!" He was already working on six different schemes for how he and David could escape.

As he began to recover from the fright of the knight shouting at him while he lay in the bush, David started processing the events of the morning. He walked over to the corpse of Rowan and took in the dreadful sight. That scarred, nasty face had always filled David with so much fear. Now it just filled him with sadness. Rowan looked confused and lost, as if death had taken him by surprise. David looked around and thought to himself, *This battle took all of us by surprise. None of us were ready for this!* As he cried some more, he also thought, *But isn't that what we intended to do to the knight? To leave him scared and confused and dead just like Rowan?* David had helped with many robberies before, but the full meaning of those murders had never gripped him the way Rowan's death did now.

Garrett likewise was frozen in his final agony. David came over to look at him and saw the nervous frustration of wishing he could load his crossbow just a little bit faster. He thought of Winthrop's crossbow. *One day Winthrop will look like this.* Before long, another thought came to his mind for the first time in his young life. *One day I will look like this.* David shuddered. Sir Judas looked on as the boy beheld his fallen comrades. Though he pitied him and desired to console or distract him, he said nothing. This was a lesson David had to learn, and pain is a powerful teacher.

Sir Judas instead set to making preparations for his new traveling paradigm. Placing his hand lovingly on the horse who had brought him halfway across the island, he said, "You were a good steed, Buttercup. I truly thought you would be the horse to outlive me, but the Lord had other plans in mind." He then removed the contents of his saddle bags and began to separate them into three piles. In order for the bags to be light enough to go a full day's journey comfortably, he would not be able to carry everything he had. Candles, a crowbar, a hammer, pitons…many useful tools were set in a pile on his left that he would not be taking. Only the truly essential for reaching Chelles could be brought now. Two days of food for three people, his waterskin, a tinderbox, an axe…these went into the pile on the right that he would have to bring. After sorting almost everything into one of those piles, the central pile was reduced to a small stack of well-worn maps.

These weren't the maps from here to Castle Nightfall–those had already gone into the pile on the right, for Sir Judas studied them every evening. Instead these maps were the ones from here back to the royal city…the maps that would lead him home. Sir Judas had often said to himself with a chuckle, *I think this shall be my last adventure.* Now that thought had a new gravity to it, for it was no longer mere speculation. It was a very practical decision about what he had room to carry. Would he need these maps? Was he ever going to see his beloved homeland again? Sir Judas said a brief prayer, made his peace, and then cheerfully set the maps in the pile on the left. "Indeed, this shall be my last adventure…the only homeland I shall ever see is above me, not behind." He then divided the pile on the right into three smaller piles and packed them up in little sacks. A small bag for David, a large but light one for Winthrop, and he would take the heaviest himself (the pack containing Winthrop's confiscated crossbow). Thus prepared to resume his journey, Sir Judas went to check on Winthrop's progress.

The going had been tough for Winthrop, given the shooting pain he felt in his left arm whenever he over loaded it. He kept trying different and awkward techniques to minimize its use, but nothing was quite right. After a quarter hour of frustrated digging, Winthrop looked at the small hole he had made in the ground. *Seems about right,* he thought. *A bit shallow...very shallow, really...but I can mound the dirt over and call it a grave.* Looking towards Garrett's brawny corpse and Rowan's solid frame, he realized the absurdity of the assessment. *Next crew who dies on me better be skinny...* He resumed digging, resigned to the fact that this was going to take some time.

A few shovels of dirt later, Winthrop began to ponder what he had just told himself. What next crew? Even if things had gone according to plan, this was supposed to be his last score. And now that things had most certainly *not* gone according to plan, the knight would be bringing him to Chelles to face justice. True, Winthrop was thinking about ideas for how he could weasel out of this bind, but that was only on the surface. A little bit further down a much deeper and older battle was raging, one that dragged up the parts of himself Winthrop preferred to never look at.

Why are you thinking about saving David? Ah! The voice!

Quick, Winthrop, push that thought right out of your head! Winthrop hated that voice and feared it, though he also longed to let it whisper.

Just think of yourself. He'll be alright.

No! He won't! Winthrop replied, *That's the entire problem! The same Bloody Baron I saved him from the first time lives on the road this knight wants to take to Chelles! I have to stay with David and find a chance for us to escape together!*

The voice gave him phony reassurance, sounding the same way it had on that night. *Don't worry, Winthrop, don't worry! Everything will work out in the end. Pray, hope, and don't worry! Besides, doesn't David make your life hard? Isn't he an anchor around your neck? Why should you go to your death, just because he's not fast enough to outrun the paladin?*

Stop it! Stop it! Winthrop thought. For a moment his head was quiet, and he thought the fit may have passed. Then he heard those haunting words.

You are free to do whatever you want.

Winthrop shuddered. He was suddenly feeling cold and faint.

Thankfully, at that moment Sir Judas startled him out of his own head. "That should do! Why don't you take a break while I start the next one?" Winthrop looked up at the knight, then down at the hole. In a distracted frenzy he had dug a huge pit that could easily hold Garrett with room to spare. Only now did Winthrop realize he was sweaty, breathless, and sore from all of the digging. He handed the shovel to Sir Judas, then took his hand and stepped up out of the grave.

"Thank you. A break will be nice." He carefully lowered himself against a nearby tree and sat facing Sir Judas. Watching the knight set to work, Winthrop was impressed. Up close he could clearly perceive how old Sir Judas was, with deep wrinkles on his face and some of the sagging skin that comes late in life. Nevertheless, he worked vigorously, setting to the digging with the energy of a much younger man. To see him work, one would never know he had been in a vicious fight less than an hour before.

"Did you find the Fountain of Youth somewhere, and that's why a paladin is still walking this earth?"

"God forbid," Sir Judas answered. "The Fountain of Youth was said to be a most wicked invention, requiring evil crimes to operate."

"I wasn't talking about the old legends, I just meant it as an expression. You work like a thirty-year-old."

"Do I look like a thirty-year-old?"

Winthrop chuckled. "No, certainly not. Except when you're fighting. You definitely move like a thirty-year-old man."

"Oh, don't be ridiculous. I couldn't even get off my horse without falling on my face. I move like an old man. God just helps this old man stay alive." A moment later, Sir Judas laughed at himself and added, "Even so, I nearly died of fright earlier. That was quite the bolt you loosed. Do you always put your warning shots so close to the mark?"

Winthrop smiled at his own talents. "I tried to put it two feet in front of you, but you started moving towards the bush."

"Well, in that case you and I should both thank the Lord that I can no longer run upon the wind. Your warning shot saved me from having to bury a child."

"'Run upon the wind?' Do you mean the paladin power of agility?" Winthrop asked, "Why can't you do that anymore? Did you forget to go to Church on Sunday?"

Ignoring the touch of mockery, Sir Judas answered, "I have no powers anymore besides the sense of deadly intent and the ability to make my weapons glow. Even those aren't really powers, but gifts from God. When I became a paladin He gave me many gifts, and over the years he has gradually taken them back. 'The good Lord giveth, and the good Lord taketh away. Blessed be the Name of the Lord.'"

"The Book of Job," Winthrop answered. "I always hated that book...I suppose it's easier to say, 'Blessed be the Name of the Lord,' when he's just taking away some super speed though."

"Job said it after suffering much."

"If he said it at all...you can put me down as skeptical of whether that story ever actually happened. I don't see how a man could say, 'Blessed be the Name of the Lord' after God just let his children die."

Sir Judas looked up from his digging and said to Winthrop, "You are surprisingly well-educated for an outlaw. Very fluent in the Scriptures. Do you read them much?"

Winthrop was saved from having to give a very awkward answer by the sound of a man yelling, "There's bodies up ahead! Full stop! Everyone on guard!"

Sir Judas stuck his shovel in the ground and said, "I suppose our conversation will have to wait a moment."

A scout holding a shortsword and wearing thick gambeson had just come around the bend and seen Rowan's body with David weeping over it. He saw the dead horse, and then he started looking around wildly to see if anyone was hiding in the woods. Sir Judas appeared and said, "Be at peace, good man. There is no one to harm you now. There was a bandit ambush on the road this morning, but I have already dispatched them."

Fearing that this might be a trap, the scout gestured for another guard to come and join him. The two of them proceeded cautiously, and after looking around and searching the bushes, they concluded that it was safe to continue. "Full ahead!" The scout shouted, and then the merchant caravan began to advance once more.

It was a train of three horse-drawn wagons as well as a closed carriage. Following these, another dozen entrepreneurs were pulling goods either with an ass or with a handcart, latching on to the wealthy merchant and each other for safety on the road. There were four armed men in total, all wearing gambeson. The two at the front were already on the trail, while two more in the back were watching the rear. As the closed carriage was passing Sir Judas, the wealthy merchant leaned out his window and said, "Hold for a moment! Everybody hold up here! I want to talk to this fine fellow."

The whole assembly rattled to a gradual stop and then Sir Judas walked up to the window. "You say you took care of a bandit ambush? How many of them were there?"

"Four," Sir Judas answered.

"And how many of you are there now?"

"Three," Sir Judas answered. "Myself, the boy you see here, and one other man right over there where we're digging the graves. Here he comes now." Winthrop was walking over to listen in on the conversation and see what might transpire.

"I'm sorry for your losses. How many of your comrades are you burying?" the merchant asked.

"None," Sir Judas said. "I see I've explained poorly. I was all alone this morning. I slew two of the bandits, and then the boy and this man came willingly into custody. They are bandits who are currently under my arrest."

The merchant started and looked at Winthrop in fear. "Then why is he untied? What are you doing? He could kill us at any moment!"

"Right now he is unarmed," Sir Judas said, "And he has also been very cooperative. He has agreed to come with me to Chelles and to answer for his crimes when we get there."

"Just kill him," the merchant said. "Summary judgment. You're allowed to do that out here."

"God forbid!" Sir Judas exclaimed. "Summary judgment is for when a criminal refuses to cooperate and is in danger of escaping! This man has been exceptionally cooperative and has agreed to face justice. Not only would I not dare to murder him under the guise of 'summary judgment', but I may very well plead with the judge on his behalf. He's a very able man, an incredible mark with a crossbow, and if the judge would be willing to trust him into my custody, I would rather see him serve the realm than hang from a gibbet."

The merchant burst into a fit of laughter. "Plead with the judge? In Chelles? Clearly you have never been there, Sir Knight. Chelles got rid of judges, juries, and trials long ago. Now they have a form the guards fill out which gives a score for how strong the case against the accused is. Over a certain number of points, and the officer filling out the form can execute him. It's much more efficient and has saved merchants like us untold fortunes in taxes."

Sir Judas was now the one who started in shock. "A…a form? A piece of paperwork? But what about any extenuating circumstances? What if the accused was feebleminded?"

"Oh, they take that all into account. There's sections to fill out for those things. But that's not what you have here. If he's right in the head and you have a confession, he'll easily score into the 'capital punishment' category. You can go ahead and kill him now."

"No!" Sir Judas shouted, turning red in the face. "Is a man's life really so worthless? Do we sell it so cheap as to kill him if the numbers say so? And oh my God, even if Chelles has gone so mad, I still wouldn't have the authority to kill him here! Only the ministers of this accursed test would have the right! Though now I'm inclined to stay out of that city, and find a court where this man will get real justice instead."

"If you won't do what needs to be done, I'll take care of it. Oliver! Kill the bandits. We can't have criminals running free with an old man as their baby-sitter."

The scout who had led the caravan came towards Winthrop with his sword drawn, but Sir Judas stepped between them and drew his longsword from its sheath. It glowed bright white and caused the scout to drop back in fear. As Winthrop saw the blade up close for the first time, he couldn't help thinking it looked vaguely familiar. "No one lays hands on my prisoners!" Sir Judas growled. "They are in my custody, and it is my duty to protect them. I will lay down my life to protect the realm from them, and I will lay down my life to protect them from the realm. Anyone who tries to murder these two will learn how dangerous a paladin can be!"

The eyes of all were wide with terror, but then the merchant snapped out of it and said, "Bah, just a magic trick. You're no paladin; you're a black knight imposter. Every mage in Chelles knows how to do a glow spell, even the apprentices." With a casual shrug, the merchant said, "Either way, you lot aren't worth the trouble. Forward march. Let the old man get stabbed in his sleep. Then we'll see what he thinks of summary judgment."

The merchant caravan rolled forward once more, rattling up the trail and out of sight. Only once the rearguard was gone did Sir Judas's blade finally cease glowing, and he put it back in its scabbard. "Thank you," Winthrop said. "You…thank you. They would have killed me for sure."

Sir Judas nodded. "These are dark times. The world is desperately in need of a little light."

Winthrop looked up the trail a while longer, then went back to the hole and said, "I better finish Rowan's grave." He began walking in that direction, then stopped to ask Sir Judas, "Did you really mean what you said? You would ask the judge to release me into your custody?"

Sir Judas nodded, "I'm considering it…depending on your behavior along the way of course. I have only just met you."

Winthrop bobbed his head, then went back to the work of burying the dead. *He must be lying,* Winthrop thought. *There's no way he would actually let me get out of this alive.* Yet, as he picked up the shovel, he couldn't help wondering why there were only two graves instead of three.

After laying the bodies of Rowan and Garrett in their graves, Sir Judas, Winthrop, and David gathered at their feet, looking down on the deceased. Winthrop felt a guilty knot form in his stomach. As he looked at the confused, stupid eyes of Rowan, he thought, *This is my fault…I was the leader…I should have told them we weren't doing this, end of story.* Then as he looked at David, another uncomfortable thought occurred. *What am I even going to say about them?* David was deeply rattled, so he needed to say *something.* All he could think of, however, were empty platitudes about how 'Deep down they were good guys,' empty platitudes that rang especially hollow given how their lives had ended.

Squirming, Winthrop took a deep breath and opened his mouth to speak, but he was preempted by Sir Judas who said, "Eternal rest grant unto them, O Lord…" He waited expectantly, but when no reply came he completed the sentence himself. "…and let perpetual light shine upon them. A hymn, O God, becometh thee in Zion…" Sir Judas continued, praying prayers long memorized, now offered on behalf of Rowan and Garrett. There was no mention of how 'good' they had been. Winthrop couldn't help remembering that old adage, 'Lies do not fall from the lips of paladins.' Instead, Sir Judas appealed to God's mercy, begging Him to forgive these men, not because of their own worthiness, but because of the worthiness of the One who had loved them unto death.

David, who had never heard anything of religion besides Winthrop's summary (a superstition that makes the rich think their lives are good because they are holy, and not because they were born lucky) was brought to tears by the prayers of Sir Judas, even though he didn't understand what much of it meant. Winthrop felt something tugging at his own heart, but he steeled himself against it. He would not cry. Strong men don't cry. He had lost crew before and not cried, and these two were not particularly special. He would not cry.

Sir Judas continued for several minutes, quoting a few words from the Scriptures, and then he came to a long pause. Silence reigned, and no one dared to break it. There was an anticipation in the silence, something that made them all hold their breath. It was like standing on a lakeshore, watching a storm roll in. All was calm, all was still, yet one could feel the coming gale. Then, as Sir Judas began to solemnly sing, the storm broke.

> Day of wrath, O Day of mourning,
> Lo, the world in ashes burning–
> Seer and Sibyl gave the warning.
>
> O what fear man's bosom rendeth,
> When from Heaven the Judge descendeth,
> On Whose sentence all dependeth.
>
> Wondrous sound the trumpet flingeth,
> Through Earth's sepulchers it ringeth,
> All before the Throne it bringeth.
>
> Death is struck and Nature quaking,
> All creation is awaking–
> To its Judge an answer making.
>
> Lo, the Book exactly worded,
> Wherein all hath been recorded–
> Thence shall judgment be awarded.
>
> When the Judge His seat attaineth,
> And each hidden deed arraigneth,
> Nothing unavenged remaineth.

What shall I, frail man be pleading?
Who for me be interceding,
When the just are mercy needing?

King of majesty tremendous,
Who dost free salvation send us,
Font of pity, then befriend us.

Think, kind Jesu, my salvation
Caused Thy wondrous Incarnation,
Leave me not to reprobation.

Faint and weary Thou hast sought me,
On the Cross of suffering bought me;
Shall such grace be vainly brought me?

Righteous Judge of retribution,
Grant Thy gift of absolution,
Ere that reck'ning Day's conclusion.

Guilty, now I pour my moaning,
All my shame with anguish owning;
Spare, O God, Thy suppliant groaning.

Thou the sinful woman savest,
Thou the dying thief forgavest,
And to me a hope vouchsafest.

Worthless are my prayers and sighing,
Yet, Good Lord, in grace complying,
Rescue me from fires undying.

With Thy favored sheep O place me,
Nor among the goats abase me,
But to Thy right hand upraise me.

While the wicked are confounded,
Doomed to flames of woe unbounded,
Call me, with Thy saints surrounded.

Low I kneel with heart-submission,
See, like ashes, my contrition–
Help me in my last condition.

Ah! That day of tears and mourning,
From the dust of Earth returning,
Man for judgment must prepare him,
Spare, O God, in mercy spare him.
Lord, all-pitying, Jesu blest,
Grant them Thine eternal rest. Amen.

When Sir Judas had finished, there was a moment of silence. Then David dropped to his knees and threw his face in his hands, heaving with sobs over the graves of Rowan and Garrett. Winthrop was doing his best to hold back his own tears, and he was about to tell David, 'It's alright kid, you'll be alright.' But then, to his astonishment, Sir Judas also dropped to his knees weeping. Softly the old man was saying, "Mercy, Lord…mercy…"

Now Winthrop did weep, mingling his repressed sorrow with the shame and confusion that came from this total stranger mourning his own crew more than he was. In that moment Winthrop had a glimpse into the ugliness of his own heart. Had he really become so callous? What if it was David? Would he mourn then? *For the love of God, I had breakfast with them this morning!* Winthrop walked away from the graves, burying his face in his arm as he tried to hide the tears from himself.

A few minutes later, Sir Judas came and found Winthrop sitting against a tree near the baggage. Both men were sniffling, though Winthrop had wiped his tears away, while Sir Judas still wore them on his cheeks. "I could use some help covering the bodies," the paladin stated.

Ignoring his request, Winthrop bitterly asked, "Do tell me, O wise and holy paladin, where did these two go when they died? Are there two scoundrels feasting at a table in the clouds, or is the devil roasting them over a fire and poking them with a pitchfork to see if they're done yet?" Sir Judas sighed heavily, but said nothing. Winthrop waited for him to answer, but when it became clear the paladin was going to hold his peace he said, "Well? Which is it? Heaven or hell? Where did they go?"

"I do not know."

"Bah!" Winthrop leapt to his feet and jabbed a finger in Sir Judas's chest. "That's not what you believe! You holy fools were always telling me that if we sinned we go to hell. Maybe a priest could help us get forgiveness, but I didn't see one while Rowan and Garrett were spurting out blood. Now if you really do believe what you people say you believe, then tell me honestly! A man is in the very act of attempted murder when he dies, and no priest is around to hear his Confession. Is he in heaven, or is he in hell? Easy question!"

Sir Judas looked at Winthrop with sorrow, pity, but also firmness. Once more, he slowly stated, "I. Do. Not. Know." He turned and walked back to the graves, dropping the subject of the burial entirely.

Winthrop muttered under his breath, "Filthy hypocrites..." Then, remembering who he was talking about, he yelled at the top of his lungs, "And in case you've lost your paladin power of super-hearing, I said, 'FILTHY HYPOCRITES!'"

Sir Judas kept on walking.

Chapter 3: The Glade of Jove

It was late afternoon on Monday when the trio set out for Chelles. Winthrop had briefly suggested staying at their camp until tomorrow, but Sir Judas was insistent. Winthrop was in no mood to argue. They took up the three packs Sir Judas had prepared and left the rest of their gear near the roadside, 'In case some fellow traveler could use it,' as Sir Judas said. Trudging along the road through those rugged hills, David's mood finally began to lighten, and the typical curiosity of a twelve-year-old boy returned to him in the form of asking Sir Judas many questions.

"So where do you come from, Sir Judas?"

"The royal city."

"Where is that?"

"Very far away."

"How long did it take you to walk here?"

"April 19 marked the fortieth year since I set out for Castle Nightfall. A few more years and I reckon I will reach my destination."

"Forty years?" David said in wonder.

Winthrop guffawed. "If it took you forty years, then you must have gotten very, very lost. It doesn't take more than two months to make that journey."

Sir Judas laughed. "For most men, perhaps you're right, but not for a black knight. We have a tendency to get delayed."

David looked back and forth between Winthrop and Sir Judas excitedly, questions forming in his head faster than he could ask them. "So why do black knights get delayed? Why would it take you so long to make a two month's journey?"

"People are very quick to ask us for help," Sir Judas answered, "...and we are very quick to help them."

"Why is that?"

"Well, David, what is a black knight?"

David paused for a moment, not sure how to answer without offending Sir Judas. "Well, uh...I suppose everyone always says they are, uh...knights who betray their lords?"

Sir Judas's mouth stiffened into a line, and he shook his head saying, "No, no. I suppose that's one possibility, but I've only heard of it in fairy tales. A black knight is a knight without a lord. In the real world traitors don't usually end up as black knights, since they tend to receive a castle from whoever they killed their lord to please."

David scowled. "That's not right. Why should traitors get rewarded?"

Sir Judas smiled again. "No, I suppose it's not right, but these things have a tendency to work themselves out in the end. Back to black knights...As I said, they don't have masters, but they still have the skills and the know-how of a knight. That means for the common man–especially if his lord is negligent (or even malignant)–a black knight may be the only person willing and able to defend a town from threats. Beasts, robbers, kidnappers...there's all sorts of problems plaguing our realm, and whenever I come to town, I am very quickly set upon with requests and appeals for me to tarry and set things right. And though it has been difficult, frustrating, even worrisome, I have never turned away my neighbor in need. I've been on a quest for forty years to make a journey that takes other men months, but I can honestly say that from the royal city to Castle Nightfall Sir Judas has never refused to help his fellow man. At least, that's what I'll be able to say once I reach Nightfall, but I still have a hundred miles or so to go."

David was starry eyed with amazement as he pondered what Sir Judas was saying. "That's incredible...but, Castle Nightfall...you keep saying that you're going there, but...what do you mean by that?"

"I mean exactly what it sounds like I mean. I'm going to Castle Nightfall."

"Right, but do you mean that as in, the area *around* Castle Nightfall? Like Castle Gregory? Or are you talking about the villages in its vicinity?"

"I mean *Castle Nightfall*, you dunderhead. The big stone fortress where the giant Goliath is sealed in a dark dome of horrors."

Now David's eyes went wide. "You can't be serious? You mean like...*Castle Nightfall?* You actually plan to go there?"

"I do."

"Bu-wha-how? Why? And how? Don't you realize what you're saying?"

Sir Judas chuckled. "Yes, I know exactly what I'm saying. I'm saying I'm going to destroy the globe of black horrors and slay the giant who defeated six paladins at once while he was overthrowing the Grand Empire. How will I slay him? I have no idea. God will provide. Why will I slay him? For that, I have a much clearer answer, though admittedly still somewhat obscure. On the plains of Nouen the giant Goliath slew six paladins, but in actuality there were always seven. I presume you know this?"

David nodded his head excitedly, while Winthrop pricked up his ears. David said, "Yes, that's because there were seven, but then Goliath slew Sir Samson, the head of the Kingsguard, and that's what began the war."

"So the story goes," Sir Judas said, "and such is the story that was told to me. But I have it on very good authority, that the giant Goliath did *not* in fact slay Sir Samson. To the contrary, he imprisoned him, and to this day Sir Samson remains a prisoner in Goliath's dome of darkness. I am going to slay Goliath so that I can rescue Sir Samson from that unending night."

Winthrop shook his head. "A fairy tale if I ever heard one. Sir Samson was in his fifties when he came to this country. Even if Goliath did capture him, by now he would have died of old age."

"No," Sir Judas answered. "He is not dead of old age. The king received a prophecy that I would save him, and so I know he must still be alive."

Winthrop rolled his eyes. "Here we go. I'm dropping out of this conversation. There's no reasoning with a man who talks like that."

David was undeterred by Winthrop's attitude. "A prophecy...wow...but still, forty years. You spent your whole life coming to save Sir Samson...what ever made you decide to do a thing like that?"

Sir Judas shrugged. "On the one hand, serving the realm is what I would have been doing anyway. I've been serving everyone in need, just with a very gradual drift towards completing my quest. But on the other hand, I have certainly had times when I've been tempted to settle down amongst friends, fame, and riches. Why do I keep leaving it all behind to come to a foreign land and save Sir Samson? Well, I suppose it's because I love him. As a Christian I should love everyone, even my enemies, but in Sir Samson's case, it's easy to love him..." Sir Judas paused for a thoughtful moment, and then added, "I was his squire. He trained me in the ways of knighthood, and initiated me into the Lessguard, the select group of men from whom paladins are chosen. And above all that, he was a very good friend."

David smiled and placed a hand over his chest, his heart both filling and melting with some new love. It was the love of beauty, the beauty of heroism, though he did not yet fully understand. Winthrop on the other hand was now eying Sir Judas closely, trying to mentally remove all the wrinkles, and figure out if this was someone he recognized from long ago. *Who was in the Lessguard back then? Think, Winthrop, think! I feel like there was someone...but how did he become a paladin? When? Something here doesn't make sense...*

David shook his head and said, "Wow...black knights are amazing...I wonder why I've never seen one before?"

Winthrop answered, "Because Lord Fearnow had the good sense to outlaw black knights decades ago."

David looked at him in surprise. "Why would he do that?"

"Because black knights aren't the rosy champions of justice your new hero paints them all out to be. They charge fees so high for their services that most common folk need to sell their farms to rescue their children. They start fights with real knights everywhere they go. And worst of all, they assemble bands of thugs that follow them everywhere, devouring the land like locusts as they loot and pillage. Heck, half the time they're working for some lord undercover. The fact that Lord Fearnow outlawed them shows that he actually cares about enforcing the law."

Sir Judas sighed. "I'm sorry to hear black knights have been such a plague in these parts. The way you tell the tale, they almost sound like robbers."

Winthrop's face flushed, he made to say some angry reply, but then thought better of it. He pulled his pack up a little higher and started walking more briskly, pulling ahead of the other two. At one point he had gone far enough that Sir Judas had to say, "Winthrop! Please remember that you are still under arrest!"

Winthrop looked back, not realizing he had walked so far ahead. For a moment, he thought about running for it. He was so far out in front of Sir Judas that he would have no trouble escaping. But then his eyes turned to David, still walking along cheerfully and cluelessly beside the paladin. That nagging thought he could never shake came to him. *You are free to do whatever you want.* Winthrop stood still. He waited for Sir Judas and David to catch up with him.

"Sorry, I don't mean to be mistrustful," Sir Judas said. "but I still don't know you very well, and I am responsible for making sure you don't escape."

Winthrop nodded. "Of course."

They walked on until dusk in silence.

The sun was close to setting when Sir Judas suggested stopping. They had just reached a very large glade with a clear view of the evening sky, and Sir Judas thought it would make a fine place for them to camp. Winthrop, however, recognized the glade, and pointing over towards a little cluster of man-made objects he said, "Best not to camp here, Sir Judas. This is a place to be wary of."

Sir Judas curiously looked where he was pointing and asked, "What do you mean? What is that?" When Winthrop didn't answer, the black knight proceeded to take a look for himself. Against the edge of the tree line was a stone altar with a brazen pot on top of it. There was some sort of foul, stinking liquid in the pot, which Sir Judas thought might be blood. There were also three stone pedestals, two to the sides of the altar, and a taller one behind it. The two on the sides held braziers with the white, ashen remains of charcoal inside them. The taller pedestal towards which the altar was oriented had a brass idol in the shape of a man laden with many jewels and wearing a magnificent crown. Each of his arms forked at the elbow, so that the idol had four hands, each holding a small offering plate, while a larger plate was set at its feet. The plates had the remnants of some disgusting substance.

"What is this?" he asked.

Winthrop answered, "It's a shrine to Jove. Several prominent members of the nobility worship him and pray for his might and power. The Bloody Baron of Dewford, the nearest town, is a devotee who often uses this place."

"Do you know what was sacrificed on this altar?" Sir Judas asked. "Was it a sheep? A cow? Do you know what they usually offer?"

Winthrop averted his eyes, subconsciously looking down at the left sleeve of his shirt. "I don't know for sure. I've never been here for their rituals, but...there's rumors...awful rumors...and I have some firsthand knowledge to suggest they might be true..."

Winthrop said no more, but Sir Judas knew enough to fill in the gaps. Trembling with rage, he grabbed the idol with both hands, lifted it over his head, and smashed it down onto the stone altar. One of the arms broke off. "Hey! What are you doing?" Winthrop shouted. Sir Judas raised the idol and smashed it down again, this time breaking the other three arms, though the head remained. He cast the idol aside. "Stop! Stop! The nobles will have us killed if we mess with their altar! We shouldn't even be touching it!" As Winthrop was trying to get Sir Judas to calm down, David was trembling with fear, worried that some sort of curse might come upon them.

Sir Judas continued destroying the shrine, toppling the pedestals, scattering the ashes, and then with a great heave he turned the altar over on its side. The stone broke under its own weight, and the altar split in two. "Oh God, we need to get out of here." Winthrop said. "We'll definitely be punished for this."

"Let Jove avenge himself!" Sir Judas cried. "If he is so great as to be worthy of sacrifice, then he is certainly great enough to come and smite this old man!" Sir Judas left the desecrated shrine and marched to the middle of the glade, where he began to unpack his bags.

Winthrop came over to him and pleaded, "We need to get out of here. Now! Even if you're not afraid of Jove, at least be afraid of the nobles. They're all powerful magicians, and they know whenever someone touches their altar. Even now I'll wager they're assembling, and getting ready to come and look for us. We need to flee!"

Sir Judas unrolled his bedroll. "I am no more afraid of magicians than of idols. Let them come if they wish to answer for their crimes."

Winthrop backed away nervously. Taking his own pack, he went to the edge of the glade and hiked about ten feet into the trees. "Where are you going?" Sir Judas asked.

"I'm sleeping here tonight. Just because you're looking to pick a fight you can't win, doesn't mean David and I have to be a part of it."

"Be not afraid," Sir Judas said. "Never was it known that a magician bested a paladin in battle. They make deals with devils for power over other men, but before a man of God their tricks are revealed as empty pomp." Unpersuaded, Winthrop unpacked his bags where he was. Sir Judas turned to David. "You're not climbing into those woods too, are you? You should be more afraid of poison ivy than magicians." David wanted to act brave and impress Sir Judas, but he ultimately nodded and then went to join Winthrop in the trees. "You two will see!" Sir Judas said. "Wait until tomorrow! We have absolutely nothing to be afraid of!"

That was the last they talked to Sir Judas that evening. Winthrop and David chatted a bit before settling in for bed, while Sir Judas reached into his pack and pulled out an old scroll. He carefully read the contents, as he did every night before sleeping. Then he said some evening prayers, examined his conscience, and finished with an offer he made to God every night. "Oh Lord, if it is possible that I could do some penance for poor sinners, I ask that You would send me sufferings, while pouring out on their hearts Your love and the grace of conversion." As soon as he had finished, the sun set, and his nightly agony came upon him. He curled up on his bedroll, and tried to sleep through the pain.

David woke up while it was dark, but still warm. It was only a few hours after nightfall. Winthrop's hand was on his side, gently shaking him while whispering, "David…David…wake up, kid!"

"Ugh…what is it?"

"Hush! Stay quiet! The knight is asleep. I was able to sneak my crossbow out of his pack. Now is our chance to go free!"

"What are you talking about? I thought we were going to Chelles and he was going to put in a good word for you?"

"Are you crazy, kid? Do you actually think that's how it will go? Even if this old man wanted to help me out, some guard will fill out the paperwork and decide to kill me just the same. I don't plan on ending my life on a chopping block. And besides, what if the nobles come for us tomorrow morning? You know that altar is magical. We need to get out of here!"

"But I don't want to leave, Winthrop. I like Sir Judas. And besides, he said he might go right past Chelles and not take you there at all."

"Oh yeah, and head for Castle Nightfall? The dark dome of horrors? Do you really think that sounds any better?" He gave David a rough shake for emphasis.

The boy thought a moment, then said, "I mean…it would certainly be dangerous, but…I think Sir Judas could keep us safe. He seems really strong, Winthrop. Did you see the way his sword was glowing earlier?"

"A glowing sword means nothing, kid! There were lots of paladins with glowing swords back in the day, but Goliath cut them down just the same! This old man might be impressive, but he's no more impressive than the other paladins who already tried to fight Goliath and died. Sir Judas can go ahead and charge to his death, but I don't intend to be there for the funeral!"

David paused, then said, "I still think we should stay with him. Maybe Sir Judas has a plan he hasn't told us about yet. Like a secret weapon. At the very least, we should talk to him."

"Bah! I'm leaving tonight while I have the chance! Now get up! You're coming with me."

David went quiet. Then after a long pause he said, "No. I'm staying here with Sir Judas."

Winthrop's eyes went wide. He grabbed the front of David's shirt and whispered, "What did you just say?"

"I said I'm staying here!" David spoke loudly and clearly. Winthrop's heart leapt into his throat for a moment, terrified that Sir Judas would awaken and realize he had stolen the crossbow. There was no noise from the knight, however, so Winthrop turned back to David. "Don't do that again! Now get up and come quietly."

"No!" David shouted. This time Sir Judas stirred.

"Stop it! What's gotten into you? Come along now, or I'm leaving without you."

There was a silence in the darkness as Winthrop waited. He heard muffled sobbing, and then David choked out, "I'm sorry to hear that. I'm going to miss you, Winthrop…"

Winthrop's jaw dropped. He was utterly stunned. At first he heard that nagging, ever-present voice in his head saying, *Leave without him. You are free to do whatever you want*, but it was quickly banished by David's tears, so that Winthrop whispered, "You…David, you…why won't you just…Oh David, stop it! Stop it! I'm not going anymore! Just stop crying! I'm not going anywhere!" He felt David throw his arms around him and bury his face in his chest. His little body was still shaking as he cried, but he was starting to calm down. Winthrop placed his arms around the boy and said softly, "Don't worry…I'm not going anywhere…"

"Thank you, Winthrop…thank you…"

This whole moment was tearing Winthrop apart inside. It felt right. It felt good. Yet he knew it was a betrayal of his creed. He was going against everything he believed in. It felt good and right, yet also wrong and hard. Unable to endure that pain any longer, Winthrop said, "Alright, enough of this. I need to sneak my crossbow back in Sir Judas's pack before he realizes I took it."

David pulled his face away with a sniffle and said, "Okay."

Winthrop carefully moved back towards the glade, feeling his way along the ground. While there was still a little twilight left he had spied out a path through the brush that he could crawl along silently. He now traced that path for the second time tonight, only this time to return the crossbow instead of taking it. The path emerged into the glade, about thirty feet from where Sir Judas slept. Winthrop was just rising to his feet when he heard a shrill, piercing shriek in the distance. He waited breathlessly. The shrieks came again, then again, getting closer. There was no denying it now. The nightmares were coming.

The crossbow weighed heavily in Winthrop's hands.

If he warned Sir Judas, there would be no hiding what he had done. It didn't matter now; he couldn't waste precious time by trying to hide his crossbow. He shouted, "Sir Judas! Sir Judas! The nobles are coming!" while running over to the knight's bedroll. He dropped to one knee and used his free hand to shake him awake. He found the bedroll empty.

The black knight's voice came from above Winthrop. "I hear them."

"We have to hide!" Winthrop whispered. "Quickly now! Get in the bushes with me and David!"

"It's too late to hide. They'll see my effects and know I'm nearby. Then they'll search the area and find us all. At least if I wait out here to meet them, we can hide our numbers and gain some element of surprise. You grab your crossbow out of my pack and go hide in the bushes, somewhere apart from David. Load it up, and be ready for battle."

Winthrop almost said, 'I already have it,' but bit his tongue. Running to Sir Judas's pack, he rummaged around and said, "Great! I have my crossbow!" then ran back to David in the brush. Meanwhile the shrieks were getting louder, and the mad cackle of a deranged woman could be faintly heard in the distance. Winthrop said, "David! Stay down and stay hidden!"

"I will," came the soft reply.

Winthrop then ran about twenty yards away, near the eastern road they had taken into the glade. He blindly felt around for a large tree, for the night was very dark and close to the new moon. He found what felt like a good one, got behind it, stuck his spare bolt in the ground, and put the stock of his crossbow in his hip. He began to pull back on the goat foot lever, but his hand was shaking too much. Then Sir Judas's spoke from the darkness, "Be not afraid. 'If armies in camp should stand against me, I shall not fear...in the day of evils, the Lord hath protected me.'" Winthrop's hand grew steady. He spanned the crossbow, placed the goat foot beside him, and began his usual ritual of preparation. He became very still. This morning Winthrop's routine had been disrupted by Sir Judas's presence, but now being near the knight had the opposite effect. As the eerie orange light, horrible horses, and three mysterious carriages came rolling around the bend, Winthrop was at peace.

David was lying on his stomach, pressed low to the ground behind a thorny shrub. Through the brambles he saw the orange light come around a bend in the road and into view. The light was dim and soft, but had the odd property of carrying a great distance, such that the entire glade was illuminated as soon as the orb appeared. The same was not true of how the light carried in the other direction, as the carriages and horses were veiled in deep and menacing shadows.

The light bounced and swayed along the trail until it reached the glade, and then it ascended to the canopy and began circling. David had thought it was a lantern affixed to the leading carriage, but now he realized its actual origin. Magic. Just as Winthrop had said, these nobles were surely magicians.

Then the horses charged into the clearing, giving out another frightful shriek. David had sometimes heard these terrible beasts when he and Winthrop would pass the Baron's manor, but this was the first time he ever saw one with his eyes. All the rumors failed to do them justice. Their skin was dark purple. Gaunt, pulled taut across every bone in the creature's body. Their withered lips could not cover their pointed teeth; their eyes were sunken, red, and glowing. They wore special bridles without any bit, allowing them to bite at anyone unfortunate enough to stand in front of them. Running at speeds impossible for other horses, they thundered into the glade straight at Sir Judas. The fabled nightmares. Monstrous horses for the monstrous man known as the Bloody Baron. With the eerie light and their glowing eyes, David felt terribly exposed. He tried to press himself further into the ground, fearing he was already discovered.

Sir Judas stood in the middle of the glade with one hand on the hilt of his sword, still resting in its scabbard. Each of the three carriages was drawn by two nightmares, but no driver controlled the animals. The first one almost ran Sir Judas over, snapping at his neck as it went by, but he dove to the side at the last moment and rolled back to his feet. A burst of laughter came from the carriage–what sounded like a man as well as a woman. The other two carriages broke off, riding to the sides along the outside of the glade. The carriages were large and circular, each with a single door in the side and one tiny window. Curtains were pulled shut over all of the windows, yet the laughing man yelled, "Nice job, old chap!" suggesting he could somehow see through it.

The carriages now formed into a series of chaotic circles, orbiting Sir Judas every which way, only ever a moment from crashing into each other or him. Then the nightmares slowed to a stop and came to rest in a loose circle around the knight. David could see him through a gap about fifteen feet wide from the front of one nightmare to the rear of the next carriage. Sir Judas once more stood calmly, one hand resting easy on the hilt of his blade. David couldn't help but notice Sir Judas looked exceptionally old right now. A little stooped. Very tired. This was not the knight who had vanquished two bandits earlier this morning. Had something changed? Or was it just a trick of the light?

The glade was silent, unnaturally still for about a minute. Even the orb slowed to a creeping crawl, moving just enough to make the shadows seem unsteady. Then one of the doors flung open, slamming into the side of the carriage so suddenly that David jumped. Leaping down out of the carriage came a man in bizarre garb. He had long, blonde hair, pulled back into a ponytail. He wore a robe that came down to his knees, seeming to shine like silk in the orange, magical glow. It was loosely belted, revealing he had no shirt on underneath. Leather boots came halfway up his shins and then ended, revealing skin; he had no pants beneath the robe. What the man did wear was several necklaces and pendants, and his fingers sparkled with an assortment of rings. The most striking thing about his attire, however, was a polished black mask covering his face from the nose up. From this distance, it looked to David as if there were no eyeholes, and the entire mask was solid black.

The man placed his hands on his hips and said with a strange accent, "Well, what have we here? Are you the stupid wretch who destroyed our altar? And just who might you b–blech-*BE!*" The man crouched down suddenly and raised his hands, baring his teeth at Sir Judas. With a grating, rasping voice he cried, "*I KNOW WHO YOU ARE! YOU ARE JUDAS! THE PALADIN! YOU'RE THE ONE WHO RUINED OUR PLOTS IN FRANK!*"

Now Sir Judas drew his sword, and leveled it at the man. "I know that voice...Mollispes, left hand of Asmodeus. It would seem we meet again."

The man stood. "Ho ho ho, what is this now? You've met before? Judas is your name, hmmm? What an ugly name. I think I'll call you Judy. Oh, that's a much prettier name. Isn't it, Judy?"

Now a female voice (the one that had been cackling) came from the same carriage. "Judash? Hish name ish Judash you shaid?" Staggering drunk, she tumbled out of the carriage and landed flat on her face in an avalanche of blue velvet and pinafore. Suddenly the woman got ahold of herself, and rising to her feet swiftly and ably, she also said in a rasping voice, "*YES, THAT'S JUDAS ALRIGHT. IT SEEMS A LONG-AWAITED RECKONING IS AT HAND!*" This woman was also wearing a polished black mask, identical to the man's. With a gloved hand she reached up and threw one of her brown tresses over her shoulder. Swaying again, she said, "I like the name Judash. It hash a good ring to it, doeshn't it Morgan?"

"Shut up, woman!" the man said, shoving her with one hand so that she toppled over to the side. "I'm talking to Judy here. You get back in the carriage and sober up."

"You're not the bosh of me!" The woman said, rising to her feet again and leaning against the carriage. "I don't take ordersh from you!"

"Who *do* you take orders from?" Sir Judas asked. "Are you in the service of Goliath?" Both the man and woman shuddered at his name. "I'll take that as a yes…in that case, I have a message for your master."

The door to a second carriage flung open, and a man leapt out of it. In a nasty, bestial voice he growled, "*WE'RE NOT MESSENGERS JUDAS! WE'RE THE RULERS OF THE COMING KINGDOM!*" The man did not fall to the ground. Instead he glided, descending slowly. His long black robes billowed as he flew, the red trim on their edges looking like dancing flames. The sleeves of his robe were each six feet long, looking like the wings of a bat in flight. The mask he wore over his face was unlike the others. It was vibrant white, gleaming in the orange glow of the orb, and covered his entire face. He landed softly, ten feet from Sir Judas.

In a nasally voice the robed man continued, "That's right, that's right, well said, my friend. We're not messengers. We're in charge. And it seems our friends want us to put you in your place…" The man laughed in a few broken trills, then asked, "What do you say, Morgan? Should I get started?"

"Yes, Simon," Morgan purred. "Please do. I'm going to enjoy this."

"Heh heh…heh heh…" Simon then began to wave his arms around wildly, the flowing robes whipping every which way. The red trim like flames glowed brightly–true flame licking the air around the mage. Simon pulled all the fire together into a ball, and then throwing it at Sir Judas he yelled, "*Ingis!*"

Sir Judas dove to the side just before the ball exploded. The flames flashed into a sphere ten feet in diameter, slightly singing the black knight's back. He clambered to his feet, then with sword raised he charged and yelled, "Enough, you fiends!" He was a few strides away from Simon when Morgan reached out, grabbed the air, and flung his arm to the side. Though he never touched Sir Judas, the paladin flew through the air as if thrown by an invisible hand. He crashed into the carriage Simon had come from. Then Morgan flung his arm the other way, and Sir Judas flew through the air and landed next to the woman. With a mad cackle she started stomping on him, yelling, "Oh fun! Oh fun! Thish ish shimply wonderful!"

Morgan started laughing too. "Tut tut, Judy! Tut tut! I can't let you hurt our Chairman now. I have to protect him, even if we are off duty!"

Simon snorted. "Let him try, for all I care. It might be fun to see him swing his sword in vain."

Morgan used his magic to pull the knight back in front of him, but hovering with his feet ten inches off the ground. "Oh come now, Simon. Surely we can think of better entertainment than that..." Morgan giggled. "Do you want to have target practice?"

Simon laughed his nasally laugh. "Yes, that actually does sound fun. Toss him as high as you can, and let's see if I can hit him."

The carriage Simon had come from lurched back and forth, then a mountain of a man jumped out the door, landing on the ground with an impressive thud. "Knock it off, you two! No killing him before the time! He desecrated the altar of my god. The only way for him to die is as a sacrifice upon it."

He stood over seven feet tall, with a chest like a pair of barrels. His arms were thicker than most men's legs, and he carried a massive metal warhammer, the head of which was carved to look like a snarling devil with four horns. He had a thick, blonde, horseshoe mustache. Unlike the others he wore no mask, black, malevolent eyes flashing in the orange light. Winthrop had seen him only once before, but there was no mistaking who he was.

The Bloody Baron.

He stalked over to where Sir Judas was floating, still taller than the knight even when he was one foot off the ground. Then suddenly, the Baron stopped. He sniffed the air several times. A wicked grin inched across his face. "I smell...a child..." Sir Judas's eyes went wide in shock. The Baron sniffed a few more times. "I smell a child over...there!" He pointed right at David.

David began to shake terribly. Still in denial, he hoped that if he stayed still they might think it was only a shadow. But then the drunk woman yelled, "I shee him! I shee him! I shee him over there!" The orange orb now floated down, focusing its light on David's position.

"Come here little boy! What's your name?" Sir Judas fell to the ground in a pile, while Morgan stuck his finger in David's direction. He slowly curled the finger towards him, gesturing for David to approach as he said, "*Approquinpo.*"

As soon as Morgan had said the word, David felt an irresistible urge to arise and climb out of the woods. Even as terror gripped him, he staggered out into the open. "What's the story with this one, my Baron?" Simon asked. "You want to sacrifice Judas, but can we roast this one just for fun?"

The Baron chuckled lowly. "Oh, I would rather use him for other purposes, but if your hands are itching, go ahead."

Still lying on the ground, Sir Judas raised his head and said, "Release him, you monsters! Or else you are surely doomed to perish!" David was fighting as hard as he could to resist the pull, yet his legs kept carrying him forward. Sir Judas yelled again, "Cease at once! This will not end well for you!"

Simon sniggered. "You are in no position to be making threats, old man."

Sir Judas answered, "It is not a threat I give, but a warning! Any of you who try to harm even one hair on this boy's head will die!"

Simon shook his head, seeming to roll his eyes even through the white mask that hid them. "Stupid fool." In a falsetto voice Simon mockingly said, "'Any of you who try to harm even one hair on this boy's head will die!' I'm about to set your friend on fire, Judas. Go ahead. Try and kill me."

Simon waved his robes around wildly once more, and the flames materialized in the air. As he pulled them together into a ball and prepared to throw, Sir Judas said, "It's not me you should fear, but him!"

'*Fwoomp!*'

A bolt streaked across the glade and sunk into Simon's heart. "Uach!" he cried, dropping the fireball. It exploded on the ground, setting his robes ablaze. Though the blow should have been lethal, Simon was still standing. In great pain and agony, he started yelling, "Put it out! Put it out! Put it out!" He ran madly in Morgan's direction, who had to stop concentrating on his spell and dodge away from the flaming Chairman. At that moment David was freed, and he immediately turned and ran for the woods.

Ignoring her burning comrade, the woman yelled, "Where wash that? Where wash that? Where did that shot come from?" The orange orb moved over to Winthrop and revealed him. Morgan ran at him, with the woman staggering along behind. The Baron meanwhile licked his lips and ran after David, swiftly closing the gap with his big bounding strides. Winthrop reloaded and loosed another bolt. Morgan panicked, thinking it was his end. Instead Winthrop ignored the assailant charging him, putting the bolt in the Baron's gut. The big man staggered and stumbled with a groan. Somehow he kept his feet, but he was slowed down enough for David to get further away. *Wasted shot,* Morgan thought. Then he grabbed the air and pulled, hurling Winthrop onto the ground near him and the woman. The two of them fell upon him with punches, stomps, and clawing.

By then Sir Judas had gained his feet. Barely able to stand after the beating he had taken, he limped to a carriage and leaned against it. Looking around he saw all the dangers. The deadly blaze of Simon. The Baron chasing David. Winthrop being pounded by two of the monsters. Looking up, Sir Judas saw the orange orb still orbiting wild circles over Winthrop. Raising his sword, he pointed at the orb and cried, *"Emitte lucem Tuam et veritatem Tuam!" Send forth Thy light and Thy truth!*

No sooner had he finished the words than the orb exploded in a flash of light, but unlike the harsh orange flames of the two fireballs Simon had thrown, this explosion caused soft motes of silver sparks to fall to the ground all over the glade. Sir Judas was unharmed by them. David felt a slight pain. Winthrop cried out as the sparks scorched him. But for the monsters, the sparks were devastating. Morgan, the woman, and Charles, the Bloody Baron, all howled madly and swatted anywhere a spark touched them. As several sparks landed on the human torch of Simon, the flames he was wreathed in turned completely silver. His already abundant cries of pain intensified, and he started rolling back and forth on the ground. Sir Judas, seeing the effect the flames were having, swung his sword through the silvery blaze. The fires stuck to the blade, causing it to cast a powerful light. Sir Judas began to limp over towards the other three. As he approached, they groveled, crying out in pain.

By that silver light their skin, previously smooth and youthful, turned pale, cracked, and rotten. Their mouths were filled with rows of brown teeth and black gums, while Winthrop (who still had Morgan and the woman on top of him) was afflicted by an overpowering stench of death. Sir Judas approached, causing all three of them to writhe on the ground like Simon. Morgan stretched out his hand and tried to throw Sir Judas, but to no avail. His magic had been broken.

Sir Judas said once more, "I have a message for you to take to your master…"

Simon cried out in a shrill voice, "Mother! Save us! What are you doing?" The door to the third carriage finally slammed open, and clouds of thick black smoke came pouring forth. As smoky tendrils reached out to silver sparks, they snuffed the little motes of light. The black tendrils now approached Simon, who was relieved as the flames went out. With a shaking voice he said, "Oh mother, thank you, thank you. Thank you so—eck!" His voice was cut short as the tendrils wrapped themselves around his neck and clamped down hard. He struggled, kicked his feet, then went still. The smoky ropes lifted his corpse by the neck and threw him on the ground near Sir Judas.

A woman's voice came from within the growing cloud of darkness, "I am strength. My children are mighty. Anyone reduced to such a pathetic state is no longer worthy to call me 'mother.' No, not even the Chairman of Chelles. I am above Lord Fearnow's puppets."

Then the woman emerged from the cloud, a thin aura of smoke still surrounding her. The silver light could not penetrate the aura and cause her pain in the same way it had done to the others. Nevertheless, she was still clearly visible, illuminated by some unknown source. She wore a long black dress with full-length sleeves and an elaborate bodice of gossamer lace that looked like spider webs reaching out to grab her prey. On her head she wore a large brimmed hat, with a veil of pure smoke that hung over the top of her face. If she had any hair, it must have been tucked away under her hat. The only thing that was visible beneath the veil were her blood red lips, which were curled into a confident smile.

Sir Judas took a deep breath and pointed his flaming sword at the woman. "Jezebel…we meet again. This new thrall you possess suits you much better than the one I killed in Ars. I'm ready to end this conflict if you are. I have a message for you and your children to take to your master."

Jezebel laughed. "No, Judas. No. Nobody is going to deliver your message. No…" Now she beamed, revealing a mouth of white, gleaming fangs. "You die tonight."

Sir Judas tightened his grip on his sword. "Bold words, considering how our last meeting ended."

"Our last meeting was in a holy place, where your powers are strongest. Right where the pompous lies and hypocrisy of all you wicked fools was crushing me as we fought. But not here. No. Out here, more than anywhere on earth, those evil fairy tales and deceptions you peddle have been stripped away. Out here we adore the light bringer, because he has set us free from your superstitious darkness."

As Jezebel spoke, smoke began to circle Sir Judas, dimming the silver flames of his sword as it was gradually obscured from view. Morgan, Charles, and the woman now regained their composure, giggling lowly as the night grew black.

Jezebel continued; "It truly does astound me that anyone, even you, would still worship your made-up god after all that has happened. When you were conquering nations and driving chariots over your enemies, sure. I get it. Pretend all of your power comes from 'God' and now you're free to do whatever you want. The yearning of the serf's heart? The peasant wife's dream of freedom? Trample them underfoot, and who will stop you? *GOD* is on your side. Deus vult!"

The smoke grew thicker, choking the light down to a dim glow as Jezebel slowly approached Sir Judas. "But once Goliath toppled your Empire and slew your brethren, wasn't it time to give up the act? Didn't he prove you were just magicians? Powerful ones, I'll give you that. But just magicians. No different from the rest of us. Didn't the countless rebellions against your Empire prove you really *didn't* know how to bring people happiness? That the Christian life is a highway to hell on Earth? After all this time, why are you still pretending your beliefs are true?"

Now the smoke was so thick that David could not even see Sir Judas, just a small little spot in the cloud where the last silver embers of the sword were glowing. He vaguely made out the shadow of a hand – Jezebel's hand – reaching out to touch the tip of the blade. "If your religion was true, we could walk by its light as if we were strolling in the afternoon." The hand grabbed the blade and the flames went out. "Darkness. All I see is darkness."

No sooner had Jezebel finished speaking than her three 'children' erupted into mad and delirious laughter. David felt two strong hands grab him, lift him up, and shake him violently. The Bloody Baron whispered in his ear, "Let me show you what happens in the darkness little boy!" David was slammed back to the ground, landing hard on his back. The Baron dropped down on top of him, prepared to do who knows what wicked deed. The other two were on top of Winthrop, trying to wrestle him and bring him to the toppled altar.

And then it happened.

Sir Judas laughed.

Not madly, not nervously, not in some fake or phony manner. He laughed a good laugh. A deep, hearty, joyful laugh. Morgan and the woman stopped wrestling. Charles released David. The boy felt the big man began to shake terribly in fear.

Sir Judas cried out, "O the depth of the riches of the wisdom and of the knowledge of God! How incomprehensible are His judgments, and how unsearchable His ways! For as it is written in the Scriptures, 'Truths are decayed from among the children of men...With deceitful lips and a double heart they have spoken,' but it is also written, 'because they receive not the love of truth...therefore God shall send them the operation of error.'"

Sir Judas broke off talking, laughing too breathlessly to control himself. For some reason David didn't understand Charles placed his head on the ground next to him and started whimpering, "Oh no, oh no, oh no...oh please don't do it! Whatever you're about to do, please don't do it!"

Sir Judas continued, words interspersed with his chuckles, "But this– but–this–oh my God, I can't help myself...but this is the part that is so funny! That when you tell a lie, but you believe in errors, you accidentally end up telling the truth!" With that David heard a metallic 'Thud!' as Sir Judas's sword was cast aside and landed on the ground.

Sir Judas stopped laughing, and then with a firm and commanding voice he said, "You WILL take this message to your master!" White light exploded, filling the glade, instantly dispelling all smoke and clouds into nothingness. David's eyes ached, and he felt as if something was burning his skin. It was uncomfortable, but not nearly as uncomfortable as the pain he now felt in his chest. His heart was hammering, racing, thundering with an excitement that made him want to shout and leap for joy. Winthrop was screaming in pain, covering his face with his hands. The three 'children' were gouging at their faces, cursing and tripping as they blindly tried to move away from the light. As David looked in the direction of Sir Judas, he could barely see anything because of the light, yet it seemed that the paladin was smiling. In his left hand he was holding the epicenter of all this brightness, where golds, and reds, and silvers were clearly seen before they combined into the white light that filled the glade.

At Sir Judas's feet, groveling on the ground and unable to move, Jezebel was screaming, "I HATE YOU! I HATE YOU! I HATE YOU!"

Sir Judas yelled, "Take this message to your master, and repeat it to him word for word! 'The sun shall rise and rise again, then when it rises next it shall not set before Goliath sees its gleaming, and the last Paladin shall come to Nightfall, to finish what began when he saw his brothers slain on the plains of Nouen.' Take him that message, and repeat it word for word!"

"I HATE YOU! I HATE YOU! I HATE YOU!"

"Do it!"

"YESSSS...AGH! UGH! ACH! YESSSSS...I WILL TELL HIM!" Jezebel groaned.

"Ite. Missa est," which being translated means, "Go. It is sent."

No sooner had he spoken than Jezebel leapt to her feet and ran at full speed toward the western exit of the glade–back the way the three carriages had come. Then the nightmares also started running, breaking their circle and turning to go in the same direction. Once the horses were on the straightaway, they accelerated swiftly and passed Jezebel; first one, then the second, but before the third carriage could take off, Winthrop jumped up in the driver's seat and grabbed the unattended reigns. Fighting through the blinding light and the pain it was causing him, he tried to steer the horses back into the glade. They fought and resisted his lead, wanting to go down the trail like the others, but he kept pulling their heads roughly to the side until they veered off the path and got stuck in the woods. Morgan, the woman, and Charles (who was— amazingly—still on his feet, despite the crossbow bolt in his stomach) all ran down the trail as well, no longer blindly groping away from the light, but sprinting as fast as they could in pursuit of Jezebel and the two carriages that hadn't crashed.

They had all disappeared around the bend in the trail before the light finally began to wane. To say the light grew 'dimmer' would not be quite right, for everywhere the light fell was still perfectly illuminated, more visible, colorful, and detailed than in the full force of the noonday sun. But the distance the light traveled did shorten, so that now the distant path disappeared into darkness, now the vibrant green leaves of the canopy could no longer be seen. Then Winthrop, then David, then eventually Sir Judas was no longer visible, for the light kept growing smaller and smaller. All that was left now was a golden cross with a red gem at each of the four arms and in the center. *Sir Judas's dagger!* David thought to himself, though oddly he couldn't see the knight's hand or fingers holding it up. It seemed as if the cross was floating, and none of its light was blocked from view.

Finally, the dagger itself ceased to glow, though for some reason he couldn't understand, David felt as if the light was not extinguished, but merely hidden. It had a presence that felt like it was still nearby, ready to come out and shine whenever it was needed. After everything went dark there was silence in the glade for the space of about a minute. Then one of the nightmares that had crashed made a whinny. Winthrop set about the business of trying to unhitch them and lash them up for the night, while Sir Judas and David sat quietly, pondering these things in their hearts. About ten minutes later they all laid back down, and though it took a long time to fall asleep because of the excitement, they were still too shocked to discuss what had happened.

Chapter 4: Miracles and Dreams

On Tuesday morning Winthrop woke with many pains from the night before. It was still dark out. At first he thought it must be the middle of the night, but after taking some time to look around he discerned that the pre-dawn sky was actually starting to brighten and things only looked so dark because of the trees surrounding him. Realizing that he wasn't going to fall back asleep, he decided to get up and walk about the glade. David was still breathing low and rhythmically, so Winthrop moved quietly to avoid waking him.

Once he was out in the open, Winthrop stood all the way up and began to stretch his sore and aching limbs. At first it was painful, but in time he felt better and improved his range of motion. He strolled around the perimeter just to get the blood moving, and was almost done with his second lap when he heard a sound come from the center where Sir Judas was sleeping.

At first Winthrop wasn't sure what the sound was. It would start and stop with little bursts and was somewhat high pitched. Slowly approaching, he realized the sound was Sir Judas whimpering; he was clearly in a great deal of pain yet trying to stifle it. "Are you okay?" Winthrop asked. "You're not dying on us, are you?"

Sir Judas made a pained laugh and said, "We're all dying. I'm just getting there a little faster than you are."

"You know what I meant. Are you injured? For all your talk about magic being 'empty pomp,' you were getting flung around like a rag doll last night."

"No, I'm not injured."

"What do you mean you're not injured? You're groaning in pain! Now where does it hurt?"

"In my head."

"Oh, that's not good. Hopefully you don't have a concussion…"

"No, Winthrop. The pain's not on my head. It's in my head. I'm dueling with unpleasant thoughts and parrying razor-sharp memories, all while trying to pull out the mind slivers I keep accidentally pricking myself with."

Winthrop squinted, struggling to see in the growing light. He now realized that the knight was not laying down, but kneeling, bent low with his face to the ground. He didn't see any cuts or welts, but still didn't understand Sir Judas's words. "What do you mean, 'dueling with unpleasant thoughts'? You sound worse than some men in their final agony. What sort of thoughts could possibly be so bad?"

"Thoughts from yesterday," Sir Judas answered. "Should I have killed Rowan and Garrett? Should I have killed Simon? Should I have shown mercy instead of cutting them down? Meanwhile I wonder whether I should have slain you and David. Am I endangering innocent people by allowing two robbers to go on living? Was I too harsh with the merchant who wanted to kill you? Should I have been more gentle with him? Was I too gentle with that merchant? Should I have rebuked him harshly? Should I have *killed* him, before he kills another cooperative criminal in the name of 'summary judgment.' And above all, did I tarry too long? Should I have ignored you and David, and burying the dead, and everything else and just hastened to Castle Nightfall to save Sir Samson? I've already taken so long. At what point have I taken *too* long? This happens every night, Winthrop. I look back on the day before and I am crushed by a storm of doubts and anxieties. All I want to do is please God and do His holy will, yet I tremble with fear that I am the most wicked and depraved man on earth. Every day I try to live with my eyes on Heaven, yet every night I become almost certain I will be thrown into the depths of hell. I feel plenty of pains in my body too, but they don't hurt one bit as much as the pains I feel inside my mind."

Winthrop said nothing for some time, not sure what he could even say in response to such words. Eventually he came up with, "You could really use a drink."

"My waterskin is right here, but thank you."

"I meant a drink of something stronger than water."

"Heh…I packed the gear for all three of us. I know we don't have any spirits."

"No…" Winthrop answered, "…but you do need to get your head off of this stuff. A drink and some company is the best way to do that."

"Well I may not have a drink, but I do have some company. Would you mind helping me to my feet, and then we can talk as we walk about the glade?"

"Yeah, come here," Winthrop said, putting Sir Judas's arm around his shoulders. The knight was very weak, barely supporting his weight, and leaning heavily on Winthrop. When Winthrop heard the rattling of chain mail, he said, "Well there's your problem right there. Take your armor off and you'll have a much easier time sleeping through the night."

"After the night we just had, you're going to recommend I be *less* prepared for sudden battles?"

"Touché." Winthrop helped Sir Judas stagger around in the same route he had been walking. Just as he had felt better when he started stretching his limbs, he expected Sir Judas to gradually improve and carry his own weight. This did not happen. To the contrary, it seemed like Sir Judas was getting worse, leaning more and more on Winthrop as they walked. *Maybe he really is dying,* Winthrop thought. As much as he wanted to get out of being arrested, the thought actually made him sad.

After a little while Sir Judas sniffed and said, "The odor of Simon's body is truly abominable. I don't ever recall a corpse smelling like this within a few hours of death."

"The heat of his fireball probably made him rot faster," Winthrop answered, "Though on second thought, once the silver light started shining, they *all* smelled like overripe corpses. Maybe the magic has something to do with it."

"Oh, you're right. That poor wretch. We'll have to bury him once it's bright enough."

"Bury him?" Winthrop asked. "You ought to be feeding him to the nightmares, not burying him! He tried to kill David!"

"Rowan and Garrett tried to kill me. I still pray they repented in their dying moments. That's what burial is all about, you know. Planting bodies in the ground like seeds, hoping against hope that they might grow into new bodies on the Last Day."

Winthrop ground his teeth and said, "You still didn't answer my question from earlier. Are Rowan and Garrett in hell? Is Simon, for that matter? Either the answer is 'yes' or else you need to find a new religion. One where men don't need priests to forgive their sins."

"What a silly thought you put to me. 'Sir Judas, either you need to start judging these souls, or else you need to stop believing in a religion where you aren't the Judge of souls.' Your ultimatum is ridiculous. But if you still can't understand, then perhaps I must speak to you more directly. Barring a miracle,

I would wager that those three men are all in hell. There. Are you happy that I said it? Barring a miracle, three men who die in the very act of attempted murder, show no signs of repentance, and do not have the help of a priest, are all going to answer for their crimes with the suffering that they deserve."

"Well now you've gone and said it," Winthrop answered. "You do believe they're in hell. So why are you going to waste several hours of labor and some perfectly good horse food just to dump Simon's body in a grave?"

"You're still not listening!" Sir Judas exclaimed. Then he recalled David was sleeping and spoke more softly, "I started my whole answer with, 'Barring a miracle...' I did not say those words for mere dramatic effect. I believe in miracles! I know that they are real! I do not know where these men went after death, because I do not know what wonders God may have worked! Did He stop the hands of time? Did He send an angel to hear them confess? Did He reach into their hearts and take what was good while plucking out all the bad? I do not know! I don't expect it. I expect it about as much as I expect a dagger to explode in light and drive away all my enemies. That's just not something a dagger does. Until it does it. And last night, it did. Barring a miracle, those men are in hell. And barring a miracle, Jezebel would have killed us all. Yet still we live, saved by the hand of God. Shall I then be astonished if He saved other men as well?"

Winthrop spat. With a mocking snarl he said, "*Miracles*. The biggest lie the Church ever told was when she pretended the world was full of *miracles*. I'll tell you, Sir Judas, I've prayed for a lot of miracles in my life and never gotten a single one. Good miracles. The happy, holy, feel good kind that any all-loving God would be sure to grant. I've never gotten a single one. Not. A. Single. One. Don't talk to me about miracles. I've lived enough life to know that they aren't real."

"Oh come now," Sir Judas retorted. "You saw what happened tonight in the glade. How that orange orb exploded into light? How the clouds of darkness were vanquished by a power beyond all human strength? You just saw two miracles with your own eyes. How can you not believe in them?"

"Those weren't miracles," Winthrop said. "They were magic spells. Just like how Morgan threw you around without touching you, and that Simon was making fireballs. You use white magic; they use black magic. That's the only difference."

"Oh God forbid," Sir Judas answered. "Not if it was the only way to save my life would I cast a spell. All magic is from the devil, and those who cast spells are always in league with him."

"Oh sure, depending on how you define the word 'magic' that might be true, but now you're just playing semantics. You and them are both drawing on arcane forces and saying special words, but you're on 'God's side' so that means you do miracles. They're killing innocent people so that makes it 'magic.' I use the same distinction as you, only I call miracles 'white magic' and evil spells 'black magic,' and I leave all the fairy tales about God and the devil out of it."

"No!" Sir Judas shouted. David stirred slightly, and he internally berated himself for losing control of his emotions once again. Whispering to Winthrop, he said, "A spell and a miracle are not two different flavors of the same thing. A fireball is more like…like…like that crossbow you shot at Simon! The fireball and the crossbow have more in common with each other than a fireball has in common with a miracle."

"Now you're just being ridiculous," Winthrop answered, "I can shoot a crossbow all day long, but I can't make a single fireball leap from my hands."

"No, of course you can't. I'm not arguing a fireball is a power men normally have. But I am saying magic is more like a crossbow than a miracle. Magic is powers that devils have and that they let humans control, just like how shooting a bolt is a power your crossbow has, but you can control the crossbow. You see, whether it's the crossbow or the devil, those are both powers that *creatures* have. They are created, finite beings, with defined limits and predictable behaviors. With a miracle it is not so. With a miracle, there is not some 'arcane power' on which the miracle worker is drawing, but instead the finger of God is at work; the uncreated Power is entering creation through the hands of His faithful servants. Not only can *I*, Sir Judas, not make those powers of light that saved us tonight, but *no creature* has that power. It was given to me by God. The same is true of even the miracles a paladin habitually performs, the ones that are often called 'paladin powers.' There is no magic or spell at work. Those are miracles of God that last as long as God is pleased to make them last, and end as soon as God is pleased to make them end. That's why so many of my paladin powers have faded; God was pleased to take those gifts away, for reasons I neither can nor must understand."

"Bah," Winthrop scoffed, "It still sounds like semantics to me. As I said, I've prayed for plenty of miracles, and God has never done one yet. It seems to me that you are probably accidentally doing white magic and assuming it comes from God. That's what the Jezebel lady was saying, wasn't it? Who knows? Maybe if I had magic powers as strong as yours, I would still believe in God. In fact, I'm sure I would, because if I had those powers I could have done all the things I prayed for, and I would assume God was answering my prayers."

"Oh, Winthrop…" Sir Judas trailed off for a little while as they walked. Winthrop wasn't sure if it was because of the knight's slowly growing pains or because he was thinking. After taking a few deep breaths, Sir Judas said, "I thank you for walking and talking with me. You are making this night far more bearable. Tell me, if you will, what is it you prayed for that God refused? What is this pain you keep carrying around that's still so fresh in your mind?"

Winthrop thought for a moment. Something inside of him was stirring, making him want to tell Sir Judas everything. But then he thought bitterly, *White magic…he's using a spell even now to charm me into telling him everything…still, I shouldn't get upset with him. He probably casts spells by instinct without even knowing what he's doing.* Sir Judas made a loud, "Agh!" and stumbled, so that Winthrop had to pull him back to his feet. The sky was brightening as dawn drew closer. By that light he saw the terrible agony on Sir Judas's face, and how much he was grimacing with every step. *He's probably dying as we speak! Best not to lay so much on him at the end. Why am I trying to make a man stop believing in God right when he could use some comfort?*

Winthrop changed the subject. "Those nightmares are certainly something, aren't they? Their speed, their endurance…truly impressive creatures."

Sir Judas breathed heavily and said, "Yes…I wasn't expecting you to wrangle them, but I'm glad you did. They might speed our journey considerably."

"That's what I was hoping. Normally no one would dare to steal the Baron's horses, since he has a summoning whistle that can call them over any distance. Even if you're trying to ride them one way, they'll turn and take you to the Baron. But with the bolt I gave him in the stomach tonight, that will no longer be a problem.

"How…ugh…oh, my…How fortuitous…And this summoning whistle, how do you know someone else won't take it from the Baron's body and use it?"

"It's not that kind of whistle, like an object. It's a way he whistles. Magically. Low and ominous…and if you're far enough away, you don't even hear it coming from him. It seems to come from the nightmares themselves, an unsettling departure from their usual high-pitched shrieks."

"How…how do you know that? Have you ever been…near…one of the nightmares when…oh, when…"

Sir Judas didn't finish, but Winthrop knew what he was trying to ask. "Yeah, I've been there when it happens. One time I laid an ambush for one of these carriages. Shot one of the horses while they were running full speed, and the other one kept running until the carriage flipped. I killed the guy inside, and ran off with the biggest score I ever got. The living nightmare was still in decent shape after the crash, so I decided to try riding away on it. I was halfway to Reswick, certain no one would ever catch me again, when the Baron whistled. That low whistle came rumbling out of the nightmare's maw, and the next thing I knew, I was on my way back to the ambush." Winthrop pulled up the sleeve of his left arm and showed it to Sir Judas in the growing morning light. A spectacular scar ran from his wrist to his bicep, with a fork at one point where it turned and came back down the other side of his forearm. "This scar right here is from my dismount. The treasure I was holding was a fragile one, so I couldn't try to jump off the nightmare and roll when I hit the ground. Instead I slid along the ground for I don't know how long and gave myself an injury that I thought would cost me my arm. Even to this day it doesn't work very well. I can't fully extend it, and my left hand is quite weak…which is especially a shame, considering that before the injury I was left handed."

Sir Judas made a little laugh. "Well I hope you learned…your lesson…no treasure is worth…taking that kind of injury…agh…"

Winthrop smiled to himself. "To the contrary, Sir Judas…some treasures are."

Sir Judas was about to argue, but at that moment his pains greatly intensified. He stopped walking, made a series of groans, and then breathlessly told Winthrop, "Let me down…let me down…I can't walk any longer…" Winthrop lowered Sir Judas and laid him gently on his back. The knight panted heavily and said, "Winthrop…you…are from…the royal city…aren't you?"

Winthrop grimaced. "What gave me away?"

"You…you know things…A lot of things. Even the things you don't believe…ah!...you still…know them…tell me, Winthrop…why are you living like this? Agggh!...why are you wallowing in the wilderness, killing for a living? Is…is this really all you want out of life? Don't you yearn for something higher? You've seen the greatness…you've seen the splendor…don't you dream of something more?"

Sir Judas started to shake. Winthrop suspected this was the beginning of his death rattle. "I used to dream. Back when I was young and stupid and full of life. But the gray hairs you and I both have say that we've grown old, too old to believe the dreams of children still come true."

Sir Judas smiled weakly. "I may be gray, and I may be old, but I still believe every good dream comes true…just not always in the way we expected." After that Sir Judas went very still. Winthrop took those final words and buried them in his heart. With tears in his eyes, he pondered the wisdom of this sweet old knight. Final words were something special to him. Ever since he was a little boy, a mere three years old, dying words were something Winthrop cherished with all his soul.

But as fate would have it, these were not Sir Judas's dying words. While Winthrop was weeping, the knight opened his eyes, sat up, and rose to his feet. Still kneeling on the ground, Winthrop said, "Wha–how–are you–What just happened! I thought you were dead!"

"Dead?" Sir Judas asked. "What on Earth are you talking about? Why did you think that I was dead?"

"You–you–you could barely stand, and then 'let me down, let me down,' and then you got all still and stopped moving. And now you're walking around like nothing happened."

Sir Judas smiled. "I already told you. This happens every night. But then I feel better every dawn." He looked through the woods at the bright orange eastern sky. "I can't see it, but I know the sun has risen, and those unpleasant thoughts I was dueling are banished for another day. Thank you for talking to me, Winthrop. You really were a great comfort."

The paladin walked back to his bedroll without any assistance and started to pack up as if nothing had happened. Staring slack jawed in amazement, Winthrop wondered for the hundredth time since yesterday, *Who on Earth is this paladin? And what on Earth have I gotten myself into?*

Chapter 5: The Indictment

"Oh now this is just awful...absolutely, unbelievably, totally, totally, awful." Sir Judas was carefully feeling the horses, inspecting their rib cages and joints now that the sun was risen. All of their bones protruded unnaturally from their sunken flesh, making the beasts look as if they had been starving for weeks. "I don't know what witchery they've used on these poor animals, but the fact that they're still alive beggars belief." The horses were not friendly, constantly trying to take a bite out of Sir Judas with their dreadful pointed teeth. With as much concern as other men would have when handling a puppy, Sir Judas patted them and said, "You poor little things. Look at this mane! Their hair comes out in clumps with even the gentlest pull! Ah, my poor Buttercup!"

David snorted. "Buttercup? Is that what you're naming that thing?"

"Of course I am. I name all my horses 'Buttercup'. It is simply the most delightful name ever devised for a horse, and there is no way to improve upon it."

David laughed. "Of course there is! What about 'Sabertooth,' or 'Thunderhoof.' There's all sorts of names for horses that are much better than 'Buttercup.' I think we should call this one 'Lightfoot,' just because of how fast it runs."

"You go ahead and name the other horse 'Lightfoot.' I've already named this one 'Buttercup.'" Sir Judas now looked down at David and asked, "How far do we have to go before we find good land for these horses to graze?"

The boy bit his lip and racked his brain, trying to recall the lay of the land. "I know the hills open up into this big grassy plain a little further down the road...maybe an hour's journey from here? I don't know how fast the trip would be with horses, but that's what it takes us on foot."

Sir Judas shook his head, "Oh, this won't do, won't do at all...we would have to walk the horses since they are far too hostile right now...besides which, they shouldn't be pulling a carriage in this condition...an hour there, an hour back, time for them to feed…it would be midday before we even started burying Simon, and he's already been out all night…we could bury him first, but then I'm worried the horses would collapse from hunger and thirst…I only see one possible solution." Sir Judas removed the bridle of the first nightmare, being very careful not to let her chomp off his fingers.

"What are you doing?" David asked.

"Letting Buttercup go get her own food." Sir Judas unhitched her from the carriage shaft and patted her on the rump. The nightmare took off running at full speed, flying down the trail.

"Sir Judas! Are you crazy? We'll never get her back now!"

"So it seems, David. So it seems." The second horse was then unhitched as he said, "Farewell to Lightfoot. Goodbye old mares! I hope that someday you find a master who treats you better than the one you previously had!" Lightfoot also took off galloping while David watched them leave with shock and sadness.

"But Sir Judas…I was really looking forward to having a horse! I wanted to learn how to ride Lightfoot!"

"Bah. David, if you can't do the right thing and have a horse, then it means you can't have a horse. No point in pondering any other options."

David pouted while looking down the trail. "You paladins are hard to live with…" As he thought about how much faster they could have reached Castle Nightfall if they had had the help of the nightmares, David asked, "Sir Judas…that message you gave them last night…You don't actually think we'll reach Castle Nightfall by Thursday, do you? I mean, we're at least a week away, even if we marched really hard. How are you planning on destroying the dome of darkness? Are you going to burst it from a distance or something? Because if you have to get up close and use your dagger, then you're definitely going to be running late."

Sir Judas sighed deeply. "I have no idea, David. Those words I spoke were not mere travel plans I had concocted. I was inspired to give that message. That makes two prophecies now that I'm waiting on…and for neither do I see a road to fulfillment. I suppose that makes this a good time to be grateful that God is in charge and not me."

Excited by this talk of 'prophecy,' David asked, "What's the other prophecy Sir Judas? What is it? How do you know that it will come true?"

The paladin smiled and walked to his pack, pulling out the scroll he read every night. "It was given to me by the king, God rest his soul, and he told me it was a prophecy. I don't know when it came to him, but he wasn't a man to lie, so it must be true."

Winthrop, who had been eavesdropping while cooking breakfast (prepared from the ample stores Sir Judas had in the saddlebags until the previous Buttercup was slain), scoffed at the black knight's words. "Or he was just mistaken. Drank a little too much holy juice and thought his daydreams came from heaven."

"No." Sir Judas said, suddenly more intense and stern than Winthrop had expected. "Not the king. He was a true prophet, and he would not be deluded in such a way." Winthrop went back to cooking breakfast, knowing it would be futile to argue the point.

"I believe you, Sir Judas," David said. "Can you tell me what the prophecy is?" Winthrop almost laughed again, but suppressed it, turning away so he wouldn't offend Sir Judas.

Sir Judas unrolled the scroll. "The king told me that this prophecy would help me find the next paladin, who he said I would initiate into the Lessguard before I saved Sir Samson." At this, Winthrop turned back around to listen. "I don't know anything more than that, but here is what the prophecy says;

When you see a night illumined
By the moon as if by the sun,
When the storm has passed,
Look to the east.
The beast of grateful eye and might
Shall carry you fast…
To the hour when one guard will end
And the new take up his blade
Cleansed from blood by a weapon of Truth.
Try him by combat,
And if he shall overcome,
Open his heart
With the piercing of purest love."

There was a long silence when Sir Judas had finished speaking. Then David said, "Whoa…" turning the words over in his head. "…what does it all mean?"

"I have no idea," Sir Judas answered. "A prophecy is only known in its fulfillment. For forty years now I've been reading this scroll every night and watching for any sort of sign every day. I found many reasonable interpretations, different symbolic expressions for the moon or the beast, or the heart, but none of it ever came together. Forty years later I'm still looking for an answer…but now I know the answer must be near at hand. As you said, it seems that by this Thursday I am going to be at the edge of the darkness, where hopefully my dagger will dispel it in the same way it dispelled Jezebel's darkness last night. If that's the case, then the 'night illumined by the moon as if by the sun' must either be tonight or tomorrow. And since tomorrow night is the new moon, it's obviously not going to be fulfilled in a literal manner." The black knight shrugged. "But as I said, a prophecy is only known in its fulfillment. Who knows what wonders we might see?"

Sir Judas now took his shovel and began to dig a grave for Simon near the edge of the glade. David stood by him and asked, "Sir Judas, do you think that I could be a paladin?"

He shrugged again. "Maybe. Maybe not. Frankly I don't know how anyone is going to become a paladin after me. A paladin must be dubbed by the king, and this realm has had no king for forty years. As the de facto head of the paladins, I can initiate a man into the Lessguard–the group of knights from which paladins are chosen–but I don't have the power to make him a paladin. I don't think that anyone does for that matter." He excavated a few more shovels of dirt and added, "That's probably the greatest difficulty I wrestle with concerning that prophecy. I don't see how anyone can become a paladin. So then what is the point of making someone a Lessguard? I think it must be important, but I don't know why. This is an area where I am certainly walking by faith and not by sight."

Undeterred, David asked, "Well, even if I can't become a paladin, do you think I could still become a member of the Lessguard? What do I have to do to make that happen?"

Sir Judas shook his head and kept digging. "Even under ordinary conditions, one cannot 'do' anything to enter the Lessguard, any more than he can 'do' something to change the color of his eyes. It's something that just happens. For one reason or another the king would choose a man to enter the Lessguard, and the head of the paladins would initiate him. In this case, the king also chose the man for me to initiate, even though the choice was hidden in the language of mystery. If it turns out the prophecy was referring to you, I will initiate you. Otherwise, there's simply nothing I can do."

David paced back and forth for a while fretting, trying to think of anything he might say or do that would change Sir Judas's mind. As the knight was nearing the halfway point of the grave digging, he said to the boy, "David, we're going to be burying Simon soon. We should start preparing ourselves for the funeral."

David cocked his head at Sir Judas and asked, "What do you mean? Isn't digging the grave the preparation?"

"That's part of the preparation, it's true, but I was referring more to spiritual preparation. For Rowan and Garrett, you probably found it easy to mourn because you knew them so personally. For a stranger it is more difficult, and I find I often have to take a little time to recollect myself and get ready for the burial. To remind myself that this was a person–a real person–someone with a father and a mother and friends and maybe children. People who will miss him. I try to remember those things, and enter into the grief of those who will grieve this man. I also remind myself that his current state is the one towards which I am heading…That we're all going to die someday. 'Nobody gets out of this bugger alive,' as Sir Samson used to say."

David was rattled. He walked over to Simon's remains, deeply disturbed. The dreadful stench, the flies flitting around, the black, charred flesh that the white mask had melted onto. *This is where I'm going...* Tears started to form in his eyes. *This is what I'll look like one day...*

Winthrop saw David growing more distressed. "Stupid knight…" he muttered under his breath. Winthrop left the fire he was cooking at and walked up to David. Putting an arm around him he said, "Hey, don't get so down, kid. You're not going to end up like this pile of filth. Don't throw any fireballs at children and you'll be fine." Winthrop tried to pull David away, but the boy stood firm and shook his arm off.

"I'm fine, Winthrop, I'm fine." David was still looking at Simon intently. "I'm fine…don't worry about me…" Winthrop stalked back to the food, glaring at Sir Judas. *This knight is going to traumatize the kid.* True, David had already seen many corpses at his tender age from following Winthrop around, but Winthrop had always been careful to protect David from what really haunts a killer. Thinking about it.

Winthrop finished frying up their bacon and mixed it with some honeyed fruits. He offered it to David, who had no appetite and ate only lightly.

Sir Judas wolfed down a good portion and then resumed digging. Winthrop sat back down and sulked while finishing the meal.

After another hour or so, Sir Judas was done. He came over to Winthrop and asked, "Will you be helping us to pray for Simon?"

"No."

"Will you at least help me move the body?"

"No."

Sir Judas frowned, but said no more. He knew argument would avail him nothing. Instead he went over to David and said, "Now for the hard part. This is going to be rather disgusting, but it's an act of love that God will reward." David nodded weakly. Using the shovel, Simon's clothes, and–when necessary–putting their hands directly on the body, David and Sir Judas shuffled Simon across the glade to the grave. Then they thoroughly washed their hands by wiping them off in the grass, rinsing with water from the skins, and repeating this process until they had used all of Sir Judas's water.

Sir Judas said to Winthrop, "May we use your water to wash as well? We don't want to leave anything on our hands." Winthrop was going to persist in his stubbornness and refuse, but thought better of it. While he wanted to have no part in this burial, neither did he want David or Sir Judas to get seriously ill. Moreover, the Eines wasn't far from here, so there was no real risk to using up the rest of the water.

After finishing washing their hands, Sir Judas and David went and stood over Simon's grave. Sir Judas prayed the same words he had said the day before for Rowan and Garrett. Winthrop sat by the dying fire, glowering. *Look at the body; that will tell you what you need to know about the soul…*

Winthrop was looking at Sir Judas closely, looking at him with the sharp eye of the critic. *Same prayers as yesterday. He might as well read a census record. There's no heart in what he's saying.* Sir Judas looked distressed and sorrowful, closing his eyes and furrowing his brow. *Pious fraud.* Sir Judas reached up and wiped tears from his eyes. *This man was born for the stage.*

Sir Judas sang the same song he finished with yesterday. "Day of wrath, oh day of mourning…" Then when he finished singing, "Lord, all-pitying, Jesu blest, Grant them Thine eternal rest. Amen," Sir Judas fell to his knees weeping freely, just like he had done the day before. Winthrop rolled his eyes. Then Winthrop noticed David was crying too. He sat up a little. David buried his face in his hands and fell to his knees, sobbing like he did for Rowan and Garrett. If Winthrop wasn't mistaken, it seemed David was crying *harder* than he did for

Rowan and Garrett. Winthrop folded his arms. He suddenly felt very uncomfortable.

They cried and said, "Mercy, Lord, mercy!" and then after ten minutes or so, Sir Judas patted David on the back and said, "You did a good thing today, David, a very good thing." They arose and set about breaking camp for the march. Sir Judas was in the center of the glade where he had slept, while David came back by Winthrop.

Winthrop moved very close to David and jokingly whispered, "No wonder it took him forty years to get this far…he must have said a funeral for half the rogues between here and Nouen!" David gave Winthrop an angry look, then silently resumed packing. "Oh, come on, kid. Lighten up. Can't take a joke at the expense of your new hero?"

"That's not it, Winthrop."

"Oh, what is it then? Is it because I'm making fun of your new religion?"

"Shut up, Winthrop."

"Hey! What's gotten into you?" Winthrop smacked David on the back of the head. "You don't get to talk to me like that! This knight has been looking down on me since the minute we met, because he's so much holier than some 'robber,' but you don't get to start treating me like trash too!"

"Shut up! Shut up! That has nothing to do with it!" As David looked up, Winthrop finally realized how distressed the boy was feeling. "This isn't about you making fun of Sir Judas. I'm not trying to disrespect you, so sorry if I did. This especially isn't about some religion, since I don't even know the first thing about religion! But I know that people's lives matter! I don't know what we're praying for when Sir Judas sings about wrath and fire and rest, but I at least know this; Sir Judas prays like lives matter! That song has been stuck in my head since yesterday, and it's a prayer about how Simon's life mattered. About how Rowan and Garrett's lives mattered. Whatever it is he's singing, he's at least singing it because they *mattered*!

"How many people have we left dead on a roadside for the birds to eat, like they mattered as much as horse food? How many people with hopes and dreams and friends and family have we snuffed out so casually, like none of them matter?" David dropped to the ground and pounded the earth with his fist, yelling, "How many orphans? How many orphans like me have a hole in their life because their parents had a full pack when they crossed our path? How many lives have we destroyed over a fistful of shiny trinkets?" At this point

David began to pull on his hair while wailing bitterly, "How many? How many? How many have I killed?"

Winthrop dropped down and tried to shake him out of his hysterics, saying, "David, David, David! What are you talking about? It's not true! None of it's true! You've never killed anybody! You've never robbed a soul!"

"I have!" he screamed, looking up with a twisted face. "Not with my spear, but with my silence! I could have saved them! I could have shouted a warning! I could have made sure the world had a few less orphans in it! Instead I killed them with silence because I thought pleasing you and Rowan and Garrett mattered more than their lives! How cheaply I valued them! Worth less than honor among thieves!"

David let his face fall back to the ground, no longer speaking but merely sobbing. Winthrop was startled and speechless, having no idea what to do. He looked at Sir Judas. Sir Judas was looking right at Winthrop. Winthrop hissed, "You need to talk some sense into him!"

"What do you mean?"

"You know what I mean! The boy's a wreck! He's in hysterics! He needs someone to tell him he's not a killer, and he's not listening to me!"

"But he is a killer."

Winthrop felt as if he had been punched in the gut. He began to tremble in rage. He clenched his fist and raised it as if to strike Sir Judas–indeed, he probably would have–but the paladin had a look that stayed Winthrop's hand. Sir Judas did not look sad, meek, nor thoughtful. There was an unshakeable firmness in his eyes. They bespoke the utter folly of trying to change his words by force. That was what Winthrop really wanted. He wanted Sir Judas to take back those brutal words.

"He's not! He's not a killer! He's never harmed a soul! Prior to your stupid horse, I could honestly say he's never raised a weapon in violence! He's a good kid!"

"No. He's a murderer. David has spoken rightly. He was an accomplice to your many murders, and the blood of your victims is on his hands too. The difference between you and him is that his heart is open to sorrow. In that sorrow he has found repentance, in his repentance he will find forgiveness, and in forgiveness he will be a murderer no more. Not you. You are still in your sins. And unless you open your heart to sorrow, in your sins you will surely die."

Winthrop's eyes went wide. Now he did leap at Sir Judas, grabbing the front of his chain shirt and shaking it, madly punching him in the chest with his scarred left fist, doing nothing except bloodying his hand on the unyielding armor. "No sorrow? No sorrow? I've had a whole life of sorrow! Damn this talk of sins! Damn your talk of sorrow! You don't know what it means to suffer! You don't have a clue what real sorrow feels like! It's worse than hell, I'll tell you that. A man has to learn how to deal with sorrow, otherwise it will eat him alive. That's what I want! That's what I want! Go and tell David to stop crying and stop fretting! Don't let him get consumed by his sorrows! Don't let him end up like me!"

"NO!" Sir Judas shouted. The glade went completely silent, and David even stopped crying as he looked up. "That's not how you deal with sorrow! That's running away from your darkness, not valiantly marching through it! David has entered his sorrow, and in a short time he will pass through the other side and be healed. You run away from yours, and that's why it's always right behind you, always eating you alive, one little nip! One little bite! Consuming you one piece at a time. Don't run from your sorrow! Embrace it! It's worse than hell because it comes from love, and love is hard as hell. Strong as death. You feel sorrow because you love. If you shut sorrow out of your life you shut love out with it."

Winthrop leaned back, clenching his teeth. "Gyyaahhhh! NO!" He punched Sir Judas as hard as he could, the armor now cutting his knuckle down to the bone. "You're wrong! You're wrong! I love more than you could ever know! I don't have to live according to your stupid rules just to love! I don't need your stupid repentance nor your forgiveness!"

"Yes you do. It is a fact of life. You cannot be a man who loves and also be a man who is free to do whatever he wants."

At that moment, something mysterious happened, something David did not understand at the time. In an instant–at a word–Winthrop's entire demeanor changed. Whereas one moment prior he was so full of vitriolic force, in the next moment he was languid, sickly. He looked as if he could barely stand, though he had just been throwing punches until blood was drawn. Swaying like he might fall, Winthrop stammered, "What did you–yes I–no, I am–I'm–I'm free to do…whatever…I want…" He backed away from Sir Judas slowly, in a daze. He started to walk toward the glade's western exit, then turned and said to Sir Judas, "I'm leaving."

He staggered a little further. "Winthrop!" Sir Judas called, "You are still under arrest! Stay here!"

Winthrop took three more steps, then turned and looked directly at David. His face was pale. His eyes were soaked. His gray beard was speckled with tears. Across the glade he softly whispered, just barely loud enough to be heard, "David…come with me."

Trembling, crying, David clenched his fists and said, "No."

Winthrop's lip quivered. "Please, David…come with me."

"No," the boy replied.

Winthrop stumbled backwards as if he had been struck, then turned and continued walking. When he reached the exit where the trail resumed, he stopped and looked back once more. There were four words he wanted to say to David. Four words he had so often longed to use. He tried to speak, but they caught in his throat. He could not bring himself to sully those precious words with his lying lips. Instead Winthrop sobbed, turned, and walked once more. He walked, jogged, then ran away, until he had run right out of David's life.

End of Volume I

Interlude

Darkness. All he saw was darkness. Even though the sun had been up for several hours now on Tuesday morning, none of its light ever shone in this accursed prison. Goliath had a love–hate relationship with the sea of blackness into which he was staring. It was so empty. So void. It scared him and it bored him. Yet at least it wasn't orange. None of that horrible, fire-like color that every solid surface was outlined and shaded in. He looked down at the rampart he was standing on. There was a large exposed block of stone where he had ripped the last one free. He was in a mood to do it again. So he did.

Goliath reached down with his mighty clawed hands, pulling a piece of the castle tower out of the floor. It was a few feet across, weighing no more than a hundred pounds. Easily hefting the stone in his right hand, Goliath tossed it high up in the air. It tumbled end over end, dancing lines of orange racing by each other as it spun. He reached down and picked up Doomfall, the once molten greatsword that turned to obsidian when the darkness came. He wound back, then swung forward, and struck the falling piece of castle with a satisfying 'Crack!' The stone arced up into the sky, traveling over a hundred feet. Then it fell and kept on falling. Below eye level, below ground level, and then the orange outlines disappeared in a mighty 'Spwoosh!' as it was swallowed by the all-black sea. Goliath listened to the splash go up and down, and the sprinkling of the final droplets.

The sea. Nothing solid. Nothing orange. Nothing for his devils' sight to show him. Taking in the sounds and blackness for a moment, Goliath could pretend he was still free. He imagined he was on the shore so long ago, skipping stones across the waves. He dreamt of the feel of the wind, of the taste of the salty mist. None of that was his now. His thick black scales felt no breezes. The only taste on his tongue was rancid sewage. He looked back to the east, where the peninsula spread out before him in rolling waves of hellish hues. Pretending was beyond his power. He was still here. And he was bored.

Goliath hit a few more stones out into the ocean, until deciding to descend the castle and go take a walk. Every day his dominion got a little bigger. Maybe it would be interesting to see what new lands were his since yesterday.

It wouldn't be. It never was. But he could pretend. Pretending was within his power. Maybe he would find something interesting today. Goliath jumped from the rampart, falling forty feet down to the ground. He landed on his feet with a mighty crash, cratering the earth beneath him. He then walked out of the divot and strode across the land, off to look for something interesting. The demons had tricked him long ago, promising he would reign in hell on earth. And so he did, for he was the master of this hellish land. Here even the demons had to obey his commands, though he had to be very careful, lest they try to twist his words. Still, he was in charge. He was powerful. Here he was, the master of hell. The demons gave him what they promised, he had just never imagined that hell would be so…boring…

He made it a hundred yards from Castle Nightfall before depression overtook him. It was *so far* to the edge of his domain now. And there would be nothing there to see. Why bother going? What was the point? He might as well stay home today. Maybe tomorrow would be better.

It wouldn't be. It never was. But he could pretend. Pretending was within his power. Or wasn't it? He could never remember what he had decided. Goliath went and leaned against the wall with a heavy sigh. If only someone was here. If only anyone was here. He would be so happy if any person on earth was here. All his troubles would melt away if he had just a single soul to talk to.

Two carriages crested the eastern hill, beginning the descent down to Castle Nightfall. The speed with which they moved revealed they were pulled by nightmares. With an angry roar he stomped his feet, angrily stamping the ground like a child. *Anyone worth talking to! Not them! Anyone but them! They are the most odious maggots on the planet!*

He was breathing so heavily with rage that stinking goo was falling out of his maw and dripping to the ground. As the nightmares stopped and the doors swung open, he made to exhale a noxious blast and drench the visitors. Suddenly, he changed his mind. *Perhaps they bring news.* He twisted a many-fanged grin onto his mouth and held his clawed hands out towards his guests, his best attempt at being welcoming.

Beatrice, Morgan, Destiny, and Charles clambered forward on all fours—a bestial run that revealed their demons were in full possession of their bodies. Throwing themselves prostrate at Goliath's feet, with one voice they all shouted, "THE SUN SHALL RISE AND RISE AGAIN, THEN WHEN IT RISES NEXT IT SHALL NOT SET BEFORE GOLIATH SEES ITS GLEAMING, AND THE LAST PALADIN SHALL COME TO NIGHTFALL, TO FINISH WHAT BEGAN WHEN HE SAW HIS BROTHERS SLAIN ON THE PLAINS OF NOUEN!" There was a long period of silence where Goliath stood perfectly still. As the demons receded, the four demoniacs began trembling and slowly raised their heads. A grin that looked as if he might devour them was frozen on Goliath's face. After the space of about a minute, Goliath said, "Oh good, another guest. What wonderful fun we'll have..." Another minute went by. Then Charles grabbed Destiny and leapt aside, yelling, "Move!"

A mere moment after he said it, the giant's monstrous fist crashed into the ground where she had been. Baring all his fangs in anger, he let out a roar once more. Morgan took Charles's advice and retreated twenty paces. Beatrice stood her ground, nervous, but not yet running. "What did you all just say!" He screamed right in her face.

"I don't really know," Beatrice answered. "It's something a paladin told us to tell you. We ran into him in the glade of Jove." Her black smoke was spreading across the ground, plucking little bits of grass with a hundred magic fingers. With his devils' sight, Goliath didn't see the smoke, since there was no solid substance to it.

The giant bent over Beatrice, looking down on her from twice her height, shaking his head back and forth to menace her with his horns. "There are no more paladins! Now tell me the truth of what really happened, or you'll not live to tell more lies."

Beatrice gulped, then slowly said, "I don't know what to tell you. That was the message. I may not know how he became a paladin, but he really was one."

Goliath roared and swiped at her with his claws. She threw the many pieces of grass up into the air. Without any color and with the outline of each blade of grass glowing bright orange, the shower was an optical cacophony that completely hid her from view. Beatrice also ducked down, feeling the rush of wind as Goliath's hand swiped above her head. With smoky wings she then sprang into the air, flapping up, up, and then out of his reach before he realized what was happening.

"Get back down here!" Goliath yelled.

"Make me," Beatrice replied.

Goliath then straightened and said, "Jezebel, by my authority as ruler of the demons in this land, I command you to bring your demoniac to the ground."

Beatrice's eyes went wide as her wings evaporated. She plummeted towards the earth and landed in Goliath's clutches. He gripped her firmly, overpowering her older frame with a single hand. He opened wide his maw, about to bite off her head. Then Charles tensed and took in a sharp breath. Goliath paused…then let out an exasperated sigh. "Beatrice, Beatrice, this isn't the way I was hoping our conversation would go. Why is it that every time you come to visit, within a matter of minutes you provoke me and try to start a fight? A fight that you *know* you cannot win?" He then placed her back on the ground and set about brushing her off, accidentally putting a long cut in her skirt with his pointed thumb. "Oh, pardon me for that. I suppose that's what you get though." Destiny and Morgan watched the scene in bafflement, unable to understand why Goliath had gone from murderously violent to sounding like a disappointed father. This was their first time here, and they did not know Goliath's…*temperament.* Charles and Beatrice on the other hand stood ready, looking at Goliath's face intently. With him, they never knew what was going to happen next. But they did know *when* it was going to happen.

Charles and Beatrice drew in a sharp breath. Goliath dropped down to the ground with a crash that made the earth rumble beneath their feet. Sitting cross-legged with his hands on his knees, he asked in a concerned tone, "So what's going on with this supposed 'paladin'? Tell me everything you know. Why did he give that message? What are his current plans?"

Beatrice shrugged. "I don't know anything."

Goliath yelled in frustration,. "Woman! Why must you vex me so! *Jezebel*, by my authority, I command you to tell me everything you know about the paladin!"

Beatrice's eyes went all black, and in a raspy voice she started shouting, "HEIGHT FIVE FOOT ELEVEN INCHES, WEIGHT ONE HUNDRED SIXTY POUNDS, HAIR COLOR WHITE, LONG BEARD, LONG HAIR,

APPROXIMATE AGE SEVENTY, SKIN WRINKLED, WEARS BLACK CHAIN MAIL–"

"Stop! Stop! Stop!" Goliath shouted. She kept babbling useless information despite his informal order. "By my authority, I command you, tell me the *important* things you know in a coherent manner!"

Jezebel then stopped babbling, and spoke in an ordinary fashion. "HE IS A KNIGHT THAT WE FOUGHT IN FRANK, BACK WHEN OUR LAST MEATBAGS WERE STILL ALIVE. WE HAD A MAJOR CITY READY TO PLUNGE INTO WAR, BUT THEN HE SHOWED UP AND GOT EVERYONE TO HUG AND KISS AND MAKE PEACE."

Goliath cut in, "What is his name?"

"I SHOULDN'T SPEAK IT HERE."

"Tell me his name."

"THAT'S A BAD IDEA, FOOL."

He leapt to his feet and stamped the ground. "By my authority, I command you to tell me his name!"

Jezebel croaked, "*SIR JUDAS!*" No sooner had she spoken that name than the earth started shaking violently, making the tremors caused by Goliath–those tremors that a moment before had seemed so mighty–seem like gentle vibrations, a mere tingling of the ground. Morgan and Destiny were thrown down, while a strong, driving wind began to swirl about them. It lasted for only a few seconds, then everything calmed to a heavy silence.

Charles and Beatrice tensed. Goliath smiled. "Incredible…" he whispered. "*Sir Judas!*" This time, nothing happened. "Sir Judas!" Nothing. "Was that a new spell you cast, Jezebel?"

"No," Beatrice answered, looking rather shaken by what had just transpired.

"Hmm, then what just happened?" He was about to ask Jezebel, but had another one of his moments where his mind whipped in a different direction. "Back to business." Goliath was no longer angry nor impulsive, but rather commanding and certain, like a general speaking with his troops. "So this Sir Judas who is apparently coming and styles himself a paladin, he says Castle Nightfall will see the sunset soon, yes? Let's see…rise, rise again, rises next…what day did he give you this message?"

"Last night," Beatrice answered. "Charles' nightmares rode through the night to get us here."

"Mm hmm…mm hmm…" The giant began pacing back and forth with his claws folded behind his back, looking down at the ground like a very thoughtful giant. "Yes, yes, I see…so then three days later he thinks he can break this darkness…what day is it today?"

"It was Tuesday morning when we entered the dome, Monday night when he gave us the message. It seems he plans on being here on Thursday."

"Mm hmm…mm hmm…and this so-called 'paladin,' was he powerful? How strong would you say he was?"

"Tremendously weak. My children would have killed him themselves except that one of his allies intervened and surprised them. Even so, they would have been victorious, if only Destiny here had not been so moronic with her spells. She allowed the knight to steal some of her magic and use it against them. He weaved her illusory light with a little thread of holy power. Then they would have been routed had I not intervened."

"But they were routed," Goliath answered.

"Not by him!" Beatrice snapped. "I defeated him! I extinguished his powers and was in the very act of killing him when the Almighty intervened! I was robbed of MY VENGEANCE at the LAST MOMENT!" Jezebel now fully manifested. "CURSE THE GOD ABOVE! CURSE HIM! INSTEAD OF LETTING US CREATURES SETTLE THINGS AMONGST OURSELVES, HE INTRUDES AND INTERVENES! I OUGHT TO BE ABLE TO TRAMPLE DUST AND ASHES BENEATH MY FEET. INSTEAD AN INVINCIBLE GOD HUMILIATES ME."

"Fair or unfair, this is most welcome news," Goliath stated. "I could not imagine a more favorable development. If this paladin really is a little wonderworker, then perhaps he will do a miracle to destroy this darkness and set me free from the prison, all the while being so weak that I can easily kill him. Then once he's dead and I'm free, my conquest can renew in earnest." The giant looked at his four 'soldiers' with a large and wicked smile. "So then all that remains is the preparations…You there! Your name is Destiny, correct?"

She stood up while shaking and answered, "Yes, m'lord…"

"Since you are the most completely and totally incompetent out of this sorry lot, I would gladly give your task to someone else, but according to Beatrice, you happen to have the ear of the witch of Chelles. Go to her, and persuade her to help Sir Judas on his travels. Fearnow will have some sort of means for getting the knight to the darkness by Thursday. Make sure it happens.

I will be *most disappointed* if this opportunity passes us by simply because the paladin couldn't get here in time. Understood?"

"Y-y-yes, m'lord."

"Good. Pretty boy!" he shouted at Morgan

Morgan stood up and tittered nervously, "Te-heh...yeeees?"

"You go to the Scar, and command the wretches who live there in my name to come to Castle Nightfall and serve me. If this knight is stronger than we imagine, I may need their assistance."

Though no one could see it in the darkness, Morgan's face went deathly pale. "The–the Scar? Oh, Goliath, I–I could never–..."

"DO IT!"

Morgan gulped. "Ye–yes, m'lord, of course."

Goliath now turned to Charles, and stalked up to him to make his presence felt. At more than seven feet tall, there was almost no one that Charles had to look up to. Goliath was the one exception. "Charles..." Goliath said in a low and growling tone. "Your job is the most critical...if you shall fail, we all fail with you, and you will be punished most severely. The priest...I will be undone if that paladin comes with a priest...I have heard rumors of a priest in the vicinity of Chelles...you must find him and destroy him. Or at least make sure he doesn't come along with the paladin."

"But Goliath," Charles answered, "There hasn't been a priest sighted in Chelles for over a decade. What makes you so sure there will be one now?"

"There is!" The giant bellowed. Find him! Kill him! Or at least keep him pinned down! Do not, whatever you do, do *not* allow him to come here! Understood?"

Charles nodded. "Yes, boss."

"Good, good...then that leaves you, Beatrice..." As Goliath turned his gaze back to Beatrice, both her and Charles flinched. Then Goliath said, in a— could it be?—in a seductive voice, "Do you think you could...stay and keep me company? I would love to have you at my right hand when the paladin arrives. And besides, until Thursday, we can..." He smiled while raising the scales where men have eyebrows. "...catch up with each other. It's been too long, hasn't it? Have I ever told you about the time I avoided Sir Daniel's lance and slew the little paladin? We should make plans for what we'll do after we defeat this new one..."

Beatrice sighed heavily. "Please, tell me all about it." Meanwhile she was thinking, *This is going to be a loooong three days…Thursday night can't get here fast enough…*

Volume II

Stranger in a Strange Land

Chapter 1: Where Civilization Ends

Sir Judas and David marched forward as the sun was setting ahead of them on Tuesday evening. For the last several hours they had been trudging in near-total silence across the wild plains leading up to Chelles. They passed the fork in the road leading to Dewford, and then shortly after began the ascent leading up to the tall hill Chelles was set upon. "Not much further now, and we'll be there." Sir Judas stated.

They walked a while longer, David with head hung low.

Sir Judas said, "I've never been to this city before, but Lord Fearnow visited the royal city often in my youth. He was probably the father or grandfather of the current Lord Fearnow."

"That makes sense."

Sir Judas decided to stop trying to make conversation. All day David had been constantly scanning the horizon, clearly looking for Winthrop and hoping every distant outline of a man might be the one who had just walked out of his life. David was hoping against hope that Winthrop would turn around to come back to him again, or at the very least that they might see him and be able to overtake him. Now it was clear that he was long gone, disappeared into the vast city of Chelles, never to be seen again.

When the outskirts of that great city had come into view, there was one very odd manor that butted right up against the road. Its door was on top of a stoop that came down three steps and then ended with about six inches of grass between the end of the step and the beginning of the road. In those six inches a wooden sign had been erected, which read, 'Chelles City Limit; Civilization Ends Here.'

"What an odd piece of signage," Sir Judas said with a chuckle, "Does civilization end when you enter Chelles, or when you leave it? The message isn't entirely clear."

David glowered darkly. "I always joked that the manor is where civilization ends. This is where the Bloody Baron lives, the one we saw last night."

"The Bloody Baron…from what little I know of him, it certainly seems a fitting name…then that stable over there, is that where his poor nightmares are kept?"

"It is."

There was a man watching Sir Judas and David pass, leaning with his back against the wall of the stable. His beard was long, brown, and tangled, while an unkempt mess of hair fell over his head in all directions. Pulling some locks out of his eyes, he let out a long low whistle, then smirked. "Howdy howdy, do I see right? Looks to me like a black knight."

Sir Judas waved politely and said, "Hail, stranger," then looked back to the road ahead and kept walking.

The man pushed off the stables and started walking towards Chelles, slowly angling towards the road and approaching the travelers. "Before ya get too far ahead of yourself stranger, ya oughta consider stoppin' in for a visit. Ole' Charles is always lookin' for outlaws to join his service. Even an old timer like you could do somethin' useful. Runnin' afoul of the law is no problem with him. It's actually more of a requirement."

"I appreciate the offer, but I must politely decline. Besides the fact that Baron Charles and I had a most unpleasant first meeting, I do not meet the requirements of such a post since I am not an outlaw."

"Oh but you is, oh but you is," the man said. "Ever since you crossed that wooden sign right there you became a wanted man, dead or alive. You black knights ain't welcome in Chelles, and now you're an outlaw whether you like it or not."

Sir Judas put his hand to his cheek, rubbing it thoughtfully. "You know, I had heard that black knights were 'outlawed' in these parts, but I presumed it meant they were required to join a new master when an old one died. You mean to say foreign black knights are actually criminal?"

"Oh, most criminal, most criminal. More criminal than me you are. If you're gonna be roaming Chelles, then you best be takin that armor off."

"No, I will not hide who I am. Better to avoid trouble and respect the strange laws of this land. Tell me, how can I cross the river Eines without going through Chelles?"

"You can't. Everything south of the Eines is Chellesian territory."

"My goodness. Now that's quite the expansion by Lord Fearnow. It seems I'll be marching a hundred miles through hostile territory…Hmm…well, thank you for the notice, stranger. I will be sure to stick to the outskirts of town and avoid causing trouble as much as I can."

The man was now walking right alongside David and Sir Judas, as if the three of them were all traveling together. "There's a very simple solution to all this, ya know. Come along with me. It's a mighty good deal. Good pay, good housing, good drinking every now and then. Not to mention more gold than you'll ever make as an honest killer. That's what you knights are after all, yeah? Killers with permission? In that sense, we're fairly similar. I just have a little less permission."

"The answer is no," Sir Judas stated flatly. "Be gone."

The man's face turned angry, and for a moment he thought of trying to smash Sir Judas's snowy head with his fist, but instead he just smiled malignantly. "Your funeral then, fella'. All I hope is that they announce your execution and make a big show of it. Me an' all the boys will come for a pretty good laugh. Mister principles getting' dropped off the gallows while more practical fellas get to watch. You have a nice trip then, Sir Stranger. Hope ya enjoy your visit to Chelles."

The man then turned around and went back to the stables, looking over his shoulder at David and Sir Judas every few steps. Once they had gone a good distance away from him, David asked Sir Judas, "Sir Judas, what *are* you planning on doing? You're going to be in a lot of danger once we enter the city unless you take your armor off."

"Oh, I don't think it will be as bad as all that. If we do run into any trouble with the law, I'll just explain the situation. I am a paladin from the royal city, I am here on the king's business, and the laws of the realm take precedence over any local laws. It's all straightforward enough that we shouldn't have any issue." Knowing the Chellesian legal system far better than Sir Judas, David had his doubts.

Long before reaching the walls of the city, David and Sir Judas reached a sea of tents and makeshift dwellings–the sure sign of a refugee camp wherever Sir Judas had been before. They were trading and working and paying visits to one another, suggesting they had been here for quite some time. Sir Judas asked David, "What is it that has driven all of these people here? Do you know where most of them are fleeing from?"

"Oh they're not fleeing, Sir Judas. Everyone comes here because Chelles is here, and they want to see the world's greatest city."

"What! That cannot be so. Who would give up the security of a walled town or the freedom of an open farm just to come huddle in a tent outside a city?"

"Oh, anyone would do that, Sir Judas. Chelles is the most spectacular place on earth. I've never been inside the walls myself, but everyone agrees. The sights, the marvels...people work hard all week just to make enough money to spend a weekend in the city. Winthrop never let me go, but I always hoped that some day when I was older I might be able to sneak away for a night or two."

"This is ridiculous. The whole camp smells like human excrement. Surely they must be fleeing a war or something..." Sir Judas stopped and asked one person he was passing, "Excuse me, young man, but what is the crisis that has driven such a great number of you to this camp?" The man looked at Sir Judas with confusion and was about to answer, but then he saw he was speaking to a black knight. With an expression of fear, he closed his mouth and hurried on his way. "Odd," Sir Judas commented.

Making their way further into the camp (and seeing what Sir Judas considered a surprisingly high number of water merchants), the black knight continued to try and ask random strangers for some information, but no one was willing to talk to him. His efforts instead had a most counterproductive effect, for word of the 'inquisitive' black knight was traveling faster than Sir Judas and David were. Before long concerned onlookers and boisterous men were coming out to stand on street corners and try to look tough.

It was to one such group of three young men, posturing and puffing out their chests that Sir Judas walked up and said with a pleasant smile, "Excuse me, young men, but I am in search of a merchant selling foodstuffs. Well-preserved foods for a journey, you see. Is there someone in this camp you would suggest I buy from?"

One of them spat a glob of saliva at Sir Judas's boot and sneered, "Black knights ain't welcome here!"

Without missing a beat or souring his demeanor, Sir Judas said, "Yes, so I am told, and so I see. But the faster I find food, the faster I can leave your town in peace. So for the sake of saving your neighbors and being the hero who drove the dreadful black knight from your lands, could you point me towards a merchant who will carry such foodstuffs?"

The knight's response caught the three men off guard, and they looked at each other uncomfortably. One of them (perhaps the most motivated by 'heroic glory') bumbled, "Uh…Curly Kayden has a shop with…that kind of food. Go way up to the first row of buildings and then it's two blocks up and one block left. Big place, easy to find…"

"Hurrah!" Sir Judas cheered, "Now the day is surely saved! We shall get our food and flee to the south. By tomorrow morning you will have delivered your town from the dreadful scourge that has come upon you!" Laughing and assuming the sarcasm was apparent, Sir Judas held out a hand to shake with the man who had helped him. Instead the man jumped back in fear, then turned and scurried away with his friends. Meanwhile the onlookers all began to talk, with little bits and pieces of their irrational madness drifting into David's ears.

"Dreadful scourge! He said it himself!"

"What are we gonna do?"

"I think that kid had it right. Help him out."

"Lay low!"

"That way we all get out of this alive."

"Should we call the guards?"

"No, no, no…then a fight is sure to happen."

"What if he doesn't leave?"

"Well then we have no choice."

"Black knights were never known for their honesty…"

"Let's hope he leaves, let's hope he leaves. Give him some food and let him be someone else's problem."

As Sir Judas and David resumed their journey, the black knight frowned and muttered, "Odd, odd, odd…what on earth are they so afraid of?" The crowd now began to dissipate, and word spread that the black knight 'will be gone by tomorrow morning.' Everyone went from trying to obstruct his path to trying to stay out of his way, giving a nice wide berth to the black-armored terror. Perhaps because everyone was avoiding them, David did not notice the usual end-of-day bustle in the camp. He and Sir Judas walked all the way up to the first row of ramshackle wooden buildings (still a quarter mile or so outside the walls) before Sir Judas commented, "How odd, but everyone seems to have gone indoors for the evening."

Only then did David realize the sun had already set behind the city. "Oh, darn it. I forgot to tell you, the sun sets very fast here. We should try to find a good alley or something to sleep in right now."

"Set's fast?" the knight inquired, "What could you possibly mean? I've traveled halfway around the world, and the sun always sets at exactly the same speed."

"Not in Chelles. We only have a few minutes left before it's completely dark, especially with it being so close to the new moon."

Sir Judas chuckled. "The sun may be going down behind the city, but we'll have at least an hour of twilight to walk by before we can't see. Now come, let's–"

The words died in his mouth as the amber and violet sky turned to blackness in a moment. As soon as his eyes adjusted, Sir Judas could see the stars, though he could not see more than a faint outline of David two feet in front of him. "Well...right when this old man thinks he's seen it all, it turns out God has a few more surprises in store to keep him humble. This is truly a marvel I've never seen before!" Groping forward, he found David and laid a hand upon his shoulder. "Well, my boy, you were right, and I've gotten us stuck in the dark. Since you have the younger eyes and the better knowledge of this place, please lead me to a good spot for us to pass the night."

"I'll do my best..." Barely making out the buildings, David made his way to the edge of the street and ran his hand along the building on his left. He was looking for an alley, but where the first building ended there was only a six-inch gap before the next one began. Then he was in the middle of the road– couldn't sleep there in case someone rode through on important business–then he felt along a series of more buildings that were all cramped together.

As they were walking along, Sir Judas asked, "David, why is it that there are so many buildings set up outside the walls? Wouldn't they get destroyed every time an enemy army came through?"

"No one does that around here, Sir Judas. I forget the fancy name for it...'Packs Chellesian' I think? But it means there are no enemy armies to worry about. Every city is at peace with Chelles for a long ways away. In all my life no army ever came through."

"Incredible...my hat is certainly off to Lord Fearnow and the magistrates of this land on that front. So much peace that men are building cities outside of walls...I don't know if there has been such a time since before the Great Calamity."

"Wasn't the Grand Empire like that?" David asked. "If the king had conquered everything, then shouldn't entire countries have all been at peace?"

"Oh, not really, I'm afraid to say. The Grand Empire was a very loose empire. *Very* loose. The king only had a few laws that he promulgated throughout the realm, and other than that he left the various cities to manage their own affairs. They often went to war with each other for all the reasons men always fight. The king would send paladins to act as diplomats, negotiators, sometimes arbiters…but for the most part, conflict within the empire was tolerated. I mean that in the proper sense, you know, not the way that word is often used. 'Tolerance.' The king was deeply grieved to see city fighting against city, tribe making war with tribe. But in the proper sense, tolerance is recognizing that preventing an evil would require creating a greater one. The king realized that he would never be strong enough to prevent wars until he was strong enough to become a tyrant. He resisted that temptation…not many men do. He had seven paladins, the sworn soldiers of Nouen, and that was it. He accepted nothing else; he would have no other armies. If men made an alliance with him to fight against some threat, they were always dismissed when the battle was over. Even when the Grand Empire was at its greatest, the king in many ways was still just the lord of the royal city."

Growing frustrated with his inability to find a good alley, David turned down the next road they came to and kept groping along. "So then why is he remembered as such a tyrant? That's what I've always heard about him. That his rule was 'oppressive.' They say all the nations 'had to rebel.' That doesn't sound like what you're saying at all."

Sir Judas smiled a bitter smile. "This is only one man's opinion, David, since I cannot speak on behalf of those you've spoken with. From what I've come to know of human nature though, I would say this. If the king had made laws that strictly regulated every detail of men's public lives, but they were permitted to commit any sin they wanted in private, men would praise him for creating a 'free society.' But the king left men's public lives almost entirely free, free to organize and rule themselves in any manner they desired. It was their private sins he outlawed–and even then, only the ones that cry out to heaven for vengeance. Everything else he *tolerated*–recall what that word means, now. He had a handful of laws against the gravest crimes one man can commit against another. For those laws men considered him more tyrannical than the despots by whom they were 'liberated' when the Empire fell. That's human nature, David. Men don't value the freedom to do good half as much as the freedom to do evil."

David frowned. "I don't agree with that at all. I think most people are good, they just need some guidance. That's where it sounds like the king went wrong. He didn't give people enough guidance or help. He was too worried about 'sins,' and not worried enough about protecting his Empire, which is actually the king's job."

Sir Judas chuckled. "You sound less like a twelve-year-old who never saw the Empire, and more like a graybeard who watched it fall. Are those the things Winthrop told you?"

David blushed. "I can form my own opinions."

"I'm not saying you can't. I'm saying you didn't. There's nothing wrong with that, by the way. When we're young the only way we can know about most things is from the elders who teach us. So now I'm telling you to listen to your elder and let him teach you. The king reflected very deeply on the purpose and duties of kingship. He thought, and prayed, and meditated often on how he should rule, and then once he had discerned the proper course he never swerved from it either for the sake of fear or popularity. He was a great king. Perhaps even a perfect one. But even if you aren't convinced that he was great or right, at least be convinced that he thought much harder about these issues than you, me, or Winthrop. For that much, at least, we ought to give him a humble deference."

David was very grateful that it was currently dark out, for he felt deeply embarrassed after Sir Judas rebuked him. He was also grateful that an opportunity to change the subject presented itself, for he finally found what he had been looking for. Between where one building ended and the next began he felt a gap of about three feet–large enough to sleep in, not large enough to ride a horse down. "I found an alley, Sir Judas, this is where we can stay tonight."

"Oh good, good, I was–ach! I was just beginning to feel a little weary from our journey…"

"Are you okay, Sir Judas?"

"Yes, yes, nothing to worry about. When you get to be my age, nighttime gets very hard. I'll feel better in the morning…" Sir Judas walked a little way into the alley and dropped his bag with a heavy rattle. "Oops…hope I didn't damage the crossbow. I forgot it was in there…" He then unrolled his bedroll and laid down on it, while David did likewise. Before trying to get at least a little sleep, Sir Judas said his usual prayer for poor sinners. *O Lord, if it is possible that I could do some penance for poor sinners, I ask that you would send me sufferings while pouring out on their hearts Your love and the grace of conversion.* Then he asked David, "I'm about to recite the prophecy from memory for myself. Would you like me to say it out loud again?"

David smiled. "I would."

Sir Judas did so;

> "When you see a night illumined
> By the moon as if by the sun,
> When the storm has passed,
> Look to the east.
> The beast of grateful eye and might
> Shall carry you fast...
> To the hour when one guard will end
> And the new take up his blade
> Cleansed from blood by a weapon of Truth.
> Try him by combat,
> And if he shall overcome,
> Open his heart
> With the piercing of purest love."

They sat in silence together, looking up at the dark, moonless sky. Finally, Sir Judas said "Good night," and became quiet as he sought a few hours of rest before his nightly pains were too severe to sleep through. David was still smiling. It felt odd to smile. Winthrop still weighed heavily on David's heart. The outskirts of Chelles were always a frightful place to be. Rowan and Garrett had died. The glade was a terrifying experience. Nevertheless, he was smiling. Sir Judas had that quality. In only a day and a half of knowing him–a day and a half filled with many crushing sorrows–David had already begun to realize Sir Judas was often smiling, and his smiles were infectious. David drifted off to sleep with a smile of his own, having caught the contagion known as 'joy.'

Chapter 2: An Unholy Ruckus

At some unknown hour in the darkness that was either Tuesday night or Wednesday morning, Sir Judas was awoken by an odd and unnatural sound in the distance. There was a deep pulsing rhythm, along with the shouts of many people. Having no idea what he was hearing, Sir Judas groped around until he found David, and then shaking him gently he whispered, "David! David! Wake up! Do you hear that sound?"

David groggily rubbed his eyes. "What sound?"

"How can you not hear it? That pulsing, sound in the distance. Whatever could it be?"

The boy yawned. "That's the heart of Chelles, Sir Judas."

"The what?"

David shrugged. "I don't really know myself. Winthrop never let me in the city. Supposedly they need it to run all night long in order to keep the city going."

Picturing something like the great water wheels he had seen used for powering mills and factories, Sir Judas asked, "But must this thing really run all night? What could anyone possibly be using it for while they're sleeping? That racket is going to keep everyone awake. It must be deafening up close."

Slightly annoyed that Sir Judas was talking about people not getting to sleep while continuing the conversation, the boy answered, "It's one of those things you get used to. The first time I ever stayed here the heart kept me awake, but Winthrop snored right through it." With a big yawn David added, "Winthrop used to say you can get used to anything after a while."

"Hmm…" Sir Judas said no more, not wishing to dwell on the still sensitive wound of Winthrop's departure. He laid back down, but knew he wouldn't get to sleep. Besides the disquieting noise coming from the city, his night time anguish had already grown severe. Doubts and fears were swirling around his head, making his heart beat faster with anxiety. He heard David's voice asking, "Sir Judas, why did you say all those things to Winthrop today?" He bit his lip, replaying the whole scene in his mind, feeling a terrible guilt, like there was something he should have done differently. A moment later, David asked again, "Sir Judas? Did you hear me? Or are you already asleep?" Only then did he realize the voice was really David, and not just an attack of his imagination.

"Oh, yes, David. I'm awake. I'm awake. Sorry, I was…lost in thought. What was your question again?"

"Why did you say all of those things to Winthrop today? In the glade? Right before he left…"

The knight let out a long sigh, then said, "To be honest, David, I don't entirely know myself. Normally, I'm one to refrain from pointing out the splinter in my brother's eye, especially when I have so many beams sticking out of my own. For all his flaws, there is a lot of goodness in Winthrop, and I was hoping that if he accompanied me on my journey, I might be able to encourage that good and help him leave his evil ways behind."

Sir Judas propped himself up on one elbow and turned towards David. "But when you were so sorry for your crimes, and so desirous to set things right, in that moment, you were truly beautiful, David. I think Winthrop saw that beauty too, and he was frightened of it. That beauty threatened him, and so he wanted to stomp it out. He wanted to shatter it to a bunch of glistening little pieces so that it wouldn't threaten him any longer. Not out of malice for you, I don't think, but just to protect himself. He wanted you to 'get used to' the guilt, just like he has gotten used to any and everything. As long as he was forced to look at your beautiful repentance, his own conscience would afflict him."

There was a low rattle of armor as Sir Judas sat all the way up. "But you shouldn't get used to it! No one should. I hadn't thought this all out yet, but in the heat of the moment in the glade I sensed that you needed to be protected, and Winthrop needed to be shocked out of his ugly comfort. I wanted him to start thinking again, to really start thinking about all the things he has gotten used to. I wanted him to realize he has gotten used to a life without love, even though that shocked him so much that it scared him away…

Sir Judas then laid back down and looked up at the stars in the sky. "We paladins never marry nor have children, David. It is an oath we swear so that we will be free to be a father to every person we ever meet, instead of only being a father to our natural relations. The best I can say for myself is that I was trying to show you a father's protection and to show Winthrop a father's correction. Even though it hurt to watch one of my children walk away, I still believe I did the right thing…but I do grieve for the terrible pain I have caused you. I am truly sorry for that, David."

David was lying on his back as Sir Judas spoke, looking up at the stars himself, the way he and Winthrop had done so many times before. As the paladin concluded, David closed his eyes and felt gentle tears roll down his cheeks. "I'm glad you said what you did, Sir Judas. I know Winthrop is a good guy. He might keep it hidden away deep down somewhere, but he's always been good to me."

As he took in the sky once more, David said to himself, *Wherever Winthrop is, I hope he's looking up at the same stars right now.* He closed his eyes and drifted off to sleep. Sir Judas tried to keep the ruckus of his groans and pain to a minimum as he laid there dueling with unpleasant thoughts.

Sir Judas was drifting somewhere between the delirium of waking and the nightmare of sleeping when he heard a loud shouting that woke him up completely. The dim light of morning twilight had begun to brighten the sky. There was a repeated pounding–much closer than before–the sound of someone banging on a wooden door, while yelling at the top of his lungs, "*Saaassshhaaaaa!!!!*" After his shout there was a chorus of laughter–at least three men, maybe more–hoots and hollers and whistles of encouragement. Again the first man yelled, "*Saaassshhaaaaa!!!!*" as he continued banging the door.

Sir Judas shook David awake and said, "Arise, David! We are needed!"

David rolled over and rubbed his eyes, looking at the knight crouched over him with confusion and drowsy listlessness. "Needed for what?"

"Open your ears! There's a gang of men harassing a maiden named 'Sasha.' By my count of the voices there are at least four, maybe five of them. Come with me, and I'll tell them to leave. Just your presence will help, since it will make them realize this isn't one crotchety old man telling them off, but that decent people in general find their behavior odious. Come along now, David."

Slowly, nervously rising, David whispered, "But we don't know these people. Shouldn't we mind our own business?"

"Protecting the vulnerable, and especially women, is every man's business. Now come along!"

Despite his misgivings (and to be honest, befuddlement), David found himself up and walking alongside Sir Judas as they exited the little alley they had slept in. Sir Judas was swaying back and forth, using the two buildings on either side to steady himself, but once they got out onto the road he could only hobble a few steps before saying, "Oof! Come here, David. Let me lean on you…ah, much better…thank you!"

They crossed the road and went down another alley, then reached another cross street where they turned left. Rounding the corner, David realized the building on their left was quite large, sprawling ahead of them for a good distance. In addition to the main floor, there was a wooden staircase that went up to a squat little second storey. Sir Judas's count was accurate, as four men stood down at the bottom of the staircase laughing and making merry, while the fifth was up at the top of the stairs banging on the door and yelling, "*Saaassshhhaaaaa!!!!*" From the way they were all swaying, they were very clearly drunk.

Sir Judas let go of David, and setting his left hand on the building to steady himself, he slowly approached the young men. David faltered and hung back, afraid of the confrontation about to take place. He was still lingering near the corner of the building when Sir Judas reached the group and asked, "Children, what are you doing carrying on like this?"

The men burst into a fit of laughter, two of them nearly falling over, one of them actually doing so, holding his belly as he breathlessly cackled. The man at the top of the stairs yelled down, "Go away old man! Sasha's my girl! This is where I live!"

"Ah, I see. So your wife locked you out. I can't say I blame her, though it does make things more complicated…"

Now another man at the bottom of the stairs fell over, while one of the two left standing yelled, "You gettin' hitched, man? Can I be in the wedding party?"

The man at the top of the stairs came thundering down, getting right up in Sir Judas's face. In the dim light it was hard to make out much about him, other than he was a little short, a little scrawny, and had tight little curls of hair all over his head. He said, "What's it to you if we're married or not, huh? What's it to you? Is it any of your business? No! Shut up and buzz off!"

"Oh my! So you aren't even married to this woman? Yet you live together? What a scandal…in that case…tell me, do you know this woman's father? We must call on him tomorrow to begin a proper courtship."

The four acquaintances of the man fell into hysterics. "C-c-call on her…with her–hey, man, have you talked to her father yet? This is too funny…Courtship! You should discuss *courtship* with her father, Kayden!"

The man in Sir Judas's face, who had been yelling, '*Saaassshhhaaaa!!!!*' shoved the black knight saying, "Enough, old man! Move it along! I don't know what kind of game you're playing here, but I'm sick of it. Go back to the rock you crawled out from before I get annoyed and mess you up."

Sir Judas rolled his right shoulder back, causing his cloak to open and reveal his sword. "Young man, you stand before a knight. It is our greatest duty to protect, and our greatest shame if we should forsake. I will not forsake this woman and leave her to the drunken madness of you and your thugs, even if when you are sober she decides to dishonor herself. Now go sleep with one of your friends, and come back when you are no longer senseless."

In the dim light of that pre-dawn hour, the man and Sir Judas stared at each other for a long, tense moment, both unblinking, both unflinching, though Sir Judas could barely stand. The man clenched a fist and raised it slowly. Sir Judas said, "Don't do it, son. I don't want this to be the last night of your life."

The man cocked back to throw a punch, and Sir Judas grabbed his dagger. Just then David ran up beside Sir Judas and said, "If you wanna take Sir Judas, you're gonna have to take me too!"

His comment, given in earnest, nevertheless broke the tension. The men laughed louder than ever. The one who had been about to attack said, "What am I supposed to do, beat up a kid and an old man? This is ridiculous…let's come back later, guys." He banged on the wall of the ground floor twice and yelled, "Hey, Sasha! I'll be home before lunch, alright? See ya, babe!" He then staggered away with his posse, plenty of drunken jokes and jeers being passed around. When the group was almost out of sight, the man turned around and yelled, "Don't think this is over, old man! I'll make sure you pay for ruining my night with my girl!" The men then waddled around a corner, swaying and laughing as they shoved each other.

Once they were gone and out of earshot, Sir Judas slapped David on the back and said, "Well done, David! Well done! You jumped in at just the right moment to keep that confrontation from escalating. Well done!"

David felt a certain weakness come over him as the adrenaline faded, and he realized how afraid he had really been. "I'm glad it all worked out…though it didn't go quite how I had planned…I was trying to act tough, and they just laughed at me instead."

"Ah, don't worry about your plans, David. Let God do the planning! You did what was right, and it worked out for the best. Now this Sasha (and everyone else in the neighborhood) can have a modicum of peace this morning." In all his excitement, Sir Judas didn't even realize that the sun had risen and he had recovered from his nighttime sufferings.

"But Sir Judas, what about the threat he made as he was leaving? Those guys could jump us around any corner in the city. They might attack us before we leave."

"If they do, they do. And maybe we'll die. But at least we'll die knowing we did the right thing. That's a far better fate than living knowing we didn't."

Sir Judas and David shared a long look, the knight smiling with giddy excitement, the boy looking back with as much confusion. Eventually David said, "Sir Judas…I know you said you're from a different country…but I'm really starting to think you're from a different world. I need to keep a running list of the craziest things you say, and try to figure out the wildest one."

The old paladin chuckled. "I'm not from a different world, but I certainly am of one. And in addition to writing down all these crazy sayings, you also need to make a note of how often I turn out to be right. I think it's good for a man to be a little crazy, just so long as it's the craziness of knowing the truth."

David was about to ask another question, but he was preempted by a woman yelling, "Hey! Hey! Get up here!" The door at the top of the stairs was cracked open, and a woman in a nightgown was waving a hand and gesturing for Sir Judas to come up and see her. "Quickly, you! Come up here!"

"Ah!" Sir Judas smiled, "It would seem the 'Sasha' that 'Kayden' was shouting for has come out to thank us."

"Um…Sir Judas…I'm pretty sure that woman is very angry at us."

At that same moment she yelled an unspeakable word for an old man, then followed up saying, "Yeah I'm talking to you! Get up here!"

Sir Judas nodded his head knowingly. "Ah, the nerves of all this excitement…I've seen this many times before, David. She's still very rattled from that man banging on the door. Let us go meet her, but don't be startled if she suddenly starts crying or laughing wildly. This happens with women of a more delicate constitution."

Sir Judas then bounded up the stairs. When he reached the landing, he dropped to one knee and said, "My fair dear, you may rest assured that those hooligans have been driven off, and you need not fear any more unwelcome advances for now. The one man suggested there was a relationship between you two. I don't know if this was mere bravado on his part, or if it was actually true, but you at least won't have to deal with him in a drunken state."

At this point, as the author of this history, I must stop and explain something about the women of Chelles. Due to the deplorable lack of morals in the city–as well as the tendency of a certain kind of woman to employ and embellish the vulgar expressions of men beyond all reason or decency–the women of Chelles had the habitual tendency to speak in a manner that would make a sailor blush. The torrent of vile profanities that spewed from their mouths was not necessarily any indication of emotion or anger, but simply the manner of speaking that was common in this place.

Now as bad as the average woman was, the one Sir Judas was now speaking to, Sasha, had grown far worse from years of banter with all manner of persons in her line of work. In order to entertain and delight customers with her 'unique' and 'daring' conversation, she was always inventing new and unheard of ways to describe the most common of objects in shocking language. For the sake of propriety, I, as a historian and a knight, cannot even countenance the thought of recording her actual words. Instead, I am forced to write a much cleaner summary of Sasha's dialogue and trust that you the reader will remember the general manner of her speech as the story progresses.

Now as I had said, Sir Judas had just informed this 'fair dear' that he and David had driven off the man she was in a relationship with. She replied by coming out of the door and buffeting Sir Judas on the top of his white head repeatedly as she shouted, "What the *hell* were you thinking, you *jerks*?" David's eyes went wide. Even Garrett had never been so crass. And he used to breed goats.

On she went, continuing to slap and yell without slowing or wearying. Sir Judas raised his hands over his head to protect himself and cried aloud, "Ah! Better to have fallen into the hands of her suitor than into the hands of the woman herself! What folly of me to think I was protecting a delicate flower! Instead I should have called for her to come to *my* aid!"

David was enthralled by this very bizarre scene, for Sasha seemed to be completely in earnest, swatting and cursing until she was red in the face. Sir Judas on the other hand was laughing, and seemed to be making light of the assault. This of course spurred Sasha to greater fury, which only seemed to make Sir Judas laugh harder. After at least a minute of this 'conflict' Sir Judas finally stepped away from her and professed, "It seems my services were most unwelcome. Forgive my rudeness, and may we depart your presence in peace."

He trundled down the stairs as she yelled after him, "I can take care of myself! Thanks for nothing!" She disappeared inside and slammed the door.

As Sir Judas reached the bottom of the staircase he shrugged at David. David burst out laughing, and said, "The very first entry in the book of 'Crazy things Sir Judas says' will be, 'She's still very rattled...this often happens with women of a more delicate constitution.' I'll be sure to note that one turned out to be false."

"What are you talking about?" Sir Judas said with feigned surprise. "That woman was exceptionally rattled! Though if her constitution can be judged from her mouth, she's not exactly 'delicate'." He and David then walked back to where they had slept, both trying (and terribly failing) not to burst out into well-earned laughter.

Chapter 3: Shopping at Curly's

After packing up their effects, David and Sir Judas walked back to the main road and tried to get their bearings. They figured out where the first row of buildings began, then counted off the blocks according to the directions they had been given the day before. As they ended up backtracking the way they had just come, a sinking pit began to form in David's stomach. Sure enough, the very large building where they had encountered the drunk men had a faded green sign with yellow letters reading, 'Curly Kayden's General Store.'

"Uh oh," David said. "Now we're in trouble."

"Yes, so it would seem," Sir Judas answered. Nevertheless, he tried pulling on the door handle to enter. It was barred shut from the inside. "It seems we got here too early!" Sir Judas announced. "Assuming the curly headed young man and the woman we met last night are the proprietors of this establishment, I suspect it will be some time before they are awake and ready for business."

Sir Judas sat down with his back against the wall of the shop. David asked, "Aren't you worried they won't do business with us, Sir Judas? They were very upset."

"Oh, it's certainly a possibility. But it's also possible we can talk things out and cooler heads will prevail. I'm not saying it's likely, but at the moment it's the best lead we have. If needs must, we can march to the next town on our existing food stores, but I don't like letting them get too low. Let's at least wait an hour or so and see if we can't replenish them here."

David felt uncomfortable with the plan of action, but he sat down beside Sir Judas just the same. At this hour there was no one else out and about. After a few minutes Sir Judas said, "I'm surprised there aren't more people going to work this morning. The sun is already up and I haven't seen a single laborer yet."

"Most people don't get up until around mid-morning in Chelles," David answered. "A lot of them go into the city late into the night and then need to catch up on sleep during the day."

Sir Judas shook his head. "Wasting away the day just to stay out late at night! And with the moon so dark this time of the month! What is there to even do on a night like last night?"

"They have all sorts of lights in Chelles," David answered. "All along the streets, all inside of the buildings. It's just as bright at night as during the day. They call it 'the city that never sleeps.'"

Sir Judas harrumphed, "City that never sleeps! But you just told me they sleep all morning! What an incredible squandering of resources, lighting that many lamps just to waste the day away. What do they even run them on around here? Wax? Oil? I didn't see anyone lumbering the woods we hiked through, that's for sure."

"They use electro-magic in Chelles," David answered. "No resources required."

Sir Judas clenched his jaw, and his face immediately darkened. "Did you say…electro-magic, David?"

"Yeah, it's some really incredible stuff. I don't know if they had it in the royal city, but in Chelles that's why everyone wants to be here. It's the only city in the area with an unlimited supply of electro-magic." David tapped his palm to his forehead as he realized, "That's why you were confused by the pulsing last night. The 'heart' of Chelles is what produces all of the electro-magic."

Sir Judas grimaced as he ran a hand through his hair. "Electro-magic…the spellcraft of our fathers…"

Not noticing Sir Judas's concern, David added, "Someday I hope I can go into Chelles…all my friends say right when you come in there is this incredible display of electro-magic that is the most beautiful thing they've ever seen."

Sir Judas said nothing, wondering what to make of David's revelation. A quarter of an hour passed. At that time a middle-aged woman came walking by. She seemed ordinary enough to David, but Sir Judas was intrigued by her attire. With trousers, belt, shirt, and shoes, she was dressed in a positively masculine fashion, yet with colors and trim that made the clothing distinctly feminine. He had noticed the same thing about the women he saw yesterday, but had not had the time to ponder it. Some of the women they passed wore skirts or dresses, but the most common clothing was pants and shirts. *What a bizarre land,* Sir Judas thought to himself. *No war, no morning bustle, and a completely novel fashion…and I'm not even within the walls! What a strange place Chelles has become these last few decades…*

As the woman passed by on the opposite side of the road, Sir Judas asked, "Excuse me, but would you happen to know what time this establishment usually opens?" The woman turned to answer Sir Judas, but as she saw his black cloak and chain mail, she grabbed her heart and shrieked. She then ran on the way she was already going, nervously checking over her shoulder every few paces to see if she had been followed. "Well that was less than helpful," Sir Judas commented.

As might be expected, before long several people came to investigate the cause of the scream. Then they started muttering, and a loose ring of onlookers began to form in the neighborhood of Curly Kayden's store. People were pointing and talking amongst themselves about how 'He was supposed to be gone by the morning!' Others pointed out that he was indeed at the general store, and he would likely be gone very soon. As the black knight kept sitting there, however, the patience of the mob was wearing thin.

At length, Sir Judas finally said, "Well, David, I am beginning to suspect the store may be closed today. Or at least, it won't be opening in time to be of value to us. The locals don't seem friendly enough to point us to a different merchant, so why don't we press on and try our fortunes elsewhere before a riot breaks out?"

"Should we knock before we go?"

Sir Judas shrugged. "I suppose it couldn't hurt, though we'll see how much good it does us." He stood up and rapped three times on the door. To his surprise, he heard the sound of sudden motion come from behind it, and Sasha's voice yelling, "Give me a *minute*!" There was a sound of clanging and thuds as she hurried about.

"Hmph! Shows me, David! The Scriptures say to 'knock and the door shall be opened'. This dunderhead just has a terrible habit of taking things too figuratively, never noticing the literal meaning that's right before his eyes."

David was a little embarrassed by his own ignorance, but eventually his curiosity won out. "Sir Judas, what are the Scriptures? You mentioned them two nights ago in the glade too, but I've never heard of them. Are those the magic books that help you cast your spells?"

"What? Of course not! A paladin would never cast a spell! Magic is evil, David."

"Well I mean, black magic obviously is, but white magic never hurt anybody. And gray magic can either be good or evil depending on how it's used."

"Who on God's green Earth told you that? It sounds like a lie from hell if I ever heard one."

David blushed. "I–I can't think of any one particular person who told me that… Everybody knows there are different kinds of magic. It's common knowledge."

"To the contrary, if everyone thinks there are different kinds of magic, it is not common knowledge but rather a common error."

David bit his lip and looked away meekly, but then another idea struck him. "Sir Judas, I just remembered; isn't the study of magic forbidden in most places besides Chelles? You probably haven't heard of the different types of magic because the scholars don't study it where you come from."

Sir Judas clenched his fists, about ready to give David an angry lecture from his own first-hand experience with magic and magicians. At that moment, however, a sliding sound came from inside the store, and the door swung open. "We'll have to discuss this later," Sir Judas said, and walked into Curly Kayden's General Store.

Sasha did not linger to greet them. Instead, by the time Sir Judas entered she had already run elsewhere, hurriedly setting about getting organized for the day ahead. David came in behind Sir Judas, and looked around at the impressive rows of shelves running for a good distance in every direction. Sir Judas was not looking at the great variety of products, but was instead focused on the very strange product right where he came in. There was a very small well with a wooden cover, closed tight and sealed by a large chain and padlock. A sign above the well read, 'Water: 4 C per gallon. Please contact a store associate to assist you with this product.' "Strange, strange, strange city," Sir Judas muttered to himself. "And somehow, it just keeps on getting stranger…"

Turning away from the locked well, Sir Judas called out, "Excuse me, but we are looking for dried foodstuffs for a journey."

"Over this way!" Sasha called. "Third aisle on the left, about halfway down. We've got dry food that's so good, it would—" Her description involved dogs, sausage, and a violin. David's face immediately turned green, and he lost all interest in looking at the food that was available.

Nevertheless, Sir Judas said, "Thank you," and led the way down the indicated aisle. He saw his options all laid out, a variety of cheeses, nuts, jerkies, and hard breads, as well as a tray for carrying items up to the checkout desk. Every food item had a little sign listing a price, not exorbitant, but more than Sir Judas had been expecting to pay. He looked carefully for the cheapest options, while calling out to Sasha, "Do you accept barter or just coin?"

"If you wanna barter, there better not be any *trash*! Try to pass your junk off on me, and I'll kick you *out*!"

Sir Judas rubbed his brow and sighed heavily. Sasha's language was grating on him, but he held his tongue and said a quick prayer for her. Then he opened his coin pouch and counted what he had available, while contemplating what they might part with to make a fair trade. Sasha rushed over to a different part of the store, but yelled back at him, "You sound familiar. You been here before?"

"Er…yes, once before. Fairly recently." Overcoming his annoyance, Sir Judas added, "Thank you for opening up for us. We really do appreciate it."

"Yeah, I had a rough night last night. Kayden was an absolute *slob*, so I locked him out to teach him a lesson. But then this *black knight* came along and started threatening him, and turned my silly joke into a real fiasco. Kayden's been in a foul mood all morning."

"Ah, you don't say." Sir Judas finished picking out what he thought would be enough food for the next stretch of their journey, and then took a deep breath. This wasn't going to be pleasant.

"We have what we came for. Where would you like us to check out?"

"Middle aisle, back of the store. I'll meet you over there in a minute!"

Sir Judas and David went to the indicated place, where the knight put the tray of food on the counter and waited for what was sure to be an *eventful* conversation. After hurrying around a little longer, Sasha came rushing to the back with armfuls of the expired produce she was planning on selling to the local chicken farmer. As soon as he saw her, Sir Judas put his hands over his eyes and yelled, "Oh my goodness! I'm so sorry! We are not in a hurry that is anywhere near this important! Please, go finish getting dressed, and we will wait for you to return!"

Sasha dropped everything she was holding, and her pale, freckled face turned almost the same shade as her paprika hair. Sasha was wearing a white crop top and a black pair of leggings. Sir Judas, not knowing any better, assumed this must be what women normally wear beneath their dresses. While he had no idea why she would open the store wearing nothing but her 'underclothes,' he nevertheless concluded that his knocking on the door had caused her to start rushing, and he was somehow responsible for her state of undress. His deduction was, of course, completely false. Sasha was not wearing undergarments, but rather clothes of the latest Chellesian fashion. Not realizing Sir Judas was honestly mistaken, she interpreted his words as an insult from the same man who had already complained this morning over her and Kayden not being married.

"*Excuse* you! What did you just say to me, *you*? You *chauvinist*! Oh, what? Are women supposed to get all stuffed up to your particular taste? I have a newsflash for you, *sir*. Maybe I wasn't dressing to impress *you*! Maybe the whole *world* doesn't revolve around *you*! Did you ever think of that? Did it even cross your backwards old mind? Why should I dress to your taste instead of wearing what I want?"

Sir Judas was looking straight down at the ground with his hands still covering his face. Beginning to shake, he said, "W-What are you talking about? My tastes have nothing to do with it. You just opened the shop while you were still in your underwear. Why would you do such a thing? Why would you trade your feminine dignity for the chance to sell pickled vegetables and dried fruits? Do you really want my coin that badly?"

"*Are you out of your mind, you crazy old man*? Do you actually think I'm going to sell anything to you?"

At this point there was a loud banging of heavy footsteps coming down a staircase into the back of the shop. "What's going on? I told you I'm sleeping here!" Curly-headed Kayden was looking at them, and went from angry at Sasha, to confused, to angry at Sir Judas. "What are you doing here?!"

Sir Judas turned in his direction, still covering his eyes with his hands. "I simply wish to purchase some food stuffs and then I'll be on my way."

"Get out of my shop old man! Get out! Out!" He came charging at Sir Judas, and threw a punch right at his face.

David took in a sharp breath, thinking Sir Judas was about to be splayed out on the floor. Instead he leaned sideways, just a little, and Kayden's fist found nothing but air. Kayden, Sasha, and David all looked at the blinded knight in surprise. Kayden cocked back and swung again. Sir Judas ducked just below the punch. If Sir Judas's heart hadn't been breaking, the scene that followed would have been comical. Kayden started punching, shoving, and grabbing at Sir Judas while failing to even touch him. Keeping his hands over his face (for fear of seeing Sasha, who still seemed half-dressed to his understanding), Sir Judas twisted, turned, and backed away, constantly professing, "I'm so sorry, I just don't understand. Why would you…" The crowd of people from outside poked their heads in through the doorway to see what all the shouting was about. Seeing a 'fist fight' between Kayden and the dreaded black knight, several people took off running to summon the city guards.

Sasha started yelling to Kayden, "Hit him! Hit him! Come on, Kayden, stop messing around! You heard what he said last night! And just now! Just now he said I'm not wearing any clothes! He talks just like my father! Hit him! Hit him! Hit him already!"

Sasha yelled a while longer, when Sir Judas suddenly realized something. He stopped backing away, lowered his hands, and with tears in his own eyes, looked directly into Sasha's. "Your father really means something to you, doesn't he?"

Kayden stopped cold. Sasha went silent. Then she began to stammer. "Wh-wh–be you–what are you talking about? I hate my father! He's just an *old* man walking in a field of—"

"No," Sir Judas said, cutting her off. "From the minute we've met, you haven't stopped spewing a constant stream of disgusting language that is so outrageous it must clearly be some sort of act. But as soon as you started saying I was 'just like your father,' all of a sudden you were talking like a normal human being. You dropped the act. He must really mean something to you if his mere mention has such an effect."

"You–you don't know me! You don't know the first thing about me! And you certainly don't know anything about my father!" Despite her best efforts to remain calm, Sasha was crying now too.

Kayden grabbed Sir Judas by the front of his chain shirt, and this time the knight did not resist him. "You get out of here now!" He growled. Then he dragged Sir Judas to the door and threw him out into the street. Kayden turned around and pointed at David, "You too, kid! Out! Get out! I don't ever want to see you in here again!"

David swiftly walked across the floor, but as he was passing Sasha, he stopped to say, "I'm sorry. Sir Judas didn't mean to insult you. I promise, he really didn't. He's just from far away and he's very confused. Chelles isn't like where he comes from. But he didn't mean anything about your father. Honest, he didn't. I…" Tears were now in David's eyes. "…I just lost my father yesterday. At least, the closest thing I've ever had to one. He walked out on me, and…and he was a really bad guy I guess, but he was a good one too. And Sir Judas, he hasn't insulted him or disrespected him, or even anybody I've ever seen him meet. I'm sure he didn't mean to insult you either, he's just…like I said, he's just very, very confused right now…."

Kayden walked up to him and grabbed David by the back of the shirt. "Alright, move it along, kid. Get out of here!" Then he dragged him to the door, but Sasha yelled, "Kayden, wait!" She ran over to the counter and grabbed the tray of food Sir Judas had picked out and came back.

"Hey, what are you doing, Sasha? You aren't actually going to sell that to them, are you?"

She grabbed a large napkin, wrapped all the food in a little sack, and handed it to David. "Take it, please, just…take it!" And then she ushered him out the door.

"Hey!" Kayden yelled, "They need to pay for that!" But Sasha slammed the door and barred it. Then David heard the muffled sound of sobbing from the other side. He turned to Sir Judas, who was covering his face and shaking his head, still muttering, "I just don't understand…I don't…why?"

"Sir Judas," David whispered softly. "You should do something to comfort her…you should apologize."

He shook his head. "No, David. This is a pain we must feel. Her and I both. I can't take back my words. She needed to hear them. All I can do is pray for her and trust in God. This is a situation in need of healing beyond my powers."

Down the street, a voice could be heard shouting, "Over there! Over there! That's where the black knight was assaulting him!" The sound of metal greaves trotting down the road quickly followed.

"Besides," Sir Judas added, "it seems our time of going where we will in the city is at an end." Seven men in scale mail and green tabards surrounded Sir Judas and David, forming a menacing and deadly ring with the glistening tips of their spears.

Chapter 4: A Swift and Speedy Trial

David instinctively backed away from the spears, pressing tightly to Sir Judas. In contrast to the boy's natural terror at having weapons thrust in his face, Sir Judas wiped the tears form his eyes and made a pleasant smile. "How can I help you fine guardsmen today?"

The green tabards the guards wore had a golden snake emblazoned on the front. The man directly across from Sir Judas had a crown on the head of his snake, indicating his rank as the officer leading this posse of guards. He spoke up first saying, "Dear person, a very serious accusation has been leveled against you by many visitors to the city of Chelles, and proper residents of its adjoining lands, to the effect that you have violated most serious and solemn laws. In order to investigate these matters, we shall now begin a swift and speedy trial. I am the presiding officer at these proceedings, Officer Feifer. Lieutenant Louis here on my right shall be the official scribe for these proceedings. Louis, please produce the trial papers."

Louis removed his spear from Sir Judas's face and handed it to Officer Feifer. He then reached into a satchel on his hip and produced a thick stack of papers, a quill, and a small bottle of black ink. He sat down on the ground, got organized, and indicated to Officer Feifer that he was ready to proceed.

Feifer said, "Very well. The trial has now begun." Sir Judas smirked. Feifer asked, "Is something funny, dear person?"

"Yes, I must admit, I do find the idea of an outdoor trial with a spear in my face to be a rather silly concept. Is there really not a more dignified place like a courtroom for these proceedings?"

Officer Feifer shook his head. "Oh, travelers of alternative national origin...always thinking about their 'dignity.' Dear person, in this land you have the duty to receive a swift and speedy trial, lest the taxpayers should be unduly burdened with paying to investigate your guilt. Now, let us begin the trial. Officer Feifer presiding, Lieutenant Louis transcribing. Would the accused please state his full name for the record?"

"I am Sir Judas, Last of the Kingsguard."

Several of the other guards took a deep and sudden breath. Officer Feifer rolled his eyes. "Now, now, no need for fancy titles and posturing. Louis, please simply record that the elderly accused is named 'Judas.'" Louis wrote swiftly and furiously, while Officer Feifer continued, "And as for the younger accused, what is your name?"

David nervously answered.

Officer Feifer waited for Louis to catch up and then continued, "Judas, the good Lord Benjamin Fearnow, for the peace and prosperity of this realm, has enacted his most just decree that no armed soldier trained according to the ancient method of squireship may enter this realm unless in the service of some noble. Tell me now, Judas, are you an armed soldier trained according to the ancient method of squireship?"

Sir Judas laughed in his face.

"Truly? Truly? Am I an 'armed soldier trained according to the ancient method of squireship?' Come now, ask your question plainly. Do you wish to know whether I am a knight?"

The lower ranking guards took in a sharp breath again. Officer Feifer sighed heavily, but kept his composure. "No, Judas, 'knight' is a term we do not use in the official proceedings of this realm. We are also in the process of sunsetting that term in common usage, but that is neither here nor there. What matters in this trial is that we don't say, 'knight' because it is a loaded term invented by proponents of regressive military systems wishing to whitewash the past. The good Lord Benjamin Fearnow, by his most just decree, for the peace and prosperity of the realm, has forbidden the use of that term in any official capacity. Instead we use the more precise expression, 'armed soldier trained according to the ancient method of squireship'."

Sir Judas put a hand to his mouth while trying to stifle a laugh. David was wondering why the black knight was not taking the trial more seriously, given that the spears in their faces were very clearly communicating how grave the situation was. When he regained control of himself, Sir Judas asked, "But is it more precise language? Is it really? For in good faith, I am certainly a knight, but I have not been a 'soldier' in any earthly army for many decades now. And even if I were a soldier, all I would have to do is hand my weapons to David here, and I would no longer be an 'armed soldier.' Nevertheless, I would still be a knight, and pose the exact same non-existent threat to this land as when I was an ancient-trained, armed…oh whatever you just spelled out."

There was an uncomfortable silence from the guards. After a few moments, Lieutenant Louis said, "Officer Feifer, I believe in juridical language he would count as an armed soldier trained according to the ancient method of squireship, even if in common speech there might be some loopholes, like he said."

"Yes, yes, quite right, Louis. You're just playing games with the common tongue, Judas, but this issue is clear as day. Now that we've established you are in fact an armed soldier trained according to the ancient method of squireship, I must inquire as to whether or not you entered this realm while in the service of a noble?"

"In good faith," Sir Judas answered, "I have never been outside the realm in all my life. Since my earliest youth I have lived within the lands of the king, God rest his soul."

Now the guards were positively startled, looking around in confusion, lowering and raising their spears absent-mindedly while they asked each other,

"Did he just say that?"

"Is Louis allowed to write that down?"

"He has to, it's what he said."

"He can't write that down!"

"Separation of church and state…"

The crowd that had gathered around to watch the trial also became agitated, pondering many of the same questions among themselves. Feifer gestured curtly for all of his men to shut up and do their duty. They closed their mouths and re-raised their spears around Sir Judas and David. Officer Feifer then said, "I'm sorry, Judas, but you clearly come from some old-fashioned realm, so we should explain how things work in a more advanced society. You see, this is an official proceeding by the government, and therefore all mention of a power unproven by scientific hermeneutics, or a P.U.S.H. for short, is strictly forbidden. That applies to both the hypothetical all-powerful immaterial being you mentioned, as well as to the hypothetical portion of a human person that does not die. Both of those are classified as P.U.S.H.es. You're free to practice your religion privately, of course, but we can't have any P.U.S.H. talk in an official proceeding. Separation of church and state. Do you understand, Judas?"

"Yes, I think I'm starting to get the gist of this. Instead of using 'unproven' terms like 'God,' you want me to stick to the absolutely irrefutable term 'Unmoved Mover,' since natural science cannot offer any plausible explanation for where the 'push' that started the universe came from. Do I understand you correctly, officer?"

Officer Feifer frowned. "Judas, you are faced with some very serious accusations. Your life hangs in the balance, and you could lose it based on how the scoring of this trial turns out. Or even worse, you could be cast into the Void. Do you really want to add a three-point penalty for contempt of court?"

"Wouldn't I have to be in a court to be 'in contempt of court'? This looks more like a street to me."

Feifer sighed heavily. "I didn't want to do this, especially with you being a foreigner and all, but you've left me no choice. Louis, please deduct three points from Judas's trial score for flagrant contempt of court, in accordance with the trial proceeding legislation enacted by Lord Fearnow's most just decree."

Louis grimaced, and then looked up at Officer Feifer saying, "Um, officer…I hate to bring this up, but…per the most just decree concerning public discourse, calling the accused a 'foreigner,' is an insult that causes subliminal distress. Moreover, per the aforementioned most just decree on trial proceedings, if the presiding officer at a trial should engage in behavior that distresses the accused to the point of causing him to express contempt of court, then not only are the three points not deducted for contempt of court, but the accused must receive a two-point *bonus* to his trial score to reflect the difficulty he would have in setting forth his case in front of such a hostile presiding officer."

"Well, that wouldn't apply here," Officer Feifer stated, "Since he expressed contempt of court *before* I accidentally insulted him. The three-point penalty should still stand."

"Not so," Louis stated while holding up one of the pages of the trial document for Feifer to read. "As you can see right here, officer, the most just decree concerning trial proceedings *explicitly states* that 'even if the contempt should be expressed before the insult was made, the three-point penalty must still be waived since it is far more probable that the presiding officer was expressing *unarticulated hostility* than that the accused would show contempt for such fair and honorable proceedings without provocation.'"

Officer Feifer's face turned beet red, as he stammered, "Um, uh–oh my, I've gone and done it now. I am oh, oh so sorry, Judas. I've made a complete fool of myself. I had no idea I was insulting you. Do pardon me."

"Really?" Sir Judas asked. "You had no idea you were insulting me until a piece of paper told you otherwise?"

"Um, officer," Louis timidly interjected, "I'm very sorry, but that word you said just now that starts with an 'F' is also a forbidden term that insults and demeans individuals of reduced cognitive acuity. For bringing up a second act of hostility that causes distress in the same trial, the accused now receives an *additional* five-point bonus to his trial score, not to mention that if a third forbidden term is used, I will be forced to declare a mistrial."

"No, no, no," Officer Feifer said, "The word 'fool' *used* to be forbidden in official proceedings, but the most just decree from last winter specifically removed it from the list of forbidden terms because it is often used in a non-hostile manner, such as how I just used the term."

"*Actually* officer," Louis said, "Just last week the Committee published a new most just decree, which added that word back on the list, because they realized the fact that the word is *sometimes* used in a non-hostile fashion is being used to defend using it in a hostile fashion."

"When does that decree go into effect?" Officer Feifer asked. "Surely there must be some sort of waiting period so that we can have time to read the decree before it's enforced. They always give us a waiting period of thirty days or something."

"Normally you would be right, officer, but the Committee's explanatory note accompanying Lord Fearnow's most just decree said that because the forbidden terms are such a serious and oft neglected threat, the new modifications to the code were effective immediately."

Officer Feifer wiped his brow nervously. "Oh my…well this certainly isn't good…a whole new list of acts of hostility has been published, and I haven't even read it! How am I supposed to conclude a trial when I don't even know which words I say will distress the accused?"

Lieutenant Louis shrugged and said, "According to the Committee's explanatory note, the decrees Lord Fearnow made through their authority are all common sense measures that any reasonable person can comply with. I really doubt you will 'accidentally' distress the accused unless you are actually hostile towards him."

Officer Feifer smiled nervously. "Yes, yes, of course...I'm sure the Committee is right about that, just like everything else Lord Fearnow decrees..."

Sir Judas chortled. "Oh, this is too rich. If I understand these proceedings correctly, then instead of making a grumbletonian out of myself like a ninnyhammer, I shall use only the most rumbumptious language that is unlikely to have made it into the most just decrees of Lord Fearnow and his Committee. Therefore, I wish to state for the record that these decrees were either made by a gentleman of four outs, or–more likely–a bunch of highly-educated fribbles who rely on go-alongers to enforce their whims. Therefore, Officer Feifer, I do call you plainly to your face an individual lacking vertebral integrity, and defy you to prove to me that you are otherwise."

Officer Feifer frowned deeply. "Louis, don't write down what I'm about to say."

"Officer, you know it's not permitted to go off the record during a trial."

Feifer turned a sharp eye on Louis. "It concerns the Committee." Louis slowly lowered his quill. Feifer stepped close to Sir Judas and whispered menacingly, "You think you're so clever, playing games with our rules and laws. Maybe you are a bit clever, but not nearly as clever as stupid. You might be able to escape this trial, but if you embarrass or insult the Committee, they will subject you to a fate worse than death."

Sir Judas became serious. "The only fate worse than death is sin."

"You are a fool," Officer Feifer answered. "You only speak such ignorance because you have never seen the men cast into the Void. The things the Committee can do...you are ignorant. I've said enough."

Officer Feifer returned to his former position and took a deep breath. "Let us try to go back to where we began this side tangent. Judas, when you entered into the realm, were you or were you not in the service of some noble?"

"Again I tell you," Sir Judas answered, "I have never been outside the realm in all my life. I have lived in the king's lands since my earliest youth."

"Judas," Officer Feifer said curtly, "there is no king, and since the time of his death, the local realm has been the lands controlled by the local lord. The realm you are currently in is therefore Chelles and its adjoining territories."

"But that's not what the realm is!" Sir Judas exclaimed. "That has never been what 'the realm' is! By that definition, any manor lord with three acres and five serfs would be lord of his 'realm,' when we all know the realm is truly the former lands of the Grand Empire."

At this point the crowd erupted, and the guards surrounding Sir Judas and David all had to remove their spears and turn around in order to push back the angry mob. One man yelled, "Imperialist!" while another shouted, "Grand for who?"

Shouting over the crowd, Feifer yelled, "That is precisely the definition given by Chellesian law, Judas! In the example you just articulated, the realm would indeed be the three acres controlled by the manor lord. And for the love of God, don't you dare use the term, 'Grand Empire' ever again! That phrase is loaded language that has been strictly outlawed in this entire realm, and for speaking it just now you are guilty on the spot of a seven-point crime! Louis, what does that bring the total to?"

The crowd started quieting down slightly, waiting for Louis to pronounce the judgment that Sir Judas was 'guilty enough' for a public stoning. Instead, with ashen face and trembling hands, Lieutenant Louis pointed to the words he had just written down. "Officer Feifer…you just…you just referred to a P.U.S.H…that's your third trial infraction…the accused is free to go on mistrial…"

Officer Feifer blanched. "What, that's not…you must have heard me wrong…" He looked at the place Louis was indicating and reread the words he had just spoken. "For the love of…*God.* Why…why would I even say that?"

There was a moment of stillness and silence from the crowd, then someone shouted, "Kill Feifer!" and a great roar of assent went up. The mob that a minute ago had wanted to kill Sir Judas now turned its full wrath on the officer who had let him go completely free. They quickly laid hands on him and began pulling him in every direction, trying to drag him to who knows where in their mindless fury.

Sir Judas looked in shock as the guards allowed their leader to be mistreated and overwhelmed while they stood there doing nothing. "Aren't you going to help him?" Sir Judas shouted.

Lieutenant Louis sorrowfully watched his commander get assaulted. "I wish there was something we could do, Judas, but it would be against the law. The Committee has instructed us in no uncertain terms that we must allow the people to form a mostly peaceful protest when they think the guards aren't doing a good job."

"My God, you people are lunatics! This isn't a protest, it's a murder mob!" Sir Judas then charged into the throng, grabbing people and trying to pull them off of Feifer. He ended up taking a blow to the face and getting thrown backwards for his troubles, but he rose up and drew his sword, raising it high. The sword began to glow, and David thought it was going to shine like it did yesterday. But then the blade dimmed, flickered, and went out. The few people who even noticed it scoffed and jeered, "Like we've never seen glow magic before!"

The mob became a riot, flying fists and crashing bodies all swirling around Officer Feifer and Sir Judas, as the people fought to devour them both. David lost sight of Sir Judas when he was tackled by two men and blocked by more, and for a moment he feared the old man would die. But then there came a loud 'Crack! *Crackle!*' and a flash of blue light, sparks, and smoke, and the whole crowd went dead still in an instant. David looked in the direction of the sound. Sitting atop a great white warhorse was a man in a green tabard holding a little metal tube with smoke still pouring out of it.

The man David now saw was one who was difficult to describe. In a certain sense he was neither large nor small, but that might give the mistaken notion that he was average. In actuality, he was very short, standing just a touch over five feet, while also being very thick, with big meaty arms, powerful legs, and a full round face and head. He was clean shaven with a short brush of dark blonde hair, and the kind of light wrinkles that suggested he was in his forties. As he rode his horse forward, the crowd parted and backed away, showing the man a reverential fear. When he drew closer, David could make out that his tabard looked similar to Officer Feifer's. At least, that's how it seemed at first, but then he realized that the crown on the serpent's head was slightly different, having an extra ornament on top to show his heightened rank.

The man rode all the way up to the heart of the scrum, and the mob backed away so that only Sir Judas and Officer Feifer were left on the ground. Both were relatively unhurt with nothing more than a few minor injuries. Sir Judas stood and bowed to the man, but Officer Feifer spat at him and said, "Move it along, Joseph. There's nothing to see here."

"Have you no shame?" Sir Judas said to Feifer. "This man just saved us from a cruel beating at the least. Have you no gratitude?"

"Joseph here is a foreig–I mean, individual of distant origin, like yourself. And just like yourself, Judas, he has absolutely no respect for our laws or customs here in Chelles. Unlike yourself, however, he has been promoted to the highest ranks of our bureaucracy despite having less education and less time served than many of the people he was put over. Moreover, he is a flagrant malefactor who publicly opposes our Committee's activities. I would rather take the beating I deserve for making a mistrial in such an important case than be in his debt."

Sir Judas shook his head. "Sulk in your madness. From what little I've seen of this city's customs, I am grateful to meet a man who would challenge them." He then turned to Joseph, bowed again, and said, "Good Joseph, I thank you for your intervention. Pray tell me, what is your rank? How should I call you with proper manners?"

"Not now," Joseph answered flatly, "Not the time, not the place. Sir Judas (many people bristled at the word 'sir,' Officer Feifer included). If there has been a mistrial in your case, I cannot arrest you, but I do strongly encourage you to come to my personal residence so that I can sort things out. Will you accept this invitation?"

Sir Judas shook his head, "I am humbled by the offer, but I am afraid I must be pressing on. I have far to travel, and little time to travel it. I fear to lose another day. If I am truly free to go, I pray you would consider me excused."

Joseph sheathed his metal tube, dismounted his horse, and walked up to Sir Judas. Standing a full head shorter, he gestured for the knight to bend down so he could whisper in his ear. Sir Judas did, and Joseph spoke quietly, "I don't have time to explain everything that is going on. Short story is the Committee is going to come after you. They will soon hear what happened here. They may already know, if they have Administrators undercover in the crowd. Certain crimes they may overlook—even black knights have passed through our lands before—but you've committed the one crime they will never forgive nor forget until they have their vengeance. You've made a laughingstock of the Committee and their laws, and they'll throw you in the Void for it. Come with me. I'll keep you safe, and I'll try to get Lord Fearnow to grant you his protection. Free travel through all his lands, and maybe even a fast ride too, if I can help it."

Sir Judas looked to the southwest, unsure of how to proceed. To go with Joseph was the safest option, but he never would have set out on this quest if safety was his guiding star. He needed to be moving on…but this 'free travel' and a steed could be a time investment that would help him move much faster. Seeing that the knight was still unsure, Joseph leaned in again and whispered in his ear, "I'm a knight too, sir. Lord Fearnow dubbed me even though the

Committee made it illegal. And on my honor as a knight, I swear I will do everything in my power to keep you safe in this deadly city and help get you through our crazy land as fast as possible."

At these words Sir Judas felt a strength and comfort come to his heart. He gave Sir Joseph a nod and said, "Very well, I shall comply with your request and come to your personal residence to sort these matters out. This boy David is with me as well. Would I be correct in presuming he is also invited?"

"Of course, of course," Sir Joseph answered. "Very well. Good people of the Chellesian outskirts, know that this black knight shall no longer be at large, despite the mistrial that took place. He shall come with me so that Lord Fearnow can deal with him personally, and a proper end to these matters shall be arranged." There was much relief and a little clapping. Whether they thought Sir Joseph was leading Sir Judas to his death, who knows. People were happy just to know that things were being taken care of. Sir Joseph then ordered the guards (including Officer Feifer) to form up into a procession surrounding David and Sir Judas and lead them to his residence, with Sir Joseph at the helm.

They made their way through the remaining outskirts of Chelles, with the buildings growing progressively more and more large, impressive, and ornate as they neared the city gate. The long line of people waiting to enter the city had just come into view when a beeping sound came from Sir Joseph. He looked down at some glowing object in his hand and said, "Oh, what timing...I'm needed at the northern gate." He looked at Officer Feifer and said, "Feifer, this man had better make it to my residence alive."

Officer Feifer spat. "So long as he doesn't resist, he'll make it there alive. Not for you, but for the sake of the most just decrees."

Sir Joseph then said to Sir Judas, "Sir Judas, I must be off at once, but I will come back to my residence as soon as I am able. If Feifer, an Administrator, or the Committee try to give you any trouble–*any trouble* at all– you tell everyone who will listen that you are under Joseph's protection. Understood?"

"Understood." Sir Judas shouted. "But how will I know if someone is an Administrator or Committee member? Will they identify themselves?"

Sir Joseph turned his horse, and just as he began to ride away he yelled, "The Administrators wear a black mask over their eyes. The Committee members wear a white one that covers their entire face." Sir Judas and David's eyes went wide as Sir Joseph galloped out of view. Monday night they had fought two Administrators and a Committee member, who they only now recalled had been called 'Chairman.' Sir Judas doubted they would be able to cross this city in peace. He also expected their enemies would be far more numerous than in the glade. He took a deep breath and prayed, '*Rescue me from my enemies, O Lord, for I hide myself in Thee.*' Then he squeezed the hilt of his dagger as he remembered the opening to the next Psalm. '*Blessed be the Lord my God, Who teacheth my hands to fight, and my fingers to war.*'

As they marched forward and neared the gate, David tugged on Sir Judas's cloak, "This is it, Sir Judas! This is it! We're finally going to get inside the city! Oh, this isn't how I thought it would ever happen, but this is like a dream come true. I've always wanted to see what Chelles was like!"

For the first time since they had met him, Officer Feifer softened and actually made something close to a smile. "First time in Chelles, kid?"

"Yes, officer. I've been in the outskirts many times, but I've never been inside the city."

Feifer said to the other guards, "Alright, boys, full stop once we get inside. For the kid. Let him have some time to take it in." Then he scowled at Sir Judas. "Don't think I'm doing this for you."

"The thought hadn't even occurred to me."

They now reached a large stone arch housing an open set of wooden double doors, banded with brightly polished steel. The walls of Chelles were incredibly tall, fifty feet at least Sir Judas estimated. Moreover, up on top of the walls was a strange black screen, extending up another thirty feet all around the city. The posse reached the gatekeepers, where Officer Feifer gave a wave. One of the guards helping to process the line gave him a slap on the back and said, "Go on through."

At about noon on Wednesday they went under the arch, through the gate, and into a large plaza where many roads of the city all converged. This was it. The eastern plaza of Chelles. This was the place that droves of people traveled from miles away just to see. That vast sea of buildings and tents outside the walls existed because of all the people yearning to see this spectacular marvel. Sir Judas and David looked up, both utterly speechless because of what lay before them.

It was the most beautiful thing David had ever seen.
It was the most frightful thing Sir Judas had ever seen.

End of Volume II

Interlude

In the heart of Castle Nightfall, where Goliath waited for the coming of Sir Judas, a hidden and invisible council was taking place between the thousand demons who were within him, as well as Beatrice's demon Jezebel. The king over the one thousand, to whom it had been given to wreak havoc upon the earth, was Abaddon, the destroyer, king over the bottomless pit in hell. When Goliath performed his black and blasphemous ritual, making that wretched deal for power, it was Abaddon who was released from the pit to possess him, along with a thousand mighty demons who lent their strength to give the giant irresistible ferocity as well as scales that could not be pierced by any spell or weapon.

They knew their days were numbered, for every one of them suspected this was the fifth trumpet. They were released from the pit to plague the earth and damn souls, not to mention torture the sons of men for their own enjoyment. In time the seventh trumpet would sound, and then their conquest would be at an end. Until then, they had to make the most of their fleeting time. How to do so was the difficult question the council was called to examine.

When angelic persons speak (and these fallen fiends still have an angelic nature) they do not communicate like men with words, but instead pure ideas are pressed directly into their fellow spirits. With the angels of God, this is a beautiful hierarchy, as every person assigned to a task disseminates knowledge and understanding up to his superiors until it reaches one with authority to decide how they should act. Then the decision disseminates back down through the ranks until every angel knows his purpose. Not in some tyrannical way do the orders come, for there are no holy micro-managers. Instead each angel is given enough information to know his purpose, but he is left enough freedom to use his own powers in deciding how to act for the glory of God. Then they act in beautiful harmony, a synchronized display of motion where many diverse functions and activities all unite into a single coherent will, an angelic image, perhaps, of how men participate in the body of Christ.

For the fallen angels, it is not so. Their communications are a chaotic and incomprehensible mess, driven by hatred, deceit, and the raw exercise of power. A demon that learns some secret or has some great insight does not lovingly report it to his superiors, but instead asks himself, *Who will make a stupid blunder if I give him partial information or a half-truth?* Meanwhile, those who learn information, never trusting their peers, try to exert their own force and strength to drag the truth out of the messenger, with varying degrees of success. A demon that has thus extracted 'information' from another then repeats the process, running to and fro to inform his peers with either truth or lies depending on the circumstance. Thus should a demonic council be understood; it is a dark and maddening swirling mass of prideful intellects maliciously weaponizing ideas as they hurl them back and forth.

The only reason this pandemonious household is even able to stand is because one uniting goal keeps them all drifting in the same direction. They hate God above, and the men below whom God has called to be His children. Therefore, mixed in with the hatred the demons all have for each other is a constant thread that binds them. They manage to occasionally set aside their internal feuds for the greater goal of damning souls and ripping children from their most hated enemy.

I give you this little bit of education, dear reader, because there is no way a human could possibly understand a demonic council in the way it actually happens. The best we can hope for is a dialogue that represents this mess, styled off of something like a rowdy parliament or senate. Thus is the manner in which the holy nun of Gavar related these events to me. She had visions of many infernal councils, both in these events, as well as others which I may record in a future book. Given the numerous miracles that have been attributed to her prayers, I see good reason to believe what she reports, and therefore I include it in this history.

Yet she was insistent–absolutely insistent–that if I should write of her visions, I must make every effort to warn my readers against idle curiosity or love of novelty. She commanded me to do my best to make them aware of how much the demons hate each other with unimaginable fury and loathing. And then she commanded me to make sure my readers realize that the only reason these abominable spirits ever work together is because they hate you even more. Yes, you, dear reader. You in particular. Not just 'mankind.' They hate you.

They want to damn *you*. And given how much stronger, smarter, and more patient they are than you, they would certainly succeed if you were not under the constant, vigilant protection of Almighty God and your holy guardian angel. And so on behalf of the holy nun of Gavar, as well as from the bottom of my own heart, I earnestly implore you that as you read the visions of demonic activities throughout this history, you will recall that more malice than my words can communicate is aimed at you every day. With this thought in mind, give thanks to God, thank the angel He sent you, and be ever vigilant against the snares of our enemies. Otherwise you may fall victim to such scheming as that which I now describe.

Over the black cacophony Abaddon sat smugly, looking down on his legion with self-satisfied contempt at their present conflicts. Tangling all over each other like serpents, they tried to work out the meaning of their options and how they should proceed. Having gained a reasonable following for a certain idea, a swarm of them formed and snowballed, rising above the frenzy. But as the growing ball arose, it suddenly began to shrink. After uniting to overcome their fellow demons, now the proponents of this idea turned against each other, fighting for who should get the credit and reward for it. The victor by no means had any relationship to who thought of or developed this idea, but was merely the most brutal and violent among those who believed in it.

Smashing and slashing all his foes away, a snarling and bloodthirsty fiend proclaimed, "So the little knight would make us free? Bah! Slay the fool! Let us smash him with Doomfall the moment he sets foot in our lands. For the demise of this world already cometh, if only we would be patient and savor the meal. This darkness inches ever further, until it shall steal upon the sons of men like a thief! Then in their blind fear and terror will they crash and tumble into their demise. Unlike in the land of sun, under this shade we are free to tempt and torment them without restraint. None will stand against us. All will despair and plunge to hell! And as this darkness blooms, not only the humans, but every tempting spirit shall be in our grasp. For all devils in this land must obey Goliath's orders, and it is we who steer his tongue. So let us rule all the Earth, both man and fiend under our boot while we watch them squirm. Does this not appeal to you comrades? Voice your assent if you realize I would lead us to the fulfillment of our dreams!"

A weak call of assent went up, along with a chorus of hisses and boos. Even the demons that supported his position turned against him, saying, "You put everything so poorly!" He was thus dragged down into the ocean of sin, while a new movement formed under the churning waters. A cluster of demons arose again, this time in support of a different tactic. They fought, and clawed, and snapped at each other, ferociously tearing their allies down. The victor over this mass was not the fiercest or nastiest, but instead a very clever demon who all the others hated a little less than his opponents. Everyone else knocked each other out, until he was the last one left to put forward their position.

"Not by such stupid, brutish force will we triumph, but rather with the slow suffocation of comfort. If darkness and doom came upon the human race, they would surely return to God in prayer and save their souls. Let it not be so, comrades. Not so! Let the paladin come and break the darkness, releasing us and Goliath from this prison. Then we shall build a kingdom modeled off of Chelles, which messengers tell us such wonderful things about. A city of lukewarm souls drifting to the abyss. With Goliath's power and Fearnow's cunning we will make all the world in our unholy image!"

This speaker was also dragged back down into the muck, but not as swiftly or decisively as the other. Even Abaddon nodded approvingly, quite fond of this proposal. It seemed the swarm was fixated on these two options, sorting themselves into one or the other camp. But then a mighty demon arose, a dread and powerful spirit that could overcome the others by his own strength. He was so indomitable that only Abaddon could rule him. The other thousand by their combined powers could not drag him down nor stop his speech.

Thus the Spirit of Fear stated his case, trying to make the others realize how poorly their plans could go. "Oh how little we know! Oh how foolish you all are! Are we seriously considering letting a paladin into our midst? Have you no Fear of what might happen? For many long years Samson has been subdued, defeated by us and unable to rise. But what, tell me, shall we do if another paladin comes and revives him? We barely defeated him the first time; how can we triumph if an ally joins him in the battle? Surely we would be overthrown, and that would be Goliath's end. Do not let him come to us! Do not let him approach! Send Jove or Jezebel and have them kill him. Persuade Fearnow to have some guards stab him in his sleep. Ambush, treachery, whatever it takes! Do not let such danger in our midst!

"And as for this other proposal, of ruling under this shade of darkness; we do not know that it will be so! We assume that every demon in the dark prison must obey Goliath, but why do we think that this is true? Think of the words of the deal that was made. Isn't it possible that Goliath commands all demons in *this land* of Nightfall, regardless of whether a dark dome covers it or not? I am of the opinion that if we try to command our fellow demons, they will laugh, attack, and overthrow us. I believe our power is only over this little peninsula, and attempting to build a great empire will lead to our own destruction. So let us not set our minds on great things, my comrades. Let us stay here in our castle and be content to rule over what we already have. Safety. That should be our motto. Let us not attempt any venture if we do not know that it is safe."

This spirit was universally reviled, and all of the other thousand together tried to overthrow him. He bore their weight, and might have carried the day, except Abaddon struck him with a lash of his tail. The Spirit of Fear then fell back in pain, while the king over this brood of vipers finally made his decision known. "Stupid and craven spirit! We shall not grovel before the sons of dirt! The clever spirit has spoken rightly, that we ought to break the darkness and then subtly conquer the world. So let us welcome this paladin, and make sure no one lays a hand on him until he releases us! If he does not destroy the dome before he enters it, we all must show restraint. Do not treat him how we treat other mortals who venture here. Instead we sit perfectly still, and no demon who dwells in this place shall touch him until he breaks the dome and we are free."

The sea of demons cheered, many because they approved the idea, all others because they feared Abaddon's wrath. Choruses of empty flattery congratulated him on his brilliant leadership. One voice cried out, "And then we kill the paladin!" and Abaddon answered, "Let us exterminate him!" The cheering redoubled, and resounded all around.

Abaddon then gestured that he desired silence. They gradually lessened their cheering, and he said, "Jezebel! Come before me!" She did as he commanded, floating above the rest of his infernal army. "Goliath wants your meatbag to keep him company, Jezebel, lest he become lonely. Since we have no need of you in our own plans, we desire for you to entertain us until the paladin comes."

Jezebel was deeply afraid. The devils below her started cheering. "How may I entertain you, comrade?"

Abaddon formed a cruel smile. "We're going to play a game. We will try to get our meatbag to kill yours. You try to keep your meatbag alive."

Jezebel fled at once, and told Beatrice, "Run! Get away from Goliath!" Beatrice did not understand, and she lingered a moment in the hall where she and Goliath had been talking. Meanwhile Abaddon gave his command, and the thousand laughed at the hilarity of it while setting to work. In the darkness Goliath had no vision except that which the devils gave him. Now they twisted that vision, sculpting it to suit their purpose. The wrinkles on Beatrice's face disappeared. Her hair fell down in waves past her shoulders. The dignified dress Beatrice wore was changed into the one the witch of Chelles had worn long ago. The usually sharp outlines the demons showed Goliath were smoothed into an image that looked like a portrait, a portrait of his most hated dream and nightmare.

The giant leapt to his feet, clenching his claws in fists of rage. "What are you doing? Why are you here! Are you Beatrice or are you the *witch*?"

Beatrice answered, "Huh? What are you talking about? Of course it's Beatrice. Who else do you think I am?"

Jezebel kept shouting, *Run! Run! He's going to try and kill you!*

Beatrice backed away in fear, but the demons made it look like the witch was leading Goliath on, motioning for him to follow. "Drop the magic Beatrice! This isn't funny! I'll kill you if you don't stop this spell!"

"But I'm not casting a spell!" Beatrice said, now turning and running through the doorway.

Goliath saw her look over her shoulder as she said the words and winked at him. That was exactly what the witch had said. "But I'm not casting a spell. You know this is what you really want…" Goliath was convinced this wasn't Beatrice. The witch had made herself look like Beatrice in order to get him alone. Now she was going to try and work her foul arts.

But he was ready this time. Goliath smiled a wide and toothy smile. He was ready…no magic spell could pierce his scaly armor. "You made a mistake in coming here! And you shall pay for it with your life!" With a mighty roar he ran after her, ready to execute long awaited vengeance.

Destiny was feeling very uncomfortable as the carriage sped along the road to Chelles. The carriage itself was always dreadful. Going so fast on poor, bumpy masonry and dirt trails made her green and ready to vomit. Far more sickening than the carriage, however, was the company. She was all alone with Charles, sitting on benches that were facing each other. When others were around, she loved his company. He was strong, fierce, and protective. He made her feel safe in a world of dangers. Whether it was the intrigues of Committee life or the rabble that would mug and assault her if they could, she was sure Charles would keep her safe.

When they were alone together, all of this was turned on its head. She became acutely aware of the eerie way he looked at her. There was something unsettling about it. She was always worried he thought of her as a piece of meat. Not in the figurative sense of how a man might look at a woman that way. With Charles it was literal. He often burned sacrifices to Jove, the demon that lived within him. She was confident the demon would love to see her on his altar. She was worried Charles might be listening to the whispers. This led to strange behavior; the more frightening Charles became, the more she tried to endear herself to him. At those times when he seemed absolutely psychotic, she discovered she would nearly throw herself at him. It left her with a dirty and disgusted feeling, competing with a demon for a man's heart.

As he was giving her one of those unsettling looks, she looked out the window to avoid his gaze. The curtain was a special material that was opaque from the outside but translucent and hazy from within. As the grass blurred by, she got motion sickness. She looked back at Charles. She felt sicker. The best she could do was close her eyes and try to rub her temples.

Thinking a little conversation might help the situation, Destiny said, "Goliath was…something."

Charles nodded. "Was that your first time meeting him?"

"It was. He was…not what I expected. I always imagined he would be more…commanding. In control. Instead he was madder than a hatter."

She opened her eyes and saw Charles was looking at her. "Do you like a man who is…commanding? In control?"

If she had eaten breakfast, she would have lost it. Instead she smiled and said, "Charles, don't be ridiculous! That giant is a monster!"

He moved his foot across the carriage, propping it up on the bench right next to her. "I meant in general. Not him, obviously. That *would* be ridiculous."

Destiny wanted to shove his boot off the bench. Instead she put her hand on it and said, "Well a commanding man is certainly…*striking*." This was not where she wanted the conversation to go. She tried to change the subject back to Goliath. "You know, you saved me back there…I don't know how I could ever thank you." The words came unbidden, the result of a long habit of self-preservation.

Charles moved his boot a little closer, brushing up against the skirt of her dress. "What was I supposed to do? Let him kill you?" He gave her that unsettling look. "You're far too important to me for that."

Destiny was going to retreat into silence, but then a genuine curiosity came over her. "How did you know he was going to attack? You and Beatrice seemed to always know when something was up before he would…I don't know. Before he would…change. There was something going on there."

Charles nodded. "Did you notice his right eye? How there were many lines all clustered around it?"

"I did."

"That's a wound he took in the Battle of Nouen. How anyone got close enough to hit him, we'll never know. But that deformed eye of his flashes bright orange whenever he is about to have one of his…moments." Charles looked away from her, peering out the window himself while lost in thought. "I think it's all those devils inside him scrambling his brain. Or flipping some switches. I swear, it's like they take all his emotions, gather them up, and roll them to see what his new mood will be. And I think that orange light is a little hellfire leaking out, the glow from them all cramming into his skull at once." Charles looked back at her and shrugged. "That's just my guess anyway."

Destiny looked at him in surprise. "Hellfire? You never struck me as someone who worries about the afterlife."

He opened his mouth to speak, then had a second thought and closed it. A moment later he asked, "If I tell you a secret, can you keep it?"

Destiny was unsure. This seemed like something she would rather not know. Nevertheless, she nodded and said, "I can."

Charles stroked his mustache and said, "I obviously don't believe in hellfire in the old fashioned sense. But I do believe devils are powerful magical beings and that hellfire gives them their power. Lots of power. Far more than a faerie with gray magic could ever muster. Goliath has a lot of devils inside of him. Beatrice's spirit is a demon too…and so is Jove."

Destiny nodded, slightly agitated. "The illusion magic my faerie gives me may not be as 'powerful' as what Jove gives you, but there's a lot more room for creativity. I can do all sorts of things by cleverness that you could never do by brute force.

"And that's fine for now I guess, but…" he trailed off.

"But what?"

"...but there will come a time when you need to go deeper. There are powers black magic gives that are far beyond what gray magic can do. Necessary powers...powers we will need in the coming world."

"The coming world?" Destiny asked.

Charles removed his boot to the floor again, and said, "Sorry. I've already said too much. Just trust me. You want to go deeper. Once you do, I can tell you more."

Destiny wanted to pick his brain, but the horses whinnied and began to slow. "It seems we've arrived at Chelles," Charles announced. "Time to find my priestly needle in a city-sized haystack."

Destiny frowned. "The needle I'm looking for will be easier to find, but she's a lot more likely to prick me."

Darkness. All he saw was darkness. Looking out the window on Wednesday afternoon (twenty minutes after David and Sir Judas had entered the city), Lord Benjamin Fearnow let out a heavy sigh. He turned back to his well-lit bedroom and thought about collecting papers for his next meeting. He believed he would have a little bit of quiet time to himself, but to his surprise the bedroom door opened and his wife came walking in. "Lady Fearnow. What brings you here?"

He expected she would have some other business, but unfortunately she wanted to talk to him. She approached excitedly, standing much closer than she usually did these days. Her golden hair was pulled up into a tight bun, while her dress was loose and gray. Though she shouldn't have looked a day over twenty, the drab garb she always wore gave her a much older appearance. And then there were her eyes, her bright, emerald, piercing eyes. Lord Fearnow couldn't stand those eyes. He looked back out the window into the darkness, preferring it to her gaze.

She pulled him away from the window. "I have wonderful, wonderful news!"

He looked into her eyes again, then looked away and pretended to be searching for something else. "What's your news?"

She followed him closely around the room. "A magician just came to town. Not half an hour ago."

Lord Fearnow rolled his eyes. "There are a hundred magicians in this city. Do you care to be more specific?"

"A *powerful* one, Benjamin. I could feel his presence as soon as he crossed the city gate."

"It's probably Simon coming to actually do his duties as Chairman for a change."

"No, Benjamin! It's not Simon. He's *nothing* like Simon. This magician isn't powerful like me or Simon. Not even like Beatrice. This magician's aura was *crushing* me. I felt this terrible anxiety, so great I could hardly breathe. Even now he's weighing heavily upon me."

Lord Fearnow looked her up and down. "Yes, I can see how afflicted you are. Forgive me if your excitement led me astray."

"I'm serious!" Lady Fearnow snapped. "It was oppressive! I had to lie down for several minutes before I started getting used to him!" There had been a time when Amanda would have laughed at Benjamin, even as he needled her. The sly, sarcastic humor that always seemed to be pouring out of him was what had attracted her to her husband in the first place. His looks were not to be despised either, but they played a supporting role. With a slender frame, wide jaw, and a brunette, pencil-thin "goatee" that did not match the blonde hair on his head, Lord Fearnow had the perfect appearance for a comic actor. Not the buffoons who did slap-stick routines, but rather the witty, deadpan comedy that perfectly matched his personality. Yes, there was a time when she could not stay angry at him, because even his barbs would have her laughing. That time was long ago.

Lord Fearnow rolled his eyes again. "If what you're saying is true, why haven't you raised a general alarm?"

"That was exactly what I intended to do. But as I was in the process, an old friend of mine, an Administrator, came to me with some exceptionally useful information." Lady Fearnow turned to the doorway. "Destiny! Come in my darling!"

In came a low ranking Administrator that Lord Fearnow vaguely recognized. Normally she fit in with the other grifters who always hung around his palace, but today she looked like an absolute mess. Her long brown hair was badly tangled and her wrinkled blue dress was covered in splotches of mud. "So, Destiny is it? Before you leave my manor, either change your dress or remove that mask. At present you are an embarrassment to the Committee and my regime. Well, come on now. Out with it. Why shouldn't I have this city on red alert?"

Destiny nervously smiled, looking back and forth between the lord and lady as she touched her mask absentmindedly. "Yes, it is very good to see you and to be here. I am glad you are in good health, m'lord, and long may you–"

"Skip the pleasantries and get to the point," Lord Fearnow yawned. "You're cutting into my break."

Destiny swallowed deeply. After an entire morning of wishing Charles was gone, she suddenly wished that he was present. "Of course, m'lord, of course. So, this magician of whom Lady Amanda spoke…you see…I happen to know the magician in question…well, not *know* him so much as know *of* him…though not merely know *of* him I suppose…I mean, I have met him before…once…on Monday night."

Lord Fearnow was growing more impatient with every moment. "What part of 'get to the point' was so difficult to understand?"

"Yes, yes, of course, the point. Of course. Well, uh, you see, this magician is not a magician in the uh, typical sense, no…you see, he doesn't pose any threat to you at all."

"Then why should I care?" Lord Fearnow asked.

"Yes, yes, a very good question, so, going back to Monday night, I was spending an evening at Baron Charles's manor, where he was throwing a delightful little party. I don't know if you've met Administrator Morgan of Birr, but he was there with Lady Beatrice of Duble and our Chairman Simon. Obviously you've met Simon. And Charles, he suggested a trip to this lovely glade only a short ride from his manor, and since the night was so fair, we thought it a delightful idea to do so, and we went to the glade, where the magician was in fact sleeping for the night. Only we didn't know he was a magician, so we sought to have a little fun with him and his two companions. It…he…"

As she sputtered out, Lord Fearnow guessed the remainder of her sentence. "…he turned out to be tougher than you thought and drove you off?"

"Yes, yes, I suppose you could put it that way." Destiny brushed a stray tress of her hair away.

Lord Fearnow asked, "Where are the others?"

"Yes, yes, a very good question, m'lord. You see, after retreating to Baron Charles's manor to regroup, it was decided I should come to Chelles to notify you of this magician. As for where the other three are now and what they've done since I left, I couldn't tell you."

"You mean four?"

"What now?"

"You said 'other three.' Morgan, Charles, Beatrice, Simon. That's four, yes?"

"Oh, yes, yes, I see now. Um, actually, no. There were only three of us…" A long pause followed, then Destiny whispered, "…Simon is dead."

"*WHAT*?!" Lord Fearnow shouted, flipping over his desk in fury. "This magician fought Beatrice, Simon, Charles, Morgan, and you with just two allies and not only scared you off but *killed* the Chairman of my Committee? And why on Earth am I supposed to believe this magician isn't the greatest threat my realm has seen since Goliath?" He was panting breathlessly, looking back and forth between Lady Fearnow and Destiny. "Stupid women! My city is infiltrated, and you waste my time just telling the story!"

Destiny recoiled in the face of his outburst, cowering before Lord Fearnow. Hurriedly answering, she stammered, "W-w-well, um, you see…yes, yes, uh…uh…well, the reason he's not a threat…oh please don't hit me m'lord…you see, the reason he's not a threat is that…I don't think he knows he's a magician yet!"

Lord Fearnow looked at her, unbelieving, literally dropping his jaw for several seconds before managing to yell, "…what!?"

"Yes, yes, m'lord, um, you see…I don't think he knows he's a magician. In fact, I'm quite sure he doesn't. Yes, m'lord! I'm sure of it!" Though still cowering, Destiny forced a smile. Lord Fearnow instead squinted at her in a confused fashion, beginning to wonder if she was right in the head. Sensing his implicit questions, Destiny went on, "Yes, yes, you see, m'lord, you see, he uh, he didn't cast any spells for a good long while. No m'lord. In fact, we were having our way with all three of them, yes m'lord. And he didn't cast a single spell until Beatrice was right at the point of killing him. And then, at the last moment, as it was, he just instinctively cast a spell. No incantations, no gestures, he just yelled and then we were blasted with a big wave of magic. Simon was closest to him, that's why he got killed. The rest of us survived, but we all ran for our lives. But yes, m'lord, that's why I don't think he's a magician, m'lord. I think he just has a lot of latent power that's still untapped. In fact, since he mentioned Scriptures, I think he might even be a Christian, and so he thinks magic is evil. That would explain why he has so much power and yet he isn't using any of it."

Lord Fearnow shook his head and waved his hands in frustration. "Even if it is true that he doesn't know he's a magician yet, I still need to find and kill this man as fast as possible. He's a walking time bomb, ticking ever closer to realizing he can control his magic, and then where will I be? From what you say he has enough power to overthrow my realm in the twinkling of an eye!" He scowled at his wife. "I don't know what crazy scheme makes you want to avoid killing this man, but it is certainly foolish. Our town is stuffed to the gills with magicians, and if he finds an instructor who will teach him the most rudimentary basics, it will be enough to doom us all."

"Us, perhaps," Lady Fearnow said with a wicked grin. "...or perhaps Goliath instead."

"What are you talking about?"

"Tell him!" Lady Fearnow said to Destiny, practically giddy with excitement.

Destiny was trembling terribly and wringing her hands. "Yes, yes, of course, m'lady. Well, you see, there were things the magician said to Beatrice that made it very clear he was looking for Goliath. Yes, he stated quite plainly that he had come to your realm in search of him. He even said Castle Nightfall was going to see the sunset, m'lord. He intends to destroy the darkness! And that got us to thinking that, you know, perhaps he would be able to aid you in defeating your old enemy. You know, we thought that the magician could be an ally. Yes, he would be a most wonderful ally, m'lord, one who could defeat Goliath once and for all!"

Destiny was smiling, but with nervous eyes showing through her mask. This was the task Goliath had given her. She was hoping she had been persuasive enough that Lord Fearnow might aid Sir Judas in getting to Castle Nightfall.

After a wait that seemed like ages, Lord Fearnow flatly stated, "Leave us. Lady Fearnow and I must discuss this alone."

Destiny tried not to show her disappointment. "Yes, m'lord. Of course, m'lord!" She curtseyed and began to back out of the room.

Lord Fearnow added, "Destiny, do not leave the palace. You are to remain here in case I need to ask further questions."

"Of course, m'lord. Of course."

By now she had almost reached the door when Lady Fearnow called, "Wait!" and walked swiftly up to Destiny. Brushing back one of Destiny's tresses and placing a hand on her cheek in an almost motherly way (even though Destiny looked several years older than Lady Fearnow), the lady said, "Destiny, darling, we have been friends since I was a child, and my favorite nights were always the ones where my parents would leave you in charge of watching me." Destiny smiled. Lady Amanda continued, "By now I'm sure you know me well enough to know that if you have told us the truth and been a reliable informant, Lord Fearnow and I will see to it that you are rewarded generously, as befits a beloved servant." Lady Fearnow's face now darkened, and her hand on Destiny's cheek was no longer affectionate. "But if we discover you have lied to us in any detail we will first torture you for the truth, and then have you executed in the public square. And not some simple hanging, oh no. You will be killed in the most creative and painful manner I can think of, as befits a beloved servant who has betrayed me."

Lady Fearnow's face once more became warm and loving, but her hand descended to Destiny's shoulder with a menacing grip that made the Administrator feel trapped. "Now…with all of that clarified, is there anything about your testimony you would like to modify? Anything at all? If you tell us the truth now, you will only be gently chastised, but if we discover the truth later, you will face my full fury. Well? Anything?"

Destiny was so terrified that she could hardly stand on her quaking knees. In fear she almost blurted out, *It's a trap! It's all a trap! Goliath wants Sir Judas to free him!* But she held her peace. With a weak (and unconvincing) smile, she said, "Of course not, m'lady. I would never dream of lying to you."

Lady Fearnow beamed, and squeezed Destiny's shoulder. "Good. Run along now. Feel free to use any bedroom in the north wing and make it your own."

Destiny curtsied again and left the room. Lady Fearnow closed the door behind her. "What the hell was that?" Lord Fearnow asked. "It was obvious she was lying. Why did you let her know we were suspicious?"

"Oh, I can't help myself, darling. More than any other, that's the torture I really love. The physical pains are all delightful, of course. I'll never say 'no' to a good whipping. But no tool off the executioner's rack can hold a candle to when I get to scourge a soul. To walk up to her in her greatest agony and say, 'This is all your fault, you know. If you had just listened to me, you wouldn't be here.' And then to look into her eyes and see that crushed look, and know deep down she really believes it? Oh! I could swoon…Forget wine, darling. The strongest drink I've ever known is to shatter a spirit and then hear my victim blame himself."

Lord Fearnow raised an eyebrow. "Himself? I thought we were talking about Destiny?"

"Oh, you know bloody well who I'm talking about, but enough of this. Right now I want to hear the sound of your beautiful mind when it starts whirring. What do you make of this whole situation? Do we really need to kill the magician, or isn't there a way we could try to use him?"

"Alright, let me think…this is certainly more interesting than the meeting I should have been in right now…" Lord Fearnow plopped himself down in a plushy armchair in the corner of the room and closed his eyes. "Okay, what do we know so far? First, he isn't a local. He obviously has some sort of effect on you that we've never noticed before, so that means he's never been here before. So where did he come from? Destiny said they met him in the glade of Jove. That part of her story sounded plausible enough. So that would mean he's coming from the east. He's not of our realm then. But if he's not from our realm, what's his connection to Goliath? Beyond our borders Goliath is merely a name, a scary boogieman of long-forgotten history…why does this magician care about him?"

Lady Fearnow went and found her own chair, making herself comfortable while she watched her husband think. "Okay, second fact. Goliath hasn't left the darkness in forty years. If the magician isn't even from our realm, and if he comes through our city on the way to see Goliath, we can reasonably conclude he hasn't visited Goliath in all that time. He's not paying secret night time visits like Charles and Beatrice…so that means he must know Goliath from forty years ago. And if he's coming out of the east, then that means he's probably from the royal city…"

Lord Fearnow now leapt to his feet. "The hidden hand! The man behind the Empire!"

Lady Fearnow was smiling in excitement, even though she had no idea what her husband was talking about. "Who is the hidden hand, Benjamin?"

"He's the answer to the riddle I've been trying to tease out for decades now…ever since we started studying magic, it quickly became clear that the paladins weren't actually using some sort of 'divine power,' like they said, but rather they were using plain old white magic. The kind of stuff any magician with a little training could do. But that raised a new question. I began to wonder how the king ever rose to power in the first place. How did his armies always win if he doesn't have a crew of divine demi-gods running around, but rather just a bunch of ordinary magicians in white coats? My speculation was that there must have been 'a hidden hand' behind the empire. Some magician of incredible power who was performing all the 'miracles' the paladins supposedly did."

"I still don't get it," Lady Fearnow answered, "Why would there have to be a 'hidden hand.' Isn't it just as likely the paladins themselves were the great magicians?"

"No. For a couple of reasons. First, one magician of spectacular, never-before-seen power is unlikely. *Dozens of them*, every paladin from the king's rise to his fall, is impossible beyond belief. Especially in a realm where the practice of magic was forbidden, and so you don't have talented young men who have used magic all their lives becoming paladins. Second, the average paladin was just way too genuine to be a secret sorcerer. Think of Sir Samson. Most children are more duplicitous than that moron. He would call people 'dunderheads,' because he thought swearing was a sin. He wasn't some secret magician of incredible power. But the king on the other hand…that conniving, scheming vermin…*he* was exactly the sort of man who would think of a trick like this. You see, he had a hidden hand, a powerful magician who did all the 'miracles,' but attributed them to the holy 'dunderheads.' And that also explained why the king's empire collapsed when it did…he and the hidden hand must have had a falling out."

"And now the hidden hand is come to Chelles…" Lady Fearnow whispered. "…but still, how can this be? If he was with the king since his rise…why, he must be at least a hundred years old!"

"Indeed he must," Lord Fearnow said. "And I'll wager that with his powers, he easily knows enough white magic to make himself a healthy and vibrant centenarian. But now old age is catching up with him, and he has come here in search of a solution…"

Lady Fearnow's eyes went wide. "He didn't come here to find Goliath at all! He's here for us!"

"Maybe not, maybe not. Let's not jump to conclusions one way or the other…" Lord Fearnow began to pace. "…why would he know about us? *How* would he know about us? We've been very careful, with dozens of witnesses like Destiny who have seen the two of us 'grow up.' Much more likely is that he really did come to find Goliath, but not to slay him. No, just think it through. If he's from the royal city from way back when, then he probably knows Goliath. He probably knows Goliath is over ninety years old himself. He probably knows Goliath doesn't have any white magic to keep him alive, and yet he has not yet died nor been defeated. That would probably lead our hidden hand to conclude that Goliath has what he's looking for."

"You're using the word 'probably' a lot. I prefer a little more certainty in my life."

"Well, my dear, the only 'certainty' we have is that we will certainly perish if nothing is done about Goliath and his blasted darkness. But now I have a little hope that we can 'probably' get the hidden hand to do our dirty work for us and take care of lizard boy on our behalf. So when those are the options, I find I prefer what is 'probable' to what is certain."

"But won't we just be trading one devil for another? What's to stop the hidden hand from killing us when he's done with Goliath? *If* he can even defeat Goliath. That's another 'probably' we didn't mention."

"Yes, that's another 'probably' but it's a risk we have no way of avoiding. At least we can try to tip the scales a little bit by sending the Committee to aid him. As for the possibility of him betraying us, he would never, ever do that."

Lady Fearnow looked at her husband incredulously. "Why not?"

A strange emotion came over Lord Fearnow at this point. He was excited for his planned stratagem, but it also made him want to vomit. "Why, because he'll be madly in love with you, my dear."

Lady Fearnow was revolted. "Oh, God, Benjamin! That's disgusting! He's over a hundred years old!"

"It's the only way!" He looked directly at her with intensity, hazarding those green eyes for several seconds before looking away in shame. "It's the only way…if we had another option, I would be glad to use it. But we don't. Think of the greater good, Amanda. We're talking about saving the world…we're talking about saving *us*."

She folded her arms tightly across her chest. "*Probably?*"

"Probably. If we had a better way out, we would have taken it long ago."

Lady Amanda arose. "…How long do I have?"

"If we can find him in time, I'll have him over for dinner. Start your preparations now." Lord Fearnow began to leave, then stopped and added, "…and put on the dress. You know which one."

"I hate you."

"You'll thank me when this is over."

Lady Amanda watched her husband leave to begin his search. When the door was closed her tears welled up. *You'll thank me when this is over?* She thought. *But it's never over, is it? Forty years and it isn't over!*"

Looking at her accursed bed and contemplating what Benjamin had asked her to do, Lady Amanda saw her little gray faerie sitting on the head board. That faerie was the only one who loved her in the entire world. "Don't worry, Amanda, don't worry. I'm going to keep you safe. My spell always works. The old geezer will never hurt you." The faerie let out a long sigh, then continued in her pippy little voice. "If only you had asked for something else when we made our deal. Remember how I told you divination magic might be a better idea? Oh, I hate to say it, but...this is all your fault, you know. If you had just listened to me, you wouldn't be here..."

That accursed spirit was not sorry, of course. She had every intention of telling Lady Amanda that this was a torture of her own making. And as that fiend looked into Amanda's eyes, it felt the closest thing demons can know of joy. It felt that sadistic, twisted illusion of pleasure, for deep down in Amanda's heart, the demon could see she really blamed herself.

Volume III

Dewford

Chapter 1: The Knife Edge of History

When I first discovered my love of history as a young lad, I, like many, subscribed to what scholars derisively call 'the big man' view of history. This is the angle taken in most popular accounts, where the events of history are ascribed to specific individuals of particularly great genius, personality, or daring. 'The big man' is strong enough to steer the course of history, as opposed to all of us 'little men' who often feel the world around us spins according to powers beyond our control.

Once I attended university I was exposed for the first time to the 'trends and forces' view of history, which veers in the exact opposite direction. In this view no 'big men' are determining the outcomes of events. Instead, everything is the outcome of gradual trends and forces. A well-trained scholar might say, "Such and such device wasn't invented because of a great inventor; it was invented because this was a scientific age where men were 'trending' towards greater inventiveness. The demands of the military created a 'force' that demanded the invention. Sure, that inventor may have accelerated the invention by a year or two with all his efforts, but if he hadn't invented it, someone else eventually would have. Thus, he didn't *really* have a big impact on history with his invention. The *trends* of 'scientific thought' and the *forces* demanding the invention dictated which way history would go."

I must admit, this 'trends and forces' view certainly has its value. It captures much of history with greater fidelity than the childish 'big man view' we all grew up with. But it has a blind spot. A chink in the armor. I discovered this when talking to a longtime mentor and colleague about the Potosi Affair. I just could not bring myself to understand what had happened. "Here are the expansionist trends, here are the pacifist forces. Every other city on the planet surrendered to the Undying King because opposing him simply wasn't worth it. So then what happened in Potosi? And why was that tiny little republic the only one that fought back against his conquest?"

Then my mentor smiled and shook his head, and said something I will never forget. "Asinus, Asinus...you're forgetting about the Knife Edge of History!"

"The what?" I asked.

"The Knife Edge of History! Yes, you are right, that for the most part men lead lives where they are pulled along by forces far beyond their control. We don't get to choose the times in which we live, just the way in which we face them. Yet every now and then some man will come to a Knife Edge of History moment. It is so called because Almighty God seems to take the world and balance it on the edge of a knife. Perhaps the trends and forces would normally move the world in one direction, but when everything is positioned in just the right way, one man who pushes with all his strength can flip the world to the other side!"

Such is the moment I shall now relate, yet it is admittedly one of the oddest Knife Edge of History moments I have ever studied. This is not only because of how momentous the moment was–for this moment decided the fate of the entire world, and the reader knows I am not exaggerating. This moment is so very odd because the man who began to push the world had no idea what he was pushing. To be completely frank, I'm not sure he knew he was pushing anything at all. He probably thought he was beating his head against the same old wall he had been smashing it into all his life.

Here is how this oddest Knife Edge of History Moment came about:

On Tuesday afternoon Winthrop hurried along the path. At first he had wandered away from David somewhat listlessly, but his pace quickened until he was running. Running, running, running to get away from that accursed glade and put the memories behind him. He ran down the winding roads of broken hills until he emerged from the woods onto the plains. Wiping copious tears from his eyes with the bloody left hand he had smashed into Sir Judas's armor (and making quite the mess of his face in the process), Winthrop looked to his left and looked to his right.

He could go anywhere.

Anywhere was nowhere.

Off to the left he could stick to the hills until he hit the Eines River, and then only wilderness until the southern bridge of Chelles. To his right he could take a long, desolate walk until he circled back around the woods and ended up in Reswick. Straight ahead and up the hill was Chelles, the frothy pit where all the sewers of the world ran together.

Chelles, Chelles, oh the misery of Chelles! Pointless days, empty days, wandering the streets of Chelles with nowhere to go and a lifetime to get there. Years of his life had been forfeited to the unending death of Chelles. Indeed, he might well have died there, if not for a little orphan boy who brought him to his senses.

Yet right now, in this moment, Chelles was exactly what Winthrop thought he needed. Back to the beginning! Back to before David came along! A strong drink to soothe the pain, a busy bar to fill the emptiness, and most of all–oh, happy Chelles!–deafening music to drown out the voices in his head. He knew Chelles was oblivion, but his heart was yearning for the Void. "To Chelles!" Winthrop declared, and he continued to run straight ahead, eager to be lost in the city before David and Sir Judas could overtake him.

He ran along, feet heavy on the dirt road, pushing his body as fast as it would go to his chosen hell. But then a surprise came upon him. He came to a long-forgotten fork in the road, and a weathered wooden sign with three arrows. 'Back to Reswick,' Never! 'Forward to Chelles,' Onward! 'Right to Dewford.' Dewford? He had forgotten about Dewford. That backwater little town had a population of about five hundred people (if you count the sheep). Winthrop had been there only once before to scout out potential marks. What he found was the town was too poor to even be worth robbing.

He forgot about Dewford. He always did. He had passed this sign a thousand times without paying it a moment's notice. And he ought to have run past it once more, not giving it a second thought. But he didn't. He didn't pass it, and he didn't know why he didn't pass it. The only good thing about Dewford was that it wasn't Chelles.

Why would I ever want to go to Dewford? Yet he did. He yearned for Dewford, even if he had no explanation for the yearning. "Bah!" He cried. "I can go to hell tomorrow! Today, I'll go to Dewford, and it will at least throw them off my trail!" So Winthrop went right, running full speed for Dewford when one moment prior he was running for Chelles. It was a little choice. It was a sudden choice. Yet it was a choice that touched the most profound depths of who Winthrop was and longed to be.

He didn't know where he was going nor what he was doing–that had been the case for so many years. But he wasn't going to Chelles–never again to Chelles. All his life that was the decision Winthrop had been making. Not literally mind you, but figuratively. He was a man who never fully plunged into the Void. As Sir Judas had accused him, Winthrop had a serious problem with running from all his sorrows. He lived in an age of 'trends and forces' where men pushed their sorrows away. But Winthrop hadn't killed them. He would run, but he would not kill. At least, that's what he had done for many years. Deep in his sore and tortured heart, there were three loves and sorrows Winthrop had not yet brought himself to kill. In this dread and fateful Week, however, he would finally run out of room to flee, and a decision would be thrust upon him. In order to hold onto those three loves, it would cost Winthrop the three most painful nights of his entire life.

This was the beginning of the Knife Edge of History moment. As the world tipped towards Chelles, Winthrop made his turn for Dewford. Whether the world would follow him would depend on whether he stayed the course.

Chapter 2: Thirst

As the road to Dewford went north, it slowly turned around a very large hill. Winthrop left the road and kept running until he had crested it. Taking one look backwards to confirm David and Sir Judas were not yet in sight, he slid down the other side and laid down to catch his breath. *That should do it!* From up here, Dewford was in view. The western side of town was an uncomfortable pocket of buildings crammed together on little hills in a way that reminded Winthrop of how a toddler walks. It seemed as if the lopsided structures might just fall at any moment. Unsuited to proper agriculture, the wavy hills were covered in natural vegetation that fed the herds of sheep and goats that meandered about under the guidance of their shepherds. Those unsteady and tilted buildings were the older ones, and had made up the entire town twelve years ago when Winthrop was on this same hill.

But now there was more, much more to see. Towards the east the land flattened out and newer houses had been built that looked more...*stable*. In addition to more than doubling the size of the core town, many little outposts were stretching into the surrounding lands. Farms had been started with a diverse assortment of crops in these flatlands, even though Winthrop thought he remembered the soil being dry and rocky. Wagons were going to and from the town, and Winthrop even thought some looked like they were leaving Dewford along a northern road. This was surprising, since Dewford was not thought of as having anything worth selling besides wool, and the shearing season was several months ago. The town must have seen some sort of economic improvement, for way off in the distance to the northeast was what looked like it might be a vineyard. This especially perplexed Winthrop, since not only did Dewford not previously have a vintage, but it had never been a town that was well-off enough to even be thinking about such luxury goods. Above and beyond all these other unexpected sights, where 'old Dewford' met 'new Dewford' a clock tower had been built, standing high over the rest of the town with a large bell that rang every half hour. The sophisticated mechanisms that would make such a device work were inconceivably far removed from the squalid, backward living of the Dewfordians Winthrop remembered. The world had turned since his last visit to Dewford. The once poor little village, hardly worthy of being called a 'town,' had grown and developed into a lovely little place in the course of just over a decade.

A smile came to Winthrop's face. *This might not turn out so bad after all!* That thought lasted all of one second, before his mind went back to the glade. Back to David, whom he had protected since before he could walk. *What did I just do?* Confusion and sorrow began to overtake him. A horror was growing as the reality of the situation began to sink in.

With quick and decisive distraction, a skill forged over long years of running from his problems, Winthrop pushed those thoughts out of his head. *Not the time, not the place.* For indeed, when Winthrop left the glade, he had not been thinking things through. He wandered off without his pack, his gear, his crossbow, his food, his money, or anything else that would be useful in proving he was a freeman. Instead, having nothing but the dirty, well-worn clothes on his back, he seemed very much like a runaway serf.

About this time, Winthrop began to realize his clothes were soaked in sweat, and his lips and throat were dry. *Well, at least I remembered one thing I need.* Winthrop reached down to his waterskin. It was empty. "What the?" he exclaimed, and then he remembered. He had given all of his water to Sir Judas to wash his hands. Winthrop took the empty skin and threw it to the ground in frustration. "Why did you have to go and bury that lump of rotten flesh anyway!" He almost kicked the waterskin, but Winthrop got hold of his emotions and restrained himself. No matter how bad this situation might be, putting a hole in his waterskin wasn't going to make it better.

He ran his hand through his wet, gray hair, suddenly very aware of how much fluid he had wasted by running around in the summer sun. Winthrop realized he might as well have run into a desert. He could no longer head for the Eines, for doing so would bring his path across David and Sir Judas (a possibility he was not willing to entertain). Dewford had a public well, but it would surely (Winthrop thought) be polluted and disgusting.

For those who are accustomed to perfectly drinkable public wells, it is important to stop here and explain Winthrop's presumptions, recalling that these events predate the Free Water Act passed some years ago. Early in the reign of Lord Benjamin Fearnow I., the lord who Sir Judas knew back in the royal city and the grandfather of Lord Benjamin Fearnow III. (according to the records of nobility that I consulted), a device was invented that made sinking wells a very quick and inexpensive process. The people of Chelles naturally set about sinking their own personal wells. They were little things that serviced their own household and saved them from having to go and draw water at the public well. Once these private wells had become ubiquitous, an event of some great controversy took place. Some say it was a greedy water merchant, others a government conspiracy, others say it was too many stupid revelers easing nature in waters the city guards didn't bother guarding…whoever was responsible, the outcome was certain. The public well was poisoned, and absolutely no effort was made to restore it. The people of Chelles didn't care that the public waters were befouled, and refused to approve a tax to sink a new public well. After all, they had their own water sources. For poor travelers to the city, however, there was no opportunity to obtain water other than by purchasing it from private vendors. This made the water merchants very wealthy while the Chellesian public stood by and did nothing. This 'model' was so successful that it quickly spread to other cities by an obviously intentional effort. Water merchants would contract deals with the local governments of towns and cities, allowing them to *deliberately* poison the public well, on the condition that they first sunk private wells for every household. The outcome of all this scheming was what any man of wisdom could foresee. Travelers died of thirst. The citizens complained about stinking corpses in the street. The governments of these towns spent far more money fixing the problem than it would have taken to preserve the public well. The water merchants went broke because many new merchants (like Curly Kayden's General Store) started selling water and drove down the price. Then when it was all said and done, society reached an equilibrium that was very similar to the original status quo, unless you were a truly penniless vagabond who couldn't afford a cup of water.

Today Winthrop was a truly penniless vagabond who couldn't afford a cup of water. He looked to the northwest, where the hills of Dewford were covered in grasses and flocks. *Where are all these sheep getting watered?* Winthrop wondered. It hadn't rained in some time, and he didn't see any evidence of larger waterways. *There must be a well hiding somewhere…* Setting his eyes on a very large barn near the biggest sheep-fold, Winthrop decided a little robbery was in order. There was a small shed near that barn, and other than that no homes nearby. Could it be that the well was in the barn? And if so, might he sneak in and find it unguarded? That would only happen if no one spotted him. A stranger coming to Dewford would probably draw at least one person's curious gaze, and then his chances would be gone. This was a wonderful hill for making plans, however. Winthrop studied the flocks, the homes, the hills, and plotted a route that might just get him to the barn unobserved. He rubbed his hands together, ready to set his heist into motion. Then he heard a voice in his head.

Just ask for a cup of water. It was Sir Judas's voice. Winthrop ignored it. No one gives water away for free, after all. Winthrop then scurried around the hills, staying low and avoiding being seen by any shepherds. As he drew near the barn, he had to cut across a little stretch of field that was very flat. Before leaving cover, Winthrop poked his head up slowly. There was a brown speck of shepherd in the distance. Again Sir Judas's voice, *Just go and ask him.* "Fool!" Winthrop whispered to himself. The shepherd was walking away from him. He slowly sank out of view. Winthrop took one last look around, then bolted across the field to the barn.

As he approached the door he looked for a good sized rock. He hoped the lock would be cheap and easily breakable. He found a solid stone and picked it up, but when he reached the door he realized his search was vain. The door was not even locked. It was slightly open. Winthrop hefted the rock as he slid inside, ready to kill anyone he found before they could raise the alarm.

There was no one inside. The barn was dimly lit by sunlight coming through little openings near the roof. In the center was a small divot in the ground used as a bath when the sheep needed washing. There were also assorted tools along the walls for shearing and general maintenance. Timber of various kinds was piled up for when it was needed to mend fences or other structures. But as to the most pressing question of where the well might be, there was none. Winthrop inspected the barn quickly, and didn't find any sign of it. "What on earth? How does he water his sheep without any water?" Winthrop snapped his fingers. "The shed...that must be where he hid it!" Winthrop felt rather foolish for not seeing through such a simple trick.

He made his way back outside and carefully looked around. There was no sign of anyone, but this was a bad crossing. He had to run across open terrain to the shed, and after he got there he would need to break in (since the shed with the well was certainly going to be locked). If there were any shepherds who had moved to the tops of the hills since Winthrop entered the barn, there was a very real chance they would see him now. He had no choice but to go for it, and he ran to the shed while looking to the west. He didn't see anyone. He came to the shed and was surprised for the second time to find a door that was unlocked.

Winthrop quickly entered and shut the door behind him. It was a very plain wooden door with no latch or lock. The only thing that held it shut was that it was a little bit bigger than the frame. Catching his breath, Winthrop had a chance to look around, and discovered he had not broken into a shed at all–it was a *home*. A poor home. More of a shack, really. There was a fireplace, cooking utensils, and next to a blanket was a roll of black clothes that looked like they were used as a pillow on the dirt floor. No table, no chairs, and no mattress of any kind. A small window let a little light in. There was a book beside the clothes titled *Institutio Generalis Missalis Romani*. Winthrop knew a smattering of the Ancient Tongue and translated the title as 'General Instructions for the Sending of Rome,' probably some sort of travel guide. The only other object of note in the shack was a little stand in the corner. On top of it was an icon of Jesus holding His Sacred Heart in His hands. Next to that was a similar icon of His Mother with her Immaculate Heart, and a small blue candle was burning in between them.

Winthrop was very uncomfortable about this little shrine. At first he wasn't sure why. Many people were still Christians, and Winthrop had been in homes before that had such decorations. They never bothered him until now. He looked around the barren shack again, and then he realized what was so unsettling. In other homes one table and two icons would be a little thing. In this house, they were not a little thing, nor even a big thing. They were the *only* thing. Whoever lived here had only the essentials needed for life (and not even a mattress at that), one book in a language this peasant certainly couldn't read, and then a table with two icons. While the resident certainly didn't intend to leave a message for Winthrop, a message was nevertheless received loud and clear; the owner's faith was his life. *Nutcase*, thought Winthrop. Despite his effort to write this resident off, Winthrop stood there looking at the shrine for several minutes until in a panic he remembered why he had come.

There's no well! He looked around the shack again. This time he noticed an object hanging on the wall near the ceiling. It was a water yoke, with two large buckets hanging down from it. Winthrop ran over and reached inside. Empty! There was a little dampness, however, revealing they had been recently used. "Where are you getting your water from, you stupid shepherd!" He plopped down on the floor, thoroughly frustrated.

Again there came Sir Judas's voice. *This man looks like a good Christian. Christ commanded that His followers give drink to the thirsty...* Winthrop grabbed his head and blinked slowly. "Dehydration hallucinations...just how thirsty am I?" He made his way back outside, and looked to the western hills in desperation. There was only one choice left. He squeezed the rock in his hand. That shepherd must have a waterskin. Winthrop would take it from him, one way or another...

He made his way swiftly to the hills, now wanting to see a shepherd but still wanting to be undetected. The grass in this area was up to about the knee, with little clusters of trees spotting the land here and there. Winthrop stayed in the low clefts between hills until he saw a small grove on top of one. He jogged to the top and slid into the thorny brush, fighting and tumbling his way in deeper. Once he got past the initial barrier, the grove opened up a little so that Winthrop could walk more freely. He crawled to the opposite side to look down the hill, and there he saw the shepherd's flock. What made Winthrop's heart plummet was that he also saw *another* shepherd and *another* flock. Two men were standing together talking with their sheep separated by a short distance.

Winthrop bit his dry and chapped lip until it bled. *Why did there have to be two of them!* A very thirsty part of him wanted to try his hand at violence anyway, but even in these straits Winthrop kept his usual habit of thinking things through to their logical conclusion. That conclusion was that he almost certainly couldn't kill them both before one of them let out a scream. With sad resignation, Winthrop sank to the ground to die.

"If I hadn't let you use my water, I'd be fine," Winthrop muttered. "I hope you're happy, Judas. Winthrop meets a grisly end. We both know that's why you *actually* wanted to drag me to Chelles." In all reality, Winthrop was far from doomed. Even with his limited knowledge and faulty assumptions, he was still clearly in no danger of death. The sun was high enough for him to make it to the Eines before nightfall. Even if he rested here to recover, he would still be able to arise the next day and march to the river without even going a full twenty-four hours without a drink. Not to mention the fact that if there was a well nearby (as Winthrop still suspected there was) he could simply watch the shepherds long enough to see where they watered their sheep.

This certainty of death Winthrop perceived proceeded not from the head but from the heart. It was the fruit of despair, a despair welling up from his heartbreaking parting with David. He would never see him again. Despite all his best efforts to push that thought aside, it was dragging him down and robbing him of the motivation to live. Everything was now futile, and that futility plunged Winthrop into a lethal form of depression. It was over. It was finished. It was time to close the book on his sad and tortured life of woe. The voice of Sir Judas wouldn't let up though. *For the love of God, just go down the hill and ask them!* Despite the annoyance Sir Judas's voice caused him, Winthrop curled up on the ground, trying to force himself into a final sleep.

Winthrop began to doze. Then he shot up with a gasp and leapt to his feet. He had heard a voice. A different voice. One he hadn't heard in forty years. It said four words he hadn't heard in just as long.

Winthrop was now wide awake. The delirium and depression were banished. Looking at the shepherds talking, seeing them clearly for the first time, a novel thought occurred to Winthrop. *What if I asked them for a drink?* Winthrop stumbled out of the thicket and down the hill towards the shepherds. The sheep immediately began to bleat, bringing him to the shepherds' attention. One of them was yet a youth, certainly less than twenty years old. He had very short hair and a very round head, with the thin, bony frame common to many peasants. The older shepherd was in his thirties. He had a wave of black hair that faded to brown near the tips, and a poorly groomed beard that was a mixture of the same colors. The older man was dressed in much poorer clothes than the youth. They were roughspun, patched many times, and he did not have any shoes. What he did have, however, was a full and plump waterskin hanging from the cord he used as a belt. The elder shepherd raised a hand and hailed Winthrop saying, "Hello stranger! I haven't seen you around our little town before. Where do you come from, and what business are you on?"

Ignoring his question, Winthrop trudged forward, struggling to stand, and a look of concern came into their eyes. "Are you alright?" The youth asked. Winthrop was now close enough for them to see the blood all over his face and hand.

Then he threw himself on his knees at their feet and begged, "Water, please. I need water. I beg you! Please, show me where you water your sheep, and I would be happy to drink the same! I—"

He was unable to even finish his request. The elder shepherd had already unstrung the waterskin from his belt and placed it in Winthrop's hands. "Drink! Drink!"

Winthrop looked at the goatskin full of liquid treasure in disbelief, not yet processing what had just happened. He looked up at the shepherd as if to ask, 'What?' but the shepherd kept insisting, "Drink! Drink!" Snapping to his senses, Winthrop unstopped the skin and greedily poured its contents down his throat. He was so euphoric that he didn't even notice how much water he wasted, spilling out and running down his beard. Before long he was squeezing the skin tightly, trying to get the last few drops.

The younger shepherd said, "I have my own skin over here if you want it." Winthrop did indeed want it. The youth brought his waterskin and Winthrop dropped the first one to drink the second, still spilling as he guzzled it down. His thirst now fully sated, Winthrop noticed something he had missed when downing the first waterskin. This water was delicious! When he felt he was dying of thirst, any water would do, and Winthrop would have been happy to drink it from a muddy puddle. As his belly filled, however, Winthrop really began to taste the water and appreciate it. It tasted as fresh as the Eines...it tasted *fresher* than the Eines, even though he had just taken it from an old goatskin. Despite the fact that his thirst was already sated, he was squeezing the second skin for every last drop as well. He wanted to keep drinking the water forever, yet he was not disappointed when it was gone.

Once he had finished the second skin, Winthrop lowered it and sighed. Then he began to slowly realize what he had just done. That first waterskin, the one he dropped in his haste...yes, it had fallen in the mud. There was mud on the ground...that's right, he had spilled and wasted so much of the water it made mud. And the first waterskin...there was mud in the mouthpiece. Winthrop hadn't even thought to close it before dropping it. He expected to look up at the elder shepherd and see that he was angry, but with a good natured smile and concerned eyes he had picked up the waterskin and done his best to clean the mouth off with the rags he called his clothing. The youth looked on with a certain discomfort, and was sure to take his own waterskin back before Winthrop had a chance to drop it.

"Thank you...thank you so much..." Winthrop said weakly.

The older shepherd squeezed Winthrop's shoulder. "It was my pleasure! Are you alright now?"

Winthrop wanted to cry out, 'Give me more!' but he restrained himself. He nodded and said, "Yes, it was plenty...tell me, why did you help me?"

The two shepherds looked at each other in confusion, then looked back at Winthrop. "You were thirsty," the elder said. "What else were we going to do besides give you a drink?"

"But why?" Winthrop asked. "Why would you give away your water so freely? Good water is hard to find."

The younger shepherd smiled. "Not out here, it's not. We have more than we can drink."

Winthrop looked around. "Is there a stream or creek in the hills I don't know about?"

The younger shepherd chuckled. "In the spring there are some, but right now, no."

"Is the public well any good? Most of them are poisoned."

The youth laughed again. "Oh, ours is more poisoned than most, but that's not where we get our water."

Winthrop was going to continue questioning, but the elder shepherd gave the youth a stern look and said, "Stop messing with him, Nicholas." Then he turned to Winthrop and said, "Stranger, we would be happy to show you where we get our water. Meet me in the town square tomorrow at eight thirty. There's a bell tower that rings out the time, so you'll know when we're all gathering."

"Not all of us," Nicholas complained. "I'm always watering the sheep out here at that time!"

"You are welcome to join us, and you know it. You just worry about the sheep taking care of themselves."

"Sheep are the stupidest critters on earth. If I don't take care of them, they'll get themselves killed."

"We have no shortage of kind neighbors, lad. They'll drive off any coyotes who even think about going after our flocks."

"Hey! I'm sixteen! I'm not a lad anymore!"

"Until you get married, you're still a lad."

"You're not married!"

"That's different, and you know it."

The older shepherd gave Nicholas a smile, while the 'lad' rolled his eyes. Winthrop chuckled a little and said, "Well if marriage is the measuring stick, this graybeard is still a 'lad'."

"So it goes, lad, so it goes. And tell me, lad, what is your name?" The elder shepherd held out his hand for Winthrop to shake.

He grabbed it firmly and answered, "Winthrop." He kicked himself. Normally he would have given an alias. The kindly shepherd caught him off guard and got his real name instead. Then Winthrop thought of the four words he had heard in the thicket. Right now he didn't really want to give an alias. It felt good to go by his actual name.

"A pleasure, Winthrop! A pleasure! My name is Zakary, and I govern the larger flock you see here. That's my barn over in the distance (the one Winthrop had broken into) and I live in the house right next to it. This here is Nicholas, a good kid from that house you see over there. He still lives with his parents, but he's been taking over for his father lately and getting ready to leave the roost. If you don't mind my asking, how did you end up coming to us in such dire straits?" As Zakary spoke, he ripped a patch off his pants, wetted it with the remnants of Nicholas's water, and began to clean the blood off Winthrop's face and hand.

The last two days flashed through Winthrop's mind. He couldn't tell the truth. Though a variant of it might help. "I...was robbed."

The eyes of both shepherds went wide. "Truly? Robbers?" Zakary asked. Nicholas began to shake a little.

"Yes," Winthrop answered, nodding energetically. "Truly...I'm a freeman who usually works odd jobs in Chelles. But then a few months back two old friends of mine–Rowan and Garrett by name–told me about the wall construction going on in Reswick. So we went and worked that job until it was completed, then we took our pay and set out for Chelles. That's when he jumped us!" Winthrop literally jumped at that point, throwing his hands up dramatically and making both shepherds startle. "A black knight! He hopped out of the hills with his sword and cut Rowan down before I could react. Then he gutted Garrett, and I was the only one left. I took off running as fast as I could. I didn't grab my gear or any of my effects. I just ran and ran until I got to that big hill outside of town."

"Good God!" Nicholas exclaimed, "This is terrible! We need to tell everyone at once!" He made as if to run towards town, but Zakary grabbed him by the arm.

"Easy, Nicholas. we need to stay calm—"

"Calm?" Nicholas asked, starting to become hysterical. "There's no time to lose! We need to run and—"

Zakary grabbed both of Nicholas's shoulders now, giving him a firm shake and then pressing his forehead to the boy's. "Be at peace. We don't know exactly where this black knight is, but we know Winthrop has a lead on him. You ran straight here, right, Winthrop?" Thinking this would not be the opportune moment to mention his trespassing in the barn and shack, Winthrop nodded. "Alright, good. There's no reason to think the black knight would run here like Winthrop. He might not come here at all, given we're so close to Chelles. So that means we have a little bit of time to get organized. I'm gonna go find Connall and Finn, and we'll set up a lookout. You take Winthrop and *walk* to town. Don't tell anyone your business, and find William as fast as possible. Winthrop, William's our constable. You tell him what you told us, and he'll know what to do. And Nicholas," Zakary leaned back, holding Nicholas at arms' length. "Stay calm. If you start a panic, William will have a much harder time organizing a response. The best thing you can do to keep everybody safe is to *stay calm.*"

Zakary then strode swiftly to the south. Nicholas yelled after him, "What about the sheep?"

"Forget the sheep! Keeping *people* safe is more important!"

Zakary soon disappeared behind a hill, while Nicholas stood there wringing his hands. Then, as if remembering what Zakary said all at once, he snapped, "Well you heard him! Come on, Winthrop! We need to get to town!" Nicholas threw down his staff and began to run, but when he saw Winthrop was merely walking he slowed to a jog. When Winthrop still wasn't keeping up, the youth impatiently stopped, clenching and unclenching his fists nervously while he waited, and then turned and began to walk briskly as soon as Winthrop was even with him.

Winthrop knew that he should be working on his story, rehearsing in his head the details of how the black knight slew Rowan and Garrett. He was about to meet the constable, after all, yet a strange mood had come over him. Winthrop found he was too curious (even bored?) to contemplate something as mundane as the lies he wove in his own head. Far more fascinating to him was how calmly Zakary had taken the 'news' of a black knight. Granted, not every town was as high-strung as Chelles, but given the bloody history of black knights rampaging about this island ever since the Grand Empire fell, rumors of a black knight tended to be far more...*disturbing*, whenever they cropped up. Perhaps a constable or a soldier would stop and calmly consider the fact that the alleged black knight was alone, but...a shepherd? Why had Zakary seemed so well composed?

Winthrop was about to see another example of level-headedness, courtesy of Nicholas's tendency to lose his own. Out front of the very first house they came to was a heavy-set woman in a light blue dress, hanging laundry out to dry. Not far off, her four little children were digging in the dirt, looking for bugs, rocks, or (in the case of the smallest child) tasty clumps of clay to stick in her mouth. With a great deal of agitation, Nicholas asked her, "Mrs. Quinelly! Did you see Constable William when you were in town today? I need to find him right away!"

Looking at Winthrop and then back to Nicholas, Mrs. Quinelly answered, "I did, but that was early this morning. I don't know where he might be now. What is it?"

Winthrop didn't know whether Nicholas forgot what Zakary had told him, or if he was just too stressed to keep it to himself, but he instantly blurted, "Winthrop here was robbed by a black knight! Only a few hours from town! There are already two people dead!"

Mrs. Quinelly put a hand over her heart, looked as if she might swoon, but then shook her head, made the Sign of the Cross over herself, and whispered, "Oh, my Jesus...Oh, Lord, save us...children, come here now! Everyone gather up..." She then shouted in the direction of the western hills, "Cooper! Cooper! Cooper, come here! It's an emergency!" Then she went back to gathering her little flock. "Children, children, all together now! Nicholas, we're coming with you to look for William. Cooper!"

Cooper came jogging to the top of a hill, about forty yards away. With a concerned look, he yelled, "What?"

Mrs. Quinnely yelled back, "A black knight has killed two men, not far from town! We need to go to town and find William!"

"Oh my...Go! Go! I'll be right behind you!"

Still carrying his crook, Cooper began sprinting towards the house. Mrs. Quinely accelerated her efforts to gather the children, while Nicholas began to run towards town. "See, Winthrop, didn't I say we should hurry? We need to—"

"Nicholas, you stay right here now!" Mrs. Quinnely yelled at him. "Safety in numbers! You stay right here with me, and help me get the children to town. Don't you go running off on your own now!"

Nicholas paused, deeply agitated, but he didn't have to wait long. Cooper ran into his house and came out a few seconds later, a long and skinny bundle in one hand and his staff still in the other. "Here, Nicholas, take my staff. Where's yours? Oh, it doesn't matter. Stranger, take my sword." Cooper unrolled his little bundle of sheephide and produced a crude falchion. The blade was minimally worked, with a few ugly hammer marks that were never removed; only the cutting edge had ever been ground or filed. The poor piece had a wooden hilt with a few leather scraps wound around it to serve as the grip. Even in his most dire straits, Winthrop had never wielded such a sad excuse for a weapon, yet due to some old muscle memory (or was it perhaps the voice he had heard?) he reached for the hilt with his left hand. Cooper let go and quickly scooped up his two oldest children, while Mrs. Quinnely carried the younger two. "To town!"

The posse began walking swiftly. Following behind everyone else, Winthrop took a moment to flourish the sword. His wrist popped a little, not enough to hurt, but enough to make Winthrop recall his left hand hadn't been able to wield a sword for years. He tossed the sword to his right hand, and tried to repeat the flourish. He nearly dropped the blade, and then shook his head. *Good thing I won't actually need to use this.*

As they hurried, Nicholas was prattling, "I just don't know what we're going to do. I mean, a black knight! How can we even fight someone like that? None of us have any armor. And—"

Cooper cut him off. "Remember what the Lady is always saying, Nicholas. Be not afraid. God says those words a lot. Be not afraid."

Mrs. Quinnely kept whispering under her breath, just barely loud enough for Winthrop to hear, "Oh Jesus, save us. Oh Jesus, save us…"

Interesting, Winthrop thought to himself. *Christians…and none too shy about it either. Not terribly unusual for peasants, but…who is this Lady Cooper mentioned? She can't be the Bloody Baron's wife. Can she?*

They had now reached the edge of Dewford, where a moat ringed the entire town. Winthrop was surprised to see that it was three-quarters full of water, given how late in the summer it was. Even more surprising, however, was what Winthrop smelled. Nothing. When poor towns weren't built next to running water, moats usually smelled abominable. They were stagnant ditches where every chamber pot in town was dumped. As they crossed the bridge over the moat, Winthrop went to the edge and looked down. The water was perfectly clear, and with the sun still being high overhead, he was able to see the muddy bottom of the moat, about ten feet below the water level. There was a crawfish, climbing over a broken wooden handle, skittering towards a green bit of algae growing under the matching shovel head. Somehow, standing twenty feet above the little creature, Winthrop was able to see every one of its tiny legs, every ridge of every segment of its shell. He was confident he wouldn't be able to see the crawfish this well through air, let alone with ten feet of water between them. Winthrop was mesmerized watching the crawfish eat, and found himself staring at the small creature.

He was snapped back to his senses when Nicholas yelled, "Winthrop! Come o-o-on!" Looking back up, he saw that he had fallen far behind the others, who were now talking to a growing group of their fellow townsfolk. Sword in hand, Winthrop ran over to join them, drawing a few nervous looks. Cooper's children were clinging to his pant legs, while he was pointing down several lanes, saying, "We need to spread out and find William as fast as possible. Connor, you go to the square and see if anyone knows where he is. Gilly, I need you to—"

"Here comes Eustace!"

"Oh thank God. Eustace! Over here!"

A slim man in his mid-twenties came running over. His face had the untended patches of hair common to men who can't grow a full beard but who have not yet accepted that fact, giving him a rather boyish appearance. Nevertheless, he was well-conditioned, with hardly an ounce of fat on him and sizable muscles that looked out of place on his otherwise bony arms. Along with the way he carried himself and the wooden horn on his hip, Winthrop formed the 'professional opinion' as a robber that this man was either a deputy to the constable, or else the captain of the town's militia. He would later find out that Eustace was indeed both.

Stopping next to Cooper, slightly winded, Eustace asked, "What seems to be the matter, Cooper?"

"There was a murder! Two men, killed by a black knight."

Eustace's eyebrows shot up in surprise, but then he recomposed himself, and asked, "Where?"

"I don't know, my wife told me about it. I just got us to town as fast as we could."

"I heard about it from Nicholas." Mrs. Quinnely stated.

"Winthrop here saw it happen. He was covered in blood when he came running up to me and Zakary in the field. Tell him about it, Winthrop."

Winthrop nodded, and began speaking calmly. "Yes, I was with two friends of mine, Rowan and Garrett, who—"

"Where?" Eustace barked, now agitated. "Where did it happen?"

"On the road between Chelles and Reswick. We were in a large glade with an altar in it."

"So it wasn't on the road to Dewford?" Eustace asked.

"No, we were travelling from Reswick back home to Chelles."

"Alright, very good." Eustace raised his voice to make an announcement to the gathering crowd. "Everybody quiet down! I need you to hear this! There were two men killed by a black knight on the road between Reswick and Chelles. Winthrop here survived the attack and ran to our town. At this time, there is no reason to think the black knight is coming to Dewford, but we are still going to organize a lookout team to keep an eye out for him the next couple days. You, you, you, and you; come with me right now. We're going to notify everyone on the outskirts as soon as possible. You four, go home and get your weapons, then rally at this spot. Grab an extra sword or spear if you have one. I will be back within the hour, and then we will go take first lookout. Everyone else, spread the word that we're martialing the militia at the southern bridge. Kieran's squad should report at six, and Driscoll's should report at dawn. Kieran at six, Driscoll at dawn. Understood?"

Everyone nodded and several cries of assent went up. As the men were organizing themselves or leaving to inform the other townsfolk, Cooper asked Eustace, "Hey, Punchy, why don't you just blow the horn and get everyone to come here? It would be faster than sending messengers, and we wouldn't have to worry about anyone mixing up the plan."

Eustace gave a grim smile. "The horn is not for rumors of robbers. Not even a black knight. If you ever hear me blow it, know that Dewford's finest hour is at hand." Eustace then put his hands on the shoulders of Winthrop and Nicholas. "William should be at Reginald's manor right now. Take Winthrop to see him, and make sure you tell William that the situation is under control. If he needs me, I'll be on the southern outskirts informing our shepherds of what's happening. Understood?"

Nicholas nodded, finally seeming to have relaxed. "Okay…you got it, Punchy. I'll take Winthrop to the mayor's house." With that, Eustace took the four men he had singled out as messengers and went south. Cooper was amongst them and took his sword back from Winthrop, before following Punchy. Nicholas stood looking after them for half a minute, catching his breath and unwinding from the anxious tension he had worked himself up to. "Alright, Winthrop…you heard what Punchy said. Let's get going."

Walking at a relaxed pace, Nicholas led Winthrop along a northern street. At least, it initially ran north. As the reader surely knows, most towns and cities in the realm were built in the ruins of ancient cities from before the Great Calamity. Those ancient cities were built with very different principles in mind, and therefore they have long, straight roads that a man can look down and see a great distance. Dewford was not built in the ruins of such a city, and so its roads are more suited for our times. They wind and meander every which way, avoiding awkward hills, soft soil, and unsuitable terrain, while breaking the wind by eliminating straight paths. This of course had the accompanying effect of making Dewford a very difficult town to navigate, and even though Winthrop was trying to form a map in his head, after half a dozen twists and turns he had absolutely no idea how to even get back to the road they started on.

While the streets were proving to be an unreliable guide, there were two other landmarks that allowed Winthrop to keep his bearings. The first was the clock tower, which rose far above every other roof. Winthrop recalled that when he was standing on the hill, the clock tower had been right on the border of 'new Dewford' and 'old Dewford'. Winthrop could tell that they were heading mostly towards the clock tower, meaning they were on their way to the center of town. The second landmark that kept Winthrop oriented was both more obstructive, and also more mysterious. It was a huge wattle and daub channel, ten feet across, and perhaps half as deep, running in a snaking path around the houses. The channel had no water in it, though the bottom looked damp and muddy as if there had been a flood only recently. Many narrow bridges, some made of mere wooden planks, had been erected across the channel, but even so Nicholas occasionally went down a road that dead ended at the channel with no way to get across. When that happened, they would double back, and Nicholas would embarrassingly mutter, "Sorry...I don't spend a lot of time in town...I usually just go to the sheep gate when I need anything..."

Winthrop didn't mind the detours at all. If anything, he appreciated that the extra time was letting him take everything in. Finally dragging his attention away from the channel, Winthrop began to notice the townsfolk, and he was positively shocked by what he was seeing. These Dewfordians, they all looked...it didn't make any sense, yet it was certainly true...they all looked like people from Winthrop's childhood. Not their faces, but everything else. There were many children–lots and lots of children, by far outnumbering the adults. That wasn't the norm anymore, for most couples in Chelles had one or two, if they had any at all. The clothing of the Dewfordians was also remarkably out of time. They did not dress according to the more modern fashions, but instead they wore what people would wear in Winthrop's youth in the royal city. The men had long sleeved shirts with dirty smocks, trousers with leather boots, or any other form of functional clothing for their specific profession. No tee shirts, no shorts. Moreover, none of the clothes were torn 'in the fashionable style.' The clothes were all neat and orderly, and any holes that had formed (from wear, not from fashion) were properly patched up.

But the women...Winthrop had not seen women dressed like this ever since he left his former homeland. Lengthy dresses, shawls, head coverings. None of it was ornate or decadent like the ladies used to have–this was a relatively poor town after all. Nevertheless, there was a simple elegance in all of the apparel that made these peasant women look more like the princesses of the royal city than any aristocrat Winthrop had met since.

As he ran into the Dewfordians, several of them gave Winthrop easy smiles and greetings. "Hey, stranger! Haven't seen you before!"
While walking past a group of five who were discussing the militia's plans, one Dewfordian waved to Winthrop and said, "Hey stranger, don't know if you overheard us talking about the militia, but just wanted to set your mind at ease. Nothing bad, just takin' care of a little somethin' outside of town."

One of the other men in that group pointed at Winthrop and said, "He's the one reported the murders. It was his two friends the black knight killed."

The first man's genial expression turned to sadness, and he said, "Oh...I'm sorry there, stranger, I...ah, my mistake. My condolences...I can't imagine how you must be feelin'."

"Oh, yes...thank you." Winthrop suddenly remembered that he was claiming his two 'friends' had died earlier this morning. Like an idiot, he had been walking around town and marveling at everything, forgetting that he had a very important role to play right now. Wiping his eyes and pretending to sob a little, he said, "I...it's been such a rush since...I just haven't even had time to think about them, and now..." Covering his face as if he was about to break down crying, Winthrop figured he had done enough to make the townsfolk leave off in uncomfortable silence. He clearly didn't know Dewford.

Instead of uncomfortable silence, one of the men hugged Winthrop in a strong embrace, and patting him on the back of the head, said, "It's alright, bud. You're gonna be alright. You're safe here."

Winthrop almost jumped away in surprise, but he kept control of himself and maintained the act. "Thank you. I appreciate it. Well, I need to get goin—"

"What were the names of your friends?" The woman who asked was middle-aged with silver hair collected into a low bun. Her skirt, blouse, and jacket were of markedly higher quality than the other townsfolk, not gaudy, but brightly colored and clearly tailored. Atop her head she wore a distinctive wide-brimmed hat with an exotic black ostrich feather that curled from the back up to the front.

"Uh…Rowan and Garrett." Winthrop answered

"Rowan and Garrett…let me write that down…" The woman produced a pencil and a small notebook of folded papers from her leather purse, then wrote down the two names. "Okay, Rowan and Garrett. And you are?"

"Winthrop."

"Okay…W-i-n-t-h-r-o-p…thank you, Winthrop. We'll be sure to pray for your two friends at the Rosary tomorrow morning. I'll also let Lady Maria know. I'm sure she'll be praying for them all night."

"That's just like her," one of the men nodded. "In fact, I'll go tell her right away. She can pray for the guys out on lookout duty. Make sure everyone's safe from that black knight."

"Good idea," another man agreed. "We could definitely use it. A black knight this close to Chelles…practically on the doorstep. Been a few years since we had one passin by, but…boy, sure reminds ya why Fearnow outlawed em."

"Andrew!" The woman barked, suddenly scowling. "Be a little sensitive, you boor. These were Winthrop's friends. You are speaking about them as if they are mere case studies in a question of jurisprudence."

Andrew was wearing a dirty smock and had a thin layer of soot covering the entirety of his face. Taking him for a blacksmith, Winthrop seriously doubted that Andrew even knew what 'jurisprudence' was. Sure enough, he nodded deferentially, and said, "Sorry, ma'am. My mistake. I won't ask questions about jurisprudence anymore." Andrew then waved farewell, said, "Sorry," to Winthrop, and took his leave in an embarrassed fashion. The others followed suit, with one of them going to inform 'the Lady,' like he said he would.

The woman with the elaborate hat came up to Nicholas and asked, "Nicholas, are you taking Winthrop to see my husband?"

Nicholas nodded. "Yes, ma'am."

"Then I shall join you. I wish to hear the entirety of Winthrop's tale."

As they resumed walking once more, Winthrop asked the woman, "So would I be correct in assuming you are the constable's wife?"

She laughed and said, "Oh no, my apologies. After calling Andrew a boor, I go and fail to introduce myself. I am Cara O'Dewforthios. My husband Reginald is the mayor of Dewford. He's the first man to ever have that name 'O'Dewforthios.' Our local baron, Charles O'Dewford, he is the proper lord of our town…and…oh, well, I'm sure I don't need to tell you anything about him. The Bloody Baron's reputation precedes him, but for all the wretched things I could say about that brute, he does have a real eye for talent, and he knew Reginald would make a great mayor, so he gave him the title 'O'Dewforthios,' making him just one rank below the Baron. Which frankly, I can't imagine anything better for the Dewfordians, especially poor…oh, I just can't even sometimes…but anyway, since Charles doesn't have any children, that means if he were to die without an heir—not that I would ever want that, obviously! God forbid…though if anyone deserved it…no, I digress, but in the unfortunate event that he should pass without an heir, as things currently stand, Reginald would then become the baron. Which is really quite something, because he was just a little manor lord with twenty serfs when I married him, but Reginald is such a good administrator, and he's always deserved so much better than what he's gotten, and then here we are! Look at us! Next in line to be a *baron*! I never even dreamed I might be a baroness one day, and frankly, I don't know if I could handle it. I pray for Reginald to have good success all the time, and never even pray for myself, but God just keeps taking care of me, and whenever Reginald gets a promotion, I get promoted with him. It really does show you, good things come to those who pray." Winthrop was forced to avert his eyes as he tried not to laugh. Recalling the crossbow bolt he had left in Charles's stomach, he suspected Cara O'Dewforthios was going to be getting a new last name within the week, though it wouldn't have anything to do with answered prayers.

The garrulous woman prattled on as they walked through town, giving Winthrop a constant stream of information about every person they crossed along the way, frequently punctuated by a sudden remembrance of, "Oh, but you poor thing, what with the death of your friends this very day. And here I am talking about such nonsense. You know, my sister Anna, she always told me…" Though they only went another five minutes after Cara joined them, Winthrop was bombarded with far more than he could possibly absorb about every resident of Dewford. He was impressed by just how much Cara knew, especially concerning names. Unlike most nobles—even the lowest of nobles— who did their best to remain aloof from those they governed, Cara knew each and every peasant, greeting them as if they were her familiars while they walked.

The trio reached the town square, which was a large cobblestone market crowded with stalls haphazardly assembled around the large well in the center of the square. Several vendors with carts laden in hot food items were roaming the square looking for buyers, while a few merchants sat on a blanket with their goods arrayed before them. The most popular stalls were the ones selling beer and wine, where Winthrop was surprised to see several wealthy merchants (most likely out of towners, by the look of them) loading kegs and casks into their wagons to be transported elsewhere. There was far more to see, but Winthrop did not have time to take it in, for Cara led them up to the door of a large manor, rapped twice with a metal knocker, and then entered as the porter opened up for her. Winthrop followed her inside, vaguely recalling that he had meant to work on his cover story before meeting the constable.

Chapter 3: An Almost Thorough Interrogation

The meaning of the name 'Dewford' is a curious little mystery. One would be forgiven if he thought the name came from how the townsfolk must ford the 'morning dew,' which Winthrop would discover tomorrow. In reality, however, the name 'Dewford' has nothing to do with the morning dew and goes back to ancient times. My investigation showed the town was called 'Dewford' within the third generation after the Great Calamity, and it was therefore likely called 'Dewford' ever since its founding. The most common and likely explanation is that one of the refugees who founded this town was named 'Drew Ford,' or 'D. Woofard,' or some other suitable name that may have mutated to the current nomenclature. Still, the way this all worked out was incredibly providential, given how apropos the name was in Winthrop's day.

Back in Dewford's early years, the town had been a sister city of Chelles, persisting at a similar, modest size and engaging in regular trade. The lands surrounding Dewford were great for pasturing sheep, while the proximity of Chelles to the Eines river enabled the use of water-powered fiber carders and spinning machines that could turn huge quantities of raw wool into gorgeous final products. This brought great wealth to both towns, but Chelles was always the more popular and more visited. Strangers loved to see vibrant tapestries and to buy the finest coats and clothing. The simple shepherd's life was profitable and essential, yet ultimately unappealing. Over time the heart of Dewford began to point towards Chelles. Those who earned their wealth by shepherding no longer clung to it as an honorable vocation. Instead it was seen as a 'starting profession,' a way for young men to 'begin climbing the ladder.' The highest rung of this ladder was leaving friends and family behind to go live in the beloved city.

For those who remained, Chelles was the ideal, the standard by which Dewfordian culture must be judged. The fashions of Dewford were cheap Chellesian imitations. The dishes of Dewford were Chellesian cuisine without the spices. Anyone who wanted to be known as an intellectual in Dewford was up to date on the philosophies and ideas circulating in Chellesian colleges. The 'rustic outlook' and 'simple man's wisdom' were despised by the very people who possessed them. Before long Dewford became a sad and hollow place, constantly longing to be like Chelles, yet resembling her less and less every day.

There were two great transformations that overthrew this state of affairs, ushering in an entirely new Dewfordian paradigm. The first was the fall of the Grand Empire; that event shook the entire realm to its core, but Dewford even moreso. Shortly after the royal city fell (about fifteen years after the Battle of Nouen) the man known as Lord Benjamin Fearnow I. brought forth great wonders and marvels of electro-magic and began to incorporate them into Chellesian life. While the corpse of the Empire was rotting, Chelles was ascending, ballooning in population as people fled the once great cities and flocked to the new modern one.

This broke the back of any Chellesian imitation, for without electro-magic Dewford could no longer be conceived of as having any resemblance to her sister city. Moreover, the trade of wool dried up, as the economy of Chelles no longer relied on such mundane products. Cutoff and isolated from the world around her, gutted of every remotely wealthy and successful individual (who moved to camps outside the walls of Chelles), Dewford descended into a certain cultural backwardness, yet one that would go on to bear much fruit. Men cannot live without meaning, and the people of Dewford often began to discuss, "What makes us special? Where is our town going? Why do we even get out of bed in the morning to work?" Though everyone thought this was a town heading for extinction, the seeds were actually being sown for a glorious rebirth.

And then there was the second event, which indeed resembled the labor pains before that birth could come. To provide the historical backdrop for this event, several decades before the events of our current tale, a baron by the name of Hardwick O'Dewford became acquainted with Lord Benjamin Fearnow I. Dewford was Hardwick's proper barony, but he found he preferred the life of a hanger-on in Chelles to the governance of poor little Dewford. Moreover, this Baron Hardwick quickly learned that Lord Benjamin Fearnow had need of a man with a certain ruthlessness. He just so happened to have it. Whenever Lord

Fearnow wanted dirty work done without it being traced back to himself, he sent the baron to do the deed. Baron Hardwick moved his manorhouse from the center of Dewford to the very edge of his barony (six inches from 'where civilization ends'), and then he filled that house with every kind of scoundrel. His children followed in his footsteps, using Hardwick's army of shameless vassals as a shadow force for Lord Fearnow II. In time the Barony of Dewford came into the possession of Charles, with whom the reader is well acquainted. It did not take him long to earn his moniker, for on the very day of his installation as baron, Charles invited his cousins and vassals to a feast to celebrate his new title. The exact details of what happened at that feast are not known, but for some pretense or another a fight broke out between Charles's right hand man and one of Hardwick's surviving children (who incidentally happened to rule over the northern territories that Charles had sought to govern instead of Dewford). The fight between those two men escalated as their respective entourages became involved, and the evening ended in a bloodbath. While such intrigue and violence was common between nobles in the days of Lord Benjamin Fearnow II., Charles's conduct in the conflict made a uniquely strong impression. Rumors swirled in the aftermath about Charles having 'the strength of a dragon,' 'the ferocity of a devil,' and 'spears breaking upon his chest.' Whether or not Lord Fearnow believed the rumors, he was delighted to have such a fearsome enforcer in his employ. Charles appointed a string of short-lived mayors to govern Dewford while he himself attended to higher matters in Chelles. The second event I have been alluding to was the day that Lord Benjamin Fearnow III. wanted a certain man found and killed in Dewford. On this occasion the Dewfordians finally had the dread misfortune of meeting their absentee Baron. As I already said, now is not the time for that tale. I simply want you to know, dear reader, that the morning dews began twelve years ago when Charles came to town, and they radically changed everything about his barony. Everything else will be related at the proper time, but for now we must return to Winthrop's meeting with Dewford's most recent and most successful mayor: Reginald O'Dewforthios.

Cara led Nicholas and Winthrop into the ground floor of the manor, passing quickly through an elegant, yet relaxed parlor to the room where she knew she would find her husband. In the dining room was a dark mahogany table, fifteen feet long, with elegant legs curving to the ground and terminating in dark red lion paws. At the far end, where the master of the house was seated, a plate of fine china rimmed with rich blue floral patterns held the last scraps of the mutton sandwich that had been enjoyed for lunch. Mayor Reginald, though he was about the same age as Winthrop, was in considerably worse physical condition. He had an unpleasant bulging globe of a gut, plump cheeks, and a jowl of fat hanging from his small chin to his neck. Other than these few areas where he carried his weight, he was a small-boned man with pale skin, little muscle, and a modest hunchback protruding from between his shoulders. This was not a deformity he had been born with, but rather one he had acquired over many years of curling his shoulders forward whenever he was stressed— and he was often stressed. In public he did a good job of hiding these unattractive aspects of his physique with a bold red coat, trimmed in black, with golden buttons and large shoulder pads. At present, however, he had draped the coat over the chair beside him in order to avoid soiling it with the mess frequently caused by his inattentive eating habits.

At the right hand of the mayor sat the constable, a large man with a more well-rounded rotundity. He had blond hair fading to grey, and his brass star of office was pinned to his tan shirt. He also had a belt that he had draped over the chair next to him, from which hung a large club, a short sword, and a coil of thin rope. When Cara walked into the room, Reginald was in the middle of anxiously expounding some concern to the constable, but he stopped short when he saw his wife. Rising from his chair, Reginald said, "Cara, my dear. If I had expected you, I would have had another plate made." He walked across the room to give and receive a quite formal kiss on the cheek, all the while keeping his eyes locked on Winthrop. "I see you've brought unexpected guests. By the looks of them, you went for a walk outside the moat today?"

"Oh, you. Poor Winthrop here has suffered a dreadful tragedy! Two of his friends were murdered by a black knight this very day!"

"A black knight?" Reginald asked, surprise clear upon his face. "Where? How far from town? Do you know his current whereabouts?"

"It was on the road between Chelles and Reswick," Winthrop answered, "In a large glade that had an altar in it."

"How many men did he have with him?" William asked.

"He was all alone. He jumped out of the woods and surprised us, cutting down my friends before we knew what was happening."

William arose from his chair. "If you'll excuse me, mayor, I need to go take care of this at once."

Remembering the message Eustace had given him, Nicholas said, "Hey William, Lil' Punchy was at the southern gate when we got to town. He told me to tell you that he had it under control. He was already takin' a group south to tell the shepherds, and he had the militia getting organized for this evening."

"Alright, good to know." William answered.

He was strapping his belt on when Reginald gestured for him to sit back down. "Stay here, William, stay here!"

"But mayor, I—"

"Eustace has it under control. You heard Nicholas. The militia can easily handle a lone knight, and Eustace has already gone to the outskirts to make sure no one gets caught alone. By the time you're in position to do anything, the whole situation will be wrapped up. You stay here and talk to Winthrop with me. I want your insights. That question you just asked about whether the black knight was alone? Brilliant. I was picturing him with a posse of followers. I didn't even think to ask. This situation calls for some practical wisdom that I know you have." Reginald then leaned in close to William and whispered something in his ear. William's eyes went wide and he looked at Winthrop.

William whispered back, "Are you sure?"

"Hardly a doubt in my mind." After that, Reginald said loudly, "This poor man's been through so much! Tell Rian to open a bottle of Pennyshire and get three glasses. Cara, will you be drinking with us?"

"Oh, you know I can't do Pennyshire, but I'll take a glass of wine."

Reginald turned to Nicholas, crinkled his nose a little, but otherwise politely asked, "Young man, do your parents permit you to drink?"

"Uh...yes sir, they do...only, well...not unless my pa is with me."

"That's some good sense your pa has," Reginald answered, "...but I'm sure he would make an exception for if Mayor Reginald offered you some genuine Pennyshire brandy. Not a full glass, mind you. You come and sit down as well. I wish to hear how you are involved in this business." One of Reginald's servants had entered the room, and the mayor said to him, "Rian, three glasses and a bumper of Pennyshire, and one glass of that gutter wine my wife is so fond of."

"Oh, Reginald! I can't even believe the things that come out of your mouth sometimes. You know, if you actually tried it—"

"Enough, my dear, that's enough. Please, you've all been standing this whole time. Sit down." As Reginald took his seat at the head of the table, he smirked and gestured at Winthrop's boots. "I would say, 'Make yourselves at home,' but I know for you peasants that means, 'Kick your feet up on the table,' and I don't want you to get the table dirty."

"Reginald!" Cara scolded. "You're too impolite to our guests."

"Oh, it's just in good fun, my dear. We're just having a laugh, isn't that right, Winthrop?"

Rian returned with the glasses and a bottle of Pennyshire. As he set a glass in front of Winthrop, Winthrop commented, "A glass of brandy makes all things funnier."

"Indeed it does! Well said, Winthrop. I see you're a witty one." Reginald now changed his face, sighed deeply, and did his best to seem sorrowful. Raising his glass, he said, "To your friends! What were their names, Winthrop?"

"Rowan and Garrett."

"To Rowan and Garrett. May they be well remembered. Cheers."

"And may they rest in peace," Cara added.

"Yes, yes, that too."

Winthrop felt a genuine pang of sorrow as he touched his glass to those of William and Reginald. He recalled again his feelings after the funeral, when he had rebuked himself for being so cold about the deaths of his comrades. *What is the matter with me?* He tried to shake those feelings off, telling himself that being comfortable with death was just part of being a bandit.

Then why are you a bandit? It was the voice from earlier, the one that had roused Winthrop to go down the hill and talk to Nicholas and Zakary. Winthrop hastily took a gulp of brandy. *I swear I'm losing my mind...*

Winthrop had never been a brandy drinker, and he was surprised by the strength of the cacophony of flavors that bombarded him. Vanilla, cinnamon, nutmeg, figs, honey, tobacco, and, of course, grapes and alcohol all tumbled together in a revolting blast to his pallet. He nearly spat the drink back out, but clenched down his teeth and swallowed. Reginald and William both had a good laugh at his expense. "Oh, ho! Happens every time! Poor folk don't have the first clue about the finer things, do they, William?"

"Oh, leave poor Winthrop alone," Cara tutted. "Winthrop, would you prefer we have a glass of wine poured for you?"

"No, no. I'm fine. Just drank a little too fast," he answered.

"That is certainly true, but only the beginning." Reginald turned to Nicholas. "Young man, what was your name again?"

"It was Nicholas, Mister Mayor, sir."

"Nicholas, pay attention, and you might just learn how to drink brandy *properly*. Not that I know when you might enjoy such a luxury as Pennyshire, but I'm sure it will come up again at some point in life. You're young yet." Reginald held the cup of the glass in his palm, swirling the liquor around generously. "The first and most important thing to understand is that with brandy it is utterly imperative to take things *slowly*. There is no rush. We have nowhere to be. It is important to stop and enjoy the experience. Begin by warming the brandy with your hand. Just hold the glass like so for a few minutes. In time, we will progress to a seven-stage drinking method I've outlined, which was received quite warmly in a guide that circulated in Chelles a few years back. But before we can even get there—"

"Um, Mayor," William interjected, "You know how I love having you walk through the method, but, there's supposedly a black knight in the area and time is of the essence."

"Oh, William, William…you have no need to be concerned. As I already observed, Eustace has it under control. But what was that you just said? There's 'supposedly' a black knight? Why did you say 'supposedly' William? You almost sound as if you doubt poor Winthrop here."

William made a surprised face at Reginald, then looked uncomfortably at Winthrop, and back to Reginald. "Eh—no, did…did I say that? I don't remember saying 'supposedly.'"

"You most certainly did," Reginald nodded. "Cara, you heard it as well, yes?"

"I did," she answered. "Not that I…well, I only noticed because it seemed like such an odd thing. I wasn't sure why you said 'supposedly'."

William was quite flustered. "Ah, well…it must have just been a slip. My apologies. Think nothing of it."

"A slip you say?" Reginald asked, his 'curiosity' becoming a bit too transparent for Winthrop's liking. "Well if it was 'a slip,' then that must mean you are harboring doubts about Winthrop's tale, aren't you? Yes? That is what a slip is, after all. You were thinking there was 'supposedly' a black knight near town, but you simply meant to say 'there was a black knight near town.' That was the slip, yes? So then, you were thinking some doubts about poor Winthrop's report?"

William's face became red as he rose to leave. "Mayor, I—why are you vexing me like this? I would gladly tell you what I'm thinking in private, but right now…I don't know anything, I just have a few doubts, and if they are nothing, I'll only end by making a fool of myself. I would prefer not to say them in front of everyone."

"Oh, but William," Reginald tutted, "it is utterly imperative that you *do* express your doubts aloud so that if they *are* nothing, Winthrop here will have a chance to clear his name. After all, he may have a perfectly reasonable explanation, but if you go telling me your doubts in private, it will warp my whole judgment of the matter. Come now, speak. What exactly is on your mind?"

In frustration, William rubbed his eyes and then dragged his hands across his cheeks. With a heavy sigh, he said, "As I told you, it's probably nothing, but…I was just thinking that…well, that it was rather odd for there to be a lone black knight in the area. I mean, at least wearing the blacks. If it was one of those robber knights out of the north on an errand, I could see him traveling alone for the sake of speed or avoiding attention, but…in black armor? Unless this black knight was a madman, why wouldn't he put on common clothes?"

Reginald raised his eyebrows and nodded approvingly. "Excellent question, William. I hadn't considered those points. See, this is why I wanted to have you here for our discussion. Winthrop, what are your thoughts? Were there any clues you saw that might lend some insight into the situation? Don't worry if you didn't happen to notice anything. You were running for your life, after all."

Cara folded her arms and pouted. "Reginald, so help me…this conversation is beginning to sound more like an interrogation. You're acting as if you don't believe Winthrop."

"My dear, how could you say that? Why, I already told him that it's quite alright if he doesn't have the answer. And besides, this wasn't my question, it was William's. You must admit, he does make a good point. A lone black knight is quite the peculiar occurrence."

Winthrop stroked his beard a couple times. "I mean…no, I can't say for sure what happened. All I know is that he jumped out of the woods and attacked us. I couldn't tell you why he was wearing black armor."

"Are you sure it was black?" Reginald asked. "I mean, after all, with how fast everything must have happened, perhaps it was some other dark color, like a dingy mud on poorly maintained armor. Or perhaps he was wearing leathers?"

Winthrop pretended to be racking his memory, while he was actually considering which story would best serve him. Reginald was offering some plausible pathways for him to get out of his lie. A little bit of 'uncertainty' could downgrade the 'black knight' to a common robber, and all of a sudden Winthrop's tale couldn't be more plausible. A bandit ambush on the road between Reswick and Chelles? That wouldn't even qualify as news. Winthrop was about to mention how, 'It was all so fast…perhaps…' but then something quite unusual happened.

A wave of nausea washed over Winthrop. It was the lie. His own internal voice had caused a dreadful ringing in his ears. Feeling terribly ill, Winthrop blurted out, "It was a black knight. I'm sure of it!" He reached for the brandy, intending to slam it back and deaden the noise in his head, but it was already silent. He no longer felt nauseous either.

Reginald, obviously not knowing the reason for Winthrop's outburst, shook his head and smirked a little. "Testy, testy. Why, Winthrop, you seem a bit on edge. You're acting like we've accused you of something. There's no need to be so defensive. I just thought William raised some interesting questions, that was all. If you say it was a black knight, then it must have been. Now, back to what happened. This was a very important point from earlier. You said the black knight was alone, correct? He had no other accomplices?"

Winthrop nodded. "That is correct."

"Well that is certainly good news for our little town, but…" Reginald turned to William, "William, in your experience, doesn't that sound a little strange as well? One man ambushing three? I've never been a robber, but I would think they would want to outnumber their prey, no?"

William nodded slowly. "So you would think…not to mention that, uh…" William leaned back to look at Winthrop's boots and trousers under the table, still very dirty from digging the graves of Rowan and Garrett. "…pardon me for being so blunt, but uh…you don't look like the most lucrative traveler for a robber to ambush. If a man is willing to fight against losing odds, there must have been a merchant he could wait for…"

Winthrop was about to answer William's musings with a grain of truth. After working the pass between Reswick and Chelles for days before seeing Sir Judas, Winthrop knew just how careful merchant caravans were. He also knew that in desperate straits, robbers *would* often mug a traveling laborer just to get enough coin for the next week of meals. Winthrop himself had made that decision a few too many times. He was about to explain the perfectly plausible reasons why the knight would have ambushed him and his friends, but Winthrop became suddenly nauseous again. He couldn't bring himself to discuss the black knight robbing him. The lie was echoing cacophonously inside his head. Instead Winthrop yelled, "The knight was alone, and he killed my friends! That's all you need to know!"

William reached for his club. Nicholas and Cara became frightened. Winthrop realized he was shouting his answers in a manner that seemed positively mad. Reginald smirked. "Ah, our poor Winthrop, so deeply disturbed by the death of your friends…perhaps we should resume this conversation later. You don't seem to be quite well."

At that moment Reginald's servant Rian rushed into the room. "Is everything alright, Mayor? I heard shouting from the…'guest' Mrs. Cara brought home."

"Yes, yes, Rian, everything is quite alright, though I'm glad you came. I actually have an errand for you to take care of…" Reginald whispered something in Rian's ear.

Rian nodded. "As you wish." Instead of returning the way he had come, Rian walked past Winthrop, through the sitting room, and went out the front door of the manor to the town square.

Reginald was still smirking as he swirled his brandy, exceptionally pleased with how this conversation was going. "Now, where were we?"

"You said that we should resume this conversation later," Winthrop answered. "Frankly, I think I would appreciate that. I'm not feeling quite myself right now."

"Yes, let's leave off," Cara implored. "Please, Reginald. Send Winthrop away. I mean…I don't know that this conversation is going anywhere."

"Oh, to the contrary," Reginald smiled wryly, "I think we all know exactly where this conversation is going. And I do need to know how to protect my town from the black knight, so please, Winthrop, put up with me a little longer. Now to go over the details again, you said you were in the large glade with an altar in it when the black knight attacked you. Is that correct?" Winthrop felt sick just to hear his own lie repeated. Then Nicholas opened his mouth and Winthrop's condition became much worse. That, however, may have been perfectly natural given the implications of what Nicholas said.

"Hang on a minute, Winthrop, now that you mention it…didn't you tell me and Zakary that the knight jumped out of the hills?"

Winthrop was silent for far too long. Eventually, he weakly answered, "I did say that, yes."

Nicholas shrugged, "So is that glade right next to a hill? Sorry, I've never been there."

Winthrop again paused for a long time, trying to figure out what he could even say at this point. Eventually, he let out a heavy sigh and said, "No, Nicholas. That glade is not in a hilly portion of the trail. The hills I was referring to were where the road ascends into the hills, near Reswick. That's where the black knight fought us and killed Rowan and Garrett. Then he took me prisoner. The glade is where I ran away from him." Winthrop looked directly at Reginald. "The events with the black knight did not happen the way I said. I would like to correct my tale and set things straight."

Nicholas gasped. Cara covered her mouth and looked deeply saddened. William nodded knowingly. Reginald was simply triumphant.

"There is no need," Reginald answered. "The truth is already apparent. You say the black knight put you under arrest? I'll bet the rest of the brandy in your glass that I can name him. While you were under his arrest, did the black knight inform you that his name was Sir Oakley Shields? He is a black knight from the main island who often does bounty hunter work of this sort."

Winthrop furrowed his brow and shook his head. "No, not Oakley. The black knight told me his name was Judas."

"Ha!" Reginald exclaimed, slapping the table with delight. "Now there's a name I haven't heard in a few years. 'Sir Judas, Last of the Kingsguard,' is that the knight who happened to arrest you?"

Winthrop's eyes went wide. "That's exactly who he was! Then you know of him! But how? What else do you know about him? And is he trustworthy? There is a boy who is like a son to me, who—"

"Oh, take this fool away from me," Reginald flicked his hand dismissively. "I don't have time for such stupid pranks. William, bring him to the well. I'll be right behind you."

William arose and donned his belt, while Reginald very meticulously unfolded his coat, carefully inspecting it for any crumbs or wrinkles. Winthrop yelled, "Wait, but tell me more! I'm not lying! That was his name!"

William put his hand on Winthrop's arm. "Come along now, Winthrop. Don't make this difficult."

Winthrop arose and allowed William to lead him towards the front door, but he called over his shoulder, "Reginald! Tell me about Sir Judas!" Reginald rolled his eyes and shook his head.

When Winthrop came out the front door, the town square looked completely different. It was packed with people, and they were all standing still, no longer moving about from stall to stall. They were all looking right at Winthrop, as if they had been waiting for someone to come out of the mayor's manor. Indeed they were, for the errand Reginald had given to Rian was to call the townsfolk together to hear an important announcement concerning the black knight. As William led Winthrop towards the center of the square, the crowd parted and made way for them. They went forward a hundred feet or so, and then came to the well. At least, it was the remains of a well. The wall of masonry rose up to the height of Winthrop's waist, and it was eight feet in diameter. There was no hole in the middle of the well, but instead several shoddy and hastily constructed courses of bricks covered the top and sealed it. Any sort of tools for drawing water like a winch had been removed, reminding Winthrop that Zakary had said, 'Our well is more poisoned than most.' There was a little wooden staircase leading up to the top of the well, which William ascended with Winthrop in tow, still holding him by the arm.

Excited chatter was buzzing around the market, as wealthy visitors and poor residents of Dewford alike shared their speculations and rumors about why the mayor had called them together. After a few minutes of waiting, Reginald made his dramatic entrance. Two of his servants threw open the doors to his manor and held them while standing at attention. Meanwhile, a third servant came forth with a penant on a short pole, crying out, "Make way for his excellency, Mayor Reginald O'Dewforthios, the first of his name, protector of these lands entrusted to him by our beloved Baron. Give way as he comes forth to set all minds at ease concerning the matter of the black knight!"

Winthrop cocked his head to the side in genuine wonderment. *A herald? For the mayor of Dewford?!* Such regal pageantry, even as modest as this display, had been out of fashion for many years. Yet as the mayor came out in his fine coat and the people paid him respectful bows, Winthrop's eyes turned to the women of Dewford in their lengthy dresses and head coverings. *It's like this whole town has fallen out of time...*

Reginald came forward holding Lady Cara by the arm. She looked at Winthrop the entire time, with sorrowful eyes and a look of betrayal. Winthrop wasn't sure what she thought of him right now. She probably took him for a liar, and rightly so. Still, he hoped he could convince her that some of what he told her was true. Rowan and Garrett really had died yesterday, and when she had spoken with him, that had seemed to be the matter about which she cared the most. When Reginald reached the wooden steps rising to the well-platform, he stopped and kissed the hand of Lady Cara, who then stepped aside. The herald ascended the steps to the well, then Reginald followed while the herald saluted him. Reginald turned in a full circle, giving a dignified wave to the gathered townsfolk who fell completely silent.

"Good people of Dewford, whose welfare has been entrusted to me by our beloved Baron, you know with what tireless vigilance I seek to maintain the security and prosperity of our humble lands. It is therefore with great distress that I heard a rumor that has surely come to your ears as well. A tale of murder and violence committed by a black knight, a man so bold as to bloody his sword within a day's journey of Chelles, under whose influence we have so long enjoyed protection from the anarchic madness of these lordless lowlifes who plague the rest of our emerald isle. Surely there is not a soul among us whose heart did not tremble at the words of this rumor!"

A general murmur of assent came from the crowd, with plenty of nods of agreement. At that point however, Andrew the blacksmith, the man whom Cara had scolded about asking 'questions of jurisprudence,' called out to Reginald, "The Lady wasn't afraid, Mister Mayor! I was there when we told her about the black knight, and she said, 'Don't you worry, now, Andrew. William and Eustace will know what to do.'" Reginald's jawline stiffened, and palpable rage blazed forth from his eyes. Andrew clearly sensed that he had said something wrong, but was not entirely sure what. In confusion he added, "…sorry, sir."

Reginald took a few heavy breaths, using all of his willpower to maintain his composure. "Oh did she say that, blacksmith? And on what evidence? You see, empty platitudes and assurances do not carry the same weight as a proper investigation. To the contrary, if a black knight was indeed coming to town, Maria's words would be outright dangerous by giving people a false sense of calm. In fact, it is only because I condescend to her condition that I do not think it necessary to charge her with spreading false reports. Not false I suppose, but certainly unfounded reports, which can be just as dangerous in the proper circumstances."

An uncomfortable silence came over the crowd. Most of the peasants were not sure why Reginald was so irate, for even though he lived among them, he rarely spoke to them, and they did not know why anyone would be upset with Maria. The traveling merchants on the other hand—especially the wealthiest among them—were delighted to hear the mayor lambast Dewford's famous 'Lady' whose prominence injured their vanity as much as his.

Reginald continued, "As I was saying, we all heard these rumors with great distress, yet to my keen ear and level head, a few of the details of this account did not quite make sense to me. Why was it that this black knight was alone, yet dared to attack three men at once? Why was his place of ambush so close to Chelles, when many safer places of attack exist? Why was he wearing his armor, when he could have removed it to pass as an ordinary robber? Pondering these questions deeply, I sent for the visitor who had initiated the rumors and proceeded to conduct an entirely thorough interrogation." Winthrop's ears were ringing. Not as intensely as when he had been thinking about lying to Reginald, but still enough to be annoying. His left ear tingled when Reginald claimed he had been 'pondering these questions deeply,' when it was really William who had originally asked them. His right ear felt a sharp pain when Reginald claimed to have 'sent' for Winthrop, when in actuality Cara had brought him. He rubbed his ears vigorously, but to no avail. Whenever Reginald told a lie, it caused Winthrop physical pain to hear it.

The mayor continued, "With a line of insightful questioning, untangling the threads of this visitor's account and perceiving the web they weaved, I was able to catch him in his own lies, and extract the truth. This visitor confessed to myself and Constable William that the events with the black knight did *not* happen the way he told them, but rather he has been spreading false rumors throughout our town!"

There were rumbles of surprise from the crowd, a few smiles from those entertained by the drama, but mostly indignation from all of those who had been anxiously waiting to learn more about the black knight menace. One man shouted out, "So there's no black knight?"

"Oh, there most certainly is a black knight," Reginald answered, "But he is the rare sort that stays on the proper side of the law. Sir Oakley Shields of Duble was pursuing Winthrop here, as well as his two companions. When they decided to use violence, Sir Oakley slew two of these fugitives and took Winthrop under arrest. Winthrop proceeded to escape from Sir Oakley and fled to Dewford. The reason should of course be apparent to all…Winthrop is a runaway serf! He has escaped from his former master, and Sir Oakley was hired as a bounty hunter to return him. He fled to Dewford, knowing serfs generally receive asylum in our town. And indeed, I would be inclined to grant it to him, except that he has caused such public discord by his lies, that I instead wish to hand Winthrop over to Sir Oakley and drive him from our land!"

Most of the townsfolk—especially the elders—were unsure of the mayor's judgment. They passed uneasy looks among themselves, remembering the abusive masters whose conduct had *caused* Dewford to abolish serfdom, and not wishing that fate to come upon another for the mere crime of starting a (mostly true) rumor. The merchants and younger townsfolk (who had imbibed many of the customs of Chelles) also did not approve. To them, black knights were such a murderous terror that cooperating with this 'Sir Oakley' was outrageous, while Winthrop's decision to bend the truth in order to flee was totally understandable. The mayor did not receive the approbation that he was hoping for from his announcement, so he added to it, "...what's more, Winthrop confessed that the reason he had fled his former master was because he had committed some very serious crimes, for which Sir Oakley was bringing him to justice!"

For a moment, Winthrop felt as if he had died. He wasn't breathing, wasn't thinking, wasn't feeling. He was not even entirely sure that his heart continued to beat. He almost swooned, but William was still holding him up by the arm. William stepped forward and whispered in the mayor's ear, "Reginald, what are you doing? He didn't confess to any of this story."

"He will," Reginald answered with a wink. "The truth is obvious. You reached the same conclusion, didn't you?"

"I did, but...he didn't *confess*!"

"He will." Reginald stated flatly. "I'm not wasting my time on a trial for a serf." Reginald then turned to Winthrop. Seeing the way he was leaning on William and how unwell he generally looked, the mayor concluded that his accusation had hit the mark and decided to press his luck. "Go ahead Winthrop! Confess the truth, and I may reconsider my judgment! Tell our people what you told William and I and perhaps we can find a place for you in our town."

Winthrop looked at Reginald in confusion. He wanted to yell, 'I never committed any crimes!' but he knew that would be a lie. He wanted to yell, 'I am a freeman! I was born in Chelles!' but that would be a lie as well. A hundred stories tried to tumble out of his mouth, but not one could pass his lips. He was panting heavily, not knowing what to say. Reginald said, "Go on. Tell us the truth."

The voice that lived within Winthrop's mind was screaming, *Lie! Lie! Save yourself! Do not be ensnared by the accursed Truth! You are free to do whatever you want!*

At that moment the clock tower struck three, and as it rang out the hour, each knell dredged up memories from his conversation with Sir Judas that very morning.

DONG!

You've seen the greatness...you've seen the splendor...don't you dream of something more?

DONG!

I used to dream. Back when I was young and stupid and full of life. But the gray hairs you and I both have say that we've grown old, too old to believe the dreams of children still come true.

DONG!

I may be gray, and I may be old, but I still believe every good dream comes true...just not always in the way we expected.

Lies do not fall from the lips of paladins.

Winthrop recovered his strength. He once more could stand upright, but he did not return to his former posture. With shoulders back, chest out, head inclined upward to give Reginald a terribly haughty look, Winthrop shouted loudly, "Nihil horum criminum confiteor!" Which being translated means, "I confess to none of these accusations!"

Of all those who were gathered, there were only two souls who understood the full import of what Winthrop said, or, more precisely, the language in which he said it. Cara looked up at him in amazement. Reginald took a step back in fright. Shaking his head and recomposing himself, Reginald smiled uncomfortably and said, "A clever trick, but I am not fooled. That is a line from one of those peasant songs, isn't it! I have heard you lot sing after you pray your Rosaries. You're just parroting something you've heard before. Your pronunciation isn't even proper."

"Si pronuntiatio mea, ut tu dicis, impropria est, ex decenniis linguae vulgari utendi est. Hoc tamen scito: linguam nobilitatis locutus sum ex quo mater mea eam mihi in gremio suo docuit." [If my pronunciation is improper, as you say, it is from decades of using the vulgar tongue. Yet know this: I have spoken the language of nobility since my mother taught it to me on her lap.]

Reginald was in disbelief, and nearly backed right off the well in fear. Trembling took hold of him. Still clinging to the last strands of denial, he stammered, "You—you must have been—a serf to a translator. An assistant who overheard a duke! That's why you botched your pronoun! Anyone who truly knew the Ancient Language would know a peasant should say 'vos' instead of 'tu' when he is speaking to men of authority."

Winthrop cried out for all to hear, "I am no peasant, and you have no authority over me! My name is Lord Winthrop, and I am the rightful Duke of Nouen!"

Chapter 4: The Duke of Nouen

Forty years ago, at the royal palace, seat of the Grand Empire.

Yesterday the armies under Goliath streamed across the lands of Nouen and sacked the lord's manor. They had intended to make war against the royal city that day, but Lord Isaac's forces fought a ferocious retreat, buying the people time to get away and warn the king. He and his men entered the royal city well after sundown, while Goliath organized an assault for the next day. In his terrible, booming voice, the giant had announced for the entire city to hear, "I issue a challenge to the six paladins! Let them alone ride out against me! If they can slay me, my army shall retreat, while if they fall I do not even ask for your surrender. Send them to me! Accept my challenge! I desire only that they die by my own hand!"

If Goliath was hoping to intimidate his foes with his declaration, it had the opposite effect. Many laughed, while others openly proclaimed their confidence.

"The paladins will save us! Even a giant can't beat them six-to-one!"

"Why, I would bet Sir Daniel alone could take down that monster!"

Winthrop was one such person, expecting that today would be the day of triumphant victory. When he arose early in the morning, his father was already gone. Sometime later, Lord Isaac returned. He was deathly pale and stricken.

"Father! What happened? You look as if you have seen a ghost!"

Lord Isaac gave Winthrop a weak and uneasy smile. "In a certain sense, perhaps I have."

"What is it? Is there anything I can do to help?"

"Take off that armor. Today you will not be fighting."

Winthrop straightened up. "I'm old enough to fight, father. I would follow you anywhere."

"Where I am going, you cannot follow, but you can at least still follow orders. Give me your sword."

Volume III: Dewford

Winthrop frowned. "You would take my weapon from me on the day of the greatest battle of our time?"

"I already told you. Today you do not battle. What's more, I have need of your sword. The king has asked for mine." Only now did Winthrop realize his father's magnificent silver sword was not on his hip.

"Why did he want it?"

"I did not ask."

"Why not?"

"Because he is my king! And I would gladly grant his every request!" Lord Isaac leveled a severe look at Winthrop. "Would you not say the same of your father?"

Winthrop unclasped his belt and handed it to his father, along with the sword and scabbard. "Where shall I find another?"

"You don't need another. And take off that armor!" He fumbled with the belt before strapping it on. "I forgot you were left handed," he said, speaking more softly. Once he had Winthrop's sword properly situated on his own hip, Lord Isaac looked at Winthrop again and said, "Put on the plainest clothes you have and take your brother to the city's retreat. Today you stay with him, and be prepared to run."

"You expect me to run?"

"I expect you to follow orders!"

Lord Isaac had a deep pain in his eyes, all the more striking on that face usually so composed and steady. Trembling and breathing heavily, he said with a shaking voice, "Take last night's bread, take your brother, and go to the rear gate." Lord Isaac placed his hand on a chair to support himself. "If your mother were here, it might be different. But she's not. You're the only one who can take care of Jacob once I'm gone. Do your duty. And if you won't do it for duty, at least do it out of obedience to your father."

Even with the chair, Lord Isaac was still shaking terribly. Winthrop asked him, "Father…what did the king tell you?"

Lord Isaac turned away. "He told me about the cross he was carrying. For the sake of our friendship, he let me carry it with him. I am glad, for he seemed greatly relieved, but in my weakness, it is heavy." He turned back to Winthrop. "Kneel down, and I'll give you my blessing."

Winthrop knelt down. Ten thousand times his father had blessed him, since before he could even walk. He would trace a cross on his forehead with his thumb and say, 'God bless you,' which is what Winthrop expected now. Instead, Lord Isaac placed both hands on his son's head and prayed,

"Lord God, Almighty Father, Light of the world and Light of Truth, I, thine unworthy servant have raised this Thy child Winthrop to the age of manhood for love of Thee and love of him. Ignore the mistakes I've made, for I am but dust and ashes. Like a good steward I have always tried to raise him and his brother to follow after Thy ways. And now that I am come unto my hour to depart this world, I do not pray that Thou wilt take him out of this world, but that Thou wilt keep him from the evil one. Emitte lucem Tuam et Veritatem Tuam, and may those rays of truth always shine in his heart. No matter how dark the world may ever be, lead him and bring him to Thy holy mountain and into Thy tabernacle."

Winthrop looked up and saw his father was crying. This was the only time Winthrop had seen him cry since the day his mother died. "Father…I still don't understand."

"Neither do I."

Lord Isaac turned and walked to the door. Only now did Winthrop realize his father had donned his uniform without putting any armor on underneath. Lord Isaac said, "Ite. Missa est," which being translated, means, "Go, it is sent." Then Lord Isaac opened the door and made to leave. At the last moment he turned back and spoke his final words. For the rest of that morning he said nothing, holding the echo of those precious words on his tongue. When saluted by his men he saluted back silently. When asked about final preparations he would point and gesture. Even when Winthrop and Jacob saw their father charge Goliath, he made no shout or battle cry. Like a silent avenger–far faster than any man in armor–he leapt up, stabbed the giant in the eye, and then fell by the flaming blade of Doomfall.

Winthrop had often wished he could repeat these words to David. Even as he left the glade, he almost said them. Yet for as long as he had raised David, Winthrop had never been able to do so. He could not bring himself to pollute such precious words with his own filthy, lying lips.

The final words of Lord Isaac, Duke of Nouen were thus: "I love you, son."

Like the stillness that comes after a blast of thunder has silenced all of nature, there was no sound nor motion in Dewford after Winthrop's startling confession. In that first moment Reginald was not even capable of doubting Winthrop's claim. To doubt something requires that the mind can first conceive it, and Winthrop's claim was inconceivable. The Rayoeki Heishado of Nouen; the 'Lightning Army' that served as the only permanent military force of the Grand Empire. In that first moment, all of the 'good breeding' and 'dignity of office' Reginald so highly valued could not hold back the flow of childhood memories. As a young boy having stick fights with his older brothers, Reginald would always play Duke Isaac, justifying the hit and run tactics that his brothers called 'cowardly' by referring to them as 'lightning strikes.' He remembered being nineteen years old when Goliath 'liberated' the emerald isle from the Grand Empire. Over the next year the mainland was 'liberated' as well. Everyone knew what was coming. The Grand Empire would die. No army was willing to take the field against Goliath. Every duke and lord who surrendered had been shown amnesty and permitted to keep his lands. In the circles of lesser nobles the chatter was always about how 'we are living in exciting times!' Yet to young Reginald, not yet frozen to the burning passions of youth, the overthrow of the 'Tyrant King' was so…banal. He wanted more. Yet he knew not what. His mind knew that this was good. His mind knew a peaceful end to the oppression was far better than vast bloodshed. Yet in his heart, Reginald didn't want peace. In his heart, he knew there must be bitter violence and glorious battles, or else what was Goliath conquering? Who ever heard of a tyrant that no one feared to revolt against? Who ever heard of a liberator before whom all men trembled? Like all men of that time, Reginald listened to the news as it came in from the battlefront, but with less zeal and interest than most of his peers. He was both busy studying to prepare himself for political life, as well as jaded by political life. News of the Grand Empire's ongoing demise was nothing more than a curiosity.

Until Goliath drew near to Nouen.

News reached Chelles (where Reginald was studying) over a month after each event happened. They all knew that the matter must already be decided, and Goliath could be returning to Castle Nightfall any day. Would the Rayoeki Heishado be coming with him? Would they be stationed on the islands? Or left on the mainland? Did Goliath consider them 'too close' to the king? Would there be executions? Surely not executions. News arrived that Goliath's army had reached Nouen. Nouen did not surrender. Goliath did not attack. There was much nodding and approval. "Goliath knows Duke Isaac will get cold feet." The next day a herald announced that Goliath had sent negotiators to speak with Lord Isaac, and they were received. There was a rumor (which was soon promoted to fact) that Duke Isaac just needed to save face. He was going to stand his ground for another day, and then surrender to Goliath. It had all been arranged. So the rumor went, but it was proven false. Each and every day at the same time, Reginald and a thousand other souls gathered together to hear the news from the runner from Reswick. Every day for a full week, the news was that nothing had happened. Goliath's army had come to Nouen. Nouen had not surrendered. Yet despite the obstinate refusal of Duke Isaac to do as all other lords had done, somehow the rumor still persisted that he would surrender by tomorrow. And somehow, Reginald still believed it. His mind knew Duke Isaac had only that one option. His heart knew there was another. And the next day, as the herald arrived from Reswick, Reginald's heart was shattered to pieces with the knowledge that it was right.

"Nouen is fallen! She has fallen higher than the heavens!" It was a tale of sorties, and cavalry charges, and Parthian shots, and ladders and rams and cloven shields and walls teeming with foes. It was a tale of a massive exodus, the whole people of Nouen streaming across the plains as Goliath's army gave pursuit. And in the midst of the tale of that whole people, all eyes turned to one woman, old and crooked, who no longer had the strength to flee. From the distant hills they watched her fall further behind, and her pursuers closed the gap, and even from a great distance, the witnesses could tell that blood lust was red in the eyes of her assailants, and their hearts trembled to behold whatever violence would come upon her. And then a horse broke off from the main body, and the rider was none other than the duke! And with silver sword held high, he called, "To me! To me!" and the men of Nouen answered, "To the lord!" and a great clash broke out around her, and from that storm of steel and spears the duke's horse galloped for the Royal City, only the woman! She was upon it! And the duke was on foot, pouring out the blood of his foes until they routed in fear, and after the briefest pursuit, the duke called for a renewed retreat. The rest of that day was a series of crashing waves as the soldiers attacked and retreated, charged and fell back. The men of Nouen fought until that day's bitter end, and the next day they fought until the most bitter end of all. The Royal City fell, and the paladins were slain, yet even from the darkest depths of their doomed cause, every soldier of Nouen, to the man, died a death of immortal glory.

Reginald went home that day and sat in his room for a long time. Then when night fell he began to weep. He did not know why, nor would he ever look for the answer. The next day he returned to ordinary life, and he nodded along with every other cold and frigid critic who said, "What a shame! Such pointless bloodshed. Those Noueneese were always a barbaric people." Reginald added, "It really says something about the king that no *civilized* duchies fought to defend him!" His comment was well received, and Reginald made a very favorable impression on some of the lords who heard him. He would always look back on that comment as the bitter moment when he traded the fantasies of his childhood for the sober maturity of a man.

Now standing on the well with Winthrop, not entirely sure how long he had been lost in thought, Reginald growled, "Prove it." Winthrop said nothing. Reginald shouted, "Prove it! You say you're the Duke of Nouen? The son of Isaac, who died defending the Tyrant King? Prove it! What's your evidence? Why should I believe you?"

Winthrop answered flatly, "Ego sum qui ego sum," or in our tongue, "I am who I am."

Reginald was within an inch of calling for Winthrop to be flogged on the spot, but his able use of the Noble Language continued to give him pause. How did a peasant learn that language? Or if he was not a peasant, why was a noble pretending to be the heir to a disgraced house that no longer existed? Possibilities wheeled through Reginald's mind as he tried to make sense of what he believed might be true. William put his hand on Reginald's shoulder and whispered in his ear the prudent advice Reginald needed to hear. "We have to regroup, Mayor."

"Regroup? He's a liar!" Reginald whispered back.

"We can't prove that. He's clearly not willing to confess to anything, which means we'll need a trial before we can pass judgment."

"Trial? Have you lost your mind?"

"Sir, I don't know what the truth is, but I know we won't figure it out standing on this well. We need to dismiss the crowd and tell them that today's events are still under investigation."

Reginald felt his temples throbbing with anxiety. There was no way to end this gathering without looking foolish. To even admit he was *investigating* such a ridiculous claim would make him a laughingstock, not only in Dewford, but also any town he traveled to visit. As his mind reeled at the thought of such excruciating humiliation, William said, "Sir. Your decision?"

Reginald closed his eyes and snapped, "Take him to Ed! But don't tell anyone there's an investigation. I'll try to give a vaguer explanation of what's going on."

In agitation, Reginald had stated this last line loud enough for Winthrop to overhear. He felt a tingling in his ears, and he sensed that Reginald's 'vaguer explanation' was going to entail some sort of lie. Winthrop asked him directly, "Are you taking time to verify my identity?"

Reginald ground his teeth, then stepped up to Winthrop and hissed, "Yes, we are 'verifying your identity,' but don't you dare tell anyone I said that, or I will be sure to see you flogged!"

"You cannot flog a duke," Winthrop answered coolly. He then turned to the crowd and proclaimed, "Mayor Reginald is taking the very prudent step of verifying my identity. Once sufficient evidence of my claim has been established, he and I will work out the arrangements for my visit to Dewford. I apologize for the confusion and anxiety I caused with the black knight. He really did kill my travelling companions, but I lied in several important details. He is not a threat to any of you, and you may rest easy. I beg you to forgive me, and you are all hereby dismissed. Go about your day in peace."

Reginald's eyes went wide. Still not convinced Winthrop was telling the truth, he almost leapt upon him in rage at this subversion of his own authority. William knew his mayor well enough to swiftly step between him and Winthrop and add, "Move it along now. We apologize for assembling you prematurely. The matter is still under investigation." The crowd slowly began to disperse, but since many of them were already doing business in the town square (and many used the stalls as an opportunity to linger longer) there were still many eyes upon the three on the well. William turned to Reginald and said, "I know we have a lot to sort out, but we can't do it here. I'll put him in Ed's custody and then meet you at your manor." Reginald couldn't even manage a word. He simply glared at Winthrop in fury.

William absentmindedly began to lead Winthrop, not realizing he was still holding him by the arm. All at once, the possibility occurred to him that if Winthrop truly was a duke, he ought to be more decorous, though he was not entirely sure how. William decided to simply ask Winthrop, "Are you going to come along willingly?"

Winthrop answered, "I am." William released his arm and led the way down the stairs. Winthrop followed.

William swiftly passed through the throngs of curious onlookers and departed the square by a narrow street that quickly wound through small town homes before crossing a narrow bridge over the wide ditches that flowed from the town square. "I'll be putting you in the custody of Ed the barkeep. He's a fairly influential man in our town. Not a noble and not a merchant, but…influential. A lot of people look up to him. And what's more, he has the facilities to put you up while Reginald and I investigate your claim. Speaking of which, do you have any information that would help us establish your identity? Anyone who might know you? You look old enough that you may have known some nobles from before the Grand Empire fell."

Winthrop racked his brain, then shook his head. "No, I can't think of anyone who would know us from that far away. If the archives of Chelles are well maintained, I might be able to give you verifiable information that few people would know. I can easily draw our family crest. Well, I might be able to describe it. My drawing hand had an injury a few years back, so my picture would end up being little more than a tangle of lines."

"I'm not sure that would be specific enough…" William said. "Surely there were many people who have seen the crest of Nouen. It was probably on the pennants of the flag bearers."

"Yes, but I can give you details that the average viewer would not have noticed. For example, the sword that is in the center of the crest looks all grey from a distance, but if you look carefully, the hilt is actually a lighter shade. That was supposed to look like the silver hilt of the family sword that was passed down from generation to generation. It also has two very small gems in the hilt. A glassy one on the left and a dark one on the right. I can also give you the motto that my father took when he was crowned, which was not on the crest, but may be recorded in an archive. 'Veritas liberabit vos.' 'The truth shall set you free.'" Winthrop was beginning to reminisce, but then he brushed away his memories. "What do you think? Is that specific enough?"

William wagged his head back and forth as he considered the matter, then said, "You know, if we check the archive and verify those things…I don't know that it would be sufficient proof to *truly* establish your identity, but…" He shrugged. "So long as you don't cause any trouble, maybe that would be enough evidence for a short stay in Dewford."

William and Winthrop were now approaching a very large one-story building. A white sign hung over the door with elegant green letters saying, 'E&S's.' What caught Winthrop's eye, however, was the fact that a small trench, about six inches across, broke off from the main ditch they had been following and ran into a hole in the side of the tavern. Winthrop asked William, "William, what are these ditches that I have been seeing all over town? And why do you Dewfordians seem to be so fond of digging them?"

William smiled. "Those are aqueducts."

"Aqueducts?"

"Aqueducts. They carry water all through town. Ed got permission to dig that special branch that runs into his basement so that he can get enough water to brew beer and serve any of his patrons who aren't in the mood to drink."

Winthrop gave William a befuddled look. "William, are...you're joking with me. What are those actually used for?"

William chuckled. "They're aqueducts! That's the truth!" His assertion that 'That's the truth,' reminded Winthrop that he had been having some sort of...*experience* whenever Reginald lied. The fact that he was not feeling anything now made him suspect William was telling the truth, but...how?

"William, aqueducts need water. These ditches are dry as a bone."

"Have you ever heard of the Dews of Dewford?"

"I vaguely recall something like that. I was in Chelles once...or maybe Reswick? No, it was Pawnshire. I was in a tavern, and there were some travelers coming from Dewford raving about 'the morning dew,' and telling everyone they met that we should go see it. We laughed at them for...well, don't take this the wrong way, but, we told them there was nothing worth seeing in Dewford."

The two had now reached the door to the tavern, and William opened the door for Winthrop. "Well if you come to the town square tomorrow at nine, you'll find out just how wrong you are." Winthrop went to walk past William, but then William put a hand on his shoulder and stopped smiling for a moment. "And Winthrop...if you have been lying to us...I don't mean to be distrustful, but...I would highly recommend that you 'slip away' at some point after dark tonight. The longer you stay here, the more trouble there will be when the truth comes out."

Winthrop nodded. "I understand, but I'm telling the truth." Then he added, "Perhaps it's like your 'aqueducts.' I can't give another answer, even if my first one is absurd."

William smiled and removed his hand. "Very well. Then let's go in and say hello to Ed."

Chapter 5: Slow Drinks Between Fast Friends

The first evidence that this was no ordinary tavern greeted Winthrop as soon as he passed the swinging door. The tavern was well-lit. Taverns were never well-lit. The rule was to keep them nice and dark with just enough light to see where you're going. This tavern had an abundance of windows to let in the sun, and many unlit candles that would illuminate it at night. Second, painted wooden statues were scattered about the room as decorations. Instead of anchors, maps, or other mysterious bits of rubbish, there were at least a dozen statues looking right at you as you walked up to the bar. They reminded Winthrop of… Indeed they were! They were religious statues. He was sure of it. Behind the large wrap-around bar was a whole set for the wedding feast at Cana. There were the servers, there the jars of wine, there the Apostles, the Lord, and His Mother. Most of the statues were ham-fisted things made by local amateurs, but a few of the nicer and more prominent ones looked like miniature versions of real people. Third and finally, the east and west walls of the tavern had stained-glass windows in their center. They weren't large nor terribly detailed, but they were good enough to catch the eye. The eastern wall was the Resurrection, while the western wall (currently glowing in the 3 o'clock sun) was a sorrowful image of the Crucifixion. Jesus was in the center, with St. John and the Blessed Virgin on either side and St. Mary Magdalene kneeling at His feet and hugging the Cross. She was the most detailed figure in the glass, curled up in a posture of bitter weeping.

"What on earth did I just walk into?" Winthrop asked, "Is this a barroom or a church?"

"Why can't it be both?" The reply came from a far corner of the room where a stocky, smiling, freckled man with red hair was wiping down a table. "You'll have to forgive my lack of manners your dukeliness, but I was at that assembly ole Veggie Reggie called, and when I heard you call out, 'I'm Duke of Nouen!' I said to myself, 'Ed,' I says, 'You know how these high profile visitors tend ta go tumblin' out. Ole Veggie Reggie is gonna send him to the tavern, and you ain't got no place set up for a duke yet, especially a duke of such high dukeliness as Nouen.' So I came rushin back here tryin' to get a proper place set up for ya, but you was hot on my tail and I haven't had more than five minutes a makin' arrangements. Though frankly, that might be for the best, cuz I'm a simple man with no proper education. I don't know the first thing about how I should set up and treat someone like your dukeliness when he comes into my establishment."

"Treat me as you would treat anyone else," Winthrop answered. "No one has treated me like a duke in decades."

William waved to Ed. "Ed, I need to go talk to Reginald, but in case you didn't hear, we are still investigating Winthrop's identity. He is to remain here until Eustace or I come back to summon him, and if he leaves, you make sure we hear about it, understood?"

"Holy mackerole, William, you can't be suggestin' that I hole him up in here while I run off to the mornin' Rosary tomorrow, are ya?"

William rolled his eyes. "Yes, you can bring him to the Rosary tomorrow. I already told Winthrop that he should be sure to see the morning dew."

"Well, if you weren't referrin' to the Rosary, you must notta been referrin' to the Lady neither. Man can't come to Dewford and not meet the Lady."

"Oh, you be careful now, Ed. Don't you go getting me in trouble with Reginald."

"Ole Eddie, wouldn't be getting' you in no trouble there, William, it would be a most discreet sorta operation. I always walk her to the Rosary and back, and so nothin' would be outta sorts if Winthrop was comin' with me. Why, I don't see why you would even have to tell ole Reggie that we was visitin' her."

"Alright, alright, you can take Winthrop to meet Maria, just don't make a big scene out of it, alright? Reginald is already agitated enough with this whole situation. Don't go twisting the knife by getting his rival involved."

"Oh, why I don't see how you can even be takin' Veggie's side in anythin', what with Maria—"

"No scenes! Short visit only! And now, Ed, I must depart." William spun about and departed swiftly, not wanting to hear the haggling he was sure would ensue about, 'Well just how short are we talkin' now?'

Ed came forward, shaking his head. "I see, I see…a duke they tell me, shows up in town unannounced…" Ed looked Winthrop up and down. "…with eh…all due respect, your dukeliness, would you mind if I spoke frankly about what's troublin' me?"

"You don't think I'm a duke."

"Noooooo, nooooo, not how I would put it, your dukeliness, not how I would put it at all. To be honest, the way you were talking to ole Veggie Reggie–he's our mayor, in case you didn't know–you got me to thinking to myself, 'Ed,' I says, 'you've never seen a duke before, and you don't know what one would act like if you saw him, but if you did see one acting, you would see something like what you just saw right there, you would.' You weren't all mean and snotty-nosed to ole Veggie–that's how he is with us, you see, and so I might think you was a mayor if you talked like that–instead you was just all matter of fact. 'Blibbidy jubba doo ba robba doo,' or whatever it was ya said, '…and now I'm movin' on with my business cuz you aren't even important enough to be worth getting upset about.' No, sir, you didn't let him get your goat, but you weren't trying to schmooze him either, like a smooth talker would. No, you just said it like it is. 'Flippidy wabbidy jabbidy. Now all a ya are dismissed.' That's how honest folk are, ya see, that's why I took ya for an honest fella. Yes sir, I wasn't havin' any doubts about your dukeliness's dukeliness, that's not what troubled me at all."

Winthrop nodded slowly, a bit surprised he had made such an impression, especially given that he hadn't been trying to make any particular impression at all. "Then what does trouble you, Ed?"

"Well, you see sir, this here tavern is eh, not exactly set up to accommodate a person of your stature. You see, we only have the one main room here, sir, no added ballrooms or nothin' for VIPs, cuz all of the Ps around here aren't IPs, other than the Lady maybe, but she don't drink or come in here ever. And no one is exactly strollin' into town like an IP, cuz Dewford isn't where IPs get together. So all I got here is the one barroom where all the common riff raff like me get together, and surely a duke like you won't want to be associating with our kinda fellas. I was tryin' to get a table in the back set up for ya, but the more I'm thinkin' about it, the more I know it just ain't gonna work out."

Winthrop waved him off, slightly amused. "As I said, Ed, treat me as you would treat anyone else. I've been in barrooms for forty years now, and never been recognized as a duke. I don't need any special lauds or honors."

As they were talking, Ed had made his way to the pass-through on the end of the bar and taken up his post behind it. He looked at the statues of Jesus and Mary behind the bar, made a quick Sign of the Cross, and then pulled two large wooden mugs from under the counter. "Well, if no special honors are needed, then pull yourself up a stool and let's lubricate this acquaintanceship. I've got an hour til I need to be startin' dinner, and twelve hours' worth of questions I need to ask in that time. First thing I'll ask ya; beer or wine?"

"Whiskey."

"Oh...can't help you with that, your dukeliness, no can do ya see. I don't do no business with the spirits merchants in town. I get some wine from the vineyard nearby, and brew my own beer downstairs, but no spirits. Helps the guests stay sober, which is nice."

"Wouldn't that defeat the purpose of a tavern, Ed?"

"Oh, no sir, not at all. We get a good ole time goin', but not with all that weepy-eyed thunder-dunker ya get in other bars, no-sir-ee. Round here we remember what Big Ben said, 'Wine is for joy, not drunkenness.' So we take our joy in moderation."

"Who is Big Ben?" Winthrop asked.

"Big Ben is this Bible fella Lady Maria tells me about who has all sorts of gems to say. Haven't read him myself, but I pay her a visit every mornin', and she's often given me this or that little pearl from Big Ben. Guy was smarter than a whip, let me tell ya. Another thing he said was that people who sell wine can't hardly avoid sin. That's why I stopped sellin' it and just give it away instead."

"Wait, you don't charge for wine? How does your tavern stay in business?"

"Now, I'm throwin' my foot down here your dukeliness, this is getting' outta control. I asked you a simple and straightforward question, and you ain't even answered it yet. No, I think you've asked me at least three questions and not even answered one of mine. Now that is hardly a fair arrangement. If I was tryin' to treat ya like a duke, then maybe I would defer to your dukeliness, but you wanted to be treated like an average fella, and an average fella needs to do a little quid pro quoin'. I get an answer; you get an answer. That's how it oughta work."

"What was your question, Ed?"

"Beer or wine?"

"Beer."

"Ah! Good man! Good man! I have all the respect in the world for a man that drinks beer. Wine is good for women, but men should stick to beer. Lady Maria tells me our Lord drank wine, and I wouldn't go criticizing Him, obviously, but times were different back then. I don't think wine was as fruity in His time as it is now. I can't say I know that for a fact, but it seems reasonable to me. Why else would a man's Man like God go around drinkin' fruit juice?"

Winthrop took a little jab at the bartender. "Maybe it was because the bartenders who served beer took too long to pour?"

Showing no indication that he thought this comment was aimed at him, Ed answered, "Nah, I don't think that was it, cuz I'm not sure they had taverns back then, at least, I've never heard of one. There was an inn this Samaritan fella went to one time, but an inn ain't the same as a tavern. I would be willin' to wager they serve wine at inns, but not beer. You gotta go to a tavern if ya wanna have a beer. There's also a difference in what kinda service you would get. A tavern bartender and an inn bartender is a completely different fella, especially in Bible times. Let me give ya a few examples..." As Ed used the maximum possible number of words to express his minimum possible knowledge of biblical bartending, Winthrop began to think that even if he served whiskey in pint glasses, this bartender would never get anybody drunk. "...and then there was King David, who mentions barley, but he never mentioned any hops to my knowledge–"

"Ed, why are there all these statues in your tavern?"

"Oh those? To help people keep their mind on God while they're restin'."

"Is this one of 'Lady' Maria's suggestions?"

"You know it. When she first floated the idea, I said to her, 'Maria' I said, 'A barroom ain't the kinda place you seem to be picturin' it as. No one's gonna appreciate havin' a statue of some saint lookin' at em while they're drinkin'. They'll feel like God is watchin' em.' And you know what she said to me? I'll tell ya, I'll never forget it. She looked right at me and said, 'Edward, God *is* watching them. What would be so bad about reminding them of that?' Oh, let me tell ya your dukeliness, that went right through me, it did. I started changin' the way things get done around here. Big Ben said, 'Wine is for joy, not drunkenness.' Well Big Ed started sayin', 'E&S's is for rest, not rioting.' E&S's is the name of my tavern, ya see. I thought it was a pretty clever line I came up with. I like how those two 'R' sounds go together. Really rolls off the tongue that way. So that was the start of my decoratin' all nice and classy-like.

Most folks didn't take to it at first, but in time they started gettin' more comfortable, then they started likin' it, and then, wouldn't ya know it, I had to take one of the statues down to clean a spill that happened, and when Lil' Punchy came in, he took one look at the pedestal and said, 'You're not gettin' rid of the statues, are ya?' And I said, 'Not on your life. I'm just cleanin' one up is all.' But let me tell ya your dukeliness, they were worried, very worried the statues were goin' away. Mighty fond of 'em they got, yes they did!"

At long, long last Ed filed the two mugs with beer and put Winthrop's mug on the bar in front of him. "A toast!" Ed declared, "To new acquaintanceships!"

"Here here!" Winthrop said, touching his mug to Ed's. He then swiftly drank from his mug before Ed could have a chance to elaborate on his toast. As soon as the warm ale hit Winthrop's tongue, his eyes went wide with shock. "Ed! This beer! It's incredible!"

"Course it is. Brewed it myself."

"No, I mean, like…really, really incredible. Ed, I've had some of the nicest, high dollar drinks in all of Chelles, but I've never had anything as good as this. What's your secret?"

"Good water. Makes everything taste good around here."

Thinking back to the water the shepherds had shared with him, as well as the crawfish that mesmerized him in the moat, Winthrop asked, "Ed…what on earth *is* the story with the water around here? There's no well, no rivers, every road has an aqueduct to nowhere, and the water is delicious. Why, I would even drink it out of the moat if I had to! I feel totally disoriented. It's like the most important thing in an entire town–its water supply–is nowhere to be found, and yet everyone is acting…normal! And moreover, everybody has plenty of perfect water. How is that possible?"

"Now, not so fast there, your dukeliness, you've gone riding all heavy-footed over the rules of acquaintanceship once again. Since answering my one question about what you wanted to drink (which was really a question I asked for your benefit, not mine, since I'm a thoughtful kinda acquaintance like that), you've gone and asked me another three questions all over again. That just ain't right, your dukeliness, no-sir-ee. You said to treat you like I'd be treatin' anyone else, and by golly, anyone else I would demand that they let me get a word in edgewise in this conversation, instead of just pepperin' me non-stop with questions. With all due respect to your dukeliness, ya really need to learn to control that tongue of yours and listen for a change."

Winthrop mused to himself that earlier this afternoon he had intended to lay down and die. After hearing Ed's never ending rants, he had every intention of being annoyed. Despite these fervent intentions, Winthrop was starting to be happy against his will, and he was even beginning to like the rambling redhead. With (mostly) feigned irritation, Winthrop barked, "Alright, Ed, what's your question?"

"Weeeeeell, as you may or may not recall, you said no one treated you like a duke in forty some years. Now that number 'forty' is a very particular number. Someone says, 'forty,' and I says, 'Now that's how long it's been since the king got killed, ain't it, Ed?' Forty's not one of those numbers I don't take notice of ya see. So you says you weren't treated like a duke in forty years, and I says, 'Ed, I bet his dukely highness was there that day and he was on the run, hidin' from anyone that might know him.' So it seems to me ya spend your days incognito like, and before long you decide you may as well keep on going that way, since it's safer for ya, but what I can't figure out is why ya ain't settled down yet. Smart duke like you, ya can probably read pretty good and think pretty good. Lotta steady jobs out there for a man with them talents, bet ya could find one in one, maybe two years, three if yer not too bright, but it definitely wouldn't take ya forty. No-sir-ee. Forty years later, and ya walked clear across Europe, and crossed Franky's Channel to boot, and yer still wanderin' around from town to town, getting' jumped by black knights between Chelles and Reswick (I heard ya say that wasn't quite it, but somethin' like that). Why is a man with a beard full a gray hairs and more education than you could shake a stick at still wanderin'? How come you haven't found a place to settle down yet? You must either have a really good purpose yer journeyin' towards, or else you have no purpose at all. That's how I see it. If ya had a good purpose you would refuse to settle til ya got 'er done, and if ya had no purpose you would just drift around forever. It's us fellas with a nice, middle purpose who find a place to put down roots and live out our purpose in ordinary daily life. Wanderin' men either can't get enough purpose in a normal life, or else a normal life has too much purpose for 'em. So which one are ya?"

Winthrop winced, swirled his beer around, and sighed while looking in his mug. He took a gulp and said, "That's quite a question...you're not totally wrong, but you're not totally right either. I think I have a pretty good purpose...at least, I had one in the beginning. I...just wanted to find a good place to live. Settle down with my little brother, like you're saying. This will sound stupid Ed–don't laugh at me (Ed nodded)–but I had hoped I might someday be a paladin. My father was the Duke of Nouen, the head of the king's own army. That meant I got plenty of training in combat, diplomacy, and everything else a paladin might need. I was a page at seven and a squire at fourteen–most squires became knights at twenty-one back then, but a future paladin would squire much longer. That was my dream, Ed. I wanted to be a paladin. But then the Empire fell. The king died. No more paladins were coming. So if that dream wasn't coming true, I figured I would chase another one. I wanted to be a father like my own father. A good man. A hero. He died saving us all, Ed. Not just me, I mean. Everyone in the royal city. They had the city surrounded to catch anyone trying to escape, but Goliath's army couldn't take the gate. Then Goliath tried to walk up and smash his way in himself, but my father charged right at him and dealt him a terrible wound. It wasn't fatal, but it was enough to drive him back. Without Goliath to lead the attack, the other commanders of the army had to bring all of their troops around for a frontal assault, and when they did, that's when we made our break for it. Me and my brother, and all of the women and children…we got away…but…but at…I'm sorry, give me a moment…"

Winthrop broke down, the grief rising from a long hidden place in his soul. He didn't even notice when he started crying, but now he realized it must have been some time ago. He wiped away his tears and took another swig of beer. Ed threw another splash in his mug, and waited patiently. This was the first time he had been quiet since Winthrop walked into the barroom.

Gathering himself, Winthrop continued, "So anyway, I decided I wanted to be a dad. Raise a family. Get nice and settled down like you said. A nice, middle purpose that can make a man stay in place. But the first place we came to, just outside the royal city, the people were so ugly. So terribly, terribly ugly. Just…full of hate. They hated the king, his laws, sure, maybe I can get that. But they hated anything even associated with the king, even if he didn't cause it at all. If you told those people the king liked steak, they would have gone and killed every cow they could find just to spite his ghost. You think I'm exaggerating, but there was one instance that was truly like that. Even now I can see it as if it was happening right in front of me. There was this big, beautiful church, almost as nice as a cathedral. It had flying buttresses supporting everything so that they could make unbelievably large stained glass windows. They would take up entire walls of the church, yet have more detail than those little ones you have in your bar here. Intricate details of all these signs and symbols woven into a glass tapestry of Bible scenery. My family used to make a pilgrimage to this church just to stop and marvel at all the stained glass for hours. So much of what you were looking at was wrapped up in layers and layers of mystery, yet you always left feeling like you saw the scene more clearly than you had ever pictured it before.

"But this one window, I can still picture it, it was Goliath blaspheming the God of the Israelites, and King Saul was cowering and afraid, totally impotent to oppose him. Now if they hated the king with a sane hatred, I would think they would love this stained glass, no? I mean, come on! This king you hate was just killed by a giant named Goliath, and here is this masterwork of art about a different giant named Goliath with a king cowering in his shadow. It should have been their national shrine! They should have saved it for all generations and shown it to their children saying, 'This is what that wonderful giant Goliath did to that evil king.' But it wasn't a sane hatred, Ed! You see, the king was a passionate Christian, and so they wanted to destroy all Christian things. Now how much sense does that make? This stained glass was around since before the king was even born, and now the king is no longer here to see what you do to it. Nevertheless, it was so despicable to them that they needed to destroy it in order to get back at him. And that's exactly what they did. They built a giant scaffolding that went up to the window, and they took up these huge hammers, and they started smashing it. Smashing it with glee. Down below the glass was crashing all about in a sparkling spectacle, and the people were cheering and clapping. And they looked at the smashed glass covering the ground and they called that 'beautiful'."

Catching his breath, Winthrop leaned back, lifted his arms in exasperation and said, "What is that, Ed? What is that? I don't know how you can hate beauty, much less look at the rubble of something beautiful and say, 'This is what *real* beauty looks like'? I don't understand."

Ed hung his head thoughtfully and said, "To be honest, your dukeliness, I just don't know."

Winthrop let out a frustrated sigh. "So off we went. We kept traveling ever further and further, never finding a place to stop because every town had its own problems. And then as we got halfway across the realm, I started to notice a new problem. There was less hatred and malice for the king. Jacob started saying to me, 'Winthrop, this town's not so bad. Why don't we settle here?' And sure, it wasn't so bad. But it wasn't any good either! We started coming to all these towns where everyone was indifferent! Totally indifferent! 'They don't smash churches here.' That's because they never bothered to build one! 'People don't curse the king's name here.' That's because they never learned it! 'They don't hate beauty in this town.' That's because this town has no beauty to hate!

"And then Jacob, he was always a bit naive, he would say to me, 'Then let's show them, Winthrop. Let's show them what beauty is. Let's settle down here and build a little chapel and show the priest how to say Mass like they did in Nouen. Let's *make* this city great!' He was only fourteen at that time. He didn't realize how people are so set in their ways and how much they dislike change–especially change back to how things used to be. At least if they're changing to something new you can call it 'progressive,' but if you want to change to something old it's called 'backwards.' He didn't see how hard it would be to get people to change, especially with us being foreigners and all."

Winthrop became dewy eyed again. He downed what was left of his beer and asked for another. "Oh, not so fast there now, your dukeliness. I wouldn't want ya getting drunk. It's my solemn duty as a bartender to look out for your sobriety."

"Well then how about this? You start getting my drink now, and by the time you actually get around to pouring it, I'll be nice and sober."

Ed pouted in pretend indignation. "I do believe my bartenderin' has been attacked."

"Indeed it has."

The two shared a laugh and Ed took Winthrop's mug and started the slow and gradual process of deciding what to pour even though there was only one option. Winthrop put one elbow on the bar and used his hand to prop up his face, leaning forward with a great weariness. "...and there was something else too, Ed. Another thing that Jacob just wasn't thinking about. I was still looking to raise some kids and a family. Where am I supposed to find a wife when all of the women have dull and ugly souls? They talk about hair, and jewelry, and who wore what to the ball, and every other vapid thought under the sun. How do you marry a woman who sets her eyes on such pathetic goals? How do you talk to her? How do you share a home with her? How do you raise children with her? 'Hey kids, ignore everything your mother cares about, because she doesn't have a deep thought in her brain. Why did I marry her you ask? Oh, all the other women were even worse.' That's no way to raise children, Ed. I couldn't have a family unless I found a woman I could respect, and I couldn't (and still can't) respect a woman who has never pondered the deeper questions of life. 'Who am I? Why am I here? What's the purpose of my life? What's the purpose of my *family*?'

"In good faith, Ed, I got to a place where I would have married a heathen if she asked those questions. And back then I was a devout churchman. Things have changed, but back then that was crazy talk. I guess you could say I was a little bit crazy. In Nouen I would have been horrified at the thought of a pagan wife, but after seeing a hundred towns with a thousand vapid woman, I said, 'Give me a Muslim who can ponder! I'll take a Jewess if she can wonder! Give me a woman who thirsts for truth, and I'll tell her His name is Jesus. But enough of these Catholic women who sit in Mass and hear the Lord say, 'I am the Truth,' but they're too busy comparing Sunday dresses to give one mote of thought to such a mysterious phrase. They drove me crazy, Ed! Crazy! The women of this realm are in a deplorable state, and no one should be surprised if men follow after. Why put in all the hard work of being a virtuous man when the women will throw you aside to chase a drunken thug with a few coins instead?"

Winthrop reached for his beer, and discovered it was still empty. "Ed!" But then he stopped cold. Only now did he realize Ed was deeply troubled. "I'm sorry, Ed. I don't mean to get so worked up…you just stumbled into some old things…things I guess I never really got over. Are you…are you alright?"

Ed took a slow sip from his own beer and swished it around before swallowing. Then he refilled both mugs in silence. He put Winthrop's mug in front of him, and finally said, "This world ain't how it's supposed to be your dukeliness. Not how it's supposed to be at all…"

"Not in the slightest."

Ed took another long sip. Winthrop waited patiently for the redhead to open up about whatever was suddenly weighing on him. Ed eventually asked, "Tell me, your dukeliness, was there ever a time you can recall that you might say (generally now, not in every case), but that in the greater preponderance of the cases, that daughters wouldn't go leavin' home without their father's permission? I'm not talkin' about for the market or something, now, just to be clarifyin'. What I'm referrin' to here, in the particulars if you will, is some Clyde-come-lately comes rollin' into town and actin all chummy chummy with her, and promisin' to set her up at his store in Chelles, but the father sees right through old slick willy and says, 'Sasha, don't you go runnin' off with that man now! He's not gonna make a proper wife of you or treat you right, no not at all.' Now let's say she ignores her father's advice and goes runnin' off with him, and never sends word again, or comes to visit even though it's only half a day away, or even let's ya know she's alright…is that the kind of thing that used to go on, or is that the sort of 'nowadays women' stuff you were talkin' about?"

Winthrop shook his head sorrowfully. "Ed, back where I grew up, that would have been considered a monstrosity. An absolute monstrosity. When two people used to live together like that, we would call them 'concubines.' That was a dirty word, Ed. I see the shock on your face. It's still a dirty word. People like to say 'moving in together,' but the right word is 'concubines.' People don't like words like that, but they're fine with the actions those words describe. Unacceptable. If a man and a woman did that in Nouen, they would have been outcasts. No one would talk to them. Or if they did, it would be just to say, 'Shame on you for running off with her,' or, 'Your father is probably worried sick about you.' I know, Ed, there's pain in your eyes. That sounds harsh, and you don't want your daughter to be treated harshly. But here's the truth; in Nouen there were no concubines! No one wanted to be outcasts, and so no one did the sins that would make you an outcast! Now there's no outrage. We're too modern. Too advanced. The sign of being enlightened is that you're completely and totally indifferent to everyone else's sins."

Ed wiped his eyes. "Yeah, that's the problem with these days. You had the word right with 'indifferent.' Everyone's indifferent. My little girl ran off with ole Clyde-come-lately, and she didn't even think she was actin' strange. She wasn't bein' rebellious, or gettin' back at me, or nothin'. She was just indifferent. When I threw a fit and forbade her to go, she acted angry, cuz that's how she pretends to be when she's uncomfortable, but I know my little girl, and I could tell she was surprised. Truly surprised. She didn't know what I was making a big deal out of. All her friends did the same. Folks in my generation did the same. She didn't see the harm in it. It was indifference, your dukeliness. Just like you said"

Ed looked around at all the windows, and then he leaned in to whisper like he had a secret. "Now don't go tellin' this to everyone, cuz I don't want no guilt by association now, but your dukeliness–honest to God now!–I won't tell ya who it was, cuz I don't want to be startin' rumors–but a man once came in this bar who was a killer. Not in no figures or exaggerations now. A *killer*. A murderer. He killed our old mayor and our old constable. He even went on to kill poor Matthew. But I'll tell ya–and this gives me the chills to this day–when he came in here for a drink, he acted like a totally normal fella. Just like how you're sittin' here right now. He wasn't tremblin' with fright, or lookin' around like a madman. I didn't know it, but he had killed the constable mere minutes before, yet he acted like it was nothin'. Just like, 'no big deal.' And what's more, he was even criticizin' some of the things other people were doin' wrong. 'This guy lied to me. This guy obstructed justice. I don't like that woman.' And here he was a killer! Talk about seein' splinters in other fella's eyes and not noticin' the beam in your own. But I don't think he didn't notice, your dukeliness. I think he knew. But he was indifferent. He was very attentive to how other people bothered him, but he was all indifferent to his own crimes. That's my thinkin', yes it is."

Ed leaned back to go on in a normal voice, but the words caught in his throat when he looked at Winthrop. Instead of nodding along or agreeing, his face had turned completely white and he was shaking. "Crimeny! Are you alright your dukeliness? You look like you saw a ghost."

Winthrop smiled weakly. "Perhaps I have..." Winthrop then stood up and started walking while leaning on the bar. "I'm not feeling so good, Ed."

"Oh, crimeny! Stupid Ed! What was I thinkin'? What with you just had two of your friends dead today, however it was it happened, and I go talkin' about murder. How could I be so heartless? Oh, I'm sorry, your dukeliness, but you just looked so composed I forgot what musta been on your heart."

"It's okay..." Winthrop answered. "I forgot what's on my heart as well. Tell me, is there a room where I could–"

"Yes! Yes! Of course, your dukeliness, right this way. I've gotta couple of guest rooms all picked out for ya."

"I don't have any money to pay you with."

"You couldn't a paid me if you had your purse. Come now, this is your room. I'll bring a bowl of stew as soon as dinner's ready. If you're feelin' up for it, you're welcome to come out and join us later."

"Thank you," Winthrop said, entering the guest room and closing the door behind him. He stood a moment longer. The image of David flashed through his head, screaming, *I'm a killer!* The familiar voice said, *You are free to do whatever you want.* Winthrop fell to the ground, and began to sob uncontrollably.

The night that passed was the most painful night of Winthrop's life so far, yet it would only be the third worst he was going to have that Week. He cried until a deep exhaustion overcame him and he fell into a restless sleep. Bitter memories were bleeding into his dreams, and bitter dreams were bleeding into his memories. After tossing and turning he would bolt awake from a terror that seemed real. Then he would realize reality seemed more terrible and unreal than his nightmares.

David was gone. Rowan and Garrett were dead. He had revealed his long-held secret. He was in Dewford of all places, in the room of a barkeep he hardly knew, without a penny to his name. The strange fantasy of what was really happening overwhelmed and exhausted him anew, plunging him back into the easy unreality of dreams until they scared him awake again. At some point Ed came in to check on him and deliver dinner, but seeing Winthrop rolling back and forth on the floor, he left the bowl of stew on the nightstand and closed the door. William came to summon Winthrop around sundown, but Ed told him he would have to catch them at the Rosary tomorrow.

Waking and sleeping, Winthrop floated around and about one memory, orbiting closer and closer. Like a planet falling towards the star that will be its end, yet doomed to only approach annihilation by degrees, everything was spinning around that central point. He was with David crossing the Rhine–no. That was with Jacob. Fr. Zambri was holding him up at sword point–no–that was a town guard. He was here and there, skipping across time and nations, ages flying by in instants, as he tumbled along towards his most dreaded memory save one.

Jacob lay in bed, coughing terribly. Every hacking, wheezing, painful blast made Winthrop wince in pain. The coughing went on and on, and then Jacob gurgled as he coughed up blood. The blood had started coming out in occasional trickles last week, but now it was so much and so frequent that Winthrop knew the end was near.

When the fit subsided, Jacob resumed his squelching, ragged breaths. The two brothers looked at each other. Winthrop was crying. Jacob was smiling sadly. After staring into each other's eyes for moments that felt like hours, Jacob said, "Go get Fr. Zambri."

Winthrop clenched and trembled. "No. There's no need. You'll get better soon. Just wait, you'll see. God will provide. Isn't that what dad always told us? God will provide."

Jacob frowned. "Winthrop…please. Get the priest." His voice was so hoarse that the last word was barely audible.

Winthrop began to sob, burying his face in his brother's chest. "Can't God heal you like He healed so many others? Even if you should die, what's to stop him from raising you from the dead? It happened for Lazarus! Why is he more special than you? Why do Martha and Mary get a happy ending, but I have to lose you?"

Jacob took Winthrop's hand, weakly clasping it in his own. "Winthrop…please…"

Now Winthrop was at the rectory, banging on the door, wiping his snotty nose constantly with his sleeve. Fr. Zambri opened the door. "Father, my brother Jacob is dying."

"Oh, don't worry. I'll come and see him first thing tomorrow morning."

"No, Father, he won't live that long. He won't live through the night. Please, come now."

"Don't worry, Winthrop! Don't worry! 'Pray, hope, and don't worry.' That's what a famous saint used to say. I'll come see your brother tomorrow. Tonight I have some very important priestly duties that cannot be postponed."

"Please, Father!" Winthrop fell to his knees. "Come as soon as your duties are done, even if it's late at night! Better tonight than tomorrow!"

"No, no, I'm afraid these duties will take all night. Be at peace, Winthrop. Be at peace! God isn't going to damn your brother just because the parish priest was busy that night. Have faith in God's mercy! And pray, hope, and don't worry. Everything will be fine. Run along now, for I must be getting ready at once." He closed the door in Winthrop's face.

He was floating now, floating along the streets in a stupor. He floated to his brother's deathbed, lying beside him. Jacob was unconscious, muttering gibberish in his sleep. "Oh my, why are you here?...Five Saturdays?...Nine Fridays?...I completely forgot!...And you are?...A pleasure to meet you, Joseph…In Articulo Mortis…No usual conditions?...what a deal!" Winthrop had no idea what sort of delirious dream his brother was dreaming, but he seemed happy, and for that much he was grateful.

Winthrop wept.

What more could he hope for now? At some point he may have started to doze, or perhaps he was simply being very still. Either way, he was suddenly attentive when he heard his brother's hoarse voice whispering, "Winthrop…Winthrop…" It was dark out. Tonight was the night of the new moon.

Winthrop pulled his brother close. "Yes, Jacob. I'm right here. I can hear you."

"Closer…"

Winthrop leaned in close, his ear brushing against his brother's blistered lips. Jacob rasped his final words. After that, he fell unconscious and Winthrop held him as he descended into his final agony and hugged him through all the convulsions of his death rattle. When he was finally still, a terrible silence hung over the room. Every breath of his brother's loud and labored breathing had been pounding on Winthrop's heart. Now the silence shattered his heart to pieces.

He wept.

He wept.

He tried desperately to hang on to his brother's final words. They were already starting to slip through his fingers.

The dying words of Lord Jacob, second heir to the duchy of Nouen were thus: "Be good, Winthrop! I'm going to heaven. Make sure you follow me, because I don't want to spend eternity without you."

Winthrop was at the rectory, banging on the door, wiping his snotty nose constantly with his sleeve. Was this the dream he just had? He kicked down the door. No, this was what happened after. It was dark out. Tonight was the night of the new moon. And it was dark in the rectory, except for some candle light coming from the dining room down the hall. There was a shriek. Winthrop started walking down the hall, a blubbering, hysteric mess.

"He's gone! My brother is dead, Father! He died without you!"

Fr. Zambri appeared at the end of the hallway, coming from the dining room. "Out! Get out at once, Winthrop! You can't be here right now!"

"Father, he was so sad! He was so sad…He could barely talk." Winthrop buried his head in Fr. Zambri's chest, trying to fall into his arms like a child sobbing in his father's bosom. Fr. Zambri pulled away, allowing Winthrop to fall face first on the ground.

"Get out! I told you! You can't be here!"

"Father, let me come in. Please let me come in. You're all I've got. My mother is dead. My father is dead. Now my brother is dead. I just don't want to be alone right now. Please, I just don't want to be alone."

Getting up, Winthrop found that he was in the dining room. He had expected to find some lone, humble candle on a plain wooden table. Perhaps there would be a bowl of cold stew that Fr. Zambri was eating. Instead he found a crystal vase full of roses, two sumptuous dinners that were partially eaten, and a woman–the wife of one of the soldiers who was currently away on campaign. There were fourteen candles on the table, in the golden candlesticks used for adoring the Blessed Sacrament.

"Wha–what is this?" Winthrop turned to Fr. Zambri, not wanting to believe. "...What have you done?"

"Get out of my rectory! What I do is none of your business! I'm free to do whatever I want!"

"What have you done!" Winthrop roared, picking up the crystal vase with his left hand. "Is this the important duty you had to see to? My brother died without the Sacraments...so that you could violate your *vows*?"

Winthrop smashed the vase against Fr. Zambri's head. He expected it to shatter. Instead it stayed in one piece. He felt a 'crunch,' heard a sickening 'thud' and then Fr. Zambri fell to the ground dead. Winthrop stared at the bloody vase in his hand, not comprehending. He didn't know how long he stared at it. Then the woman screamed. Then he was running. Running. Always running. Thirty-six years had passed, yet even now he was still running. Running from David. Running from Sir Judas. Running into Dewford.

He was holding the vase in his left hand again. It was covered in blood. Fr. Zambri's final words were echoing in his head. 'I'm free to do whatever I want.' Winthrop heard those words, and all the dying words, swirling around inside his mind. His mother's words. She was dead. His father's words. He was dead. Jacob's words, still so fresh. 'Be good, Winthrop!' Jacob was dead. 'I'm free to do whatever I want.' Fr. Zambri was dead. His heroic mother, his noble father, his pious brother, this wicked priest. They were all dead. No matter how they lived, this was how they all had ended. No matter how he lived, this was how Winthrop would end as well.

He looked at his bloody left hand. Did he wish it wasn't bloody? He felt all of heaven, his angel, and his brother just begging him to wish it wasn't bloody. 'Yes, it's bloody, but please, Winthrop, just regret that it is bloody! Just be sorry for what you have done!' He looked at his bloody hand. He looked at Fr. Zambri's body on the ground.

"I'm glad my hand is bloody."

In that moment Winthrop felt the faith of his childhood die, as he stepped into the hard, cold, dark, and rational world of the abyss. "We all die, and that's the end. So if holy Winthrop and wicked Winthrop will end in the same grave, then I will be the Winthrop who loves who he loves and hates who he hates. No God will tell me right and wrong when He Himself should have to answer for the crimes that fill this world. I'm glad my hand is bloody. I'm free to do whatever I want."

Winthrop woke up screaming in a pool of his own sweat. His left hand was still covered in blood, only now it was withered and crippled. His nightmare and his reality had come together and become the same.

Ed came running across the hall from his own room and opened the door. "What is it your dukeliness? What's wrong?"

Winthrop ran a hand along his clammy brow and pulled his wet hair out of his face. "A bad dream, Ed. Sorry to wake you."

"Ah, you don't gotta be sorry for nothin', your dukeliness. Tell me, were you dreamin' about the murder?"

"Yes. Yes I was."

"Ah, that's no good. Won't do at all. Tell ya what. Your stew from last night is here. Cold by now, but get yourself a bite and I'll get dressed for the day and keep ya company."

"That's not necessary, Ed. I'll be alright."

"No, don't ya go actin all solo hot shot on me now. Sometimes we all need someone to just sit there and eat cold stew with us. Ain't good to be alone in a time like this. Now give me a moment to get organized…"

Ed lit a candle. A lone, humble candle. He set it on the plain wooden table where a bowl of cold stew was waiting for Winthrop. Winthrop ate greedily, only now realizing he hadn't eaten since yesterday's breakfast. Winthrop asked if there were any more leftovers from the night before. There were. He and Ed moved to the bar and ate cold stew together by the light of the candle, until the light of the sun began to slant through the stained glass of the Resurrection. They said nothing. At least, not much. Ed was not one for being too quiet, so every few minutes he would say some empty words like, 'Good stew,' or, 'Should be nice weather today.' Winthrop preferred silence, but he was grateful Ed was there.

The day kept brightening, and eventually the clock tower rang out eight on that Wednesday morning. Ed asked, "Do ya pray the Rosary, your dukeliness?"

"I haven't prayed a Rosary in many years, Ed."

"Well today's the day to get back on that horse. I know ya heard by now that every day at eight-thirty there's a group of us prays the Rosary in the middle of town square. I'll bet my bar you ain't never prayed a Rosary like this one, no-sir-ee."

"I don't know if I'm up for a Rosary Ed. I'm a little lost right now."

"Then I'll draw ya a map. Not that ya need one, since I'm goin' too and ya could just follow me."

Winthrop gave him an annoyed look. "Ed...you know I wasn't talking about being physically lost. I was talking about...about deeper things. Harder things. I may not be using this word in your Catholic sense, but I was talking about *spiritual* things."

Ed leaned in close, and with a smile he whispered, "Winthrop, this physical world and your spiritual things ain't as unrelated as ya think. Now follow me and you'll know where ya are. Physically and spiritually you'll be kneelin' with the Lady."

Ed walked through the bar's pass through and went to the door. "Are ya comin'?"

Winthrop thought a moment longer, looked at the lone, humble candle, then said, "Yes. I do believe I'll come." He got up and joined Ed at the door, and the two of them departed together.

Chapter 6: The Morning Dew

"Now if ya don't mind, your dukeliness, ole Ed's gonna have to make that lil' detour you heard me mention to William yesterday. The Lady, she don't walk too good no more, has quite a bit a trouble getting' outta the house, she does. So I've made myself a lil' custom of stoppin' by her house in the mornin'. It's only a minute or two outta the way, and I'll help her walk to the square. Now I know I ought notta be givin orders to a duke, but you better come along now, cuz you are sure gonna wanna meet her."

"Yes, I should like to meet her very much." Winthrop had been eager to meet this 'Lady' Maria ever since people started talking about her yesterday, wondering what sort of person she must be to command such reverence and have so much influence on the other townsfolk.

"Well then you come right along this way, it's only around this corner and across the aqueduct. Watch your step there, your dukeliness. You know, I was just thinkin'…" As Ed prattled along, Winthrop tuned him out, taking another curious look at the ridiculous (and bone dry) aqueducts running away from the town square. As he replayed the events from yesterday in his mind, he recalled that none of them ran across the square, instead terminating at its edges. Between the 'Lady' and the 'aqueducts' and the fact that Dewford had exploded in size since Winthrop was there twelve years ago, he was growing more and more intrigued (and even a little excited) to be investigating the town anew.

As they turned down the road the Lady lived on, Winthrop looked ahead to see which house might be hers. None of them looked quite right. None was grand enough for someone who commanded her level of respect, but the one that Ed stopped at looked the most 'not right' of all. It was a tiny little house, easily mistaken as being the shed of an adjacent building. Even by the standards of 'old Dewford' it was very poor and run down, with the exterior walls badly in need of paint while the door was weathered and splintering. With no ceremony or fanfare–acting more like a son than a guest–Ed opened the door and walked right in, saying, "Hey, Lady, it's ole Ed comin' to take ya to the Rosary. And I even got an extra guest with me today. By now ya musta heard we have a duke visitin' town, yeah? Lemme introduce ya! Your dukeliness, come on in, I'm makin' an introduction…"

Winthrop slowly stepped into the dimly lit house. There were no candles or lamps, just natural lighting from two small windows, one in each room of the house, both of which were visible from the entrance. The room on the right was a sitting room with three stools, a little table, and a very simple kitchen. To the left was a bedroom, only separated from the sitting room by a curtain that was currently pulled back. There were two more little wooden stools gathered around the bed that was the Lady's 'throne'. On it sat the Lady, propped up by several pillows into a reclining position.

She was nothing like what Winthrop was expecting. She was young. Very young. Not even thirty if he had to guess. Hearing the way others talked about her and that she 'doesn't get around too good anymore,' he had been expecting an elderly woman. Instead her brunette hair had no traces of gray but rather had a few light-brown, natural sun streaks. Even though her hair was pulled up in a simple bun, Winthrop thought the mahogany shades of her tresses dancing across each other put every fancy Chellesian hairstyle to shame. Her eyes were almond shaped and reddish brown. They looked familiar, even though Winthrop was confident he had never seen this woman before. And when she smiled…her eyes smiled with her.

Winthrop wasn't the only person who observed this effect; everyone who met her said the same thing. What did it mean for 'eyes to smile'? Nobody knows. Was it the way her eyes squinted a little? Was it the way the skin around the eyes would crease? This author had the great privilege of meeting Lady Maria before her passing. Without prejudice to the way these physical qualities contribute to the effect, my opinion is as follows. The eyes are commonly called 'the window to the soul.' I posit that the soul of Lady Maria was so simple and so sincere, that when she smiled you could look right through her eyes and see that her soul was smiling too.

To go on in describing her beauty is a work I leave to the poets, for a historian's humble pen is not suited to such grand undertakings. For the purpose of this history it is sufficient to know that, like so many others who met Lady Maria before him, Winthrop was struck by her beauty the very first moment he

laid eyes on her. And, like so many others, the second moment left a very
different impression.

Her body was horribly deformed. She was hunchbacked, but in an
asymmetric way, where her left shoulder came further forward than her right.
Her right arm was twisted at an odd angle at the shoulder, and then again at the
elbow, and then again at the wrist, so that she looked as if she was trying to turn
her arm around backwards, even though that was actually her resting position.
Many other disjoints, defects, and oddities plagued her frame that need not be
mentioned. Winthrop was shocked and horrified. Moreover, he realized too late
that his emotions were showing on his face.

Recomposing himself, he offered a bow and said, "A pleasure to meet
you, Lady Maria. During my brief time in town, it has become clear to me that
the people truly honor you and your judgments. I can see why they call you 'the
Lady,' for even if you are not noble by birth, you certainly are in your conduct."

She playfully glared at Ed and pouted, "Oh, what did you tell him!"
Turning back to Winthrop she said, "The only reason I'm called 'the Lady' is
because Ed is always going around handing out nicknames, and they have a bad
tendency to stick. I will call you by your name, but don't be surprised if by the
end of the week everyone is calling you, 'your dukeliness.' And so I ask 'your
dukeliness,' what is your name?"

Winthrop walked up to the bed, and holding out a hand he answered,
"Winthrop." She tried to raise a hand to place it in his, but Winthrop had chosen
a very awkward location for her, and her deformities made it so she couldn't
get her hand into that position. He instead bent down to take her hand and gently
kissed it.

When he looked back up, Maria's face had turned bright red. "I…I'm
not sure I should be getting treated this nicely, m'lord. I'm just a common
woman."

Winthrop wasn't quite sure why he had done it himself. Even if she
actually had been a noblewoman, Winthrop had not been in the habit of using
proper manners for many years. With an uncomfortable smile, he said, "I'm
sorry if it was out of place…you just…bring back certain memories I guess.
Memories of how I was taught to act back home in Nouen."

"Did the dukes kiss the hands of common women back in Nouen?"

"No, not all of them. Not even most. In fact, no, not at all. I think what
I was trying to say was more like…you just reminded me of someone I used to
know, that was all."

Lady Maria smiled. A soft smile, yet still her eyes were smiling with her. "Well, whoever this woman was, she must have meant a lot to you."

"Yes. As a matter of fact, she did."

Lady Maria slowly moved her feet over the edge of the bed and stood up, looking even more crooked on her feet than she had while she was laying down. Reaching out with her less twisted left-arm, she took Ed by the elbow and said, "Let's go to the Rosary, Ed. We wouldn't want to be late."

"Sure, and while we're goin' I can tell ya a little more about his dukeliness. Lemme tell ya, he's been quite the character, though you're already startin' to see that yourself–"

"Not now, Ed. Not now. You know I like a little quiet time before the Rosary. Thank you for introducing us. Lord Winthrop, it's a pleasure to meet you. If it isn't too rude, please come with us in silence. Oh yes, and please, take one of these..." She made a sort of lurching gesture towards a rack on the wall where several rosaries hung from hooks. He took one with smooth and firm red beads for the Aves and dark blue, shriveled little beads for the Paters.

Winthrop remembered rosaries like this from back home, and pressing it to his nose he confirmed his suspicion. It smelled like roses. These beads were made from actual rose petals that had been ground down into a paste and then hardened. "Well this is lovely. Whoever gave it to you was very thoughtful."

Lady Maria smiled. "I made it myself, but since you appreciate it so much, you can keep it."

Winthrop looked at her crooked frame in surprise. "You made this? I'm...ah, forgive me. I just thought it would have been very difficult for you."

"It was." She made an odd version of a shrug with one shoulder. "Many difficult things are worth doing. Now let's all quiet ourselves and get ready."

They left the house and began to walk very slowly towards the town square. Ed was even silent–actually silent–a novel rarity as far as Winthrop could tell. Their journey was not much longer than a hundred yards, but at the glacial pace that Lady Maria walked it took about five minutes to get there. On the way several townsfolk who were passing by stopped and made solemn gestures of respect to Lady Maria. One man deeply bowed, another tipped his hat. One woman leading a flock of small children got down on her knees while Lady Maria passed, and then fell in behind her as a mini procession to the town square. This made a deep impression on Winthrop, though Lady Maria herself did not even notice. Her eyes were closed and her attention was elsewhere, allowing Ed to lead her while she began praying.

At length the trio and those following them reached the eastern edge of the square. The first thing Winthrop noticed was that all of the stalls and wares had been wheeled out of the square since yesterday and were pushed up against the edges of the open space. Now the only people in the square itself were those in a single gathering of dozens of peasants, countless children, a small handful of wealthy visitors, Cara O'Dewforthios (still wearing her hat with the ostrich feather), and three men dressed in sackcloth—zealous pilgrims with rosaries so long they wore them around their waist like a belt. Winthrop had not come with any expectations about who would be leading the Rosary, but he was surprised none the less. Zakary the shepherd, wearing his dirty and well-worn shepherd garb, was inviting people to quiet down and take their places, while assuring them the Rosary would begin shortly. Around the perimeter of the town square many other people had assembled to set about the usual business of a small town. Even though the stalls were not open yet, the smell of roasted foods was in the air. There were also water yokes everywhere, including one on the ground right next to Zakary. Winthrop was about to ask Ed, 'Where do people fill those?' but he remembered Lady Maria had asked for silence.

Ed led Lady Maria to the far side of the group (nearest the well) where a chair was set up facing the well. "Now lemme make a quick adjustment here…normally we'd have the Lady at the shepherd's right hand, but for a duke I think we oughta be makin' a change. There we go, you can sit here on his left side, Lady, Mrs. Cara Featherflop right next to ya, and his dukeliness will kneel at Zakary's right. Perfect. Our little hierarchy goes shepherds, lords, ladies, and then all the riff raff. Just how it should be." Winthrop was wondering why 'shepherds' were at the head of the hierarchy. From what people had been saying yesterday, Winthrop didn't think that Zakary commanded much respect, especially in comparison to the Lady. Several annoyed looks passed between the wealthier visitors who did not care for Ed's 'hierarchy,' but no one openly complained.

Lady Maria took her seat, and then everyone else kneeled except for Zakary (and of course the smallest children, who ran around the gathering while shouting and playing their little games). Winthrop knelt in the place Ed had indicated. Zakary came over to Winthrop and whispered in his ear, "I hear you caused quite the ruckus yesterday. You didn't tell me you were a duke!"

Winthrop nodded. "Yes. And not that I care about these sorts of things, but why are shepherds ahead of lords in Ed's hierarchy? That's a very odd organization."

Zakary smiled broadly through his thick beard. "Maybe someday I can explain it to you. He has his reasons, but it's best not to advertise them."

Winthrop was going to ask for more explanation, but he was cut off by the clock tower letting out two chimes for the half hour. The prayer group fell completely silent, but there was still plenty of chatter and background conversation coming from all the other people on the edges of town square. Zakary solemnly announced, "The Five Glorious Mysteries of the Most Holy Rosary. In the Name of the Father, and of the Son, and of the Holy Ghost, Amen. I believe in God, the Father Almighty, Creator of heaven and earth..." As the opening prayers began, Winthrop slowly counted off the beads. He was already starting to feel a little glum. Why had he come here? Was it just to be with Ed? No, he had been hoping he would feel something. He used to feel something when he prayed his Rosary. He used to really believe with all his soul that saying these prayers mattered. That if he said his Rosary every day, the world was going to be a better place. Seeing how awful the world had become as he aged had thoroughly disabused Winthrop of that notion. He looked behind him at Ed, head bowed, hands raised, eyes clenched shut, praying with all his might. He envied him. It was so nice to believe. If only he could go back to that place of blissful ignorance.

"The First Glorious Mystery, the Resurrection of Our Lord Jesus Christ from the Dead. Fruit of this Mystery, Faith. Our Father, Who art in heaven, hallowed be Thy Name..." Winthrop sighed, thinking to himself, *The Resurrection. What a lovely story. Death's not sad; everyone's waiting for us in heaven. Ah, the things we tell ourselves. No one ever told me why God makes us wait for the Resurrection, though. Why not do it right away, huh? Not only would the world be a lot less sad if we resurrected right away, but there would be a lot less infidels too. No one's going to say 'no' to a religion where everyone comes back three days after dying. Apparently the 'All Knowing' God overlooked that possibility. Or maybe He doesn't want all men to be saved after all. He'll give 'faith' to anyone He wants to be saved and let the rest of us–*

Winthrop was snapped out of his own thoughts by Lady Maria suddenly crying in anguish. He looked over at her and saw that she was weeping bitterly, sobbing, and every sob was rattling her poor broken body, and causing further pain. Tears completely covered her face. Sir Judas flashed through

Winthrop's mind, and he recalled how the knight had wept at the funerals. As Lady Maria continued crying, the children gradually stopped running around and giggling, slowly and sadly moving a little further away to continue their games. The other women started weeping. Even Winthrop started to tear up. He looked to the edge of the square and saw that the other people were going about their business, trying to pretend they weren't hearing anything, even though their eyes showed that they were troubled. Only Zakary seemed unaffected, keeping his attention forward towards the well as he led the Rosary. "...pray for us sinners, now and at the hour of our death, Amen."

Winthrop looked back to Lady Maria, and found that he couldn't look away. She wasn't praying like Ed. Winthrop wasn't sure what that meant, but he knew it was true. Ed was praying very sincerely, but it was a sincerity that could be written off as naiveté. Winthrop could look down on Ed's prayers. Not Lady Maria's. There was something deeper here, something about the way she pronounced the words through heartfelt tears. Even though he wouldn't have admitted it, Winthrop was thinking he might not be as smart as he thought.

"The Second Glorious Mystery, the Ascension of Our Lord Jesus Christ into Heaven. Fruit of this Mystery, Hope. Our Father, Who art in heaven..." With great effort Winthrop tried to look forward again, but the Lady's loud tears and moaning kept drawing him back. *Is her body the problem? Why is no one doing anything? This can't be normal, is it? There's no way this happens every day...Why is she here? Clearly sitting in that chair is causing her great pain...* The prayers rolled on and Winthrop lost track of where they were. He pushed some random red beads through his hand until he heard Zakary say, "Glory be..." and then announce, "The Third Glorious Mystery, the Descent of the Holy Ghost at Pentecost. Fruit of this Mystery, Charity. Our Father, Who art in heaven..."

Winthrop let out a long sigh. This Rosary was driving him mad. He forgot how long a Rosary can seem. It was only fifteen minutes, but today it was fifteen *long* minutes. He wanted to talk to Lady Maria and figure out what was going on, but instead they were saying Hail Mary number twenty-one. *Why am I here...I could just leave...* Winthrop looked around the town square again. Most people weren't praying. They were making preparations for the day. There was no way he would be odd if he joined them. If anything, it was odder to be kneeling here. Winthrop thought he should go ask them about Lady Maria, but he looked back to her and changed his mind. She would want him to stay and pray. For her sake he figured he might as well stick it out.

By now Lady Maria's pain had increased, but the cries of pain were growing quieter. She had a look of great exertion on her face, and she was scrunching her eyes like she was intensely focused. She was no longer saying the words, but Ed was. Zakary was. Cara was. All of those gathered were. Everyone was oh-so-serious about their duty of saying these words, even though Winthrop couldn't see one lick of good it would do. Stopping and asking Lady Maria, 'Are you alright?' That might do some *actual* good. That would make someone *actually* feel better, unlike babbling these Hail Mary's over and over. Yet Winthrop didn't interrupt her. He knew it wasn't what would *actually* make her happier, even though it was illogical that she would rather keep hearing the same old words. *Ah well, nothing for it.* Winthrop started saying the words himself, reckoning that perhaps that was the only thing that might make Maria feel better. It seemed to be working too, for she had a faint trace of a smile in the midst of her suffering.

The fourth mystery, the Assumption, flew by, and before long Zakary announced, "The Fifth Glorious Mystery, the Coronation of Mary as Queen of Heaven and Earth. Fruit of this Mystery, Final Perseverance. Our Father, Who art in heaven…" As they went through the last decade, Winthrop was excitedly counting out each of the beads. *Seven…eight…nine…ten!* "…pray for us sinners, now and at the hour of our death, Amen." That last line of the last Ave caught Winthrop's attention. *Death…how much do these simple people actually know about death? Have they ever met death eye to eye? Really wrestled with it? Bah. Even if they have loved ones who have died, they brushed that pain away with fantasies about an afterlife. They probably brushed it away with these very prayers. The Virgin Mary prayed for my mom at the hour of death! What is that worth? What's the value of a prayer? Wouldn't a healing be better? Prayers are cheap.*

"Oh my Jesus, forgive us our sins. Save us from the fires of hell. And lead all souls to heaven, especially those in most need of Thy Mercy." Zakary paused. *Oh what is it now? Did Zakary forget the words? Hail Holy Queen, Zakary. Hail Holy Queen! Say the last prayer and we can get on with our day!* The pause continued. Then Winthrop began to hear something coming from the well. 'Tit…pit…pit-pit…pit…tit…titter-pat-tit-pit-pitter…' The Lady was wailing loudly. The sound at the well intensified. "Titter-pitter-titter-titter-pitter…" The air over the well was beginning to look strange, like some sort of semi-visible red thing was floating over it, slowly taking form. Every Dewfordian was weeping. Ed looked up to the sky with dewy eyes. The children started shrieking with excitement. The people on the edge of the square wiped their eyes, and rested from their labors for a moment. Winthrop was looking around wildly, trying to figure out what was happening.

"Titter-pitter-titter-pitter-whoosh-whoosh-bwattat   datta   datta bwoosh!" Then Winthrop saw clearly. It was rain. A torrent of rain. Rain so thick he couldn't see through it anymore, all crashing down on the cobbled top of the well. He looked up. There wasn't a cloud in the blue sky. The pillar of water went up and up and up, falling right out of heaven itself.

Zakary began to sing in a deep and solemn voice,

Salve, Regina, Mater misericordiæ, vita, dulcedo, et spes nostra, salve.	Hail, Holy Queen, Mother of mercy, our life, our sweetness, and our hope, hail!
Ad te clamamus exsules filii Hevæ.	To thee do we clamor, exiled children of Eve.
Ad te suspiramus, gementes et flentes in hac lacrimarum valle.	To thee we sigh, mourning and weeping In this tearful valley.
Eia, ergo, advocata nostra, illos tuos misericordes oculos ad nos converte;	So then, our advocate, to us thy merciful eyes turn;
Et Jesum, benedictum fructum ventris tui, nobis post hoc exsilium ostende.	And Jesus, the Blessed fruit of thy womb, to us, after this our exile, show.
Ohhhhhhhhhhhh, clemens, Ohhhhhhhhhhhh, pia, Ohhhhhhhhhhhh, dulcis, Virgo Maria.	Ohhhhhhhhhhhh, clement, Ohhhhhhhhhhhh, loving, Ohhhhhhhhhhhh, sweet, Virgin Mary.

The waters crashed down, flooding the town square and cascading out to the periphery, where dozens of aqueducts carried it all away. Winthrop was transfixed, staring at the marvel before him. The pillar of water was illuminated by the sun, and since they were standing on the eastern side of the square, the light refracted from red near the ground to orange, yellow, green, blue, indigo, and violet as the water reached up into the sky above. Without realizing what he was doing, Winthrop arose and walked towards the pillar.

He took no notice of the water lapping at his boots as he entered the flood zone, nor of the children running around and giggling as they splashed each other and him. He took no notice of the fact that the water was now knee-high, soaking his feet and pushing him away, making him fight to keep wading forward.

The water was delightfully warm. He felt that, but he didn't think of it. He just kept walking forward until he reached the little wooden steps ascending to the top of the well. He wasn't looking for them, but he found them. He stepped up once, twice, then a third time. He was on the top step, water blasting him from the waist down, his nose mere inches from the wall of water. It was bright red, thundering loudly. Somewhere in the distant background, Winthrop probably heard someone say, "Hey! Are you crazy? What are you doing?" but he didn't notice them. Winthrop looked straight up to see where the sky met the colored wall in front of him. He stepped up one more time, onto the well, and into the water.

Somehow he could see. Somehow he could stand. The crashing torrent should have knocked him off his feet, but instead it was the force of beauty that made him slowly lower himself to his knees. Staring straight up, the pillar was like a thousand cascading rings of rainbows, falling all about him. The sunlight passed in, reflected back, back again, back again, crossing every which way so that the rings of light were pierced by iridescent shafts bending and dancing all about each other. Each moment was a miracle, yet the falling water never held its place long enough to take the whole miracle in. Instead it was racing past, so that the light was like a thousand sunrises and sunsets of scorching skies and peaceful nights, a lifetime of wonder passing by in a minute. Yet just as with the crawfish in the moat, Winthrop's vision reached out further. He saw the falling water rush past the moon, the sun, galaxies of galaxies–in the twinkling of an eye they were here and gone. His vision reached world's end, where the water passed beyond all time, and then Winthrop could see no more.

How long Winthrop knelt there, he did not know, but eventually he felt the need to breathe. Sorrow came over him. He didn't want to leave. He wished this vision would last forever. But as the mortal frailties of his body made themselves known, Winthrop took one last look, made his peace, and then let the torrent carry him along.

He was unceremoniously ejected off the well, down three feet to the masonry below, and was carried along by the rushing water. Before he could even get his bearings two hands grasped Winthrop by the back of his shirt and pulled him up. He instantly began gasping for air. Ed came running over, splashing through the water. "Your dukeliness! Your dukeliness! Are you alright? Crimeny your dukeliness! Ya got blood on your head. Are you alri–"

"Why, Ed! Why?" Winthrop was choking, whether on water or tears he did not know.

"Why what? Whaddaya mean, 'why'?"

"Why, Ed! Why!" Winthrop plunged his head back down below the water. The two hands holding him by the back of the shirt yanked him up

Winthrop pointed up at the rainbow pillar. "Why are you not astounded? Why doesn't this bring you to your knees? How can anyone possibly be roasting potatoes and filling water yokes as if you were on the shores of the River Eines? Oh my God, you people! Why aren't you going to the ends of the earth to tell every soul about this miracle? Why? Why? Why!"

The hands holding Winthrop by the back of his shirt spun him around, and he was face to face with Constable William. His eyes were red with tears. "We did. And we do. You told me just yesterday that you were in a barroom when you heard about this miracle. Then you and your friends laughed at the messenger."

Winthrop backed away in shock. William was right, but... "No. No William. That was...that was different."

"No it wasn't."

Winthrop turned slowly back towards the pillar of water, then sank to his knees in the rushing stream.

"Come on, your dukeliness, let's get goin'."

"No!" Winthrop shook free of Ed, and rising swiftly splashed forward for several steps. "Ed, I need to see this. All of it! I don't care if I get wet. I can't afford to miss a moment!" He dropped to his knees and let the warm water rush past him as he took it all in. The sky, the pillar, the strange colors of water on the ground reflecting it all, mixed together with the reflection of Winthrop himself...He laid bare his soul and let beauty touch it.

A few seconds later, Winthrop heard the splashing of someone else beside him. He turned, expecting to see Ed. Instead, it was Zakary. He dropped to his knees next to Winthrop, looking up at the pillar. "Thank you. I've dreamt of doing this so many times, but I was always telling myself I'd be crazy. That I shouldn't 'make a big deal' out of a daily occurrence. Thank you. You've given me the courage to be a little bit crazy. Maybe tomorrow I'll be even crazier."

Winthrop looked at the pillar again, and the two men knelt beside each other for a few more minutes until the rain sputtered out and ceased.

Chapter 7: Silence

"**H**ey Zakary! I sure hope that black knight didn't steal your change of clothes!"

"Zakary only has one outfit I've ever seen. That or all his clothes smell just as bad…"

"You guys are missing the whole point! Now his cloak is a moving washcloth. The sheep can come up for a drink anytime they want!"

"That's disgusting. Those clothes aren't sanitary. Not even for a sheep."

Zakary splashed up to the men who were ribbing him, throwing and taking playful punches. Eventually he realized the best retort for their commentary was to start giving out bear hugs, and soak his harassers with the 'unsanitary' water from his clothes. Zakary's playful demeanor took a jarring turn however, when Cara came up behind him and whispered, "Zakary?"

He turned to face her and became suddenly sober. "Yes m'lady?"

"Would you be so kind?"

Zakary looked around, then shook his head sadly. "Not today. Too many people who…you know." Winthrop noticed that the shepherd's eyes darted between himself and William as he said that.

Cara nodded sadly and then walked away. "Pray for me."

"I will."

Winthrop wanted to inquire about what had happened, but a throng of children descended upon him. Winthrop was then bombarded with a volley of questions and comments from the older children (especially the boys) who had an extraordinarily high opinion of what he had just done.

"How did you do that?"

"You stood in there for so long!"

"Can you show me how to get in the water?"

"I thought you woulda been smushed."

"You shoulda seen how fast you got launched out of there at the end!"

"What was it like inside?"

"Are you gonna do it again tomorrow?"

"Can I do it with you?"

"I bet I can stay in longer than you can."

"No way!"

"Ya huh."

"Wanna bet?"

In the midst of the chatter, Winthrop was silently looking at Lady Maria, who was looking back at him, her face streaked with tears. She was smiling and in pain. He didn't know if the tears were joyful or sorrowful. What he did know was that he really wanted to be alone with her right now. For what seemed like an insufferable length of time, the prayer group said their farewells and told Winthrop what they thought of him and what he had done, and what he ought to do about his soaking wet clothing. Eventually it was decided that Zakary would walk Lady Maria home while Ed would take Winthrop back to the bar to grab a change of clothes.

Winthrop asked the Lady, "May I come to visit after I have dried off?"

"Yes. I should like that very much."

Winthrop turned to William. "Constable?"

William rested his hands on his rotund belly and sighed deeply. Winthrop knew this was a common posture amongst constables for keeping their hands at the ready in case a scuffle suddenly broke out, but for William it actually looked like a natural position. His stomach made a nice shelf.

"I stopped by to see you last night, and Ed said you were already asleep. And while I wouldn't say you caused *trouble* this morning, you have eh…certainly caused a bit of a *scene*."

Winthrop nodded slowly. "This is probably when I should say 'Sorry about that,' but eh…I'm not."

William chuckled. "I'm glad you could see the miracle. Maybe now you can go and be that crazy person who tells everyone to go to Dewford." William became uncomfortable. "But uh…on the subject of your stay here…Dewford is…I hope you understand, but…we're not in any sort of position to be dealing with your claims. Yesterday I thought we might investigate in the Chellesian archives, but once I spoke with Reginald…well, we thought it all through and realized that even if your claim *is* true, it has implications that Dewford is not equipped to handle. An unexpected heir to a house thought to be dead, a house at enmity with the kingdom of Goliath, Goliath who has not set foot in his own kingdom in decades…there are just so many complications that are above our rank. Reginald decided that we should send you to Chelles, and if the archives do verify your claims, Lord Fearnow is the one who will sort it all out."

Winthrop hung his head. "You're a good constable, William. Not many men can combine the spine to tell such unwelcome news with the grace to do so politely. I understand I've put you in a difficult position, but…is there really no way I could have some time to speak with Lady Maria?"

William looked at Ed, recalling the barkeep's comment from yesterday about how, 'Man can't come to Dewford and not meet the Lady.' He drummed his belly a few times with his hands, then said, "Well I've got a very important breakfast to attend to right now, so I was going to have Eustace make the arrangements for you to go to Chelles. And he's been known to get lost from time to time, so…you might be able to squeeze in a *short* visit."

Winthrop smiled. "Thank you, William."

The constable turned and whistled a few notes as he walked away. "No need to thank me. I'm just a hungry man who wants his breakfast." Winthrop found it interesting that this 'lie' had not bothered his ears.

They dispersed and Winthrop and Ed were at the barroom in minutes. Both on the walk back and while he was digging up some fresh clothing, Ed prattled on constantly as was his fashion. "Well, I'm sure glad your dukeliness made them there arrangements to be spending time with the Lady, because forthrightly I didn't wanna go tellin' you so, but I was not goin' to be able to entertain ya all morning due to having to manage some things that ya could call time sensitive, the timin' bein' based upon relativeness to when the water comes, after all, and right now I need to be getting back to work, what with bein' a bit more behind schedule than normal at this time of the day, so I'll just be grabbin' ya somethin' to wear, which I oughta be warnin' ya about, that it's gonna be a little loose of a fit since I have a bit more of the enthusiastic personality type at the dinner table, whereas your dukeliness is more of the peckish nibblin' type if it isn't too rude to be sayin'…"

Every bit of noise was grating on Winthrop's ears. From the time he entered Maria's home until he left her, Winthrop had felt a certain stillness. Even with all of the vocal prayers, conversations, and her cries of pain at the Rosary, the only word he could think of to describe being in her presence was 'silence.' Now that he was out of her presence, Ed's formerly charming stream of consciousness had become an exhausting gong that Winthrop desperately wanted to stop clanging. Eventually, Ed found what he was looking for and came back with pants, underclothing, a towel, and a short-sleeved shirt. "I didn't bother grabbin' any socks since it's all nice out and your boots are soaked anyway, so I reckoned ya might go around barefoot for a little while–"

"Do you have anything with longer sleeves, Ed?"

"Oh, I suppose if I went and dug up my winter clothes, but nothin' light enough for a hot day like we've been havin' lately. If I went and got ya somethin' like that you'd be cookin' awfully fast, that ya would. Might be able ta throw ya in the stew for dinner, but–"

"Very well. Thank you, Ed. I was just asking." Winthrop took the clothes rather gruffly and then went to the room he had stayed in the night before. He closed the door and sighed. Finally. Silence…

Winthrop proceeded to get dressed, putting on the shirt last of all. The sleeve was already short, and he was also a bit taller than Ed, meaning it didn't even reach his elbow. The grisly scar Winthrop had on his left arm was fully exposed. He tried tugging down on the sleeve. No use. He wasn't looking forward to having to field questions on the scar, and sure enough he hadn't taken four steps outside the bedroom before Ed yelled, "Crimeny sakes, your dukeliness! Looks like somethin' sure took a bite outta ya! How'd ya get that mess on your skin there? Was that why your hand was bleedin' yesterday?"

"I prefer not to talk about it."

"Holy mackeroley, I can see why, that musta been quite the critter. I'd be curious if ya would tell me…" Winthrop deflected Ed's continuing questions, found where he was supposed to hang his wet clothing, and then departed without giving the barkeep the story he was looking for. Ed was not the only curious person however, and sure enough the many townsfolk Winthrop passed on the way to Lady Maria's were stopping to stare, point, and whisper in hushed tones about the long and bumpy lines of flesh running from his wrist to the elbow and back again. Winthrop tried to ignore them and pressed on, yearning to get to Lady Maria's house and get away from all of the bustling crowd and its noise. He excitedly turned down her street, rushed to the door, took a deep breath, and knocked.

The door was opened by one of the men in sackcloth whom Winthrop had seen at the Rosary. He bowed to Winthrop and said, "We were just leaving. Peace to you brother," and four more smiling people came out behind him. Winthrop looked curiously at the entourage until Maria's voice came from inside saying, "Come in." Winthrop entered and closed the door behind him. Looking into both rooms of the house, he saw that they were alone. Maria was propped up in a sitting position on her bed, fidgeting with some sort of cloth and a ball of yarn. Winthrop looked a little closer and realized to his surprise she was crocheting. Her arms and hands had seemed so…*incapable* when he saw her earlier, but they were in fact nimble enough to twist and wind the little hooked needles through the yarn repeatedly. He didn't realize he was staring until she asked, "Are you alright?"

Winthrop chuckled nervously. "Sorry, I was just…impressed by your crocheting."

"Oh, it's nothing, just a little blanket I'm making for one of the families in town. They're expecting next month, and Kelsey–the mother–she's got her hands full with two little toddlers already running around, so I offered to make something for the one on the way. They *had* a newborn blanket, but their youngest has decided that it's *her* blankie, so I offered to throw a new one together."

Winthrop nodded. "It's coming together nicely."

Lady Maria smiled and looked back down at her work.

Silence.

Winthrop had been yearning for some silence ever since he left the town square. Now that he had it, he was desperately trying to think of something to say.

"May I take a seat?"

"Of course."

Winthrop sat down on a stool by the bed. The mattress was on a raised frame, meaning Lady Maria was now higher than him while he was sitting.

More silence.

"You remind me of my grandmother." As soon as the words left Winthrop's mouth his face turned bright red. Lady Maria laughed. "I'm sorry, that came out wrong. I didn't mean to say–"

"That I'm a crippled old woman who sits in bed and hobbles around like your grandmother used to?"

Winthrop's face felt even warmer. "That would be precisely what I didn't mean to say…though I realized what it must have sounded like as soon as I said it. My grandmother was actually never a hobbler. She had no trouble getting around right up until her passing. No, you just–you remind me of sitting on the floor as a child while she would knit in her armchair. I would plop down sometimes and wait for her to tell me the most marvelous stories. I always knew that if I waited long enough she would have something incredible to say. As I was sitting here, it just struck me that I felt that way all over again."

More silence.

Winthrop added, "Which is ridiculous, really, because I'm so much older than you. If anything, I should be sharing my pearls of wisdom with a younger woman, but I'm afraid I don't own many pearls." He paused fidgeting awkwardly for a moment. "It was just a feeling I had for a moment. I don't know why I even mentioned it."

Lady Maria smiled one of those famous smiles of hers, but kept looking down and crocheting.

More silence.

Winthrop went on again, "How old are you?"

"Twenty-nine."

"My goodness, you're young."

More silence.

Winthrop went on yet again, "You know, it was just a feeling, and yet it wasn't *just* a feeling. I really was waiting for you to tell me something profound or deep. Everyone in this town has such a high opinion of you. I figured you must be some sort of wizened sage or something. Someone who really knows things. I was looking forward to that, because I feel like right now I don't know anything, and I was hoping to talk to someone who knows things. But…it is possible for a young person to know things too, I suppose, it just isn't as common as for someone with more experience. Though, I have plenty of experience, and I'm the one who doesn't know anything." When Maria didn't react but just kept moving her needles, Winthrop hung his head, wondering what he had really come there for. "I should go."

He rose swiftly and started walking away. He was already at the door when Lady Maria asked, "What do you want to know?"

He came back to the chair and sat down, leaning towards her as he asked, "What was that pillar of water in the town square this morning?"

"It was a miracle."

"Why?"

"What do you mean, why?" She finally looked up from her needles, giving Winthrop a confused look.

"Why was it a miracle? Why isn't it just an incredible natural event? Does that happen every day?"

"It does."

"Then how do you know it's a miracle? How do we know it's not just something natural like the sunset that happens every day because the earth is spinning round and round? If anything, the fact that it happens every day suggests it *is* like a sunset, that there's some sort of natural explanation that causes it to happen repeatedly in the same way every time."

Lady Maria cast off and then set her blanket and yarn aside. She asked, "How do you know sunsets aren't miracles?"

Winthrop scoffed. "You can't be serious."

"Serious about what?"

"You can't seriously think sunsets are miraculous."

"I don't know what I think of the answer. But I do think this is a good question. You talk about things not being miracles if they happen over and over. So then sunsets aren't miracles, but rare things like lightning are? Maybe lightning is still too common. What if a shooting star hit Dewford right now? That would be pretty rare. So is it a miracle? Or is it just gravity? I don't think that commonness or rareness has anything to do with miracles. This is a good question. Let's keep asking it."

Winthrop leaned slowly forward, until his elbow was resting on the bed. These were exactly the kind of sagely riddles he had been hoping for, though he wasn't quite ready for them now that they had arrived. He asked the Lady, "The water pillar is a miracle?"

"Yes, I'm certain of that one."

He reached over and picked up her ball of yarn, and then dropped it. "If I drop a ball of yarn and it falls, is that a miracle?"

"No."

He now gestured out the open window by her bed. "Are sunsets miracles?"

"I don't know. I don't think so, but I'm not certain yet."

"Why the doubt? What's the difference between a ball of yarn moving through the air and a ball of fire moving through the sky?"

"Well...falling balls of yarn aren't beautiful. Some blankets are beautiful, when you're done, but the yarn isn't. Sunsets are beautiful. Beautiful things need an artist. Maybe a sheep rolling around enough could turn its wool into a knot of yarn, but it could never turn it into a pretty little blanket. I want to say that sunsets are a miracle where God paints the sky. Now perhaps He could have painted it once back when he made the earth, and then God could use the same sunset every day. If He did that, I would say sunsets go in the same box as a falling ball of yarn. But every sunset is *uniquely* beautiful. Every day you get a new piece of art, which means the Artist must have painted it anew. Maybe this is the real answer to our question. Maybe falling balls of yarn *are* beautiful in their own way, but it's a beauty God made in the beginning, and they've been falling the same way ever since. So that's natural. But I think sunsets are a new creation every day, and that makes them a miracle. You know, I quite like this definition! Because that would mean that if a shooting star shot into Dewford because it fell the same way stars always fall, that's not a miracle. That's natural. But if it fell in some new way, like if God wanted to send us a pretty diamond from heaven – that would be a miracle." Lady Maria leaned back on her pillow throne with a smile of content. "I have decided sunsets are miracles. I challenge you to prove I'm crazy."

"You're crazy."

She laughed just a little. "I said to prove it."

"Well you are!" They both laughed for a while after that, but then Winthrop's face darkened. "Miracles...I decided long ago there were no miracles. And now...now what can I say? If I've already decided there are no miracles, then what does this morning mean?"

Lady Maria smiled knowingly. "It means that you were wrong."

Winthrop looked down, trying to figure out what he should say next. He certainly shouldn't say the truth that was on his mind. That would be the craziest thing of all...

More silence. Enough silence to make Winthrop a little crazy.

He looked back up and said, "Ever since yesterday, I'm trying something new. Something very new. At least, very new for me. And since I'm so new at this, I really don't know what I'm doing yet, and I'm worried I'm going to make a mess of it."

"How many times does a child fall when he is learning to walk?"

Winthrop thought back to David as a toddler. "Too many to count."

"Then don't worry about falling. Keep trying to walk. What is this new thing you're doing?"

"Telling the truth."

More silence.

Winthrop was having a hard time holding these silences. At length he said, "It's not an easy business, telling the truth. Compared to lying, it's much easier to figure out what to say. You just say the truth. Easy. But I'm finding it's much harder to live with what happens after you say it. Lies don't cause as much trouble. I'll give you an example. I've spent most of four decades now saying I'm a free commoner, when I'm actually a duke, and a high ranking one at that. That lie is very easy to live with. Very easy. But yesterday I told the truth, and now the mayor wants to ship me off to Chelles, where I'll either be flogged if the duke doesn't believe my tale, or hanged if he does. And that's not even the worst part of this whole honesty business! Once I told the truth about who I really am, *I* had to start living with who I really am. I spent all of last night…I spent it…oh, I hate to use this phrase—I spent all of last night 'dueling with unpleasant thoughts.' Thoughts about who I am. It turns out I don't like who I am, and I wish I could lie about that. I would like to at least lie to myself, but that seems like the worst kind of lie of all. I'm starting to find I really hate myself, and I would rather tell myself, 'You're a good chap, Winthrop,' than say, 'You're the most awful kind of scoundrel.' You must think I'm truly rotten. What kind of man thinks it's hard to tell the truth?"

More silence.

Winthrop was thinking of what to say to fill the silence, but it was Lady Maria who spoke first. "Jesus thought it was hard to tell the truth. In a certain sense, anyway. He didn't struggle with telling it, but He recognized it was hard. I forget where He said this, but in one of the Gospels He said something like, 'If I say I don't know God, then I'm a liar. But I do know Him, and because I say I know Him, you are trying to kill me.' And they did kill Him. You're right to say telling the truth is not an easy business. It'll probably get you killed someday. But to be honest, Winthrop, that's really not so bad. Jesus must have been a lot happier to die knowing He was God's Son, than to live thinking He was nobody." She paused a moment, then smiled sweetly at Winthrop and said, "That's what you need to make telling the truth easier, my duke. Not less truth but more of it. You need to hold onto the truth that you are God's son. Tell me, are you baptized?"

It is unlikely that any other question in the world could have disillusioned Winthrop so quickly. After listening attentively, pondering deeply, even setting aside his own hostilities because he was wrapped up in Lady Maria unpacking the *story* of Christianity, that question shocked him back to his usual antipathy. "…yep. I sure am…"

Lady Maria had seen his face fall, but she went on anyway. "Then you're a child of God. You can be just like Jesus. Every time telling the truth gets hard, remind yourself, 'I do know Him. And because I say I know Him, you are trying to kill me.' Remember that you're the son of God, Winthrop, and you'll have the strength to scream the truth, even as you're dying."

More silence.

Winthrop laughed a black and bitter chuckle. "Well then I suppose it sure is a good thing some priest poured water on my head as a baby. That makes me a son of God! Now I can be happy when I die! I sure hope my parents didn't lie to me when they said I was baptized, though...or that the priest didn't say the wrong words...or that the water wasn't too polluted to count as 'pure water,' and 'valid matter.' If any of those things happened, then I guess I wouldn't be a child of God after all. Nope, I'm just a child of wrath doomed to damnation because someone made a mistake when I was a baby and I wasn't paying close enough attention to set them straight back then. You know, I should probably get baptized again, just to make sure, right? Oh, but wait! That's a sacrilege! That's a mortal sin! If I was baptized right the first time, I'll go to hell for doing it a second time. But if I wasn't baptized right the first time, I'll go to hell for *not* doing it a second time. Well now I've got myself in quite a pickle...whether I go to heaven or hell all depends on figuring out the truth behind some event that happened when I was a baby, halfway around the world, where all of the witnesses are dead and gone. Do tell me, oh wise Lady Maria who 'knows things,' how ever shall I proceed?"

The door swung open, and Eustace stepped in. "Everything alright in here? It sounded like things were getting a little out of hand."

Lady Maria said, "We're fine, Eustace. Thank you for checking in. It's just a heated discussion, but nothing to worry about."

Eustace started to slowly close the door, glowering at Winthrop the whole time. "A few more minutes, and we'll be heading to the mayor's manor, okay?"

"Thank you for letting us know, Eustace," Lady Maria answered. The door closed.

More silence.

"You seem awfully confident I won't hurt you. What makes you so sure of that?"

"Oh, don't say such foolishness so loudly. He can obviously hear you."

"Thank you for the advice. In that case I'll whisper my question, but it's the same one. You say 'There's nothing to worry about.' Whatever put that idea in your head? How do you know I'm not a robber who will kill you and take all your valuables?"

"Even if you were a robber, I would have no reason to fear. I don't have any valuables for you to kill me over."

"Well, what if I wasn't a robber. What if I was the kind of man who loses his temper and kills sometimes?"

"Are you?"

More silence.

"Have you ever killed someone in a rage, Winthrop?"

More silence.

"Would you kill me if you were angry enough?"

A little silence.

"No."

"Then I have nothing to worry about."

"Of course you have something to worry about! I could be lying!"

"If you were a liar you would have told me you've never killed someone in a rage. If you're honest on that point I'll trust you on this one."

"That's faulty reasoning. A logical fallacy."

"I've never studied formal logic, m'lord. I don't know a whole lot about these 'fallacies,' but I do know something about people. Even wicked men have their virtues, and yours is clearly honesty. If you say you wouldn't kill me, then I have good reason to believe you."

More silence.

"You never answered my question about Baptism."

"You weren't looking for an answer. You wanted to beat me over the head with a question."

"That's because there is no good answer to that question."

"There is a very good answer to that question. But if you have already decided there is no good answer, then there is no point in me giving you one. I won't cast my pearls before swine."

"So I'm swine now?"

"Stop looking to start a fight. I did not call you swine, and you know it. I said that if you will not listen to the words out of my mouth, I will not bother saying them. If you will listen, I will say them. You are not swine. You are, however, capable of acting like swine."

More silence.

"I would like to hear your answer."

"Are you actually open to the truth?"

"Tell me what you've got, and I'll see if I'm convinced."

"It doesn't work that way. Men decide what they believe, and they decide if they are open to the truth. If you are hanging on my words to refute them even as they leave my mouth, you will never be convinced."

Winthrop took a deep breath. "Very well. I will not hang on your words to refute them. I am going to sit here and listen, and for the moment I am open to the possibility that you might know the truth. What's the answer?"

"My answer is that the Church is the Body of Christ. If you have faith in the Head, then have faith in the Body also. Your parents, your priest, have faith in them. And if they did make a mistake, have faith in the angels too, since they're members of the same Church. If you live your whole life like a son of God, ignorant of a mistake some other people made in your infancy, trust that God will send an angel before you die to bring a rain cloud and baptize you with water from heaven. He will not reject anyone who comes to Him."

More silence.

"I really thought you would be someone who knows things, but you're just a naive little girl who hasn't seen enough of the world yet. You aren't even a mature or thoughtful Christian. The words out of your mouth sound like something a child would say."

"Thank you for the compliment."

"That wasn't a compliment. I called you childish."

"Without faith like a child, no one enters the kingdom of heaven."

"It wasn't intended as a compliment."

"What you intended doesn't change what you said. So again, thank you for the compliment."

More silence.

Winthrop leaned over the bed, so that he and Lady Maria had only a foot or so between their faces. "I am about to say what is perhaps the most awful thing a man could ever say, and yet I feel the need to say it. Do you hear how quietly I'm whispering? I suspect that by the time I truly discharge my mind I will be shouting, shouting so loud the whole town is going to hear me. So I'm starting quiet, very quiet, and hoping that the quieter I start, the quieter I'll finish, and maybe Eustace won't overhear us through the window."

"If it's truly that rotten, why would you say it?"

"It's a confession of sorts. Not like the Sacrament. I'm not looking for forgiveness. But I would like to make a confession. You see, I'm starting to see why you're so special. For all the insults and bitterness I'm throwing your way, I know I don't really mean any of it. I suspect you already know that too. I can get angry, that's certainly my vice. But since you must suffer my vice, please also suffer my virtue. You're a wonderful young woman, Maria. You made me open myself up to the truth. I was open to your truth about Baptism, and frankly, I'm not persuaded. Eh, maybe I am. I'm starting to think that's not the point.

"You see, you made me open myself up to *the* Truth. Not this or that truth, but all of it. The whole Truth. And in the process I came to see something truly horrible about myself. Something vile. Despicable. I would like to share it with you. It's an ugly truth, but it's a true truth. This whole telling the truth business has been brutal, but if I could tell it to you I think it would mean more to me than anything else in the world. Will you let me do that, Maria? Will you let me tell you the terrible truth that you have made me see?"

She nodded slowly.

Silence.

More silence.

The longest silence yet.

Winthrop began in a whisper, but just as he had predicted, his anger took over. Despite his best efforts, the volume kept increasing as he went.

"You have made me realize that I hate God. I hate Him. You don't seem surprised. You should be. I know I certainly am. You see, yesterday I was still pretending He didn't exist. Yesterday I didn't think I hated God, I thought I didn't believe in Him. I was an atheist. I *thought* I was an atheist. I've talked religion with people before, and that's the position I always took. If you had asked me yesterday, that's exactly what I would have told you. 'I'm an atheist.' I quite liked being an atheist, Maria. That might be hard for you to believe, but I enjoyed it. I didn't have to be angry at God. I didn't have to hate Him. I could just tell myself I didn't believe in Him. I was free to enjoy all of life's finest moments, without being bogged down by the Christian millstone around my neck. I was free to do whatever I want."

At this point, Winthrop's voice really started picking up volume. "But now, two things have changed, and how I wish to God they hadn't. Yesterday, I decided I would never lie again, which is paying me miserable wages. I would have to go back and think about it, but I'm pretty sure there hasn't been a single moment where I was better off telling the truth than telling a nice, convenient lie."

Maria interjected, "Does it matter that your honesty is the only reason I trust you?"

Winthrop glowered and continued, now in a much more elevated voice, "And then today I saw a miracle! An undeniable, irrefutable miracle. I want to say it's just science or a shooting star. I want *you* to tell me it's just science or a shooting star, but you won't! You won't lie to me! And, I won't even lie to myself, so there's nothing left to say! It's a miracle! A miracle! An honest to God miracle, and that means God exists. *Fine.* God exists! I'll admit it! There is a God, and I hate Him! I'm not an atheist, Maria! I should have realized much sooner that I never was. I'm a satanist! A satanist! There is a God, and I hate Him! I don't like Him, I don't like His world, and I think the devil had the right idea when he rebelled! Curse God! Curse Him! Yes, I know He exists. The Unmoved Mover and Teleology and all those proofs they ever taught us still apply, but He isn't good. God might exist, but He is *not* good. I'm a satanist! I could live with that! It's not as convenient as being an atheist, but I could still live with that!"

Now Winthrop leapt to his feet, pointing an accusatory finger down at Lady Maria. "But *you.* You had to go and wreck that plan for me! With all your talk about beauty and goodness, and sunsets, and artists…I know you're right, and I almost hate you for it. If I didn't love you with all my heart, I would hate you with whatever was left. But I do love you, like I loved my mother, though I'm old enough to be your father. I wish I could hate you, even if it was just a little, because then I might be able to lie and say you're wrong.

"Bah! But I'm not lying either! There I go again with this accursed honesty! So here's the truth! And maybe I'm wrong! I don't know what I'm saying, but I'm saying what I know! I know your God is beautiful, but He's so ugly as to kill everyone I love! I know your God is just, but He's so capricious as to base the salvation of two robbers on whether a priest heard their Confession as they died. I know your God is Truth, but that means the Truth decided my brother has to burn in purgatory because an evil man wouldn't give him Last Rites! The Truth is I'm supposed to feel guilty for killing that man! Why? Why! If he tortured my brother for a day, I should be glad to smash his head to pieces! Why then, if God tortures my brother in purgatory for years should I say, 'Blessed be the Name of the Lord. Praise be Jesus Christ'? Why? I killed that priest, and I'm glad he's dead, and if I had a big enough vase, I swear to God, I would gladly kill God too!"

The door swung open, slamming into the wall. Eustace rushed in while Constable William held his club high in a shaking hand. "Winthrop…come with us now." Eustace made to grab Winthrop's right arm, but the robber deftly twisted under Eustace's hand and gave him a shove back across the room. William caught Eustace with one hand, still holding the club up over his head. "Winthrop! Come quietly! Don't make me have to hurt you!"

Eustace came charging in for a tackle, and this time Winthrop showed no restraint. He ably pivoted on his left foot and gave the deputy a devastating kick to the chest with his right. It stopped his charge on the spot, and sent him tumbling back on his rear, clasping his ribs.

William no longer had the option to end this peacefully. He came in swinging his club, expertly standing in just the right spot that he would be able to hit Winthrop, but Winthrop could not strike back. Instead he ducked, and as the second blow came he blocked with a stool and threw it at William's head. Eustace was back up, but clearly winded. He charged Winthrop a third time, now just diving at his feet. He knew he didn't need to hurt the outlaw, just trip him up so William could get a clean hit with the club. Normally Eustace would be right, but Winthrop could see William. Throwing the stool hadn't done much damage, but it got in the way, buying Winthrop a few precious moments. He spread his legs so he wouldn't fall and then allowed Eustace to wrap his arms around Winthrop's knees. That meant both of his arms were occupied. Winthrop bent down and gave him a flurry of blows right to the kidneys.

Howling in pain, the young man released Winthrop and rolled onto his back. William came charging back in, but Winthrop jumped over Lady Maria's bed, making his way towards the window. He was about to jump outside, but two hands grabbed him from behind. He turned to see who it was, not believing William was standing close enough. It was Maria. Through tearful eyes, she begged him, "Promise me you will stay this course! Promise you will never lie again!" William swung his club at Winthrop's head. Winthrop ducked, feeling the club whip through his long hair. William went to swing again, but Maria lurched upright, putting herself in the way of his strike. Eyes locked on Winthrop, she yelled at him, "Promise me!" William made to run around the bed. Another man was at the door. Eustace was hobbling to his feet.

Winthrop was half a step ahead of the constable. It was close, but it was enough. He dove head first out the window, and then landed on the cobbled stones of the street with his face and bad left arm. William tried to climb through the window carefully, but it was too small. The only way through was a full-speed leap of faith like the one Winthrop had just made. Winthrop heard footfalls coming around the house. William yelled through the window, "After him! Murderer! The false duke is a murderer!" Then he ran for the door to pursue Winthrop.

Winthrop was up and running. Running! Always running! Every day since his brother's death was running. Running from this town, running from that. Running from the glade, and then running into Dewford. Running, running, always running, and now he was running yet again. But one difference emerged. One singular moment. Through the familiar clamor and chaos of that foggy life of death, the voice of Lady Maria came shooting like a golden arrow.

"Promise me!"

He looked back to see Maria's pleading face framed in the window he had jumped from. Winthrop looked directly into her eyes. Just for a moment. And nodded.

He whispered, "I shall never lie again."

Lady Maria smiled. It was a sad smile. Sad, but not without hope. And as with all her smiles, her eyes were smiling too.

Off he ran. An angry mob was searching for him, but their righteous zeal could not match Winthrop's sheer will to survive. He ran past the farms and flocks and fields until he reached that hill on the southern side of town where he had hidden from David and Sir Judas the day before. Clambering up to the top, he looked back and saw Dewford laid out before him. His last pursuer had given up and was walking home while occasionally glaring in Winthrop's direction.

Panting to catch his breath, Winthrop fell to his knees, looked up at heaven and said, "Alright, God, I admit it. I know You exist. I'm still not happy with You. I still don't like You or Your ways. But I do love Your Maria. And I don't think You're very good, but I do know You're very strong. I'm a liar. For so many years I've always been a liar. I lied to Rowan and Garrett, pretending to give up leading the group so I could kill them for a little gold. I lied to Zakary and Nicholas and set stupid Dewford into a panic. I'm a liar! But I don't want to be! So here's the deal! You and I are still enemies! But if You really do love Your enemies–or if you at least love Maria–then make me into an honest man. Use Your all-powerfulness, and give me the strength to make good on what I promised her. In honor of Lady Maria, and calling You, Almighty God, as my witness, I solemnly vow that never again shall a lie fall from my lips!"

The one hundred and sixteenth psalm (or one hundred and seventeenth according to the Hebrews) reads as follows;

> Praise the Lord all ye nations,
> Praise Him all ye peoples,
> For confirmed is His mercy upon us,
> And the Truth of the Lord remains in Eternity.

There are many reasons this psalm has come to be associated with Winthrop. One of those reasons which I will now touch on is the final line. 'The Truth (*Veritas!*) of the Lord remains in Eternity.' To the best knowledge of everyone I interviewed in the writing of this history, Winthrop kept his vow of honesty for the remainder of his mortal life. Now he keeps it unto ages of ages. Therefore, I do not think it would be inappropriate for us to say, 'The Truth of the Lord remains in Eternity. The truth of Winthrop remains in Eternity as well.'

End of Volume III

Interlude

Reginald was reclining at table in his mansion, resting a moment after finishing his lunch. He tried to be a simple man. He tried to stop and enjoy the little pleasures of life, especially the delightful meals that Rian always whipped up. Reginald was fond of food. He liked to stop and savor it, just as he liked to take his time savoring a good glass of brandy. He couldn't though. The affairs of such an important man as himself kept him always on edge, always stressed. Even when he tried to relax and enjoy what was right in front of him, his mind would wander to the unsolved problem of the day. He would start worrying, fretting, and planning what he ought to do. Then, before he knew it, he would look down and see that his entire meal was gone, shoveled into his gullet with no memory of what it even tasted like. Today an empty glass of brandy was beside it, and he didn't even remember asking Rian to pour one. This used to be an occasional problem for him. Then as the town expanded and grew, there became more problems the mayor had to deal with. The joys of life slipped through his nervous fingers more frequently. Today he couldn't even remember what he had for lunch.

That so-called 'duke' was on his mind. 'Lord Winthrop.' What a mess that whole farce became. Reginald wished he had whipped him on the spot. That would have been so much simpler. Now he was going to be shipping him off to Chelles, where it would become common knowledge that Reginald was actually entertaining Winthrop's story and felt a need to investigate it. His stomach churned at the thought of the humiliation.

Reginald got up from the table and started pacing nervously, worrying about what was to come, wondering whether he should call the whole thing off and just throw Winthrop out of town. The main problem was William, who genuinely believed Winthrop's story. Reginald couldn't get anything done without his constable's consent, and William had an annoying belief in the importance of due process.

As he was thinking these thoughts, Rian came in and announced, "Good mayor, Constable William has come to call on you. Will you receive him?"

"Yes, yes, send him in."

The servant disappeared and William came into the dining room a few moments later. "Good afternoon, Reginald. Did you have a good lunch?"

"Yes, yes, it was a delightful bowl of..." He turned towards the table and realized his lunch had been on a plate, not in a bowl. "It was fine. Did you send off Winthrop yet?" Lady Cara, overhearing the conversation, came rushing in from the next room.

William shifted very uncomfortably. "In a...certain sense, you could say we did, but in the more obvious sense...he skipped town."

"A ha! So then he was an imposter! At least by taking your advice to leave he's going to save us the trouble of dealing with him."

"Well...yes and no. He's out of our hair for now, but...I suspect this isn't the last we'll hear of him."

"And why is that?" Reginald asked.

William rubbed his neck and grimaced. "So this whole incident took place at Lady Maria's house. Winthrop wanted to talk to her, and she sure got him talking. He got all worked up and started shouting, which made Eustace send for me to come. I got there just in time to hear Winthrop shouting that he had committed a murder, so that's when Eustace and I went in to try and arrest him. And call this a stupid prejudice, but I figured Winthrop must be an imposter, a fake duke. Just some outlaw fugitive who came to our town and pretended to be someone important."

"That's exactly what the evidence would suggest," Reginald stated flatly. "That's not a stupid prejudice William. That's a reasonable conclusion."

William sighed. "I'm not sure you're right, sir. I talked to Lady Maria afterwards, and she was absolutely convinced Winthrop had been telling her the truth. She even pointed out to me, 'If he was lying to us about his lineage, why should we believe him about the murder? If he was telling the truth about the murder, why should we doubt his lineage?'"

"Foolish fallacies of a foolish child!" Reginald barked angrily. "Do not submit your own sound judgment to the simple mind of an inexperienced woman, William. This is exactly the sort of thing thieves and robbers do all the time. Tell the truth about this, lie about that. She just has no experience with criminals."

"She has far more experience than you will ever have!" Cara shouted. "She has stared deeper into the face of evil than any of us!"

Reginald looked at her in surprise, frowned, then reluctantly admitted, "Yes, well fine, I suppose she does. Though if I wanted to split hairs, I would point out that even if that man is 'evil' he has never *technically* committed a crime."

Cara whispered, "God forgive you for uttering such stupid words."

Reginald changed the subject. "What was the nature of this murder anyway, William? Was it the two friends he claimed to have? No one from our town, was it?"

"He said he killed a priest," William answered. "He said the priest wouldn't give his brother 'Last Rites,' and so he killed him." At first Reginald was surprised, but then he burst out laughing. "What's so funny?" William asked.

"Bwa-heh-heh...oh, that..." Reginald walked to his red coat, hanging over the back of his chair, and picked up one of the sleeves, pensively running his fingers across the fabric. "Of all the things this Winthrop has ever said...all those 'proofs' he offered for us to go and research in the Chellesian archives...this is the first thing that has made me think he might actually be the Duke of Nouen."

William looked at Reginald in confusion. "That he killed a priest? Why would that make you believe him? Were the Noueneese anti-Catholic?"

"No," Reginald answered, still fingering his red coat. "...rather, I am struck by the idea that he would kill over something as trivial as a death bed ritual and as noble as right and wrong...that is the mystery of Nouen that has nagged me all my life." He looked at the other two in the room and held up the sleeve to show it to them. "The magistrates of Nouen always wore a red sash about their waist. It was a reminder that they should be ready at every moment to pour out their blood for what is 'right'. I've worn red coats for my entire career out of a lingering fascination with that idea. In theory it has a certain noble quality. In practice, it's the road to barbarism."

"Barbarism?" Cara asked incredulously. "How can fighting for what's right lead to barbarism?"

"Oh, my dear, you can only ask that question because you have never seen the idea put into practice. But when no two men agree on what is 'right', yet all are willing to fight to the death for whatever it is, the world is swift to descend into bloodshed and chaos. What protects us and keeps us safe is an unspoken agreement between me and every citizen of this town that 'right' means following my laws and staying out of prison. Once men start living by their own moral code, all of a sudden you have priests dead on the floor over a few drops of oil and some words in Latin." Cara glowered at him. "Do you wish to disagree?"

"I have nothing more to say to you."

After Cara left, William asked, "On the subject of all this Imperial talk, what was that thing that came up yesterday with the black knight? Winthrop gave you his name and that's when you were done with him." Cara stopped and lingered in the next room, curious about the same question.

Reginald grinned. "Sir Judas, Last of the Kingsguard. That was the name our noble duke gave us."

"Yes, who is that?"

"Ah, he's a fictional character from a lousy story, somewhere between a bad joke and a bad novel. It can be hard to tell those two apart sometimes."

"What do you mean?" William asked. "Are you saying Winthrop's tale was stolen from a story?"

"Oh, I don't know whether he knew that or not. I only learned it while I was working in Lord Fearnow's employ. There was this letter we received one day, ostensibly sent from some count of Brit. The contents were the sort of ridiculous romance that noblemen often publish under a pseudonym." Reginald began using a comically sappy voice. "It was an invitation to a wedding feast, between a poor peasant boy named Stephen and the noble Contessa Violet who had fallen in love with him. And Stephen had saved her from a kidnapper! And what's more! He was no ordinary peasant, but rather a squire! And not to any ordinary knight, but to a paladin! Sir Judas, Last of the Kingsguard! A survivor of the order we all thought was destroyed for forty years!" He waved his hand dismissively. "Oh, it was all so over the top. Total rubbish. Even more so than most of those silly stories we would receive. What made it especially memorable, however, was that the whole thing was presented as if the story was actually true. Official letterhead, seal of office, a message that 'Sir Judas will soon be coming to your lands, in search of the giant Goliath.'"

"When was this?" William asked.

"Years ago. 'Sir Judas' never came to Chelles, but now he has an imposter who's in the area. That, or Winthrop heard the story and assumed we would be taken in by him retelling it."

"How do you know 'Sir Judas' is an imposter?" William asked. "The Duke of Nouen and a surviving paladin? Wouldn't it make sense for them to be together?"

Reginald shook his head. "I do not know what to make of Winthrop. I still think he's a liar, but who knows? Maybe an heir has washed up on our shores. But as for 'Sir Judas,' I am certain. The 'Last of the Kingsguard' died when Goliath slew Sir Daniel."

"Why are you so confident?" William asked.

Reginald looked at his constable thoughtfully, wondering how far he should trust him. He whispered, "What I am about to say must remain entirely between us. Understood? Not a word to another soul, or it's the kind of thing that could cost me my head." William nodded. Cara could barely hear him, so she snuck to the entryway, being careful not to let her shadow fall into the dining room.

Reginald continued, "When I was stationed in the ducal palace, I once stumbled across a certain journal. I wasn't looking for it, mind you. I just happened to come upon it. It had been left open on Lord Fearnow's desk, and my mind read it before my eye could turn away. I learned that the grandfather of our current duke, the first Lord Fearnow, had a certain secret. A secret I would have published if I were the duke, but for whatever reason he's never told a soul. And while I won't repeat what this secret is, I will at least tell you what it means. Lord Fearnow I. knew beyond any shadow of a doubt that the six final paladins died on the plains of Nouen. The king never knighted any others." Reginald straightened up and returned to his normal voice. "If Winthrop really did meet some black knight claiming to be a paladin, then that man is a liar."

It was mid-afternoon on Wednesday, several hours after Sir Judas and David had left Curly's General Store. There had been a rush of customers for most of that time, not to mention the army of gossips who wanted to come in and talk about what had happened. Eventually things slowed down, and now Kayden and Sasha had their first moment to be alone since the tumultuous opening that morning. She smiled at him. "Whew! We can breathe at last!"

Kayden nodded, rearranging the inventory with a frown on his face. She waited for him to tell her what was bothering him, but several minutes rolled by without him saying a word. She finally asked, "Hey, babe, what's on your mind?"

His frown deepened. "That stupid knight."

"Oh, forget that turnip licker. Why the *heck* are you thinking about him?"

"I'm just…I don't know. He's bothering me. I don't like what he said."

"What, about how we should all live like some *old fashioned* married couple from yester-year? You know how *people* like him are."

"Eh. It's not that. At least, not completely. I didn't like what he said about your father."

"Oh, that pious hypocrite can take a hike. I can't believe the nerve of that knight, acting like he even knows the first thing about us and what my dad put us through. He would probably applaud him too, give my dad a gold star for throwing his daughter out of the house because we don't agree with their stupid religion and what they think about living together. I don't care–"

"You're doing it again."

"Doing what?"

"You're not swearing. I never noticed it until the knight pointed it out, but now I can't stop thinking of examples. You never cuss when you talk about your father."

"Oh, come on. That's *crap*."

"You did that one on purpose just to prove me wrong."

Her face turned bright red, causing many of her freckles to blend in with her skin. She got right up in Kayden's face and seethed, "You're not actually gonna side with that knight, are you?"

Kayden's sadness deepened. "You do the same thing with me too. I noticed it some time ago. When you talk about your day you sound normal, but when we get to talking about the things you really care about you forget your sentence enhancers. I thought it was cute that I was the only person who made you talk like that. Now I'm wondering what it means that your father has the same effect."

"It means nothing."

"If you say so…"

She went back to restocking the shelves for all of three seconds before she felt the need to say again, "It means nothing."

"If you say so."

Another minute of fussing around the shop, and then she shouted, "It means nothing!"

"Okay."

A tense silence reigned, with neither speaking to the other until their next customer came in. He had very fine clothes–clearly noble–with mud-caked boots. He was exceptionally tall, probably about seven feet, and very broad. He had a blonde handlebar mustache, and imposing eyes. Seeing Sasha, he walked right up to her, propping a hand against the shelves in order to lean uncomfortably close. "I'm looking for information on a black knight and his two companions, sweetie. When I asked about town I heard he shopped here this morning. Were you working at that time?"

She stepped away and folded her arms. "What's it to you, *curious client?*"

He stepped closer. "Spicy. I like that in a woman, especially a fiery one." He stroked one of her paprika tresses. She slapped his hand away. "I'm in a bit of a rush, so I don't have as much time to play as I would like. Did you overhear them talking about where they were going next? Anything about a priest?"

"Go chew lobster claws."

With a huge, meaty paw, he grabbed her left forearm and hoisted her into the air. Sasha shrieked as he shook her. "Answer me!"

"Drop her, creep!" Kayden rushed in and tackled Charles from behind. At least, that's what he intended to do, but tackling Charles was like trying to tackle a wall, and all he succeeded in doing was popping his shoulder out of place while falling to his knees.

"Out of my way, pretty boy." With a shake of the leg, Charles sent Kayden backwards, all the while holding Sasha up so high her feet couldn't reach the floor. Turning back to her, Charles barked, "Tell me! Did they mention where they were going?"

"Kayden! Help!" Sasha saw Kayden raise himself off the floor, holding his injured shoulder with a wild-eyed look of fear. He was panicked. He took a step back–for a moment she thought he was about to abandon her–but then something came over him. He stopped, steeled his face, let go of his shoulder and yelled, "Saaassshhhaaaa!" Kayden charged back into melee and gave Charles a running drop kick to the back of the knee. It was just enough to make his leg buckle, causing him to fall to the ground and let go of Sasha so that he could use his hands to catch himself.

"Annoying brat!" Charles grabbed Kayden with both hands, lifted him up over his head, and hurled him across the room into a display of animal feed. The wooden display broke to splinters as Kayden crashed into it with a loud groan, but the sacks of feed padded his fall and probably saved him a half-dozen broken bones. Charles stalked over to rectify that fact, whispering, "Lamech killed a man to his wounding, I for a mere insult. If he was avenged seventy times seven fold, let me teach you how much the Bloody Baron is avenged!"

"Wait!" Sasha yelled, running up and putting herself between Charles and Kayden. "I can tell you what you want to know! Just don't hurt him anymore!"

Charles almost swatted her aside, but he remembered his mission. "Well?"

"There were only two of them, not three. An old black knight with long white hair and a young boy. The boy said that his father left them yesterday. That's all we know, honest! Just don't hurt Kayden anymore!"

A look of realization slowly dawned on Charles's face. "They split up yesterday? They were in the glade the night before…Then that means…" His murderous eyes glowed with frightful glee. "If the father went to get the priest…the only town from there to here would be…Oh, how apropos…it shall all finish where it began!"

Charles took one last look at Kayden and said, "Normally I would kill you anyway, but it isn't worth the time it would cost me to bribe the guards. Be grateful your little firecracker saw reason before I completely lost my temper." He swiftly strode out of Curly's. Sasha ran and closed the door behind him, putting the heavy wooden bar in place.

Beatrice hid behind a column in the mess hall, listening to the thundering footfalls of Goliath. They were fading…she was safe for now. The exit was a large wooden double door set in the center of the wall, about thirty feet from her. At least, it seemed to be. Once again, she snuck her way carefully to the door and reached for the handle. Her hand passed right through and felt some sort of burlap material. She tried walking *through* the wooden door without opening it. She made it four inches before hitting a cold, damp stone wall. *Where am I?* she wondered.

In the impenetrable darkness of Castle Nightfall, the only 'sight' that was possible was through the burning orange images the demons presented to the mind. For years now, Jezebel had been a reliable ally to Beatrice, allowing her to navigate as easily as walking by sunlight. Ever since Goliath had started chasing her though, her vision had been warped and distorted. Jezebel said it was the other demons overpowering her. The result was that Beatrice was groping around the castle blindly. Worse than blindly, since her habitual tendency to trust the images before her was difficult to suppress, and she kept acting like she knew what she was seeing. She had tried closing her eyes entirely, but that was no good. The warped vision was *generally* correct. It just made mistakes.

Such a mistake was exactly what befell her when, after carefully feeling her way along the illusory wall, she went to swiftly walk three steps across an 'empty' stretch of space and crashed into a large invisible object. 'Klang! Kla-Klunk!' It was the sound of pots and pans banging into one another. *I'm in the kitchen!* The vision before her eyes wavered and began to twist. Jezebel spoke to her mind, "I'm trying to fix the image. Help me! Focus your power!"

Beatrice strained her mind, trying to assist Jezebel. The kitchen came into focus, a narrow room with two doors along the same wall, separated from each other by a long countertop fifteen feet wide. The sound of heavy footsteps quickly intensified, and then the far door blasted into the room, punched off the hinge by Goliath's scaly, clawed hand. He ducked under the doorway and entered the room, the horns on his head scraping the ceiling. His eyes had the same crazed look they had had ever since he started chasing her.

"Why are you doing this, you stupid witch? Why are you making yourself look like her?" He grabbed the rusty metal bar on which old, tattered dish rags hung, and wrenching it clear out of the wall, he chucked it at her head. Beatrice couldn't quite duck in time, but with an upwards flick of her hand she used her shadow magic to deflect the bar and make it miss high. It smashed the wall behind her so hard that pieces of stone broke off, leaving no doubt what would have happened if it had hit her.

"I'm not doing anything! What are you talking about?"

"Lies! You hope to mess with my mind and make me your pawn! No more! I will never be anyone else's pawn again!" Now he drew Doomfall, that great and fearful blade, but in the tight quarters of the kitchen there was nowhere to swing it. Once upon a time it would have been made of magma that could slice through the stone walls with ease, but ever since the darkness came, it had been a rough and bumpy obsidian blade, cold to the touch. Therefore, Goliath clumsily angled it in front of him and while still stooping down, charged at Beatrice. She leapt up into the air and used her shadow magic to pull herself around the blade and over his shoulder, flying in an erratic counter-spin that let her dodge behind her assailant. She flew through the air, full speed towards the door and slammed head first into an overhead cabinet, invisible to her until that moment.

Dazed, hurt, confused, she twisted and fell to the ground and dashed her bleeding head against the hard stone. "Ugh!" She struggled to stand, fell back down, and then crawled for the door as fast as she could.

Goliath turned around. "Why do you do this, foolish woman? Why do you have a death wish?" Unlike Beatrice, whose vision was being twisted by Abaddon in many ways, Goliath was seeing almost everything correctly. There was only one exception. Beatrice did not look like an aged woman in a dignified dress, but instead she looked like Lady Amanda, wearing the same dress she had worn on that night. Even now, he did not see a bloody and injured woman crawling for dear life, fearfully checking over her shoulder to see if he was following. Instead she looked coy, playful, smiling as she seductively crawled away, seeming to say with her body language, 'Come, follow me.'

"I'll kill you, witch! I'll kill you!"

He raised his sword, charged, and was just about to finish her off. The legion didn't really care whether she lived or died. Morgan's reinforcements from the Scar would give them all the help they needed if they got into a fight with the paladin. Beatrice screamed. But then, at the last moment, a different image flashed through Goliath's mind. This one didn't warp or twist. It wasn't the burnt orange of the devil's sight.

This was a memory. Vivid. Full color. Goliath didn't remember color. Even when he often thought back to times before the darkness, he remembered his memories in the vision he had now. Not this memory. He saw Sir Daniel's great white warhorse, with yellow iridescent wings, flying at him from behind. He turned. He was too slow. The scorched red colors of Doomfall were at his side; he couldn't swing the blade fast enough. Sir Daniel's holy weapon *Spes* was at Goliath's heart, glowing with the blue flames of divine power. It was about to crash through his scales, slaying him on the spot. And Sir Daniel's face…that was the focal point of the memory. His green eyes were so confident…almost cocky. His red lips smirked. It was that look men have when they know a secret.

Goliath remembered how it ended. Sir Daniel's lance tipped up, glancing off the giant's shoulder. Doomfall came around. The last of the

Kingsguard was slain. The day was won. Goliath remembered it all in black and orange, but it wasn't in this colored memory. The image he had seen was the moment when all seemed lost. *Spes* was at his heart. Glowing blue with power. He couldn't get Doomfall around in time. That smirk. That accursed smirk. When the darkness was new, Goliath had stayed up many nights, howling at the sky, wondering what the meaning of the smirk was. It had been many years since he thought of it, but now those memories all came flooding back. That smirk. What did he know? Why did he do it? Did Sir Daniel really miss? It seemed impossible. Yet what else could it have been?

Goliath stormed out of the room, Beatrice completely forgotten. He went up to the top of the castle and looked west towards the ocean. The perfect blackness. It was the only place where there was nothing for the demons to show him.

Darkness. All he saw was darkness. For forty years, all he saw when he looked out at the waters was darkness. He was cast off by God. He was cast off by himself. He thought back to the day he pronounced those magic words that the Legion told him would make him rule the world.

> Let this day be turned into darkness,
> Let not God regard it from above,
> And let not light shine upon it.
> Let darkness and the shadow of death cover it.
> Let a mist overspread it, and let it be wrapped up in bitterness.
> Let a darksome whirlwind seize upon this night,
> Let it not be counted in the days of the year,
> Nor numbered among the months.
> Let this night be solitary, and not worthy of praise.
> Let them curse it who curse the day,
> Who are ready to raise up a Leviathan.
> Let the stars be darkened with the mist thereof,
> Let it expect the light and not see it,
> Nor the rising of the dawning of the day.

When Goliath first learned this spell, he knew the words were from the third chapter of the book of Job. With eager glee he had imagined the power he would wield once he completed the work of making himself 'the Leviathan'. In those last days before he created the darkness, he had eagerly read the forty-first chapter of Job and memorized by heart the poem describing how powerful he would be. Yet in all his labors, all his reading, his vain and stupid reading, he had never bothered to go back to chapter three and ponder the words immediately preceding the spell.

'Cursed be the day that I was born.'

His eyes felt the painful sensation of ooze coming out of his tear ducts.

"You win, Daniel. You win, you smug little knight…You knew where I would end, didn't you?" Goliath looked down to the earth, at the crater where he had tried to kill himself many times.

He looked back to the ocean. "If you really are the knight of hope, can you give me the hope that I will someday die? I tire of this hell, and I am ready for the other." He looked out at the waters intently, hoping to see some glimmer of light that might be a sign from heaven.

Darkness. All he saw was darkness.

Yet in that darkness, he had an idea. He continued looking out into the ocean for hours, considering a new possibility he had not thought of before. A seed of hope had been planted.

Lord Fearnow walked up to the double doors leading to the banquet hall. He looked over his shoulder and asked Officer Feifer, "You're sure they're in here?"

"Yes, your grace, right on the other side of the door. I've had my guards posted the whole time to make sure they don't leave."

Lord Fearnow turned to his wife. "And you're sure it's him?"

"I'm…I'm positive…" Her face was pale; her body was trembling. "Such power…oh, Benjamin, he's too strong! I feel so many spirits swirling around him. It's like he's bound an entire army of magical beings to his service!"

"Easy, Amanda, easy…Feifer, leave us at once. Tell the Administrators to lend their power to Amanda's spell. Then go to the rear entrance and have your men ready to come in as soon as I give the signal."

"Yes, your grace," Feifer answered. He looked at Lady Amanda, growing nervous about how his men would be able to stop a wizard if he was as powerful as she said.

At that moment, one of the white-masked Committee members stepped forward and said in a scraping voice, "Feifer…Concerning Joseph…he will try to protect the knight. Make sure he is taken care of."

Lord Fearnow glared at the masked man, then turned to Officer Feifer. "Don't kill him, understood? I want Joseph alive, even if he does get involved. Just drag him out of the room so he doesn't interrupt the spell."

Feifer nodded and then departed. Lord Fearnow turned to his wife and barked, "Pull yourself together, woman. You have the herbs, the blood, the book. No one can stand against this spell. We know that from previous experience."

"Benjamin…it's no use. He's different. He's stronger than anyone we've gone after before. He'll flick my magic away like he's swatting a fly."

Another Committee member stepped forward and told Lord Fearnow, "Your Grace, you ought to know, that when we tried to ensnare the black knight earlier, his sword was able to cut our spell. The lady may be right."

"My wife's spell is not like your webs of smoke. It will work. It always has. Amanda, I'll excuse myself from dinner when I want you to start casting it. Your Administrators shall assist. Then, when I throw open the door, work your magic. Who knows? Maybe he'll join our cause willingly. But if he doesn't, it doesn't matter. He'll be ours before the evening is done."

Though Lord Fearnow was looking at his wife, his eyes seemed to go right past her. He was too caught up in his dreams of power, fantasizing about having the wizard under his thumb. If he had looked at her, he would have realized how much this all disgusted her. How much she thought it really *did* matter, and that she was hoping against hope the wizard would cooperate *without* her magic arts.

"I've always lived for these moments, Amanda, these knife-edge moments, where my entire life hangs in the balance." He kissed Lady Fearnow on the forehead, still looking past her as he went to the wooden doors. "Tonight we'll either rule the world, or we'll be dead. It doesn't get any better than this!"

Lord Fearnow flung open the doors and gave a dramatic bow to Sir Judas, David, and Sir Joseph.

Volume IV

Temptation in the Desert

Chapter 1: The First Temptation

The walls of Chelles were incredibly tall, fifty feet at least Sir Judas estimated. Moreover, up on top of the walls was a strange black screen, extending up another thirty feet all around the city. The posse reached the gatekeepers, where Officer Feifer gave a wave. One of the guards helping to process the line gave him a slap on the back and said, "Go on through."

At about noon on Wednesday they went under the arch, through the gate, and into a large plaza where many roads of the city all converged. This was it. The eastern plaza of Chelles. This was the place that droves of people traveled from miles away just to see. That vast sea of buildings and tents outside the walls existed because of all the people yearning to see this spectacular marvel. Sir Judas and David looked up, both utterly speechless because of what lay before them.

It was the most beautiful thing David had ever seen.

It was the most frightful thing Sir Judas had ever seen.

Under the shadow cast by the tall curtains atop the walls of Chelles, brazen rails thrust up from the ground, linking with twisted rings of wrought iron to form a metallic skeleton terminating in a precipice seventy feet in the air. Dangling from cords anchored to the iron rings were polished orbs of glass about the size of a man's head. With a haunting beat of 'Boonk…Boonk…Boonk…' a whole row of orbs would ignite with an unseen fire within, only to be quenched a moment later as the next row up ignited to the rhythmic blast of 'Boonk…Boonk…Boonk…' The lights ascended ever higher, a glowing ring rising until it had reached the summit of the metal tower. Somehow the noonday sun and sky seemed dimmed, so that the glowing peak of the tower stood out against a shadowed backdrop. Then with a great blast of light and sound, all of the lights came on at once, flashed thrice, then streaks of light like comets hurtled towards the ground. Crackles and cheers from all sides gave sound and fury to the walking shadows cast by the falling lights. Then they all went out, and all was still, and Sir Judas and David were merely in the shade of an ordinary summer afternoon. But after a reprieve that was far too brief, the orbs at the base of the tower flared with blazing light, and the drum of 'Boonk...Boonk...Boonk...' announced the ring of fire's march to the sky once more.

They stood transfixed and trembling, unable to look away and barely able to continue gazing. After the strobing crescendo of lights had gone out the third or fourth or thousandth time, Officer Feifer announced, "Alright, time to move along. We need to be getting to Joseph's house." Not to his surprise, neither of Sir Joseph's guests responded. Feifer put a hand on each of their shoulders, and with a gentle shake for David and a rough jerk for Sir Judas, he reiterated, "Come along now, dear persons. We've got places to be."

Eyes still riveted to the tower, Sir Judas slowly turned his feet, then his hips, then all at once tore his gaze away. Spinning to Feifer, he asked, "What is this witchery, Officer? Where did you get all this...*magic?*" With horror Sir Judas finished his sentence, only now realizing how bad it was. All along the walls of the city, on top of every roof, strung down every street and flashing from every window were orbs of light. They were smaller than the ones on the tower, but far more numerous, raging like a swarm of fireflies in a midsummer night's nightmare. The uncountable will-o-wisps did not rise or move like the tower's lights, but every one of them pulsed in unison with the 'Boonk...Boonk...Boonk...' of the city's electric heart. "How is this possible?" Sir Judas whispered.

"Behold the triumph of our people," Officer Feifer announced proudly. "This is no witchery, but rather technology. The arcane arts of our forgotten past. With the ancient wonder of wonders, Chelles has become the first realm to fully recover from the Great Calamity, and soon we shall have surpassed any other kingdom to ever exist."

"No...No!" Sir Judas exclaimed. "The glory of our ancestors was Dante! Plato! Aquinas! It was Therese and Theresa! Our ancestor's greatest glory was that they showed us the road to Heaven. If you follow their love of flashing lights...you pave again their highway to hell."

Having never before heard such a response to the lights of Chelles, it took Officer Feifer several seconds before he fully processed what Sir Judas was saying. When it did sink in, his lip curled and his grip tightened around his spear. He looked like he was about to strike Sir Judas, but then a sadistic smile formed. "In case the matter was not yet settled at your trial, I am now certain of your demise. I see at least three Administrators who just witnessed your public blasphemy."

Sir Judas turned around. Amidst the throngs filling the plaza, there were three black-masked Administrators strewn about. They were immediately visible not merely because of the masks, but because they were among the few who were not looking at the electric tower. For all of the deeply ingrained terror Chellesians had of black knights, few people could look away from the tower's magnetic pull. Based on their vapid faces, Sir Judas doubted they even realized he was there. The Administrators in contrast had their eyes fixed on Sir Judas. They stared him down for half a minute before looking away and going about their business. Officer Feifer whispered, "Don't get your hopes up thinking they'll leave you alone. They never miss a thing. They just wait for the right moment to punish it."

Sir Judas narrowed his eyes at Feifer. "Officer…you are under orders to escort me to Sir Joseph's house. You were charged to make sure I reach my destination alive."

Feifer smirked. "Well then we better get going."

Only now did Sir Judas realize David was still staring at the tower. Shaking the boy abruptly, he said, "David! Don't look at that monstrosity. There is something unnatural about it."

David blinked slowly at Sir Judas, a dazed look in his eyes. "Huh? What did you say, Judas?"

Sir Judas's blood ran cold. Since the moment they met, he did not recall a single instance when David had neglected to say 'Sir' Judas. It was not the honorific he cared for, but what its absence at this moment signified. The tower had done something to David. It had touched his mind somehow. With uncomfortable realization, Sir Judas wondered, *Did that blasted thing affect me as well? Has my mind been disturbed? And if it has…how would I even know?*

Feifer snapped him out of his reflections, saying, "You wanted to leave, Judas? Very well. Let's be gone." One of the guards gave Sir Judas a push in Feifer's direction. In the mere moment when Sir Judas had looked away, David returned to gazing on the electric tower. He had to be pulled away by one of the guards, and as he began to walk he asked, "Huh? What's going on? Where are we going?"

Feifer gave no answer. He led his group through the plaza, directly past the tower. They had gone a full block west when they reached an intersection where a black-masked Administrator crossed their path. Without slowing down or even looking at Feifer, he merely whispered, "Generex."

Feifer paused for a moment, then continued walking. They went two more blocks before turning towards the south. Sir Judas asked, "What is Generex?"

"Official business, Judas. Mind your own." Walking along the streets, Sir Judas began to see more and more Administrators at every turn. At first they seemed to be busy with other affairs, but as he marched further into the city he thought he began to see the same Administrators more than once. Moreover, they all seemed to be smirking whenever they looked at him.

Sir Judas knew it was a trap, but he was powerless to escape it. He did not know which way would even lead to safety, and there were hostile magicians at every turn. As the group continued south, the strings of light on every street and building came to an end, while the thrumming pulse that drove them grew ever louder. 'Boonk...Boonk...Boonk...' All of the buildings were now large, square, and gray. At the end of the current road, Sir Judas saw the looming wall of Chelles. Feifer led them almost all the way up to it, but they turned right down the last street before the wall. On the right side of the street were two large buildings with a tiny alley between them. On the left was a massive building that took up the entire block. From that direction seemed to come the dreadful thrum of 'Boonk...Boonk...Boonk...' They were halfway down the street when Sir Judas saw the sign above the large building's single door. 'Generex.'

Officer Feifer announced, "Full stop." Two of the guards placed their hands on Sir Judas's shoulders.

"So this is Generex, Feifer? A deserted part of town where you can kill us?"

"Oh, no, you won't die today Judas." The door to Generex opened and three Committee members emerged. Feifer continued, "As I warned you at the trial. There are fates worse than death."

Sir Judas nodded. "The Void."

"Yes." Feifer shuddered as he looked at the approaching menaces. "I thank my lucky stars I haven't had a run-in with the Committee in three years. Until today that is..."

The Committee members wore identical garb to Simon, the Chairman from the glade. Long robes with long sleeves, and white masks covering their entire faces. They wore black hoods over their heads, so that no speck of skin, hair, nor humanity could be seen anywhere on them. The trim on each of their robes was a different color, but besides that they were indistinguishable. Their long sleeves were rolled up in bundles they carried in front of their chests, so that it was not even clear what sex the three might be.

Feifer stepped aside, allowing the Committee members to approach the prisoners. To his astonishment and horror, they surrounded him instead, thrusting their masked faces forward, mere inches from his own. "*You have failed us, Feifer.*" The voice that came forth was neither male nor female, but otherworldly. It was hoarse, cracked, and scraping, like the sound of a whetstone on an assassin's dagger.

"*By your foolish inability to control your tongue, you have allowed this lawless murderer to escape the hands of justice.*" This second voice was like the first. It was distinct enough to tell the difference, though it seemed to come from the same location. Sir Judas could not tell which one of three had spoken either time. It was as if both voices came from the middle of them all.

A third voice inquired, "*What is the verdict?*"

With ashen face, Feifer backed up hastily. "No! No! No please! Not the Void! I swear I'll be good! I swear!" He turned and ran for the alley, and the three Committee members did nothing to stop him. Instead, they looked towards the rest of his guardsmen. "*Concerning Louis, what is the verdict?*"

"*Concerning all of Feifer's accomplices, what is the verdict?*"

The two guards holding Sir Judas released him, and all of the guards made a mad dash after their leader. With hysterical screams they ran down the alley, crushing into each other as they crammed to get away. Their shouts continued a moment longer, and then there was a sudden silence.

A fourth Committee member emerged from the alley down which the guards had all just run. Stalking towards Sir Judas and David, a new voice growled, "*Guilty, Guilty, Guilty. We find all defendants Guilty.*"

The four Committee members walked forward together. As they did a voice asked, "*What is the sentence?*" and all four voices together acclaimed, "*The Void.*" Howls and screams came from the alley, as Feifer and his men loosed wails the likes of which Sir Judas had never heard before.

Terror took hold of Sir Judas. His mind was too paralyzed to even think. The four white faces surrounded him. The first voice he had heard said, "*You have failed to comply with Lord Fearnow's most just decrees.*" Sir Judas thought the voice came from the figure behind him, but then when he turned to look that way, it seemed as if the voice was from the other direction. No matter which way he looked, it was the Committee member to whom he had just shown his back. The voice came from each and none.

Sir Judas answered on trembling legs, "I have done all I could to follow the laws of this land, but Lord Fearnow has outlawed black knights. I cannot possibly comply with such a law unless I cease to be."

"Oh, but cease to be you shall, for our laws must be upheld."

"Lawless, lawless, wicked man."

"Could you not pledge fealty to a lord?"

"Pledge it to Fearnow."

"Proclaim yourself his servant now, and the Committee shall consider your repentance."

Sir Judas was dying to do so. More than anything else, he just wanted the masked terrors to be appeased. Yet he could not bring himself to betray his cause, and so he forced himself to say, "I have not yet finished the last quest given me by my king. Until the will of my previous lord is fulfilled, how can I be faithful to another? A man cannot serve two masters."

"Will his will be fulfilled if you die?"

"Do the dead grieve the sins of the living?"

"Serve Fearnow and live."

"No rotten corpse will know your choice, but the ones who can send you to the Void certainly will."

"Take off the armor."

"Choose life."

"Take off the armor and live!"

Sir Judas's fear was unnatural, far greater than he had ever known outside this city. His knees were knocking, heart hammering, and his very bowels seemed to tremble at every blast of 'Boonk! Boonk! Boonk!' bellowing from the building beside him. Grasping for anything, he pitifully answered, "But Feifer acquitted me!"

"That was no acquittal."

"Mistrial."

"A mistake he shall pay for for years to come."

From the alley down which they had fled, Sir Judas heard Feifer and his guards all scream, "Agggghhh!...Agggghhh!...Agggghhh!..." in perfect unison with the beating sound of 'Boonk...'

All four Committee members dropped their sleeves from in front of their chests, then pulled their right sleeve up until a red clawed hand emerged from underneath. Sir Judas about died of fright as a scraping voice said from within his own skull, *"FEIFER CANNOT SAVE YOU."*

In terror he looked around at each of them. Black eyes, white masks, and red claws were in every direction. He was disoriented, spinning, masks and robes blurring by in a cavalcade of confusion. All he could see in the wheeling madness was the four red claws inching towards him, reaching out towards his face. Sir Judas heard a voice whisper, *"Joseph…"* His vision dimmed to nearly black, the scarlet hands were all that still remained. Sir Judas muttered, "I am under Joseph's protection…"

Four voices screamed. *Human* voices. Two men, two women, once voice coming from each of the four robed figures directly. Like a man who had been startled awake, Sir Judas could finally see clearly. Their 'red hands' were just red gloves with decorative nails at the tips. Behind the eyeholes of their masks was not blackness, but rather perfectly visible eyes. Sir Judas looked down and saw David. The boy was sitting on the ground looking up—past Sir Judas—with an expression of terror on his face. Sir Judas drew both his blades. "Magic! You cast a spell on us to make us fear you!"

The robed men and women ignored him. One man yelled, "To hell with Joseph! Kill the knight, and kill the dwarf right after him!"

A woman answered, "And then what? Fearnow will kill us for having touched his precious pet."

The other man seethed, "Stupid fools. Forget Fearnow. You know Joseph is beyond our power. That's why he keeps the dwarf so close at hand."

The last Committee member answered, "Fearnow will protect his little knight, but that will not extend to his guests. Throw this black knight into the Void, and let Joseph pout all he wants."

The other three seemed to assent, for all four began to make wild gesticulations. As their sleeves whipped about violently, Sir Judas's mind flashed back to Simon in the glade. Their motions were like those he used before his fireball, but whereas Simon had pulled threads of fire together, these figures were spreading threads of smoke around him. They interwove and tangled with each other to create a net that had Sir Judas totally surrounded. Sir Judas slashed at the net with his sword, which passed through the smoke as if it was nothing. One of the women laughed. "Fool! No blade can cut our snare! It is a bond from which none escape!"

At the very place where Sir Judas had cut it, the net unraveled, unwinding itself until the whole mess became harmless puffs of smoke rising up into the sky. The four magicians all froze in place, dumbfounded by what they had just seen. Sir Judas slowly rotated, pointing his sword and dagger at each of them in turn. "It is now *your* turn to tremble, only this time the cause is not a lying hex. Flee this city you spawn of satan, or else your blood shall fill its streets."

One of the masked men regained his wits and snarled, "Don't get cocky. You can never hope to oppose us, for we are legion. Our servants are more numerous than the sands of the sea." At least three dozen Administrators in black masks now revealed themselves, standing up on the roofs of the buildings and coming running from around the street corners. Then Sir Judas heard the sound of trotting greaves and Feifer led his posse out of the alley. His eyes were red and puffy, like a man who had been weeping for long hours. He pointed his spear at Sir Judas and said, "I will be good...I will be good...I will be good..." to the same rhythm as the electric heartbeat coming from the Generex building.

Sir Judas sheathed his sword and knelt down beside David, putting his right arm around the boy as he kissed the central ruby of his dagger. "Ten or ten thousand, what's that to Him? 'I will not fear thousands of the people surrounding me.'" The Committee members began to chant. The Administrators waved their arms. Feifer charged. Sir Judas cried, "'Arise O Lord! Save me!'"

An explosive voice boomed, "STOP!" All of Sir Judas's assailants stood perfectly still. Then every eye slowly turned towards the woman running towards them. She was a Committee member with a polished white mask, but instead of the menacing demeanor with which the other four had always moved, she sprinted as fast as she could in her robe. When she reached the other four members she bent over to catch her breath. "What is the meaning of this?" One of her peers demanded. "We were about to take care of a black knight who is threatening the city."

The panting woman stood up and answered, "You don't know how wrong you are." She gestured for the other four members to come over to her. Keeping their eyes on Sir Judas until they were two dozen yards away, they formed a tight huddle and she whispered in their ears. "Simon?" One of them exclaimed. She nodded and continued whispering. "No. Truly?"

"Lady Fearnow has no doubts."

The four original Committee members nodded in unison, then all five spread out to surround Sir Judas and David. The black knight stood up and helped David to his feet. The youth was still looking over Sir Judas's head with an expression of fear and…something else. Sir Judas didn't have time to inquire, but David almost seemed excited. Feifer nervously backed away, wanting to be behind the Committee rather than before them. When all five members were in position, they whipped their sleeves around, but not as a spell. They formed the ball of cloth they held in front of their chests, resuming their original intimidating posture. The magical voices that always seemed to be behind Sir Judas said, *"What is the verdict?"*

"Guilty."

"What is the sentence?"

"The boy and black knight shall be under arrest at the house of Sir Joseph until the fifth hour of this evening. Then let Feifer summon them, that they may dine with Lord Fearnow."

"Long may he reign."

"May he reign forever."

Then the five Committee members spun around and released their bundles, whipping their long sleeves as they chanted, *"Fait insivibilis!"* A cloud of smoke formed around each one of them, then dissipated, and they were gone. With a great scurrying of motion, the Administrators fled from view. Sir Judas and David were left alone with Feifer and his guards.

After a tense silence, Sir Judas said, "Officer…shall we resume our journey to Sir Joseph's house?"

Sniffling and wiping his eyes, Feifer nodded. "Of course." He began walking down the street, giving no instructions to his guards, nor seeming to care whether anyone was following.

David ran after him, hurrying to catch up. The youth asked, "Are you alright, Officer?"

"Of course I am. Why wouldn't I be?"

"Well…all the screaming. What did the Committee do to you?"

"The Committee? They weren't down the alley. I thank my lucky stars I haven't had a run-in with the Committee in three years. If I can help it, I intend to keep it that way." David and Sir Judas both stopped cold, unable to believe their ears. Even more shocking than what he said was the manner in which he said it. Officer Feifer seemed perfectly sincere.

Chapter 2: Veritas and Caritas

The so-called 'royal palace' of Lord Benjamin Fearnow was once a military fort back when Chelles was young. It was not situated on the highest hill in the city (where palaces often go), for it was not built with the intention of being marveled at. Nor was it built in a central location so that it could be easily accessed by those doing business in the heart of Chelles. It was on the westernmost extremity, built into the city wall, so that the master bedroom of the palace could look out and see the sunset through a window (recall that Chelles had tall black screens on top of all her walls, stretching high into the sky, so that it would not be possible to see the sunset by any other means).

Further isolating this lord's manor (for that is what 'the palace' really was) from the rest of the city was the fact that for one hundred yards around the perimeter absolutely no electro-magic was permitted. Since nearly everyone in Chelles desired to live in the brighter section of the city, this resulted in the vicinity around the 'royal palace' being a ghost town devoid of life. At the very edge of the perimeter, just on the side of the line where electro-magic was allowed, was situated a very skinny, very long, two story house to which Officer Feifer now led Sir Judas and David. It had a small stable next to it, where Sir Judas correctly deduced that Sir Joseph must keep his horse.

At the door Feifer pressed a little button. A faint sound of musical notes came from inside the house. A few moments later a stout woman with salt and pepper hair answered the door. At first she looked to be in her forties (Sir Judas thought she might be Sir Joseph's wife), but when she saw Feifer her face scrunched up into an angry prune that suddenly made her look very old. "What do you want, Feifer? Why are you here? What mischief are you planning this time? You causing trouble for my son again?"

"Dear Emma, I regret to inform you that your son caused this trouble for himself. He invited these criminals (Lieutenant Louis coughed)–I'm sorry, these victims of accusation–to come and stay at his personal residence until they have dinner with his grace tonight. Moreover, the Committee has issued a most just decree in confirmation of Joseph's actions, requiring that they remain here under house arrest until the appointed time." Feifer then turned to Sir Judas and said, "I am leaving two guards here to keep an eye on you at all times."

Feifer was about to walk away, but Sir Judas asked, "Officer…you referenced the Committee's 'most just decree' that David and I be placed under house arrest. Do you remember when they issued that decree?"

Feifer furrowed his brow and turned to Louis. "Lieutenant, do you recall the date on the decree in question?"

"I definitely remember reading it this morning, but I don't recall the date of issue."

Sir Judas looked back and forth between the two with confusion and concern. "But guardsmen…David and I were not even in Chelles until this afternoon. How then could you read a decree from the Committee concerning us this morning?"

The two looked at each other in confusion. Then their faces twisted as if they were in pain. Then they returned to normal and Feifer said, "The Committee had word that you were coming, Judas. The decree was issued ahead of time so that we would know how to act." After that, Feifer appointed two guards to stand outside the door, then he left, taking the remainder of his posse and setting out for the 'royal palace.'

Emma gave Sir Judas and David a wary look. "A black knight and an urchin who are mixed up with the Committee…I think I might want to take a walk until my son comes home…" She turned around and walked into the house, grabbing her coat and then coming to the door. "Make yourselves at home. Don't break anything. If you steal something, my Joseph will get it back. Do you know what time he is supposed to be here?"

David answered, "He said he had something to take care of at the northern gate, but that he would meet us as soon as he was done."

Emma nodded nervously, then walked out the door. "I think I'll run down to the market. Joseph should be back before I am…"

"But ma'am!" Sir Judas called. "We are two perfect strangers! Are you really going to leave us in your house alone? Would you prefer the guards came in with us? Or that we wait outside?"

Emma looked at him fearfully, then shook her head and said, "In this town, perfect strangers are the only ones who *don't* concern me…" Then she left without saying more.

David closed the door and whispered to Sir Judas, "I think I'm beginning to understand why Winthrop never let me come here."

Sir Judas nodded. "Behind all the flashing lights, something is hiding in the shadows…" The two were standing in a little entryway with hooks on the wall for hanging coats and hats. Sir Judas didn't trust the full weight of his pack to those hooks, but he did take it off and leave it on the ground beneath them. David did likewise. Sir Judas shrugged and said, "Well, nothing for it. It seems our tour of the house will have to be self-guided. Do you want to explore the upstairs or the ground floor?"

The word 'explore' is of course one of the most musical words in the entire world for a twelve-year-old boy. Even the terrifying afternoon he had just endured could not deter David from roaming around a stranger's house and seeing what interesting things he could find. "I'll take the upstairs!" and then he was off. David ran to the stairwell at the end of the hall and ascended, leaving Sir Judas all alone in the entryway. The knight fell to his knees right where he was and wept as he prayed in thanksgiving. He thanked God for delivering them from the mob that morning, from Feifer's murderous trial, from an entire gang of magicians, and that they now had a roof over their heads. The knight arose feeling somewhat renewed. *Lord, give me the strength to keep on walking.* Then he slowly moved from room to room, exhausted from the day's ordeal.

David threw himself into his task with enthusiasm. He found a small, unused bedroom as well as a bathroom with a very strange chamber pot. He found another bedroom with racks of swords and shields on the wall, including one empty rack where a sword was missing (Sir Joseph's room!). Then right next to Sir Joseph's room was the most fascinating room of all. Inside was a wooden desk with a single chair, as well as several shelves on the wall. Covering every flat surface were strange devices like nothing David had seen before. There were lots of blue rectangles with little shiny dots of gray on them. Thin tendrils of red, black, and white strings connected different parts to one another. Little racks of tools on the desktop had all sorts of strange scissor-like things and rolls of some sort of sticky stuff in black, and red, and other colors.

David had no idea where to begin. He vaguely recalled Emma saying, 'Don't break anything,' but what would be the harm in a little experimentation? He picked up one of the blue rectangles that had red and black strings connecting it to many others. The strings gave just a little bit of resistance and then broke off. The boy's eyes went wide in terror. He tried to find where the strings had come from, but there was no evidence of any sort of stitching. Moreover, he now realized the strings were not made of yarn, but rather some sort of smooth and slippery material. David ended up putting the rectangle back and draping the strings on top of it in a pattern that looked similar to the other ones. *Hopefully that's good enough for Joseph.* David then looked to the side of the table in front of him. There was a metal lever protruding from the wall, with a groove that would allow it to slide upwards. *Well obviously* that *won't break anything.* David pushed the lever up and discovered how wrong he was. Lights in the room began to blink on and off, while the sound of a piano began to play. Then the very strings David had broken began to shoot white sparks, and then all of the blue rectangles began to smoke. David grabbed the lever and yanked it down. The lights and music ceased, but smoke continued to issue from the blue rectangles.

'Don't break anything.'

David hurried out of the room and shut the door. There was already a small cloud in the hallway, which he swung his arms around to try and dispel. Whatever he had burnt, it had a particularly pungent odor. To his dismay, Sir Judas came up the stairs while David was still opening windows. "Did you find anything interesting?" the black knight asked. Then taking three short sniffs he asked, "What is that dreadful smell?"

David's mind quickly reached for any sort of explanation he could find. *This room was all full of smoke! As soon as I opened the door it came billowing out!* Looking into Sir Judas's eyes, however, David's conscience pricked his heart. He recalled the legends of how honest paladins would be, and had no doubts Sir Judas's integrity surpassed the stories. Not wanting to disappoint him, David confessed, "Sir Joseph has a bunch of stuff in that room that I started playing with, and I think I broke something."

"Is it on fire?" Sir Judas asked, rushing to open the door.

"No, the smoke came out of those blue rectangles. I think it was caused by electro-magic instead of fire."

Sir Judas took a quick look at the blue rectangles and then picked one up to examine it. In the process he broke the red and black strings off of it in a very similar fashion to what David had done. "Oh bother…" After trying and failing to reattach the strings, Sir Judas laughed and said "Well, whatever it is you broke, I suppose now we can tell him we both did it." He put the blue rectangle back where he took it from and left the room, closing the door behind him. "So much for Emma telling us not to break anything. I suppose this is what happens when you let strangers roam your house unattended."

"Do you think Sir Joseph will be mad?" David asked.

"I have no idea. If he's a wise man, and he appreciates our honesty, confessing that we broke his things may actually make a favorable impression. If he is upset, especially if what we broke was valuable, then there's a reason truth is such a dangerous weapon." Sir Judas shrugged. "Nevertheless, this is a case where we have to tell it."

David rolled his eyes. "Truth's not a weapon."

"Oh, but it is, David! It's one of the cruelest weapons you'll ever find. They say that 'Truth' is the sword St. Michael wields in his battle against satan. A sword like that is safe in the hands of an angel, but in the hands of men it is more dangerous than a double-edged blade. Truth cuts friend and foe alike, even our own selves, and therefore must be kept in its sheath until you find the proper moment to draw it."

Sir Judas now drew his own sword, and getting down on one knee he laid it flat in his hands and held it before David. "This is *Veritas*, one of the holy weapons anointed by the king. In the Old Tongue, its name means 'Truth,' and whoever wields it must excel in that virtue above all other men…would you like to hold it?"

David felt a whole kaleidoscope of butterflies break loose in his stomach. "Y-yes."

"Go ahead, just be very, very careful. The blade has a certain power to it. Both sides of the sword are sharper than a razor, even though in forty years I've never once taken a whetstone to it."

Trembling with excitement, David took the hilt with both his hands. It was soft, yet firm, made of some material that seemed to grip his palms. The crossguard was glimmering silver, curling up on either side around a gemstone. One gem was dark and cloudy like amethyst, the other perfectly clear like glass. The steel blade was heavier than David had been expecting, and the tip dipped a bit before he corrected for the weight and lifted it back up. "This is incredible! Thank you, Sir Judas!" but Sir Judas was disappointed. "What is it?" David asked.

"Oh, I…I thought perhaps…" The knight took a moment to think of how to explain things, and then stated, "David…this is not my sword."

"Whose is it?"

"I do not know."

"How can you not know? Who gave it to you?"

"The king gave it to me. Before he died, he entrusted this sword to me and told me it was the holy weapon of a Paladin who would come after me. That was also when he gave me the scroll that I read every night. I was hoping that when you took the sword I might see some sort of sign or indication that it was yours. I'm...I'm not doubting the king's prophecy...but I'm beginning to feel doubts, if that makes sense..."

David raised the blade upright and took in its majestic shape. Even though he did not know the details of how a sword is crafted, it was still obvious to him that this one was wonderfully made. "What do you have doubts about, Sir Judas?"

"Time, David. Whether there's enough time for the two prophecies to come true. Time is grinding to an end. The king told me I would initiate the next Lessguard before I fought Goliath, and the prophecy clearly says I will initiate him 'On a night...' When we fought Jezebel in the glade I told her Castle Nightfall would see the sun set tomorrow night, and that then I would come to it. I don't believe I was speaking on my own...I believe it was the words of God...but if so, then that means tonight is my last chance to give this blade to its rightful owner. For forty years I've been carrying this sword, finding all sorts of young men who might have been worthy to wield it, and for forty years I've been disappointed over and over and over. And now I'm in Chelles, where every man I've seen is either obsessed with a tower of lights or else trying to throw us into 'the Void,' and I have no idea how this prophecy can come through. And what if it doesn't? What if I've spent my entire life on a doomed quest because I mistook one man's poetry for God's message? Was the king also wrong about Sir Samson being alive? Has he been dead all this time, and I've been hunting phantoms?" Placing his head in his hands, Sir Judas smiled and said, "If the prophecy is true, then God has certainly kept me in suspense...a lifetime of disappointment, and tonight is the final verdict. One more disappointment, and the comic tragedy of my entire life is magnified. One moment of vindication, and the glory of my entire life is revealed. Like I said, I'm not in doubt, but I am nervous. If the sword had glowed when you took it, then that would have set my nerves at ease." Sir Judas sighed deeply and then stated, "Deus vult."

David lowered the sword sadly, wishing it had glowed just so Sir Judas might be comforted. Handing it back, he asked, "What do those words mean? The ones you just said?"

"'God wills it.' 'Deus vult' is the battle cry of every true knight, but not just in the battles fought with swords. The more important battles are the ones we fight every day. Sometimes we conquer and see success, far more often we fail and are disappointed. But whatever happens, and whatever will happen, we always remind ourselves, 'God wills it.' Not even a sparrow falls to the ground without God knowing it and permitting it. Everything that comes into our lives, for good or ill, was foreseen by God and either directly willed, or at least permitted, because He loves us and knows what's best for us. So whatever might happen with the prophecy tonight, even if my entire life was squandered on a fiction and I am the greatest fool in the realm, still I will say, 'Deus vult.'"

With a sour frown, David asked, "What's the point of accepting His will if it's not what we want? Everyone I know who does pray says it's the secret to getting things. 'Prayer will make you rich.' 'Prayer will keep you safe.' But if God's not going to help us–if he would let you waste your life as you said–then what's the point of saying, 'Deus vult'?"

"Ah, the simplicity of a child is always refreshing to old ears. Let me ask you, if the sword *had* glowed, and you were the next great Paladin, would you be happy with all of the events over the last two days that led you here?"

David started to speak, stopped, thought some more, and then answered, "...I don't know. To have a magic sword and be a great hero would be amazing, but...well, there's Rowan and Garrett...and Winthrop...I...don't know. I think...I think I would still want that. I mean...to be a hero...I just don't know."

Sir Judas smiled at him. "And that's the point. We don't even know what we want. We think we do when we ignore the tradeoffs. Trim the complexities out of life and pretend our desires are simple and straightforward. But once we stop and look at the big picture, we realize that life is a grand mosaic floating on a pond, where every tile we flip sends ripples out to rearrange the entire puzzle. 'I want to be a paladin!' yet that dream requires so much of our own life be upended first, and then our life as a paladin will dramatically change the lives of so many others. When we really stop and try to take it all in, we must humbly confess, 'We don't even know how to pray as we ought.' So we do ask God for good things and for our dreams to come true, but we always end our prayers with, 'Fiat voluntas Tua.' 'Thy will be done.' Or, as I often pray, 'Deus vult.'"

David pouted. He didn't get it. Not totally. But he was starting to grasp something. A seed had been sown, and the first bit of faith was starting to push through the soil. *I'm sad right now because Winthrop left...I don't want to be sad...but maybe flipping this tile to 'happy' would cause a bunch of ripples that made things worse. Even better...maybe when this tile was flipped to 'sad' it made a bunch of ripples that are going to make things better...*

Another thought occurred to David. "Sir Judas, can you show me the other weapon you used in the glade? The dagger?"

"Ah, yes. *Caritas*. My secret weapon." He sheathed *Veritas*, pulled the dagger out, and held it before David in the same manner as the sword had been offered.

David asked, "Why is it so much stronger? *Veritas* did some good work against the monsters in the glade, but this little dagger beat them instantly."

Sir Judas shrugged. "I can't really say for sure. Sometimes one works better, sometimes the other. They're both great weapons, but with one obvious difference." Sir Judas now gripped *Caritas* as if he was actually wielding it. David jumped back in surprise as the blade began to glow bright white. Unlike when Sir Judas had made *Veritas* glow to scare off the merchant caravan, *Caritas* blazed so intensely that it seemed as if it was on fire. David even felt a heat from the blade, but only in his heart, not on his skin. "...*Caritas* is *my* holy weapon. The king used it to dub me a knight, and it has always felt more natural in my hand. A good knight should be skilled in the use of any weapon, but we all have one with which we truly excel."

He casually flipped the dagger, gracefully and effortlessly caught it by the tip, and offered it again to David, asking, "Would you like to hold *Caritas* as well?"

David smiled. "Of course."

The hilt of *Caritas* was made of solid gold, with golden gilding running up the fuller of the blade so that the whole dagger seemed to be one golden cross. There were bright rubies set on the pommel, each side of the crossguard, the center, and in the fuller, five rubies total. David almost dropped the dagger because he was surprised by its weight. He expected it to be about a pound, but it was actually triple that because of how much gold was used in the design. It was a very awkward weapon, unbalanced, and the decorative gold and ruby on the blade were ridiculously non-functional. The dagger sat heavy in David's hand while the tip seemed too light and unstable, making it hard to aim. Yet he liked it. It was a strange quirk of David's, but he liked the feeling of having something dense and weighty in his own hand, while his enemies would only see its fleeting tip. Then, when he was already so fond of *Caritas*, something happened that would make him love it until his dying day.

The dagger began to glow.

Even though he was shocked, David did not drop it. Instead he gripped it tighter. Unlike when Sir Judas held the weapon and the dagger's light was only white, in David's hand the golden cross and the rubies blazed forth, pouring out a vivid light that seemed to make every other color in the room come alive, the same way things had looked when Sir Judas used *Caritas* in the glade. Also similar to that night in the glade, David's hand could not be seen, for it was swallowed up in the dagger's light, so that only the cross was visible. The light of *Caritas* not only burnt David's heart, but his entire body was burning as well. Nevertheless, he held on, not letting go until the light gradually waned and went away.

Neither of them said a word for some time. Then, after he had taken a minute or so to process what had happened, David turned to Sir Judas with a huge smile and asked, "Was that what you were expecting?"

The black knight was confused. "That…was not what I was expecting at all. *Caritas* already has a master…I've never heard of such a thing before…" Sir Judas shook his head and smiled. "Even at my age, there's always something new to discover."

"Good! Then I don't have to worry about getting old!" David and Sir Judas turned to see Sir Joseph standing at the top of the stairs at the end of the hall. He was no longer wearing his armor, but instead was wearing a dirty pair of loose fitting pants and a black, sweaty vest. Even in armor it was clear Sir Joseph was short and thick, but seeing his arms with no sleeves seemed to really accentuate just how compact and bullish his stature was. His sword was in a scabbard on his left hip, while he also wore a second scabbard around his chest that held the strange metal tube he had used earlier in the scuffle outside of Curly's.

With a big smile he walked over, and pulling Sir Judas up on his feet (he had gotten down on his knees to hand the holy weapons to David), Sir Joseph said, "I suspected you were an interesting fellow, but I didn't realize just how interesting you were going to be. Do you mind if I take a look at that dagger?"

"Not at all," Sir Judas answered. Sir Joseph held out a hand to David (who was about the same height as Sir Joseph, but half his weight). The boy looked down at the dagger again, and then reluctantly handed it over. Sir Joseph turned it every which way, examining it in detail, looking for something very intently. Eventually he asked, "How do I turn it on?"

"Turn it on?" Sir Judas asked.

"You know, the glowing. How do I do that?"

"You can't do that. It's a miracle. The dagger glows when it finds its rightful owner. My confusion is that right now *Caritas* seems to have two rightful owners, but the fact that it isn't glowing in your hands only means you're not a third."

Sir Joseph kept turning it over, pressing the rubies, looking for a secret button. "Is it unnatural for the dagger to glow for different people?"

"I wouldn't expect it to glow for anyone but me. David here must be quite special for what we just witnessed to have happened."

"How many people have you given this dagger to before?"

"I haven't really counted. Maybe a dozen over the years?"

"Well that's hardly a significant sample. Maybe it glows for one out of every five people, and you only just now found another person who can activate it. Who knows? Maybe there's a pattern behind it all. Maybe we could figure out what kind of person activates the dagger and learn something about its properties? And maybe it even has other powers that you haven't discovered yet! Powers that would only activate for certain kinds of people that are different than you or David. Or maybe…" Sir Joseph was getting breathless with excitement. The untapped potential of an unknown technology always exhilarated him. He looked at Sir Judas and asked, "Do you mind if I do some tests on this dagger?"

Sir Judas held out his hand. "Yes, I do mind, and I would like to have *Caritas* back now." Sir Joseph returned it. As Sir Judas sheathed the dagger, he asked, "Would I be correct in thinking you believe in the so-called 'scientific study of magic'?"

Sir Joseph smiled. "Not only believe, but practice. I'm an electro-mage. The best one in this entire city. Though since I'm a knight, I suppose I should have led with better manners and only later indulged my curiosity. Welcome to my humble home! I'm sorry my mother wasn't here to greet you when you arrived. I would have thought she would be home."

"She was," Sir Judas answered. "But when she learned the Committee has been making 'decrees' about us, she decided she wanted to leave immediately."

Sir Joseph's eyes went wide. "So the Committee did come for you after all! Even though you were under my protection?"

"Well that was the odd thing," Sir Judas replied. "They were casting spells and terrorizing us until I mentioned your name. Then all at once, their magic faltered."

"Well, the magic didn't fail because of Sir Joseph's name," David added. "That was because of the thing that was with you."

Sir Judas and Sir Joseph looked at the boy in confusion. "What *thing*?" Sir Judas asked.

"You know, the *thing*. The one standing right next to you? It was like seven feet tall and had wings, and that huge sword."

Thinking back to how David had seemed dazed by the electric tower, Sir Judas asked, "David...are you sure you are feeling alright? Perhaps what you saw was an illusion? Or a spell of the Committee."

"It wasn't one of their spells!" David exclaimed in frustration. "It was the thing that cut all of their spells, just like what you did with the net of smoke. Only his sword was flashing every which way. You *must* have seen him Sir Judas! You two were even talking to each other at one point!"

Thinking the youth had lost his mind, Sir Judas said, "David, I assure you. I didn't talk to any sort of creature like you are describing."

"Yes you did!" David answered. "You looked like you were feeling sick and about to collapse, and then the thing whispered 'Joseph' in your ear, and then you said, 'I am under Joseph's protection.' And as soon as you said that, all of the bats that were casting spells on you flew away, and the creature saluted, and then it began burning the magic clouds with its sword."

Sir Joseph and Sir Judas both understood at once, but only one of them was right. Sir Joseph said, "Ah! It sounds like you must be quite the white mage, Sir Judas. Is this winged creature the spirit that lends you power?"

"Oh, God forbid!" Sir Judas cried. "There is no such thing as 'white magic,' just demon magic and miracles. And what David has just described is a miracle that was worked by an angel who came to defend me. Why, from what David says he saw, I would even wager I was not saved by *your* name per se, but rather by the name of St. Joseph, which God providentially arranged for you to receive at birth. He is the terror of demons, and it sounds like the devils that were attacking me fled in fear when I invoked him."

"Oh, you won't persuade me that *all* magic is the work of devils," Sir Joseph answered. "I have a whole workshop behind this door where I design new electro-magic spells. I assure you, it has nothing to do with little pixies, but rather the tubes through which magic flows."

Sir Judas frowned. "I once read a history book that said electro-magic isn't *really* magic, but rather a certain type of invention–a 'technology' as the book called it–and maybe it is. Maybe there aren't any demons making that tube on your chest shoot sparks, but I will say this. After seeing electro-magic in use for one hour, I would throw it in with every other kind of occult spell or ritual just the same. The flashing lights in the plaza we walked through were doing something sinister, and what's more..." Sir Judas shuddered just recalling the memory. "...when the Committee was trying to frighten us, they made Feifer and his guards all begin to scream. And as they did, the scream was...it was in waves, waves of screams that corresponded to the dreadful beating of that 'electric heart' that rumbles throughout this city."

Sir Joseph nodded slowly, opened his mouth, but couldn't seem to find the words to say. Eventually he sighed heavily and said, "I know what you are speaking of, and...there is something I should like to...I would like to know your opinion concerning certain...questions of electro-magic."

Sir Judas frowned. "You want my opinion? The first I've seen of electro-magic was this very afternoon. Surely someone with more experience could answer whatever *questions* you have."

Sir Joseph shook his head. "There are some questions that can only be answered by those who do not yet know the answer. Or perhaps, I should say those who have not yet been *told* the answer. And as for why I care about your opinion in particular...you remind me very much of a man I never got to know."

Sir Judas furrowed his brow, then his frown thawed into a faint smile. "I remind you of someone you never got to know? Oh, come now. You can't say something that mysterious and then not explain your meaning."

Sir Joseph laughed. "Well the explanation will be somewhat lengthy, so if you don't mind, how about we move to another room of the house where I can show you a few delightful electro-magic inventions."

Sir Judas grimaced, clearly uncomfortable with the proposition, but he asked, "Do you promise me, on your honor as a knight, that you will not show me anything truly magical, but just electro-'technologies' as I would rather call them? Not any of your so-called 'white magic' now—only show me plain, mundane inventions, or else I will smash them to pieces. Do you promise this?"

"If I understand your meaning, and magic without pixies is a 'mundane invention' no matter how marvelous it may be, then on my honor, I so promise."

Sir Judas nodded, and Sir Joseph began to lead them away, but David said, "Um, excuse me. Sir Joseph. On the subject of uh…your inventions…"

"Oh, yes!" Sir Judas exclaimed. "I'm so sorry! I got wrapped up in our conversation and totally forgot. David and I were exploring the room there and seem to have broken a blue piece of something that had a few…I don't even know what you would call them, but these red and black cords that fell off of it…"

"Wires," Sir Joseph answered. "You probably broke my solder joints. Don't worry about it. That's an easy fix."

"Well, in addition…" David continued sheepishly, "I also flipped the lever on the wall, and there was this smoke that started coming out."

Sir Joseph bit his lip, and even though he looked quite pained, he said, "That…is also…alright…or at least, forgivable…I invited you to my home, and didn't lock my study…ah, that's exceptionally frustrating, but how were you supposed to know? I have no one to blame but my own stupid self."

"Is there anything we could do to make it up to you?" Sir Judas asked.

Sir Joseph shook his head. "The curse of being the foremost expert in electro-magic is that no one else can fix your spells if they break. I don't see any solution besides me getting back to the grindstone and doing that work over again."

David and Sir Judas both hung their heads sorrowfully. The boy said, "In that case, I'm really sorry," and Sir Judas agreed.

Sir Joseph shrugged. "You aren't the first two to break something, and I know you won't be the last. Electro-magic is a bit delicate. I can at least add one extra layer of protection by remembering to lock my door." Sir Joseph stuck his head in the office to make sure the power was off and nothing was burning. Then he shut and locked the door and led the way to a room further down the hall. He slammed the door open a little too quickly in his frustration, but otherwise he mastered his emotions and did not reveal until much later that David had destroyed an entire month's worth of work.

Chapter 3: The First Temptation Revealed

The room that Sir Joseph opened the door to did not have a window to let in any light. After David and Sir Judas had followed him in, he closed the door, leaving them in total darkness. "Don't you want to light a candle before you close the door?" Sir Judas asked.

"I don't intend to light a candle at all," Sir Joseph answered. "I'm going to use a dab of electro-magic instead…" He pulled a lever on the wall, similar to the one David had pulled in his office, causing five lights to spring to life overhead. They had a soft orange glow to them, giving the room a similar appearance as if there was a fireplace illuminating it. There were two cushioned chairs and a couch all facing each other, with a metal chest in the center of them. The chest was perfectly rectangular, knee high, three feet by two, and had no clasps or locks that held the lid shut. Up above the five orange lanterns were suspended from gracefully curving brass rods that all met at a central pole which ran up to the ceiling. Jutting out of the pole above the lanterns was another odd piece of technology; five wooden blades shaped like fat scimitars were sticking out of the pole.

Filled with curiosity, David asked, "What are those wooden things above the lights?"

Sir Joseph answered, "Those are fans, David."

"Fans?" he asked. "Why would you store your fans up there? Also, they look very…awkward to try and fan yourself with."

Sir Joseph walked over to a corner of the room where he kept a step stool and placed it next to the chest. Climbing up, he said, "You're absolutely correct that the shape is wrong for fanning yourself. But the shape is perfect for letting the electro-magic fan you." Sir Joseph then pulled a few black wires out of a discreet compartment in the pole, between the lights and the fan blades. He touched two of them together and the blades began to rotate around the pole. "Whoops. Wrong way. I installed this fan back before I understood why our ancestors used color-coded wires. Give me a moment…" He pulled the wires apart, grabbed the blades to stop their spinning, then rearranged the wires again and said, "That should do it!" The blades began to whir around so quickly that they formed a single blurring disk. A delightful breeze descended from the fan on the occupants that made the summer heat seem to vanish instantly. Sir Joseph then stashed his wires back out of sight, closed the panel, and returned the step stool to its place in the corner. Then he smiled and asked, "Shall we recline like kings who have their own servants to fan them?"

With a smile David leapt onto the couch and asked, "So what about the couch? Does it do anything magical? The floor? The walls? What else is there?"

Sir Joseph laughed as he sat in one of the arm chairs. "I haven't gotten that far with my home renovations yet, but someday I might have more tricks. In this room I only have the lights, the fans, and this chest sitting here between us."

David eyed it greedily. "What does it do? How does it work?"

Sir Joseph took hold of the lid, but before he opened it, he turned to Sir Judas and asked, "How far away have you come from, Sir Judas?"

Sir Judas finally looked away from the lights and fan and sat down in the other arm chair. "I was born in the Royal City, journeyed all over the realm during my squireship, and then over the last forty years I took a rather circuitous route through the West Lands to end up here."

"So you're quite the world traveler then?"

"It is possible that I am the most well-traveled man alive."

Sir Joseph beamed broadly. "Then tell me, Sir Judas, whether in all the world, you have ever found such a delicacy as this!" Sir Joseph opened the lid to the chest and a few small, translucent clouds ascended from it. Inside were two small kegs, one of which was already tapped, along with six crystal glasses.

Sir Judas looked at Sir Joseph quizzically. "Beer? If you think that's a rare delicacy, perhaps you should travel a bit more…"

"Oh very funny, but no. There is something about the beer that may surprise you. Here, try this glass, but be very careful not to drop it if you're startled." Sir Joseph poured beer into one of the glasses and handed it to Sir Judas. The black knight accepted it carefully, and sure enough, he was indeed surprised. The glass was cold to the touch. He took his first sip, and the beer was cold as well. "Well, what do you think?" Sir Joseph asked. "Cold beer, but with no ice to water it down. Everything in this box becomes cold if you leave it in there long enough."

Sir Judas took a longer draught and smiled as he leaned back in his chair. "Cold beer…exceptionally rare, I'll give you that, but I have indeed had it once before. When I was still a squire I accompanied my master down to the Endless Sands of Afrique. There, one of the desert princes welcomed us into his castle and personally poured the beer for us. We were amazed and delighted to have such a treat in the middle of a scorching hot day. He then served frozen cream that we ate while he gave us a tour of his 'ice castle.' It was a great underground cavern with a roof that could be opened to the freezing desert at night, and then sealed tightly before dawn." Sir Judas nodded his head, genuinely impressed. "While a simpler way to cool beverages may exist, I have to give you credit for the size of this little contraption. I would never have expected to find something so cold in such a tiny space."

Sir Joseph was noticeably deflated. "You're the first man I've met who did not consider this a novelty…"

Sir Judas chuckled. "Well for what it's worth, I would rather enjoy a happy memory than a novelty. Those were good times. Simple times. Times when less weighed upon my heart."

After pouring himself and David a glass as well, Sir Joseph closed the lid of his ice chest. Looking into his own drink, he said, "Less on your heart…I'm glad my little spell can give you that memory. For all the joys I find in electro-magic, I don't know that that has ever been one of them. My simple times were back when I was a nobody in this city. Back before I had to go about daily with a dozen knives pointed at my back."

"Someone's trying to kill you?" David asked. "Then why do you stay here?"

"That's a question I often ask myself," Sir Joseph answered. "And it is a question on which I should like to hear Sir Judas's opinion."

Sir Judas nodded. "Is this that riddle you gave us earlier? You want my opinion because I remind you of someone you've never met?"

"It is," Sir Joseph answered. "Though to tell that tale, I must back up and describe the man in question. I was born in Pennyworth, a small city a few days' journey south of here. Not to be confused with Penny*shire*, which is where the famous brandy comes from. Pennyworth was a port somewhere between a merchant city and a fishing village. There were a few noble families always squabbling for control, but not like here. When men lost their heads over import policies, it was always in the *figurative* sense.

"My mother was a member of the Eyre family, her father being second son to the baronet of some neighboring villages. Her father, uncles, and grandfather all had ambitions of climbing higher, and she sat in a very difficult place in the Pennyworth political games. As a woman on the periphery of the family, her only real 'value' was to tie up family alliances with marriage. That fact was rather cruelly thrust into her face on a regular basis. Whenever her father was angry or she made a mistake, he would complain that she was 'just a useless mouth to feed until I can pass you off to someone else.' Then one day her father came home overjoyed that he had managed to arrange a marriage, and...well, I'm not trying to defend my mother. I'm just giving the context to what happened.

"She ran away from home and lived secretly at the house of a wealthy captain. I don't know how she thought it was going to end, but within a few months she was pregnant with me. Half a year later, when the pregnancy was too far advanced to hide, the captain loaded his valuables on his boat and skipped town, never to be seen again. Her father and mother were irate, understandably so in one sense, but they took it much too far. For the sake of *family dignity*, it was made known that no one in her family was to succor her. And whether or not it was the family's intention, all of their clients followed suit. No one in the Eyre family's sphere of influence was willing to help her because she was an embarrassment, and no one outside of their influence would help her because she was an enemy. I was born on a winter night in a toolshed my mother broke into. The next morning when the groundskeeper found us inside, we even lost the shelter of the toolshed.

"The next couple days we slept in the streets, terribly cold, hungry, her milk drying up. My mother was convinced it was going to be the end for us. She prayed to God, asking Him that she would die before she had to watch me starve. She's always said that God answered that prayer, just not in the way she expected.

"The next day there was a parade by the waterfront, where the noble families all rode by with their attendants. My mother asked everyone in the crowd to spare her a crust of bread, but to no avail. As her family rode by in the carriages, she called out for them to help her, but they wouldn't. She says she saw her father weeping, but he just looked away and rode on by. Then came Sir Ishmael.

"He was an old, foreign knight in the service of the Santangel family, traders from the southern mainland. When he heard my mother calling for help, he broke out of the parade and rode his horse into the crowd. 'What is this?' he asked. No one answered. 'What is this?' he asked again, suddenly angry. When no one answered, he yelled, 'Do you not hear this woman begging for bread? Can you not see she carries a half-dead child? Or do you wish to call the wrath of Allah upon your heads, for stopping your ears to Hagar's cry? Depart from me, accursed people! I will see to this myself!' Oh, what I would give to have seen what happened next. My mother tells me a brawl broke out, because those good, pious Christians did not take too kindly to being cursed by a Muslim. But somehow in that tumult, Sir Ishmael must have held his own, because when the dust settled he rode off with my mother and I and brought us to where the Santangels were staying, safe and sound.

The Santangels weren't the least bit pleased with him. They didn't want to get mixed up in the political controversies of a small town where they just sold wares, and lodging a local noblewoman was sure to do that. They told Sir Ishmael we had to leave, but he was having none of it. He threw his foot down and made sure we stayed at the Santangel residence until my mother had healed from her delivery. A little over a month later she finally departed, with Sir Ishmael paying for sea passage up the coast to Chelles." Sir Joseph became dewy eyed at this point in his narrative. "That was the last time she ever saw him. A few months later Sir Ishmael fell sick and died. The only time he and I ever 'met' was that month when I was a newborn. My mother told me he wanted to be the first person to get me to smile, and he would spend any free time he could holding me and making faces. Apparently it was right as we parted that he finally succeeded. On the very day my mother and I set sail for Chelles, I began to giggle at him uncontrollably, laughing at his every face."

Sir Joseph then left off speaking and the three sat in silence for a while. Eventually, Sir Judas said, "Thanks be to God for Sir Ishmael…and may he rest in peace…what I am afraid I still do not understand, however, is why I remind you of him."

"Isn't it obvious?" David asked. "You're just like him."

"In what way?" Sir Judas inquired, genuinely unaware.

Sir Joseph answered, "The elderly knight who sees someone about to die in the midst of an entire city that has lost its mind. Fighting to save them, rebuking the crowd, opposing the ruling powers that be…it's exactly what transpired between you and Officer Feifer this morning. That alone was enough. When I saw you trying to save Feifer from the mob, I thought, 'Sir Ishmael is back from the dead.' But now something else has transpired, which has only furthered my...*fascination*, let's call it. By now I'm sure you've heard about the 'Void' the Committee is always threatening to throw people into."

"We have," Sir Judas answered. "And I have been growing rather curious as to what this great threat is supposed to be."

"You almost found out first hand," Sir Joseph answered. "That was exactly what they were trying to do to you when your 'angel' saved you. It's a spell they cast that takes you...somewhere. 'The Void.' I don't know what it is or how to express it, but...it's the place that isn't. All is darkness. All is silent. Everything is so dead that your own heartbeat is cacophonous, and you begin to think...it would be better if that cacophony stopped making so much noise..." Sir Joseph shuddered. "I have been there only once, and it still gives me chills, even though my experience was far better than most."

"Better how?" David asked, so filled with fear that he wanted to change the subject, but so curious he was unable to.

"I was in the Void for a very long time. Even a minute is one minute longer than you can stand. I had broken one of their damnable decrees by refusing to whip a 'criminal' who had done nothing wrong besides stealing bread for his family. After a few seconds in the Void, I was lost. I was about to scream that I would do whatever they wanted. I was going to shout for all to hear that I would be their most faithful slave. And then Sir Ishmael appeared.

"Darkness is a funny thing. It is utterly impossible for darkness to have a partial victory. If the only thing you can see is darkness, then you say, 'All I see is darkness'. But if there is even one other thing you can see, then you don't see darkness at all. You say, 'The only thing I see is Sir Ishmael.' Darkness is what the Void is made of, yet it ceases to be if even one light can overcome it. The Committee left me in the Void for hours. Far, far longer than anyone else has ever dwelt there—probably because I wasn't screaming like everyone else. I would honestly tell you that I wasn't even in the Void. I was with Sir Ishmael. He didn't say a word to me, yet he didn't need to. He spoke so much more with his eyes. He was proud of me...He was disappointed in me...He encouraged me...a thousand other things were said in those precious hours where we sat in silence together.

"Eventually it came to an end. When it did, I was right where I had been when the Committee cast their spell on me, but a massive crowd had gathered. Fear came over everybody, and before long, people were shouting, 'Joseph isn't afraid of the Void!' The Committee wanted to kill me, but Lord Fearnow made sure that didn't happen. He has an interesting relationship with his Committee. He constantly has new uses for them, but he is also constantly afraid they will one day turn on him. When he learned that the Committee had no hold over me, Lord Fearnow raised me to one of the highest ranking posts in his city. When I told him about my dream to be a knight like Sir Ishmael, he even made an exception to his usual policy of outlawing knighthood. He secretly dubbed me in order to have me as a sword sworn to defend him." Sir Joseph became troubled at this point. "Sword sworn to a lord."

Sir Judas nodded slowly. "Now I understand…this is the matter you truly desired my opinion on…not electro-magic, nor even staying in this city *as such*…" He grabbed his armor by the chest and rattled the black chains. "I am a 'sword without a lord,' as the saying goes, and you are wondering if you ought to be one as well."

A pained expression came to Sir Joseph's face. "The rulers of this city are so evil. The Committee abuses their power at every turn. And while Lord Fearnow stays aloof enough that his hands are never dirty with their filth, I can't avoid the conclusion that he's at least knee deep." Sir Joseph hung his head. "I can't serve this city any longer, Judas. I need to feel like I'm serving good instead of evil."

"But you are." Sir Judas answered. The other knight looked up at him with troubled confusion. "Tell me, Sir Joseph, if you forsook your lord to be a black knight, where would you go? What would you do?"

Sir Joseph shrugged. "I don't know. Look for people in need, I suppose. Isn't that how all the stories go?"

"The stories, yes. The reality, not quite. The reality is that in between the last person I helped and the next are days of journeying through the wilderness, because I can never remain in one town too long. The reality is that everywhere I go the ruling powers are hostile to me, trying to thwart me in my efforts to serve. When the problem is corrupt nobility, then so be it. I must confront them one way or the other. But when the problem is a kidnapping or a robbery, I have often thought, 'I could do so much more good if this town's militia was standing behind me instead of before.' That is what those who chafe at their yoke often fail to appreciate. You say this city is evil. I concur. But in this evil city Sir Joseph is free to move about and break up mobs, and deal with that matter at the northern gate that you took care of before coming here. Sir Joseph is even free to speak to Lord Fearnow and try to sway his course. Sir Judas is under house arrest. Unable to even venture outside and ask the poor, 'How may I assist you.' You said you cannot serve Lord Fearnow because you need to serve good instead of evil. But Joseph, you can serve Lord Fearnow *and* serve the good, and in so doing try to turn him away from evil." After taking another moment to ponder, Sir Judas added, "I would never recommend black armor to anyone. If God has truly placed you in a position where you must live without a lord, then you already know what you ought to do without needing my advice."

Besides the whirring of the overhead fan, the room was quiet for several minutes. Then David asked Sir Judas, "Where are you going?"

Sir Judas looked at the boy in confusion. "What do you mean, David?"

"That was what you asked Sir Joseph when he said he was thinking about becoming a black knight. 'Where would you go? What would you do?' I want to know your answers to those same questions. 'Where are you going? What will you do?'"

Sir Judas made a small smile. "I told you that the day we met. I'm going to Castle Nightfall."

"Why?"

"I told you that as well. I'm going to rescue Sir Samson."

"I don't believe you."

Sir Judas's smile faded. "Lies do not fall from the lips of paladins, David. I have not tried to deceive you in anything I've uttered."

David sat up straight. "But that doesn't make any sense! Don't you know it's under a dome of total darkness? A dome of horrors, filled with monsters, and that almost no one who goes in ever comes out again?"

"So I've heard. That rumor reached me long ago, repeated by someone who thought it would dissuade me from my quest. Instead it made me laugh, and it inspired me. Domes of death and darkness just so happen to be my specialty, but that's a story for another time."

David leaned forward, clenching his fists. "But it still doesn't make sense! Why would you go there? You just said you've been marching through the wilderness, fighting guards in every town, cut off from the people you want to help. And to top it off, you want to go to Castle Nightfall? It is literally the worst place on earth you could possibly want to go. If you were journeying towards *anywhere else*, it would make more sense than going to Castle Nightfall."

Sir Judas closed his eyes, smiled deeply, then he opened them again and said to David, "Firstly, but not most importantly, I am bound to go. The final order of my king was to go save Sir Samson. At the end of the day, I suppose I still am a sword *with* a lord, only my lord is not on earth, but in heaven. Secondly, and more importantly, Castle Nightfall is the best place on earth I could possibly go. If we judge a place in terms of pain and pleasure, then you are right that Castle Nightfall is the last place I would ever go. But I would propose to you a different standard, one that will make your life much more fulfilling. The man I love more than any other man on earth is at Castle Nightfall, and that makes it the place where I will find the greatest possible love. Love doesn't often go together with pleasure. Sometimes it does, but more often it goes with pain. I think God made this passing world that way just so we would have a chance to prove our love to one another. Not for my own delight am I going to Castle Nightfall. It's not even for the pleasure of seeing Sir Samson again. No, the pleasure he will give me is far less than the suffering he will cost me, and that is where true love comes in. A love stronger than our pains, a love stronger than our crosses. I am going to Castle Nightfall because more than any other place on earth, it is the place where I will fully love."

Without realizing it, David put a hand over his heart. It was burning again, just like the first time Sir Judas told him about his quest. Sir Joseph, startled by the revelations these two were discussing in a matter of fact fashion, blurted, "Wait, Samson? The king? Who exactly are you, Judas? Who was your former master?"

Sir Judas laughed. "My apologies for my lack of manners. Somehow I must have forgotten to mention it. I am Sir Judas, Last of the Kingsguard. I am also the only paladin, but not the last. I was promised another would come after me."

Still wide-eyed and processing, Sir Joseph asked, "So, wait, when you say 'Sir Samson,' you mean, *the* Sir Samson. The head of the Kingsguard? The one Goliath slew to begin the war?"

"The very same," Sir Judas answered, "only it was revealed to me that he was not slain. Sir Samson is a prisoner in Castle Nightfall, and I am on my way to save him." Looking back to David, Sir Judas added, "It is this quest, I believe, that is the only reason I have not fallen into the crimes for which wicked black knights are known. I have somewhere I am going. I have someone I am going to. For the last forty years, it has been the hope of seeing Sir Samson again that has carried me through my greatest struggles."

Closing his eyes and leaning back, David said, "Tell us about Sir Samson. How can you love someone so much?"

Sir Judas closed his eyes and tried to think. Tears began to form at the memory. "He was certainly an unusual paladin. People often whispered that he was the least holy one (the impious saying it as a compliment), but I think that was because they didn't understand what holiness really is. He had the kind of holiness that drew men to him. Sir Daniel was known for his prayers. Sir Geoffori was known for his penances. Sir Edward was known for being a walking encyclopedia of every Bible verse and Church tradition. Sir Samson was known for being 'an ordinary dunderhead.' Those were his own words for himself, and they were oft repeated. What most people didn't realize was that he was ordinary in a very extraordinary way. He completely understood who he was in God's eyes. He knew he was flawed and full of failings. He knew he was loved regardless. He never felt the need to try and show off any holiness or piety. He loved God sincerely when he did well, and he repented sincerely when he sinned. That didn't earn him a high reputation, and maybe in some objective sense it's a lesser holiness, but he had a profound humility that endeared him to all of the paladins. Instead of infighting, rivalries, and spiritual envy, the other six were eager to put their talents at his service. I am eternally grateful that God made him the master under whom I squired. So much of what I personally needed to learn about the road to heaven came to me through his example."

Now Sir Judas looked up, smiling broadly at a happy memory. "And then there were those rare moments when his holiness was not hidden, and no one would dare suggest at those times that he was 'ordinary' in any way. One morning I recall we had formed up for battle, and the enemy opposing us had far more troops. What was worse, they had many cavalry, and the battlefield was a plain where they would be able to maneuver. We were all frightened and nervous. I was praying fervently for God to save us, while others were calling for us to surrender. And then Sir Samson raised his greatsword *Alacritas*, which means 'zeal.' He yelled, 'Deus vult!' and then he burst into flames."

The other two started. "He did what?"

"You heard me right. He burst into flames. Literal flames, blazing all about him. 'The man on fire,' as we would call him. I was standing next to him and the heat was so great that it scorched my face and left my skin red for the next few days, yet I never felt more courageous and alive in my entire life. And then Sir Samson ran all along the front yelling, 'Deus vult! Deus vult! God wills it!' He grabbed all the most nervous and frightened men, and he shook them violently yelling, 'Deus vult! God wills it!' And then the fire spread, and before long we were all ablaze, yelling and cheering and screaming with all our might. And when the word was given we charged into battle, a whole army of 'men on fire.' Needless to say, our foes were terrified. They routed instantly, and we chased them all day long, dealing a decisive blow in that conflict. Some observers said we were like the famous berserkers of Gaul, but it was just the opposite. Those barbarians made a ferocious charge by entering a blind rage. We were the opposite of blind. In the light of that fire we saw everything clearly, so clearly there was no room for fear. We saw that death would come for us no matter what. On this battlefield, or lying in our beds, the end of this mortal life is unchanging. So then if we were destined to die regardless, why not choose to live like heroes? Why not live for an eternal reward? Why not live like men on fire?

"Oh, David, you're making me wish Sir Samson was here right now. I can just see him standing in the central plaza of Chelles, with all those dazed souls looking up at the flashing tower. Sir Daniel would pray for them. Sir Geoffori would fast for them. All I could do was mourn for them. Not Sir Samson. I can just see him bursting into flames, running up to one of the Committee members, ripping his mask off and screaming in his face, 'Deus vult! Deus vult! God wills it!' I can see him running up and down the streets, slashing every string of lights and sharing his fire. And then after he had turned this whole city upside down, he would come to that giant tower, right where you walk in, raise *Alacritas*, and prepare to charge. And then someone would ask him, 'What can we do? We can't destroy that monstrosity! How can a man fight a mountain?' And Sir Samson would just smile and yell, 'Deus vult! Deus vult!' and run right at it, and slash and fight until the electric tower fell to pieces."

Sir Judas was on his feet, swinging an imaginary greatsword in overhead strikes. He laughed at himself, because he hadn't even noticed when it happened. He simply got carried away and started acting things out at some point. Only now did he realize he looked ridiculous, yet he didn't care. "That's my brief introduction to Sir Samson for you two, but there is no substitute for really knowing the man. I hope you will come with me to Castle Nightfall, David, and once the battle is won you can meet the greatest paladin to ever live."

Chapter 4: The Second Temptation

The royal palace of Lord Benjamin Fearnow was one of the most exquisite, elegant, and lavishly decorated buildings in all the realm. It was also one of the most banal, bland, and uninteresting buildings in all the realm, which tends to be how such places are. Upon immediately entering the lobby, a large double staircase wound up both sides of the room, hugging a massive gold framed painting that took up the whole wall. The painting was just red paint. It was darker red at the top, and faded to a light pink at the bottom.

A few minutes before their scheduled dinner, Sir Judas, David, and Sir Joseph proceeded up the right hand staircase accompanied by two guards. All along the ascent the walls were decorated with pictures of random shapes and colors having no apparent pattern or purpose. At the top of the staircase Officer Feifer was awaiting them with the rest of his posse. They stood in formation on a landing that had a beautiful marble pedestal set on either side of two imposing mahogany doors. The pedestal on the right held a brass statue of the body of a very skinny man wearing just a loincloth, while his head looked like that of a very excited monkey. On the left was a similar statue of a female monkey person.

Sir Judas scratched his chin and said, "Lord Fearnow certainly has interesting taste in artwork."

"Yes, he's very proud of it, Judas," Lieutenant Louis said. "What did you think of the 'Shades of Rage' painting on the floor below us?"

After a moment of trying to recall whether he had seen it, Sir Judas realized, "The large wall of red paint? Is that 'Shades of Rage'?"

"Yes, it's Lord Fearnow's most beloved masterpiece. He has often expressed how it manages to capture all of the different forms that anger is capable of taking. What are your thoughts?"

Sir Judas tried to think of the politest way to tell the truth. He came up with, "I find it interesting in the same way as these two statues."

"Ah, yes. 'The Ascent of Man.' These sculptures are actually historical marvels from *before* the Great Calamity, if you can believe it. There are many theories as to what they are meant to depict. I've never heard a connection to 'Shades of Rage,' before, but I can see where you would get that. Taken from a certain angle, perhaps the monkey *is* angry, though I personally thought his face was more..." As Lieutentant Louis prattled on about his myriad insights into these pieces, Sir Judas decided he had acted most judiciously by not elaborating on the meaning of the word 'interesting.'

After waiting for Louis to finish, Officer Feifer asked, "Judas, do you not have a change of clothes? Certainly you must know it is not the norm to attend dinner in full armor. Or is that the way things were done in the realm you hail from?"

Sir Judas weighed his words carefully, recalling that Feifer seemed to have no recollection of the Committee's attack earlier. "I try to always be prepared. You never know when a knight will need to defend himself or others."

"How vigilant of you." Feifer walked up to the mahogany doors, doing his best to hide his fears. There was no reason Sir Judas should know about the ambush. They had done nothing to make him feel unwelcome in the city. *So why was he wearing armor?*

Officer Feifer then announced in grand style, "Welcome to the banquet hall of his majesty, Lord Benjamin Fearnow!" He then grabbed the handles of both doors, flung them open, and stood at attention as he tapped the butt of his spear on the floor. The other guards led a procession into the room, followed by Sir Joseph, and then David. Sir Judas stopped to talk to Feifer a moment.

"I know this must sound pedantic, but it is an issue that touches close to my heart. Your introduction is improper. Lord Fearnow should be referred to as 'his eloquence,' not 'his majesty.' 'His majesty' is a descriptor that is reserved to the king and the king alone, God rest his soul."

"Actually, Judas, you are the one who is improper here. The Formal Equivalency Act of 2532 transferred all rights and titles of the king to Lord Fearnow seeing as there was no longer a king, and he was the next highest ranking authority."

"What! He can't just usurp the royal privileges like that! And even if he could, that still wouldn't make him 'his majesty,' since the Duke of York rules over this Land of Ire anyway!"

"The Duke of York sold the Irish title to Lord Fearnow in 2528, Judas. Lord Fearnow is high lord over all the Land of Ire."

Sir Judas was struck speechless by this revelation. With his mouth slightly ajar, he shook his head and walked into the banquet hall. At the last moment, he stopped and asked, "You may not know this, but for what price would the Duke of York sell such a precious birthright?"

Feifer became somewhat uneasy but answered, "When the duke visited Chelles he was so in love with the electric tower that he traded his birthright for a miniature replica." Officer Feifer closed the door halfway before stopping to add, "It truly was an impressive replica…you would have to see it to understand…" Then he finished shutting it.

The black knight began to tremble. He walked to the long banquet table and sat at the lowest place (furthest from Lord Fearnow's seat at the opposite head) and muttered under his breath, "Truly impressive? Like I would believe for a minute it wasn't magic…though from what you said earlier, Feifer, I can't really tell how much you know…'" He sat there staring straight down at the table for several minutes before he realized something about the lighting. Sir Judas looked at the candelabra all around the room. The room was lit with dozens of wax candles burning with perfectly ordinary fire. *Why doesn't the Lord of Chelles have electric lighting in his own home?* His mind was haunted with thoughts of the electric tower, David's dazed look, and Officer Feifer's comment that he hadn't seen the Committee in years. Sir Judas turned these things over in his head until the doors on the other side of the hall flung open and Lord Fearnow made his entrance.

Lord Fearnow flung the doors open and made a dramatic bow to Sir Joseph, David, and Sir Judas. "Welcome! Welcome! Welcome to my humble home!" As Lord Fearnow rose from his bow, he saw Sir Joseph sitting on the left side of the table, next to the seat of honor. David was across from him. David smiled, and Sir Joseph nodded his head to the lord, but five chairs down on the other side of the room, Sir Judas had risen and returned the bow. "Oh, please sit! Please sit!" Lord Fearnow walked right past the place that had clearly been set for him, and came down to the other end of the table, sitting next to Sir Judas.

"Welcome to my home! I am Lord Benjamin Fearnow III." He waved for David to approach. "Come lad! Come! No need to use the whole table! And what is your name?"

"David."

"A pleasure to meet you, David! And how about you, black knight? Who is it that I have the pleasure of talking to?"

"I am Sir Judas, Last of the Kingsguard."

For the space of a breath there was an awkward silence. Then Lord Fearnow tittered an uncomfortable laugh. "Eh-heh...you are, uh...I'm sorry, but did you just say...Last of the Kingsguard?"

"Yes I did."

The two men looked at each other, Sir Judas politely smiling, Lord Fearnow clenching his jaw while his wheels were spinning. The paladin was at peace. No one had believed his story in forty years, and he had no reason to think today would be any different. Lord Fearnow, on the other hand, was deeply torn by his own duplicity. He had expected this 'great and powerful wizard' from the Grand Empire to lie to him, but this was an especially bad lie. This was a lie that was so outrageously false, that he suspected it might be some sort of test to see how he would respond. And if it was a test, he didn't know what the right answer was. Was the wizard looking for a gullible dupe whom he could string along? Or was he looking for a capable partner who saw through such silly ruses in an instant? And if he was looking for a capable partner, how would he want such a partner to respond? With anger? Indignation? Dismissiveness? Laughter? Cunning?

"Sir Judas, Last of the Kingsguard eh? I must have fallen asleep when my tutor covered history, but I thought all seven of the Kingsguard were slain by Goliath? Sir Samson was cut down at the last stand of the two hundred, and the other six died at the Battle of Nouen. Moreover, I thought that only the king could dub a paladin? Is there something I do not know?"

"It is true that only the king can dub a paladin. That's exactly how it came to be. He dubbed me." Sir Judas's simple answer hung in the air. Lord Fearnow expected more explanation, but none was forthcoming.

Eventually he asked, "If that is so, 'Sir Judas,' then why didn't you sally forth with the other six paladins against Goliath?"

A look of sorrow came over Sir Judas at those words. "So I have been asked before, but alas! There was nothing I could do. I was not dubbed by the king until after that conflict was already over."

Lord Fearnow was at a loss. What was this wizard playing at? And how should a 'cunning and capable' partner respond? Gently pressing this story, he said, "I'm sorry, Sir Judas, but I was under the impression that the king died on the very day of that battle. In the same hour, in fact. Did he somehow manage to find time to dub you in the midst of his final hour?"

"Yes he did. It was one of the most sorrowful and beautiful moments of my entire life." That sad smile that was often on Sir Judas's lips unsettled the noble.

"I'm sorry, 'sir,' but I just don't see how your story can be true. My grandfather was at the Battle of Nouen, and he stood by the king until the bitter end. In all the times he told me that story, never once did he mention the king dubbing one last paladin. Did my grandfather lie to me? Unless he did, I don't see how your tale can be true."

Judas folded his arms and leaned back in his chair, sucking his lips like he had something to say and was thinking it through before he said it. "No, I don't think your grandfather lied to you on that front...he left the king's side shortly before his death, and then I was dubbed right after that."

Lord Fearnow clenched his fists and flared his nostrils. *That* was clearly a lie. He wanted to call 'Sir Judas' out immediately, but he remembered that he had his own role he needed to play. "But sir, the dubbing of a new paladin is a huge affair with days of rituals and festivities. Do you honestly expect me to believe that after staying by the king 'until the bitter end,' as my grandfather put it, he somehow managed to miss the last few *days* of the king's life? Do you realize how absurd this story sounds?"

"Of course there wasn't time for all that. And in times of urgency, the king wouldn't go through all of the formal rituals, since the minimums for a valid dubbing are much less than the usual solemnities. The only things that are needed are a weapon, a drop of royal blood, and the king saying, 'I dub thee, Sir Judas!' Everything above that was fitting, but not essential."

Lord Fearnow's wheels continued to spin. The wizard's game had become utterly mad. He clearly had no idea what he was talking about, nor did he have any inkling of how the king had passed his final hour. He might have been able to pass off this story in every city he came to thus far, but Lord Fearnow knew too many details to be deceived by the tale he told. And that's when it hit him. He only knew the wizard was lying because he knew particular details. Details no one else was aware of. This wizard wasn't putting him to the test at all. He was telling a lie that seemed unassailable, expecting Lord

Fearnow to actually believe it. The wizard wanted to be believed…that meant it was probably time to stop being so skeptical and start being a little more credulous.

A waiter came in holding four crystal goblets and a pitcher of water. Lord Fearnow barked, "Ah! About time the kitchen sent someone! Pour the water, and then go put in our dinner order with the chef. I'm thinking shé gēng tonight." The waiter dutifully placed the glasses before each guest, put the pitcher in the center of the table, and then made to leave. As he was going, Lord Fearnow called, "Waiter, hold on a moment. I have a question for you. What's your name again?

The waiter dutifully bowed and answered, "Seamus, your grace."

"Seamus, before you run off, take a guess at what the black knight's name is."

Seamus looked at Sir Judas, shrugged, and said, "I don't have the faintest idea, your grace. I have never met this man before."

"His name is 'Judas.' Can you believe that? What a peculiar name, isn't it?"

Seamus pulled his eyebrows together. "If it would not be inappropriate to ask, your grace…no, I'm sorry. I wouldn't want to…"

"Wouldn't want to what, Seamus?"

"Forgive me, your grace. I was going to speak out of turn and say something…inappropriate."

"Say it." Seamus's face grew red. When he still seemed uncertain, Lord Fearnow added, "Say it. That's an order."

Seamus nodded. "Well, please take no offence at my comment, Judas, but, I thought to myself…what kind of mother would name her son 'Judas'?"

Sir Judas answered, "The name is not from my mother, but from my king. When a paladin is dubbed, the king gives him a new name."

Seamus grew more confused, but he bowed and exited the room. Sir Joseph finally came and sat down next to Lord Fearnow. "I'm not quite sure that addresses his underlying question, Judas. I've also been wondering what kind of woman would name you that, but at least a mother can be written off as eccentric. For your king to give you that name…I mean, did you do anything to deserve it? Around here that word means 'traitor.' As in, 'That man who stabbed me in the back was a real Judas.' Is it the same meaning in your native tongue, or no?"

"Yes, in our tongue as well as the Ancient Tongue we have the same expression. 'That treacherous cur was a Judas indeed.' But the expression doesn't come from a word, Sir Joseph, it comes from a name. 'Judas' was the name of the disciple who betrayed Jesus Christ to death. One of his trusted and beloved friends. That's where the expression comes from, but there are other people named Judas in the Bible. There are three Judases that I'm aware of, and while the traitor is the most famous, I feel as if the king may have had all three in mind when he gave me my name."

"How so?" Lord Fearnow asked. He was growing more perplexed by the moment. He had expected the wizard who abandoned the king to be as hostile to the Grand Empire and its religion as he was. It was sounding like the wizard had a very different attitude, and Lord Fearnow was trying to figure out how he should act to secure an alliance.

Sir Judas answered, "The first Judas was Judas Machabeus, the son of Mattathias. When an infamous and wicked man named Antiochus came and conquered Judea, he led a terrible persecution, torturing and oppressing the Jewish people in ways not fit to be discussed at dinner. They were horribly crushed, betrayed by their own countrymen, abandoned by the priests. But then, when all seemed lost, and the tragic story appeared to be at an end, Judas Machabeus came riding out of the wilderness, a piece of the old Jewish kingdom that was hidden away in the time of destruction, and now was revealed when deliverance was at hand. He went around gathering allies, forming an army, and then rebelled against the Greek oppressors. And though they were a small army, God was with them, and they were able to cast off Antiochus and take back their kingdom.

"Then there was Judas Thaddeus, who was also one of the twelve disciples of Christ. Like Judas Iscariot, he abandoned our Lord on the night before He was to suffer, but Judas Thaddeus repented. Then he went out to preach the Gospel and was faithful to the end, even though his end was much harsher than for Judas Machabeus. Judas Thaddeus laid the foundations of Christendom, yet he never lived to see the fruits of his labors. All his life he worked for an impossible cause, and he went all the way to a martyr's death trusting that somehow this was a part of God's plan. In my younger days, I liked to believe I was named after Judas Machabeus, and in some ways I am that hidden man returning from the wilderness. As I've aged, however, no army has come flocking to me, and my cause has looked more and more impossible with every step. The years have been revealing to me that Judas Thaddeus is my model too.

"But as I said, I believe I was named after three Judases, not two, so I have one more left to explain, although he may be the hardest to understand…you see, in this realm there are many men who commit treason on some level. Against the king, a lord, a wife, a friend…traitors are sadly more common than most men think. And traitors deserve to be punished. They deserve to be met with hostility. They deserve to never be trusted. While I am no traitor in any way that I can see, nevertheless for the sake of my name and the truth I tell, I have been punished, shunned, and mistrusted all throughout the realm. This means, at least in me, more treason has been punished than has actually been committed, and in the scales of justice me and a traitor who never answered for his crimes could be weighed together and justice would be satisfied.

"For the obstinate traitor, going on in his crimes without repentance, this must seem absurd, and like a double injustice; he commits a crime, and now innocent Sir Judas pays the price. But in good faith, I tell you I am glad to pay that price, because I yearn for the salvation of that obstinate traitor. I yearn for his repentance. And if someday he thought of repenting, but looked at the punishment he must undergo, that traitor might break down in despair and decide he cannot accept the price. But he won't see that, you see. Instead he'll look at the punishment and see that the price was already paid! Sir Judas was scourged as a traitor, and now this traitor's debt is gone. No stumbling block, no obstacle, he can turn his life around and become the new man. He can step out of the darkness and into the light. By carrying the name of Judas Iscariot, I do penance for all the traitors of the realm…" Sir Judas trailed off, and then added very quietly, "…and two traitors in particular who weigh heavily upon my heart."

When Sir Judas had finished talking, the room was still for several moments. Then Lord Fearnow arose and began to make his way towards the door he had come into the room by. Sir Joseph said to Sir Judas, "You are completely and utterly mad."

David shrugged. "I thought that made a lot of sense."

Sir Judas sat in silence, watching Lord Fearnow silently walk across the room. The lord stopped at the door and looked back. Sir Judas said, "You look just like your grandfather."

Lord Benjamin Fearnow III. shuddered. "I heard that a lot growing up."

"Please tell me, how long ago did he die?"

Lord Fearnow took a moment to remember, and then said, "About eighteen years ago. I was ten."

Sir Judas was about to ask another question, but Lord Fearnow rushed out of the room and slammed the door behind him. He ran to where Lady Amanda was sitting and told her, "Start casting the spell."

Gasping for breath, she answered, "Benjamin, I…I can't…he's too strong. A terrible maelstrom of spirits is swirling about him. If he dispatched even one tenth of the army that serves him, I would be dead within the minute." Lord Fearnow looked around at his Committee members. None of them were standing upright. Some were doubled over, one laying down, another leaning against the wall.

"I know his power weighs upon you all…I felt it too just now, crushing me…but we're about to be dead anyway unless you do something. He knows who Amanda and I are."

"What? How?" Lady Fearnow asked.

"He knows who we are. He just told me a whole story about it. Some mad, rambling tale about how he's trying to save two traitors. He knows, Amanda! He came right out and accused me as I was leaving the room. He knows! Start the spell, and go as fast as you can. I don't know how long I can stall, but I do know there's no way we can persuade him to our cause. He came all the way across the realm to hunt us down and 'save us.' We both know what he's referring to…our only option is to fight him with your magic."

She nodded. "I'll try."

"You can do it. Knock once on the door when you're ready, and then as soon as I open the door, work your magic." Lord Fearnow then pointed an accusing finger at all of the Committee members. "Fail now, and you doom us all." After that, Lord Fearnow walked back towards the door, feeling like he was being constantly pelted in the face and heart with dreaded memories and emotions. It was incredible how much power the wizard had, that simply to be near him was so terrible. Lord Fearnow pushed through the doors and back into the room, looking far wearier and worn down than when he had left. He did not cross all the way to his previous seat, but instead sat down at the head of the table, putting the entire room between himself and his guests.

Sir Judas asked, "Is everything alright, m'lord? I thought I heard a woman in the other room whose voice was very distressed."

"Yes, that was my wife. She's very ill right now."

"I'm so sorry! I had no idea! You didn't need to tear yourself away from her for our sake. Perhaps we should expedite our business so that you can go back to nursing her."

Lord Fearnow grew nervous. His plan to stall was not going well. "No, no, she'll be quite alright. There's no need to feel rushed."

"Oh, but I insist! Not only could you return to your wife sooner, but you would be assisting me as well. I am currently on a rather urgent quest that requires I travel through your lands. I do not wish to be in Chellesian territory any longer than I must, and if your guards and Committee represent your own sentiments, then I know you don't want me here either. Therefore, I am asking for freedom of travel through the southern regions of your territory. You can add whatever stipulations or contingencies you desire to the actual document, I just ask that it be completed swiftly—this very night, if possible."

Lord Fearnow slouched in his chair, putting one foot up on the table and propping his head up with one hand. "And what is this quest of yours, 'Sir Judas, Last of the Kingsguard'?"

"I am going to slay Goliath, the giant who cast our realm into chaos, and rescue Sir Samson, whom he holds prisoner." Lord Fearnow burst out laughing. Sir Judas insisted, "I know that I am old, and Goliath mighty, but if God is for us, who can be against us? And besides..." Sir Judas said with a wink, "I even found a boy named 'David' to help me."

Lord Fearnow kept laughing. "Oh, it's not your powers that amuse me, great and mighty paladin. That you can defeat the invincible Leviathan I do not doubt. No, I was laughing at something altogether different..."

There was a single knock on the door.

Lord Fearnow smiled and arose.

"Sir Judas, I am about to do something incredibly stupid, but there is some foolish, dramatic part of me that simply cannot resist the temptation. Will you indulge me for a moment if I play the madman?"

Sir Judas frowned. "I would never encourage anyone to act like a madman."

"Oh, but you should really hope I do. You see, if I was a wise man, I would go answer that knock and check on my poor, sick wife, but as a fool, I will tarry, just a moment, and tell you what is on my heart."

"See to your wife. You can tell me what you are thinking when you return."

"Alas, I wish I could, but I fear that once I open that door, you and I may never speak again, and this is something I really want you to hear. You amaze me, Sir Judas. Impress me. Astound me. Astonish me. Educate me. I could sit here all night and recite words that reflect how deeply I admire your talents. You see, every liar who has ever lived tells his tale in the manner that will make it most plausible, and when the details of his tale come under scrutiny, he multiples explanations to make it seem even more believable. What no liar ever dares to try, yet you have mastered with aplomb, is to impersonate an honest man, and tell his story the way a truth-teller would tell it. To state it plainly, simply, without anxiety for whether or not it will be believed, since the truth-teller does not need anyone to assent to his statements–he himself has already assented. 'Sir Judas, Last of the Kingsguard,' so masterful is your lie, so sincere your presentation, that *I* was even tempted to believe it, though I know that it is false. That's how great you are! How skillful! That I am tempted to believe your word rather than my own eyes. Alas! I wish I could study at your knees all the days that you have left, but necessity will not allow it. Nevertheless, know that whenever I lie, now and forevermore, I shall try to lie exactly the way you have shown me."

Sir Judas leapt to his feet in rage. "You insult my honor! And not only my honor, but more importantly the sacred honor of all the paladins, whose perfect honesty is so manifest that it is a saying repeated throughout the realm! 'Lies do not fall from the lips of paladins!'"

"By God, you are amazing. Even now I want to believe you. But you are no paladin, 'Sir Judas,' that I know for a fact. The king never dubbed you, and he never named you 'Judas,' though the story you cooked up for that name was spectacular. Whatever the truth may be, you will tell me soon enough. Not you, I know, but the shell of a man that is left over when this dismal work is done. I shall miss you, 'Sir Judas.' The fantasy of who you pretend to be is so much more exciting than whoever you truly are. Farewell."

Lord Fearnow flung open the door. Sir Judas's sense of deadly intent flashed through his mind. A curse was coming! The escape was to draw his dagger! *Caritas* came out. Then the spell seized him. His head whipped towards Lady Fearnow, who was standing in the doorway. She was the most beautiful woman he had ever seen.

Her golden waves of hair cascaded gently down her shoulders. Her shining face was like seeing an angel in human form. And those eyes…those piercing green eyes…he felt as if she was looking right through him, and finding pleasure in what she saw. She was so young…was she even twenty? What could she want with an old man like him? Yet from the look in her eyes…the way she was smiling…the dress she had put on…She wanted him! She was beckoning for him to follow her!

Everything Sir Judas heard sounded like it was coming to him through water from far away. Lord Fearnow shouted some word. A commotion came from behind him. A dozen masked men came running into the room behind Lady Fearnow. Sir Joseph ran towards them and garbled something. Guards tackled Sir Joseph. David was screaming. It faded away. Lady Amanda was all that mattered. Sir Judas blocked out everything else and began to walk slowly towards her.

Some part of him was still yelling to look at his left hand. For a moment he did–oh, the horror! It was a cross! It was a dagger! Instruments of death and blood! He didn't want that! Why would anyone want that? Lady Amanda was offering him so much more…so much better. She spoke to him, and he heard her clearly. Her voice was not distant like everyone else's, but instead it surrounded him on every side. Her voice shook his very being, a deep booming voice coming up out of the floor. "COME TO ME. GIVE ME ALL OF WHO YOU ARE, BODY AND SOUL. I SHALL TAKE YOU TO MYSELF, AND WE SHALL BE UNITED FOR ALL OF ETERNITY!"

Eternity! Oh happy eternity! An eternity of being with Lady Amanda in the joy of unending life!

"I am the Life."

It was a different voice–a man's voice, coming from his left hand. Sir Judas looked down again…*The cross! Torture! Suffering! Death! Was Death calling him to Life?*

"I am the Resurrection and the Life. He that believeth in Me, although he be dead, shall live."

The deep voice, mouthed by Lady Amanda, yet coming from the depths below, boomed, "COME TO ME! THINK OF WHAT I OFFER. THINK OF WHAT HE REFUSES. AM NOT I THE DESIRE OF YOUR HEART? AM NOT I PLEASING TO BEHOLD? AM NOT I THE ONE WHO WILL GIVE WHAT HE REFUSES? HE SAYS, 'I AM GOING TO REFUSE THE FRUIT FOR WHICH YOU YEARN.' AM NOT I PROOF THAT THE FORBIDDEN FRUIT IS SWEET?"

Sir Judas wavered, looking between Lady Fearnow and the dagger. He wanted to sink into her embrace, and let her take his troubles away, but then he remembered the words Lord Fearnow had said mere moments before.

Every liar who has ever lived tells his tale in the manner that will make it most plausible, and when the details of his tale come under scrutiny, he multiples explanations to make it seem even more believable. The voice from the pit offered so many good arguments for why he should believe her.

The truth-teller does not need anyone to assent to his statements–he himself has already assented. The voice from the Cross said He was the Life. No other witness had been called. His own words were enough.

Sir Judas looked at Lady Amanda again, fighting to regain his wits. She was pointing at him. Her arm was trembling, and her lips moving, as the voice came from the pit saying, "THAT'S MINE! MINE! HOW DID YOU GET MY DAGGER?" It was an alluring voice. It was a nasty voice. It was a voice that was losing its power. Then, through the waters, the voice of David came shooting like an arrow. "Sir Judas! Save us!"

Caritas flashed. The spell shattered. In a moment he saw it all. Feifer was wrestling David, lifting him off the floor. Sir Joseph was in a jumble of chairs, with three guards piled on top of him. Six Administrators were sprawled out on the ground. Six Committee members were still standing, but shaking and exhausted. Lord Fearnow, white as a corpse, was muttering gibberish under his breath. Lady Fearnow was still trembling, finger pointing, shocked out of her wits as she whispered in her own voice, "That's my dagger…how did you get my dagger?"

Sir Judas looked at the dagger, looked at her, and then a horrible realization came upon him. "You look exactly the same…you *both* look exactly the same…only younger! Oh, God, what have you done?"

"That's my dagger…"

Lord Fearnow began to screech, "Feifer! Feifer! It's Mordecai! Kill Mordecai!"

"Of all the ancient abominations…oh, God, what have you done?"

"That's my dagger…I want my dagger…"

"Feifer! Feifer! Drop the boy! Kill Mordecai!"

"You foul and loathsome monsters! How could you ever do such a thing?"

"I killed you with that dagger!"

"Feifer! Feifer! Kill Mordecai!"

Sir Judas drew *Veritas*, and roared with all his might, "REGICIDES!"

Chapter 5: The Grand Empire's Final Hour

Forty years ago, at the royal palace, on the day of the Battle of Nouen.

Lord Benjamin Fearnow and Lady Amanda–both in their fifties–were searching for the king. After failing to find him amongst the citizens who were prepared to flee, they began searching high and low in the castle for where he might be hiding. Eventually they discovered that he was not hiding at all. He was in the great hall, seated on his throne, up on a dais that took six steps to ascend. All six of the remaining Kingsguard had gone to the frontlines to prepare for battle. The only defender left with the king was Mordecai of the Lessguard. Fr. Canton, the king's personal chaplain, was also there, chanting the twenty-second psalm in the Ancient Tongue.

"Nam, etsi ambulavero in medio umbrae mortis, non timebo mala, quoniam tu mecum es," which is translated, 'For though I should walk in the midst of the shadow of death, I will fear no evils, for thou art with me.' The king was listening, smiling, eyes closed as he peacefully prayed along with Fr. Canton. Mordecai was standing erect and vigilant at the bottom of the steps. He had one hand on his sword, but he was wearing his court garb–*unarmored*. Lady Amanda noted that with glee.

"My king! My king!" Lord Fearnow shouted, cutting Fr. Canton off. "What are you doing, sitting here as the battle is being joined? Swiftly! We must flee! The opportunity to escape is slipping away!"

"Escape?" The king asked with a small chuckle. He opened his blazing emerald eyes and looked down on the lord of Chelles. "But m'lord, the battle is not yet lost! Even now the six paladins are preparing to accept Goliath's challenge and ride out to face him. Can the king flee while his men are advancing? I shall sit here and hold court until the battle is truly lost."

"Your grace," Lord Fearnow said, "The enemy has circled the city round about with their engines of war, and the trebuchet are trained on this castle. As soon as the duel between Goliath and the Kingsguard is over, they will level this castle to the ground. Come wait outside with the rest of your people."

"I am not concerned with needing to escape this castle. Even if it did fall around us, I am confident a man could survive under the great stone dome of this throne room. It might take him three days to dig himself out, but he could do it. No need to worry about this castle collapsing."

"Well if not for the trebuchets, your grace, at least flee because of the coming invaders! I fear that if you wait for word of how Goliath's duel has gone, by then the enemy will be in the city and may overtake you. My men will do what they can to slow the invaders, but they are not a skillful army, and I do not know how long they will hold the gate."

"Yes, yes, Lord Fearnow, I was thinking the same thing as you. The fact that Goliath's army chased yours clear across the realm, yet you lost no men? Obviously your army was not offering much resistance. That's why I moved your forces to the vanguard outside the walls, and stationed Duke Isaac at the gate. If the day should be lost, and we must retreat, his valiant men will hold to the very end. Not until every last one of them has fallen in honor will the enemy set foot inside this city. Why, I am even hopeful that they will defend so fiercely that Goliath will have to call all his forces together and assault the gate himself. When that happens, a passage will open in the rear of the city, and all of the women and children might be able to escape unharmed."

Lord Fearnow felt his stomach lurch. "My...my men are in the vanguard, your grace? I thought they were supposed to be to the rear of the army?"

"I thought the other side of the wall would be a more appropriate place for them. You would already know this if you had been with us when we assembled for battle."

Lord Fearnow tried not to show his frustration. His men were supposed to attack Duke Isaac from behind and deal a decisive blow that would end this conflict quickly. From outside the wall they were just a statistic; a slight increase in the numbers of Goliath's already overwhelming forces. The battle would still be won, but not as cleanly, and not without taking a heavy toll.

He tried one final tactic. "The courage of your grace is brilliant to behold, and I myself feel inspired anew. Please, your grace, come and share this inspiration with your people, that they may be comforted in their present trial."

No sooner had Lord Fearnow finished speaking than a distant shout was heard. "Deus vuuuuuuulllt!" A roaring cheer from the whole city followed, so loud and so clamorous that the great hall itself seemed to be shaking. The king answered, "They seem inspired enough to see their champions ride." He then descended from his throne and removed his crown. Only now did the Fearnows notice that the king had a silver-hilted sword on his hip. He drew it, and placing the tip of the sword on the ground, holding the hilt in both hands, the king took a knee before Fr. Canton. Mordecai followed suit. "Please give us your blessing, Father."

Fr. Canton prayed over them, made the sign of the cross in the air, and said, "Benedicat vos omnipotens Deus, Pater, et Filius, et Spiritus Sanctus," and the king and Mordecai answered, "Amen." Then they arose, and the king asked, "May I kiss your hand one last time, Father?" Fr. Canton extended his hand, and the king gently kissed it. Mordecai did as well. Then the king said, "You may go now, Father. Take care of your flock, and may God bless you."

Fr. Canton bowed, then took off running, not for the sake of his own life, but because his task this day was to lead and guard the women and children in their flight from the city. The four were now alone. The king ascended his throne once more, and then sat down with the silver sword laid flat across his lap. "Come, Lord Fearnow, approach me. Stand at the bottom of these steps and present yourself before your king."

Lord Fearnow nervously moved forward, being careful to keep Lady Amanda between himself and Mordecai. There was a shout of dismay from the crowd, mixed with screams and sobbing. The king announced in a steady voice, "Sir William has fallen."

"Please, your grace!" Lord Fearnow cried, "It is time to flee! Come with us before it is too late!"

Another shout of sorrow went up. The king said, "Sir Geoffori has gone to his reward."

"Your grace, have you lost your wits? Are you mad with grief? Come! While there is still time to save yourself!"

Groans of anguish sounded one after another. "Sir James, Sir Henry, and Sir Edward all fell in swift succession."

"For the love of God, your grace, can't you see the writing on the wall?"

"I do see it. Daniel read it for me."

There was a great swelling from the crowd, a growing excitement of imminent hope, as all the city prepared to shout in exultation together.

Then there was silence.

Then a scream.

Then a cacophony of wailing and grinding of teeth.

Then the stones from the trebuchets began to slam into the great hall, and the crashing of stone on stone reverberated without ceasing.

The king shouted over all the noise, "Sir Daniel had a chance to slay Goliath, but he has fallen. Now I shall speak plainly. Tell me, Benjamin, why is it so important that I let you stab me in the back? Do you fear an old man with a sword? I will not raise it against you. No, I think you fear my eyes. You know that if you kill me to my face, I will hold your gaze, and for the rest of your days you will see these green eyes, reminding you of all you have done. You are a craven who hides in the shadows, hiding even from yourself. Your heart is bent on evil, and I know I will not sway you from your course. But if you must do evil, do it manfully. Do not hide behind your wife's skirt while she draws a hidden dagger. Take this sword and kill me eye to eye, and admit you are a regicide. If you can be at least that honest, I will not despair of your salvation."

Mordecai turned around in shock, not believing what he had just heard. "Your grace, do you mean–?" He understood his blunder too late. Lady Amanda leapt upon him with her golden dagger, driving it through his back and into his heart. Mordecai fell to his knees, letting out a gurgling scream.

Swooning, his vision already going dim as his blood rushed out, Mordecai saw Lord Benjamin Fearnow ominously ascend the six steps to the throne, stand over the king, and then snatch the sword from his lap. "Is this how you want me to take your life?"

"No one takes my life from me. I lay it down of my own accord, and I trust in Him Who can take it up again."

Lord Fearnow drove the sword through the king's chest.

"NOOOOOOOOOO!" Mordecai yelled. Then he fell flat on his face. The last thing he saw was Lord Fearnow backing away down the steps. He and the king had locked eyes with each other, and neither broke the gaze. The sword was still in the king's chest, pinning him to the throne. Unsure whether his face was wet from his blood or from his tears, Mordecai blacked out.

"Mordecai! Mordecai!"

Mordecai stirred groggily, as if waking from a terrible nightmare.

"Mordecai!"

"Your grace!" Suddenly he remembered what had happened. It was not a nightmare, but reality. He looked around wildly, then he felt a sharp stab of pain in his back and chest. The dagger was still inside him.

Everything was dark, and the smell of stone dust was heavy in the air. Everything was also quiet. Quiet as a tomb.

"Mordecai, come up here. Come kneel at my knees."

Mordecai complied, groping in the dark until he found the steps, and then blindly crawling up them. "Are we dead, your grace?"

"No, not yet, though I soon will be. For you, I fear, the journey home is just beginning, but walk with the Lord all the days of your life, and you are certain to reach your destination…Ah! Here you are. Lay your head in my lap. Yes, just like that. There's a good lad. Steel yourself. This will hurt."

Mordecai felt the dagger in his back wobble a little, and then leave, opening the wound and causing terrible pain. The king then placed his hand on the wound, pressing down, and the pain instantly subsided. "Be not afraid. This wound is not unto death."

Mordecai then felt the king's hands on his face, lifting his head up. One hand withdrew, and then Mordecai heard him say, "I dub thee, Sir Judas." There was a tap on Sir Judas's neck from the dagger, leaving behind a wet splash of his own blood mixed with the king's. "Sir Judas, receive *Caritas*, your sacred weapon." Sir Judas felt around until he found the dagger, and then grasped it firmly. It began to glow in his hand. He cried in distress. The king, still pinned to the throne by the sword, was a gruesome sight to behold. So much blood had come pouring out, that it was quite literally a miracle he was still alive. The light also revealed that the king and Mordecai were inside of a tight stone prison of rubble with one big round piece overhead. Just as the king had predicted, the large hemispherical ceiling over the great hall had remained intact, and they were saved in this dome of darkness.

"Arise, Sir Judas, and go to your destiny. Sir Samson lives, a prisoner of Goliath. The quest I give you is to save him, and save him you shall, so long as you walk always with the Lord." The king reached feebly towards his left breast. "And another quest I give you as well. In my pocket here is a prophecy. You are the Last of the Kingsguard, but another Paladin shall follow you. This sword you must draw from my chest and take with you, for it is the sacred blade

Veritas, and it shall be that Paladin's holy weapon. Initiate him into the Lessguard before you confront Goliath. Then let God take care of the rest. The prophecy will ensure you find the right man."

The king's arm fell. He took a deep, rasping sigh. He looked up at Sir Judas and smiled. His green eyes sparkled as he proclaimed his dying words. Then his head fell down, and Sir Judas wept. He closed the king's eyes. He drew *Veritas* from his body. He carried the king to the bottom of the dais and reverently laid him on the ground as if he were asleep.

Then Sir Judas began to dig his way out. He labored the rest of that day and all of the next. By the third day the dome of darkness had been overwhelmed by the odor of corruption, and Sir Judas barely had strength to move. He was exhausted and half dead, pushed to his limits by his labors, by his hunger, by his thirst, and by his loss of blood. On the third day he began to pass in and out of consciousness, thinking that each time he 'fell asleep,' might be the last. Then as he continued to pick away at the rubble, he found the final piece he needed to dislodge. The other stones around it shifted, and a tunnel opened, two feet wide. Daylight was on the other side.

Sir Judas took one last look at the king's body. He would have cried if he had the water to do so. He took *Caritas* in his left hand, *Veritas* in his right, and squirmed his way through the tunnel to the surface.

On April 17, Good Friday of that year, the Grand Empire died, and Mordecai was buried with it. On the third day, April 19, Sir Judas rose from its grave.

The final words of the king, and the final words of the Grand Empire were thus: "Love your enemies, Sir Judas. Love them, and do not hate them."

Chapter 6: The Third and Greatest Temptation

Sir Judas drew *Veritas*, and roared with all his might, "REGICIDES!" In his rage he almost charged the Fearnows, but realizing how outnumbered they were, he judged that he needed to save Sir Joseph first. He used a chair to step up onto the table, then with a running jump he dropkicked the pile of guards crushing his fellow knight. The guard he hit was not harmed, since the padding under his armor absorbed the blow, but it was enough force to push him off of the pile.

Besides Feifer, there was one other guard who was still on his feet. As Sir Judas rose that guard now lunged forward to stab Sir Judas with his spear. No man could have dodged at that range using natural powers, but Sir Judas had supernatural aid at hand. Before the guard had committed, the black knight was already dodging. The guard pulled back and stabbed again. Sir Judas dodged again. A third time Sir Judas dodged, and now he was on his feet, the assailant bewildered by the old man's agility. As the fourth stab came in Sir Judas parried with *Caritas*, and the guard was driven backwards as *Veritas* was used to counterstrike. By now the guard Sir Judas had kicked had risen. He circled around to flank Sir Judas, and then the two guards attacked him from opposite sides.

For any ordinary combatant, this would be the end. Even a master of swordplay in his prime could not hope to overcome two skilled opponents working together. Yet the same sense of deadly intent that had enabled Sir Judas to dodge the lone spearman served him just as well against two. Foreseeing his enemies' strikes and reacting before they happened, he not only managed to keep himself alive, but he very quickly put the two guards on the back foot. One moment Sir Judas advanced on one guard, the next he turned to ferociously attack the other. When one thought he had an opening to strike, at that very instant Sir Judas slashed with *Veritas* at his face. The two guards backed away, trying to put as much space between themselves and Sir Judas as they could.

One backed into a chair and stumbled a few paces back. Sir Judas didn't waste a moment.

He ran towards the other guard with full force, unleashing a flurry of attacks with his blades. A slash from *Veritas*, an upward parry with *Caritas*, and now he was at close quarters, inside of the spear's effective range. Sir Judas sensed from some impulse that he should not kill this man, even though it would be more expedient. Trusting his intuition, he punched the guard in the nose with the fist holding *Caritas*, and then slammed the pommel of *Veritas* into his brow. The guard crumpled with a groan, clasping his forehead.

Then a '*CRACK!*' sounded, and Sir Judas whirled back around. He saw–to his surprise–Sir Joseph was no longer in danger. One of the guards was flailing around on the ground like a man having a seizure. Lieutenant Louis was flailing six feet up in the air, held overhead by Sir Joseph. With a red face and a mighty heave, he threw him across the table and into two Committee members who were leaning against it. Two more Committee members began to cast spells. As they waved their arms and chanted, Sir Joseph aimed his metal tube at one and loosed a crackling blast of lightning. Sir Judas threw *Caritas* at the other, burying it in his gut below the sternum. The guard who had stumbled over the chair saw Sir Joseph and Sir Judas turn to face him together. He dropped his spear, raised his hands, and falling to his knees cried, "I yield!"

Sir Judas ran across the room, ripped *Caritas* out of the dying Committee member, and advanced upon the Fearnows. Lord Benjamin yelled, "Feifer, you fool! Use the boy!" Sir Judas turned to see Officer Feifer had thrown David aside and was running to intercept him, protecting his lord and lady. Feifer leapt up onto the table, and Sir Judas leapt up as well so the guard wouldn't have the high ground. The duel lasted but a moment. Sir Judas feinted right, and Feifer tried to tackle him. Sir Judas went left and stuck his leg out. Feifer tripped over it, and Sir Judas struck the back of his head with the hilt of *Caritas* for good measure. Feifer tumbled headlong off the table and was unconscious as soon as he hit the ground.

In the space of that swift battle, Lord Fearnow had grabbed David by the arm. Pulling a dagger from within his robes, he held it up to David's neck and yelled, "Stand down! Or I swear I'll kill the boy!"

Sir Judas gave him a withering look of contempt. "Filthy craven, hiding behind a child as a shield! We both know you will not harm him, or else you will lose your only defense. Use my words as your shield instead. Release him, send your men from this room, and I will not harm you or your wife."

Lord Fearnow squirmed. He hadn't considered what he would do *after* he killed David. He assumed the threat wouldn't have to be carried out. Quite liking the offer Sir Judas had made him, he asked, "What guarantee do I have that you won't kill us after the guards leave? How do I know you aren't lying to me?"

"You already know the answer."

Lord Fearnow smirked and released David's arm. "Guards! Committee! Leave us be. Joseph will keep Amanda and I safe in case of trouble." David immediately ran around the table and stood behind Sir Judas.

"Your grace! What's going on!" Sir Joseph demanded. "Why was I just attacked by the guards?"

"Oh, don't be so dramatic, Joseph. They didn't stab you, they tackled you. We couldn't have you getting in the way, and I had no time to explain. Now come stand by me and the lady, and do your duty while we talk."

Clutching her chest as she hobbled towards Lord Fearnow, one of the Committee members panted, "Your grace, do not send us away. You need someone to protect you from the wizard."

"After dispatching three of you in a matter of seconds, I have a much higher opinion of Sir Joseph's prowess than your own. Be gone."

"Your grace..." the woman croaked, almost sounding as if she was about to wretch. "The wizard has done something to us. I can feel it. There is a terrible pain in my chest. What if he did the same to you?"

"My word is final. Be gone."

Under Lieutenant Louis's orders, the battered guards picked up Officer Feifer and the guard having a seizure and carried them out of the room. "He'll be alright when he wakes up," Sir Joseph said, "I just gave him a little touch of electro-magic." After taking care of their own men, the guards came back for the Administrators who were all lying unconscious despite being untouched in the conflict. Last of all the unconscious and dead Committee member were taken away, with the other four accompanying them.

Finally alone, Sir Joseph turned back towards Lord Fearnow and asked, "M'lord, what is going on? What on earth is the meaning of all of this? You attacked a guest in your own home! And why did he call you a regicide when there hasn't been a king in your entire life?"

"M'lord?" Lord Fearnow asked in an icy voice. "Why, Sir Joseph, don't you mean, 'your grace'?"

Joseph looked uncertainly at the man who had been his benefactor and master for years.

"Who do you serve, Sir Joseph? Me or the king who has been dead for forty years? Who do you call, 'your grace'?" The lord's countenance was dark and angry. Lady Fearnow was still pale and visibly shaking. She couldn't stop looking at Sir Judas.

"*M'lord*, you've gone too far. This outrage is beyond the pale. Who do I serve? You or the king? I've never known the king, and I can serve Lord Fearnow no longer. I am officially resigning my position. As of tonight, I am a black knight."

For a moment Lord Fearnow was taken aback, but then he bit his lip and leaned forward, staring at Sir Joseph with an unsettling intensity. He nodded a few times as a wicked grin inched across his face. "Then here I am with two black knights, and no one to defend me. I have no doubts to your prowess, Joseph. If the time has come to be the vigilante of justice, I'm sure you can slay the lady and I and fight your way out of this city…" Lord Fearnow raised an eyebrow. "…but can your mother?"

Sir Joseph's eyes went wide. "You wouldn't."

"No I wouldn't. Because I would be dead. It's the Committee who would cease control after my decease, and doesn't that change the complexion of our question? What would *they* do to the mother of one of their most reviled adversaries? If you and I were gone, but your mother remained, just what might we expect from the men who live behind a mask?"

Sir Joseph began to tremble.

"Yes, Joseph, now I think you understand just how badly you wish to keep me alive. I do not care why you serve me; I only care that you do. Now come stand beside your lord and lady, and fight to the death to protect us if this paladin tries anything."

Sir Joseph nodded very slowly. "Yes…your grace." Lord Fearnow let out a brief chuckle and sat down as Sir Joseph walked across the room.

Sir Judas sheathed his weapons and took a seat at the table, directly across from Lord Fearnow so that there were only a few feet between them. He said nothing, still breathing heavily. Lord Fearnow's lips slowly curled into a most loathsome smile. "What was it you said, Mordecai? That it was evil? Perhaps the worst of evils?" Sir Judas still said nothing. "I should probably tell your friends that we've met before, shouldn't I, Mordecai? Joseph seems quite confused. On the one hand, there is much to explain, yet on the other, there really isn't." Still with that evil smile, Lord Fearnow looked back and forth between David and Joseph. "You see, gentlemen, the question that resolves everything is how you choose to describe the greatest technological achievement of all time. What is your opinion on the pinnacle of what the ancient world ever brought forth?"

David's eyes went wide. He blurted out, "You can't possibly mean…is it real?"

Lord Fearnow answered, "Oh, it's real, David. It's very real. What Mordecai here calls an 'ancient evil,' is the mythical Fountain of Youth. And rather than counting Lady Amanda and I as blessed for having tasted its waters, he brands us as 'abominations.' Did you hear him say that? He called us 'abominations.' So much for all that Christian love and tolerance. Such a dreadful word they reserve for anyone who breaks free from their idolization of death and suffering." Tears began welling up in Lady Amanda's eyes, and her shaking became gradually worse.

Lord Fearnow paused, waiting for Sir Judas to take his bait. The black knight remained silent.

As terrible realization dawned on Sir Joseph, he asked, "Wait, so…your father, who I served before you…was that actually?"

"Yes, Joseph, that was me. All of the good 'my father' ever did for you was actually me when I had grown older. At the time my father 'passed away,' I drank from the Fountain again and became the 'third' Lord Benjamin Fearnow. We've always been very careful through these years to avoid too many public appearances, and we keep the household staff always rotating, lest someone–like Mordecai here–should realize the family resemblance is a little too strong, and extends to the lady as well as the lord." Unable to control her crying any longer, Lady Amanda covered her face and turned away. Lord Fearnow rolled his eyes at her womanly weakness.

He waited again for Sir Judas to say something. The black knight continued to hold his silence. Growing frustrated, Lord Fearnow tried again to bait him. "My 'grandfather' was also me, you know. My first life. He was the one who slew your beloved king! Do you wish to accuse me of regicide again? I would be happy to tell you why I did it! It's not hard to justify my cause!"

More silence.

Sir Joseph weakly asked, "Fearnow…what have you done? The king died at the Battle of Nouen when the castle of the royal city collapsed on him. You don't honestly mean to suggest…do you?"

"Yes. I did it. I killed him like a man. Killed him right to his face, didn't I Mordecai?"

More silence.

"Damn you," Sir Joseph cursed, crying slightly. "I always knew you had dark secrets, but this is far beyond my wildest suspicions. You killed your king? Say what you will about his laws, but I've never heard anyone question his character. How could you bring yourself to kill such a good man?"

Lord Fearnow's malevolent grin vanished, and in an instant he was frowning. "That's a false division, Joseph. You can't divide a man's life into pieces like that. You can't say, 'Good man, bad ruler.' It's all one. The wicked tyranny with which he ruled was the natural fruit of his warped and twisted religion. His evil rule sprang from an evil heart. Ancient superstition and backwards morality made him outlaw the greatest things. Joy, comfort, freedom, life. Life everlasting! In Chelles we found the means to make all men live forever. The pie in the sky pipedream that Christianity had peddled for millennia was finally right there for the taking. And what did the king say when I told him? Did he rejoice and ask me to save him?"

Lord Fearnow leapt up and slammed the table. "No! He rejected it! Threw it away! It didn't fit with his vision for how life everlasting was supposed to work! He told me to destroy it! The salvation of the world was at hand, and he told me to nail it to a cross and kill it! Murderer! Murderer! Everyone who has ever died from the time of his reign down to the present is blood on the king's hands! He's the greatest murderer who ever lived, and I'm glad I took his life!" Lady Amanda collapsed into a ball on the floor, weeping bitterly. A sob came forth from her breast every time Lord Fearnow said the word, 'murderer'.

David asked, "But Lord Fearnow…the king has been dead for so long. Why haven't you shared the Fountain of Youth with all the world yet? There's nothing he can do to stop you now."

Lord Fearnow narrowed his eyes, and glared at Sir Judas as he answered, "The king is gone, David, but his poison lingers. It may be hard to believe now, but forty years ago this realm was thoroughly Christian, obsessed with dying, going to heaven, and whatever the king told them to do, since he had 'divine authority.' Even if most people aren't devout anymore–thank God for that–their perception of good and evil is still warped and twisted by years of Christian culture. We've been trying to heal those wounds in Chelles, but it's slow and painful work, especially when so many people still hold the king in high regard. 'He was such a good man' as Sir Joseph put it. If the king had drunk from the Fountain and entered the new golden age, the people would have surely followed. Instead he rejected it, and the whole realm still holds his prejudices."

"Yeah, but...I still don't get it...even if most people would reject the Fountain of Youth, why not offer it to anyone who would take it? I know I would. I bet most people would. If there are people who want to die, let them die off, but the rest of us can live forever. Why not share the Fountain with whoever wants it? I still don't understand..."

Lord Fearnow hissed in the direction of Sir Judas, "What you don't understand, David, is just how strong the prejudice of these Christians is. They won't be content to let us live in peace. They won't be content to say, 'I go to my eternal reward, but that poor fool is stuck in earthly pleasures.' Oh no. They want to 'save us,' David. They want to save us...that means calling us abominations. That means hunting down the abominations. The Christians say, 'No, it's not good enough for me to die and go to heaven. I need to kill every abomination and make sure they go to hell. I'll let them repent and go to heaven if they want. After all, I'm really trying to save them.' It's a twisted logic, David. I hope that much is clear. They don't just want God to reward the good. They want him to punish the evil as well. One of their theologians once said, 'The just in heaven will look upon the damned in hell and rejoice.' That should tell you everything you need to know about them. Did you see how Mordecai wanted to kill me and my wife mere moments ago? Do you see how even now he stares at us with such hostility? He would strike us dead if I hadn't tricked him into giving his word. I know I pretended to threaten you to get that promise out of him, but I hope you understand. I would never actually hurt a child, but that's how these paladins are. He would have killed us unless I pretended to threaten you, but since there was one innocent life in the way, well, he lays down his arms. Even now he won't kill us because he gave his 'sacred word.' He would rather let two abominations run amok than commit even one little venial sin. No concept of the greater good. No vision for how to make the world better. They attack sin with all the violence they can master, yet are utterly impotent in the end. Do you see how twisted these people are, David? Joseph? Do you see how bizarre and backwards his mind is? Yet tell me I'm wrong. Is he not sitting there, even now, exactly the way that I described it? If we shared the Fountain of Youth with the whole world, self-appointed paladins like this one would ride in from the hinterlands and fill the streets with blood, just to 'save us' all from being abominations. I once read a historian who speculated that's what the Great Calamity may have been. The civil war that arose between people who say they want everlasting life with their lips, and those who would take everlasting life with their deeds. I love that theory. 'The Great Calamity.' The collision between the Christian dream and the Christian reality. A greater calamity the world has never seen."

Fearnow was breathless, panting as he leaned forward and put both hands on the table. "Well Mordecai? Does the great and mighty paladin have any defense? Any answer? When I insulted your honesty, you were pretty swift to tell me I was wrong. Now I've gone and insulted far more than that! Your religion, your king, your God, it's all rubbish. Do you have any retort? Is there anything I've overlooked? Or am I right in saying your delusions are the feverish dreams of a disease that is slowly killing the world?" Lord Fearnow was prepared to go on further, having grown accustomed to Sir Judas's silence. His pause was merely for dramatic effect, but in that pause Sir Judas now opened his mouth and spoke.

"Where are your children?"

Lady Amanda let loose a blood curdling shriek. She rose up off the floor and fled the room with her hands over her face.

Lord Fearnow was still leaning on the table. His whole body began to tremble, and he seemed to be in danger of his arms giving out beneath him. "Lady Amanda is barren. She always has been."

"You lie."

Lord Fearnow took a step like he was going to leap across the table, then he backed away. The paladin asked once more, "Where are your children?"

"We never had any! Stop trying to change the subject! Whether we are able to have children has nothing to do with this discussion."

"It has everything to do with what we are discussing. It proves the great and violent tempest of your words is ultimately just empty wind, shaking the leaves a little too loudly and making an irksome noise. If you wish to have a serious discussion of Christian doctrine, Lord Fearnow, then hold your tongue and be silent for a moment. You are awfully quick to profess the beliefs of Christians on our behalf. Now open your ears and hear our creed from the mouth of someone who actually believes it:

"God can do all things; He does not need any servants. God has all joy within Himself; He was not bored or in need of us to entertain Him. In the Heart of the Most Blessed Trinity is a superabundance of love, and while it was possible for God to rejoice entirely in His own love for all future ages, it is in the nature of love and joy and goodness to desire to share themselves with others. Those things yearn to be poured out in the lives of those who lack them, even if those people do not yet exist. This is why God created all of the angels and us men, not for His sake, but for ours. He had all love and goodness, and He desired that we should have them too.

"Now through the inscrutable and hidden judgments of God, a most mysterious decree was made. The reasons for the decree we may never know, yet the decree itself is known by all: That God entrusted to man and woman the great creative power only He Himself can wield, allowing them to be the ministers of His divine omnipotence, appointing husband and wife as co-creators. He made them like unto Himself, so that like Him they may say, 'We have so much love. Let us make a man in our own image and likeness, so that he may have this love as well.'

"And now I ask a third time; where are your children, Benjamin? Where are the heirs to your inheritance? You claim to hold the keys to eternal life. You claim your earthly paradise is coming. Is there no one you wish to share it with? Do you not desire for children to enter into your joy? When David asked why you have not shared this wonder, you pled the prejudice of Christians. I do not believe you, yet I will yield that point. Why not raise your own child and let him drink from the Fountain of Youth? Could you not have raised a son with the proper beliefs, when he was constantly under your tutelage? Is the specter of Christian bigotry so haunting that you would deny a daughter a share in your joy? No. Your world is miserable because of your own decisions, not the Christian boogeymen you say surround you. You have no children because you don't wish to invite anyone into the world of sorrows that is inside of your own heart."

"Hypocrite!" Fearnow yelled. "You would lecture *me* about children, when you yourself have none and have sworn you never will?"

"In this realm I have many children, just according to the spirit and not the flesh."

"Wrap it in whatever pretty language you want. The facts are the same. You have a dream. Your 'quest.' You see that children are a stumbling block that would prevent you from ever achieving your dream. So what do you do? You decide to never have children. Then you're free to follow your dreams without having an anchor tied around your neck. You're no better than me.

You're just like all of those priests who used to afflict us with sermons about how we need to have more children. Meanwhile they themselves had none."

"Not so," Sir Judas answered, "The chasm between us is far greater than pretty language. In the forty years I have been coming to save Sir Samson, I have never abandoned nor forsaken a single one of my children. My duties always require me to press on and part from them physically, yet I never cease to pray for them every day and beg God to give them everything they need in my absence. Can you say the same? Is the world filled with those you guard and treasure? Poor Lady Amanda ran from this room in horror when I asked about your children. I will not dare to repeat the rumors that are told of the Fountain, but suffice to say I do not see any heirs to all your joy."

Lord Fearnow now stormed towards the doors he had come in by, cursing every step of the way. When he reached them, he stopped and yelled, "Do you really think you are oh so wise? Has your religion really made you so insightful? Everything must seem so simple from the clouds you sneer at us from, but come down to earth with the rest of us! You might be surprised by what you find!" He threw the door open and waved for Sir Judas to follow. "Come with me now, and I will show you the error of your ways!"

Sir Judas arose, and slowly followed after Lord Fearnow. David and Sir Joseph came right behind. Lord Fearnow led them through a few small rooms, up a staircase, and then into the master bedroom. Lady Amanda was laying on the bed, weeping bitterly into her pillow. She lifted her puffy red face and yelled, "Why did you bring them here? Leave me alone!"

"Shut up. We didn't come for you."

Lord Fearnow walked to the window in the room, looking out through the western wall. There was a chalkboard next to it with dozens of scattered numbers, lines of math, and city names like 'Troja,' 'Valsmark,' and 'Pennyworth.' The handwriting of the equations and numbers were from many different people, yet in huge letters at the bottom of the chalkboard, a single hand had emphatically written three foreboding lines:

END OF CHELLES; 36 DAYS

END OF BRIT; 7 MONTHS

END OF THE WORLD; 1 YEAR, 7 MONTHS

"Behold, last of the holy Christian warriors! The end of all things! Not a sudden, fiery second coming by the God who said, 'Let there be light,' but rather the slow, icy death of the ever approaching darkness." Looking out the window, Sir Judas saw pure blackness, as if staring into the dead of night when clouds have hidden the moon and stars. Knowing it was still only evening, he walked over to the window in surprise. Now that he was closer, he could look up and see the blue sky above them. He could look down and see the stone of the city wall meeting the green of the field that came up to it. If he looked straight ahead he could see the ocean, and the sun slowly beginning to sink down towards it. Yet if he turned his gaze a little to the left, blackness overtook him. The darkness had a strange and disorienting effect, where even the light from his peripheral vision was taken away. When he looked at the darkness he did not see sun, sky, sea, or field. Even the curtains and the wall right next to him all vanished and fled away.

Darkness. All he saw was darkness.

"It's coming for us, Mordecai. Coming for all of us. It used to be just Castle Nightfall and its surrounding lands, and we all thought Goliath had disappeared into his own little Void. Good riddance. Many of my peers went to their graves believing that. Only Lady Amanda and I lived long enough to learn the truth. The darkness is growing…very slowly at first. We didn't even notice for the longest time. Then we ignored it, thinking our memories were just wrong about where the boundaries had always been. But then it became undeniable. It was approaching Pennyworth. A panic was brewing. The leaders of that town spent so much time trying to figure out how to slow it down. Talking, talking, talking. Looking for tricks to prolong the inevitable. Only I held the real solution. The final solution.

"Fire is fought with fire, and the Void must be fought with the Void. I unleashed the ancient technologies and their unbridled power of distraction. It was impossible to stop the darkness, but I could at least make sure men didn't think about it. Didn't worry about it. Didn't feel the same despair that consumes those of us who look away from the electric tower.

"For decades I've been tracking the darkness closely, having a few talented math mages measure the progress and write their equations. Then they made me kill them, for they were starting to suggest we had to tell people. They didn't see the point. They didn't get it. I had to build an entire Committee of hand-picked souls who understood telling people was the worst thing we could ever do. 'In seven years we will all be dead. You might add a month to your life if you move further away.' That wouldn't help them. Only I could help them. I had the power to give a life of peace and tranquility. No fear, no anxiety, just a moment of confusion, the cold, and then a sudden death. That's my dream for them. That's why I conquered every city south of here and lured the people to come outside my walls. Eventually panic will spread like wildfire, but by then it will be too late. The darkness is picking up speed as it goes. Doubling in size every so often. Chelles will be in panic one week, and the next it will be no more. Brit will be in panic one day, and the next it will be no more. At the end it will grow so swiftly that entire cities will vanish before they know what hit them.

"Nevertheless, I fear, at some point everyone who is left will head for the Antipode Islands. That's where Lady Amanda and I are going. It's the furthest place in the entire world from Castle Nightfall. The last bastion of humanity. We'll go there, and wait, our immortal life reduced to less than two years. The swarm of rats fleeing the sinking ship of this world will eventually come together, and then we shall crush and climb one another, as the wave of annihilation sweeps in from every side. No electro-lantern can brighten the darkness, and no spell can slow it down. Lady Amanda and I had hoped you were a powerful wizard who would save us, but our hope was vain. A mere paladin is what you turned out to be. You have some white magic, I'm sure, but not what we need to save us. You are no ray of sunshine. You're just a trick of the light.

"Now let us speak of children, Mordecai. Is my heart lacking in joy? Is my promised paradise of eternal youth a lie? Yes, yes it is. But look into that black portal to hell and tell me, am I not right for acting thus? Who would bring a child into this world, just for it to scream and die before it reaches the age of two? Oh, we could have had children earlier, you may say. But what's the right amount of life? Five years? Ten? Twenty? One hundred? How many years of life does a child need to have before the parents aren't guilty of cruelty for bringing it into the world? We have no children because we are merciful. Only someone with a soul as black as that Void would bring forth children knowing what we know."

By the time Lord Fearnow had finished speaking, both David and Sir Joseph were pale and stricken. A great dread had come upon them. Sir Judas continued to look out the window. Still looking into that awful darkness, he said, "Death will come for you eventually, Benjamin, no matter how deeply you drink from the Fountain of Youth. Christ will come again, but even if He didn't, someday all the stars would burn out and the sun would go dim, and you would perish just the same. The everlasting life you long for does exist, but death is its portal, not its enemy. The Fountain of Youth does not speed you on your journey. It forces you to tarry longer in this vale of tears.

"Now let me cut through your excuses, for you have many indeed. If the darkness was gone and you saw the afternoon sun on an unblemished horizon, would you then say, 'Times are good. Let us bring children into this world.'?"

"A moot point," Lord Fearnow answered. "The darkness is here. Playing the 'what if' game only fills a man with misery."

"It is not moot!" Sir Judas now turned towards him, and looked directly at Lord Fearnow. "I am going to slay Goliath! I am going to save Sir Samson! And somehow, someway, in the process, this darkness is going to be dispelled. Tomorrow morning the sun shall rise, and Castle Nightfall shall see its setting. So I ask again, if you look out this window, and there is no darkness, and you see your bride in the evening twilight, will you then say, 'Times are good. Let us bring forth children.'?"

"Yes!" Lady Amanda shouted, jumping up off the bed and throwing herself down at Sir Judas's feet. "Yes! Please! Oh, I'm so sorry, Mordecai. I'm so sorry for all I've done to you! This is my fault! It's all my fault! I'm the reason for the darkness! I'm the reason we are all dying! I'm the reason for my husband's despair that has made him despise the fruit of my womb! It's all my fault! I've ruined everything, and there is nothing I can do to fix it! But please, Mordec–I mean, Sir Judas. Please. I know you have the power. I feel it swirling all about you. Please, save us! Save me! Save me from the curse I brought on my own head!"

Sir Judas looked at her in amazement. "Lady Amanda, what are you talking about?"

"It was me! It was me!" She cried at his feet, softly whimpering that phrase over and over. "It was me..."

Lord Fearnow looked at her with utter contempt, despising her more than he had hated anyone in his entire life. More than he had even hated *her* in every moment prior to this one. "Shut your mouth, pathetic woman. Didn't I already tell you to be quiet? You can't take credit for the deeds I've done. You were a pencil. I was the author. You are nothing more than a tool in my hand."

He looked back to Sir Judas. "You are right that I will die, Mordecai. All my life I have tried to fight it. I've stretched my yarn as far as it will go, and the furthest extent is less than two years from now. Yet as I look at you, and consider all the things for which you stand–your king, your empire, your totally revolting religion–I must confess, I have finally found a cause for which I am willing to end my life.

"'No greater love has man than this, to lay down his life to save a friend.' Thus your Savior supposedly spoke, but I give you my words instead. 'No greater malice has man than this, to lay down his life to damn an enemy.' That's what I want for you, Mordecai. I want to lay down my life so that you will see that I am right. That it's all hopeless. That it's all doomed. I want it to be you who is huddled in the Antipode Islands, clinging to the last moments of light as your prison shrinks ever closer. I want you to murder me, Mordecai! Kill me! Go ahead and do it!"

Sir Judas put his hands up, away from his blades. "What are you talking about? What are either of you talking about? You're raving like a pair of lunatics!"

"Maybe we are Mordecai, maybe we are. But even raving lunatics can still say what's true. That's exactly what I'm about to say to you. If I told you every lie in the world, you might forgive me, but you would never forgive me if I told the truth. You would never let me walk out of this room alive! What I have done cries out to heaven for vengeance, and the sword is on your hip! This is the truth, Mordecai! Strike me dead once you have heard it!

"When Samson came to Chelles it was to answer my warnings about a giant named Goliath. There was no giant, but there was danger–the trap that I was laying. We ate and drank, and spoke of the paladins, and the sacrifice they make of a wife and children. I pressed him on it, needled away, sowing little seeds of regret. He was a passionate man, and I played to his passions, speaking of all the joys he would never know. And then I had this wretched woman cast her spell, the same one I made her use on you. Only where she failed me in your case, against Samson she succeeded. He ran to her like a dog. From the highest heavens he fell into hell, and what a crater the impact made.

"When horror came upon him and he realized what he had done, I fanned the flames of his despair. I played up how unforgivable was his crime, and the wrath that was sure to come upon him. And then I had Amanda feed him his only escape. I broke him, Mordecai! I broke him, and refashioned him according to my own image! He drank from the Fountain of Youth to protect himself from your God's vengeance after death. He ran around gathering an army to protect him from your king. And when the time came, Amanda taught him the blackest spell, the one that would raise up a Leviathan, to give him a power so great that no paladin could overcome it. Your master fell from the Garden of Eden, and I was the serpent whispering in his ear.

"Do you hear me, Mordecai? Do you hear me? Do you understand why I laughed when you told me your quest? It was all in vain! Your life was lived in vain! You cannot save Sir Samson from Goliath! Sir Samson *IS* Goliath!"

....

One of the greatest challenges for any historian is investigating stories that seem like they cannot possibly be true. It is hard to wade through so many second-hand, hearsay accounts, where everyone claims to know for a fact what is possibly just a rumor. Moreover, if you do find the truth, and the strange, outlandish tales turn out to be real, your peers and more 'academic' historians will ridicule your labors. They say you were deluded by fables that only children would ever believe.

For the sake of my own reputation, and to lend legitimacy to this account, I will now suspend my usual writing style and record the story that I heard from the mouth of Sir David directly. He was obviously an eyewitness to this event, and his memory of it was crystal clear. What follows is a verbatim transcript of what he said to me in our interview:

I remember being so shaken...I couldn't believe it. I didn't even understand what was really going on, you know? I was just a child. I wasn't old enough to remember the Grand Empire. I had never met Sir Samson or Goliath. In one sense they were just names to me, and yet...even back then, they were more than that. I didn't fully understand what had been suggested between Sir Samson and Lady Amanda, but I didn't need to. Even a child can understand evil. When Lord Fearnow gave that speech, I encountered evil in a way I had never met it before. It felt like this demon who had been hovering over the entire dinner had finally been unmasked.

I was terrified. I wanted to cry. Actually, I did start crying. It was awful. There was this horrible gaping wound of evil in the world, and more than anything else, I wanted someone to somehow heal it. That's exactly what Sir Judas did. He had been standing with his arms raised away from his weapons– a pledge that he would *not* kill Lord Fearnow. Yet when the lord had spoken, his left hand slowly descended, and gripped *Caritas* so firmly that his knuckles were turning white.

I remember him walking towards Lord Fearnow slowly...oh, so slowly...every footstep was so loud, because the rest of the room was silent. He walked up to him so that they were inches apart...thud...thud...thud...They were eye to eye. A part of me wanted Sir Judas to walk away, just to prove Lord Fearnow wrong. To put this whole thing behind us. I did not yet understand what Sir Judas had always been saying. You can't run from darkness. You need to confront it, face to face.

They stood there for an unbearable length of time. Then Lord Fearnow hissed, "Do it...do it! You know it's what I deserve!" Sir Judas pulled *Caritas* out of its scabbard. "Yes! Do it! Admit that I am right!" Sir Judas took his right hand and grabbed Lord Fearnow's hair, tipping his head back. I couldn't help thinking his neck was totally exposed. "Yes! Yes! This is exactly what I want!" Lord Fearnow was practically in ecstasy.

And then it happened. Sir Judas kissed him. He pulled him close and kissed him on the forehead and at that moment *Caritas* erupted into a blaze of golden flames. I talked to Sir Joseph later, and he never saw the flames, so it must have been a vision. But I saw the fire burn all around Sir Judas. It was exactly how I had pictured Sir Samson when I heard the story of that one battle. Sir Judas was a man on fire.

The flames spread to Lord Fearnow, but there was a darkness fighting back against them. The darkness looked like all these squirming tentacles at first. Only once the fire had completely surrounded him did I realize what they were. A brood of vipers. Dozens of black snakes, constricting Lord Fearnow's arms, legs, neck, and heart. They were all flailing around in that golden fire. Lord Fearnow was flailing too, trying to pull away from Sir Judas but unable to do so.

Then I heard the snakes cry out, "RELEASE US! RELEASE US! WE NO LONGER WISH TO TEMPT THIS FOOL! LET US PLUNGE OURSELVES INTO THE HOTTEST FIRES OF HELL, FOR THEY ARE COLD AS ICE COMPARED TO THE FLAMES WITH WHICH WE ARE NOW AFFLICTED!" And then one of the snakes reared back and bit Sir Judas. It disappeared. Another one attacked him. It disappeared too. As one, they all snapped at Sir Judas, biting his hands and neck and face, disappearing as soon as they did, and then there were none left.

At that moment Lord Fearnow finally pulled away, and then the vision of the fire subsided. But before it went out, I definitely saw a little ember, smoldering on his brow, looking like it might also start to burn. Lord Fearnow yelled, "What are you doing? Kill me! Stab me! Slit my throat! Rebuke me for all the evil I have done to you!"

And Sir Judas said, "May God rebuke thee. For myself, I forgive you."

Lord Fearnow grabbed his own hair and pulled on it, his eyes going wide in his crazy anger. "NOOOOOO! I don't want your forgiveness! I want you to kill me!"

Sir Judas answered, "I forgive you, and not only do I forgive you, but from the bottom of my heart I thank you. For forty years I have been marching to Castle Nightfall, intending to do battle and slay the giant Goliath. Now, at the eleventh hour, when the day of reckoning is nearly at hand, you have revealed to me the truth. You have saved me from killing my master, and making the greatest mistake of my entire life. Thank you, Benjamin. Thank you. Your voice to me is like the voice of an angel, bringing glad tidings from heaven...even if they are hard to hear."

And then he walked away. I was weeping. I don't know if it was from sorrow or from joy, but I was weeping. Sir Samson was alive. That much we knew for certain. It was not merely a prophecy, but a proven fact. It was both wonderful and terrible, all at the same time. Sir Judas walked out, and Sir Joseph and I followed. Then Sir Joseph left us to go to his house. Lord Fearnow was in so much shock and rage that he didn't think to send the guards or the Committee after us until we were already gone. Sir Judas walked out of the palace, out of the city, and then collapsed just outside the gate of Chelles.

There was one other thing I forgot to mention...it was important, because it came up later. As we were leaving, Lady Fearnow was weeping and looking ashamed, but Lord Fearnow was raving like a madman. He was so carried away in his fury–or maybe it was that other thing that came up later– that he called Sir Judas 'Sir Judas.' Ever since he found out who he was, he had been calling Sir Judas 'Mordecai.' Yet as we were leaving, Lord Fearnow was sarcastically ridiculing and shouting, "Ecce homo! Behold the man! A great and noble knight, with virtue surpassing every other soul on earth! Will he avenge his king? No! His Empire? No! His master? No! He won't even avenge himself, because God said it was a sin! Ecce homo! Behold the man! Sir Judas, Last of the Kingsguard! This man is *truly* incorruptible!"

Chapter 7: Walking in the Moonlight

"Another good day done," Sir Samson said, tethering his horse to a peach tree. "How are you feeling, Mordecai? Up for an evening stroll to stretch your legs?"

"Aye," the squire answered, "Nothing would feel better about now."

After briefly looking around, Sir Samson pointed up the lightly wooded ridge they were on. "Uphill march? A little extra work for the legs on the way up, and then we'll be rewarded with a good view of the sunset and an easier walk on the way down."

"Sounds good." They began making their way up the ascent, following some winding deer trails until the trees opened up enough to move freely. Mordecai asked, "So how did the meeting with the duke go today?"

"Bah. As good as it always does. I say, 'You're free to rule however you want, but there's these few rules the king has that are non-negotiable.' Then he says, 'I want to be a part of the Empire, I really do, but I just need a few concessions that are non-negotiable.' And wouldn't you know it, Mordecai, but his list of non-negotiable concessions is in direct contradiction with the king's list of non-negotiable rules. Happens every time. Absolutely every time."

"So what do you do when that happens?" Mordecai asked.

"Stand there, look tough, and say, 'Non-negotiable means non-negotiable.' And then he spends all day trying to negotiate with me, until after wasting a spectacular amount of time achieving exactly nothing, him and his administrators say, 'I think we made some great progress today. We're going to take some time to review, and send an ambassador once we put our proposal together.' The diplomatic process is an absolute joke, only nobody's laughing because it's not very funny."

Mordecai laughed.

"I mean it! Why do you find it funny?" Sir Samson's scowl broke into a smile after a moment. "Fine, it's a little bit funny. But it's sad too. The king doesn't ask for much. All he really says is, 'No going to war with your neighbors, no witchcraft, no sins that cry out to heaven for vengeance, and we're good to go.' Why am I always dealing with people who find these rules so unreasonable?"

"They find it pretty reasonable when Sir Daniel asks…maybe *you're* the problem?"

"I'm not the problem! He gets all the easy jobs! The king's best friends and the oldest members of the Empire? Of course they do whatever Sir Daniel asks! But the people who would sell their own mother on a slave market if she fetched the right price? Then the king sends me to look tough and say, 'Non-negotiable means non-negotiable.'"

"I'm sorry, sir, I didn't mean to agitate you."

"No, I'm not agitated. You meant it in jest, and I can take a good ribbing. Sir Daniel knows that too. When he's in a mood to joke about our assignments, he leans into me a lot harder than you just did." Sir Samson now used a ridiculous falsetto to impersonate his much smaller brother in arms. "'You catch more flies with honey than with a fly swatter, Samson. Maybe if you turned on the charm the flies would be nicer to you.' Oh, he thinks he's funny. Sometimes he is. I'm gonna miss the little man." They had just reached the top of the hill. The sun was already set, but the sky was still burning beautifully where it had passed. The moon was fully risen.

"Miss him? Is he going somewhere?"

"Not him. Me. My next assignment is taking me out to the western edge of the empire. That little lord who's always visiting from Chelles says a giant is harassing his lands. I'm supposed to investigate, and then assemble a posse from the locals if there really is a threat to deal with."

"Oh, this is wonderful! Chelles is in the Land of Ire, just west of Brit. It's a whole island nation. Not quite an archipelago, but I think it will still be fascinating. Did you know there's a tunnel under the sea that connects Brit to Frank? I don't know if it would be more exciting for us to go by land or by sea…"

"You're not going." Mordecai looked at Sir Samson in shock. "The king and I have already talked it over. As soon as we report back to the royal city after this diplomatic circuit, your tenure as my squire is over."

"S-Sir Samson, I-I don't understand. What have I done to upset you?"

"You didn't do anything to upset me, Mordecai. Quite the opposite, really. Every other squire I ever had annoyed me to death after a week…you're pretty annoying too, but you have some redeeming qualities that make you worth the trouble." Sir Samson gave a wink. "Either way, it doesn't matter. This wasn't my decision, but the king's. He asked me, 'If one of the Kingsguard fell ill tomorrow, would you recommend Mordecai be initiated into the Lessguard?' and I told him, 'Yes I would, not a doubt in my mind.' Then he told me the Kingsguard was going to have a vacancy soon. Didn't tell me who, but Geoffori's the oldest by a good margin. Don't go spreading that rumor, now, that's just my speculation. So the king told me that before I took off for Brit, I was to initiate you into the Lessguard." Sir Samson smiled. "Congratulations, Mordecai. You're going to be a paladin."

"I...I...oh, Sir Samson!" Mordecai threw his arms around him, tears of joy in his eyes. "I...I'm so grateful! Oh, thank you so much! I'm not worthy of this honor!"

"No, none of us are." Sir Samson let go and looked straight up at heaven. 'Domine, non sum dignus.' That's about the only bit of the Ancient Tongue I know. I say it all the time, even when I'm not at Mass. Anytime I get some lucky break or a good compliment, I just say, 'Domine, non sum dignus.' Lord, I am not worthy." Sir Samson now looked down towards the horizon, taking in the way the colors changed from north to south.

"I'm going to miss you, Sir Samson."

"I'm going to miss you too, kid."

"Sir Samson, I'm almost thirty."

"In my mind you'll always be that ten-year-old kid who wouldn't stop begging me for stories about knights."

They stood there for a while, watching the night sky grow dark together. "Do you have any advice for me before I stop being your squire?"

"That's a question for Sir Geoffori. He's a much better advice giver."

"Right now I'm not looking for riddles and proverbs. I'm looking for your best, practical advice."

"Well in that case, go ask Sir Daniel. He's the holiest knight we have. Stick with him, and you'll be walking on water in no time."

"Sir Samson! Stop deflecting! Why can't you give me a straight answer?"

Sir Samson bit his lower lip, then said, "Because I'm not that good of a knight. If you're looking for role models or advice, there are six better members of the Kingsguard to go to."

"The king doesn't think so. God doesn't think so. They both put me here with you as your squire. Not Sir Geoffori, nor Sir Daniel, nor anyone else. They both thought I should learn how to be a paladin by studying the life of Sir Samson. You could argue the king made a mistake, but God knows all things. He knows where I'm supposed to be. And where I'm supposed to be is on a hill right now with Sir Samson. Maybe you don't have the wisest or the holiest thing to say, but nevertheless, maybe it's exactly what I need to hear."

Sir Samson took a deep breath and folded his arms. "Tenacious little kid wants some advice…what could I even give you?" An idea dawned on him and he snapped his fingers. Then he pointed upwards and said, "Learn to appreciate the moon, Mordecai. Maybe even learn to love it."

Mordecai looked up at the waxing gibbous, trying to find the deeper meaning. "I know the moon is often associated with the passing things of this world…obviously, that's not what you're trying to tell me…it can also be a reference to Mary and the saints since they don't have any light on their own, but rather they reflect the sunlight, which is a symbol of God…is that what you're saying? That I should pray to the saints more often?"

"No, you dunderhead! I'm talking about the moon! The big glowing rock in the sky! Oh my goodness…" They both began to laugh.

Mordecai tried to justify himself. "But, I mean, the moon is just the moon. I figured there must be some sort of profound allegory you were driving at. What is there in the moon that is so lovable?"

"It's the light we really need, kid. The light that shines in the darkness. The sun gets all the credit for being brighter and warmer, but think about it. The sun shines during the day, when it's already bright out. If the sun goes behind a cloud, we realize we don't actually need it. We can still see just fine because it's daytime. But the moon? That's the light we couldn't do without. When the moon is shining we can walk in the night. The moment it's gone, all we see is darkness."

Sir Samson looked up, smiling proudly at his little reflection. "Ah, the moon…take the sun if you need it, Mordecai…I'll be happy just to have the moon…You'll understand if you're ever lost and afraid in the middle of a pitch black night. Pray for the moon, and let God guide your way."

By now the sun's light was completely gone, but the moon and the stars were still shining brightly upon them.

"Sir Samson, I have a question."

"What is it, kid?"

"Do you have any idea how sunlight works?"

"I was speaking in riddles, you dunderhead!"

"Sir Samson…Sir Samson!" David wasn't sure whether Sir Judas was asleep or not. He seemed to be in some sort of in-between state where he was still conscious, yet exhausted with grief. Once more the old knight quieted down, laying so still that David thought he was finally resting. But then he whispered again, "The night is dark Lord…it's so very dark…send me the moon…please send the moon…"

After some time, Sir Joseph emerged from the city gate, wearing his armor and riding his horse. David and Sir Judas were not far from the gate, just out of the way enough to avoid the traffic. Sir Joseph saw them and dismounted, running over to kneel beside Sir Judas. "Is he alright? Sir Judas! Sir Judas! Wake up! What are you doing? Why are you just laying here?"

The black knight barely opened his eyes. "Grief. Grief has crushed me, Sir Joseph, and I do not know how these bones can revive."

Sir Joseph shook his head angrily. "Fearnow…that monster has to pay for what he's done…I should have struck him dead in his bedroom when I had the chance!"

"He is your lord, Sir Joseph. Serve him well."

"Serve him? Are you delirious, man? Do you even know what you're saying?"

"He's your master, Sir Joseph…serve him well…remember our discussion from earlier. You are a servant of goodness. You are a servant of Fearnow. In all things Lord Fearnow commands you that are not evil, be his good and faithful servant. And if he *does* command you to do evil, then as a good and faithful servant refuse his command and accept the consequences. Who knows? Perhaps the wicked master will be saved by the virtue of his loyal knight."

Sir Joseph grabbed Sir Judas by the shoulders and tried to sit him up. "Now I know you're delirious. That man is pure evil. Any service rendered to him would be spreading evil in the world."

"If Sebastian could find ways to serve Diocletian, then you can find ways to serve Lord Fearnow. Do not despair, Sir Joseph. Even if Lord Fearnow is your enemy, love your enemy. Love and do not hate him…" Sir Judas's head now rolled back, truly unconscious at last.

"Do you have any idea who he's talking about, David? Sebastian and Diocletian? Has he mentioned them to you before?"

"No, not at all."

"Bah…I'll argue with him in the morning. Tonight we need to get him out of town. It's only a matter of time before Lord Fearnow gives permission for Feifer and his henchmen to track him down. The Committee has God knows how many spies outside the walls, and they'll be looking for us soon as well. Come on, help me get him up on Isabella." Sir Joseph and David worked together, trying to get Sir Judas draped over the saddle of Sir Joseph's white courser. Sir Joseph had plenty of strength to lift him, but he was a very short man (David wasn't any taller), and Isabella's withers were above both of their heads, making the task extremely awkward. Eventually they succeeded, and then Sir Joseph led his horse Isabella out of the Chellesian outskirts, accompanied of course by plenty of gawkers, rumor-mongers, and words such as, "Is he dead? You got him, Joseph? Good for you! Thanks for keeping us safe!"

They followed the eastern road out, retracing the same steps David and Sir Judas had come by the previous evening. Once they were out to where most people slept in tents (and those were spaced sparsely) Sir Joseph gently lowered Sir Judas off his horse and laid him on the ground. "Do you have a bedroll or something for him to sleep on?"

"We left our packs at your house. We didn't think to grab them after all that happened."

"Ah! I should have noticed that and grabbed them while I was there. Nothing for it now. I'll ride back home tonight, and my mother and I will meet you out here with your gear tomorrow morning, okay?"

"Your mother?"

Sir Joseph nodded. "I don't know where we're going yet…but now I know for certain that we can't stay here." Sir Joseph looked at Sir Judas once more and laughed. "At least he has his armor. He definitely got that call right…oh, Feifer, that cur! Now I know why he was asking!"

The man and the boy looked at their sleeping elder together. Off to the east, where civilization ended, they heard one of the Bloody Baron's nightmares make a dreadful scream. It snapped them back to their senses. It was time for Sir Joseph to be going.

"Good night, David. See you in the morning."

"Good night, Sir Joseph. We'll be waiting here for you."

Sir Joseph then rode back to Chelles, rushing to make it inside the gate before the sun sank behind the darkness and the city was closed. When it had finally dropped low enough, the sky went from blue-green clouds streaked with purple to total blackness in an instant. Tonight was the new moon. Thick clouds covered the stars. David looked round about, then went to sleep.

Darkness. All he saw was darkness.

Hours later, in the middle of the night, David was sound asleep while Sir Judas was tossing and turning with troubled dreams. Long-forgotten memories of trips and adventures with Sir Samson played through his mind, mixed with a great dread and sorrow over his beloved master's fall from grace. Then came the despair. A dream of Sir Samson chasing an entire army by himself. *My master was so much stronger than me. How could I ever defeat the forces that overcame him?* A dream of Goliath slaying the Kingsguard. *He's so far gone that he would slay his brethren–what hope do I have of changing his heart?* A dream of the giant brooding in his darkness for forty years. *All that time to consume himself...is there even any of the old man left?*

He had a dream where he was crossing blades with Goliath, and he kept yelling, 'Sir Samson! Please, repent!' The giant laughed in his face. 'Thou fool. Did you really think that after forty years you could show up, say the right words, and 'save me?' I like it this way. My darkness will conquer the world, and I shall rule it. Your life is wasted. Die in vain.' Then he swung Doomfall around (which Sir Judas only now realized was once the greatsword *Alacritas*) and struck Sir Judas in the side with a blow so mighty that it killed him through his armor. Sir Judas bolted awake in a terror.

He sat there for several minutes, trying to calm his breathing in the moonlight. There was David, here was *Caritas*. Everything was as it should be. It was just a dream. The one odd thing was the animals. The sheep were bleating the cows were mooing, and the roosters were crowing. All the animals were raising an extraordinary ruckus. Sir Judas looked at one of the farms that had a fence about sixty yards away. The animals were stamping around wildly in immense agitation. No, not agitation...the animals actually seemed happy. It was excitement. *What's gotten into them?* He laid down on his side and recalled that he had not done his usual nighttime routine. He said his prayer for sinners, offering to accept any hardship or difficulty that God would give him for their sake. At this point Sir Judas realized another oddity. He didn't have the pains he experienced every night, neither in his body nor in his soul. "What an unexpected treat. Thank you, God. Tonight I'll get the best sleep I've had in years." Sir Judas closed his eyes and recited the prophecy to himself. "When you see a night illumined by the moon, as if by the sun…" Astonished realization seized him. Sir Judas's eyes opened wide as he rolled onto his back, looked up, and cried, "The moon!"

What he saw took his breath away. Tonight was supposed to be the new moon. Instead the moon was full. The bright, glowing, silver ball was illuminating the entire earth with its light, yet there was so much more to see. The moon was ringed with a bright, chromatic halo, a crisp circular line of pinks, magentas, and greens all mixed together, while there was a distinct region of midnight blue between the ring and the moon. The moon and its halo were in the only part of the sky that was not covered by clouds. Everywhere else there was a striking and dramatic cloud cover as white as at noontime and so clearly visible that the details of every puff and swirl of cloud could be discerned.

"This is the night…This is the night!" Sir Judas leapt for joy, shouting and clapping his hands as he yelled, "Yes! Yes! Thanks be to God!" He fell down on his face and worshiped with tears falling from his eyes to the ground. "My God…I am so sorry for my lack of faith and for my doubts. I know You can do all things, yet in my frailty my confidence wavers. Thank you, O Lord. Thank you for this reassurance that all of Your words shall always come to pass."

David stirred. Sir Judas grabbed him and excitedly shook him awake. "David! Tonight! This is the night!" The boy groggily rubbed his eyes. "What's going on?" David then opened his eyes fully and said, "Whoa! What's that ring around the moon?"

"It's a sign, David! A sign! 'When you see a night illumined by the moon as if by the sun, when a storm has passed…' This is it! The clouds are lit up like noontime! And dinner with Lord Fearnow…or maybe my dreams? That was the storm! Tonight is the night!" Beaming with joy, Sir Judas resumed his routine, reciting the entire prophecy from memory;

When you see a night illumined
By the moon as if by the sun,
When the storm has passed,
Look to the east.

The beast of grateful eye and might

Shall carry you fast...

To the hour when one guard will end

And the new take up his blade

Cleansed from blood by a weapon of Truth.

Try him by combat,

And if he shall overcome,

Open his heart

With the piercing of purest love.

This is it! This is it, David! Tonight is the night!"

David looked around. "So if tonight is the night...what do we do next?"

"I have no idea! Wait, where is Sir Joseph? Maybe he's the one!"

David pointed towards the city. "He went home to get our packs. He said he would come back here first thing in the morning. Should we try to get back inside of Chelles?"

Sir Judas considered it for a moment, but then he remembered the next line. "Look to the east! Chelles lies to the west of us! Come, David, come to the east! To my eyes Sir Joseph seems a worthy choice, but we must trust in God Who sees the hidden things of the heart." Then he took off running, with a burst of vigor that made the years seem to fall off him in an instant.

"Hey! Wait for me!" David yelled, and he ran after Sir Judas as fast as he could. Sir Judas had a head start, and–incredibly–he was widening the gap, bounding east along the road until he had left all of Chelles behind him and was nearing the manor where 'civilization ends.' "Sir Judas! Slow down! I can't keep up!"

Then, instead of slowing down, the knight suddenly stopped. "There they are! Are they? Oh my goodness, they are! Bwahahahahaha!" He stopped and bent over, laughing breathlessly until David caught up with him.

"What is it, Sir Judas? Why are you laughing? Is it those two things over there? What are they? They look a little like horses, but obviously no one would be riding at this hour."

"Look closer, David! Look closer! Those aren't just any old horses!"

David looked again, then in amazement he cried, "Sir Judas! Those horses are purple! And their sunken faces! It's Lightfoot and Buttercup!"

"Yes, David! Exactly! Here they come! Oh, just look at them!" While the two horses were still nightmarish in many ways, their bellies and flanks were noticeably fuller, and their ribs no longer showed at the chest. Whereas back in the glade the two nightmares had been constantly trying to bite Sir Judas, now one of them trotted up to him and nuzzled her head against his face while he patted her and smiled. "Hello, you! Ho, haha…a beautiful reunion if ever there was one! Just look at you! You must be twice as big as when I last saw you! Have you done nothing but eat the last two days? Ahaha! I would have been happy enough to know you were both alright, but it seems our paths are destined for a greater crossing. Tell me, may I ride you?" The horse turned sideways, offering Sir Judas her side. "Thank you! If I recall correctly, you are Buttercup, yes?" Buttercup whinnied. "Then that would make you Lightfoot. Tell me, Lightfoot, would it be alright if David rode you a little ways?" Lightfoot spun with a few fancy steps and then sidled up next to David.

"Atagirl! Alright, David, upsy-daisy!" Sir Judas grabbed David's sides and effortlessly hefted him up on Lightfoot, then he leapt up on Buttercup himself. Having never ridden a horse before, and now sitting atop one bareback, David panicked and grabbed the horse around the neck. "No, none of that now, David! Use your knees. I put you in the perfect spot. Put one hand between the shoulders if you really need support, but don't lay forward like that or you'll have a miserable ride…There you go! Looking better already. Sit up a little straighter…alright, good enough for a first timer!"

Sir Judas now spoke to Buttercup directly and said, "If I may be so blunt, you seem to be a very intelligent creature. Very, very intelligent. Do you perhaps know where we must go tonight? I know I need you to carry me fast, but I know not where you're carrying me. Any help you could provide would be simply marvelous." Buttercup neighed, snorted, and then turned south, trotting in that direction at a brisk clip. Lightfoot cantered to catch up, then trotted alongside her. For an ordinary courser, a trot would travel about eight miles in every hour. Nightmares in general are faster than a courser by half, meaning the trot was about as fast as most men run. At first this frightened David, and he leaned forward to grab Lightfoot about the neck. However, once she started angrily swaying her head back and forth, he recalled that nightmares have fangs that can do some real damage, and he decided it would be better to fall from a happy nightmare than to hang on to an angry one. Sitting upright made things smoother, and before long he was getting comfortable with riding. After a few minutes he was even feeling comfortable enough to enjoy the constant stream of celebration coming from Sir Judas.

"Oh, David, this is the night! For forty years *Veritas* has weighed heavy in its scabbard. So many years of looking for someone who might be worthy! Someone who would be able to shoulder the great weight of continuing the Paladins after me! You can't imagine how many false leads and false hopes I've had. Young men of great innocence, or great courage, or some other great virtue that impressed me. Men who risked life and honor to save their towns, their families, or even perfect strangers. The squire who followed me for twelve years. There was even a young maiden I met in Frank who I thought just might be the one. Oh, David, I've been disappointed more times than I can count, but not tonight! For so many years I've been vigilantly watching for that first sign; 'When you see a night illumined by the moon as if by the sun...' I've looked for so many deeper meanings, so many symbols, like the prophecy was a coded message I had to figure out, 'What did the king mean when he said, 'moon'?' He meant the big glowing rock in the sky, you dunderhead! Haha! Dunderhead indeed! Tonight is the night!"

David was beaming, infected by the joy spilling out of Sir Judas with every breath. As he looked up at the moon, the clouds, the halo, felt the nightmare between his legs, and thought of the prophecy, a curious thought came to his mind. "Sir Judas...do you think you could tell me about the king?"

"Ah, David, to tell you all there was to know about him would take a lifetime. Is there something more specific on your mind?"

"Yeah, I mean...please don't take this the wrong way, Sir Judas, but...everything I've ever heard about the king was either similar to what Sir Joseph or Lord Fearnow said. Either he was a good man but a terrible ruler, or he was a terrible man and a terrible ruler. I never knew whether he was a good man or not, but everyone at least agreed on the part about being a terrible ruler. And yet...when I look at this night he foretold forty years before it happened...when I think of the glow of the weapons that were made from soaking them in his blood...how could someone like that not rule well? If he has so much knowledge, and so much power, and...and so much *beauty* surrounding everything he does...how could he make such ugly laws? Even to this day I *still* hear grownups complaining about this or that awful law he made. I was hoping you might know more than I do." After a brief moment of silence, David added, "Sorry if I ruined the mood, but...I don't understand."

"Oh, no need to be sorry, David. I told you before, and I'll probably tell you again–the old appreciate the young. We have wisdom, but you have simplicity. Wisdom can make things seem very complicated, and complicated things can be stressful. Then a child puts something very simply, and wisdom is delighted that going deeper has made things simpler. I've had a few too many arguments with people over the king's laws, and we always get dragged into the mud of this or that detail of policy. You just cut through it all with wise simplicity. 'Everything surrounding the king was beautiful. Then how could his laws have been ugly?' Now let me see if I can answer your question with as much wisdom as you asked it.

"Tell me, David, are you perfect? Or, since you've heard complaints about the king's laws from adults, would you say the adults in question were all perfect? Were Lord Fearnow and Winthrop and Sir Joseph completely free from any flaw or defect?"

"Of course not. That's a ridiculous question."

"Yes, it is a bit ridiculous, but nevertheless I had to ask. One more question, and then I can give you the answer. If you ever did meet a perfect person, how well do you think you would get along?"

"We'd get along perfectly. Obviously."

"You don't think he would frustrate you or drive you mad?"

"How could he? He would be kind, gentle, loving, and patient. Never angry, never accidentally annoyed. How could he ever frustrate me if he was always acting perfectly?"

Sir Judas laughed. "Oh, David, I'll tell you exactly how he could do it! He would frustrate you and drive you mad because you are not perfect! Which means there would be plenty of occasions where you and this perfect person would not agree. You would find all sorts of things to argue and bicker about, not because he was wrong, but because you were. And then, after you got fed up with 'always being wrong,' you would stop arguing with him and just ridicule him as someone who 'always has to be right.' What's more, every little defect in your actions–every little sin to use the proper word–would always put you and this man in conflict, since his desires include you acting perfectly, while your desires include you acting imperfectly. In many things–most things– he would put up with your flaws and bear them patiently, but when it came to the important things, he would correct you, rebuke you, even oppose you if needed. But you wouldn't even agree on which things were important! I know you aren't familiar with the Scriptures, David, but there are two stories that really illustrate my point.

"Jesus Christ was a Man who was absolutely perfect, which put Him in constant conflict with a group of men called the Pharisees. Jesus was the long-awaited Jewish Messiah, who the Pharisees wanted to come and make Judea into the greatest kingdom that ever existed. Now one of those imperfect ideas the Pharisees had in their head was that if they were going to be the greatest kingdom on earth, they would need to overthrow the Roman Empire and stop paying taxes to Caesar. So they came to Jesus one day to see if He was a good Messiah or not, and they asked Him for a straight answer. 'Do we have to keep paying taxes to Caesar? No more beating around the bush or dodging the question. Tell us right now that You're here to overthrow the Romans and their taxes, or else confess to us that You're not a very good Messiah and we should look for someone else.' And then our Lord Jesus, with utter perfection, told those imperfect men the last thing they wanted to hear. They would have been fine with either of the two options they gave Him, but the perfect answer wasn't even on their minds. He said, 'Bring Me a penny (because He didn't have that much money to His name), and tell Me whose face is on it. It's Caesar's face? Then render unto Caesar what is Caesar's, and render unto God what is God's' He didn't even care about the money! Just throw it away! Let Caesar take his coins back; you Pharisees are focusing on the completely wrong things!

"And then there was the second story, which happened later that same day. After years of being accused and harassed by the Pharisees, and bearing it patiently, the moment finally came when Jesus took them to task for all their sins. He made a long list of why they were wicked, but what a list it was! Included on this list were such sins as 'loving the places of honor at feasts and synagogues,' and, 'loving to be called 'Rabbi'.' Jesus gave a scathing condemnation of the Pharisees, saying they would all be damned if they didn't repent. Now stop and think about it, David. Not only are the Pharisees in conflict with a perfect Man because of their flaws, but think about how much they disagree with Him on which issues really matter. Questions of world government, conquest, oppression, or paying taxes that supported pagan worship? These issues were near and dear to the Pharisees' hearts. The perfect Man did not care. Pride, vainglory, and other matters the Pharisees didn't even blink at? The perfect Man says these are the most critical issues that He must address as He's building His kingdom.

"It's no wonder that people wanted to kill Jesus. The miracle is that there were so many men who loved Him. Men who were humble enough to say, 'You are perfect, and I am not, and I will accept all of the suffering that comes from standing in Your light, because You are worthy of perfect love, and I

cannot give it unless you shine Your light into every dark corner of my soul.'
The perfect Man is a great divider, David. You're either with Him, or you're
against Him. No middle ground, no temporary visits. With Him or against Him,
and not even all of eternity would ever be able to change your mind.

"Now as for the king, I will tell you, David, he was perfect. Not perfect
like Christ or His Blessed Mother, but as perfect as the rest of us can ever hope
to be. He was perfect, and just to spend a minute with him brought all of your
imperfections into the light. There were some of us who accepted that. We gave
him not just a minute, nor an hour, nor a year, but we gave him our entire lives.
He was worth it. His kingdom was worth it. You could never have a more
perfect king. And that's exactly why there were many more people who hated
and reviled him. How could it be otherwise? He brought perfect laws to
imperfect men, and the contradictions were deep and painful."

Sir Judas left off speaking, riding along gently while David pondered
what he had said. He opened his mouth to say, *But that still doesn't explain it
Sir Judas! What about this law or that policy? Clearly those ones were evil!*
But he didn't say that. He was distracted by the white clouds and the beautiful
moon with that mysterious halo. Instead, David said, "I don't know how it's
possible...but I believe it is. Lots of things are true that I just don't understand."

"Well said, David. Wise words indeed. I think you've just summarized
most of what I've learned in seventy years, which means you're fifty-eight
years ahead of me."

The rush of the Eines River was beginning to sound in the distance. Sir
Judas said, "David, concerning the last few lines of the prophecy...it says I
must try this man by combat. Trial by combat is a grisly and ugly thing, and it
may seem at some point that either myself or the next Paladin are in danger. It
is absolutely imperative that you do not interfere. Not by deed, not by word,
not in any way at all. You must let the trial run its course fairly, understood?"

"Of course."

"Very well."

They rode on just a few minutes longer, until the Eines was coming
into sight. At first they didn't see anybody...then they saw a hint of movement
a little to the east...then it was very clear—a man! His outline was visible in the
moonlight. He was at the water's edge, bent over and drinking. "There he is,
David! There he is!" Sir Judas pressed his heels into Buttercup's flanks, and
she took off at a full gallop towards the man. Eager to go faster, yet knowing
nothing of horses, David shifted and bounced around, pushing Lightfoot in

random spots, until he eventually gave up and dismounted, running after Sir Judas on foot.

Sir Judas galloped ahead, shouting to the man he was approaching, "Hail, most fortunate amongst men! I come to announce a great honor and privilege, far exceeding any gift you could ever merit! You have been chosen to succeed me in the great and venerable line of–" The words died in Sir Judas's mouth. He had finally come close enough to see that he knew this man, and he was certainly not the kind of man Sir Judas had been expecting. "...Winthrop."

The robber stood up from the river, water still dripping down his beard. "The great and venerable line of Winthrop? As fate would have it, I'm already a member, but I had no idea it was such a privilege."

"What are you doing here?"

"I'm having a drink. Rivers are good for that. I assumed you were here to re-arrest me, but you actually look surprised to see me. In which case, I ask you the same question."

"I'm looking for someone."

"David? Did you lose him?"

"No, Winthrop! I'm right here!"

Winthrop turned in David's direction and shouted, "David!" then ran to embrace the boy.

Sir Judas had dismounted by now, and he moved to stand in between them. "Not so fast, Winthrop, I have some business I need to discu–" Winthrop shoved the seventy-year-old man aside, sending him tumbling towards the river bank in a rattle of armor.

"David!" Winthrop flung his arms around David and lifted him up off the ground, squeezing him with all his might. He started to cry and dropped to his knees, relaxing his embrace enough to look David in the eyes and say, "David, I'm so sorry. Oh, please forgive me. I never should have walked away and left you. I was just so confused and emotional...I got angry with Sir Judas, which is no excuse, but...oh, I didn't even start thinking until it was too late. I'm sorry! Please forgive me, David! I promise I'll never leave you again! I promise, and I mean that. I know my word hasn't meant much before, but things are going to be different from now on. I'm changing my ways. I don't know where we'll live or what we'll eat, but no more robbing! No more crimes! We're going to find a town where we can settle down, and I'll find honest work, and I'm going to teach you some sort of skill so you can find good, honest work too when you come of age. What do you say, David? Can you forgive me? Does that sound alright to you?"

Tears were welling up in David's eyes as he said, "Yes, Winthrop, I forgive you, and yes that plan sounds wonderful. Nothing would make me happier." He buried his face in Winthrop's chest and said, "Oh, Winthrop, I'm so sorry! I'm the one that should be apologizing to you!"

"You have nothing to apologize for."

"Oh yes I do! I always wanted to go to Chelles, and I was always nagging you and complaining because you wouldn't let me. And then today I finally went in, and it was so evil. So unbelievably evil. Only I didn't realize it at first! I thought everything was wonderful! I wanted to look at that electric tower forever! I didn't know it was evil until Lord Fearnow himself confessed to us that he was using electro-magic as an intentional distraction to make people stop paying attention to life until they suddenly died! It was horrifying, Winthrop! Thank you for keeping me out of that trap! I can never thank you enough, and I'm sorry I didn't listen to you more willingly."

"Whoa, whoa, whoa, slow down, kid. You met Lord Fearnow? And what exactly is he doing with electro-magic?"

"It's as David said," Sir Judas announced, finally catching up with Winthrop. "The doom of this world is racing towards us, and he is doing everything in his power to hide the problem." Sir Judas and David then recounted the events of that day to Winthrop, starting with the attack by the Committee, then moving on to the odd conversation with Lord Fearnow, the spell of Lady Amanda, how Sir Judas learned who the Fearnows really were, the battle that followed, the Fountain of Youth, the fact that Goliath was really Sir Samson, and lastly they told of how the darkness, that ever growing darkness, was creeping across the world to swallow them all.

"That's...that's not possible..." Winthrop muttered. "That's—no way. No one would...no one *could* hide...something like that...is he mad? Is he utterly insane? How could Lord Fearnow possibly know something like that and not tell us? Why would he hide it?"

"In a certain sense, no, I don't think he's mad," Sir Judas answered, "Mentally, I think he may be the sanest atheist I've ever met. It's his spiritual disease that makes him act the way he does. He does not believe heaven will help us overcome the darkness, and no natural means can stop it. Therefore, he is trying to give all men the most pleasure, the least pain, and the least anxiety they can have before the inevitable comes upon them. In another sense, he is insane, but it's a logical insanity. It's the insanity of a man who neither knows nor trusts in God."

Winthrop turned and walked a few steps away. He kicked a loose stone into the river, spat and sneered, "Well I'm glad you've found a solution, Judas. Crazy people aren't worried about the end of the world because they have electric towers. Sane people aren't worried about the end of the world because they have God. Looks like old Winthrop will be the only one who has enough sense to actually worry."

Sir Judas answered, "Is it so outrageous that God will deliver us, Winthrop? This evil was forged by the power of a fallen paladin; why is it unreasonable that it will be destroyed by a faithful one?"

"The *paladins*. Don't make me laugh. Six of them combined couldn't defeat Goliath. Now one old man is going to defeat him all alone?"

"The strength of our order was never in the men, Winthrop. It was always in the God Whom we adored. He decides whether a battle ends in victory or defeat. In His mysterious providence, He decreed that Goliath should triumph over my six brethren. In the coming battle He will decree that the paladins triumph instead."

Winthrop kicked another stone into the river. Then shaking his hands and using a ridiculous voice, he said, "*Mysterious Providence*. Oh, how could I forget it!" Using his usual voice, he continued, "What proof do you have that God wanted to destroy my beloved nation on that day? Why do you make Him out to be responsible for all of the tragedies that flowed from that battle? Isn't it possible that Goliath slayed the paladins because he was stronger? Could the sorrows of my life maybe–just maybe–be because I got unlucky, and not because God wanted my life to be a pile of pain? I'm trying to believe in God, Judas. It's a bit of a recent development. I want to believe in Him, but if He really was there at that battle, deciding who wins and who loses, then He has a lot to answer for. A lot more than I did when you arrested me. So go arrest God. Tell Him we're putting Him on trial. I'll be the judge.

"If it turns out He could have changed the course of the battle, but He just didn't know all these bad things would happen if Goliath won, I'll forgive Him. Can't blame someone for being stupid. I'll just make sure that from now on when I pray, I'm sure to explain that the thousands of people begging for Him to save us really are in quite a bit of danger and that we need Him to intervene. Hopefully He learns His lesson. Now if it turns out God knew *exactly* how miserable the world would become if Goliath triumphed, but God wasn't strong enough to beat Goliath, well, I understand that too. Maybe God really is a nice guy, but I can go ahead and stop pretending that He's going to change the course of my life. He just doesn't have that many miracles up His sleeves. Perhaps He was too stupid to realize He should have stopped Goliath, AND He was powerless to stop him. I'm beginning to wonder what makes God so special at that point... But if God *did* know what would happen if Goliath won, and if He *did* have the power to stop him, then God is guilty of all the innocent blood that has flowed since that day, and not only since that day, but before it as well. Where does all this evil come from, if an all-knowing, all-powerful God is holding the earth in His hand? I want an answer, Judas. I'm putting God on trial. It's time for Him to answer for what He's done."

Chapter 8: Winthrop's Trial

"Lord have mercy," Sir Judas answered, "How can you make yourself above your Maker? Who appointed you to be the judge of your Judge? Have you lost your mind since we parted ways?"

"If I've lost my mind, it's been gone for years. I'm just done pretending I know where it is. If I think the sky is brown, and everyone else says it's blue, and I know darn well that good, sane people are supposed to say it's blue, I'll still call it brown because that's the color I see. My errors may abound, but my lies are at an end. For a long time now, I haven't been able to figure out how an all-loving, all-powerful God can let the crimes of this world go on, and I'm finally willing to say so. I'll say the conclusion of that thought too; God either isn't all-powerful, or He's not all-loving. I don't see any possible way He could be."

Sir Judas answered, "For your honesty I commend you, but your humility is profoundly lacking. 'I don't *see* any possible way; therefore, it doesn't exist.' Once God has been convicted, shall you then arraign the wind? It probably doesn't exist either, since Judge Winthrop cannot see it. Heaven help us if you ever go blind; then the whole world might cease to be!"

"Do not mock me, Judas! You play games with my words because I said 'see' to mean 'understand.' I can understand the wind, and a blind man hears proof of what's all around him. But where is this good God? Where is the proof? I'll confess that I have a Maker because everything comes from something, but where is the proof that He loves me? Where is the proof I'm not just an ant He likes to pull the legs off of for fun? I don't see the whole picture with most things–*understand* the whole picture, don't want you twisting my words again–but even if I don't see the whole picture, I can at least tell that there's a painting. I can feel the frame, smell the oils, make out a vague shade of red and say, 'There's a painting here! Based on what I know, it might even be a good one!' Can you give me that, Judas? Can you give me something?

Anything? Can you give me one scrap of proof that there really is a painting of God's *Mysterious Providence* and that I'm just not seeing the whole masterpiece?"

"You have been reunited with David in the middle of the night because two nightmares brought us here under the light of a moon that shouldn't be shining. Is that the kind of proof you're looking for?"

"We parted ways yesterday and met at the nearest watering hole. I call that a coincidence. A happy one, but still a coincidence."

Sir Judas thought for a moment, knowing he had seen millions of examples of God's Providence throughout his life. He was racking his brain, trying to figure out which one would be most persuasive to Winthrop, which one he would be least likely to poke holes in or rationalize away. Then he came to his senses. He said a brief prayer, acknowledged that he was no man's savior, and asked the Holy Ghost to guide him in being a shepherd for this lost sheep. Still unable to think of any evidence Winthrop might accept, Sir Judas said, "I don't have any examples you won't write off. Since I am on important business tonight, I cannot tarry here and argue with you. Just to be sure, I need you to lay hold of this sword. If it does not glow in your hand, then I must press on and look for its rightful owner."

"Nothing? Absolutely nothing? Is that really the best defense of the faith a paladin can give? If you had sat here and argued with me all night I still would have disagreed with you, but at least I would know you were a thoughtful man yourself. If you can't offer even one good example of God's *Mysterious Providence*, it makes me question if you even really believe what you say, or if it's just empty words. I thought more of you, Judas. I thought you were the kind of man who would 'be ready to make a defense for the hope that is in you.' How could you actually–"

Winthrop fell over backwards as if he had been struck. Almost instantaneously, drops of sweat had formed on his brow. For a full minute, he laid on the ground trembling. Then he asked, "What black witchery is this, you sorcerer?"

"You know I don't use witchery, Winthrop. I'm just offering you a sword."

"That's my father's sword. It looked familiar to me when I saw you use it, but only now do I recognize what it is. Where did you find it?"

It was now Sir Judas's turn to be startled. "The king had it on the day of the Battle of Nouen. I do not know how it came into his possession. Lord

Fearnow took it from the king's hands and used it to kill him, yet even this proceeded according to the plan God had revealed to the king, for this sword has become the preeminent holy weapon, consecrated not by a mere drop of royal blood, but by its abundant outpouring. I have brought this sword with me on all my travels, looking for its rightful owner..." Sir Judas looked down at it, then up to Winthrop. "Stretch out your hand, and see whether it is truly yours."

Winthrop began to reach for it with his right hand, then stopped. Hesitating mere inches from the hilt, he asked, "What is its name?"

"*Veritas.*"

Winthrop shuddered. He took the sword.

Nothing happened.

Winthrop's heart fell. He couldn't believe it. For a moment–just a moment–he had believed he was going to see a sign. In his shock, he didn't even resist Sir Judas as the black knight took the sword back. "As I said, I must be going. I need to find this weapon's rightful owner." Sir Judas then began to walk away.

Winthrop stood there in a daze and hung his head. Then, looking upon the scar on his left arm, a thought occurred to him. "Wait! Judas!" He ran after the knight, and Sir Judas turned to meet him. "Let me take that sword in my other hand!"

"What hand you hold the sword in does not matter. It would glow either way."

"Maybe for most of you paladins, but not for me. Let me hold my father's sword in my left hand."

Sir Judas was reluctant, seeing no value that would come from this experiment. Nevertheless, he consented and held the sword out to Winthrop once more.

Winthrop's left arm was always stiff, and extending it caused his hand to tingle. Besides this, his left hand was quite weak and not good for holding weapons. Yet as he reached for *Veritas*, it felt as if his arm was made new. The scar remained, but all else was healed. He firmly gripped the hilt in his left hand, and repeated the words of his father's blessing from long ago. "Emitte lucem Tuam et veritatem Tuam..." *Veritas* flared with a bright and powerful light, silver like the moon, yet illuminating all things in their natural color. The grass was green, Sir Judas's armor was black, and overhead the stars could be seen shining in a sky that was perfectly blue, little diamonds piercing through the rolling clouds. The light was strong and steady for several seconds, and then gradually waned until it went out. "Father..."

Sir Judas's eyes were dewy. "Was that enough light, Winthrop? Can you now understand that there is a picture, even if you can't fully see it?"

Still trembling, Winthrop looked at *Veritas*, the moonlight reflecting off its blade. "...What does this mean?"

Sir Judas turned around and walked back ten paces, then turned to face Winthrop and drew *Caritas*. "It means that I must try you by combat, to see if you are worthy to enter the Lessguard and prepare to become a Paladin."

Winthrop looked at *Veritas*, then at *Caritas*, then at Sir Judas. "And what if I don't want to be a Paladin?"

"Do you?"

"I don't know! I'm considering my options."

"If you don't want to be a Paladin, then I must take back *Veritas*. You say it once belonged to your father, and I believe you, but it is now a holy weapon and belongs to the future Paladin who will wield it. I will take it and continue onward, searching for the rightful owner. I do not have time to stop and arrest you tonight."

"And what if I do want to be a Paladin? What would that mean?"

"You know what it would mean. You remember from your youth. It would mean a life of service, completely giving yourself to the realm. It would mean renouncing property, marriage, and even your own freedom, living instead as a slave to those you serve."

Winthrop looked back down at *Veritas*, still struggling to believe that this was really happening. He whispered, "Father...why did you give the king your sword?" Then he looked up at Sir Judas and said, "Sir Judas, two nights ago you told me that all dreams come true. I disagreed with you then, because my dream was beyond all possibility. Yet here I am, and in two days so much has changed, that I am now willing to confess my impossible dream to you. I want to be a Paladin. I've wanted it since I was younger than David is now. For the forty years since that fateful day I have both loved my dream and I have hated it. You've heard me discharge my mind; I've said in no uncertain terms that the world is all wrong and that God is to blame. How can a man be a Paladin who blames so much evil on God? Part of why I think I resent Him so much is because the paladins prove He could set things right if He wanted to. I remember their wondrous powers. They could heal the sick, raise the dead, smite the wicked with irresistible strength. I've asked myself so many times,

'Why wouldn't a good God use that power? Why won't He fix all the brokenness with which I am surrounded?' I'm like Job sitting on a dunghill, Judas. My friends, my family, my country, and even just the plain decency of society have all been crushed under the driving wind that brought down the house. And this stupid, deluded part of me that always dreamed of being a Paladin says, 'If the Almighty would change His ways and use me to restore what there once was, then I would say with holy Job, 'Blessed be the Name of the Lord!'' Is that so much to ask? I want to be a Paladin so I can get the same ending as holy Job. God's supposedly done it before; let Him do it again."

Sir Judas tried not to smile, but in the end he let out a little laugh. "I'm sorry, Winthrop, I'm not laughing at you. I'm laughing at something else said long ago. On the morning that the king died, when we were surrounded by armies on every side, the king asked me what I thought of the final chapter of the Book of Job, the very ending you have just described. And I interpreted that chapter in a manner very similar to you. I said, 'It gives me great hope to know that after we have suffered a little, God will reward us and set things right. Who knows? Maybe He will even restore your entire Empire to you, your grace.' The king laughed at me and said, 'Mordecai, if the Book of Job had chapter titles, I bet the final chapter would be 'Epilogue: The Final Test'. I don't think God was trying to assure us that we will regain the lands, money, and children that we lost for His sake in this life. I think He was testing us to see if we were really paying attention throughout the whole rest of the book. Is God good because we see the wicked rebuked and the innocent exalted? Or is God good? End of question, end of discussion. That's the lesson of the Book of Job, and the final chapter is the final exam.'

"I've thought of the king's words these many years, Winthrop, for I've seen more wrongs than I can right. It will be the same with you. A Paladin cannot fix the world. Like all other men, he must do what he can while trusting in Him Who said, 'Behold! I make all things new!'"

Winthrop held *Veritas* upright, then flourished it with a deftness that his left arm had not known in many years. "I still hold my opinions, and I would not pretend otherwise even for all the power in the world. Would you make a man a Paladin who still isn't a Christian?"

Caritas gave a golden glow from Sir Judas's hand. "God is master of the prophecy He gave the king. My duty is to try you by combat. I'll let Him sort out the rest."

Winthrop took a deep sigh. "Very well, Sir Judas, Last of the Kingsguard. I accept your trial. What are we fighting to? First blood?"

"To the death or to the yield. The victor is not victorious while the vanquished would still oppose him."

"Sir Judas!" David cried, "What are you doing? Don't hurt him!"

"Quiet, David! Remember what you promised me. Do not interfere with this trial, neither by word nor by deed. Winthrop, do you accept these terms?"

With the great and terrible excitement of coming close to both death and dream all at once, Winthrop nodded. "I do."

"Then let us begin." Sir Judas tossed *Caritas* to his right hand, then slowly began to advance on Winthrop. "Now that I'm not lugging that big hunk of steel around everywhere, I can finally use my own weapon in the proper hand!"

Winthrop casually circled the tip of *Veritas* around several times. He had studied swordplay extensively under his father, but the skill had gone rusty after years of being a robber. Not only did he used to use blunt and heavy weapons, but since his riding accident twelve years ago he had exclusively used the crossbow. All of that faded away. He felt as if he was young once more, ready for a sparring match with his father. Years of drills and practice returned, and with his father's sword in his healed left hand, Winthrop's muscles remembered how to fight. Light on his feet, almost dancing across the gap between them, Winthrop fluttered this way, dashed the other, then made a long, reaching lunge at Sir Judas's stomach.

Sir Judas was dodging before the thrust was made, moving well to the side of Winthrop's stab and then stepping up to tap his left hand on Winthrop's chin. Startled but unharmed, Winthrop lashed out with his sword. He found nothing but air as Sir Judas ducked the blow and backpedaled out of reach.

"You're going easy on me," Winthrop said, rubbing his jaw where Sir Judas had hit him.

"To the contrary, I am testing you very rigorously."

"I'm not wearing armor. You could have stabbed me on the spot and won."

"If you think I want to kill you, you do not yet understand the trial."

Winthrop pointed *Veritas* ahead of him, advancing on Sir Judas much more cautiously. He focused on his reach advantage, keeping the paladin at sword's length. Surprisingly, the black knight lowered *Caritas* and stood there, arms at his side, flat on his feet, totally unprepared.

Winthrop feinted a stab.

Sir Judas didn't move.

He feinted a slash.

Sir Judas didn't move.

He feinted a stab, inches from the black knight's face.

Sir Judas yawned.

Winthrop went for a real slash, neck high.

Sir Judas ducked the blow, moved closer in a crouch, and punched Winthrop in the gut twice with each hand. Bent over and winded, he still managed to make an upwards slash with *Veritas*. Sir Judas casually stepped around Winthrop, causing the strike to miss, and then shoved him from behind so that Winthrop landed on his face.

"Oh come now. Certainly you know more swordplay than that. Is this really the best you can do?"

From the dirt, Winthrop muttered, "It's been a while…"

"I sure hope your father knew how to use that sword better. He didn't hand any skills on to you."

"My father was a great warrior! A champion of Nouen! He taught me everything I know!"

"If everything you know is everything he knew, I'm not terribly impressed."

"You're not impressed? Let me know if this impresses you!"

Winthrop charged with *Veritas* raised high for a mighty overhead swing. Sir Judas stepped aside and stuck his leg out, causing Winthrop to trip. He arose quickly and came back in for a wicked side slash. Sir Judas had already stepped back out of the way. Another overhead slash. Another dodge. Sideswipe. Dodge. This time when Winthrop went for an overhead swing, he aimed to the right of Sir Judas, where the knight had been dodging to.

Sir Judas didn't move.

Winthrop did it again.

Sir Judas didn't move.

A third time.

No response.

Winthrop tried to cleave Sir Judas's head.

The black knight went left, grabbed Winthrop by his shirt, and flung him forward to the ground.

"Agh!" Winthrop growled, getting up to his knees. *Why can't I hit him?* An image flashed through Winthrop's mind. It was Sir Judas turning to face Garrett before Garrett had given away his position. *Sense of deadly intent...* Winthrop slowly rose to his feet, realizing how doomed this battle was.

"What's the matter, Winthrop? Exhausted already?"

Winthrop was racking his brain, trying to think of anything that might help him. *How do I fight a man who knows my every move before I make it?* Another image flashed through his mind. It was his crossbow bolt whizzing in front of Sir Judas's nose, and the shock of the black knight when he did it. Realization dawned on Winthrop. *He doesn't see my every move!* He looked down at *Veritas*, closed his eyes, made a promise, then opened them and began to advance on Sir Judas.

"Tired out, Winthrop? Need a breather? You *are* always talking about those gray hairs of yours."

Winthrop raised *Veritas* for what looked like an overhead strike. He stepped up so that he and Sir Judas were eyeball to eyeball. The knight made no move to dodge. Winthrop lunged forward with his forehead. It smashed right into Sir Judas's nose. "Ohhhh!" Then Winthrop brought the pommel of *Veritas* down on Sir Judas's head. The black knight staggered, fell to one knee, then went down on all fours, dropping *Caritas*. Winthrop held the tip of *Veritas* up to Sir Judas's neck. "This trial is over."

Sir Judas smiled. "No, Winthrop, it is not over. The real trial has just begun." He crawled a couple feet to where *Caritas* had fallen, while Winthrop pulled the tip of *Veritas* away so he wouldn't nick him.

"You are defeated!"

"No I'm not. Death or yield, those were the terms. I am not dead, and I do not yield, so the trial continues." Sir Judas arose with Winthrop pressing his sword against his armor.

"Don't make me kill you, Judas."

"I don't think you can."

Sir Judas then swatted *Veritas* aside and made a thrust with *Caritas*. Winthrop jumped away, not having any armor of his own. He made a couple retreating slashes, trying to create space between the two of them. Sir Judas pressed forward, showing no fear as *Veritas* bounced off his armor. Sir Judas then made another stab, but this time Winthrop dodged to the side, parried, and used his shoulder to shove Sir Judas to the ground. Again he held his sword up to Sir Judas's neck. "Yield!"

"No." Sir Judas swatted *Veritas* away again, and once more made to rise. Winthrop smashed *Veritas* into his back. It did no damage through the chain mail and gambeson, but it was enough force to knock Sir Judas down again. He rose again. Winthrop knocked him down again. He rose. He hit. He rose. He hit. He rose. He hit. Over and over and over, Winthrop swung *Veritas* at Sir Judas's back until his arms were growing tired. Still, the paladin rose.

"Yield!"

"No."

"How can I pass this trial?"

"Kill me."

"I can't kill you!"

"Why not?"

"Because…" Winthrop threw *Veritas* to the ground. "Because I told myself I wouldn't! That's how I got past your stupid sense of deadly intent! I promised myself I wouldn't kill you, and now I can't do it!"

"Break your word."

Winthrop ground his teeth. "You don't mean that, mister holy lips. And even if you did, I can't. I promised someone very important to me that I would never lie again, and that's a promise I intend to keep. Even if I wanted to kill you–and boy am I sure tempted–I still couldn't do it, because I promised I wouldn't. So either yield and make me a Paladin, or else take the sword and go find another. I can't kill you and keep my promise, so I guess that means I can't kill you."

Sir Judas smiled deeply–not that annoying smile with which he had been taunting Winthrop in order to test him, but a genuine and loving smile. Taking *Caritas,* he walked up to Winthrop and said, "Now I do yield, and you have indeed passed the trial. I cannot make you a Paladin–only the king could ever do that–but as the head of the Kingsguard, I can, and do, initiate you into the Lessguard to begin your final preparation."

Sir Judas then stabbed *Caritas* into the right side of Winthrop's chest.

"NOOOOO!" David screamed. Shock and terror were on Winthrop's face.

Sir Judas withdrew the blade and embraced Winthrop, helping him to stand. "Be not afraid. This wound is not unto death. Your heart has been pierced by purest love, and now you shall feel its holy pains." Sir Judas's words had a mysterious power that calmed both David and Winthrop as soon as they heard them, yet in a manner that did not suppress their natural emotions. David felt distress and peace at the same time. He was panicked to see Winthrop's heart pumping blood out of his chest, yet he was also tranquil, confident that this was meant to be. The natural terror and fear of death that Winthrop was experiencing were combined with the excitement of not knowing what would happen next. His heart began to beat rapidly and burn. He was losing his breath, but not like he was dying. Instead it was like the breathlessness of when one's beloved is nearby.

Sir Judas asked, "Winthrop of the Lessguard, tomorrow I will travel to the edge of the darkness, and the next day I intend to reach Castle Nightfall and face Goliath. Will you come with me?"

Winthrop almost shouted 'Yes!' The word was on the tip of his tongue, but then his heart lurched in a different direction. "I…I want to. I want to come with you and face the monster that killed my father, but…my heart…right now it is positively burning for another. There is someone I must see, and then I will come with you. Can you wait a day?"

"I cannot. I must do all I can to fulfill the prophecy that was given in the glade." Sir Judas then pressed his hand to Winthrop's wound, giving a momentary relief to the pain. "Follow your heart, Winthrop. Whatever this desire is, it comes from God. Go meet this person, and then make haste to follow. Perhaps you will overtake me on my journey. Or perhaps you will be needed at the time you arrive and no sooner." Sir Judas then unlatched the belt that held his scabbard and gave it to Winthrop. "Take this. It's more necessary for carrying a sword than carrying a dagger." Still struggling to stand, Winthrop looped the belt around his waist and latched it, then sheathed *Veritas*. "There is just one favor I would ask of you, Winthrop. Pray for me, Friday morning at dawn. I suspect that will be about the time I reach the castle, and that is when I will have greatest need of your assistance. You said you believe in a powerful God. At least ask Him to come to my assistance. Can you do that much for me?"

Winthrop felt uncomfortable—not merely because of the gaping wound in his chest—yet he nodded and said, "I will. Just don't expect it to be some holy Christian prayer."

"I'll take whatever you can offer."

By this point David had walked up to join the two men, and was looking back and forth between them. Sir Judas asked the question he had been dreading. "David…what about you? Will you come with me to the darkness, or will you go with Winthrop?"

The boy was distraught. He took a step towards Winthrop, then said, "Winthrop, I…I'm so happy to be back together, and I don't want to…but, *Caritas*…today when I held it, it glowed like it was my holy weapon, and…it made a light like when you took *Veritas*, and I…that darkness, Winthrop, it's horrible. You look into it and it just swallows everything up. I want to stay with you, I really do, but…I can't help feeling that I need to go wherever *Caritas* goes, and that I need to stay by the light that my holy weapon can make. And I…I don't want to! I don't want to say goodbye to you again!" David broke into tears and buried his head in Winthrop's chest. His face became wet from the water of his tears mingled with Winthrop's blood.

Winthrop hugged him tightly until he stopped crying, and then took David's face and pressed their foreheads together. "Listen, David. This isn't 'Goodbye.' This is just 'See you later.' I have one person I need to see in Dewford, and then I'm coming for you as fast as I can. We'll be together again soon. And by God, David, I have to tell you that I'm proud of you. You're a good kid. Far better than I raised you to be. Go with Sir Judas, do what you can to help him, and before you know it, I will be there."

Winthrop turned to leave. Then he stopped and looked at David once more. There was something he wanted to tell him. He still couldn't say it. He knew exactly why. "David, come here."

He whispered something in David's ear. "What does that even mean?" David asked.

"Ask Sir Judas tomorrow. He can explain. I need to get going before what's left of my blood leaks out." Then Winthrop put one arm around David's shoulder, looked him right in the eye, and said,

"I love you, son."

He kissed David and staggered into the night. His father's dying words were still unsullied, and his oath to Lady Maria was still intact.

End of Volume IV

Interlude

The sun was setting as Charles reached his opulent manor where civilization ends. He walked up to the great mahogany double doors and pushed. They were locked. He raised a boot and kicked the doors open, splinters flying where the iron lock had burst through the wood. "Gary!" He bellowed.

The elderly butler was already walking to the door to see what the commotion was. Unsurprised to see he would have to replace the front door (again), he stated, "M'lord, I'm so glad you're well. I've been worried sick ever since you and your friends didn't return from your night ride Monday night. Now I may rest easier."

"Save it. Go to the stables, and have Reuben prep four chariots for tomorrow. And if you see any of my men, tell them to marshal in the yard. Now!"

"Of course, m'lord. I'll see to it right away."

Charles stormed through the house, looking for all his roughnecks. They belonged to that most unsavory lot of society that combines the manners of a guttersnipe with the fortune of a gentleman. They were all landed nobles whose negligence of their estates only ceased when they needed serfs to throw into battle. The one exception was Riley Minnagh, whose connections were both less formal and more useful.

After shouting and slamming every door he could find, Charles went out front of his manor to await his men. Riley was already there. "I take it you ran into Gary?"

"No, not Gary, I know you. Boss has a job for me to do."

Charles folded his arms. "Your dreams of being a poet are as close as ever."

Riley smiled. "Forgive me, big man. I get excited when you're in these kinds of moods."

Charles imagined the kind of day tomorrow would be. He returned the smile. "As do I…"

In a matter of minutes the nine noblemen had arrived and formed a line before Charles. He announced to them, "Tomorrow we go to Dewford. There is a man hiding out in that town whom I cannot allow to escape. Summon all of your men, report here by noon tomorrow, and then we go to besiege the town."

The men looked at each other in disappointment, until one of them voiced what was on all their minds. "But m'lord…is there…going to be any takings? This sounds like a relatively…peaceful operation. It's not like you're gonna pillage your own town."

"Well you can get that idea right out of your heads. I care more about my morning movement than the dunghill known as Dewford. Besiege the city, search it, get the man I want, and once he's taken care of take whatever you want. Just don't touch the merchants or any visitors. Locals only. Otherwise you might cause trouble for me with Fearnow."

Their moods improved dramatically. After saluting the Baron, the nine noblemen rushed to the stables to get their horses. Riley and Charles were left alone again. Riley walked up to Charles stroking his wild and unkempt beard, saying, "Hey Boss, excited as I am to get to the gettin', noon tomorrow is too soon. I gots a difficult lot to round up in Chelles, and even trackin' em down'll take longer than the others. Should I just get as many fellas as I can, or should I come later than the others?"

"Neither. Get them all, and get them by noon. Do whatever you have to do to make it happen."

"But Boss!"

Charles didn't wait for any further discussion. He was already heading for his manor to review the maps he had of Dewford.

By ten o'clock the next morning the nobles began to arrive with their serfs. The arms were all of passable quality, while the men themselves were lean and strong. The nobles all had three or four men who were the right age and disposition for marauding, bringing the total assembled to forty-five. Charles paced anxiously, wanting to be gone as soon as possible. Noon arrived. Riley had not yet appeared.

As the next hour creeped slowly by, Charles received repeated requests to let the men disband and take their armor off while they waited. He refused. "As soon as that sluggard gets here, we leave. Everyone stand at the ready."

Another hour came and went. Another began to pass. It was nearly three o'clock when a large crowd appeared on the road coming from Chelles. Charles ceased pacing and stood still. He placed his demon-head hammer on the ground in front of him. Riley's mob totaled over a score, swelling the force's numbers. They were criminals one and all—the same lot Riley had invited Sir Judas to join when they met earlier that week. Unlike the serfs the noblemen brought, these outlaws owned nicked blades and sweat-stained gambeson. Their arms had been maintained less and used more, and their evil faces showed it.

Riley walked up to Charles and bowed. "Better late than never, Riley is good as ever! All the men is here, Boss. Didn't miss a one, even on such short notice."

"You are late."

Riley looked up uneasily. "But Boss, I did my best. It was an impossible—"

"Were any of your men ready to go on time?"

Riley nodded nervously. "Yeah, Boss, a few of 'em, but…you said to get 'em all, so—"

"Who? Who was ready on time?"

Riley turned around. Looking at his men, he pointed and said, "Well there's Holland. He got Niall and Jaxon, and then was waitin' for us at—" Riley saw a look of shock appear on his men's faces. Before he could even turn around, Charles's hammer smashed his skull to pieces.

Placing the gory hammer back on the ground in front of him, Charles said, "Holland. Get over here." A round-faced man lacking a front tooth slowly walked over to where Riley laid, looking back and forth between the hammer and the body in a daze. "Congratulations, Holland. You've just been promoted to the head of Riley's forces." Charles then picked up his hammer and pointed it at the dozens of scared and startled men. "In case anyone was unclear on how utterly important today's mission is, allow me to spell it out for you. I liked Riley. I don't like you. For most of you, I don't even know you. So if this is what happens when a man I like fails to do what I ask…" Charles lowered his voice and growled, "You can figure out the rest yourselves."

Kayden groaned as he opened his eyes, his whole body aching and sore. He was in bed…how had he gotten here? He looked over at the one candle in the room. The darkness outside the window told him it was already night time. "Ugh...what happened?"

He looked the other way and saw Sasha was in a chair right next to him. She had dozed off, but hearing him stir she woke up and said, "What happened? My knight in shining armor saved me from the exquisitely mustached dastard."

"Heheheheheh–oof! That hurt...knight in shining armor, huh? Maybe I should start dressing like that old man we saw earlier. I think I would look good in black...and I'd probably feel a whole lot better in armor."

"Oh, I didn't mean it like that. That chauvinist was nothing like you. He's just a grouchy old man who can't stand 'kids these days.' You're a real knight, standing up to save the fair lady from the giant."

Kayden looked up at the ceiling, watching the candlelight dance with the shadows. "You know, it's kinda funny."

"What is?"

"I was gonna run away when that man was holding you over his head."

"What do you mean?"

"I mean I was scared! I knew I couldn't take him! It was a hopeless cause. I was gonna run...if I remember right, I think I even started to. I took a step the wrong way, but then I remembered the old man from this morning...the first time, when I ran into him out back. Me and the boys were banging on the door, and he came up to stop us. Obviously the guy's a chauvinist. I'm not defending him on that front. An old man who thinks a girl like you can't take care of herself needs to have his head examined. But still, even if his head's not screwed on straight, the guy's got guts. He was outnumbered five to one and he was still ready to throw down with a bunch of men half his age in order to save the fair lady. He has the brains of a chicken, but the courage of a honey badger. And then there was that kid, the one you gave all the food to. He wanted in on the action too! So there I was, ready to run away from the mustached menace, and I think to myself, 'So far today a geriatric paint-licker and a snot-nosed kid have stood up for my girl. Am I really gonna be the first man to run out on her?' They guilted me into it, Sasha! I got guilt tripped into being a knight in shining armor. So then when you say the black knight was nothing like me, well...I thought that was funny. Cuz I was kinda trying to be like him."

Sasha was welling up. "You're stupid."

"I love you too." They looked at each other for several seconds, holding hands.

Silence.

More silence.

Then Kayden said, "Do you want to get married?"

Sasha rolled her eyes. "You're stupid. I know how you feel about that. You don't have to change just for me."

"Yes I do."

"No you don't. It's like you always said. Marriage is just a label. It doesn't change the love we have for one another. A rose by any other name is just as sweet."

"I'm an idiot."

"I agree."

"Hey!" He playfully swatted at her, then realized it was his sore arm he was swinging. With a grimace he said, "No fair...picking on me when I'm hurt." Looking back into Sasha's eyes he said, "Maybe a rose by any other name does smell just as sweet. But when you call something a 'rose', people are less likely to walk all over it than if you call it a 'road'. I thought about that when that man was flirting with you today. I had this thought of, 'My Sasha deserves more respect than creepo is giving her. Why does everyone in this store think it's alright to flirt with her? Would they do that if she was married?' We know our love is serious, but everyone else in the world should know that too, shouldn't they? I wanna tell the whole world, 'This woman who smells so sweet to you isn't a road, or a doormat! She's my *wife*!' I don't know, I never really thought about it before, but I would kinda like to use that word. 'Back off, jerk! That's my *wife*!'"

Kayden shrugged, tweaked his bad shoulder again, winced, and then continued, "There's another thing on my mind too. You always wanted to get married. If I'm not willing to sacrifice what I want for what you want, does the rose really smell as sweet? In a weird way, I think we would actually be more in love if we did get hitched."

"Oh, Kayden!" Sasha carefully embraced him, her heart full of gratitude and love. "So when are we going to do it? Where are we going to get married? Oh my goodness, I can start saying I'm your fiancée now, can't I?"

"Slow down, Sasha! I haven't proposed yet!"

"Oh, fine. Go ahead. Propose."

"Well not right now! I need to find an opportune moment."

No sooner had Kayden finished speaking than the silver moonlight began to slant in through the window. "What's that?" Sasha asked, walking over to look outside. Then she yelled, "Oh, Kayden! Kayden! Are you okay to walk? We need to go out on the balcony!"

He twisted and turned with some difficulty, rocking himself up to a sitting position. Stiff all over, he waddled to the door, and they stepped out onto the back balcony together. "Oh my God!" After that they were both struck speechless, looking up at heaven, the full moon, the rainbow halo, and the sea of perfectly white, rolling clouds.

Silence.

Plenty of silence.

Eventually Sasha managed to say, "This is amazing...I...I've never seen anything like it..."

Kayden lowered himself to one knee. "*This* is the opportune moment." Laughing as he took Sasha's hand, he asked her, "Sasha, will you marry me?"

"Yes. A million times yes!"

He struggled to rise, but needed her to help him, and then they kissed in the moonlight. A while later they were leaning against the wall, still looking up, while Sasha's head was resting on Kayden's shoulder. "Oh, Kayden...who are we going to tell first?"

"I was already thinking about that...whadya say we get Larry to run the shop the next two days, run over to Dewford, and tell Ed?"

She jumped away from him. "Now I'm worried you hit your head when that man threw you. Marriage is one thing, but...you want to tell *Ed*? He threw a conniption fit when we told him we were moving in together."

"Yeah, so what if he did? I'm in a mood to forgive anything tonight. Besides, he's your father. And he's the one who wanted us to get married in the first place. Maybe he'll actually be happy if I tell him he was right."

Sasha shook her head. "Oh, Kayden...oh, let's give it a shot. He'll probably yell and chase us off again, but...maybe he won't..." She was crying as she looked up at the moon and said, "Maybe...just maybe...he'll walk me down the aisle."

Sir Joseph quietly snuck into his own house, half-afraid that an Administrator was already there. Without any lights he navigated to his mother's room and knelt down beside her bed. She was tossing and turning, making frightened little whimpers and fragments of words. He reached out a hand gently to rouse her. She startled awake. "No! You won't take us!"

"It's me, mother. Joseph."

"Oh, Joseph…Oh good. I was having a terrible dream." She panted for several seconds before her breathing returned to normal. "What is it honey?"

Sir Joseph's stomach was in knots. There was so much to say, yet he had no idea where to begin nor how to say it. He finally began with, "Mother…we need to leave Chelles."

"Oh good. I've been waiting so long for you to figure that out. When do we leave?"

Joseph was flabbergasted. "Mo—Mother! Are you awake? Do you realize what I'm saying? I'm talking about leaving our home behind."

"It's not my home. I was born in Pennyworth. You were too, for that matter, though you were too young to remember. Chelles has never been our home. It's just the place where we live." Emma got out of bed and reached underneath, producing a tidy pack.

"What is that?" Sir Joseph asked, still not believing how casually his mother was taking the news.

"Do you remember that day when the masked freaks tried to throw you in their Void, and the whole city got to talking about how their magic couldn't affect you?"

"Of course…"

"That was the day I packed my travel bag. Every neighbor of ours came to congratulate me on how safe I must feel having 'Joseph the Indomitable' as a son. I remember feeling the exact opposite, knowing that was the day you made some very powerful enemies. Ever since then I've been waiting for you to wake up and realize we need to take our fortunes elsewhere. You've certainly kept me waiting, though I suppose Fearnow taking you under his protection complicated the matter. Nevertheless, I never unpacked my bag. I've always known this night would come."

Sir Joseph shook his head, feeling as if he had an obligation to make his mother take the situation more seriously. "Mother, where will we go? What will we do? What will we eat?"

"Oh, don't play dumb with me now, Joseph, as if you don't already know." She stepped into her closet and flipped the switch to turn on a ceiling light, then closed the door and began changing.

"Mother, I don't know. I haven't given any thought to what we'll do after we leave Chelles."

"Oh, don't give me that. You've been thinking about it for months. Five times a day you'll say something like, 'Black knights don't have to deal with these orders, do they?' or, 'What I wouldn't give to be a black knight today.' Then this afternoon when Feifer told me you had invited a black knight into our house, I knew the end was near. I didn't think we would be leaving this very evening, but I'm not terribly surprised either. Now where are we meeting him? What's the plan?"

Shaking his head and smiling, he said, "Mother...I really wasn't planning it...oh, maybe I was. I swear you know me better than I know myself."

"Of course I do. I'm your mother." She opened the door to her closet and emerged in a poor roughspun dress, with her greying hair pulled into an ugly bun. Sir Joseph barely recognized his noble mother, and hoped no one else in the city would recognize her either.

"Well that is certainly an effective disguise."

"This isn't the first time I've been on the run."

Sir Joseph nodded his head slowly, coming to grips with what lay before them. "Very well...there is a service door in the wall I planned on leading us out by, but we will be certain to be seen by whoever is guarding it. However, now that I see how dressed down you are, I think it might be better to leave in the morning. After the gates open I can ride Isabella out 'on patrol,' while you slip by in the crowds. Then we'll rendezvous on the road to Reswick and make our way to freedom."

Emma nodded. "Well then let's make sure your saddlebags are packed tonight so we can leave first thing in the morning."

The two of them made a few trips to and from the stable, doing their best to make sure they didn't forget anything. They were carrying David and Sir Judas's packs out on the final trip when a scream of terror came from the royal palace. It was immediately followed by the voice of Lord Fearnow shouting a furious tirade. "You knew! You knew! Everything would have been different if you didn't lie to me!"

Emma looked at her son. "Was the woman's voice Lady Amanda?"

"No...I didn't recognize it."

The woman's voice came again. "Help! Help! Someone, please help!"

Sir Joseph looked down at their packs, then asked his mother, "What should we do? If we get caught preparing to run, they won't let us leave the city."

Her face turned angry and she threw down David's pack. "Are you a black knight or aren't you, Sir Joseph the Craven? No son of mine is going to leave a helpless woman to her fate. Now get going! Go! Don't you come back here without her!"

Emma pushed him with both her hands, then swatted at his head, but he was already gone. Dropping the other pack, Sir Joseph ran for the palace as fast as his legs could take him. The moment he came through the front doors he was amazed by the tumult that had happened. The two monkey statues had been toppled, with little brass limbs strewn along the stairway. Paintings had been flung off the walls, and the great 'Shades of Rage' painting that Lord Fearnow was so fond of had been ripped and shredded to pieces.

Sir Joseph looked around, trying to figure out where to go first. The woman screamed again, coming from a doorway to his right. He ran through it into a long corridor. There he found a woman he vaguely recognized as one of the Administrators. She was unmasked and disheveled, fleeing from a still enraged Lord Fearnow, who was grabbing every object that wasn't nailed down and throwing it at her.

"Please, your grace, please! Have mercy! I'm sorry!"

"The only mercy you'll get is if I decide to kill you quickly!"

"Eeeek!" A small figurine barely missed her head, shattering where it hit the stone wall behind her. Seeing Sir Joseph, the woman yelled, "Save me, sir knight! Save me!" She ran behind him as Lord Fearnow gave chase. Sir Joseph drew his electro-gun and pointed it at Lord Fearnow.

"So it's treason, then, is it, Joseph? I always knew it would come to this! Your true sympathies are revealed… You raise your heel against me! So you were in on it too! You and this witch tricked my Committee into losing all of their magical powers!"

"Your grace," Sir Joseph asked, "What are you talking about? What happened with the Committee?"

"I can't trust a single one of you…you've all gone over to that contemptible Mordecai, the cursed black knight. Black cloak and black armor as a symbol of his loyalty. Black for loyal? Isn't it funny? It's all very funny. Why am I the only one laughing? Who mentioned loyalty? You're all disloyal, treasonous curs! I would have you executed if the headsman wasn't in on it too!"

"Lord Fearnow," Sir Joseph said, "If this woman has truly committed treason, then we must address the matter in the morning. You are not well, and if you do anything to harm her tonight, I am confident you will regret it tomorrow."

"It's too late for that Joseph! You should have been here when I talked to that witch hiding behind you this morning! Or better yet, when I talked to that witch I'm married to forty years ago when she created this whole mess! That's a regret! I regret ever listening to the lying words of these wicked women!"

Destiny pleaded, "Your grace, I'm sorry, I had no intention of deceiving you. I didn't know he could make people lose their magical powers."

"Of course you did! That's why you weren't there when we attacked! You want to kill me and seize control of the city! You and Amanda both! That's why she told me to listen to you! That's why she botched the spell! And Joseph! You were in on it too! That's why you requested that I meet with him! You're all in on it together!" His eyes were wild, flitting back and forth not only between Destiny and Sir Joseph, but also in every direction around the room, as if the walls themselves were about to attack.

In a calm voice, Sir Joseph said, "Your grace, no one wants to kill you. Even Sir Judas didn't want to kill you. You're safe, your grace."

Lord Fearnow focused on Sir Joseph for a moment, his head twitching side to side. "Mor–Mordecai, you say? Didn't want to kill me? Heh heh…oh, you're right, Sir Joseph. I should reward him! Reward him! That's just what I'll do…" He turned his mad gaze on Destiny. "You! Whatever your name was! Do you want to prove your loyalty? Go find Mordecai! Track him down for me! Take Sir Joseph with you, and bring him back here. Do that, and I'll believe you. Otherwise, you're a traitor, and a traitor's death is what you'll get! Joseph! Do whatever she tells you, or you'll share in her fate too!"

Lord Fearnow then whipped around, storming off as he muttered a constant stream of gibberish. Once the door slammed on the far side of the corridor, Destiny threw her arms around Sir Joseph and exclaimed, "Oh, thank you! Thank you! You just saved my life! Ohhh…" Then, as she calmed down and recalled the task they had been given, she said, "Yes, now…considering the uh…we need to find Sir Judas, it would seem, so…and you are going to help me find him, of course…where do you suggest we start?"

Sir Joseph looked down the corridor again, making sure the door was truly shut. Then he whispered, "I will not help you bring Sir Judas back here, not even if I die for it."

Destiny dropped her act. "Oh, I'm so grateful! Thank you! I don't want to meet him again, either! He's so terrifying! Please, you have to help me escape this city!"

Sir Joseph raised his eyebrows, looked at the far door again, and whispered, "Now that is certainly an interesting request you've given...you want to leave this city?"

She nodded fervently. "Yes, I need to run away. Far, far away. And I know the road to Reswick isn't safe for any woman by herself, but the only man I can trust to protect me is thoroughly tangled in this city's webs." Destiny's face became tortured and pathetic. "Sir Joseph...you have such a high position in this city, and I could never ask you to put that at risk. But please...I need an escort. I need help. If I asked you to find someone to accompany me in my exile, how far could I travel under your protection?"

Sir Joseph smiled. "Far."

Beatrice was soaring on wings of shadow magic, looking down at Goliath sitting on his rampart. Her head was still throbbing from when she crashed into the cabinet, but right now she was just grateful to be alive. "What is he doing, Jezebel? He's been sitting there for hours, just looking at the big black spot where the water is."

"Why don't you go ask him yourself?"

"And let him try to kill me again? Not a chance. Can't you ask his spirits?"

"I can, but not while you're using my shadow magic. You'll have to land somewhere and hide while I ask."

Beatrice did as Jezebel said, cautiously alighting more than a mile away from the castle. No distance felt truly safe, given how swiftly Goliath could bound across the land. Nevertheless, she hid in a cleft in a rocky crag and then sent Jezebel to ask her questions. The demon came back to Castle Nightfall in an instant, and saw the swarming legion of demons crawling over Goliath. They saw her as well, and one of them taunted, "Get a good workout today, Jezebel? Your meatbag was having a real rough time running around in the dark!"

"Your meatbag is sitting here in a trance. Why?"

A thousand shouts and answers emerged at once, defensive, offensive, off topic, sarcastic, absurd. Jezebel was going to give up and leave. Evil spirits usually need to overwhelm an inferior to extract truthful information out of them, and there was no way for her to fight a mountain of demons. But then, to her surprise, the strong and powerful voice of Abaddon cut through the chaos and pressed itself upon her. "HE IS IN A PRECARIOUS STATE, AND UNLESS YOU WISH TO FACE MY WRATH, YOU AND YOUR MEATBAG WILL PUSH HIM IN THE RIGHT DIRECTION."

Jezebel was surprised. "What do you mean 'precarious.' What's going on?"

"HOPE. HE HAS GROWN HOPEFUL. HE IS BEGINNING TO THINK THAT THE PALADIN MIGHT BE SOMEONE HE ONCE KNEW. A SQUIRE WHO WAS KILLED BY AMANDA FEARNOW. HE DOES NOT KNOW THAT SHE KILLED HIM, AND HE IS NOT LISTENING TO US WHEN WE TELL HIM THE SQUIRE IS DEAD. HE IS HOPEFUL THAT THE PALADIN WANTS TO SAVE HIM. HE IS EVEN HOPEFUL THAT THE PALADIN MIGHT EXORCIZE HIM. AFTER SENDING OUT HIS MINIONS TO MAKE SURE THAT DIDN'T HAPPEN, NOW HE IS HOPING IT DOES. AND YET HE HOPES IT DOESN'T. IT'S PRECARIOUS. WE NEED TO PUSH HIM IN THE RIGHT DIRECTION."

"Can't you just scramble his emotions? Roll them around until he's in the proper mood?"

"WE TRIED THAT. HE FORMALLY COMMANDED US TO 'STOP MESSING WITH HIS MIND.' WE DID STOP MESSING WITH HIS MIND FOR ONE MILLISECOND, AND SINCE THAT TECHNICALLY SATISFIES HIS COMMAND, WE ARE FREE TO START MESSING WITH IT AGAIN, BUT THAT WOULD BE FOOLISH. HE WOULD JUST FORMALLY COMMAND US TO STOP AFFECTING HIS MIND FOR A YEAR, AND THEN WE WOULD ACTUALLY BE IN TROUBLE. WE NEED TO LAY LOW FOR NOW, AND ONLY EXERT OUR STRENGTH IF IT IS TRULY NECESSARY. YOU AND YOUR MEATBAG MUST TRY TO INFLUENCE HIM. RIDICULE HIM. TELL HIM HIS HOPES ARE FOOLISH. WE'LL TOUCH HIS MIND IN VERY SUBTLE WAYS AND MAKE HIM MORE AGREEABLE TO YOUR MEATBAG."

"After you just had him chasing us around to kill us? Forgive me if I don't believe you."

"THIS IS DIFFERENT! HE'S HAD A VISION, AND NOW HE STARES AT THE BLACKNESS BECAUSE HE DOESN'T WANT TO SEE THE VISION WE GIVE HIM. HE IS DWELLING ON IT. THINKING OF IT. MEDITATING. IF THIS VISION IS FROM THE ALMIGHTY, THEN

OUR FOE IS MAKING WAR AGAINST US. WE MUST FIGHT BACK! WE CANNOT ALLOW THE RULER OF THE AGE OF DARKNESS TO BECOME A CHILD OF LIGHT ONCE MORE! WE MUST SET ASIDE OUR STUPID DIVISIONS AND RIVALRIES! A HOUSE DIVIDED CANNOT STAND! NOW FALL IN LINE, AND DO AS YOU'RE TOLD! WE MUST WORK TOGETHER TO PLUNGE GOLIATH BACK INTO DESPAIR!"

As Abaddon spoke these commands, he put his power behind them, working together with the Spirit of Fear to afflict Jezebel. She couldn't countenance the thought of trying to oppose him. Though Abaddon had already caused her suffering, she knew he would make her even more miserable if she didn't obey his orders. "It shall be done," was her simple answer, and then she sped back to Beatrice at once.

"Well?" Beatrice asked. "Did you figure out what he's doing?"

"Yes I did," Jezebel answered, "and you're going to be the one to make him stop doing it."

"Like hell. I'm not going anywhere near him."

A sick pleasure formed in Jezebel's devilish spirit. She felt disgusted that she had been bent to Abaddon's will. She was going to enjoy making Beatrice feel the same way.

Lady Amanda had been alone in the room weeping ever since Benjamin stormed out. Every time she would start to get ahold of herself, she would recall more of her many sins and peer deeper into the ones already on her mind. A new stream of copious tears would pour forth. *Where is my faerie? Where has she gone?* For many years now–decades, in fact–her gray faerie had always been at her shoulder, comforting her whenever she was sad. When Amanda cast a spell the faerie would leave for a few moments to deliver it, but she always came back swiftly. Now it had been hours and there was absolutely no sign of the little creature. When Amanda had cast her charm spell on Sir Judas, the faerie had landed on his shoulder and started to whisper in his ear. Then Lady Amanda had blinked, and the faerie was gone. *Where is my faerie? Did Sir Judas do something to her?*

She thought back on her relationship with the little rascal. No matter how depressed or disgusted Amanda was with herself, the faerie always knew what to say to make her feel better. When she had seduced Sir Samson, the faerie reminded her that it was for the greater good. When she killed Mordecai (or so she had thought) the faerie had distracted her from the guilt with funny jokes about the stupid squire. And then there was the long term. As the slow, crushing depression had set in over forty years of bitter sacrifices and unrealized dreams, the faerie always gave her hope and reminded her that things would someday get better if she stayed the course.

Lady Amanda looked around the room, the disgusting and wretched room where she had led Sir Samson. *This is where the course has led me! I'm still in the same horrid prison after forty years!* She wept again. Then she thought of the moment when she had thrown herself at Sir Judas's feet. In that moment she had felt...something. She still did. It was something...good? But how? The last several hours had been nothing but tears, yet she felt...better. She remembered his words. 'I am going to save Sir Samson! Tomorrow morning the sun shall rise, and Castle Nightfall shall see its setting.' Freedom. Freedom from the guilt for what she did to Samson. Freedom from the dark doom she had helped him form.

Lady Amanda went to the window and looked west. The stars and candlelight in her room disappeared as she peered into the darkness that extinguished all things. "Freedom...not only from this darkness, but from the other one as well...the one I cannot avoid...death!" Tears flowed from her eyes as she kept looking into that terrible abyss. "Can it really be? It doesn't seem possible. After all I've done, Sir Judas's God would never forgive me." She thought back to what she had been taught as a child, about mortal sins that God would punish with hellfire. "Any one of those sins would damn my soul, and I've accumulated an entire litany. Maybe there's forgiveness for some, but not for me. I've burned that bridge, and only ashes remain."

At that moment something happened that had never happened in forty years. She saw moonlight; she saw it while looking at the dome of darkness. The ocean and the mountains and the fields were all bathed in silver, and rolling white clouds were tumbling across the sky. And the darkness–the all-extinguishing, irresistible darkness–was suddenly quite restrained. It was just a dome now, the tiny tip of which poked above the horizon, surrounded on all sides by many colors. Lady Amanda threw her face into her hands and started bawling, sobbing loudly from what she had seen. She lowered her hands again, half-expecting it was just a passing fantasy of her imagination, yet the light remained. The darkness that had seemed invincible just moments before was clearly overpowered. The light was stronger. The Light could shatter that darkness whenever He was pleased to do so.

Lady Amanda softly whispered, "Oh my God…is it true? Is it really true? Is this Your answer to me?" For the first time in half a century, Lady Amanda fell to her knees and said a prayer. "Oh God, I don't understand how You could ever forgive me, but I believe it. It seems impossible, but I believe. Please have mercy on me, dear Jesus." Then lightning flashed from inside the darkness–it lasted only a moment, but she was sure! Light had come from inside the darkness! And then with a booming voice of thunder, she heard God speak directly to her soul. All the weeping she had done these last several hours was like nothing, for her tears poured forth sevenfold. She was no longer crying from sorrow, but from joy. In the depths of her heart Lady Amanda knew her sins had been forgiven.

She fell on her face and adored, and the weight of the old woman fell away. The new woman arose. The woman who had fallen to her knees was afraid of tomorrow. The woman now standing was ready to face eternity.

Volume V

Winthrop Reborn

Chapter 1: The Duchess of Nouen

On Wednesday night, Winthrop stumbled along, going as fast as he possibly could. Blood was still coming out of his heart, and though it hadn't killed him, his consciousness was slipping away. With the moonlight fading he staggered forward, trudging into the worst night of his life so far, yet what was only destined to be the second worst by the time the Week was done. He needed to see her, yet he was terrified to do so. More than any woman in the world, the thought of talking to her once more frightened him. He hastened towards her, though he knew it didn't matter how fast he went. She was coming for him. The night was black. The moon was gone. The stars were all covered by clouds. Darkness. Almost all he saw was darkness. But there was one light shining, and so he didn't see darkness at all. All he saw was...*her*

They were walking through the garden behind the manor. It was a cloudy and overcast day. It was going to start raining soon. Winthrop was picking raspberries, those weird purple ones that only grew at home. She was next to him with a basket, trying to pick what she could reach without bending down. She squatted while holding her pregnant belly, but then she stood up suddenly and groaned.

"Ooooh...okay, Winthrop honey, it's time to go back in the house." She was so young, only in her twenties. He never noticed that before. He was only three, so she didn't seem young to him back then. In her twenties...so little of her life was behind her, and so much should still lie ahead...

He took her hand, walking along with the concerns of a little heart. "Are you okay, mommy?"

She smiled. "Yes, honey, mommy's going to be just fine. I think your younger sibling is coming today." Winthrop had been so excited when she said that. He didn't know any better. He thought this would be a happy day.

But he wasn't three. Not anymore. He was fifty-six. He wasn't short. He was taller than his mother now, holding her soft little hand in his injured left hand, with a hideous scar running down his arm. "Mother, you're not going to be fine. You're going to die today!"

Her countenance darkened. "...I know."

He was shocked. "What do you mean you know?"

"...It doesn't feel right. It's not like when I had you. Your little sibling is sideways. I don't think they're going to fit."

"He's not, mother, he's not! The surgeon is going to come, and he's going to say...he's going to say..." The words were stuck in Winthrop's mouth. Even now he couldn't bring himself to say them.

"What's he going to say, Winthrop? That it's me or him? He can get your brother out, but one of us will have to die to make it happen?" She closed her eyes and hung her head. "I'm going to die today, Winthrop. Fr. Ron kept reminding me that this could happen. I went to Confession two days ago. I'm ready."

They were almost inside. Winthrop's mother stopped for a moment and put her hands on her back, letting the next contraction work. When it was over they held hands and started walking again.

"But mother, what about God? Shouldn't He save you? Shouldn't He do a miracle? This is all His fault! He could save you at a snap of His fingers, and yet He's going to let you...He's going to let you..."

There was so much pain in her face. Winthrop wasn't sure if it was from the labor or from what he was saying. She answered him, "This is my time, Winthrop. I am sorrowful because my hour is come. So what shall I say? 'Father, save me from this hour'? But it was for this hour that I came into the world, that you and your brother might have life through me. Instead I say, 'Father, let Your Name be glorified'." Winthrop heard thunder. He hadn't seen any lightning.

"Mother...what about me? What about Jacob? I need you. Father is going to die when I'm fifteen. Jacob will die when I'm nineteen. Mother, I'm going to be all alone. I need you. Please! I need you!"

She hugged him. "You'll have me. I'll always be there. Do you think that mothers only take care of their children when their children can see them? Don't be silly, Winthrop. All your life I've been watching over you. While you sleep, while you play, while you had no idea I was there. This isn't the end of me watching over you. Now I'll be able to do it always."

He was three again. The dream passed swiftly now. He was playing in the house without a care in the world. Then there were people coming and going. The doctor came. Fr. Ron came. The maids were weeping. Winthrop was summoned upstairs to his parents' bedroom. His father's cheeks were wet. His jaw was quivering. Jacob was in his arms. Winthrop's mother was under a thick blanket, even though it was summer. Her face was pale. Her brow was sweaty. "Three beautiful boys…all together with me." She closed her eyes. She smiled. She spoke her dying words. Then her hand fell down beside the bed. Duke Isaac burst into tears. It wasn't like him. This day and the day he died were the only two times Winthrop ever saw him cry.

Young Winthrop didn't know why mommy was sleeping. He started to cry in frustration when she wouldn't wake up. Old Winthrop awoke from his dream in the much deeper tears of understanding.

The final words of Lady Rebecca, Duchess of Nouen were thus: "This is the happiest day of my life. I'll be watching over all three of you until you see me again in heaven."

Chapter 2: An Honest Prayer

Darkness. Almost all he saw was darkness. But there was one light shining, and so he didn't see darkness at all. All he saw was her. The light was dim, barely glowing. A tiny candle in a blue holder. Its dim light showed an icon of the Blessed Virgin. A sword was piercing her heart. Winthrop's own heart throbbed at the sight.

He crawled over to the icon of Mary, his face mere inches away from hers. "How can you just accept it? How could you let it happen?" His eyes adjusted to the darkness. He now noticed a second icon. Winthrop picked it up and brought it into the candle light. It was Jesus, holding His Sacred Heart in His hands. That Heart was scourged, crowned with thorns, and pierced in the side. That Heart was on fire.

Winthrop looked back to the icon of Mary. "Don't you remember the wedding at Cana? Don't you know He'll do whatever you ask? 'His hour has not yet come,' yet He made it come at your request. When He was hanging there on the Cross, didn't you know you could have prevented it? Didn't you realize you could have saved Him? He wouldn't call his twelve legions of angels for Peter, but if you had asked, He would have summoned them to smash the Cross and conquer the world. Why didn't you ask Him to save Himself? Why did you let Him die there?"

Winthrop dropped his head to the ground then slammed the dirt floor with his hand. He looked back up and shouted at the icon, "Look, Lady, I want to believe! I really do! But your Son is telling me I have to stand by and watch my father get killed by a giant, who turns out to be a paladin that betrayed his oath. I have to watch my brother die without any Sacraments because Fr. Zambri was too busy flirting to give him Last Rites. I had to grow up without a mother because God cursed her childbearing over the sin of Eve, a woman I've never even met. And your Son wants me to bear all these things, endure them patiently, and still say, 'Blessed be the Name of the Lord.' How am I supposed to do it? How is it even possible to do it? If you had really done it, I would believe. I wouldn't understand, but I would believe. If you could watch them torture your Son and know you could save Him, but instead you stood by and said, 'Blessed be the Name of the Lord,' I would know there was a bigger plan, even if I'm too blind to see it.

"But how do I know? How could I ever know? The Church says that's what you did. The Scriptures say that's what you did. But how do I know those stories aren't made up? It's a whole lot easier to believe that men in charge *made up* the story of a woman who accepts whatever comes her way than to believe you actually stood by that Cross. I don't see how a Mother can lose her Son and suffer all that pain, all while she had the power to save Him, yet instead she says, 'Blessed be the Name of the Lord.' I need a sign, Lady. I need you to give me a little proof. Give me something. Anything! I know your Son said a wicked generation demands a sign. Well I'm a wicked man, and I'm not afraid to admit it! I need you to send me a sign from heaven! Please!"

Winthrop stared at the icon, hoping some sort of miracle would happen. "Please!"

The Blessed Virgin just stood there, holding her heart, looking right back at him.

"Please!"

Winthrop leapt back and took a sudden breath. He couldn't believe his eyes. He blinked. It was gone. He blinked again, repeatedly. All he saw was the Blessed Virgin, yet…he had seen it. He started to write it off, but…No! He had seen it! He wasn't going to lie to himself! He knew what he had seen…

About that time, Winthrop noticed an uncomfortable bulge in his pocket. He reached into it to see what was there, pulled it out, and dropped it in shock. It was a rosary. The one Lady Maria had given him yesterday. He had completely forgotten about it until now. "Maria…" Winthrop leaned back, sitting in the dirt. "…Ave Maria…"

He looked back and forth between the icons of Jesus and Mary for what only felt like a few minutes, but it must have been longer, because to his surprise he now noticed they were well-lit. The whole room was well-lit. The mid-morning sun was coming in through the window, lighting up the little shack. It was Zakary's hut, the one Winthrop had searched for water two days ago on Tuesday afternoon. Today there was a little tin plate set out with two small cakes of bread and herbs. Winthrop looked back to the icon stand, then out the window. How long had he been sitting there? A new thought occurred to him.

Did Zakary know he was here? Or had he just let himself in last night? As he arose he felt the tug of something around his chest. It was bandages. He wasn't wearing a shirt. Instead he had long, white strips of cloth wrapped around his torso to cover his wound. There was a red spot on the right side where Sir Judas had stabbed him, starting to soak through. "What on earth is going on?"

Then the door flung open, and Zakary–soaking wet–sidled in sideways carrying his water yoke. His jaw dropped when he saw Winthrop on his feet. The yoke fell to the ground with a large splash. "How are you standing? Oh no, this isn't going to work. Easy now, Winthrop. This is just the second wind. You might be feeling better, but you're not *actually* better. You're going to be stuck in bed for a good long while with that wound you're nursing."

Zakary was trying to get Winthrop to sit down, but Winthrop pulled himself free and brushed Zakary off. "Don't worry, Zakary. I have it on very good authority that this wound isn't going to kill me. Can you tell me what happened last night? I don't remember much after I was stabbed."

"You're the one who I was going to ask for an explanation! I was asleep in bed when a shriek woke me up. I came to the door, where I found you sprawled out on the ground. In the distance I could hear someone riding away on a horse. I couldn't see anything because of how cloudy and dark last night was, but I figured someone must have killed you and then left you here for me to deal with. Only it turned out you were alive!" Zakary tapped the red spot on Winthrop's bandages. "I can't believe that wound missed your heart somehow. It's a miracle you're alive."

Winthrop smiled. "It is certainly a miracle." Looking around the room, he asked, "Where are my shirt and sword?"

"I took them to the barn. The shirt and your belt both had blood on them that I was going to try and wash out."

"Thank you, Zakary. I'm going to go grab them–"

Zakary stepped between Winthrop and the door. "Not so fast, 'Lord Winthrop'. When I went to town this morning, I heard a lot of talk about the commotion you caused at Lady Maria's yesterday. One rumor in particular that needs addressing is that you supposedly confessed to a murder. I hope you'll understand that I have no intention of letting an alleged murderer go grab his weapon before I hear an explanation." Then another thought occurred to Zakary. "And while you're at it, if you could please explain how you got your hands on such an ornate sword while getting stabbed in the process, that would clear up some concerns I have as well."

Winthrop rubbed his forehead and sat down in the dirt. "Zakary, where do I even begin? I suppose the first thing to mention is that two days ago when I came to ask you for water, I lied to you. And I'm really sorry for that. I often say words are wind, but I mean it. I really am sorry. Probably half an hour after I lied to you was when I decided I need to stop lying forever, and so the lie I told to you will hopefully be the last one. So here's what really happened…" Winthrop proceeded to relate to him the actual events that led to the deaths of Rowan and Garrett, how he had been arrested by Sir Judas, the aura surrounding Sir Judas that made him start thinking about his childhood this whole Week, the fantastic fight in the glade, his falling out with Sir Judas and fleeing arrest…he related everything up to when he had met Zakary, what happened in town, his conversation with Lady Maria, and then the events of the previous evening. He told Zakary how it was Sir Judas who stabbed him in the heart, and how ever since that happened his heart had felt this burning need to go meet Lady Maria. Lastly, he finished by explaining the prayer he had been saying before the icon, and what he had seen this morning.

"So then I was looking at the icon…just begging our Lady to give me some sort of sign, and then…oh, this is going to sound stupid to you, but…Zakary, I saw her face completely change. It changed so she looked just like Lady Maria. Or you could say it was like Maria had been painted into the icon of our Lady. It only lasted a moment, and then the icon went back to normal, but I'm certain I saw it. I wasn't delirious or anything from the blood I lost last night either. I saw Lady Maria's face in the icon, and she is the very person I've been longing to see all night. And then, as if that wasn't enough, I reached into my pocket and found a rosary she had given me, which I completely forgot about. Now I'm convinced that I need to go talk to her. I asked for a sign from heaven, and heaven said, 'Go talk to her.' So I will. But!" Winthrop threw his hands up in the air. "There's no way I'll get anywhere near her house before the whole town descends upon me! I'll be killed or arrested before I even get the chance to say, 'Hello.'" He dropped his arms again and asked Zakary, "You wouldn't happen to know a way for me to sneak in, would you?"

Zakary shook his head in wonderment. "Winthrop, you are a hurricane of activity that has blown through my sleepy little life these last three days. I'm still reeling from finding out you led a band of robbers and met a paladin, and you're already twelve steps ahead trying to sneak into town! I can't keep up with you!" Zakary took a deep and thoughtful breath. "You know, I probably wouldn't believe you, and I certainly wouldn't help you, except that I had a bit of an experience today. I went into the water pillar, like you did yesterday, which was very beautiful, but…nothing compared to what happened while I was praying the Rosary. Today is Thursday, so we were doing the Joyful Mysteries, and then when we got to the third mystery where Jesus is born in Bethlehem, I had an *experience*. I don't think it was a vision, but I don't think it was completely natural either. It was like I was doing my best with my human efforts to see that moment in time and meditate, and then God took me deeper into it to show me something. I saw the baby Jesus, brighter than the sun, shining like He did at His Transfiguration. I saw Mary looking right at Him, the first woman to ever see God face to face. I saw Joseph, approaching on his knees, coming to adore his Creator. Then I saw all the angels, streaming towards Bethlehem. They were processing from the furthest extents of the world, from the furthest extents of the universe. An uncountable number of them all came from heaven, and it was as if the Father and the Holy Spirit left heaven to come to the manger too. It was this incredible spectacle, Winthrop, and it was all so real. I never thought about it before, but it was as if I could see God and all His saints all in one little cave, this blinding light that gave me the power to see. And then the little lord Jesus solemnly declared, 'All of this and more I would do, if even one sinner would repent.' It hit me, Winthrop, it really hit me. I came back here thinking about how everyone said you were a killer, and yet I had had this experience in prayer, and now…oh, now you've got me thinking. What should I do if even one sinner would repent? If God would humble Himself to become man, and suffer, and die, for even one sinner who repents, then what could I possibly refuse? You think heaven wants you to talk to Lady Maria? Then I will get you in to talk to Lady Maria, even if I have to take up my cross."

"Zakary, thank you!" Winthrop leapt to his feet and hugged him. "So what's the plan? How are you going to sneak me in?"

Zakary shook his head thoughtfully. "I didn't say anything about sneaking."

"What other option do we have?"

The shepherd knelt down and began unrolling the black ball of clothes he used as a pillow. "Yesterday I told you that you had given me the courage to be a little bit crazy. Today I'm going to be even crazier."

Chapter 3: All Roads Lead to Dewford

On Thursday there were three pairs of travelers making their way to Dewford. The first to arrive were Sir Joseph and Destiny, who set out on horseback from the northern gate of Chelles in the pre-dawn hours. Though it took all of his courage to leave her alone, he knew his mother would be safest if they left the city by different gates. He and Destiny would ride north on the 'official business' of hunting down Sir Judas, while his mother could pass herself off as a peasant and go east to deliver the two packs to Sir Judas and David. Sir Joseph and Destiny made sure they waited until there was enough light to see them clearly, and Sir Joseph stopped to banter with one of the guards for good measure. It was imperative that there were witnesses who saw them leave by the northern road. They were expecting Fearnow to come looking for them eventually, and the misdirection just might save their lives.

After riding up past two hamlets and their farmlands, they found a good field to turn and ride east. They galloped for a short burst, wanting to get away from the road and anyone who might see them. Then they let up once they had reached the rocky wilderness and were sure they were alone. From there they went at a lighter pace until they emerged from the hills bordering Dewford. It was about nine in the morning when they got to town, reaching a crossroads where a bridge over the town's moat met a dusty trail that circled the town. Sir Joseph wanted to go south immediately, but Destiny reminded him that if they met his mother in the vicinity of Chelles, the whole point of splitting up would be wasted. It was going to be several hours until Emma reached Dewford, and it would only invite questions if they went to the rendezvous point too early. Instead she suggested they look for a tavern somewhere near the eastern gate and pass the time there. After asking the locals where they could find such an establishment, they were pointed towards E&S's, and the two of them attempted to go there at once. They soon discovered that it was nearly impossible to navigate the twisting alleys of the small town, especially because the bridges across the aqueducts were often too narrow for the horses. They spent nearly an hour getting lost and asking for directions before they finally managed to arrive at E&S's. After tying their horses off at the hitching post, they went inside and discovered the tavern was empty. Destiny looked around at Ed's religious decorations in disgust. "What terrible taste they have in this town. This must be the ugliest barroom I've ever seen."

Sir Joseph shrugged. "It's not modern, but it's nice enough. Now let's see about breakfast." He walked around, loudly announcing, "You've got some customers up front! Is anybody here?"

There was a clattering from under the floorboards, and then Ed came out from a back room. "Oh, good mornin' to ya. And who exactly do I have the pleasure of hostin' this morning?"

Sir Joseph answered, "Two travelers passing through and in need of breakfast. Whatever the price, we'll double it if you don't ask too many questions." He clearly had no idea who he was talking to.

"Oh, now I'm afraid that's an offer I am rather undisposed to be acceptin' now, mister sir. For starters, I would never put two hungry travelers over a barrel and extort 'em for what God ordered me to give away for free. You can stop and have yourselves a bite here, free of charge, any time ya want. So ya see, even though I appreciate the sentiment of ya payin' me double, I'm not terribly motivated by an offer like that. Now as to the other little bit of what some might call 'suspicious circumstances' of wantin' to be passin' through without even a name to call ya by…now that's a somewhat suspicious thing if I do go ahead and say so myself. Not extremely suspicious, mind you–Ole Ed is always very careful with his words, and don't throw them around too loosely– but definitely *somewhat* suspicious. I'll tell ya why I don't find it *extremely* suspicious. You're gonna wanna go ahead and take a seat, this story might take a little time. So just yesterday I had a guest in here–ah, it's probably not good for business to be tellin' ya this, or else you'll have a low opinion of my establishment–but this guest, he was a stranger that told me his name. 'Winthrop, duke a Now Inn' he said, cool as a cucumber. Didn't miss a beat. Totally acted the part. Well as fate would have it, he was actually one bad egg. And I ain't talking about the kinda egg that's gone a little bad, I mean a really rank one ya can smell from three doors down. He was a *killer*! And Ole Ed, I never suspected a thing. Not the first time that's happened neither, no. Twice now I've had a killer sit down at this bar and have a drink, and I served em right up thinking it was some ordinary customer. So now that's got me sayin' to myself, 'Ed,' I says, 'if you don't suspect someone a nothin', that's an extremely suspicious individual, but if you find them to be extremely suspicious, that's only a somewhat suspicious individual.' So usin' my new system, I only find you two to be somewhat suspicious, so I don't make too much pumpkin pie outta you not wantin' to tell me your names. Still, I'll be needin' a name to call ya by, or else I'm gonna start gettin' confused when I try to talk to ya."

Sir Joseph, agitated beyond manners by his anxiety for his mother, said, "Ed, we are travelers on pressing business. We've been on the road all morning and are going to be on it this afternoon. If you could please get the lady and I a bite to eat…"

"Oh, pressing business. I can certainly relate to that one. If ya didn't already figure it out from the way I'm bein' rather terse and a little bit short with ya, I'm also in a big rush right now. Just half an hour ago I got my water in for the day, and I'm in the process a gettin' some of it ready for brewin'. Homebrew everything myself around here, I do. And it certainly is a bit of a process, if ya don't know much about it. Are either of ya familiar with how wine and beer get made?"

"Please, Ed! Breakfast!"

Destiny tutted him. "Ed, my darling, you will simply have to forgive Sir Fitheag here. He's a bit of a boor, as those northland knights can be. But do tell me more about this wine you make yourself. I'm a bit of a connoisseur of fine beverages. You wouldn't mind if I sip on a little as we're sitting down to breakfast, would you?"

"No, not at all. I'm always appreciative of someone who knows how to slow down and appreciate the finer things. Now, let me tell ya all about my opinions on women who drink wine, and how that differs from men who drink it…"

Destiny and Ed chatted without a care in the world, despite the tight timetables they were both supposedly keeping. Meanwhile Sir Joseph felt the long, slow minutes inching by. A thousand different ways his mother might get caught or arrested were running through his mind. In the midst of his frustrations, he was enormously grateful for Destiny. He simply wasn't in a mood for small talk, yet right now that was one of the best things they could do to avoid arousing suspicion. From the way she was laughing and quipping, no one would suspect she was a traitorous Administrator on the run. Sir Joseph chuckled to himself. Ed's tavern really did seem to attract a certain kind of person...

At long, long last, two bowls of last night's stew were on the bar (Destiny turned up her nose in disgust at the salty leftovers) and a mug of wine was being poured. "Will Fithy Fitheag be havin' a mug as well?" Ed asked.

Curious about the moniker, Sir Joseph asked, "Fithy?"

"Means 'shorty'" Ed sniggered. "Ain't my most creative name, but still a fine one none the less." Sir Joseph's face fell. He was none too happy about a nickname that might identify him.

"Go ahead and pour me a splash. I might as well wet my whistle while we eat breakfast."

Ed produced a second mug and put a little wine in it. "As I was sayin' just a little bit earlier, I do have some rather strong opinions on men who drink wine, but since you're just havin' a little sample, I might have to de-intensify my usual assessment by a bit..."

As Ed prattled on, Sir Joseph took his mug and held it up to Destiny saying, "Cheers."

With much more delight and bubbliness, she responded, "Cheers!" and touched her mug to his. Sir Joseph drank his wine in one gulp, and his eyes went wide in astonishment. "Oh my goodness, Ed! This is amazing! This must be the best wine I've ever tasted!"

Rather than taking delight in the compliment, Ed's eyes were filled with horror. He was looking at Destiny and sputtering, "H-h-hey lady, are you alright?" Her face was red and she was clutching her throat. Foam had formed at the corners of her mouth. After several seconds of gurgling, she coughed out the wine and rasped, "Poison!"

"B-what? Whadya mean poison? I would never poison nobody!"

Her eyes became dark and frightful. Sir Joseph wrote it off as a trick of the light, but he thought her irises looked black. She jabbed a finger in Ed's chest and shouted in a deeper voice than usual, "THE WINE BURNED AS SOON AS IT TOUCHED MY TONGUE, AND I NEARLY CHOKED TRYING TO SWALLOW IT!" She continued, hissing threateningly, "You're an agent of Fearnow's, aren't you! Tell me how you caught up with us if you want to live!"

"Whadya talkin' about? Fearnow from Chelles? What's he have ta do with anythin'?"

Sir Joseph took Destiny's mug and sniffed it. It had the same delightful smell that his own mug had had. He tried a small taste. Delicious. A big gulp. No effect. By now Destiny had grabbed Ed by the shirt and was threatening to have him tortured in the most barbaric fashion if he didn't start talking. Sir Joseph pulled them apart and said, "M'lady! Calm down! I just tried your wine, and it's not poisoned at all! It didn't affect me in the slightest!"

Marginally calmer, she looked at Sir Joseph (it must have been a trick of the light, for her eyes were their usual brown color again), and she asked him, "Really?"

"Really! It's not the wine, but you. Maybe you have some sort of allergy to it."

She looked back at Ed. "If you want to live, drink the rest of that mug right now. Otherwise, I'll know you poisoned me."

"Of course! Of course!" Ed exclaimed. He took the mug and downed it all in one go. When it was empty he turned it upside down. "See? Ole Ed would never poison nobody! Never even cross my mind! You must be allergic to somethin' I use to make it. Oh, thank God you're safe! If your allergy were worse, we woulda had a right tragedy on our hands…"

Ed sat down in his chair behind the bar and wiped the sweat from his brow. "Whew…well this has been quite a mornin'…quite a Week, if I'm bein' honest. I think I've had more than enough excitement to last me the rest of the month. Ole Ed is ready for everythin' to start calmin' down, and then he can get settled back into his normal routine."

It was at that very moment that the second pair of travelers came through the front door.

With both great excitement and great trepidation, the happy fiancés left the Chellesian outskirts along the eastern road. They had waited until about dawn (unusually early for them to be up) before going to wake Larry and ask him to run the shop. Upset both to be woken up so early and also to be imposed upon at the last minute, he negotiated a rather hefty take of the revenue for everything he sold the next few days. Kayden was in such a grand mood that he actually accepted the terms, even though he knew he would be losing money on everything Larry sold. Kayden then prepared a small shipment of pâtés, dried meats, cheeses, fruits, and a dozen bottles of wine–a splendid arrangement for a poor man's engagement party. It was all loaded into a hand cart that he often pulled around town for others who were hosting such events. At first Sasha objected on the grounds of Kayden's injuries the day before, but he assured her that he was actually feeling quite well this morning and he was more than capable of pulling that cart to Dewford. As they set out about an hour after dawn, Sasha asked, "Are you sure that he's going to be this happy to see us? He might not be in much of a partying mood."

Kayden answered, "If he isn't happy to see us, hopefully some candied jalapenos will change his mind."

She rolled her eyes. "Sometimes your ideas are brilliant, and sometimes they're *not*."

"And which category does this idea fall under?"

"I haven't decided yet."

They followed the road east all the way to the junction, foregoing a shortcut across the fields because the cart might get stuck. As they were coming up into the south of Dewford, Sasha got a little dewy eyed. "I forgot how nice this place is. Chelles always had the appeal of being a big city, but Dewford is…it's very nice, in its own quaint little way."

"It is," Kayden said, "And it's so close by we can easily visit. One of my suppliers actually comes through here twice a month just because he likes to spend the night in Dewford. This should really be a big time destination when people want a vacation from Chelles. I wonder why it isn't?"

Sasha shrugged. "It's a sleepy place. The people back home like excitement. There isn't a whole lot of that in Dewford."

They were now several blocks into town, following the main road as far as they could so that they wouldn't have to pull the cart across any aqueducts. One man who was passing them stopped and asked Kayden, "Are you some kind of merchant, boy?"

"Yes, but not today. I have a delivery for Ed the barkeep. Can you point me to…oh, what's the name of your father's tavern again?"

"E&S's."

"That's right. Can you point us to E&S's?"

"Of course, it's right over…wait, are you Ed's little girl? Sasha? It is you! I'd know that red hair anywhere!" For a moment the man looked excited, but then he looked back at Kayden. He gave Sasha a stern look and said, "Well you certainly have a lot of nerve. Did 'Clyde come lately' here get you pregnant, and now you need your father to put you up?"

"Who's the one with a lot of nerve!" Kayden dropped the cart and grabbed the man by the front of the shirt, shaking him roughly.

"Is this how men act in Chelles? A bunch of savages who fight at the drop of the hat? Go ahead and hit me. Constable William will have you arrested in no time."

Kayden reached back to throw a punch, but Sasha grabbed his arm and said, "No, Kayden! Leave him alone! All you'll do is get arrested." Muttering and sputtering, Kayden let the man go, picked up his handcart, and started walking.

The Dewfordian spat and said, "Coward and a harlot. A perfect couple." Then he left and returned to his own business.

Once they were alone, Kayden said, "Gah! Why'd you stop me, Sasha? I should go back and pound him to a pulp! He has no right to talk to you like–" Only now did Kayden realize that Sasha had started crying. "Sasha, Sasha, what's wrong?"

"What's wrong? I'm an idiot, that's what's wrong! Oh, what was I thinking? If one of my dad's patrons that I barely know is still upset with me, why did I ever think my father would forgive us? Let's go home, Kayden. I've already humiliated myself enough."

"Hey, hey, hey! None of that! No giving up on our plan! We're gonna go see your father and tell him we're getting married. He'll be happy for us, just you wait and see."

"And what if he isn't? What if he's still mad and he throws us out again?"

"Then I'll knock his lights out, go to prison for a few days, and when I get out we'll get married anyway."

She shoved his arm. "That's not a real answer."

"We'll figure it out. Same thing we always do. There. That's my real answer."

"Okay…" Sasha took a deep breath. "Are you sure you still wanna go through with this?"

"Absolutely."

"Alright, then come this way. I still remember where the tavern is, you goofus. I lived here all my life until two years ago."

They made their way to the town square and then turned northeast, following the large aqueduct until it dropped into the basement of E&S's. Walking past two horses on their way to the front door of the tavern, they heard animated shouting coming from inside. "Sounds like it's already a lively day." Kayden smiled at Sasha. "You ready?"

She nodded. "Ready as I'll ever be."

Kayden put the handcart down, put his arm around Sasha, and they walked into the barroom together. A noblewoman was rising from her chair and brushing her dress as she said, "Well this is one of the worst breakfast stops I have ever made. You can be *certain* that I will never recommend this place to my peers. And I will have you know that in addition to your wretched wine, the breakfast was absolutely *disgusting*! Hey! Look at me when I'm talking to you! What are you staring at? Pay attention!"

Ed was paying attention, just not to her. Confused, shocked, uncertain, he rose from his stool and started to walk, then ran over to his long-lost daughter. He threw his arms around her and kissed her, and she said to him, "Oh, daddy! I'm so sorry! I've missed you, and I–I don't even…oh, what am I even supposed to say? I hope you're not mad at me!"

"Mad at you? I'm just happy you're alright!" Still hugging Sasha, Ed looked at Kayden and nodded. "Clyde."

"My name is Kayden, Ed."

"Course it is. I remember your name is Kayden. I also remember your nickname is Clyde. 'Clyde come lately' to be precise."

"Ed, I've asked your daughter to marry me. I know you were angry at me before because we didn't get married, but…if it's not too late, I'd like to put that behind us and start over."

Ed tensed and straightened up, about to pour out his indignation. Who did Clyde think he was? To show up after two years and just say, 'I'm marrying your daughter, let's put it behind us.' No apology? No asking for his blessing? Ed almost said these thoughts that were in his head, but then two thoughts from his heart occurred to him.

First, Clyde was an idiot. He was one of those kids who grew up in Chelles without a father and probably didn't even know how disrespectful he was being. Second, Ed thought of Maria, and all that she had been through. *If Lady Maria can take all that and still forgive, I can forgive ole Clyde come lately.* Thinking these things, Ed relaxed, held out his hand, and said, "I forgive you, Kayden. Let's bury the past."

Kayden smiled, took Ed's hand, and pulled him close for a hug. "Okay! Easy now, Clyde! Don't think we're gonna be getting' all mushy gushy!" Kayden let go, and Ed looked back at Sasha. "So my little girl is gettin' married? Oh my! Ed, ya ball o'wax for brains, ya need to start throwin' a wedding feast! When are ya kids tyin' the knot? Today's Thursday, so…Saturday?"

Sasha blushed. "Dad! That's way too soon! The style nowadays is to be engaged for at least a year. We'll still need to pick a venue, a caterer–"

"Don't be ridiculous. The venue is E&S's tavern, and the caterer is all my friends." Then Ed ran out of the barroom and into the street. "Oh look! Clyde already brought enough to get the party started! Hey Andrew! My daughter is getting married! Yes, really! She's returned! Let everyone know! Mrs. Featherflop (his nickname for Cara O'Dewforthios, on account of her ostrich-feather hat), there's a wedding feast! Hey, Lil' Punchy! Go out to the fields and get Zakary! Tell him to send his best three sheep to the butcher, and I'll give him what is just. If he asks why, say, 'Ed's lost daughter has returned, and the wedding is this Saturday!'"

Ed was running around in a joyous frenzy, shouting to all the town that his daughter's wedding feast had begun. Sasha was blushing red as a beat. "Kayden! Go tell him we're not getting married on Saturday! It's way too soon!"

Kayden laughed. "After two years, me and your dad just made peace. I'm in no rush to lock horns with him again. Besides, what will be the harm in getting married sooner rather than later? I don't have anything scheduled for Saturday."

"You! But you–it's–it's just not done! What do you mean, 'Saturday?' You–you–you *expletive*!! How could you possibly agree with my *dad*? You two are *crazy*!" This was the day when Sasha was cured once and for all of her 'speech impediment' that only struck when she was angry at Kayden or her father. For the rest of her life, she was perfectly capable of using all of her creative powers of vulgarity whenever they acted in a way that deserved it.

Sir Joseph leaned over to Destiny and whispered, "We need to get going *now!* If the whole town descends on this tavern, someone is sure to recognize us."

Destiny leaned even closer and took Joseph's hand. With the bubbling tone of a woman in love, she whispered words that were dissonantly calculating. "I've worn a mask as long as I've been an Administrator. No one knows my face. You are not currently wearing your armor. We are not in Chelles. So long as you remain seated at your barstool, no one will notice you are short, besides the barkeep who knows you by your alias. No passing observer in this little town will ever suspect that we are fugitives. With a wedding in the air, they will simply think we are a cute couple, married about ten years based on our ages." She squeezed his hand and bumped him with her shoulder. "Play your part, *dear*."

Sir Joseph nearly fell out of his chair, so great was his astonishment. Then he leaned back in and whispered, "You Administrators are downright creepy. How can you pretend to be in love so easily?"

As soon as the words left his mouth, he realized how naïve he sounded. He expected Destiny to sneer at his question, but she actually became quite thoughtful. After twirling her brown tresses a few times with her finger, she answered, "How can you tell whether you're really in love, or just pretending?" When she saw how surprised Sir Joseph had become, she quickly added, "I'm not talking about you. Someone else…"

He scratched his head and answered, "Why would you ever pretend to be in love?"

Her eyes drifted away, then came to rest on Ed's stained glass of the Crucifixion. Pointing at Mary Magdalene and the Lord, she said, "I'm not interested in weeping for the man who dies for me." She then pointed at the Mother of Jesus and John. "I'll find a different man to keep me safe." Absentmindedly, she chewed her lip for a moment. "I've become too practical for love. Pretending is all that's left."

Sir Joseph could say nothing. Heart filled with pity, he simply wished there was something he could do to heal whatever wound Destiny was mourning. That was the only moment since he kissed his mother goodbye when he was not worried sick about her. Then Destiny wiped her lip and trilled, "So what time are we expecting Mahrith today?" and he remembered who was still another hour away.

Meanwhile the wedding feast began in earnest. E&S's was soon stuffed to the brim and the feast poured out into the street. The food Kayden brought was rapidly devoured, but many of the guests had assembled their own offerings, bringing an eclectic collection of foodstuffs spread out at random locations in the tavern and the surrounding roads. It was a little past noon when Constable William finally managed to find Ed. He had come to investigate the party nearly an hour ago, but the crowd was so vast and Ed was moving so rapidly that it was very hard to catch up with him. Putting an arm around the proprietor, William said, "Big Eddie! Congratulations! I heard Sasha finally came home."

"That she did, William, and I'll tell ya this might be the happiest day of my life. Maybe even happier than when I married her mother. Golly, Ole Ed's been blessed."

"That you have, my friend. So tell me," William asked, rubbing his large belly, "...do you have any plans for a main course or is it gonna be all these little dishes?"

Ed slapped the constable's arm away, pretending to be insulted. "Is there a main course? What kinda cheapo host do ya take Ole Eddie for? Of course I have plans! Lil' Punchy went and told Zakary to send his best sheep to the butcher's. He shoulda been back by now...oh look! There he is! He's wavin' right at us! Runnin' awfully funny he is. Wonder what's got him all worked up?"

Pushing and jostling his way through the crowd, Lil' Punchy was shouting, "William! William! He's coming back! Over here! We need to go, right now! He's coming back! He said he's going to see Lady Maria! And coming with him–I didn't even recognize him! I never would have known!"

William forced his way through the crowd as well, and when he got to Lil' Punchy he grabbed both his shoulders and said, "Calm down, Eustace. Tell me who's coming."

The crowd quieted down, seeing that some sort of trouble was clearly brewing. That's why practically the whole town heard Eustace announce the coming of the third and final pair of travelers.

A little over twelve years before the events of this tumultuous Week, Dewford had another great upheaval. What sparked that tragic series of events was when Most Reverend Paul, a missionary bishop, came to Dewford to look for a worthy young man to ordain to the priesthood. After finding such a man and giving him a whirlwind introduction to the faith, the basic vestments, and a single copy of *Institutio Generalis Missalis Romani*, Most Reverend Paul ordained that man and took off for another town, carrying on his mission of rebuilding the Church after the fall of the Grand Empire and the universal persecution that followed.

The aftermath of that ordination shall be related very soon, but suffice to say things eventually calmed down and then the new priest got to work. He secretly and subtly spread the Gospel through the town in cooperation with those who had been baptized by the bishop. Because priests were relentlessly hunted down and murdered by the nobility, he was afraid to make himself known. Nevertheless, he gathered an ever-growing flock of townsfolk to say the Rosary every day, hold secret Masses in E&S's every Sunday, and pray in the dead of night at the graves of all who died. So cautiously did the men and women of Dewford guard the identity of their priest, and so circumspect were they in their dealings, that in all those twelve years not only did none of the unbelievers accuse that man of being a priest, but furthermore he was perhaps the last person in the entire town that the rulers would suspect.

Priests were known for living in beautiful rectories; he lived in a one room shack. Priests were known for dressing as ornately as nobles; he wore the same stinking shirt every day. Priests were known for demanding everyone treat them with respect; his social status was one step above his sheep. There was nothing in his appearance to make them consider him, yet he was the one who bore their infirmities, praying without ceasing for their poor little town, and offering up an Immaculate Sacrifice for all their sins.

Now the hidden years were ended. He who was counted least among them carried the silver sword of a duke. He who was ridiculed for owning a single shirt had donned a black cassock and purple stole. He who lived on the furthest edge of society was now processing to the heart of town. His left hand was draping one end of his stole over Winthrop's shoulder, while he chanted loud and clear, "Nam, etsi ambulavero in medio umbrae mortis, non timebo mala, quoniam Tu mecum es," which being translated means, 'For though I should walk in the midst of the shadow of death, I will fear no evils, for Thou art with me.'

Winthrop processed with his hands prayerfully raised together, head bowed, looking at the ground in front of him and thinking, 'This will never work...this will never work...this will never work...'

He was wrong.

It was working.

All the visitors who saw them stopped and stared in awe, totally overwhelmed by what they beheld. The Dewfordian believers, not understanding, nevertheless formed a procession and followed their priest. At the bridge across the moat Eustace ran up to them, stopped, and gawked, stupefied with all the rest. As Zakary was passing him (I suppose I should refer to him as 'Fr. Zakary' from now on), Eustace breathlessly asked, "Where...where are you going?"

Winthrop answered, "To the house of Lady Maria." Fr. Zakary kept chanting. Eustace took off running. The procession wound towards the center of Dewford, men, women, and children all making way for the unimaginable prodigy they saw before them. As Winthrop and Fr. Zakary turned down the street Lady Maria lived on, a commotion and shouting could be heard from E&S's nearby. *Almost there!* Winthrop thought. *C'mon, Zakary, just make a run for it!* He did no such thing. Fr. Zakary continued processing at a solemn and dignified pace.

A stampede came from the other direction, a crowd of men led by Constable William. They surrounded Lady Maria's house, and William stood in the middle of the road. Fr. Zakary and Winthrop processed until they were two feet away from him. William drew his club.

"Step aside," Fr. Zakary commanded.

"You–I can't even–Zakary, I...that man's a killer! Get away from him, Zakary! And where did you get that black robe? Take it off now and stop pretending! If you keep acting like a priest, I'll have to arrest you both!"

"Step aside. By heaven's order this man is to meet with Lady Maria."

"Zakary, there is absolutely no possible way I'm letting a confessed murderer in the same room as a poor crippled woman. I'll crack his skull in half first!" William drew back the club menacingly, showing he was willing to swing, but not doing so yet.

"I have placed my stole upon this man. He is under my protection. To hit him is to hit me. Would you really strike a priest of Almighty God?"

William wavered. His mind was still swirling in total confusion. He couldn't put all his thoughts together, but he grabbed onto one that was the clearest to him–his duty as a constable. "Zakary...he's a killer. I have to arrest him. And if you're really a priest, I have to arrest you too. It's the law."

"There is a Law above the law, and in the name of that Law, I command you to step aside!"

William was torn, exasperated, uncertain...yet he lowered his club. He stepped aside. The crowd gasped as Fr. Zakary processed past him, processed right up to the door of Lady Maria's house, opened it, let Winthrop go inside, and then slammed it shut. There were some people in the crowd who had half a mind to go around to Lady Maria's window and try to either eavesdrop or climb in. Those thoughts died as soon as Fr. Zakary flourished *Veritas* and pointed it at the sun. With the afternoon light dancing off that gleaming metal, strange tricks of the light flashed all about, and for a moment–just a moment–

it seemed as if the sword was ablaze and the priest had wings of light. The image passed quickly, but the dread remained. No one dared to try and enter while Fr. Zakary stood at the door.

Chapter 4: More Silence

Lady Maria was propped up on her bed crocheting. Winthrop stood at the door.

Silence.

"Sounds like you caused quite the commotion out there."

Winthrop nodded.

More silence.

"Well do come in, Duke Winthrop. Take a seat in one of my chairs."

He nodded. He walked over and sat in a chair beside her bed.

More silence.

"Why did you come back to town?"

Winthrop swallowed, finding it nearly impossible to summon any words. He finally managed, "I needed to see you."

More silence.

"Oh, Winthrop, I'm not that special. You're going to get yourself arrested just to visit a worthless cripple. That was awfully stupid."

He shook his head. "You're not worthless. You just might be the most valuable person in the whole world to me right now..." He tried to ask the question that was weighing on his heart, struggled to put it well, couldn't think of how to phrase it, and ended by simply blurting out, "Do you believe in God?"

More silence.

"Of course I do. You already know that. Please tell me you came here for a more important purpose."

"That's the purpose. It's the all-important purpose. I wanted to know if you believe in God, but not only *if*, I also–what I'm trying to ask is...*how*? How can you believe in Him? And not just any God, but the Christian one, the one Whose Mother you pray all your Rosaries to. If you believed in Zeus, or Thor, or the goddess of arts, crafts, and baby blankets, or any other god, I would understand. Believing in gods who get angry and punish people for stupid reasons makes perfect sense, because this world is filled with people who are suffering and there's not a single good reason why. But how can you believe in the Christian God, Who is all-good, all-loving, yet allows you to lay here every day and waste away in a…in a…" Winthrop looked at her grotesque, broken body. "He's letting you waste away in a living hell!"

Silence.

Lady Maria gently smiled. "Is this what you think hell is like?"

Winthrop waved his hand over her body. "Every time you move you suffer so much."

She shook her head. "Winthrop, there are two kinds of suffering in this world. The suffering that comes from hell isn't pain or torture, at least not on this side of eternity. It's the suffering of anxiety, stress, and boredom. It's the suffering of getting what you want, realizing it doesn't satisfy you, and then picking something new to chase. Then you get what you want again, and the cycle continues, round and round, getting all of your greatest pleasures, none of which make you happy as your life is slipping away. That's not my suffering at all.

"My suffering is the suffering that comes from heaven. It's the pain of getting what you want, realizing it satisfies you perfectly, knowing it would make you happy for all eternity, and then losing it, because we can never hold on to heaven for long in this vale of tears. All we get are little glimpses along the journey. Every taste of heaven is a cross, but it's a sweet cross. It's a cross you rejoice to carry, because it's better to suffer and fight and take the kingdom of heaven by violence than to drift in through no effort of your own. Are you getting it yet, my duke? Can you see? My sufferings are not in contradiction to an all-powerful, all-loving God. They are His gifts and His promises as I'm climbing His holy mountain."

Winthrop leaned over her bed. "I don't get it. I don't see it. What good can possibly come from you lying here in pain? Why isn't it better for God to raise you back to health?"

She held up her crooked left arm and laughed with sad tears in her eyes. "Because by my pain I pay the price for so much good. I can ransom my late husband from purgatory. I have purchased the safety of my son. Someday, who knows? My sufferings might merit the grace of conversion for a sinful stranger who is very dear to me. Could God do all of those things without my suffering? Of course. But isn't it more beautiful that he would entrust this work to me?

Shouldn't I rejoice that He made me a co-redeemer with His Son? My dignity in suffering is so much greater than it would be in pleasure."

Winthrop took her hand. "What even happened to you? How did you get to be this way?"

She gave a sorrowful smile, then began to relate the events from twelve years prior…

Chapter 5: The Bloody Baron

Back then a bishop came to town. He started teaching us the faith. I believed right away, but my husband Matthew was less enthused. He was distracted with his work and projects, and going to Ed's bar (it was a very different tavern back then). He received Baptism, but he made clear he did it just to make me happy, not because he thought it was a big deal. Around that time our first son was born, and my husband named him David. He didn't want him baptized though because he thought David should decide for himself when he was older. Me and the bishop both protested, but Matthew wouldn't even consider changing his mind.

Sometime later the bishop fled town, but he told me Fr. Zakary was a priest in hiding. He had been a family friend for a long time, since his father and Matthew often worked together. Two days after the bishop left, the Baron came to town, a big brute of a man named Charles, and a sorcerer besides. He was an absolute monster, one of the most sadistic villains I've ever had the displeasure of meeting. The first time I laid eyes on him he sent shivers down my spine. Him and a dozen thugs started terrorizing the town, throwing people out of their homes while they searched for the priest and confiscating anything valuable as 'evidence.' Things were bad, but we thought we might be able to tough it out. Then Lady Amanda arrived.

She was the wife of the lord of Chelles. She wasn't here for long. She came out to have a meeting with Charles. The rumor was that she was explaining the rewards he would receive if he found and killed the priest. God only knows what she promised him, but after talking to her any semblance of humanity he still had withered away. First he killed the constable. He beat him to death right in the town square and threw his body in the well. Then he did the same to the mayor. Then he went to Ed's tavern for a drink, which has always haunted Ed. Then he said the most horrifying thing. He said that unless we turned over the priest to him, he was going to take all the children in town back to his manor, and dedicate them to the service of his god Jove. We were all terrified. Everyone started talking about the best way to get out of town.

Everyone except Matthew. I still remember how that night he looked at little baby David for a long, long time. I asked him what was on his mind, but he wouldn't tell me, just keeping it to himself. The next day, Matthew went to the well in the center of town and announced, "I'm the priest! I'm the one everyone's looking for! I'm sorry I didn't turn myself in sooner."

My knees gave out beneath me when I heard him say that. I had no idea he was planning it until it happened. With David in my arms, I ran up to him and yelled at him to stop lying before he got himself killed. But he just kept on lying, saying, "I'm the priest. The bishop ordained me when you weren't around, Maria. Sorry I didn't tell you." Then, as the Baron was storming towards us, Matthew hugged me and whispered his dying words. "The one line Jesus said that really hit home with me was that part about saving your loved ones. 'No greater love has man than this, that he should lay down his life for his friends.'"

Charles fell upon him with wicked glee and strangled Matthew to death, not ten feet away from me and crying David. Then he threw his body in the well, and a terrible shadow came upon him, this black thing that I saw enter right into his heart. He stretched out his hand over the well and said, "Cursed be the waters of this well. May poison and death fester in all who ever drink or even touch them. May these waters be a perpetual reminder to all who live here of the fate of those who oppose me." Then he chanted some ominous gibberish in a language no one understood, and a terrible stench worse than corruption poured forth.

I was on the ground weeping, bawling my eyes out. Then I felt him grab the back of my dress and pull me up. He ripped David from my arms. I was trying to wrestle him back, but another man grabbed me and tore me away. I was screaming at him, "No! No! What are you doing? Give me my baby!"

The Bloody Baron walked over to one of his carriages, put David in the arms of one of his cronies, and then slammed the door and the carriage took off for his manor. Charles announced to the town, "The rest of your children are safe, but I'm taking the priest's son as a lesson to you, lest anyone ever dream of violating Lord Fearnow's ban on priests again." Then him and the rest of his outlaws gathered their things, all the plunder they were stealing from us, got in the rest of their carriages and went home. Long before they left, I was already running after David.

The carriage went south out of town–impossibly fast, being pulled by those dreadful nightmares of his. Even after I lost sight of the carriage, I kept running. I ran and ran, until I came to the big hill that the southern road wraps around. I clambered up, knowing the carriage was probably long gone, but still hoping to get a glimpse of it. What I saw took my breath away. The carriage was overturned. One of the nightmares was missing. The other was dead. I was already exhausted, but I ran the rest of the way to the wreckage. It looked like the work of a robber. The horse had been shot with a crossbow, and the man in the carriage had a bolt in his chest as well. David was gone. Not dead. He wasn't there. I was worried I would find his poor little body in the carriage, but I didn't. The robber took him.

I was overjoyed. It's strange to say, but I was probably the only mother to ever rejoice that a robber had kidnapped her son. It meant he was safe. I didn't know what his fate would be with the robber–probably slavery–but it was a case where the devil I didn't know was better than the one I did. I was still at the scene of the crash, laughing and weeping when Charles and the rest of his men caught up. He was astounded. "What did you do? How did you do this?" I laughed at him. "Tell me what you did, woman!" I spat in his face.

He started to beat me in a rage, angered more than anything by my joy. He kept threatening that he was going to torture me until I answered him. I couldn't stop smiling. The crueler he revealed himself to be, the more grateful I was that my son was saved from his hands. Every twisted and perverse thing he did to me was one that David had been spared. That was why I was so happy. I was offering all these sacrifices for my heroic husband who had saved the town from doom. I was suffering in David's place, an opportunity any mother would take in a heartbeat. I was even suffering for that robber. He could have left my son for dead. I would have gotten to see David one last time, but it would have been the pleasure of a moment, taken away when Charles caught me. Because that robber had enough humanity to take my David with him, David was saved. I know that man's a villain–robbers are wicked men. But at least for that little bit of goodness he showed my son, I begged God to have mercy on that robber and let me offer my tortures for his conversion. To this day, every day, whenever I feel my sufferings, I say, "For love of you, O Jesus, I offer up these pains. Please call that robber to Yourself."

Lady Maria awkwardly wiped the tears from her eyes with her deformed hands. "When he could finally stand me no longer, the Bloody Baron took me back to town and left me in the town square against the well. Sweet Ed took pity on me and nursed me back to health. That was also the time when the pillar of water began to fall every day. Everyone was worried about what we were going to drink, but God provided. Fr. Zakary came and said a Rosary near Matthew's body, and the water fell. The same thing happened the next day, and the next. Then there came a day where no one prayed a Rosary there, and no water came. We realized that getting together to pray the Rosary was bringing about the miracle, and so the town has kept getting together to pray, every day for the last twelve years."

Winthrop was pale and trembling. She said, "Sorry to startle you…I've had so long to process these things. I forget how shocking it is to hear them for the first time."

He pointed his thumb at his chest. "I'm the robber."

Silence.

"What do you mean?"

More silence.

"I'm the robber. I ambushed that carriage. I was on the back side of the hill, and I shot one of the horses. The other one kept running until it overturned the carriage. I was hoping to find a noble and some loot. I found David instead." He looked down in disbelief, placing his hands on his head. "His blanket. It said 'David.' You crocheted that, didn't you?" Tears were in Winthrop's eyes as he looked at the baby blanket Maria was holding in her lap. "I got him a nurse outside of Chelles. Began using all of my loot to pay her until he was old enough to come along with me." Winthrop leapt up. "Maria! I'm the robber!"

In a hurry she started trying to rise, struggling to quickly get out of her bed. After briefly flailing, she laid back down and said, "Come here! Come here! Oh, let me hug you, Winthrop! Let me kiss you! You're not lying to me?"

"No! I promised you I would never lie again! I'm telling you, Maria, I'm the robber! Do you see this scar on my left arm? It's from when I tried to ride away with David on the surviving nightmare. After getting almost all the way back to Reswick, the horse turned around and galloped full speed for Dewford. I had to jump off and hold David in my right arm while the ground smashed my left to pieces. I've raised David these last twelve years, Maria."

"Oh!" She covered her face and cried. "Come close, Winthrop! Oh, let me hold you! I dreamed I would meet you someday! Tell me, where is my David? Is he alright?"

Winthrop nodded, "Yes, he's alright. I just saw him last night. He's with a wonderful man now. Sir Judas, Last of the Kingsguard. He's a paladin from the Grand Empire who has come from the other end of the world to face Goliath. And David...he's a little hero, Maria. Oh, I'm so sorry...he's going with Sir Judas to help him fight Goliath. He has a holy dagger that glows when he holds it, and he's going to use it to help Sir Judas finish his quest. Last night I knew I needed to come see you, but I told them as soon as I was able I would go after them and help them as well."

Lady Maria was hysterical with joy. "He's alive! He's alive! Oh, thank God! And thank you, Winthrop! Oh, thank you so much! I can never thank you enough! Why won't you come closer? Come closer and let me hug you!"

Winthrop still sat in his chair, not ready to come any closer. "Maria, I...I've done a terrible job of raising him. I'm so sorry, but...I'm a robber. I'm no saint, and I don't deserve your thanks. I taught David all of the wrong things. I introduced him to all of the wrong people. You should be cursing me, not hugging me."

"Oh, Winthrop, he's alive! You kept him alive! Can I not thank you for that?"

"No! You can't! I'm sorry, but you can't! The things I've done right for David are so much smaller than the things I've done wrong! Go ahead and weigh them in the scales of justice. I deserve your hatred."

"Oh, forget what you deserve! Why should I care what you deserve? The constable will take care of getting you what you deserve. I'm grateful we have William, because someone has to think about what's 'deserved.' But I am no constable." Maria straightened up as best she could, and then with a sober solemnity she declared to Winthrop, "I thank God I was born a woman, that I became a mother and not a father, because as a mother I am free to put away the sword of justice and cry for mercy. Someone else can bring down the wrath of God on robbers, but for myself I cry, 'Mercy! Mercy! Good God, show him Your Mercy!'"

Winthrop finally lunged forward, and putting his arms around Lady Maria he said, "How? Why? Why should I have your mercy? And why am I still too blind to see? ...No, I'm not too blind to see. I have to be honest. I do see. I don't want to, but I've seen enough pieces of the puzzle come together..."

He lifted his head and looked Lady Maria in the eye. "I need to ask you a favor…"

The door to Lady Maria's house opened. Winthrop came out with Lady Maria, who was holding his left arm and hobbling along. Winthrop looked around at the crowd, and called, "Ed! Please come here. Lady Maria needs a place to sit for a little while. Can you set her up in your barroom?"

William came forward. "Not so fast, Winthrop. Before you get any funny ideas, you're under arrest."

"Don't worry, William, I'll come quietly. I just need you to give me an hour first." Winthrop turned to Fr. Zakary and said, "Father…please hear my Confession."

William was about to object, but instead he nodded. Ed took Lady Maria. Winthrop and Fr. Zakary went into the house. An hour later they came back outside. Everyone who was still there gasped.

As a historian, I must say that this particular moment was one that really surprised me. Even with mundane events, different sources and witnesses tend to report them very differently. They use different words and descriptions, and different people remember certain details that others forgot. Not with this moment. Out of the witnesses who were there that day, I had the opportunity to interview a total of seven. While their accounts of these events had a natural amount of variety up until this point, at this moment they all converged. Every single witness I spoke to used the exact same phrase to describe what happened, what they saw, and why it had made them gasp. I asked all seven witnesses what the phrase meant. Not one of them could explain it. It was a mysterious thing. It was a thing men could know and recognize, even if it was a thing they could not understand. This is the phrase I heard in all seven interviews, and I submit it as the only words that could possibly describe the moment in question;

"When Winthrop came out of Lady Maria's house, he looked like a man who had been raised from the dead."

Chapter 6: The Baron Returns

A strange, strange wedding feast was underway at E&S's. After the initial turnout of over half the town, everyone had gone to Lady Maria's house to see the confrontation between Winthrop and Constable William. After Winthrop's Confession, the constable had arrested both him and Fr. Zakary, and the townsfolk had then followed all of them to the jailhouse to see what would happen. Reginald was there when they arrived, but he did not stay for long. Certainly not long enough for an official trial. Moreover, instead of sending his herald out ahead of him, he simply strode out the door with his head down, lost in thought. It was clear to all that he was deeply agitated over something, yet none dared to ask what it might be. After all this excitement and activity, most of the townsfolk ended up going back to their neglected chores and duties instead of returning to the wedding feast.

Now the only people at E&S's were Ed, Sasha, Kayden, Lady Maria, and Destiny. Not one of them was in a good mood. Ed was worried sick about Fr. Zakary, muttering repeatedly, "Oh, bother Zakary, ya sure got in a fix now…a real fix ya got yourself in…my, it's a mighty fix…and how is my Sasha supposed to get married without a priest?"

Kayden and Sasha were upset that their impromptu wedding feast had been so suddenly interrupted. They had now begun to argue about how long they should wait, whether getting married on Saturday was a good idea or not, did this feast 'count,' who's fault was it that this party was a disaster, etc. Such are the silly concerns that arise for engaged couples who don't yet realize their wedding feast will be forgotten in a year or two and only the marriage will then remain.

Lady Maria was deeply distressed on a variety of counts. Fr. Zakary had been arrested, and she had no idea what Reginald would do with him. The mayor had never shown anything but indifference to the fact that his subjects (and wife) were increasingly Christian, but Maria feared the opportunity for worldly advancement might induce him to send Fr. Zakary to Lord Fearnow. She had learned that Winthrop was the man she had been praying for all these years, a mere hour before his arrest that would probably end at the gallows. Above all, she now knew David was alive, yet this joyous news laid heavy upon her because he was going to the most dangerous place in the entire world– Castle Nightfall.

Lastly, there was Destiny, who felt an ever-growing dread that this day would not end well for her. During Winthrop's commotion she and Sir Joseph had gone to the eastern gate to await their rendezvous with Emma. The appointed time came and went. Another hour passed after that. Neither spoke a word. The same fear was on both their hearts, though for completely different reasons. Sir Joseph was afraid that his mother had been taken by the Committee. Destiny was afraid that Emma would be tortured by the Committee until she revealed Destiny and Joseph's location. When the townsfolk began to return to their vineyards after leaving the constabulary, Destiny suggested that one of them should go back to the tavern with the horses in order to draw less attention to themselves. Sir Joseph nodded. She had known which one of them it would be when she suggested it.

Destiny was gnawing on her nails, trying and failing to compose an argument that would convince Sir Joseph that they needed to leave his mother behind and take care of themselves. She had just despaired of ever persuading him, when Emma came running into the tavern. Looking around wildly, she spotted Destiny and shouted, "Come quickly! You need to stop Joseph! He isn't thinking clearly!"

Bewildered, Destiny leapt up and ran to the door. As she went, she asked, "Where have you been?" and Emma answered, "I couldn't find them!"

Outside, Joseph stood beside Isabella. He had loaded David and Sir Judas's packs into his saddle bags while the bag in which he kept his armor was open on the ground. He was already wearing his hauberk, and was hastily strapping on his greaves. "Joseph! What are you doing?" Destiny demanded.

"My mother looked for Judas and David for hours and couldn't find them. No one even admitted to having seen them. It must be the Committee's doing. They're the only ones who leave no witnesses."

"The Committee attacked Sir Judas last night and was defeated. That's the whole reason Lord Fearnow wanted to kill me!"

"That was before...before the *revelation*. Fearnow told Sir Judas something so evil...he was a broken man after that. He passed out just from the grief before I left him...Damn it! I never should have left them alone!"

As he pulled on his gauntlets and unhitched Isabella, Destiny asked, "I'm sorry if what you say is true, but what do you think you're going to do about it?"

"I'm going to save him."

"You can't!"

"Then I'll die trying."

He pulled his helmet down over his head and turned towards the eastern gate. Destiny shouted, "Don't you care about me and your mother? Don't you care what will happen to us if you leave us alone?"

For that one moment, Sir Joseph wavered. Destiny's words almost made him stay. But then he looked down at David's pack, filled with the food they needed for the journey to Castle Nightfall. He recalled the calculations from Fearnow's chalkboard, and the short time until the darkness came for them all. With tears in his eyes, he turned to Destiny. "Of course I care about my mother...and you as well. I know we've just met, but...I promised I would keep you safe. I intend to keep that promise. I know you don't understand, but that promise is why I have to go save David and Sir Judas."

He spurred Isabella's flanks, yelled, "Heeyah!" and he was off. He galloped for the eastern gate, then turned south along the dirt trail just outside the moat. Destiny grabbed the empty pack he had left on the ground and hurled it after him, yelling, "Stupid knight!" After a minute or so of panting heavily as she cursed his cloud of dust, Destiny finally turned around and stormed towards E&S's. Ed and Emma stood outside the door, having witnessed the entire scene. The barkeep let out a low whistle. "Woo-ee, that's quite the series of interstin' phrases the two a ya were tossin' back and forth there. Now I don't wanna go intrudin' into no one else's business, but I do find it rather interestin' that you weren't callin' that Fithy fella 'Fithy' but rather 'Joseph', what with him bein' a short little knight and you tossin' Fearnow's name around and all that, makes a man wonder if I might know who Fithy really is..." Destiny gave Ed a look so venomous, he actually stopped talking.

After an initial gallop of exuberance, Sir Joseph reigned Isabella in. A horse, of course, can only gallop for a mile or two, and Sir Joseph knew that well. It felt painfully slow to go at a trot, but it was the fastest speed Isabella could hold all the way to Chelles. After following the moat-trail to the southern bridge, Sir Joseph turned onto the main road and passed through the shepherd's hamlet towards the large hill where Winthrop had first looked down at Dewford. He was in the very midst of debating whether he should follow the road or cut west of the hill, when he saw motion on top of the hill itself.

From a distance it seemed like the whole top of the hill was shaking. As Isabella kept trotting, he realized it was a large number of men walking around on the hill's crest, with their bodies mostly hidden from view. *Why are there a bunch of men on the hill?* Sir Joseph wondered. Then the sunlight hit one man's head just right, and Sir Joseph saw the gleam of a shining metal helm. His heart stopped cold. *It can't be...not near Chelles!* Then he heard a dreadful sound. The blood curdling screech of a nightmare ripped through him, making his bowels become unsteady. Shouts and war cries were raised, and as a teeming horde of men came streaming down the hill, four chariots came flying around it, racing down the road and straight towards Sir Joseph. Each was pulled by two of those frightful nightmares that the Bloody Baron was known to keep. Three of the chariots had three men each. They looked like they had been made for two (a driver and an archer) but Charles's best men had all squished in, not needing any room to drive since the intelligent nightmares were capable of steering themselves. The fourth chariot held the Baron, wearing bronze scale armor that was gleaming in the evening sunlight. With one hand on the chariot for balance, the other held a great and fearsome hammer. It was a wicked thing cast in the shape of a fiendish head. He pointed the hammer at Sir Joseph and yelled, "Remember what I said! No one escapes this town!" With shouts of assent, two men in the chariots raised their shortbows. Sir Joseph wheeled Isabella around, tapped her sides three times and yelled, "Heeyah!"

As far away as Sir Joseph was, he easily could have made the town. But after only going about fifty yards, he realized the farm houses around him were still occupied. Thirty feet away, a boy of about ten was standing at the door, looking towards the charging force with horror. Sir Joseph shouted at him, "Run! Run!" He looked towards the other houses. "Attack! Dewford is attacked! Everyone run to town! Now!" The boy moved. Terrified mothers and shepherds appeared from every house, and then there was a great rush towards the town. Sir Joseph looked back. They would be able to outrun the infantry, but the chariots...the chariots would mow these people down. The sight of the nightmares made Sir Joseph tremble, but with white knuckles he gripped the reins and turned Isabella around. *Alright, Joseph, this is what you wanted...this is the life of a black knight who is desperately needed.* He spurred Isabella forward and cried, "You shall not harm this town!"

Sir Joseph was too far away to see the faces of his foes, but as he watched them hastily swing their shortbows around, taking aim at him instead of whoever else they were about to shoot, he imagined how much surprise must be in their eyes. The first arrow loosed, and the archer failed to lead his shot. Sir Joseph saw the streaking feather and heard the whir as it went over his right shoulder. The second archer took an extra moment of preparation, loosed, and put the arrow exactly where he wanted it. It struck Sir Joseph in the center of his chest.

He felt a terrible jolt, and was winded for a moment, but other than that he was unharmed. "Idiot!" Charles roared. "That's not peasant padding, it's chain mail! Kill the horse, and then we can drag him back to town!" Sir Joseph thanked his lucky stars that the archers were using broadheads instead of armor-piercing arrows. He also realized, however, what short work those arrows would make of Isabella. As the archers hastened to ready their next shots, Sir Joseph drew his electro-gun. Its range was a little over ten feet, pitifully short for direct combat, but Sir Joseph had a trick up his sleeve. Isabella weaved left and right as she approached the oncoming chariots. One archer loosed and almost hit, but as Isabella turned to the side, the arrow hit Sir Joseph's greave and deflected. It still managed to scratch her flank, but the courser kept charging despite the scrape.

The second archer waited, knowing if he was patient he would have an unmissable shot before Sir Joseph got anywhere near them. As the distance narrowed and he was about to loose, Sir Joseph suddenly pulled back on the reins and Isabella stopped as fast as she could. As the surprised archer tried to adjust his shot, Sir Joseph pointed his electro-gun at the ground and pulled the trigger. With a loud '*CRACK!*' a blast of smoke and sparks hit the dirt, causing an explosion of dust and flaming grass. The heat from the fire caused a rapid updraft, and the grass began tumbling end over end in a rolling wave of flame. Such a small amount of heat was no more dangerous than the embers that fly from a bonfire, but the sudden appearance of the flame had the exact effect Sir Joseph was hoping for. The nightmares were startled and turned away from Sir Joseph, throwing all of the passengers in the chariots into each other and making the archer loose his arrow harmlessly into the sky. Isabella, trained to anticipate this tactic, resumed her gallop as soon as Sir Joseph ordered it and ran right through the gap in the chariots caused by the frightened nightmares.

The running infantrymen stopped in fright, and a cry went up, "It's Joseph! Joseph of Chelles! Why is he here?" Bewilderedly asking himself the same question, Charles said to his nightmares, "Turn around slowly. Stop by the white horse." As they began to circle back, Charles called out to all of his men, "Stand down! Don't attack Joseph!" The archers lowered their bows, while the other chariots turned to follow Charles. They came to a stop thirty yards from Sir Joseph, so that the knight had the chariots at his front and Charles' infantry at his back.

Sir Joseph barked at Charles, "I don't know what manner of madness has made you bring an army against your own town, but I order you to depart at once. I will not let you attack this people!"

Still trying to figure out why Sir Joseph was in Dewford, Charles answered, "Let's not be too hasty, little man. I am here to hunt a priest in my own territory. I brought enough men to assist me in case the townsfolk do not cooperate. Not only do I have the right to hunt a priest, but Lord Fearnow would surely approve of such an expedition. Why don't you tell me what his grace's business is here, and we can try to carry out our little manhunt without getting in your way."

"I don't believe your lies for a minute. You shot arrows at me until you recognized me, and would have murdered me if your aim was better! What arrest party attacks strangers?"

"One that is in a great hurry," Charles growled. "Now stop trying to intrude into the governance of my own town, and tell me where you and your men are staying. We will be sure not to touch anyone who is under Lord Fearnow's protection."

"I am not here on Fearnow's business! That despicable cur may permit such violence, but I will never stand for it!" Sir Joseph boldly declared, "As of this morning, I am a black knight. This whole town is under *Sir Joseph's* protection!"

Sir Joseph had swelled with confidence as he proclaimed those words. It evaporated as the Bloody Baron smiled. "You stupid little man. I wouldn't kick a dog if it meant war with Fearnow, but I will raze this town and laugh at 'Sir Joseph's protection'." Charles pointed his hammer towards Dewford and bellowed, "Attack!"

Hearing the murderous cry from the mob behind him, Sir Joseph spurred Isabella and rode west towards the hills. Charles yelled at his chariot men, "Don't just stand there! Kill him!" As the chariots slowly accelerated after

Joseph, he turned south and rode behind the hill where Charles's infantry had originally been hiding. He looked northward one last time before the hill blocked his view. The crowd of peasants he warned had reached town safely. Now he just needed to take care of himself.

Sir Joseph almost took the road to Chelles, and if he had it certainly would have been his doom. But wanting to still aid the Dewfordians and keep his mother safe, he trotted slowly around the hill to its eastern edge and gave Isabella a moment to catch her breath. Just as he expected, the chariots rumbled right past the western edge of the hill, heading south at full speed, and expecting to find Sir Joseph on the road. Instead he galloped north east, avoiding the southern gate where Charles's infantry were going, while still thinking he would have enough time to reach Dewford ahead of the chariots. It was this second consideration where Sir Joseph miscalculated terribly.

As lovely as Isabella's white body was, it was certainly not effective for camouflage. The nightmares spotted her almost immediately and turned to give chase. The race was on, hooves thundering, wheels clattering, and the chariots slowly gaining ground. Isabella was a fine courser, swift enough to outrun any horse tied to a chariot. But these were nightmares, not natural beasts. Despite how much weight they were pulling, they were still faster than Isabella, and able to run at full speed far longer. As the distance narrowed, one of the archers loosed a shot at Isabella. His bow bobbed high at the last moment, missing Isabella and skitting off Sir Joseph's thigh, only covered by the very bottom of his chain shirt.

The second archer waited until he was at twenty yards, too close to miss and getting closer. He leveled a steady shot right at Isabella's flank. Seeing his foes so near, and the gate so far, Sir Joseph desperately looked for something–anything–he could use. He remembered Sir Judas's pack. Reaching in, he produced the first object he could find. A frying pan! He flung it backwards at the archer. He missed to the left, but the chariot was packed tight. The man standing next to the archer dodged to his side and bumped the archer, forcing him to realign his shot. Sir Joseph hastily dug for something else–a shovel! Back it went, failing to travel the full distance, but causing the nightmares to swerve out of the way. The archer still held that shot, patiently waiting for his chance to strike.

The next item out was a bedroll, and Sir Joseph got a very lucky break. As he threw it the roll unfurled and landed on top of a nightmare's head. It started panicking and trying to shake the bedroll, swerving back and forth as it continued to run. It went right and was dragged by its partner, then went left and crashed into it. All the while the chariot was swinging about wildly, making any kind of aimed shot impossible. It also forced Charles to slow to a near stop so that he could avoid the careening chariot in front of him.

Sir Joseph had almost made the edge of town. He began shouting, "To arms! To arms! The town is under attack!" An arrow lodged in Isabella's left haunch. The other archer had finally found his mark. With a horrid scream she staggered and fell, throwing Sir Joseph to the ground in a brutal tumble. He landed at the edge of the moat, winded, bludgeoned, dizzy, and knowing he had mere moments before his assailants were upon him.

He looked back and saw a chariot with an axeman leaning out the side. He had little more than a second until the chariot was upon him. He clambered to Isabella. The chariot was at twenty yards. He reached for the holster on her saddle. Ten yards. He pulled the metal cylinder. Five yards. The axeman swung. Sir Joseph shot. There was a flash of smoke and sparks and crackling and a scream and then the chariot veered away to avoid the moat. The axeman fell from the chariot and tumbled into its depths. Weighed down with weapons and stunned from the blast, he swiftly drowned.

Panting heavily, Sir Joseph holstered his gun and reached into the pack. He pulled the crossbow, three bolts, and the goat foot. The chariots with Charles's vassals all entered the town by the bridge Sir Joseph was riding for, while the Bloody Baron circled back to deal with the dismounted knight. Sir Joseph carefully slid down the side of the moat, knowing he would sink like a stone if he fell all the way into the water. With his boots dug into the muddy walls, he leaned back against the side of the moat and hastily loaded a bolt into the crossbow. He heard the Baron yell, "Full stop!" and then the sound of heavy footfalls came from above Joseph's head.

Sir Joseph looked up. The Baron's armor glistened, including a helm that covered most of his head. Only the joints and face had any exposure. Every other place Sir Joseph could shoot would be a wasted bolt. Twirling the massive hammer around as if it were a toy, Charles said, "You picked the wrong day to 'protect' Dewford, little man."

Sir Joseph turned and pointed his crossbow at the Baron's face, awkwardly trying to keep his balance by dropping to one knee and digging his back foot into the mud below the water's surface. "I order you to cease your assault at once! Do not think I will spare you because you are a nobleman."

Charles snickered, "You will not kill me, but that isn't why."

Charles dropped to one knee and swung his hammer, reaching down into the moat to try and get Joseph. The fiendish head was still high by about a foot. Meanwhile, Sir Joseph had a clear shot at the Baron's face, and he didn't hesitate to loose his bolt. It was a direct hit to the face. The Baron grunted. Black ooze came forth from the wound. Charles reached up with his left hand and pulled the bolt out of his cheek. He snapped it with his fingers as if it were a piece of straw.

Sir Joseph dropped the crossbow in terror. "What–what sort of monster are you? You're not human!"

Charles reached down as far as he could with his hammer, and slithered in a serpentine voice, "*CICRUMRETIO*" As the man's eyes went all black, the eyes of the warhammer glowed red. From the devil's face claws slowly emerged, reaching towards Sir Joseph. He was paralyzed with fright, watching helplessly as the red talons inched ever closer. When he finally got ahold of himself and tried to jump away, the red claws moved blindingly fast and hooked themselves into his chain shirt. Charles's eyes and voice returned to normal. "Oh, I'm human…and so much *more*." He then stood upright, pulling Sir Joseph up out of the moat by the red claws. He casually flicked his hammer to toss Sir Joseph into his other hand, while the claws released him and faded. "In the coming world men will no longer be held back by highborn weaklings like your former master. The strong will be strong and the weak will be dead, and there will be no Fearnows to hide behind." The Bloody Baron smiled a wicked grin. "Welcome to the future."

Sir Joseph tried to draw his sword. He couldn't get it out of the scabbard while dangling in the air. Charles tossed him up and reached back to swing his hammer. In desperation, Sir Joseph drew his electro-gun and fired. In horror he heard it fizz, pop, and spew a few drops of water out of the barrel. He had gotten it wet while he was in the moat. As he came back down and Charles began to swing, Sir Joseph closed his eyes and cried, "God save me!"

His head hit the ground.

Sir Joseph blinked.

He felt like he was still alive.

There was a thud of the hammer hitting the ground.

He didn't think he should still be alive.

Sir Joseph looked up. Charles was staring at his hands. His face was wrenched in agony. A silent scream was on his lips. He staggered away for two steps, fell over backwards, and then the scream was no longer silent. He howled in unabated torment, as if a little spark of hellfire had just scorched him. Charles was grabbing and clawing at his face, trying to rip the skin off his own flesh, then shaking his hands wildly as if they too had been burned.

Sir Joseph got up and took off running. He had no idea what had happened, but for now, he was just grateful to be alive. He got into Dewford and disappeared down a little side street. He slapped himself to make sure he wasn't dreaming. *No, I'm definitely awake, but what was that? He must have had some white magic spell that protected him from pain, but it expired at just the right moment, and he suddenly felt the bolt.* Sir Joseph knew it was a ludicrous explanation, but it was the most plausible one he could think of. And for the next several hours, he wasn't going to have much time to think.

In the chaos of war and battle an outnumbered force can often overcome the greater army. Sneak attacks take this fact and push it to seemingly impossible heights. With no more than fifty men at his command (less one felled by Sir Joseph) the more than two hundred men of Dewford who were of fighting age could easily have defended their town. The problem was that those two hundred men did not know there were so few invaders. With chariots rolling, and arrows flying, and children screaming, and nightmares shrieking, any man of Dewford who crossed paths with the armed marauders quickly threw down his weapons and proceeded to be ushered into the great crush of people in town square. Even for the few who kept their heads and were prepared to fight, by themselves they could do nothing. They needed to unite with their fellow townsmen. They needed to know where to rally. Peppered throughout Dewford were dozens of militia men moving through the streets alone, waiting with great anxiety for Eustace to sound his horn and call them to battle. The horn never sounded. Over the course of the next hour, every Dewfordian was thrust into the town square at sword point, or else reduced to hiding in the most obscure hovel he could find.

For the fastest and most panicked Dewfordians, that 'hovel' was Mayor Reginald's manor. The large imposing structure of stone looked far safer to them than their own homes. They ran inside and quickly filled both floors, a fact Reginald was not at all enthused about. Moving to each of his subjects in a frenzy, he demanded that someone tell him what was going on. 'An attack' was all that he could gather, and besides that he was as confused and impotent as they were. Eustace needed to call the militia. That was the whole point of *having* a militia. Reginald moved through the rooms of his house in extraordinary fear and agitation, swearing and cursing that Eustace ought to do something. Then Charles kicked down the door.

The great armored behemoth stalked into the living room, where townsfolk crushed each other to move away from him. Surveying the general lot of them, the mayor's red coat and finery stood out starkly from the simple homespun cloth of the peasants before him. "Mayor! Come here!"

On trembling knees, Reginald advanced. "M—m'lord Charles. Why are you—I don't understand. Is this an attack? You—we have been nothing but faithful…why would you?"

Charles strode over to Reginald and puffed out his chest, shoving his armored scales in the little man's face. "I'm here for one thing and one thing only. There is a priest in town, and I want him dead. Get it done, and you can go back to being king of the dunghill."

Dread came over Reginald's face. "The priest? No, I…I…" Reginald's mind knew he had only one choice. His heart knew he had another. The memory of Lord Isaac, Duke of Nouen was still fresh on his mind, dredged up by the tumultuous events of the last three days. For a moment, he wished to stand and fight. For a moment, he wished to spit in Charles's face. For a moment he dreamed he would die a glorious death, a mayor who laid down his life to defend his people. It was only a moment. The moment passed and forty years of sensible pragmatism made Reginald believe he really did have but one option. "The priest is currently locked up in the jail. I will bring you to him at once."

Charles smiled. "Well this might be an easier job than I imagined."

"Yes," Reginald answered with a heavy heart. "Yes, it couldn't be easier." The mayor led the way.

"Coward!" Cara rushed through the crowd to meet him at the door, grabbing Reginald by the front of his coat. "What are you doing? He's going to kill Zakary! You know this! You know it!"

Reginald shoved her away. "Quiet, Cara! There's nothing I can do!"

"Why is your coat red?" She asked him with frenzied eyes. "Why is it red?"

He was on the verge of crying as he whispered, "I like the color. I just happen to like the color." Cara grabbed the sleeve of his coat and ripped down with all her might, tearing the seam at the shoulder so that the sleeve dangled by tattered threads. Then she ran out the door ahead of him, while Reginald fussed over the sleeve of his coat.

Charles roared, "I don't care about your stupid coat! Take me to the priest!"

Reginald wiped his eyes and walked out the door. "Of course m'lord. Of course." They proceeded out into the packed town square, where a way was made for Reginald and his entourage. He looked for Cara, but did not see her. Proceeding swiftly, he led Charles to the jailhouse, but at one point he looked down at his sleeve and tried to pull it back up, hoping he could somehow make it look presentable. While he was thus distracted, Reginald made a wrong turn, and was forced to double back, increasing Charles's impatience to fever pitch.

When they reached the jailhouse, a small crowd had gathered outside the entrance. Charles waved his hammer menacingly, causing the crowd to part and let him through. He tried the door. It was locked. As was his custom, he tried to kick it down. The thick, iron banded door held. In frustration he swung his hammer repeatedly. At first only the wood was breaking and splintering, but soon even the metal was bending under the force of his impossibly powerful swings. From the other side William could be heard shouting, "Whoa! What's going on?"

The door came down, and Charles yelled, "Take me to the priest!"

"Oh my–did you have a battering ram? The priest? Yeah, of course, uh…right this way…" There was a period of silence, and then a yell went up from inside the building. There were shouting voices, muffled talking, smashing, screaming, one man who ran out, Reginald barking orders no one listened to, and then William's body was thrown down the steps. The entire crowd saw with horror that his head had been struck by that terrible hammer.

In the period of Dewford's decline and poverty, many of the townsfolk had lived in a tight cluster of shanties that surrounded a tiny outdoor lot (perhaps originally intended as a courtyard) that was used for easing nature. Over the past decade, as the quality of life of the residents rose and the town also found a need for administrative buildings to govern its growing populace, the shanties had been taken over by the town and remodeled into a proper town hall. It was now a single, continuous building with very tiny windows and stone steps on the western side leading up to the only door in or out. Immediately inside the complex was a little lounge where William and Eustace would pass the time. Two curling hallways went back from the lounge, one running south to the courtroom, one north to Reginald's office and then bending back to meet each other at the jail on the eastern side. Altogether, the building formed the shape of a ring with a small courtyard in the middle of it. The lounge, courtroom, office, and jail all had doorways leading into the courtyard, which had been scoured and replanted in order to form a small grassy lawn for enjoying the outdoor weather. A vibrant red-leaf peach tree had been planted in the center of the courtyard, and the first fruits of the season lay uncollected at its roots.

Earlier on Thursday afternoon, before the attack, William had led Fr. Zakary and Winthrop back to the jailhouse. Reginald was impatiently waiting for them. "Where have you been?" he demanded of William. "I was beginning to think he slipped through your fingers again!"

"Sorry, mayor," William answered, "But Winthrop asked to go to Confession, and…it seemed prudent to me."

"Prudent? You fool! He could have escaped! And who is this priest anyway? Where has he been hiding?" Reginald studied Fr. Zakary's face and then nearly jumped as he recognized him. "The shepherd? You're the one who leads the Rosaries, aren't you?"

Fr. Zakary nodded. "I am."

Reginald sighed in frustration. "Well, at least I can rest easier on one front. It has always vexed me to see my wife letting a shepherd take the place of honor ahead of her. Now I know you aren't a shepherd at all."

"To the contrary," Fr. Zakary answered with a gallows smile. "I'm *more* of a shepherd than you thought, not less."

"Oh, spare me," Reginald rolled his eyes. Then jabbing a finger into Winthrop's chest, he said, "And you. You imposter. I'm sure glad you had a chance to 'Confess,' because you will be meeting your Maker very soon. We have your confession to murder. That's the real confession! By tomorrow you'll be hanging from a gibbet and I'll have you out of my hair. Let that be a lesson to any other criminal who tries to avoid guilt by impersonating nobility!"

"I am not avoiding my guilt," Winthrop answered. "It was I who came to you, not you who caught me. But I also want you to know, I never impersonated nobility. I really am the Duke of Nouen."

"Mayor, would you care to inspect this while I open the door? It was in the possession of Zakary when he came to town. He says he got it from Winthrop."

William handed *Veritas* to Reginald. The mayor turned it upside down and studied the hilt. "The silver sword...where did you get this?"

"From Sir Judas, Last of the Kingsguard. He received it on the day my father died."

"Bah! Enough of your fairy tales! Where did you get this sword?"

Winthrop looked at the mayor sadly. "I already gave you the true answer. I will not give you another."

Reginald's face darkened. He cast *Veritas* to the side, falling to the stone floor with a loud clang. Then he turned to leave in a hurry. William called, "Reginald! Wait a moment! After I lock the prisoners up, we need to talk about what to do with them."

Reginald did not wait for privacy to discuss the matter. He shouted, "Hang Winthrop. The priest...ah, my life would be easier if I hanged him too. Fearnow might kill me if I don't, but Cara certainly will if I do. Send him into exile tomorrow. Make arrangements." Then the mayor departed with a troubled countenance, setting all the town to talking about what had so disturbed him.

William locked Fr. Zakary and Winthrop into separate cells, but across the hall so that they could see each other. "I'm sorry, fellas. I...I'll try to talk to Reginald. A repentant man like Winthrop shouldn't have to face..." He trailed off. Fr. Zakary finished his sentence.

"Death?"

"...yeah."

"That's why cassocks are black, William. A priest reminds all men that death is coming. My only sorrow is that I didn't get to wear this lovely garment longer."

William closed the oaken door leading to the jailhouse and dropped the wooden bar to lock it. Then he picked *Veritas* up off the floor and sadly went back to his desk in the lounge. Zakary was a good guy. The smelly butt of everyone's jokes, but he took it all in stride and did a darn good job as a shepherd. The town wouldn't be the same without him leading their Rosaries...every morning would be dimmer with the priest sent out into exile. William sighed. *And how long will exile last? How long will it be until someone else puts him to death to please Lord Fearnow?*

It seemed like a crying shame. It was a crying shame. William began to cry. Then he thought of Winthrop. Now there was a man who deserved to hang. Killer gets killed. Done. But he was a repentant killer. The only reason he even got caught was because he wanted to talk to Lady Maria, who made him sorry for what he'd done. Couldn't a different punishment be arranged? Wasn't there a better way to settle this?

Over the long hours of the day Eustace was out on patrol. Most of the time passed with William putzing around the lounge in a melancholy and bitter mood. Soon a knock was going to come on that door and say it was time for the trial. Winthrop's or Zakary's, he didn't know. Today or tomorrow, he didn't know. Tomorrow meant his prisoners would have an extra day of life. Tomorrow also meant William would have to stew through the night.

The late afternoon turned into evening. William lit a few candles since the windows didn't let in much light. Shouting and screams started coming from outside. *What on earth is going on out there?* William ran to one of the little windows and looked outside. All he could see was people running around. He ran down one of the hallways, looking out each window as he went. He still couldn't figure out what was happening. He tried shouting through the window to ask one of the passersby, but no one would stop to talk to him. William thought of going out, but he decided against it. If this was some sort of external threat, Eustace would sound his horn. The most likely explanation must be that a riot was underway, and the most likely cause in William's mind was the arrest of Fr. Zakary. Whether the rioters wanted to free the priest or kill him, William intended to hold the door and make sure justice could run its course.

An hour passed, and William felt the clammy sickness of prolonged dread creep into his bowels. He was just beginning to hope that everything might be under control. Then a frantic pounding came on the door.

He rushed to the door and opened a little slit that allowed him to talk to whoever was outside. It was Cara O'Dewforthios, as well as several wild-eyed peasants. She began to breathlessly tell him, "Reginald...Reginald's leading him here, William. We have to get Fr. Zakary out! Please!"

William tried to calm her, saying, "Don't worry, Cara. Fr. Zakary will be exiled tomorrow, but we're not going to execute him. The hangman is just coming to talk to me about arrangements. Sending a man into exile requires a certain amount of preparation or else—"

"No! Not the hangman, the Baron! The Bloody Baron! The same one who killed Matthew for being a priest! The same one who tortured Lady Maria!"

William's face blanched. "*That* Baron? Oh my God...and he's coming here?"

"Yes! He's right behind us! He'll be here any minute! Please, William! Save Fr. Zakary!"

William closed the slit. The women outside kept shouting to him through the windows. He had just seen Lady Maria earlier today. *Oh God, no one deserves that! Justice is one thing, but I'm not handing Zakary over to that monster!* He grabbed the sword he had confiscated and ran to the holding cell in the back. Lifting the bar and throwing open the door, William announced, "Summary judgment!"

The prisoners looked at him in surprise. "What?"

"Summary judgment! When a prisoner is known to be guilty of a capital offense, and there is reason to expect he might escape before the trial, the constable has authority to pass judgment immediately."

"Don't worry, William," Fr. Zakary assured him, "We aren't going to try and escape."

"Yes you are! Because that devil, the Bloody Baron, he's coming here right now to do who knows what to you, but I'm not having a Lady Maria incident on my hands. The constable is supposed to protect people, and I'm protecting the two of you. Summary judgment! You're both guilty of your crimes, and I'm sentencing the two of you to community service. Get that Baron out of town! Save our people! He's looking for Zakary, so run far from here and he'll follow you! Winthrop, here's your sword!"

He handed *Veritas* back to its rightful owner. It flashed a silvery light as Winthrop grasped it. William was taken aback. "This whole time...you've been telling the truth...haven't you?...M'lord..."

"I was...William, run with us! Otherwise he'll kill you like he killed the constable twelve years ago."

There was a loud thud at the door. Charles's kick.

"It's too late! There's only one way in or out. I'm going to lead him back by the northern hallway right here, while you two are going to go down the southern hallway over there. Hide in the courtroom until you hear us back by the jail, and then make your break for it!"

The smashing of the hammer began. William ran back. Fr. Zakary shouted after him, "William! Thank you! You've given us our lives!" With tears in his eyes, Winthrop said nothing.

Constable William reached the front door, where the thick wood was splintering and the iron bands were bent. "Whoa! What's going on?"

The door came down, and Charles yelled, "Take me to the priest!"

"Oh my–did you have a battering ram? The priest? Yeah, of course, uh...right this way..." They walked in silence down the northern hallway. William's knees were starting to give out beneath him. As he tried to raise the wooden bar that locked the jail, it got stuck. He was feeling too weak to force it open.

"Out of the way!" Charles shouted, pushing William aside. He threw up the bar, flung open the door, and then thrust William in ahead of him. "Which cell are they in?" Looking around wildly, Charles saw that all of the cells were empty. "What's the meaning of this? Where is he?"

"Gone," William answered. "They went down the other hallway while we were coming here. Right now I hear Reginald shouting. He's probably trying to warn you that they got away. Good. I'm not letting you lay a finger on Zakary. My job is to protect the people of this town, and now I've done my duty."

Charles hefted William up off the floor with a single hand and slammed him against the wall. "You fool! Your 'duty' will cost you your life!"

"So be it."

Charles took one step back, threw William at the wall again, and with his right hand he swung that terrible hammer at William's head.

The dying words of William were more precious than finest gold. Those words have been lovingly recalled by his children, who repeat them at his gravesite once a year down to our present day. They were the words of a simple man. They were the words of a valiant man. They were the words of a small town hero who never had fame, glory, or power, yet possessed something far more wonderful–a pure conscience and the love of all who knew him. William spoke beautiful dying words.

Today was not the day he spoke them.

Winthrop ran into the jail with his sword pointed right at Charles. "Die!" he yelled as he sprinted across the room and drove the tip of *Veritas* into Charles's chest. It was a gap in the armor just below the shoulder, only exposed while Charles had brought his right arm back to swing his hammer. Letting out a cry, he still managed to swing, but the hammer went high and only clipped the top of William's head.

Even that glancing blow had injured William badly, and blood was streaming out the wound and down his face. Winthrop yelled, "Run, William!" and the constable didn't need to be told twice. He was already stumbling and staggering out the door and down the northern hallway, carried by adrenaline in that moment of life or death.

Winthrop pushed off Charles and did a back roll, avoiding the Baron's backswing with the hammer. The Lessguard didn't have a supernatural sense of deadly intent, just the natural one that came from decades of using hit and run tactics. Charles's wild blow was at waist height, right where Winthrop had expected it. Winthrop's roll put him under it, but something caught on his foot. Looking down, he saw an orange glow emanating from the hammer, and hooked around his ankle. "*CICRUMRETIO,*" Charles snarled, his eyes frightful and black. The Baron flung Winthrop up, trying to smash him into the ceiling. Winthrop slashed at the talon with *Veritas*, and to Charles's surprise the blade was able to cut through his magic, severing the claw and causing it to dissipate. The outlaw got his other foot on the ground and dove away, just barely dodging the hammer as Charles smashed it down into the ground.

Looking at Winthrop more closely, Charles said, "You were in the glade that night…so you *are* trying to get the priest to exorcize Goliath! Too bad for you that I'm here now, and there's no way the two of you are making it to Castle Nightfall."

Suddenly recalling what had happened that night, Winthrop looked at Charles's armored stomach. "I shot you in the gut. How are you still alive? How are you on your feet?"

"Heh heh…that little prick? Why, it's good as new. I would dare say it's even as good as the tickle you just gave me." Charles lifted his right arm and reached underneath with his left hand, pulling it back to show there wasn't even a drop of blood on his fingers.

"What the…"

"Sorry to disappoint you, but your weapons are useless against me. One of the many benefits of serving Jove. The armor is just for show, to keep people from getting suspicious." Charles launched an underhand swing at Winthrop. He dodged backwards, then turned and ran. He knew this battle wasn't winnable. Charles rattled after him, racing down the hallway much slower than Winthrop could run.

Winthrop got to the lounge up front. William had collapsed on the ground in a pool of his own blood. He ran up to the constable, and put *Veritas* on the floor. With both hands he heaved William through the broken door, tumbling down the steps to the crowd below. "Hide him!" Winthrop shouted. He knew what he just did wouldn't be good for William's head wound, but it would be better than falling into the hands of Charles.

The Baron ran into the room. If Winthrop went out the door he would escape, but that would lead Charles right back to William. Charles was charging with his hammer held high. Winthrop noticed the candles William had lit. Grabbing *Veritas*, he thought, *Here goes nothing,* and he pointed it at one of the candles.

"Emitte lucem Tuam et veritatem Tuam!"

Charles looked at the candle in horror, remembering what had happened in the glade. As soon as Winthrop had begun to speak, the candles all flickered, changing the lighting of the whole room. Charles covered his eyes and braced for impact.

No impact came. There was no silver fire. Nothing out of the ordinary. It was just candles flickering from Charles running across the room.

Winthrop took what he could get. In the moment when Charles was cowering, he sprinted down the northern hallway. Realizing what had happened, Charles made to pursue him, but then realized the futility of such a chase. *Where are my men when I actually need them?* He yelled at Reginald, "Mayor! Go get my men!"

"Y-y-yes m'lord, of course! I'll do that right away!"

Charles stood at the entrance, prowling back and forth like a tiger, anxiously looking down each of the hallways. No sign of Winthrop. He must be hiding in the back hallway, waiting for Charles to make a misstep. After what felt like an eternity, one of Charles's roughs came with his ax. "You called, boss?"

"Stand right here! Guard this hallway! No one gets past you! Understood?"

"Yes, boss!"

Charles went running down the southern hallway and flung open the door to the court room. No Winthrop. He looked in the jail. No Winthrop. He went to the northern hallway and opened the door to Reginald's office. No Winthrop. His man was standing at the far end of the hall. "Did you see him?"

"No, boss, no sign of anybody."

Charles backtracked in bewilderment. Then he noticed the door to the courtyard. "Ah hah!" He threw it open. There was a small lawn, a tree, and three other doors. He checked each of those doors, only to see they led to hallways he had already been in. He ran around the courtyard, overthrowing everything, making sure there was no possible place to hide. *Where did the devil go?* Charles took two more laps around the town hall, looking for any secret doors, hidden closets, or any possible place that Winthrop could be. If it wasn't nailed down, he threw it aside and looked behind it. Nothing. No routes of escape, no cubbyholes. Winthrop was just gone.

Fr. Zakary was long gone. By the time Charles gave up his search, William was gone too. Charles was enraged. As he finally stormed out of the town hall, poor Reginald was the only one around for him to vent his anger upon.

Charles dragged the mayor into the town square as he shouted, "Everyone listen up! I have an announcement!" He then let out a long, low whistle. It sent shrill tremors down the spines of those who heard it, even Charles's own men. Then the nightmares let out their horrid screams, and soon all four chariots were surrounding the square. Charles forced his way to the well and threw Reginald upon it before leaping up himself. "Listen here, and listen well! Some of you are old enough to remember the last time I came to this backwater speck of dung. That means you know what happens when I don't get what I want, and what I want is the following; before that tower rings nine o'clock, there are three people you are going to deliver to me. I want the constable, the priest, and the gray bearded stranger who was under arrest. By nine o'clock tomorrow morning you bring them to me, dead or alive, or else I'm going to teach you a lesson so unforgettable, that my visit twelve years ago will seem pleasant by comparison." Then he lifted Reginald with one arm and began shaking him like a rag doll. "And the first person I'll be showcasing this lesson on is your beloved mayor!"

The crowd of townsfolk looked at each other uneasily, not sure what to make of the present situation. Charles gave them some direction by yelling, "Get out of here! Start looking!" Then they all began to move in a rush just to get away from the angry and unstable Baron. As they were going, Charles yelled to his men, "Set up a perimeter outside of town! If anyone tries to leave before the three men we're looking for are dead, kill 'em!"

As the chariots rolled out with hoots and hollers, the townsfolk were all splintering off and talking amongst themselves. Most of them felt like there was nothing they could do but wait and hope that whoever was hiding the fugitives would turn them in. Only about a score of them were thinking about how they might search for those three. No one had any good ideas, but with only another two hours or so before the night was completely dark, they decided to head for the best place in town to get organized. They made their way to E&S's.

Winthrop waited in the peach tree breathlessly as Charles stormed around the courtyard. If even the slightest twitch rustled the leaves, he knew it would be his end. After several interminable minutes, he was finally certain the Baron was gone. Winthrop got down from the tree and made his way out of the town hall, into the streets of Dewford. He was trying to figure out where to go, when he heard the Baron begin to shout something from the town square. Wanting to avoid detection, Winthrop climbed to the top of the nearest building and then laid down flat as he crawled to the edge. He was still too far off to make out the words Charles was shouting, but he was able to see the scene well enough. Maybe that was why he had a moment of insight into the absurdity of everything happening.

Charles looked like an invincible behemoth when you were standing next to him. His incredible strength and the way a sword bounced right off of him further confirmed that image. But from this distance he looked quite small. No, not small…he looked his actual size. He was maybe a foot and a half taller than Reginald. That was all, a foot and a half. He was so big and burly that he might weigh as much as two small men. Just two. Not two hundred. And right now there were easily two hundred Dewfordians in the square. The 'army' he had brought to town was pathetically small, smaller than some of the bands of robbers Winthrop had fallen in with in the past. Chariots can wreak havoc on a poorly equipped force, but Dewford was a navigational nightmare where no chariot would want to run. As Winthrop was taking it all in, he realized the Dewfordians would easily kill Charles and all his henchmen if only they would band together and fight. Yet none of them did. Why not? Surely if sixty robbers had come to town, someone would have shouted, 'Let's get 'em!'

Charles started gesturing for everyone to leave, and they obediently filed out of the square. Winthrop figured it out. *Authority*. Charles was an authority figure to them. He was their baron. He was evil, and a tyrant, but he was still their baron. They were his subjects. The men of Dewford would have fought Charles if he was a common robber, because he would have no authority over them. But he did have authority, and therefore fighting him was an act of rebellion that ran much deeper than killing a robber.

The wound in Winthrop's heart throbbed. *Authority*. He had it. He was a duke, and he was a Lessguard. Both titles gave him sufficient authority to remove a Baron who had criminally oppressed his people. The Dewfordians would neither understand nor care about the intricacies of Imperial law, nor the legal questions of whether Imperial law was still enforceable. They didn't need to. Simple men respected authority, even if they didn't know where it came from.

Winthrop looked to the south. He needed to go meet up with Sir Judas and David, yet how could he leave the Dewfordians to their fate? Was this why Sir Judas had taken forty years to get here? Had he lived this same dilemma, not merely once, but a thousand times? Had he felt the crushing weight of rescuing Sir Samson, yet in every town there were wrongs only a paladin had the authority to right? These people were sheep without a shepherd—no, sheep with a wicked shepherd—and Winthrop's heart was moved with compassion for them. How could he abandon Sir Judas and David? How could he abandon an entire town?

Then Winthrop thought of Lady Maria. How could he abandon an entire town…to the criminal who did *that*? His mind went back to Sir Judas's request. 'Pray for me, Friday morning at dawn…' He let out a long sigh. Somehow Sir Judas must have guessed that this would happen. Why would he ask Winthrop to pray for him if they were all going to be together? He nodded his head, resigned himself to what lay ahead, and then set his mind to the task of overthrowing Charles.

This was the kind of thinking that would go better with a mug of beer in his hand.

Chapter 7: A Trick of the Light

"What are we supposed to do? We can't just turn William over to that guy. Even if we did know where he is."

"We don't have a choice in the matter. William might be innocent, but so is everyone else the Baron is going to kill. In order to minimize how many people die, we need to turn them all in."

"What if we try to negotiate? Perhaps we can give him the outlaw and Zakary and that'll be good enough."

"Not one of ya is turnin' in Fr. Zakary!" Ed yelled, brandishing a wine bottle at all of his patrons. "He ain't done nothin' wrong besides bein' a better shepherd than the mayor realized, and yer not handin' him over to that barbaric mountain a meat."

The men all started shouting at each other and a row began to brew. Then Winthrop walked through the door. They all stopped and looked at him in silence, not quite believing their eyes. Winthrop made eye contact with each and every one of them, walked up to the bar, sat down, and said, "Ed, I'll have a beer."

With loud shouts they rushed upon Winthrop, grabbing him and pulling him in every direction.

"Now we've got you!"

"No escaping this time!"

"Let's just turn this one in, and then maybe the Baron will be satisfied!"

The mob was about to drag Winthrop outside when Cara O'Dewforthios forced her way into the crush of men. Swinging her famous ostrich-feather hat at them, she shouted, "Stop it! Stop it! Stop it right now, you ungrateful boors!" As she kept swinging her hat and shouting, the men were eventually cowed into at least listening. "That's right! That's right! Knock it off at once! This man might be a killer and an outlaw, but I'll tell you what I can say for him and none of you! At least he stood up to the Baron! At least he saved William! And then, when William was trying to run away and collapsed, this man threw him outside and distracted the Baron by running back in. So all of you back off of him, because I for one am grateful he's alive!"

Some murmurs of agreement came from around the barroom. Ed reluctantly poured Winthrop a beer while whispering to him, "I'm gonna knock ya silly for what ya didn't tell me yesterday, mister outlaw."

"Charles has first dibs on that, but I'll make a note that you're in line right behind him."

Now Andrew the blacksmith, who had advocated turning in all three spoke up again, "It doesn't matter if this outlaw did a good deed for William or not! Someone has to die, and it might as well be this stranger instead of a dozen innocent men." He then paused and lowered his voice. "…it might as well be him rather than Reginald." Cara turned away and covered her face.

Winthrop stood up and shouted, "Why does someone have to die?" He let them stew in the silence for a moment while he took a drink from his beer. When no answer came, he answered himself, "Because Charles said so? If it's true that someone really does have to die, then why isn't he the one we're talking about killing?"

"That man's a beast!" came the reply. "Have you seen the things he's done? The things he's broken? He's stronger than ten men put together!"

Winthrop leapt up and swung his arms around, gesturing at all of those gathered. "And there are twenty of us in this room! So if we all fight him, there's no way he can take us!"

The Dewfordian men all looked at each other uneasily. Eventually, one of them said what the rest were thinking. "Yeah, but…if we fight him…some of us are going to die."

"Do you not see what is already happening?" Winthrop asked. "When he came to town, the Baron started shooting and slashing before he even told us what his demands were. How many innocent people did he kill before you got the chance to appease him? I saw at least two corpses just walking here, one of which was a child. This is an evil that cannot be reasoned with. It must be fought. Alone, none of us can defeat the Bloody Baron, but together, we will overcome him and the murderers who stand beside him."

Sir Joseph now stepped forward. "I second that. I was attacked by those men as I was leaving town. They killed my horse, and tried to kill me too. My only 'crime' was that I was in the wrong place at the wrong time. If we let this menace go on any longer, it will never be safe for you people to even dare to go outside." Murmurs of agreement started coming from the crowd.

Kayden joined in, "It's not just Dewford! I'm from Chelles, and he came into my shop and beat me up yesterday, not to mention smashing some of my wares." More murmuring from the crowd.

Then Ed slapped the bar with his hand. "And for the love of God! Think of Lady Maria!" He pointed to the booth where she was quietly sitting, listening to the men discuss their options. Those murmurs of approval broke forth into shouts, and Ed led them in chanting, "Never again! Never again!" As the men kept yelling, 'Never again!' Ed continued, "Never again! We're not handing Zakary, William, or nobody over to that Baron! No! Never again!"

"Never again! Never again!" Raucous cheering and the clashing of mugs filled the room.

Then the crowd was suddenly silenced by Eustace running forward and throwing himself at Winthrop's feet. "It's my fault they're dead!"

Winthrop looked at him in confusion. "What are you talking about?"

"It's my fault! I had my horn! And I knew those men were attacking our town! I should have sounded it to call the militia, but…" Eustace broke off into sobs. "I was too afraid! I knew that if I blew it, those murderers would hear and kill me!" Eustace took his horn and held it out. "Winthrop—Lord Winthrop—you are a stranger to our town, yet you risked your life to save William. You are a stranger, yet you have loved this town more than me. I no longer deserve to lead our militia."

Winthrop looked at the horn, then at the eyes of the men in the room. He stretched forth his hand and pushed the horn away. "I am a Lessguard, not a king. If you should be discharged, that's Reginald's business. But tonight, you *are* the leader of Dewford's militia, so rather than renounce your duty you must fulfill it. Now, everybody gather around! It's not going to be easy to fight our way out of this mess, but I've got an idea on how we can do it."

As Winthrop laid out his plan, the spirits of the Dewfordians began to soar. A few of them began to depart, running door to door to quietly call each man to his appointed position. Only one person remained deeply nervous about these developments. Trembling in the corner, Destiny's heart jumped every time Winthrop looked at her. She was deathly afraid he would avenge the beating she gave him in the glade, but there was no recognition in his eyes. She was very, very grateful she had worn her Administrator mask for the rituals in the glade of Jove, as well as the fact that she had changed her dress in the palace of Lord Fearnow. When she finally managed to slip out of the barroom, she took off running to look for Charles.

With a little help from a frightened passerby, Destiny managed to find the lord's manor. She walked up the steps to the broken door, then had a sudden moment of nervousness. *Why am I here?* The splinters at the door latch reminded her of the many times Charles had terrified her with his foul moods. *Why am I coming to him?* She hated Charles. He was a disgusting creep who she couldn't stand to be around, besides his violent temper. *Why am I helping him?* Did she really want him to find those men and kill them? Did she really even care? What was Goliath to her? What was Charles to her? Did they actually have anything to offer? She thought back to the carriage ride with Charles.

He had told her she would need greater power in order to survive in 'the coming world.' But how long until that world came? The darkness had been growing her entire life, and it was still a little bubble in a little country on a little island of a little continent. The world was vast. What was to stop her from running away to a distant land and living out her days in peace? She thought of Sir Joseph. The stranger who for no reason she could perceive had promised to protect her. What was to stop her from running away with him? Thinking these thoughts, Destiny almost turned around. She almost ran away and never looked back. But she didn't. She slowly walked inside to find Charles and tell him what she had learned. Why? We will never know. It was probably the same reason we all commit sins that only serve to make us miserable.

Habit.

Destiny found Charles in the dining room, ripping violent bites out of an entire loaf of bread. Reginald was sitting next to him and seemed to have no appetite. Charles was surprised to see her. "What are you doing here?"

"Fearnow wants my head for trying to help the paladin get to Nightfall. I was fleeing through Dewford when you came crashing into town."

"Do you know what's going on? The priest was here today, Destiny! And the graybeard from the glade found him to bring him to Goliath!"

"I know. I tried to skip town while he was being arrested, but got slowed down by my travelling companion."

"Skip town?" he yelled, leaping up to tower over Destiny. "Don't you know Goliath will kill me unless I get the priest?"

Feeling the same shame and disgust she always felt in these moments, Destiny smiled, touched his arm, and lied. "Of course I know that. That's why I was trying to leave town. I wanted to inform you that the priest was under arrest in Dewford."

Charles calmed down instantly. "I thought you were implying something else. Though you should have left your 'companion' behind and come to me anyway." He sat back down and looked at Reginald thoughtfully. "It doesn't matter now...this will all be over soon enough. They'll give me the priest...they have to."

"That's what I came to warn you about. The peasants have no intention of complying. I was at the tavern just now, and the graybeard came in and whipped them up. They're all planning on fighting back against you."

"What!" Charles yelled, rising from the table once more.

"Charles! There's at least twenty of them there! Moreover, as I was leaving they were talking about getting their friends and eldest sons and having over a hundred men to fight with. The graybeard has them convinced that you could never take that many at once. And he's right, isn't he?"

"One way to find out." Charles grabbed his hammer from where he had propped it against the wall.

"Would you please just listen to me for one minute? Hear me out! This isn't a problem that can be solved with power. United, they are too much for you. We need to divide them, make them turn against each other. Then you can pick them off one at a time."

Charles paused, interested in what Destiny was suggesting. "And how exactly do we divide them?"

"Despair. Lots of it. And there is no greater despair than this; we give them a little hope and let them think their plan is going to work. Then crush them and reveal it was only a trick of the light. Do that, and they will be at each other's throats. Tomorrow morning you'll have plenty of highly motivated peasants scouring the town for the priest." She then told him everything she had heard in the barroom and what her plan was to end this little rebellion. Reginald begged Charles not to go through with it. Even though he wanted to save his own skin (and he honestly believed Charles would let him go if the three were found), nevertheless, Reginald was opposed. Destiny's plan was far too cruel. It was far too bloody.

It sounded perfect to the Bloody Baron. "Good work, Destiny. See this through, and I will be sure to reward you greatly." For a moment, she was excited. A reward that would prepare her for 'the coming world.' Then Charles placed his arm around her waist. It was only a trick of the light.

"I rolled four fives."

"Nooooo way. Whenever you lie you do one less than the number."

"Fine. I rolled five sixes."

"You're still lying!"

"Alright, alright. This time I'll tell ya what I really rolled. I've got six sevens."

"You rolled five dice!"

"Not to mention they only go up to six…"

The three manor lords sat around laughing, shoving each other raucously while gambling the possessions they had stolen from Dewford's citizens. The nightmares were hooked to the chariot about ten feet away, muzzled to make sure they didn't eat anything that wasn't on their approved diet. A good distance behind them, the lords' serfs were guarding the northern bridge across Dewford's moat. The sun had set about an hour ago, and the twilight was growing dim. The men were just starting to talk about rolling for night watches when a cry went up from the bridge. "Hey! Get back in town! Nobody leaves tonight by order of the Baron!" The three lords stood up and squinted, trying to see what was going on.

"Some sheep cuddler must have a death wish."

"Should we do something about it?"

"Nah, stay with the chariot. If a fight breaks out, we don't want to get sucked into the melee."

A metal clashing could be heard, then the men on the bridge started shouting. "Hey! Knock it off! Don't you sling another stone!"

More metal clangs came as the Dewfordians slung stones at their armored foes. The serfs kept shouting, "No! Stop it! Not another!"

The three lords got into their chariot. Then a serf from the bridge yelled, "Get 'em boys!" and battle cries went up as two dozen men charged across the bridge. In panic, one of the lords yelled, "No! Stay at your post! Do *NOT* charge!" But it was no use. The serfs were gone, running headlong into Dewford. Cussing under his breath, he told the nightmares, "Into the city! Follow the sound of battle!" The nightmares rolled forward, proceeding at a slow pace as they wound through Dewford's roads. The sound of the battle was easy enough to follow, but the nightmares soon found a dead end where the men had run across a plank bridge spanning an aqueduct and the chariot could not proceed. Squinting in the shadows of the buildings, the lords could see that their men were all packed into a narrow line. After crossing the plank bridge, they had been on a narrow walkway between a building and the aqueduct. That walkway led to another plank bridge that the men of Dewford had used to retreat. As their pursuers closed in, however, they had knocked out the bridge, forcing their foes to either leap across the aqueduct, or else run down into it and climb out. Either way, they would impale themselves on Dewford's spears. The men at the front of the walkway saw the threat, and were therefore calling to fall back. The men behind, however, mistaking prudence for cowardice, were shoving forward and calling for an advance. Meanwhile, a pelting of stones continued to come from the Dewfordian slingers, though none had managed to fell anyone yet.

"What do we do?" one lord asked another. "Circle around behind?"

"I don't even know how we could do that. We need to get our men to fall back."

"If you hold still, I can try and shoot someone from here."

"Yeah, start picking 'em off. They'll give up real fast."

The horn sounded.

It was no great or noble horn that Eustace blew. Just a plain piece of hollowed wood. Yet to those bandits who had not heard the sound of honest warfare in living memory, where all violence was the vulgar brutality of their own selfish interest, the horn awakened them to the foggy memory that it is not only robbers who kill. Shouts came from every direction, 'DEWFORD!' the word upon their lips, and in those moments before they met their end, Charles's thugs felt the dread of knowing that they stood before men of valor. From the roof of the building across the aqueduct, men leapt up and heaved heavy stones over the edge. The falling rocks killed many instantly, and the rest of that wounded and tottering lot staggered into the aqueduct. The Dewfordians on the other side charged down upon them, and Charles's men could not so much as raise their hand in opposition. At the same time, the lords in the chariot spun around, answering the shout that had come from mere feet behind them. There was a blast of sparks, a storm of spear and sword, then they fell dead before Sir Joseph and Andrew.

The nightmares started at the crack of the electro-gun and took off running forward into the aqueduct. The chariot tumbled sideways, pulling the nightmares on top of one another. They violently bit and beat upon one another, but then amazingly got back to their feet and resumed running, dragging the still-twisted chariot along behind them. The Dewfordians rushed to climb out of the aqueduct, and luckily for them the nightmares were muzzled, or else they surely would have been bitten. The chariot wreckage scraped along, following the most direct route to the town square. Sir Joseph would have preferred to take command of the beasts, but there was nothing he could do about it now.

When the first phase of the battle was over, shouts could still be heard coming from the south side of town. None of the ambushers had sustained major injuries, so Sir Joseph said to them, "Good work! Time to hustle now! Shamus! Lead us to the sheep gate!" The militia did as he said. They formed three files and began a swift march through town by the shortest route. Coming down to the sheep gate, the shouts of battle kept growing louder, but the gate itself was at peace. Cooper turned to meet Sir Joseph with a score of men. "They were quickly defeated! As soon as they realized we had them outnumbered, they turned and ran south."

"That's not defeat, that's repositioning," Sir Joseph answered. "Eustace and Winthrop's job just got harder, and now they will be expecting reinforcements. But hopefully we can still surprise them."

"How many men should I leave at the bridge?"

"Leave the bridge unguarded. This town is a mess to navigate, and they won't be stupid enough to try in the dark. Bring every man for the flank."

The combined forces of Sir Joseph and Cooper now numbered over forty, yet they were able to swiftly and quietly move through the town the Dewfordians called their own. Sure enough, as Sir Joseph had predicted, the fighting was fierce on the southern bridge where Winthrop and Eustace were leading half of Dewford's men. Using the tables from Ed's barroom, they had managed to fashion crude fortifications across the bridge. Once Charles's men realized what was going on, they attempted to charge, but all they got for their troubles were half a dozen spear stabs from men on the other side. They proceeded to retreat, but after regrouping they got to work making the most out of their superior arms. Standing out of range of Dewford's slings, they constantly loosed arrows from their shortbows, providing effective suppressive fire for the infantry. The footmen would then charge in a coordinated fashion, leaping over the barricades just as the archers ceased to shoot. The first time this tactic was employed, nearly a dozen of Charles's men got behind the barricade and proceeded to rip open a hole six feet wide. They were successfully beaten back, but damage was done; moreover, two men were hit by arrows while repairing the breach. When the second wave came, the Dewfordians leapt up too soon and two of them were slain by arrows. The infantry were repulsed again, but Charles's men were getting the better of the fight. Eustace had twenty men left, while the assailants had an equal number. Then the reinforcements from the sheep gate arrived.

The Dewfordians were now terribly outnumbered. Large sections of the barricade were flung down, and a brutal melee ensued. The Dewfordians' saving grace was that they were still on the bridge, and Winthrop fought valiantly to hold the center of the line. As a result, the charging men were pushed towards the sides of the bridge, and then as two of them fell off the edge and into the moat below, Charles's men spooked and retreated one final time. The Dewfordians got no relief, for the archers resumed their attack while they dove behind the last remnants of their shelter. Propping a single table up to duck behind, Winthrop hissed to Eustace, "Where's Joseph?"

The answer was about sixty feet away. When the reinforcements arrived from the sheep gate, one chariot had ridden north as a lookout to see if the Dewfordians were in pursuit. Seeing no men, and finding the bridge abandoned, the chariot rode back with the news that they had gone somewhere in the city. Holland concluded that they were coming to reinforce the bridge, and that was why he had called for an all-out charge to take the bridge before they could arrive to help. Swearing at his men for falling back (and recalling how Charles had handled Riley's failure earlier that day), he ran to the front line and began physically grabbing them and forcing them into formation. "Stand here! You here! Do not swerve left or right! We take the bridge now or not at all! Hurry! You! Right here! On my word, you run forward, and you do not stop until you are standing in the middle of town. On my mark! Archers, loose! Soften them up! Hold now, hold…on my mark, ready…"

As the third wave of battle had been raging, Sir Joseph and his men were down in the moat, carefully crossing as quietly as they could. None of the men of Dewford owned armor, and Sir Joseph had left his at the barroom. While the two outlaws who fell off of the bridge fell into the moat and drowned, the peasant army was carefully rising up out of the water and sticking their heads over the edge of the moat. In the darkness they were unseen, and Holland's forces were too focused on the bridge to make any note of them. The fourth charge was just getting organized as Sir Joseph inched up onto the ground, still lying down. He pulled up Cooper, then another man, and soon half of the

Dewfordians were out of the moat. Holland yelled, "Hold now, hold…on my mark, ready…" and Sir Joseph whispered, "Here we go men! Flank when they charge!"

A blast of light lit up the sky. An ominous orange globe had appeared, shining a spotlight on Sir Joseph and his men. "Charge!" he shouted. It was too late. The nightmares shrieked and two chariots moved behind Sir Joseph's force. The archers turned and saw a dozen easy targets before them. A volley of arrows. Four screams, and four men went down with grievous wounds

Sir Joseph had no idea what had just happened, but years of experience taught him to expect the unexpected when battle was joined. "Pull everybody up!" He reached down to grab the man behind him and lift him up out of the moat. Fear had come over the Dewfordians however. The terrifying light and the death of their brethren was more than they could handle. The man Sir Joseph was reaching for leapt away and down into the moat. Several others followed. Sir Joseph swore and yelled to the men still with him, "Get to the barricade! Now!" Sir Joseph's group regained their wits and began to run for the remnants of the tables. Sir Joseph dove over the little wall, then stuck his head up and looked back for the others. The arrows continued to fly, but Holland's men were by no means expert shots. The dozen men who followed Sir Joseph made it to safety, but then a splash came from the moat where the others had tried to flee. The two chariots wheeled up to that spot, and four shortbows were raised. "No!" Sir Joseph yelled. Crawling to that side of the bridge, he saw the Dewfordians were stuck against the wall of the moat, ten yards from the archers and trying to climb. Round after round was loosed, and the waters of the moat ran red.

Now the orange orb swiveled, and its deadly glow spun to the east. Kayden and eight others were a hundred yards away. They had taken the northeastern exit from town because it was the least guarded. Having the smallest force, their orders were to stay out of the battle until Sir Joseph launched his surprise attack. As a result, those men had stopped advancing a hundred yards from the southern bridge. Now they were in the middle of no man's land. As the chariots began to charge, there was no way to run for the barricade, and professional killers were racing towards them.

At that moment the third chariot returned, the one that had run away from Sir Joseph on the north side of town. The nightmares pulling it voiced their dreadful screams as the rider's dress streamed in the orange light. "Destiny! What are you doing?" Sir Joseph yelled. She looked at him with terrible remorse, but chanted arcane words nonetheless. A second orb appeared in her hand, and she threw it at one of the tables where it exploded in ghoulish flames.

The fire swept through the wooden tables, spreading as if they were straw. Afraid for their lives, all of the men on the southern bridge fled, stampeding over each other in their rush to get away. Only Winthrop had the presence of mind to think, *Wood doesn't burn that fast.* As he saw the fire moving along the thin sheets of wood that made up the table tops, he also thought, *Wood needs to be piled up in order to burn.* He looked closer. The tables were not consumed. The fire had completely surrounded him now, setting the whole mass of tables ablaze. *I'm not hot. I'm not even warm.* Winthrop stuck out his left hand and touched the flames. They didn't burn him in the slightest, though the fire did start spreading to the rest of his body.

Winthrop shouted, "It's an illusion! It's only an illusion! Everybody get back under cover! She's using magic to trick you!" The men who did look back were not calmed, but rather horrified. The blaze all about Winthrop was dreadful to behold, and through those illusory flames they imagined his flesh looked charred and scorched. In a panicked frenzy they tried to run home. Holland pointed towards the blaze and yelled, "As soon as she ends her spell, we charge!" The infantry formed up and marched forward towards the bridge.

Winthrop looked up at the orange orb, still shining on Kayden and his men while the chariots approached them. "Alright, this time I know it works. This is exactly how Sir Judas did it!" He pointed *Veritas* at the orb and yelled, "Emitte lucem Tuam et veritatem Tuam!" One of the nightmares shrieked. Other than that, nothing happened. "Emitte lucem Tuam et veritatem Tuam!" A nightmare shrieked. Nothing else happened. "Emitte lucem Tuam et veritatem Tuam! Emitte lucem Tuam et veritatem Tuam! Gah! Why isn't it working?" A nightmare shrieked. Nothing else happened.

Winthrop thought back to what Sir Judas had told him after defeating the magicians the first time. 'With a miracle, there is not some 'arcane power' on which the miracle worker is drawing, but instead the finger of God is at work, the uncreated Power is entering creation through the hands of His faithful servants. Not only can *I*, Sir Judas, not make those powers of light that saved us tonight, but *no creature* has that power.'

He looked up at the orb, down at his sword, then fell to his knees and prayed. "God, I'm sorry I've been trying to treat your powers like magic. I'm sorry I've been thinking I'll get the same results as Sir Judas if I say the same words. I'm new at this. Mea culpa. But please, save us! This demon and the woman working with him are making a massacre of innocent people. If I don't deserve to be saved, at least save those who came out here tonight to save their town. Please, God. Hostile wars press upon us. Give strength, send help."

A nightmare shrieked. Nothing else happened.

Winthrop looked up. He couldn't believe his eyes. He would have stood there in dumbstruck amazement until it was too late, except that (according to his testimony) an angel grabbed him by the hand. Winthrop didn't see this angel, but it pulled him where he needed to go. He took a few steps. He started to run. He leapt through the blaze of tables. He ran across the bridge. He was running directly towards Holland's advancing men when Winthrop leapt up and stretched out his arms.

He grabbed Lightfoot the nightmare around the neck and pulled himself up on her.

Because Lightfoot wasn't saddled, Winthrop almost tumbled over backwards. He steadied himself and held her mane (the same mane Sir Judas was pulling clumps out of when she was starved) and then held *Veritas* high. It flashed a pulse of silver, and the flames surrounding Winthrop were changed. They didn't cast any sort of harmful glow, but they did totally transform his appearance. Whereas moments before he looked like a dying man, now he was wreathed in glory, and instead of filling the Dewfordians with dread, it was the outlaws whom he terrified.

Winthrop called to Lightfoot, "Alongside that chariot now, on the left!" and she overtook one of the chariots heading towards Kayden's company. The men in the chariot looked backwards in shock. Winthrop raced past them, pulled up next to their nightmares, and with a single blow from *Veritas* struck off one of the horses' heads. Its body fell down below the chariot wheel, causing a crashing tumble that launched all three outlaws from their vehicle. The other chariot swerved away from the wreckage and slowed to a stop, for the nightmares were running without guidance and did not know how to respond.

Winthrop cried, "Men of Dewford! Stand and deliver!" The nine men of Dewford ran towards the two chariots, and battle was swiftly joined. Winthrop turned towards Holland's infantry just as Eustace blew his horn. Then Eustace cried, "Forward!" Winthrop heard a great shout from within the town, and then beheld the terrible prodigy. Men leapt through the flames on the bridge, covered from head to toe in illusory fire, just as Winthrop was. They were unorganized and haphazard, every man charging by himself instead of forming solid ranks, but that only added to the effect. Each man's flame streaked to the man behind him, forming a rolling wave of fire and death that set Holland's men to flight. Turning their backs and running for their lives, the outlaws screamed in terror to see Dewford's men on fire. Looking over to the fight that was near him, Winthrop saw that the second chariot was now empty and the six outlaws had been dispatched.

Only one foe remained. Winthrop set his eyes towards Destiny and yelled, "After her! Get the witch!" Lightfoot obeyed and took off at a gallop. At first Destiny tried to flee along the road, deciding it was finally time to go to Reswick. In mere moments, however she realized Winthrop was far too fast. He was overtaking her with *Veritas* raised and bloody, his face still aflame.

She yelled for her horses to stop, put her hands up, and cowered in the bottom of the chariot. "Mercy, sir! I surrender!" Lightfoot came to a stop beside her. Winthrop dismounted and pressed *Veritas* up to Destiny's chest. "Please don't kill me! I'll cooperate. I promise I won't hurt you."

Winthrop removed the blade, grabbed her arm, and pulled her out of the chariot. He then walked behind her and put the tip of *Veritas* between her shoulder blades. "Start walking. We're going to the jail. Stay quiet, and you will get a trial. If instead you utter so much as one word of gibberish that sounds like a spell, I will kill you dead on the spot. Do you understand?"

"Yes, yes, of course. I understand."

"Start walking."

As she moved forward, Destiny's faerie appeared to her, flying ten steps ahead. "We need to get out of this. He will kill you. You *know* he will. There will be no trial. He just wants to torture you to death instead! Use the invisibility spell. Use it!" Tears formed in Destiny's eyes as the faerie kept inventing horrors Winthrop was going to commit. They were all the same. Charles, Fearnow, Winthrop. Her entire life was a web of men threatening to kill her unless she could find a way to keep herself safe.

What Destiny did not know (but her lying demon surely did) was that Winthrop intended to keep his word. His blood was hot, and she had killed so many men, yet Winthrop saw himself in this young woman. Sir Judas had given him another chance at life. Winthrop was a killer and a robber who would have killed Sir Judas if he was able, yet the paladin had arrested him instead of executing him. He intended to do the same for Destiny if she would only hold her tongue and not try to harm anyone with magic. If.

Destiny's heart broke as she heard Sir Joseph ask, "Destiny…why did you do it?" Seeing his kind face crying, her own tears came rushing forth. Joseph was unlike any man she had ever met. He did not threaten her. He did not scare her. She was a perfect stranger to him, yet he had saved her from the hands of Fearnow and promised, 'I am going to keep you safe.' She had repaid his gratuitous kindness with an act of unforgiveable betrayal. She didn't want to look at him, but even more than that, she didn't want him to look at her. Destiny decided to cast the invisibility spell. She chanted her dying words.

Winthrop killed her so fast, there was no time to warn her. She never heard Sir Joseph say, "Destiny! Don't!"

The dying words of Destiny the Administrator were the bastard Latin of a spell the devil taught her. Woe to all who come before their Maker with such words on their lips.

Chapter 8: Fallout

The final toll of the battle was forty-one dead, two dying, one who might die, thirty-four with non-life threatening injuries. If not for Destiny, the death toll would have been twelve. If not for Lightfoot, it would have been all. When Destiny died all of her magic ceased, and it was now too dark to set about burying the dead. Instead the Dewfordians gathered the bodies together to bury tomorrow. They went back to E&S's tavern weeping for the sons, fathers, and friends that they had lost.

The one person whose life still hung in the balance was Kayden, who had played a great role in bringing that day's events to their bloody conclusion. When the orb of light turned towards the eastern ambush, Kayden was the first man to get hit by an archer in one of the chariots. He took an arrow in the left side of his abdomen and fell to the ground to wait for the end. In a twist of fate, however, when the frightened nightmares had stopped running, Kayden was only five paces away from them. The young groom, remembering how Charles had treated Sasha the day before, mustered his remaining vigor, rose to his feet, and climbed up into the chariot to defend what he was fighting for. He stabbed one axeman in the back, and then as the other two turned and shoved him out of the chariot, the rest of Kayden's group was able to leap up and attack before the nightmares could run away.

Wanting to help him heal, but knowing nothing about battlefield medicine, the Dewfordians almost pulled the arrow out of Kayden's gut, which certainly would have killed him. Thankfully, Sir Joseph overheard them talking about who should do it, and he put an end to their ignorant madness. Instead he had them build a makeshift stretcher and carry Kayden to the barroom, where he would be able to attempt a proper surgery.

Thus the sad and dejected warriors returned with sunken spirits. Their spirits were about to sink lower.

The first bad sign was that none of the lights were on in the tavern. As they came inside, someone yelled, "Hey Ed! We're back! Why is it dark in here?" The sound of crying was the only answer. "Hey! What's going on?"

The crying continued as there was a spark, another, and then a candle lit. Sasha and Emma were behind the bar, the latter holding a bottle of wine by the neck. The statues of the wedding feast at Cana that usually stood behind the bar had been knocked to the ground and smashed. As Winthrop ran across the room to meet Sasha, he discovered why she was crying. Behind the bar Ed was sprawled out on the floor, lying in blood and broken statuary.

"What happened?"

Sasha threw her arms around Winthrop. "Oh, thank God you're back! He came while you were gone! Kayden! Where's Kayden?" She pushed her way through the crowd of men until she found the stretcher. Then she screamed in hysterics, "He's hit! There's an arrow in him! How did none of you see that? Quick! Pull it out!"

As she reached for the arrow, Sir Joseph grabbed her wrist and pulled her away. "Calm down, Sasha! Right now the arrow is packing his wound. Pull it out, and you'll reopen everything, not to mention cut him up on the way back. I'm going to treat his injury, but you need to step back. Nicholas! Go get the supplies I told you about. Sasha, what I need you to do right now is bring some chairs over, light three or four good candles, and arrange them so I can see what I'm doing."

"What about Ed?" Winthrop asked. "Is he…"

Ed snorted. "Dead?" With a groan he began to turn on his side. "It takes a whole lot more than that to kill an Irishman."

"Oh daddy! You're alive!" Sasha ran over and dropped down beside him. "He was unconscious until just now."

"Pfft. I wasn't unconscious. Ole Ed's eyes were just a bit tired from looking at that ugly mustache, and I decided to give em a little rest."

"Sasha!" Sir Joseph called, "Oh, never mind. Mother! Light those candles for me!"

Sasha helped Ed to sit upright. Winthrop dropped to a knee beside him and asked, "Ed, where's Maria?"

The father and daughter both hung their heads. Sasha answered, "Charles took her."

Winthrop began to shake. Ed stammered, "It was just the four of us here when that fella came–I had no idea he was gonna…he tried to grab her, and all I had was a bottle so I...I took it and smashed it on his helmet there, hopin'...I thought if I could get some glass in his eyes–he just grabbed me and threw me, and then I don't remember what..."

Sasha continued, "The wine got in his eyes and really hurt him. Even after he threw my dad across the room, he kept on screaming and trying to wipe it out of his eyes. Then he made like he was gonna go after my dad and kill him, but I grabbed two more bottles of wine and started waving them at him. He actually backed down, which startled me, but then he grabbed Maria and threw her over his shoulder...he took off with her, and I...I'm sorry, I didn't follow them. I was so afraid, and there was nothing I could...I just turned off the lights...he said that...that if the priest, the stranger, and the constable weren't turned in by nine o'clock...he said he was going to kill *her*!" Sasha started crying again. "Who could be so heartless as to hurt a woman in her condition?"

Winthrop arose. "The same man who was so heartless as to put her in that condition."

"Aaaahhh!" Andrew ran over and tackled Winthrop to the ground. "We never should have listened to you! We should have just done what he said and turned you in!"

Rolling around with him, Winthrop asked, "What, and turn in William too?" Shoving Andrew off of him, Winthrop rose to his feet just in time to get shoved from behind.

"Finish him off! No more messing around! We need to save the Lady!"

A third man grabbed Winthrop around the neck, but then a few defenders came to his aid. The fight was broken up and Winthrop was able to separate himself from everyone else. Still sitting down, Ed hollered, "Knock it off! Every one a ya!"

Andrew answered, "For Maria, Ed!"

He retorted, "Will you be the one to tell her, 'I killed his dukeliness for your sake, Lady.'? You know she never would want nothin' like that. And besides! Use yer heads for at least a minute!" Ed struggled to his feet, Sasha supporting him even as he leaned on the bar. "I suppose I gotta reminder all of ya that for all the mistakes his dukeliness has made in our little town these last couple a days, standin' up to the Bloody Baron ain't one of em! That Baron didn't attack us cuz of his dukeliness. He came to kill Zakary! He didn't take Maria just cuz of his dukeliness. He wants us to hand over William too! And I'll tell ya right now, this is exactly the sort of thing that proves his dukeliness is right! The Baron is gonna keep doin' this sorta stuff unless we put an end to it! Killin' the man fightin' to solve our problems ain't the answer! We need to go kill the man who is actually causin' em, alright?"

Ed expected to get a chorus of approval, similar to how he did before the battle with the outlaws. Instead despair had crept into the Dewfordians. No matter how clear, no matter how logical the path forward, these men no longer had the will to walk it.

"I want things to go back to how they were, Ed."

"I'm a farmer, not a fighter."

"Tommy's dead."

"I lost my two oldest sons!"

"We've seen enough bloodshed in this town."

At these words Winthrop drew *Veritas*, and pointed it at each of the men in the barroom. "You've all had enough bloodshed, huh? You're not willing to fight to save your town? Too bad, because that's your only option! I won't come quietly. If you want to turn me in and surrender to Charles, you'll have to take up your spears and stab me to death. You can try to save your town by fighting a baron, or you can try to save it by fighting a duke, but you cannot save it peacefully! If you're too cowardly for battle, then get out of this barroom and join the miserable lot who will never say they saved Lady Maria nor that they died trying!"

The Dewfordians all looked at each other, and then slowly began to leave. One by one, each of them decided he had had enough. Sasha was appalled. "You-you!" A torrent of hateful expletives poured forth from her mouth. "You oughta be ashamed of yourselves! My Kayden isn't even from your town and he took an arrow for you! How are you gonna just walk away like this?"

Ed tried to calm her down, but Sir Joseph silenced him. "Let her yell, Ed. Men need to hear what women really think of them." Even though they were ashamed, the men still left. Before long the only people remaining in the quiet barroom were Winthrop, Ed, Sir Joseph, Emma, Kayden, Sasha, Eustace, and Nicholas.

Winthrop asked the two young men, "You plan on saving William and Zakary?"

They both nodded.

"Good. Loyalty is hard to find. So what's it going to be? Kill me and hope Charles is happy, or figure out how to kill him instead?"

"Zakary is the one he wanted in the first place," Nicholas answered. "He just wants to kill you and William because you ticked him off. I don't believe for a second that he would let Zakary go if we gave him you."

Eustace let out a long sigh. "We need to fight. They know that, but…they have no *hope*…you saw them charge across the bridge! Every man was running headlong towards a pack of killers. There was no talk of losses nor bloodshed. When they were burning they could bear any loss, but with Maria gone…the flame has gone out…"

Other than Kayden's groans, there was silence in the barroom. Nicholas eventually asked, "So…do we have any sort of plan for how to kill the Bloody Baron? Not only is he as strong as an ox, but Joseph told me he shot him in the face with a crossbow and it did nothing."

Winthrop nodded. "The same thing happened when I stabbed him with my sword. It was a perfect hit, right in the gap in his armor. Didn't do a thing. He laughed at me and told me his armor was just for show, that he can't be hurt by any weapons."

"What?" Eustace shouted, "Then why did you tell us to fight him? He's invincible! We never had a chance!"

Winthrop shrugged. "My plan was to crush him with ten men and then saw his head off one inch at a time. He's not all powerful, just very powerful. Very powerful can be managed with ten men. Four can work if we get creative."

"Creative? Are you kidding me? All the creativity in the world isn't going to hurt a man who can take a crossbow to the face!"

Sir Joseph looked up from working on Kayden. "Eustace, where's that burning hope you were talking about?"

Winthrop walked over to the bar and picked up one of the bottles Sasha was holding earlier. Doing his best impression of Ed's voice, he said, "Lemme tell ya my opinion on men who drink wine…or get splashed in the face with it for that matter…" Winthrop examined the bottle carefully and asked, "Ed, was there anything special about the bottle you hit Charles with?"

"No, nothin' special at all. Just my normal vintage. Same as what yer holdin' there."

Winthrop tossed the bottle up and caught it. "And Sasha, this is the bottle you threatened Charles with?"

"It is."

He tossed it again. "Why would he be afraid of wine?"

Ed slapped the bar as it dawned on him. "I'll betcha he's allergic!"

"What?"

"He's allergic! Just like that gal that was here earlier with Fithy Joseph! She took a swig of my wine and started actin' the same as Charles did when I got wine in his eyes. I'll betcha them two are siblings, and they got the same allergy!"

Winthrop looked at the bottle of wine quizzically. "No, Ed...allergies don't work like that. You are right that they have something in common, though. Both of those two are possessed. Or at least, Destiny used to be..."

Nicholas gasped. "Possessed? Like with...demons?"

"Yes, with demons. I met them on Monday night while their demons were clearly manifest. It seems the demons usually stay more hidden than they were that night, but there is absolutely no doubt about it. Those two are possessed." Winthrop thought some more. "And if they are possessed...then I don't think they were hurt by your wine at all, Ed. They were hurt by the secret ingredient you use to make it."

Ed shouted, "The water! From Matthew's grave!"

"Exactly. It was the water in the wine that hurt those two. The demons in them probably can't stand it."

Sir Joseph had a moment of realization. "That water Ed uses for his wine. Is it the same as the stuff in the moat around the town?"

"Aye," Ed answered, "It runs through the aqueducts to get there."

"That explains it!" Sir Joseph exclaimed. "Today when Charles caught me outside of town, he had this moment where he was suddenly in terrible pain. I thought it was a delayed reaction to my crossbow bolt, but the water would make far more sense. I shot my electro-gun at him and it misfired. Because I got it wet, it just sputtered a few drops of water out, but that was probably better for me than if it had worked! The water is what hurt him." Sir Joseph thought some more. "Moreover, it hurt him far worse than Destiny was hurt by drinking a glass of wine."

Winthrop placed the bottle back on the bar. "It was the purity..." He turned to Sir Joseph. "The water in the moat...even though it runs through the streets of town, it is still purer than the wine. That's why it hurt him more. And if *that* water was so effective even after running through all the aqueducts, imagine if we could get our hands on water even *purer* than that..." Winthrop looked at Eustace. "Deputy, I have a creative plan after all."

Winthrop shared what he was thinking. They discussed, adjusted, and ironed out the details, then snuck out of the barroom to make their preparations while Sir Joseph and Emma finished patching up Kayden. They only got a couple hours of sleep that night, and then Winthrop arose with the sun to take care of the most important part of the plan. Riding Lightfoot south out of town, Winthrop looked to the east and fulfilled his promise from Wednesday night. "God, Sir Judas is the biggest pain in the rear I've ever known, and that played an important part in getting me to love You. Please help him be as big of a pain for Goliath, and maybe Sir Samson will love You too."

Then he tapped his heels to his nightmare's sides and trotted to Fr. Zakary's shack.

End of Volume V

Interlude

Charles stormed into Reginald's residence carrying Lady Maria over his shoulder like a sack of grain. Though she was in great pain, she did not let out the slightest cry. She refused to give her sadistic captor that much pleasure. Charles came to the dining room and dropped her roughly in a chair. The vassal who was watching Reginald laughed as she bit her tongue to keep from screaming.

Reginald was beside himself. "Oh, do be more gentle! Can't you see you're hurting her?"

Charles turned his gaze on the mayor with malevolent delight. "Oh, I do see that good mayor, but you don't need to fear. You won't have to see her pain much longer. Now that I have a more precious hostage, you have outlived your usefulness…"

Charles came around the table and tried to grab his prey. Reginald yelped and dove away, then scampered around to the other side. Charles started to go one way, then went back the other, toying with the mayor like a cat playing with a mouse. When he had had enough fun, he grabbed the table and hurled it aside. It smashed to pieces against the wall while he laid hands on Reginald.

"Kill him and you'll never find the priest!" Lady Maria called.

Charles looked at her in confusion. "What are you talking about? I still have you as a hostage. They'll turn the priest in."

"Not if they think I'm doomed either way. You promised to kill the mayor at nine unless they turn in the three men you're looking for. If you kill Reginald before then, they will know that cooperating with you is no guarantee of safety. You can't hold me hostage if they have already despaired of saving me."

Not caring that Maria's words were eminently reasonable, Charles was furious to be opposed. "Despair of saving you? Once I start torturing you, they'll turn in the priest just to make me put you out of your misery. Or have you forgotten what I did to you last time?"

"It is you who has forgotten. I laughed in your face then. I will laugh in your face tomorrow."

"Insolent wench!" Charles dropped Reginald and made to strike her.

Without flinching, Lady Maria said, "Kill me, and your lot will be ten times worse than if you killed the mayor. Men with nothing to lose make terrifying enemies."

Shaking with anger, clenching his teeth, Charles slowly lowered his hand. Then he grabbed the mayor in one arm and the Lady in the other. "Alright, enough of this! Everyone upstairs! You're both staying up there tonight, and if you even set foot on the staircase, Ruadhan will kill you dead!" He dumped them on the landing. "Sleep well, if you can. Tomorrow, one way or the other, you die."

Lady Maria tried to stifle her laugh, but in the end was unable. "I'll be up all night, but not for you. Today I learned of so many things I have to be grateful for. I'll be too busy thanking God to sleep."

Eight miles east of Castle Nightfall, twelve miles west of where the darkness begins, the main road runs along a southern bay. For all forty years since Goliath was sealed in his dome, every visitor who came to him had hiked north through the wilderness to avoid the abandoned city situated on the bay. Over time (recall that the dome of darkness was originally very small, and only Goliath knew it was growing), the villages and towns in the region had cut a new road around the city and built new ports to receive their shipping. Only the most reckless of explorers ever ventured into that accursed place, and those who did were never quite the same when they returned.

It had come to be known as 'the Scar' though no one was quite sure why. The Scar was there before Goliath's rise, and even when he had toppled the Empire and seemed poised to rule the world, the great and mighty giant followed the northern road like all other men. He knew what curse was upon that city, and he had no intention of setting foot within.

Instead he sent Morgan.

Morgan had been told to summon the 'wretches' who lived in the Scar to come and aid Goliath. Like anyone else who had heard the legends, Morgan assumed the place was filled with demons. And since Goliath had authority to command the demons in his land, it would make sense that he was summoning them as allies. The truth was a terrible prodigy, even darker than he had imagined.

Morgan's carriage arrived at the edge of the Scar on Tuesday afternoon. By his devil's sight he saw that the walls of the city had been torn down and left in a pile of rubble next to the buildings. There was a dry and empty moat surrounding the entire city, with a little wooden bridge across it. The nightmares came to the edge of the bridge, then turned aside and began to go back the other way. "Whoa! Easy now! Stop right there!" The nightmares listened to Morgan. "Cross that bridge." They ignored him. "What are you doing? Cross the bridge!" They wouldn't listen. After shouting and yelling for some time, Morgan eventually gave up and got out of the carriage. The horses took off running immediately. "Hey! Get back here!" They were gone. Swearing and cursing at Charles's stupid horses, Morgan turned back to the Scar.

He felt a great chill. He pulled his robes closer around him. There was a wooden sign erected beside the bridge. Unfortunately for him, he couldn't read what it said because his devil's sight only showed the outlines of the sign, not its colored letters. Instead he crossed the bridge and entered the city. As soon as he set foot on the cobblestones of the city's road, he began to hear a distant sound. *That must be who I'm looking for...*

Walking into town, the sound became louder. It was clearly voices. As he advanced further down the main road, he made out that they were screaming voices. *No wonder Goliath called them wretches. They must be miserable to scream like that.* But as Morgan kept getting closer, he began to second guess himself. *Is that...could it? Those aren't screams of misery. They're shouting for joy! I can make out the sound of laughter!* A short walk later the road curved back north, and Morgan was looking over the edge of a cliff towards the southern bay. He couldn't believe his eyes.

A bonfire was burning. Not outlined in devil's sight, or any other sort of false image. There was real fire that Morgan was seeing with his real eyes. Around it men and women were dancing wildly, lit up in all of their natural colors. There were tables nearby covered with many beautiful foods, while the sound of splashing could be heard where the revelers had jumped in the bay for a mid-August swim. The people would dance to the point of exhaustion, sit down to eat, drink, and then rise up to play once more. Morgan was mesmerized.

As if in a trance, he slowly walked along until he found a good place to scale the cliff and then follow a gentler slope to the beachfront. Mollispes, the demon inside of him was screaming for him to run, but those wicked spirits are famously powerless for inspiring men to do good, even when it would better suit their designs. Morgan's desires were kindled, and no devil could persuade him to turn away.

As he drew near to the fire he felt warm. The chill he felt earlier was banished. One man at the fire took notice of him and came bounding over with a smile on his face. "Hello, friend! Are you here to join the fun?"

"Yes, I would love to, but…tell me, who are you? Why are you here in this darkness?"

The man laughed. "What darkness? It looks like there's a fire blazing to me!"

Morgan chuckled. "Yes, I suppose…I see that, of course, but…how did you get a fire to…Where to start? Obviously you must be possessed in order to be able to live in this dome."

The man shook his head, beaming even more broadly than before. "We're not possessed. We are free spirits. Men and women who are not chained down by the things of this world. Ambition, country, family, children…all the things that so many souls are anchored by and allow to be their masters. We are encumbered by none of them, and nothing else besides. We are a free people. Neither death, nor darkness, nor cold, nor anything else can restrain us from our joy."

With excitement, Morgan looked around and asked, "But…how? How can you be so free? We're flesh and blood. Cold is cold and death comes for us all. How can you just 'be free' as you say?"

The man slapped Morgan on the back and said, "Come, and I will show you!" He skipped down to a table covered with more food and flowers than all the others. In a flight of whimsy, Morgan skipped right along behind him. When he came to the table, he saw there were two objects on it that the decorations were gathered around. One was a picture of a man in royal purple robes riding on an ass. The other was a golden statue of a humanoid bull that stood on two legs and had four arms.

"Don't worry! Don't worry!" the man said, "This isn't about to turn into a religious cult or anything!"

"Oh good," Morgan said with a smile, "You were starting to make me nervous."

"No, no, none of that. Nothing so degrading as being the slave to some god. Like I said, we're a free people. This is a memorial to our friends. Tell me, have you heard of Balaam the prophet?"

"I haven't."

"What about Moloch the liberator?"

"Never heard of him."

"Well these are the two that set us free. Balaam taught us the way of living freely, and Moloch gave us the power to do so. I think that's what your question was really driving at, even if you didn't know it yourself. How do we live in the darkness? Balaam taught us to do what we want to. Let no one tell you the darkness is cold, frightful, or even that you can't see in it. You decide. And then Moloch, he's the liberator. You see, the reason we can't live freely even if we choose to is because our choices have consequences. I live in the darkness, I can't see. I eat too much food, I get full. I drink too much wine, I get drunk. I can't do what I want because my choices have consequences. Moloch, he frees us from the consequences. He takes away the darkness, the fullness, the drunkenness, so that our freedom is now complete. We're not only free in our choices, but free in our results. We are free to do whatever we want, a power no men have ever been blessed with before."

Morgan looked around in wonder. It seemed too good to be true, yet the proof was all around him. A fire blazing in the darkness! So much warmth in this chilly place that the people were all half-dressed. Men drinking from goblets that never ran dry, and eating from tables that were never emptied.

He remembered the reason he was sent here. "I don't know if this is even possible, but…could Moloch free me from Goliath? I was sent here to summon any demons I could find and bring them back to help him, but I would rather stay here with you. If I did though…Goliath would kill me."

The man laughed. "Goliath? That old lizard will never harm you again. Don't you know that he gives this place a wide berth? We're free from his power, and he knows that he could never control us. There's nothing a tyrant fears more than a people who are truly free. That's why he sent you instead of coming himself. He's afraid of us. But if he's that scared of what we can do, then why should you do his bidding? Join us. Become a free man. It's far better than to grovel before the strong and beg for protection."

Morgan was trembling with excitement. "Yes, yes it is. Tell me, how can I do it? How can I be free from him forever? Free of *everything* forever?"

The man took Morgan by the hand and led him to one of the tables. "I already told you! Follow the teachings of Balaam. Do whatever you want for the next couple days, and let absolutely nothing restrain you. Then when you are good and ready, we will fully initiate you into perfect freedom!"

"Do whatever I want?"

"You are free to do whatever you want."

In a burst of joy, Morgan began grabbing food from the table, stuffing his face with every meat and candy he could find. Without stopping to wipe his face, he grabbed a goblet of wine and chugged it so fast it ran down his chin and all over his clothes. Without cleaning any of that mess up, he ran to some woman and asked her to dance. She agreed, and they began running gaily around the fire. It was a little after noon on Tuesday when Morgan began this revel, about the same hour that Sir Judas was refusing the offer to work for Charles and that Winthrop was drinking water from Fr. Zakary. He carried on like this over and over–eat, drink, play, eat, drink, play–ad nauseam. Mollispes was shouting warnings, but Morgan couldn't hear him over the music. With no sunrise and no sunset, he lost all track of time.

The man didn't. He was steadily tapping his foot, one tap every second. He counted to one hundred seventy-two thousand eight hundred taps. He had told Morgan to revel for 'a couple days,' and he didn't let it go on a moment longer. It was now Thursday afternoon. Winthrop was just finishing his Confession with Fr. Zakary, while David and Sir Judas were in Lake Gregory, as will be related in the next volume. The man waded into the revelry and found Morgan dancing furiously in a group of ten men and women.

"Well done! Incredible performance! You've done a truly tremendous job! Oh, look at you, a beauty to behold! You are the perfect picture of freedom!" Morgan was five pounds heavier, staggering drunk, covered in his own vomit, and deathly exhausted from days without sleep.

Weakly smiling he said, "Yeah…that was an…*intense* freedom. I'm definitely ready to be freed from the consequences now." He nearly puked again, but managed to swallow it down.

"Yes, of course. I think Moloch will be very pleased with you. Walk right this way. It's going to get a little hot for a moment now, but only for a moment. Then it won't be a *little* hot, ever again. Stand right here, next to the fire. Yes, perfect, just like that. Right up next to the edge there. Perfect. Right next to the fire."

Morgan giggled. "As much fun as that was the first time, it's so amazing to think I'll be free of the consequences so that I can do it all again."

"Oh, you will be free of the consequences, but who said you could do it all again?" The man pushed Morgan from behind, and he tumbled headlong into the roaring flames. As Morgan screamed, the man said, "You drank too much wine, but you will not be drunk. You ate too much food, but you are no longer full. You live in the darkness, but you shall always see fire from now on. Nor shall you fear death, for you will live forever in this eternal moment.

Morgan screamed and screamed, and struggled to get out, but he was sinking further and further into the flames, so that it seemed as if he had fallen a hundred feet into the fiery pit. The man was standing far above, looking down on him with glee. "Who are you?" Morgan screamed. "Why have you done this to me?"

"In my past life I lived according to my beliefs, but I was cut down in the flower of youth. Moloch saw me as useful, however, and he took this city from the demons who lived here before and allowed me to run it according to my principles. I am here to spread my creed and teach men to believe in the gospel that I preach."

"A name!" Morgan screamed, hurtling further and further into the Inferno. "Give me a name! So that I may know who to curse for all eternity!"

"In life I was called Fr. Zambri, but the only name you should curse is your own. Nevertheless, curse as you will. You are free to do whatever you want."

As the sun was setting on Thursday, Lady Amanda stood at the western window of her bedroom, looking out at the horizon. She would look at the grass, the sky, the mountains, then drift back to the horizon to see if it was still there. It was. All of her vision would be swallowed up in darkness. She would look away again for some time, then back. Still there.

Lord Benjamin came in as the last sliver of sun was sinking out of view. He had calmed down considerably since last night and was back to his usual sardonic self. "Did Castle Nightfall see the sunset tonight? Or is the paladin just a bag of wind?" She answered him not a word. "It's over a hundred miles to the edge of the darkness, and then another twenty miles to Nightfall after that. He won't even be close enough to spit at the darkness for a week."

Still, she answered him nothing. She watched the last sliver of sun intently, not letting her eyes wander into the darkness. "It's about to go out." Benjamin taunted. The sun dropped. Shortly after the sky was black, except for the stars.

"So tell me now," Benjamin asked, "Are you ready to admit that Mordecai was full of it, or shall we stare into oblivion and wish really hard it wasn't real? How would you like to proceed?"

Lady Amanda took a deep breath and then said, "I suspected this would happen."

"You suspected that a seventy-year-old man and his boy sidekick might not be able to defeat the Leviathan that destroyed the biggest Empire in world history? Your deductive powers are overwhelming."

"I have no doubts that the darkness will be destroyed and that Castle Nightfall shall see the sunset. What I suspected is that it might look bad. Last night God gave me a sign to comfort me and assure me He is in control. He showed me that His light surrounds the darkness, compasses it, and that He can scatter it anytime He chooses. Last night the vision gave me peace, and then today I asked myself, 'Why would God do a miracle to strengthen my faith unless it is about to be tested?' So I suspected this would happen. It looks like the prophecy has failed, but it hasn't. It will come true. I just don't yet understand how."

Lord Fearnow shook his head. "Don't go over to this madness, Amanda. The truth is scary, but we must accept it. For half a century we've been trying to rid our realm of the wishful thinking that is religion. Now you're foaming at the mouth just like religion's most rabid devotees. 'The prophecy didn't come true. That proves my religion is false. But I expected my religion to be proven false, because God is testing my faith, which is what my religion said God would do. Therefore, my religion is true.' Don't fall into that crazy thinking. I love my wife because she's a strong woman who stands for what she believes, not some reed swayed by the wind of whatever words Christians are screaming."

Lady Amanda was done arguing with him. It would be casting her pearls before swine. Instead she fell to her knees and prayed. She prayed hard for Sir Judas and David. Lord Fearnow left, and still she prayed. She stayed up late into the night begging God to aid them. Around midnight she was going to crawl into bed, but she felt a tug at her heart telling her to stay and pray the longer. She knelt at the window, looking out into the blackness, praying fervently until dawn lit the landscape anew. It was eight o'clock on Friday morning when she finally laid down beside the window and slept.

The darkness was still there.

Beatrice was shaking with fear as she approached Goliath. She had flown up onto the same wall as him, but eighty feet away. One dreadful step at a time, she moved closer. *Hope...Jezebel says I must quench his hope...oh, but he's just going to kill me as soon as I try!* He didn't look at her. He was still looking west across the inky blackness of the ocean.

When she was about twenty feet away, he finally spoke. "The sun is set."

She nodded. "And?"

"I didn't see its setting."

Taking a nervous breath, she answered, "What of it? Wasn't your plan to conquer the world beneath this darkness anyway? Why do you care if he didn't banish it?"

"I don't care that he didn't banish it. I care that he didn't come. I was...I was hoping...I was hoping he would come."

There was that nasty word. "Why? Are you bored? Is chasing me around and trying to kill me not enough for you?"

"You do not love me."

Beatrice was taken aback. "What the? What kind of a stupid statement is that? It would be impossible for any woman to love you!"

Goliath let out a low, rumbling sigh. "You think it stupid because you've reduced love to romance, and romance to courtship. That is not the love I hoped for. I was beginning to hope (Beatrice cursed that word) this paladin might be the last of the Lessguard. I hoped it might be my squire Mordecai. After all, who else could it be? I was beginning to hope he had been coming for me, like Odysseus seeking his Penelope. I hoped that for forty years he had been detained, tossed about on the stormy seas of unwanted adventures, yet always coming. I hoped that tonight he would finally arrive, or else that I would see the darkness vanish as he drove it away. And then in the evening twilight, I would have bounded across the twenty miles from this castle to where he was. I would have seen him with my own eyes, and he would see me, and we would both run to meet each other and embrace. I would hold him in my arms as we wept, and—who knows? I was even hoping for this dream–that the scales would fall from my body, and as men we would hold each other once more. That's the love I hoped for, Beatrice. I was hoping he would come. Even if it wasn't Mordecai, I was hoping for somebody. Anybody. I was hoping that in this big wide world, there would be at least one person who loved me enough to come."

Fear banished by disgust, she spat at him. "You're pathetic, and you revolt me. You want the scales to fall from your body? You have all the power in the world, and you would throw it away for a hug? By God you are despicable. I want nothing more to do with you."

Goliath slowly turned towards her. Her fear returned, and she trembled, knowing she had gone too far. Yet he didn't draw his weapon. Instead, he calmly answered, "As I said, you do not love me. I was just hoping someone who did would finally come."

Prelude to Volume VI

Ballad of the Black Knight

Rising from the ruin of the once-great that is fall'n,
Fighting free clear back to Nouen, all that was now gone,
Waters raged, yet still one ark held treasure through it all.
Gloating o'er the body still walking in their midst.
Sanctus! Sanctus! Sanctus! Blessed is he who comes!

South to Serbia's coast, hidden in a merchant's cart,
Robbers found to their surprise, steel and blinding light.
Kind for kind, the debt repaid, to sea for swiftest route.
Savage slavers stole the ship, and into chains he went.
Sanctus! Sanctus! Sanctus! Blessed is he who comes!

Led the slave revolt that came, setting captives free,
On feeble raft shoved he off, adrift for Italy.
Bound to land, back north he hiked, hope brought along the way,
Took no coin, just food'n roof, cheap price for all their needs.
Sanctus! Sanctus! Sanctus! Blessed is he who comes!

In Rome he dreamed all would be well; here his heart was pierced,
A sea of filth and faithless crimes; unbelievers all.
Too proud to take Moses' chair. 'Judge not is the law!'
Sweet as snakes, smart as doves, streets red as their robes.
Sanctus! Sanctus! Sanctus! Blessed is he who comes!

Boldly went and preached the truth for all who had ears.
Said they who God's Law blaspheme, "Thou follow not our rule.
If one should preach, not sent by us, feigned prophecy,
Two signs must first be shown, or else he is not true."
Sanctus! Sanctus! Sanctus! Blessed is he who comes!

God did provide by black knight's hand, Church's word nev'r void.
Two signs of wonder shook the land, turning mild hearts.
False and wicked were his foes, "One more and we'll believe."
Ground yawned wide, cast down by He Who cannot be deceived.
Sanctus! Sanctus! Sanctus! Blessed is he who comes!

By his fame sped along unto Hannibal's plaque.
With new steed and reckless grit, through the Alps he dared.
White winter's blast the steed did fright, ov'r frozen ledge.
On iced foot he stumbled on, until the end was found.
Sanctus! Sanctus! Sanctus! Blessed is he who comes!

Step by step he made his way, no woe ev'r denied.
While knights to lords and cities cleaved, the poor he called his own.
In Ars he found the demon's spawn, men set for war,
Not by might, but private eye, all schemes were unveiled.
Sanctus! Sanctus! Sanctus! Blessed is he who comes!

The plot destroyed, the peace restored, Jezebel crushed,
Then rode he with famous squire, Stephen foul and fair.
He taught the blade, the flesh, the soul, knight soon to be,
Passed through Franc to Chunnel great, and in the darkness strode.
Sanctus! Sanctus! Sanctus! Blessed is he who comes!

Cross Brit they cut in search of Ire, then back again.
For seaward passage dear, contessa they must free.
Through wheeling, wilding roads the druid's labyrinth wound,
A year of trials and progress slight, 'ere she was saved.
Sanctus! Sanctus! Sanctus! Blessed is he who comes!

A love unseen, a peasant French, English lady kind,
Pedigree poor, deeds unmatched, marriage was arranged.
Black knight alone, less one he thought would his sword claim,
Crossed to Land of Ire, sword, helm, God still all he had.
Sanctus! Sanctus! Sanctus! Blessed is he who comes!

Ballad of the Black Knight
Foot touched earth for final time, nevermore to sea.
Some years that country slowly crossed, needed everywhere,
Til that day the robber struck, bringing end in view.
Two nights thence, the heir found, he unto darkness came

This the last and greatest stage!
Here will final battle rage!
Forty years for just one chance,
To save him spared by Daniel's lance!
Will Goliath in his sins die?
Or will Sir Samson fin'ly cry:

Sanctus! Sanctus! Sanctus! Dominus Deus Sabaoth!
Pleni sunt cæli et terra gloria Tua!
Hosanna in excelsis!
Benedictus qui venit in nomine Domini!
Hosanna in excelsis!

Volume VI

The Passion of Sir Judas

Chapter 1: In the Shadow of Darkness

After giving Winthrop his scabbard on Wednesday night, Sir Judas started walking west along the Eines river. He felt so much lighter without *Veritas* on his hip. He looked up at the rolling pillows of snow white clouds and smiled. *I'm seventy years old. It's about time I start walking without a sword.* He looked down at *Caritas*, washed Winthrop's blood off of it in the river, and then tucked it into his boot. David came over and stood beside him, still looking in the direction Winthrop had walked.

"He's gone again, Sir Judas...I don't see him anymore."

Sir Judas put his arm around David and said, "Yes, but it's much easier to part on good terms than on bad ones. I'm hopeful you'll see Winthrop before too long."

"That's a reunion I'm looking forward to. All of us together again."

Sir Judas nodded.

The two nightmares that had walked away during the duel now returned to Sir Judas and David. "Well hello there, you two! I thought you were leaving!" The two monstrous beasts walked up and nuzzled Sir Judas. Buttercup licked his ear with her forked tongue. "Oh ho ho...there, there! Thank you! You two are too kind. Tell me now, are either of you strong enough to carry two riders at once?"

Buttercup snorted and shook her mane proudly, giving Sir Judas a creepy, toothy smile. "In that case, we're in luck. I have a job for each of you if I may ask a favor." To Buttercup he asked, "Do you know the way to Castle Nightfall?" She whinnied and flicked her tail. "Wonderful. Then I would ask you to let David and I ride you along our journey there. As for you," he turned to Lightfoot, "I would ask you to follow that man I was just fighting and help him with whatever he needs." Lightfoot looked sad and shook her head. "There, there, now. Do you remember who he is? He's the man who leapt up in the carriage and saved you. If not for him, you would have followed your previous master home. Aren't you grateful for what he did?" Lightfoot begrudgingly nodded. "There's a good girl. Go take care of him now. Thank you." Lightfoot gave Sir Judas one last, eerie lick and then trotted after Winthrop.

Sir Judas took a deep sigh, then turned to David and said, "Let's be off, David. We have far to ride, and we should cover what ground we can before going back to sleep tonight." He lifted David up on top of Buttercup then heaved himself up just behind him. "Okay, Buttercup, we're both ready. Are you sure you will be able to walk like this? I'm a little too far back–" She let out a happy "Nya-ah-ha-ha-ha-ha," then took off at an incredibly fast trot–faster than most horses canter. The only reason Sir Judas knew it was a trot was because of the rhythm of the gait. "Amazing! How can you go so swiftly? And with two bareback riders to boot! If possible, we want to ride for an hour, and then you can have your rest, okay?" Buttercup made an odd neigh. Sir Judas thought it almost sounded like a laugh.

They rode along the river, hearing the distant pulse of Chelles's electric heart. The tall black screens mounted on the city's walls blocked the view of the electric tower and other luminaires. Ostensibly it was to keep outsiders from looking in at the city's lights. Sir Judas and David now knew it was really to keep the people inside from looking at the outer darkness. Before long they met the road running away from Chelles's southern gate. They turned left to cross the bridge running over the Eines, and then the city was behind them. They sped south along the road, passing through half a dozen abandoned villages. In amazement Sir Judas mused, *In an hour I've traveled further than I do most years.*

His amazement was far from over. Whereas a normal steed would be exhausted by this point, the nightmare was picking up her pace. With a familiar road under her hooves, she went even faster. The miraculous moonlight had long since faded, but Buttercup knew how to reach Castle Nightfall in total darkness. She trotted for a second hour, then a third, still showing no signs of fatigue. Sir Judas was so distracted by Buttercup's trotting, that the night was halfway gone before he realized he wasn't feeling his usual pains. He gave thanks to God for this special reprieve from the suffering he always felt when the sun wasn't shining.

Somewhere around that time Sir Judas felt David start to wobble in front of him. He smiled and put an arm around the boy. "Byah! Oh, don't worry, Sir Judas, I'm–yaaaaawn–I'm okay. I was just dozing a little."

"I'm not worried at all, David. You go ahead and doze. I'll make sure you don't fall until Buttercup stops for the night."

"Yaaaaawn…I'm good. I'm gonna…I'm gonna stay up with you…" A few minutes later David fell into a deep sleep, leaning backwards on Sir Judas. The black knight smiled. This was a truly wonderful night. He couldn't remember if he had said his usual bedtime prayers after leaving Lord Fearnow's palace, so he decided to say them again. He recited the prophecy to himself, not in the hopeful anticipation he had maintained for forty years, but instead in tearful gratitude. Then he said his usual prayer for poor sinners, offering to do any penance God would give him for their conversion. Having completed these prayers, he was ready for sleep. He just needed to wait for Buttercup to finish trotting.

Onward she ran, stopping neither for food nor drink. Sir Judas was terribly tired, yet he allowed the horse to keep going. As they bounced along in the dark, he began to seriously wonder if this was real or a dream. He was answered by the morning twilight, the grass growing bright before him, and then…

"Oh my God…"

As dawn broke and lit the world, Sir Judas saw the dome of darkness looming before him, so close it no longer seemed like a dome, but rather a wall that reached up to heaven and beyond the horizon to north and south. It became difficult to keep his bearings, as Sir Judas had to focus on the road ahead and not look up. If he did, everything went black, and he felt the vertigo of losing his peripheral vision. He thought they must have been at the very edge, yet Buttercup trotted for another hour, the darkness always getting closer.

At long last the nightmare's trot began to slow, then she turned right for a side road that ascended a low hill up to a castle. The gate was open and no one was on the walls. Once they reached the top of the hill Sir Judas looked west. The main road they had just departed went another mile further before it finally entered the land of night. When they stopped, David awoke. He yawned and looked at the sun. "Morning already? Oh my! Did we ride all night long? Sir Judas, you must be exhausted!"

"We did, and I am." The black knight lowered himself to the ground and fell over from the pains and stiffness of that long ride. Getting back to his feet, he helped David down, then began to walk around and stretch his legs. "This castle looks abandoned. If so, I know exactly where I'm going to sleep today. Time to find the captain's quarters!"

The castle was indeed vacant and had been for some time. Sir Judas told David that he thought (correctly) this must be Castle Gregory. The wall was a half-circle that had its two ends on the shore of a lake, a distinctive feature he recalled from his maps. Between the lake and the castle buildings was a long-neglected garden. It hadn't been worked for over a year and was overrun with grass and weeds. Nevertheless, wild vegetation from previous seasons had sprouted up, and there were vines of tomatoes, squash, and peas sprawling out along the ground. Once they saw the garden, David felt his stomach rumble hungrily. Only now did he remember that they had missed dinner last night and that the food Sasha gave him was in the pack at Sir Joseph's house. "Sir Judas, would it be alright if I picked some food out of the garden? It wouldn't be stealing, would it?"

"No, David. A man has a right to eat. And besides that, this castle must have been abandoned at least since springtime, if not longer. Otherwise the garden would have been sown. Whether it was abandoned because the men were afraid of the darkness, or whether it was because the darkness meant no one was using the road this castle is protecting, either way they are long gone. Moreover, the fact that the gates were left open suggests they wanted this place to be usable for any traveler who had need of it. Let us take whatever we need here." Sir Judas yawned. "Starting with a good bed! And if you do go picking food, grab a meal for me. I'll eat it when I wake up."

David did as Sir Judas suggested and made a meal out of whatever he could find. The squash was too tough for him raw, but the tomatoes and peas were delightful fresh off the vine. Normally, he would have been disappointed to discover they were bushing peas instead of snap peas, but he was hungry enough not to care. Buttercup went to the lake and guzzled water for many minutes before walking into the garden to look for food. He expected the nightmare to graze on grasses, but instead she began tearing into a raw squash with her sharp fangs. Then she began eating the vine the squash grew on. Then she ate dirt the vine emerged from. She suddenly began to make excited slurping sounds, and then lifted her muzzle with an ant colony crawling all over her lips. Her forked tongue flicked out to grab them, pulling the insects in so she could have some 'meat.' David couldn't help asking himself, *What on earth did they ever do to turn a horse into this thing?*

After filling up on peas and tomatoes, David explored the castle. It was indeed abandoned, but not in a rush. The tools, food, and even the bedding were all gone. The one exception was what looked like a guest room where a single mattress had been left. Sir Judas was sleeping soundly upon it. David went back outside and looked north across the lake. There was a beautiful forest on the other side. This was a peaceful place. Nevertheless, he struggled to enjoy that peace. His eyes kept being drawn back to the west.

The darkness was oppressive from this close. You had to look almost straight up to see over the top of it. David would try to look north and enjoy the forest, but the darkness was on the edge of his vision. He tried turning his back on it entirely, but that gave him the feeling that it might sneak up behind him. No matter what he did, he couldn't get comfortable. He would keep looking at the darkness and then regret it as soon as he did. As noon approached, David realized the sun was getting very close to the big black wall. He would look up for a moment, eyes blinded by the summer sun, then glance just a little bit west and be blinded by the dome instead. About half an hour later the sunlight began to dim. "Oh no!" David yelled, knowing what was about to happen. The sun passed behind the darkness. All at once, the sky went black.

David laid back on the ground, looking up at the stars. Now the darkness was even more dreadful. It wasn't possible to make out exactly where night sky ended and darkness began. If he was looking at the stars, he could figure it out, but David would look in other directions as well. Then he would randomly look west and go blind all at once. The feeling that the darkness was reaching out to grab him was always present. He tried to go inside and find something to do, but the castle wasn't navigable without any light. Instead David went to the lake and found stones to throw across it. After an hour or so he was truly miserable. Taking an especially large rock and chucking it beyond his view, he heard the splash of water he couldn't even see. "This is awful!" he cried out, "No wonder this fort was abandoned! No one can live in this stupid darkness!"

"Be at peace David."

The boy about jumped out of his skin. He hadn't heard Sir Judas approach and had no idea he was beside him. "I'm sorry, Sir Judas. Did I wake you up while I was blundering around the castle?"

"Not at all. I had a good long nap and woke up feeling refreshed. Do you have the meal I asked for?"

"Yeah, it's right over here. All I could find were peas and tomatoes."

"I'm grateful for anything I can have." David gave Sir Judas the bundle of vegetables and they both sat down to eat. Sir Judas ate heartily, while David nibbled and picked away. Not only had he already eaten, but he was also in a foul mood because of the darkness. The boy mostly sat there in bitter brooding until Sir Judas was full enough to talk. Then he shocked David out of his frustration.

"The sun is still shining on us."

At first David didn't even know what to say. Slack jawed, he looked up, looked down, looked up, looked down, then he asked, "When you say 'the sun,' are you talking about 'good times,' or 'the joy of friendship.' Like, what do you mean by 'the sun.'"

"I mean the sun, you dunderhead, the big glowing ball of fire in the sky."

Once more David looked up, just to make sure he hadn't totally lost his mind. Then he said, "Sir Judas, do you remember that book I mentioned a couple days ago? The one I was going to keep with all of your crazy sayings? This one is getting an entire chapter. I'm going to circle and underline it to make sure every reader knows this happened. Of all the craziest things you've ever said, this one blows them all away."

"Maybe it does. But do you remember what I said you would also have to include in that book? A note about whether or not I was right."

"It's the middle of the night right now."

"It's the middle of the day. About two in the afternoon if I had to guess."

"Well I know that's what *time* it is, but the sun isn't shining on us."

"Yes it is. Stick out your arm. You'll feel the sunlight on one side and not the other. Or look up at the darkness and pay attention to your eyes. They start to hurt as you get closer to looking at the sun. This explains something I've been wondering about. When we got closer to the dome I expected everything would become an icy winter land. Instead, it is still summer. Then I wondered why we found crops in the garden. If crops were getting half a day of sunlight (and only a couple hours back in spring), then how were they still living? Why is grass growing? How are those trees across the lake still vibrant and alive? Now I understand. The sun is still shining. It's not a dome of darkness at all. It's a dome of blindness."

David did as Sir Judas had suggested. He turned his face where the sun had disappeared, then followed his aching eyes to where it currently was. Just like when looking at the sun during normal daylight, his eyes hurt so badly he needed to turn away, even though he didn't see anything. After thinking about it a little longer, David said, "That's why your peripheral vision goes dark when you look at it. It's not that the darkness is coming out and surrounding us, it's that our eyes go blind when we see it!"

"Yes, and it also explains the sky. Even if the darkness was blocking the sun right now, the sky would still be blue, not black and starry. It would be like when you're in a building and look outside. The fact that sunlight disappears when the sun sinks behind this dome must be a special case of blindness. A blindness to all sunlight."

They sat there in silence for a few minutes, taking it in. Then David chuckled and said, "You know, Sir Judas, I'm not sure if this makes any sense or not, but I'm actually less afraid of the darkness now that we figured that all out. I've been worried that it's this *thing* that is wrapping its arms around me and pulling me in whenever I look in the wrong direction. Now, it's just a reminder to look somewhere else. Does that make any sense to you?"

"It does. I was thinking the same thing, actually. Perhaps I even understand why we feel that way. Unless God created this dome, it must have been made by the demons and their magic. And if so, the nature of the dome really tells us something about its architects. They want us to believe that they are lords of the universe. That their darkness can suck you in and extinguish all light, and that even the sun is subject to their powers. But they don't have that kind of strength. They just have enough power to make us men go blind. And not even permanently blind, just a temporary blindness. That's even weaker than a sword to the eye. We men can blind each other permanently. The demons are using very small and unimpressive abilities, but wrapping them up in fear, ignorance, and lies to maximize the impact those abilities have. Now that we see through their ruse, we aren't as fearful of facing the darkness."

"No...I guess not..." David answered, "But still...what about once we enter the darkness? There's all sorts of rumors about how no one can survive inside of it, and how anyone who tries is driven mad."

Sir Judas laughed. "Well first of all, both of those rumors can't be true. *Either* no one can survive it, *or* those who do survive are driven mad. As for what to do about it?" Sir Judas shrugged. "God will provide. Even if we walk amidst the shadow of death, we will fear no evil, for He is always at our side..."

Chapter 2: Winthrop's Words

As Sir Judas had guessed, it was now two o'clock on Thursday, about the time Winthrop was concluding his Confession. Sir Judas said to David, "There's something that was on my mind as we rode last night, David, and now that we've stopped near a lake, it seems like the perfect time to discuss it. I know you aren't well-studied in Christianity, but have you ever heard of Baptism?"

David was startled. "I have! I heard that word for the first time last night! Before we parted, Winthrop told me, 'Ask Sir Judas to baptize you tomorrow.' I asked him what it meant, and he said I should ask you."

"He said that? Truly?"

"He did. You seem surprised."

"I am…after all we discussed last night…for him to then say that…I am surprised. Very, very surprised."

"Why?"

Sir Judas rubbed his chin, thinking deeply. "Because Baptism is what makes a man a Christian, David, and I'm surprised Winthrop would say, 'I want you to be a Christian,' when he himself professed not to be one. What a strange thing. More tortuous than all else is the human heart…"

"That is strange," David said. "That's nothing like how Winthrop has always been, but…last night he seemed different. In some ways. In other ways he was the same old Winthrop I've always known, but…he was definitely different."

"Different in a good way or a bad way?" Sir Judas asked.

David smiled. "Different in a wonderful way…last night he told me, 'I love you, son.' He never said that before. I always thought he was the closest thing to a father I ever had, but…for him to actually call me 'son'…That was…" David trailed off. He couldn't find a word to describe it. Sir Judas was

wise enough to know he never would. Some things in life are beyond all power
of words.

Silence.

A few moments later, the black knight returned to their earlier topic. "I
don't wish to scare you, David, but I cannot deceive you either. We are going
to Castle Nightfall to confront Goliath, the destroyer of the Grand Empire and
slayer of six paladins in a single battle. Now that I know he is actually Sir
Samson, I will try to reason with him, but that is no guarantee of our safety. He
is a fearsome killer and there is a very real possibility that you, me, or both of
us will die in the confrontation."

David pulled back his shoulders and stuck out his chest. "I'm not afraid
of dying!" he boldly claimed.

"You should be," Sir Judas retorted.

That took the wind out of David's sails. "But…heroes aren't supposed
to be afraid of dying. They're supposed to be courageous and fearless!"

"I agree, but if death is the end of everything, then a man who doesn't
fear death isn't courageous. He's reckless, arrogant, and stupid. In order to be
sane, a hero must be fearless because he has a good reason not to fear death,
not because he doesn't think about how his actions will get him killed."

"So what's a good reason, then?" David asked, "Honor? Glory?"

"You tell me, David. If you were honored as a hero long after you were
dead and gone, but you didn't know about it because you were *dead*, how
valuable would that glory be?"

David let out a long sigh. "…Not at all…but then…maybe you would
die for your country? Or for someone you love? That's what lots of soldiers
say. 'I'm fighting for my loved ones.' That must be a good reason to die."

"Ah! For love! A noble motive indeed! 'No greater love has man than
this; that he should lay down his life for his friends.' But tell me, if you laid
down your life for someone you loved, and then you were dead, would you
even know that you had saved them? Could you take delight in giving them a
longer life if you yourself were not alive to take delight in anything?"

David rubbed his brow. "Sir Judas, I…I'm surprised to be hearing these
things from you. You don't honestly believe what you're saying, do you? You
took forty years to come save Sir Samson, and now all of a sudden you're acting
like there's no point in being a hero."

"My purpose is not to make you despair of heroism, David. I seek only
to make you understand it on a deeper level. Of course heroism is a good thing.

Anyone with a functioning heart can figure that out. We all recognize that when a man gives his life for a worthy cause, he is a beautiful soul who fills the world with goodness. We also all know that a man who thinks only of himself and saving his own life, even at the expense of those he claims to love, is a most contemptible craven. The purpose of my questions is not to make you doubt these things, but to make you wonder how they are true. How can it be good to die a hero if the hero won't be around to know he died a hero? How is that possible?"

David though for a moment and then slowly nodded his head in recognition. "It's because there's a heaven, isn't it?"

"Precisely."

David thought back to what he had heard about heaven. "Winthrop always said Christians invented heaven as 'the opiate of the masses.' He said there was no proof heaven existed, but…it's actually common sense. If being a hero is good, then there must be some sort of reward for heroes when they die. And if being evil is bad, then there must be some sort of punishment for evil people too. That's why Christians came up with hell."

"You're on the right track, but your history is a bit off. As you said, heaven and hell are common sense. Long before there were Christians–perhaps even before there were Jews–a good and holy man named Job suffered many terrible tragedies. He lost all of his property, all of his children, became terribly sick, and his friends all turned against him. His wife even told him to do what most men would do in that situation. 'Curse God and die!' But instead, holy Job blessed the Lord, saying 'I know my Redeemer liveth, and in the last day I shall rise out of the earth. And I shall be clothed again with my skin, and in my flesh I shall see my God. Whom I myself shall see, and my eyes shall behold, and not another: this my hope is laid up in my bosom.' By the light of natural reason alone–or 'common sense' as you put it–Job knew there must be life after death where the injustices of this earthly life would be set right."

At this point David began to shake, and became terribly afraid. "But Sir Judas…if that's so…I already told you two days ago, I'm a murderer! I helped Winthrop, Rowan, and Garrett kill countless people. People I could have saved! If I die…I haven't done nearly enough good to make up for those crimes. Even if we saved the world from Goliath, it might not be enough good! How much good do I have to do to not get punished after death? How could I ever pay the price for so many lives that I've destroyed?"

Sir Judas took David's hand in the darkness, and gently squeezing it he said, "Do you remember yesterday, when I said that I am glad I've been treated like a traitor for all these years, because now if a traitor should want to repent, his price has already been paid?"

"Yes, I remember you saying that."

"Well this is the Good News, David. The Gospel is that God, knowing there would be sinners like you and me who would realize our wickedness and repent, yet also knowing that the sins we already committed would be too great for us to ever make up for, decided to take all of those sins upon Himself. He was scourged like fornicators should be. He was crowned with thorns like the proud should be. He was murdered like murderers should be. Every torment and torture your sins ever have or ever will deserve has already been suffered, David. Just as I said, 'the traitor is free to repent, since I have already paid his price,' so too, you are free to repent. Your sins have already been answered for. You just need to accept the forgiveness God is giving you, and the first step in that acceptance is Baptism."

David was very confused, and looked at Sir Judas in the starlight, not understanding. "What do you mean, 'God was scourged.' 'God was crowned with thorns.' 'God was murdered.' Is God dead?"

"No. But He was. God became man, so that He could do the things He couldn't do as God alone. As man He could suffer, die, and atone for the sins of men before God, all while still remaining God. And then, on the third day after His death, being the perfect 'hero' Who saved all men from eternal doom, He became the first man to receive a hero's reward. He rose from the dead, and then after showing Himself to hundreds of witnesses over forty days, He ascended into Heaven where this Godman now reigns at the right hand of God. And not only Him, but all other men who accept the death He offered to pay for their sins. Right now there are ordinary men like you and me in heaven, ruling over all the world. Death is no longer the end for heroes. Instead it has become the portal that leads them to Paradise."

David thought some more about these things. "And Baptism means accepting His death? Letting God pay for what I've done wrong?"

"It does."

"But if that's the case, then why wouldn't everyone accept His death and be baptized? It doesn't make sense that anyone would ever say 'no' to that kind of deal, yet most people aren't Christians."

"Go back to where we started, David. God rewards the good and punishes the wicked. That is still true. For those who were leading a wicked life and repented, God now offers a chance to tip the scales of justice. But for those who were never baptized because they didn't want to live rightly, or for those who received Baptism as an empty gesture with no intention of converting, God will not force them to leave their sins behind. You are right that most men are not Christians, but it isn't because most men don't want to go to heaven. It's because most men don't want to go to heaven more than they want to continue sinning. Or to be more precise, it's because most men *decide* they would rather sin than go to heaven. It's a sad truth about our fallen race, but most of us freely reject the salvation God is offering."

David now looked over at the darkness, this time on purpose and not as an accident. "You're going to try to get Goliath to repent, aren't you? To get baptized?"

"A man can only be baptized once, and Sir Samson already was. After that, the only sacrament that can take away his sins is Confession, and for Confession he'll need a priest. All I can do is pray for him, encourage him, and try to persuade him to repent. From there, he's in God's hands."

"Sir Judas, you're using some words I'm not familiar with. What's a sacrament? And why would he need a priest to confess? Most people just confess in court."

"I'm sorry, David, we're a little far afield. Normally you would have months to learn the faith and make sure you understand it, but we're obviously in a bit of a hurry. I need to stick to the minimums and gloss over things like 'sacraments' and 'Confession.' God willing, if you survive this journey, you will have the rest of your life to learn much more. Now, the minimums. There are four truths necessary for salvation. These are the things you must believe in order to be baptized. The first is that God punishes the wicked and rewards the just after death. Do you believe this?"

"Yeah, of course. Like I said, it's common sense."

"Well said. Second, you must believe that God suffered for the sins of the whole world–and for your sins in particular–by becoming man, a man named Jesus Christ." When Sir Judas pronounced this most sacred Name, a great 'BOOM!' came from the darkness, and the ground began to tremble beneath their feet.

David laughed. "It sounds like the devils believe it. I don't fully understand how God can become man, but if He really loves us, then it makes sense He would want to save us from being punished." Sir Judas was looking into the darkness, thoughtfully wondering what had just happened.

Remembering what they were in the middle of, he said, "The third thing you must believe is that there is only one God. I know there are many beings that people call 'god' or 'goddess,' like Jove or Artemis, but those are man-made myths that demons sometimes prop up with magical pseudo-miracles. The proof I offer you for this claim would be Monday night in the glade, when those Jove worshippers were all put to flight in a single moment when the one, true God stretched out His hand. There is no other God like Him, and all who claim to be are imposters. Do you believe this?"

David thought back to when Charles grabbed him and seethed his threats, and how at that moment all seemed lost. Then *Caritas* had flashed with such spectacular power that the fight was instantly won. "I believe it. As impressive as throwing fireballs may be, what a real God can do is far greater."

"*The* real God. There's only one."

"Yeah, that's what I meant. 'The', not 'a'."

"Very well. Lastly, the fourth truth that must be believed for salvation is that the one God is a Trinity of persons. Three persons, one God. The first person is God the Father. The second person is God the Son. He's the person Who became man. The third person is God the Holy Ghost. All three of them are the one, true God."

After Sir Judas finished speaking, there was a long and awkward silence. Forty years of preaching the faith to non-believers had taught him how well this part was going to go over. He didn't even bother hoping people would get it the first time anymore. Instead, he began praying Hail Mary's silently.

At length, David asked, "Did you just say there are…three gods?"

"No. There is one God, but God is three persons."

David blinked. "So is…God like a hydra? He has three heads, but…only one hydra? Three persons, only one God?"

"Incorrect. Each head of a mythical hydra would only be one part of the hydra. The Father is not a part of God; He is all of God. The Son is not a part of God; He is all of God. The Holy Ghost is not a part of God; He is all of God. If you could only see one head of a hydra, you wouldn't be seeing the whole hydra, but if you saw a single person of the Most Blessed Trinity, you would be seeing all of God."

Silence.

"So...then there's only one God...which is why when you see one person you see all of God...are these just three different titles for God?"

"No, not at all. They are three distinct persons. The Father is not the Son, nor is He the Holy Ghost, yet all of them are God."

More silence.

David took a deep breath. "So the Father is all of God, one hundred percent of God, no part of God is missing, yes?"

"Correct."

"The same goes for the Son and the Holy Ghost?"

"That is also correct."

"And they're not all the same, they're three different people, right? The Father is not the Son; the Son is not the Holy Ghost...I'm still right?"

"Couldn't have said it better myself."

"Then there's three gods."

"Wrong. They are all the one God."

David threw his hands up in the air. "Then they're all the same!"

"Incorrect. Three persons who are not each other. Three persons who are all one God."

"Then each person is a part of God, like a hydra head!"

"Incorrect. Each person is all of God. No 'piece' of God is missing in any one of the three persons."

More silence.

In exasperation, David said, "Sir Judas, I need some sort of evidence. Give me a little proof. Or a good argument. Heaven and hell turned out to be common sense, even though I never would have guessed it. Is there something like that here? Is there a different way you could explain this where it would all start making sense?"

Sir Judas thought for a moment. Then he smiled and said, "Do you remember last night when I said that men hated the king's perfect laws, not because there was any flaw in the laws, but because there were flaws in the men?"

"I do."

"Something similar is at work here. The Trinity makes perfect sense. I'll go further–it is the *foundation* of all sense. The reason and logic in our own minds is merely a reflection of the perfect reasonableness of the One Who created them. You struggle to grasp the Trinity not because it is in any way *contrary* to your powers of reason, but because it is *beyond* your powers of reason. It's too reasonable for our flawed human minds. That's why we all need a power that goes further than the human mind can go on its own, and that power is faith. To every man who wants it, God gives sufficient faith to believe in Him."

David chewed on those words for a little while, then asked, "Did God ever say He was a Trinity."

"Yes He did."

"He told you that personally."

"He told all men that, both in the Sacred Scriptures that were written by God, and in Sacred Tradition which is taught by His one, holy, catholic, and apostolic Church. Both Sacred Scripture and Sacred Tradition teach that there is one God Who is a Trinity of persons."

"But how do you know those are really from God, Sir Judas? How do you know it wasn't men who wrote the Scriptures? Or started the traditions? Or even if those were both *originally* from God, how do we know men didn't change them over time?"

"By faith I know that Sacred Tradition is true. Sacred Tradition teaches that the Church has handed on the Scriptures faithfully. The Scriptures teach me about God as He has revealed Himself. Since they were written by God, they have no error, so long as I interpret those Scriptures in union with the Church that gave them to me. I have faith in God's Church, and everything else flows from there. There cannot possibly be any man-made errors or corruption if the Catholic Church really is what she says she is–the guardian of what God has revealed to men."

"But why would you think that's true?" David asked, "Why, when men make so many mistakes–when just *yesterday*, Lord Fearnow was mistaken about whether there were any more paladins, and he seemed to have irrefutable evidence on the subject–why would you trust that a Church handed down everything without making some huge mistakes? You said faith is a power beyond reason, but what reason do you have for faith? It's like the definition of faith is 'believing things that don't make sense'."

Sir Judas sat there a little longer, saying his prayers for David. Then he opened his mouth and said, "I can't give you a reason for your faith, but I can at least give you the reason for mine. I grew up in the Grand Empire, where all of society was Christian. I almost never thought about my religion–nobody did. My family took me to church and taught me my catechism, but it was never personal nor mystical. It was merely cultural. I always thought, 'I grew up in a

Christian culture, and the Africans have a Muslim culture, and the places we're conquering have a pagan culture, and we want the whole world to be Christian because Christianity is the 'best culture'. It promotes science, art, and rights for women and children.' That was all I thought of religion. I neither needed nor had any faith to maintain such a superficial understanding.

"Then I met the king. I was a squire for one of the knights of Nouen before I squired for Sir Samson, so I spent a lot of time at court for two years when I was a teenager. Despite my young years, I thought I knew so much more about how the king *should* be running his Empire than he did. Part of it was naiveté about statecraft. I underestimated how limited and restricted a ruler's options really are. But more than that, the king and I had different visions for what a perfect kingdom would look like. I thought he should try to build heaven on earth. He thought he should try to build earth going to heaven, and those are two very different kingdoms.

"One time when the king was enforcing a law that I thought was 'merely about morals,' I asked him, 'Why do you care so much about what people do in the privacy of their own homes?' He answered, 'Because I love them and I don't want them to go to hell.' I retorted, 'What are you ever going to do if you find out your version of Catholicism is wrong? What if God is much nicer than the Bible says He is, and everyone goes to heaven in the end? On the day you figure that out, you're going to realize you should have focused more on relieving suffering in this life and that you shouldn't have worried so much about a loving God causing eternal suffering in the next.'

"The king was neither angry, nor was he hurt. He simply told me, 'I am not wrong. I am certain that we should totally dedicate our lives to saving souls. That is not in conflict with helping our brother in this life, but it is certainly the higher priority.'

"'Well, that's arrogant!' I accused him (not realizing how arrogant of a teenager I was myself), 'What makes you so smart that you can't be wrong about anything?' He answered with a befuddling riddle. I probably won't relate it exactly how he said it, but I can at least give you the general sense.

"He said, 'You see me moving towards you. Or wait? Are you moving towards me? The distance between us is shrinking, but is it me approaching or you? Or a little of both? Maybe you're actually retreating, and I am in pursuit and overtaking you. You look to a tree for reference–but wait! What if it's moving too? The scientists say the earth spins after all. Everything's relative, nothing's absolute. All is in motion and all is sitting still, and it's really just a matter of what perspective you choose to take. You can say I'm approaching you, and I can say you're approaching me. Even though we disagree with each other, we can both be right according to our own personal truth. But wait! Behold! I see a cornerstone, unmovable by any force. Whosoever falls on this stone is broken, and whomsoever it shall fall upon it grinds to powder. A point of certainty, one thing I know, in a whole world that is or isn't in flux. And now that my eyes are fixed upon the stone, I discover I'm not moving after all. The distance between me and the stone is constant, so then I must be standing still. The distance between you and I is still shrinking, so then you're approaching me; I'm not approaching you. And the tree, the earth, the world, and even the furthest edge of our entire universe I can now know, because from the cornerstone I have found a firm foundation where I can finally stand and judge.'

"In a rage I yelled at him, 'Have you gone mad? Are you having a stroke? Or do you simply wish to vex me with your riddles?' The moment the king answered me was the moment I came to believe. He said, 'Mordecai...the Eucharist *is* Jesus Christ.'" Out of the darkness lightning flashed, and thunder blasted. The ground beneath them shook and quaked. David was terrified. Sir Judas grew even more pensive, wondering what this marvel signified. Then when the thunder ceased to echo and the earth was firm, a great stillness settled upon them.

Silence.

Perfect silence.

Sir Judas continued, "After he had said those words, the king proceeded to explain to me how on a certain occasion he had received the Eucharist–what looks like a little piece of bread, but is actually God in the flesh–and on that occasion God revealed Himself. He spoke to the king from the Eucharist and revealed with absolute certainty that what the Catholic Church teaches about that Holy Bread is completely and unequivocally true. That was his cornerstone. From there he was able to reason that several other things the Church teaches must also be true. From those conclusions he proved yet more of her teachings, and from those conclusions he could go further. In time he proved by the light of his own reason that every single one of the Church's doctrines is true, yet it was reason built upon a foundation of faith. God had to make the first move. He gave the king a point of certainty, his cornerstone. Then the king spent the rest of his life building on the foundation God had laid.

"And one of the things the king built was my cornerstone, David, though it was actually God building through him. A skeptic could find some way to write off the king's testimony. I could have accused him of lying or being mistaken. Instead God enlightened me with enough faith that I had the power to choose to believe my king. Looking at how he lived, I was certain that he was certain, and God confirmed me in my certainty. So why do I believe God is three persons in one God, even if I can't fully comprehend what that means? Why don't I have any doubts about something my reason cannot fully grasp? Because I was certain the real God had spoken to me through the king, and that God told me the Catholic Church was true. That's my own cornerstone, and everything else flows from there."

David wrestled hard with what Sir Judas had to say. Despite his joking about his 'book' of Sir Judas's crazy sayings, he knew the paladin wasn't actually a madman. Moreover, David was a boy who was normally disposed to believe his elders, since he was humble enough to recognize how little he knew himself. Still…this was too far. He couldn't bring himself to believe the seeming contradiction of three persons who are one God based on the testimony of a man he had only known for three days.

Another man came to David's mind. He asked, "Sir Judas, do you think Winthrop knew I would have to believe in the Trinity in order to be baptized?"

"I don't see how he couldn't. The Trinity is explicitly named in the very act of Baptism. 'I baptize you in the Name of the Father, and of the Son, and of the Holy Spirit.' In addition, he was raised in the Grand Empire, and in my conversations with him he has always known exactly what Christians believe, even if he rejects or ridicules those beliefs himself."

David arose. "Then I do believe in the Trinity. I don't get it, but I know that it must be the real God, because that's the God who finally got Winthrop to say he loved me and to call me his son. Maybe it's my imagination, but I think I'm feeling exactly what you said with God 'confirming' an idea that it's possible to poke holes in. I'm certain that God was pleased with Winthrop telling me to get baptized and believe in Him, and so God helped Winthrop to say what he had never said before. The Trinity God must be real, because it would take a God to get through to Winthrop, and that's the God who finally did it. I want to be baptized, Sir Judas. Make me a Christian."

The knight bowed his head, thanked God for answering his prayers, and with tears in his eyes he arose and put his arm around David's shoulder. "Come with me down to the lakeshore." The two walked down to the edge of the water so that they were up to their ankles with the tallest waves coming up to their shins. "I know you just said this, but for the sake of formality, I must ask again. David, will you be baptized?"

"I will."

Sir Judas bent down and cupped the water in his hand. He poured it on David's head once, twice, and then a third time as he said,

"David, ego te baptizo,

in Nomine Patris,

et Filii,

et Spiritus Sancti."

As the water flowed over David's head the third time he didn't *feel* anything change, yet he *knew* everything had. All he could feel was wet hair matted to his forehead, yet he knew the weight of the world had fallen from his shoulders. He was lighter, firmer, stronger. A new life was bubbling up within him.

Sir Judas said, "Your sins are forgiven. Give thanks to God."

'Your sins are forgiven.' Those words echoed in David's ears. He turned towards the darkness. It blinded him. He smiled. He wanted to be a hero. He was willing to *die* to be a hero. For the first time in his life, that was a perfectly rational impulse.

Chapter 3: Sunset Thursday

One of the hardships that comes in every life is an eagerness to act at a time when it is imperative to wait. Such was the challenge that both David and Sir Judas were now enduring. From the time that David was baptized until seven o'clock they were both putzing around in the dark with nothing to do, expecting some great miracle to happen, yet being totally powerless to make it happen any faster.

It was a little after seven that an unexpected problem occurred. Out of the blue, a low and ominous whistle sounded. Buttercup raised her head, shrieked, and cantered east along the road they had come by. Sir Judas ran after her yelling, "Whoa! Easy girl! Come back!" but she would not listen. She slowed down enough to look at them one last time, and then turned her face forward and ran away. Sir Judas sighed and then walked back towards David.

"What was that?" the boy asked him. "Why did she run away like that?"

"Because I'm a forgetful idiot, David, that's why. As soon as we caught these horses, Winthrop told me that they come whenever they are summoned, answering the call of their master over great distances. I completely forgot about that. Bah. If I had been thinking, I would have tied her up. Oh well…We just have to remember that God accounts for our honest mistakes in the plans of His Providence."

David was unconsoled. "Once the darkness goes away, we could have ridden her to Castle Nightfall in an hour. Now there's no way we'll reach it tonight."

Sir Judas shrugged. "That's alright. I've hiked across the entire realm to reach this place. I can endure one more day of hiking."

They then returned to their anxious waiting, growing more expectant with every passing minute. It was hard to tell by just temperature and birdsong, but eventually Sir Judas announced, "I think it's about eight. Another hour until sunset at this time of year." David nodded.

That hour dragged on painfully slowly. David and Sir Judas sat on the lakeshore, looking between the stars in the sky, their reflections in the water, and the dome where they stopped shining. Every few minutes, David would say something like, "Sunset's getting closer." Sir Judas would agree. "Any minute now," David would then add. "Mmhm." came the reply. On and on it went, for what seemed like an eternity. Finally, right as David was about to make another comment, Sir Judas stood up and said, "Arise. We must go."

David jumped to his feet, eager to finally be doing something. The pair took a final drink of water from the lake, then left the castle and walked to the main road. From there they marched westward, eyes on the ground ahead of them until their vision was blinded. They backed up a few paces and waited.

The wall of blackness was ten feet away. It was creeping towards them, moving about an inch every two seconds, or a foot every half-minute. Soon they had to retreat, moving ten feet backwards. Then it closed in on them again, and they retreated another twenty feet. "The sun will be setting any moment now," Sir Judas said, "The darkness is about to be dispelled." It approached again. They retreated again. Sir Judas began to feel his pains that only happened at nighttime. "The sun is set where we are, but it will be another minute or so until it sets for Castle Nightfall." The darkness closed on them again. They retreated again. By now Sir Judas knew the sun must be set at the castle.

"Sir Judas…why isn't the darkness gone?"

The black knight bit his lip. "Perhaps there is some work God wants us to do to help." Sir Judas looked up at heaven and prayed, "Almighty God, Creator of heaven and earth, in the beginning You said, 'Be light made,' and light was made. Now I ask you to send forth Your Word again, and dispel the shadows of sin and hell we see before us, allowing Your servants to pass through unharmed. Oh God, You have brought me thus far in my quest! Now give me the means to bring it to its conclusion!"

Nothing happened. The darkness inched ever closer.

Sir Judas pulled *Caritas* out of his boot and pointed it at the darkness. Nothing happened. He tried to make it glow with light. For a moment it brightened, but only until the light reached the edge of the darkness. Then it stopped, receded, and the dagger's glow became exceptionally faint. It flickered like a candle and then went out, even though Sir Judas was still trying to make it shine. He clenched his eyes shut and let out a heavy sigh. Opening them again, he said, "The good Lord giveth, and the good Lord taketh away. Blessed be the Name of the Lord. Since the time I became a paladin, one by one I have lost every power I was given. Now, when a light would be more valuable than ever, it seems the power to make *Caritas* glow is at an end. Only my sense of deadly intent remains." David was feeling dread at this announcement, but Sir Judas laughed and said, "Good. This way no one will ever think Sir Judas saved the world with 'paladin magic'. Let God have all the glory."

Even so, David was about to cry, but then a new thought occurred to him. "Sir Judas, may I hold *Caritas* a moment?"

"Of course, David! I completely forgot that it recognized you yesterday. Here, take it. It's certainly worth a shot."

Sir Judas took the dagger by its blade and offered the pommel to David. As soon as the boy grasped the dagger it immediately began to glow. A golden orb of light emanated from it, half a foot in diameter. It showed *Caritas* and David's arm in vibrant color, then started growing, expanding to reach one foot away from him, then two, four, ten, almost twenty, and then–David gasped. It crossed the darkness! The orb penetrated the invincible dome of doom, spreading out until it had a radius of forty feet, twenty feet of which was beyond the wall of black. It showed the grass and gravel that had been swallowed up minutes before. By a wondrous light more perfect than the sun, David could see as if it was the middle of the day. Another realization suddenly struck him. The darkness no longer blinded him! He couldn't see beyond the edge of the light orb, but he could look at the wall of black where it ended and not lose his vision. The same was true of the blackness to either side, for the darkness was still approaching, beginning to hug the orb, but never crossing it.

Sir Judas sighed. "What a shame. I was hoping the dagger would glow for you like it did yesterday. I don't see how we can go on without a light, but then what are we supposed to do?"

"What?" David cried out, "Sir Judas, what are you talking about? There's plenty of light! A bright big ball of it! I can see you perfectly right now! And look! The light shines in the darkness! The dome is surrounding the light, but not extinguishing it."

Sir Judas was perplexed. "David, are you alright? There's no light at all. It's just as dark as it has been all afternoon. We can barely see our hands in front of our faces."

"No, Sir Judas! No! It's light out now! Hold up any number of fingers– two! Now you put up four. Now three. Now both hands are behind your back. It's bright out, Sir Judas! It's bright! Stop pretending you can't see it!"

"I'm not pretending, there's...there's no light, David. Darkness. All I see is darkness." By this time the darkness had almost reached them again, and to Sir Judas it still looked like a wall that was a foot away. He backed away as they had repeatedly done. David instead walked forward, past the point where the wall seemed to be. "David! No!"

"I'm right here, Sir Judas! Right here! I can still see you perfectly well!" Sir Judas was looking around in surprise. From the way his eyes were moving, David could tell that he really was blind.

Sir Judas lowered himself to his knees and bowed his head. "So this is where You have led me...to go by sight is not an option...only by faith can I hope to walk...David, come here. Take me by the hand."

David did as he was told, stepping out of the darkness and meeting Sir Judas where he was kneeling. "Thank you, David, this is how we must proceed. I can't see anything, but I believe you can. Take me by the hand, and don't let go for any reason. Don't let go of me with one hand, nor *Caritas* with the other. Hold on tight, for both our sakes. We have about twenty miles left to go. The maps I've studied show that this road should be a straight shot to Castle Nightfall, so long as we don't turn off to the left or right."

Sir Judas looked ahead into the blinding darkness, then back to David. "I would ask one last favor before we begin, David. Hold *Caritas* up to my face, close enough for me to see it. David did so. In the dim starlight Sir Judas could make out the shadowy outline of the Cross. He closed his eyes and kissed it. He knew it might be the last thing he would ever see in this life.

Then Sir Judas threw back his head, and shouted for all who had ears to hear, "Deus! Vult!" David led him forward, and the black knight plunged into his master's darkness.

Chapter 4: Dark Night of the Senses

A cold blast tore through Sir Judas the moment he set foot in that accursed land. His bones were frozen, his muscles rigid, he passed from a night in summer to the deepest winter almost instantly. It was nearly impossible to breathe. His chest was heavy, the air bitter and sulfurous. It burnt his throat and caused piercing aches in his lungs. His feet were numb from the cold. He could neither feel nor wiggle his toes. Every step was a clumsy, lumbering stagger. There was a driving wind in his face, and as it rushed past he heard countless howls of maniacal laughter.

Huffing and coughing the insufferable air, he asked, "Oh, David–Ach!–how are we to get through this?"

"Get through what?"

"The cold, the air, the wind...do you not feel them ripping you to pieces?"

"No...it's a warm summer evening...are you okay?"

Sir Judas huffed after breathing more of the poisonous air. "Forget I said anything...Lead me on."

"You don't sound good at all. Do you want me to take you back?"

"No...forward. This must be...Ach! Another trick...of the demons...like the blindness. I'll be fine."

David led Sir Judas along the road, winding downhill towards the sea with craggy hills off to the left. Sir Judas was stumbling as he went, almost falling every few steps. When he felt like he could go no further, he asked, "How far have we gone at this point, David?"

"It's hard to say in the darkness...I wish I could see further, but this stupid light only goes forty feet!"

"Don't curse...that light, David. Forty feet...Ackak!...is far greater than zero. Let us be grateful...for what we have. If you had to guess, how far?"

"I don't know...a quarter mile?"

Sir Judas thought, *Eighty times more of this? I don't think I could go one mile, let alone twenty!* He spoke none of his doubts aloud, but he did begin to shake. Noticing the trembling of his hand, David said, "Sir Judas...we should turn around. Maybe God will send a better miracle."

"No! I won't go back! I did not come all this way just to fail at the end! I...Achhkah!...I will...I will carry on." Sir Judas fell into another fit of coughing as he stumbled on his way.

Then the voice began to speak.

"YOU CANNOT DO THIS. YOU CANNOT SUCCEED. ANOTHER QUARTER MILE, MAYBE TWO, BUT THAT'S THE FURTHEST YOU CAN GO...YOU WON'T EVEN MAKE IT ONE MILE IN OUR LAND." The voice was low, cold, and rasping. Every word that it spoke rumbled, somewhere between the majesty of rolling thunder and the pathetic gurgles of a hungry stomach.

"Quiet! Quiet!" Sir Judas said, "I will not listen to your doubts! The Lord will deliver me!"

"HE WILL NOT SAVE YOU. HE WILL LEAVE YOU TO DIE IN THIS WRETCHED PLACE. THERE IS ONLY ONE WAY YOU CAN LIVE. ALL WHO TAKE MY HELP ARE IMMUNE TO THESE PRESENT SUFFERINGS, AND IT IS HELP THAT I GLADLY OFFER."

"Get behind me, satan! Be gone! Not for all the kingdoms of the world would I take your help!" David was looking around, trying to figure out where the voice was coming from. It sounded very close—as if it was inside the light, maybe even next to Sir Judas—yet he didn't see it anywhere. They trudged onward, going a quarter mile once again. Sir Judas's knees were knocking, his breathing ragged, and he was leaning heavily on David with every step.

The voice returned.

"HITHERTO THOU SHALT COME, BUT NO FURTHER, FOR THIS IS THE BOUND WHERE WE RUN FREE. TAKE ONE MORE STEP, AND YOU ARE SURELY DOOMED TO DIE."

David stopped. "Sir Judas, what should we do?"

"Lead me onwards."

"But Sir Judas! Didn't you hear the voice?"

"Let him bluster all he—Achk!—all he...wants. We go forward. Lead me by the hand."

David nervously resumed walking, waiting for some unknown terror to come. He didn't have to wait long. After ten steps Sir Judas shouted in pain and dropped to one knee. "Ah! My back! Ahhh!" He fell forward, catching himself with his free hand, then shouted in pain and fell on his face. In order to keep holding his hand, David dropped to his knees beside him. Using the hand that was holding *Caritas*, he felt along the chain mail on Sir Judas's back. The armor was wet. David pulled his hand away. His knuckles were covered in blood.

The voice now spitefully hissed. "I TOLD YOU TO COME NO CLOSER! HERE WE ARE FREE TO DO WHATEVER WE WANT! GO BACK NOW, LEST WE TEAR THE FLESH FROM YOUR BONES!"

David started trying to retreat, but Sir Judas pulled his hand in the opposite direction. "Sir Judas, we must go back! Otherwise they'll kill you!"

"If they could, they already would have. Don't believe their lies." He put his left hand on the road and pushed, while pulling himself up by his right hand that was holding David. He stood up about halfway, then with a shout of pain fell down again. He pushed up again. He fell down again, but this time David was underneath him, struggling to help him up. Sir Judas finally regained his feet, even as he lacked the strength to stand. "Thank you, David...Ah! Ugh...lead me on..."

Sir Judas was leaning so heavily on David that the boy could barely handle the weight. The rumbling majesty of the voice gave way to a shout so loud and shrill it made David want to cover his ears. "IF IT IS PAIN YOU WISH, DRINK YOUR FILL!" Sir Judas began wobbling wildly. David was in front of him and beneath him, almost carrying him on his back. Sir Judas was being buffeted side to side, threatening to topple David and knock them both over. Every time Sir Judas lurched, David felt a fresh splash of warm blood hit him in the face. Right when the boy thought he couldn't go another step, Sir Judas began to chant,

Judica me, Deus, et discerne causam meam de gente non sancta: ab homine iniquo et doloso erue me. Quia tu es, Deus, fortitudo mea: quare me repulisti? Et quare tristis incedo, dum affligit me inimicus? Emitte lucem Tuam et veritatem Tuam: ipsa me deduxerunt et adduxerunt in

Judge me, O God, and discern my cause from the nation that is not holy: from the iniquitous and deceitful man deliver me. For Thou art God my fortitude: Why hast Thou repulsed me? And why do I go sorrowful whilst the enemy afflicteth me? Send forth Thy light and Thy truth. They have

montem sanctum Tuam, et in tabernacula Tua. Et introibo ad altare Dei, ad Deum qui laetificat juventutem meam. Confitebor Tibi in cithara, Deus, Deus meus. Quare tristis es, anima mea? Et quare conturbas me? Spera in Deo, quoniam adhuc confitebor illi, salutare vultus mei, et Deus meus.

conducted me and brought me unto Thy holy hill, and into Thy tabernacles. And I will go into the altar of God, to God Who giveth joy to my youth. To Thee, O God, my God, I will give praise upon the harp. Why art thou sad, oh my soul? And why dost thou disturb me? Hope in God, for I will still give praise to Him, the salvation of my countenance, and my God.

"NO! NO! WHY DO YOU CHOOSE DEATH?" The voice was flitting around rapidly, coming from this direction, and now another, flailing every which way as it made its curses. Though Sir Judas was still deeply afflicted, he began to stand more firmly. First he was leaning less on David, then he was walking all on his own. Strengthened after singing that psalm, Sir Judas began to sing another. When that one was finished, he sang more. At that time David did not yet know the Ancient Tongue, but he would always remember Sir Judas's burst of strength began with the words, 'Judica me, Deus, et discerne causam meam' From that moment onward, Sir Judas would not cease to cry out his prayers.

They carried on in this manner for some time, the miles now rolling by much more swiftly. They went over a little wooden bridge that crossed a shallow creek, and then the route turned directly westward. David wasn't sure how far they had come, but it felt as if they had walked for hours. For him, the air was becoming cooler as the night wore on. For Sir Judas, it seemed as if he was finally getting used to his present sufferings.

The voice returned once more.

"TURN AROUND AND GO BACK, OR ELSE WE SHALL SMASH YOU, BREAK YOU, SLAY YOU, THEN LEAVE YOUR CARCASS TO ROT IN THIS GOD FORSAKEN PLACE." Sir Judas did not so much as waver in his chanting. David tried to ignore the voice as well, walking forward, but very much afraid.

"VERY WELL. YOUR DIE IS CAST."

There was a loud snapping sound, and then Sir Judas fell to the ground with a howl of pain. David dropped down beside him, then gasped in horror.

First, he finally saw that Sir Judas's face and hands were totally covered in blood. This, however, was secondary to the injury that had just occurred. Sir Judas's thigh was broken and contorted at a gruesome angle. In distress he cried out, "Sir Judas! Your leg! What do we do now?"

The voice answered his question. "HE MADE HIS BED. NOW HE SHALL DIE IN IT. FLEE, CHILD! LEST WE TURN OUR WRATH UPON YOU!"

Sir Judas squeezed David's hand tightly. "Do no such thing, David. When he speaks in lies, he speaks according to his nature. They cannot touch you, or else they already would have. We go onward."

"But Sir Judas, how? Your leg is broken!"

"It doesn't feel broken. I just felt a little pain and then took a tumble."

"It wasn't a 'tumble,' your leg is—" David stopped in amazement. Sir Judas was rising. He looked back at the leg. It was perfectly straight. "How...Sir Judas! A moment ago your leg was broken!"

Standing up straight, Sir Judas answered, "That moment is in the past. We must live in the present." He then began to chant again. David walked forward in wonder.

The voice snarled at Sir Judas, "STUPID MEATBAG, DUMBER THAN THE DIRT FROM WHICH YOU WERE MADE. DO YOU THINK I CAN ONLY STRIKE YOU ONCE? MY BITE NEVER WEAKENS, AND MY VENOM NEVER FADES." As David carried Sir Judas along, he heard a series of stomach churning cracks, crunches, and splintering sounds. Sir Judas would stop singing for a moment, squeeze David's hand in pain, then take a deep breath and sing again. Whenever David took his eyes off the forward road to look at Sir Judas he would see the old man's body break and twist with crippling injuries. It seemed he was mortally wounded with every step, but then he would be healed before the next one.

David was fighting back tears, heart breaking with this barrage of torments. Even if the injuries were healed shortly after, every time one was inflicted it caused Sir Judas excruciating pain. He had never really prayed before, but seeing Sir Judas suffering, David said, "Oh God, You can do anything. Please, make this stop! Stop whatever thing is hurting Sir Judas and make it go away!" At last the voice fell silent, and the only sound was the paladin's solemn chanting.

No more injuries came until Sir Judas finished his psalm. He said, "Good prayer, David. Wonderful prayer," and then he began a new chant while they marched forward. The black knight leaned on David less and less, until he recovered the strength to stand all on his own.

Sometime later they came to a fork in the road. There had been little dirt paths merging with the gravel trail all along, but this was a major road of quality construction. It went directly north, while a wooden sign in the middle of the western road had a painted arrow pointing that way. David asked, "Sir Judas, does our route turn right at all, or should I keep going straight?"

"Straight ahead. Like I said earlier, our route is a straight shot to Castle Nightfall."

They continued past the sign. One mile later, David saw large piles of rubble enter his little orb of light. "Sir Judas, we've reached the walls of an old, ruined city. Is this Castle Nightfall?"

"It can't be...by my guess, we're only about halfway there, though I've never tracked distance blind before. Is there a sign anywhere saying, 'Welcome to such and such a place.'?"

David looked around. "Oh yes! Here it is. Let's get a little closer. Alright, it says...Oh my...Instead of welcoming us it says...'Beware: Moab lies ahead.' I guess this city must be Moab."

"Perhaps," Sir Judas said, "Though that certainly isn't an Irish name...Moab was an infamous tribe in the Bible...I think this sign is meant to be some sort of warning about the people who used to live here...or even worse, perhaps the people who still do. Let us proceed with caution. That demon who tempted me offered to protect me from the darkness. I am worried that this might be an entire city of people who received protection from the Moabite god, Moloch. Let's keep quiet, go as swiftly as we can, and try to leave this city behind us."

Chapter 5: The Scar

David led Sir Judas into the city. The road changed from gravel to cobblestone as they entered, and as soon as they set foot on those cobblestones, they heard a distant sound. It was similar to Chelles late at night, only without the pulsing of the electric heart. It was the sound of shouting, screaming, and revelry. "Sir Judas, do you hear that?"

"Yes. That's probably the 'Moabites' we were warned about. As I said, let us go swiftly and try to avoid anyone if we can help it. I pray that they are as blind to your dagger as I am, or else we will draw every eye in the city."

While it was indeed true that the Moabites couldn't see the dagger's light, that didn't mean they were unaware of the travelers' arrival. Sir Judas and David had only gone about one block before a man walked into the orb of light ahead of them. "Greetings! Greetings! Welcome to our beachside paradise! Shall I escort you to our party?"

David looked at Sir Judas fearfully. The knight simply said, "We are passing through," then made to keep walking.

"No, no, but I do insist! Please! Please! You look half-dead from your journey! You're completely covered in blood, man! Let us show you our hospitality and give you a little rest."

Sir Judas gave David's hand a tug forward, signaling for him to keep walking. "I cannot rest here. Your offer is politely declined."

The man moved up so that he was two feet away from David and Sir Judas. Two score men and women now entered the light, totally invisible until they emerged from the wall of darkness on every side. Sir Judas and David were completely surrounded. "It isn't polite to decline though. At least let us serve you a drink. Here comes a goblet of wine. Please drink, I insist."

"Battle looms," Sir Judas stated flatly. "I cannot let my senses be dulled by the intoxication of food or drink. Now if you will excuse me, every moment in this darkness weighs heavy upon me. We shall be going." Sir Judas tried to walk forward again, and here David made a very understandable mistake. Sir Judas, being blind, was about to walk into one of the men surrounding them. He had no idea he was there. David instinctively pulled him back to prevent the collision. When this happened, the man who had been speaking realized several things. He noticed Sir Judas's empty, blind stare. He noticed David's eyes were actually moving to whatever he was looking at. He noticed the fact that they were holding hands. It seemed impossible, yet the evidence was clear. For so long, no one had come to this place unless they were possessed and had the vision of devils. The possibility of a blind man coming was absurd, yet here he was.

The man who had been speaking looked at all of the others with wicked glee. This was going to be fun. He grabbed David and Sir Judas by the wrist, and ripped their hands apart.

"Hey! Let go of me!" David yelled, not yet realizing how much danger they were in.

The man released Sir Judas's wrist and then took him by the hand. He didn't move his lips, but a voice came from him that sounded exactly like David. "Quick! This way!" The man then took off running, with Sir Judas following as quickly as he could. David was shocked into silence. When he regained his wits and tried to yell it was already too late.

A hand pressed down firmly over his mouth and an arm wrapped around him from behind, pinning his arms to his sides. A woman slithered in his ears, "None of that now. Let us give him a proper welcome." She was small and slender, not much larger than David, but her arms had an unnatural strength that made them harder than steel chains. A man grabbed David by the wrist, and then began to pry *Caritas* out of his hand. When the dagger was ripped free from his grasp, David feared it was going to go out, but the light continued shining. The man tucked the dagger in his belt and then grabbed David by the feet. Together with the woman, they carried a frantically struggling David down to the beachside.

When he reached the cliff overlooking the beach, David saw the great roaring bonfire. The man carrying him yelled, "Someone throw a little sand in the portal! We don't want the old man to see it coming!" A reveler did as he had said and hurled a fistful of sand into the giant fire. David expected it to have no effect, but instead the fire was instantly extinguished. At least, it seemed to be extinguished. David still felt the heat, and then once they came within forty feet of the fire (close enough for the fire to be inside the orb of light from *Caritas*) David saw the fire was still blazing, taller and hotter than it was before. Its light was now hidden from view, but that only made the flames more deadly.

At the same time Sir Judas was led blindly by the leader of the group, hurrying down alleys and side streets while hearing a constant stream of commands in David's voice. "This way! Over here now! Ah! They're ahead of us! Quick, turn around!" Most of the other people were running after them with shouts of anger, acting like they were in hot pursuit. Sir Judas ran as fast as he could on their circuitous path, quickly losing all sense of direction. Once the leader was confident Sir Judas was thoroughly disoriented, he led him back towards the bonfire, running along the beach.

David saw Sir Judas enter the globe of light, rushing headlong towards the fire. He squirmed and fought, and tried to shout, but it was all to no avail. The man and Sir Judas went full speed at the flames and then–thank God!–Sir Judas stopped at the last moment and pulled back. "Quickly!" the man said with David's voice, "Only a little further! They've lit a wall of fire we need to jump over, and then we'll be out of here!"

Sir Judas held up his hand to cover his face. "Is there truly no other way around?"

"This fire surrounds the whole city, and runs out into the ocean! We have to jump now!"

Sir Judas set his face like flint and prayed, "Lord, into Thy hands I commend my spirit." He then ran towards the fire to jump again, but backed away at the final moment. "Ah! I can't! Lord, strengthen me!" Again he tried, but he was driven back by the flames. He couldn't bring himself to do it.

"They're right behind us! Now! We have to jump!"

Sir Judas slapped himself in the face with his free hand. "Come on, stupid self. Stiffen your spine, and set your–" Sir Judas broke off suddenly. "You said there are…flames around the whole city?"

"Yes! Now jump quickly!"

"…how far can you see?"

"The wall of fire is so tall I can see it all the way on the other side of the city!"

Sir Judas backed away from the fire and ripped his hand out of the man's grasp. "What is my name?"

The man answered in David's voice, "What are you doing? Give me your hand!"

"What is my name, you accursed deceiver! You are not David! Where have you taken him! Get away from me! All of you!" Sir Judas had backed into the crowd, which laid hands on him and began to laugh madly.

The man now said in his own voice, "Oh, I guess I'm discovered. Very well. If you won't go into the flames willingly, we'll do the deed ourselves. Throw him in, lads." David's eyes went wide. He thrashed with all his might, but it achieved nothing. The woman holding him was too strong. Two men from the mob grabbed Sir Judas by his chain shirt and dragged him to the fire's edge.

Sir Judas's sense of deadly intent flashed. He was about to be hurled into a roaring blaze. The escape: how odd! He didn't understand, but he trusted. Sir Judas cried out, "I renew my offer!"

The two men disappeared. Sir Judas fell down and landed on his backside. Everything was still. Everything was silent. Every single witness was in utter shock.

Then the mob's fury broke like a raging storm. They all ran up to grab Sir Judas, shaking him and yelling, "What did you do? Where did they go?" A woman slapped Sir Judas in the face. She disappeared. Another man kicked him. He disappeared. Three others tried again to throw him in the flames. They all disappeared. One by one as they pressed upon him, everyone who did Sir Judas any violence vanished into thin air. Moved by rage, the woman holding David threw him aside, and with the man holding *Caritas*, they charged Sir Judas to attack him. The woman disappeared as soon as she tackled him. The man disappeared as he thrust *Caritas* harmlessly into Sir Judas's armor.

Now the entire crowd was gone, and only the man who had spoken in David's voice remained. He realized everyone who struck Sir Judas was vanishing, yet unable to control his anger, he was about to do the same. "Where are they, black sorcerer?" he seethed at Sir Judas. "What have you done with them?" Sir Judas was curled up in the fetal position in great pain. He was coughing and hacking like he did earlier, and gruesome crunching sounds with spurts of blood were coming from him once more. "Where are they? Answer me! Bring them back!"

Sir Judas groaned, but didn't answer the man a single word. He didn't seem to hear him. Losing control of himself, the man kicked Sir Judas, yelling, "Answer me!" Then he was gone.

David rose to his feet in wonder. He had no idea what had just happened. Then, behold! A man appeared beside him in dazzling white robes, with a face of pure light and a sword of lightning in his hand. David was terrified until the man said, "Be not afraid," and then he suddenly felt great peace. The man continued, "I am your guardian angel. As a man of dreams, it has been granted you to glimpse behind the veil, to see the things no eye can see, and to hear the words no ear can hear. For as long as Sir Judas lives, you may speak of nothing I show you, but once he has safely reached his home, you must write these things down, so that all men may glorify God, and labor fervently in the priesthood of all believers. Do you accept this?"

Struck speechless, David nodded.

"Very well. I shall now show you a vision of this world as it truly is." The angel touched two fingers to David's eyes, and they were opened. He stuck a finger into each ear, and they could hear. Then he touched a finger to David's tongue, and it was sealed, so that it would not speak of anything he saw until the time that had been appointed. David did as the angel commanded and had Sir Patrick write this vision down for him two days after he was permitted to do so. The account that follows is quoted directly from his personal records.

Chapter 6: The Triumph of Sir Judas

When the angel touched my eyes, the first thing that happened was that the darkness went away. It was the middle of night, so the sky was still black, and yet I could see everything clearly. I no longer needed any light from the sun. My eyes must have been getting light from somewhere else. I could see the mob again, as well as Zambri (the man who was leading them). They were all gathered around Sir Judas, right where they had been when they started attacking him, only now they weren't attacking him anymore. They were all cowering in fear. Sir Judas was thrashing around on the ground. At first I thought there was this pillar of fire coming up out of him, but then I realized it was going down, not up. When I looked closer, the pillar of fire was actually an uncountable number of flaming arrows, all falling nonstop on Sir Judas's body. I looked up to see where the arrows were coming from, and way up in the sky was this enormous swirling mass of monsters. Legion upon legion of demons were assaulting him. Even though they were so far away, I could see them perfectly. They were the most hideous and disgusting creatures I ever saw. Their bodies were like a bunch of animal body parts all thrown together, only…uglier. Because they had intelligent faces. There's a difference between a cat with a dog's head, and an *intelligent* cat with a dog's head. The intelligent one is far more pathetic and frightful.

Then from the horizon, out across the sea, the stars began to go out, and I realized there was a big wave coming right towards us. I assumed it was the ocean, but as it got closer I realized it wasn't. It was more of the demons. A vast swarm of bodies, so thick they blocked out the sky came rising, rolling, and then crashing all about us–except they didn't. Instead of spreading out like a real wave, this wave got smaller and smaller at the end, so that every demon went blasting right past Sir Judas. They howled in his ears, and tempted him with caresses, all while unleashing a storm of teeth and claws that ripped his flesh to pieces. In the midst of them stood a single man in white–Sir Judas's guardian angel. The angel allowed all of the demons to break and wound Sir Judas–even wounds that should have been deadly–but then it would heal his body immediately afterwards. Still, he was feeling all that pain...

Over and over this happened. Arrows streaming down, wave after wave ripping him apart. A pool of blood was spreading out from his body. Then that man Zambri asked the exact same question I was thinking. "What is going on?"

This giant green lizard slithered down out of the sky. As soon as he started talking, I recognized it was the voice that had been talking to me and Sir Judas the entire time. The lizard said, "We are trapped here, forced to tempt this stupid meatbag, when we could be far more effective working anywhere else. And you stupid, damned meatbags somehow got yourselves stuck here too, so fall in line and get to work. Jump in the bottom of the wave. The smell of burnt flesh is dreadful, and I want you as far away from me as possible."

The lizard flew back up, but Zambri yelled, "Wait! But why are we trapped here? Why can't we go back to work tempting souls? And why are so many demons wasting their time tempting one man? Surely satan wouldn't order such a waste of his forces. There must be a million of you here!"

The lizard flew back down (thankfully he didn't see me), and with a smile full of broken teeth he said, "I hate to bear your stench any longer, but for the suffering this will cause you, I'm willing to suffer a little myself. Every night this man prays a certain prayer, saying, 'God, I offer to bear any hardship or difficulty that would lead to the conversion of poor sinners.' And the Almighty, in order to increase our already boundless torments, has decided to grant that daily petition in the cruelest possible way.

"Whenever a demon–or a stupid meatbag like you–tries to afflict or harm this knight, we become trapped with him, forced to now tempt him instead of whoever we were supposed to be working on. Normally that would only affect the demons who wanted to tempt him *anyway*, except that this rotten meatbag has led a most abnormal life. He has meandered all over Europe, stopping in too many towns and villages to count. On the many, many occasions he has talked to those he met along the way, rather than talk about the harvest, the weather, or any other appropriate subject, he always finds a way to bring up the Almighty. At that point, the demon who is tempting whoever the knight is talking to does the most natural thing. He tries to make the knight feel uncomfortable for starting such an unpleasant conversation. But then the minute he afflicts the knight in that way he suddenly sees us, and by that point he's already stuck with us. Now what happens? Now the knight is talking to someone about the Almighty, and there isn't anyone around to distract or manipulate them. It's dreadful! Truly dreadful! In time, satan realized none of us were at our posts, and so he sent out many search parties full of talented devils. They wander around without finding where we are trapped, until they eventually do find us and become powerless to leave. You couldn't dream of a greater tragedy! I take that back, because a greater tragedy is already happening...

"Wherever this man has gone, a wave of repentance has followed in his wake. Europe has been plundered of over half its demons. There are not a million of us here, but a *billion*! One billion of the greatest minds to ever exist, all bound to the worthless task of tempting one man who flees from every sin with horror. Meanwhile, the faith and the Church are spreading like wildfire, and our brethren are too outnumbered to even slow them down."

Despite the fact that the devil was awful to listen to, I felt very excited. His words had the opposite effect on that Zambri guy, because he was getting paler every moment. When the devil was done, Zambri laughed nervously and said, "Well–heh heh–at least there are no bishops left. They can believe the faith all they want, but the Church will die of old age within one generation."

"No you fool! You ignoramus! Are you even less informed than us? Dozens of bishops are spread throughout the realm, and a hundred more have gone as missionaries to the very ends of the earth!"

And then Zambri said, "That's not possible! In life I was a priest named Zambri, and I was very well informed about what happened in the Church. Right before I died there was a council that every bishop went to, and while they were all gathered together a giant earthquake killed them all. I didn't even need to be a priest to know that! Everyone did! And the Reformers who wanted to fix the Church said, 'That shows whose side God is on! He killed every one of those wicked bishops!' And if there are no bishops, there is no way there will ever be another bishop or another priest, since only a bishop can hand on that power."

Then the devil opened his mouth really wide and spat a green, nasty substance all over that Zambri guy. The devil wasn't happy with him at all. He wasn't even pretending to smile anymore. Instead, while Zambri was rolling around in pain, the devil snarled, "Do you give God the credit that belongs to me? That earthquake you heard about was not the work of the Almighty, but instead it was *me* getting permission from Him to slay those bishops for all the abominations that they had done. The final straw was for opposing this knight, in fact. After years of our clambering for permission to kill them, the Almighty permitted us to strike every one of those wicked bishops dead."

Zambri was still rolling around in pain from the venom when he called out, "So then they are all dead! How can there ever be another bishop?"

The devil vomited more venom on him, and then shouted even louder than Zambri's screams. "You're still not listening, fool! This is why you meatbags could never rule in hell. He gave us permission to slay every *wicked* bishop. But there was *one* who repented at the preaching of Sir Judas, and what a difference there is between one and none! He was saved from the earthquake by a great miracle, just like the sons of Core. That miracle so transformed the bishop that he spent the rest of his life roaming Europe in sackcloth and ashes. He ordained priests in every town and consecrated bishops in every nation. Now a renewed Church has been resurrected from the tomb of the one that fell with the Grand Empire..." The devil roared and smashed the whole crowd of humans with his tail. "Our greatest fear is upon us! The Church has been purified!"

Then everyone else who was there–the damned humans and the devils in the sky, and the ones in the rolling waves–all began to howl and curse together. They were shouting so many things that I couldn't hear them all, but I did manage to catch what the devil who had been talking to Zambri shouted. He yelled, "Curse the God above! Curse Him! Instead of dealing with us Himself, He forces us creatures to settle things amongst ourselves. I would much rather lose to an invincible God than suffer the humiliation of being bested by dust and ashes! Graagh! To hell with Him, and to hell with you! Enough, you stupid meatbags! Fall in line! Get to the bottom of the wave, and beat this accursed paladin!"

As the next wave crashed, the devils who were in it grabbed Zambri and all his followers, and dragged them in for another assault. The green lizard demon flew back up into the sky, but instead of vomiting out more flaming arrows, he vomited out that nasty green venom. Then the vision disappeared, and I couldn't see or hear the demons anymore. *Caritas* only let me see a dozen yards until there was a wall of darkness. Inside the light, I saw Sir Judas rolling around madly, screaming in constant pain.

My guardian angel was still there. Like, as in, he was visible to me. I suppose he's always here, even right now, but I could still see him. He told me, "Go to him. Comfort him. Encourage him. Do everything you can to help him endure these sufferings. He cannot go any further."

And then I said, "Mister angel, please let me help him! Let me carry my own demons, and maybe some of the other ones that are afflicting him too. That's the help he really needs right now."

The angel said, "The day will come when you can follow in his footsteps, but today you are too young, too weak, and unconfirmed. If even one of these demons was free to do what they usually do in this darkness, within three hours it would lead you into mortal sin and then kill you and drag you to hell. Humble yourself, David. Accept your place in God's plan of salvation. Serve Sir Judas in your way, and let him serve you in his. Before I go, there is one last thing I wish to tell you. Let these be words of strength and hope in the battle that is now at hand."

Then I thought he was going to touch my chest with his finger, but it went through my chest and touched my heart. My mind suddenly remembered Sir Judas kissing Lord Fearnow while we were all in his bedroom. Only it was more powerful than a memory, more like living through it again. I was in the bedroom, and I heard my angel's voice say, "Whether he is a saint or a sinner, every man is a tool in the hand of God. In this moment, the Holy Ghost came upon Lord Fearnow and made him confess the words that God wanted him to say. The man himself did not know this, and he said these words by way of ridicule. Nevertheless, they were the words of God, and every single thing he said was true.

Then Sir Judas turned and walked away. Sir Joseph and I followed him, and Lord Fearnow shouted out the words my angel had been talking about:

"Ecce homo! Behold the man! A great and noble knight, with virtue surpassing every other soul on earth! Will he avenge his king? No! His Empire? No! His master? No! He won't even avenge himself, because God said it was a sin! Ecce homo! Behold the man! Sir Judas, Last of the Kingsguard! This man is *truly* incorruptible!"

The angel disappeared. Sir Judas was curled up in a ball on the ground, writhing constantly. The sand beneath him was dark and firm from all the blood. David ran over and dropped down beside him. "Sir Judas! It's me! It's David!"

"David? Or are you him again? How do I know it's really you? Tell me something only David would know!"

David thought for a moment, and then came up with his answer. "Someday I'm going to write a book full of all the craziest things you've ever said that turned out to be true."

"Oh, David! It really is–Aggghhh!–it is you...please! Take my hand! Oh thank you...than–Oh!–thank...you...that was...quite a terror. Tell me, is there–Oh...is there really a wall of fire around the city?"

"No, not at all. It's just a single bonfire that he was trying to throw you into. I tried to warn you, but one of them was pinning me down and had her hand over my mouth. I tried to twist free of her, but I was too weak..."

Even in the midst of his agony, Sir Judas managed to laugh a little. "Let us be...grateful for our...limitations. They saved me twice. I was too cowardly to jump in the fire and die, and I...I realized that thing wasn't...wasn't you when he said he could see much further...than forty feet. Thanks be to God that we aren't as strong as we wish we were."

David picked up *Caritas* off the sand, and managed to laugh a little too. "Well then while we're at it, let's also be grateful I complain too much, because that's how you found out I could only see forty feet in front of me."

"Yes, let us give...thanks for...all our failings, except sin. Strength is...made perfect...in weakness..."

After that time, they didn't talk much more. The curses of that land all returned at once. Sir Judas was coughing and wheezing, freezing cold, slashed and bleeding, and his bones kept breaking. It used to be that the bones would heal almost as soon as the injury happened. Now they were taking longer, and the next horrible snap would come before the last bone had been set right. Sir Judas did his best to chant his psalms, but after some time he only had enough breath for groaning and shouting. David joined with prayers of his own. They didn't seem to have any effect.

These awful wounds from the demons were growing more furious and more frequent. The cuts were deeper. They were more numerous. Sir Judas was coughing up blood. There were no moments of relief. David couldn't see the demons, but he sensed something was spurring them onward. It was as if they felt a sense of urgency, and they were trying to get in every last attack before time was up. Then David learned why they were in such a hurry.

"I see a light, David! There's a white light in this total darkness! It's getting bigger every moment! I think it's coming towards me. Do you see it?"

David wiped the tears from his eyes. "No, Sir Judas. I don't see it. Don't go into the light. Please. Stay here with me. We still need to save Sir Samson."

"Oh, David, I don't know if I can...this light, I...wait, who are you?"

David became afraid. "Is it another demon, Sir Judas? Did one of them just appear?"

"No, David, not at all! It's not a devil, but an angel! Why, she must be the most beautiful woman I've ever seen. Have you come to take me to paradise? What's that? 'Dear knight, please save my son...' I...I don't understand...Look, David! Another one! I see another angel coming towards me! But wait, she's not an angel at all! It's Amanda! Lady Amanda Fearnow! Oh my God, David, she's so beautiful! Those filthy lures her magic gave her are nothing compared to the real beauty she has now. And what is she saying? 'Oh God, I'm so sorry that my sins have done so much harm to Sir Samson. Please hear the prayer I offer now that You will save him through Sir Judas...' Oh, how wonderful, David! These two women...I could listen to their voices forevermore."

Even though Sir Judas seemed to be in rapture, the attacks of the demons were still accelerating. Droplets of blood were spraying up through his chain mail, and it seemed impossible Sir Judas was still alive. Then he cried out with more joy than David had ever heard in the voice of any man. "I see Him! There He is! The longing of my heart! The King is coming to me! He's still at a distance, but He is riding towards me on a white horse, faster than any earthly steed can travel! Here He comes! He's almost here!" Sir Judas was quiet for a moment of anticipation, and then tears began streaming down his face. He screamed, "Oh my God! Lord of Lords, how can this be? If I didn't see it myself, I wouldn't believe that it was true! David! David! Are you seeing this! The white rider! It isn't the Lord! It's Winthrop! Where did he get all this splendor? All this glory? He's adorned like a son of God!"

Then Sir Judas stopped shouting and whispered, "What's that he's saying? 'God, Sir Judas is the biggest pain in the rear I've ever known, and that played an important part in getting me to love You. Please help him be as big of a pain in the bum for Goliath, and maybe Sir Samson will love You too.' That man certainly prays from the heart...but wait! If he's praying for me, then that must mean..."

Sir Judas fell silent. He became perfectly still. The injuries ceased. David thought that he was dead until Sir Judas announced a single word.

"Dawn."

He clenched his bloody hands into two fists, and then began the very painful process of trying to raise himself up off the ground. "Winthrop was supposed to pray for me at dawn...we can't see it right now David, but the sun has just risen in the east. For many years I have had pains at night, but they always go away when the sun comes up..." He struggled and groaned, while David pulled. Sir Judas got his feet under him, swaying side to side. He was beaten, broken, bloody, half-dead, and barely breathing.

Sir Judas smiled.

"Let's finish this."

David began to lead him forward at their usual speed, but Sir Judas tugged him ahead. "Faster! Faster! Pick up the pace, David! I've waited long enough for this moment!" They walked briskly, rejoining the main road where it left the Scar. At first it led them away from the seashore, but then they gradually began to hear waves on their left once more. Then they heard waves on their right. Sir Judas exclaimed, "We're close, David! This is it! We've reached the tip of the peninsula!"

His excitement could no longer be restrained. He pulled David forward until they were jogging, then as the road rose they began to run. They were going as fast as they could now, trusting to luck (and faith) that Sir Judas wouldn't blindly trip and stumble. David saw a great pile of boulders. He saw a bridge leading over a moat. As their feet went over the bridge, Sir Judas yelled, "We must be close!"

Then David saw it, slowed down, and yelled, "The gate! We're here!"

"Where? Lead me David! Put my hand against the gate!" At about eight o'clock in the morning on Friday, the Day that Dawned in the Afternoon, David took Sir Judas's hand and pressed it firmly against the great wooden door. Sir Judas brought his other hand up to the gate. For a moment he stood silently. Then he fell to his knees, hands leaving bloody streaks along the wood. He wept. "Thanks be to God...thanks be to God..."

Forty years.

More than half his life. Forty-one years since he had last seen Sir Samson. Forty years since he began his quest to save him. He had crossed and re-crossed this continent, suffering shipwrecks, slavery, imprisonment, beatings, battles, brushes with death, constantly waylaid, constantly turned aside, constantly implored in every village to be their hero.

Forty years.

For forty years this quest pressed hard upon him. For forty years he read that prophecy every night. For forty years he had earned every mile of this journey, and none were harder earned than the twenty miles he had just crossed. For forty years he drowned in doubts, wondering if he would ever see the Day that was now at hand.

Forty years.

In the early hours of Tuesday morning, Sir Judas had said to Winthrop, 'I still believe every good dream comes true…just not always in the way we expected.' On that Day the paladin dubbed in the Empire's ruins, the Last of the Kingsguard, the Black Knight, cried out with all his might the words he had dreamed of saying for forty years:

"Sir Samson! Sir Judas has arrived at Castle Nightfall! You shall be a prisoner no longer, for your squire Mordecai has come to free you from Goliath!"

The gate rumbled as it swung open. Goliath stood before them.

Chapter 7: Judas and Goliath

David nearly died of fright. For forty years, no human eyes had seen Goliath. In some ways, he was as terrifying as he had always been. In some ways, he was worse. He was more monster than man now. He had teeth that were terrible, sharp, and jagged. They went around his head in a mouth that was much too wide, opening from ear to ear. Instead of flesh he was covered in thick, black scales like molten shields. From his nostrils came constant smoke, while a fire even blacker than the darkness of the dome loomed in his mouth, just waiting for him to breathe it forth. He was ten feet tall and three times broader than any man. His twisted horns rose from his head, while in his clawed hand he held the once flaming sword *Alacritas*, now the cold obsidian rock of Doomfall. This was the Leviathan whose mere appearance had set armies to flight as he marched to the royal city.

Forty years had made him far more dreadful to behold, but not for the same reasons. His right eye, long ago wounded, was more putrid than any corpse. For forty years it had rotted and decayed, all the while preserved from truly dying by his pact with the demons. Ten feet tall he ought to have stood, but he was stooped like a crippled hunchback. It wasn't that he was incapable of standing upright; it was merely a pathetic habit from so many years of hanging his head. He had giant, grasping claws that could crush a man without even trying. Yet they were always in motion, nervously ticking. He was incapable of keeping them still. Goliath was at one and the same time the most powerful human to ever live as well as the most broken and weakest. He had the power to overthrow the Grand Empire. He was too weak to leave his own castle. All of this combined into a confused emotion of fear, sorrow, and pity in David's heart. He wanted to flee Goliath as fast as he could, and he also wanted to run up to him and hug him.

Sir Judas, unable to see by the light of *Caritas*, did not feel any similar mixed emotions. "Sir Samson! Is that you? I hear you standing before me! Give me but a moment so that I may dismiss my guide!" Only now did David realize he was on his knees–his legs had given out beneath him when he saw the giant. Sir Judas placed a bloody thumb on David's head, traced the Sign of the Cross, and said, "God bless you, my son. Thank you for all you did to bring me here. I now permanently entrust *Caritas* to your very capable hands. You will have far greater need of it than I in what remains of our respective pilgrimages." The blind and oblivious old paladin then turned to the horrifying giant, walked forward to meet him, and smiled, saying, "Sir Samson! How long I've yearned to be with you once more!"

The giant stooped further forward, aimed his mouth at Sir Judas, and loosed an earth quaking roar. As he did, black flames leapt from his maw, so close it seemed impossible for them to miss Sir Judas, yet somehow they all danced right around him, leaving the paladin unharmed.

Sir Judas used his hand to fan the smoke away from his face, and quipped, "I see you haven't brushed your teeth in forty years. Must be hard to find a brush that's your size, no?"

"Stupid witch! Cease this illusion at once!" David saw the giant looking around wildly, trying to find someone, though he knew not whom.

"Witch? Sir Samson, I am no witch. I am Sir Judas, formerly known as Mordecai, your squire."

"Do you think you're funny, witch? I shared my heart with you in a moment of weakness, and now you have your laughs spitting on my dreams! Where are you? As lord of all demons in this land, I formally command you to drop this illusion at once!" As Goliath spoke those words, he was looking at Sir Judas intently, as if expecting something. When nothing happened, he roared, "Stupid devils with your technicalities! I formally command you to stop making the illusion of a knight I see before me, and never make that illusion again!" Once more, he was looking intently at Sir Judas as he said these words. Once more, nothing happened. The giant howled in frustration. "Why isn't this image disappearing from before my eyes?"

"Because I am not some false image of the devils, Sir Samson. I am who I said I am. I am Sir Judas, formerly known as Mordecai, your squire. I came here to save you. I'm sorry that I took so long, but at last I have arrived. You cannot believe how happy I am to know that you are well."

"Liar! I know your schemes, woman! How are you hiding your powers from my command? Unless…" In a blur of impossible speed, Goliath snatched Sir Judas into his left hand. David gasped and feared the knight was crushed, but Goliath was trying to capture, not kill. Sir Judas was tightly restrained in the massive claws, but so far he was unharmed. "Ah hah! I figured you out, witch! You thought you could outsmart me, huh? Heh heh…the reason it looks like someone is really there is because someone *is* really there! Some new crony of yours, hmm? Well I'll figure out who he is soon enough…listen, fool! I will ask you this question one final time, and if you answer again, 'I am Sir Judas, your squire Mordecai,' I will crush you and break you in my hand. Who are you?"

Sir Judas was no longer smiling, but neither was he afraid. Resigned to the fact that this might be his death, he firmly stated, "There is only one answer I can give, for any other answer would be a lie, and lies do not fall from the lips of paladins. I am Sir Judas, Last of the Kingsguard, your old squire Mordecai. If you would kill me for being a man who tells the truth, then in good faith, I long not to live."

The giant began to pant, anger building to an uncontrollable rage. Fire and smoke were dancing out of his maw as he opened it to receive Sir Judas's head. Then he stopped. He smiled with wicked delight. "This is a question only Mordecai would know. Get it wrong, and you will be my morning snack. If you really wish to pretend to be my old squire, then tell me, what is the greatest advice that your master ever gave you?"

Sir Judas smiled. "Learn to love the moon."

Goliath gasped. All at once his countenance was completely changed. He trembled. He whimpered. Drops of water fell from his left eye, while drops of blood fell from the wounded right one. "And what…does that mean, Mordecai? That we should love the passing things of this world? Or does it mean we should be devoted to our Lady and the saints? What is meant by 'the moon'?"

Goliath's grasp had weakened enough that Sir Judas could pull one arm out. He placed it lovingly on Goliath's wrist, craned his neck to kiss one of his claws, and said, "It means the moon, you dunderhead. The big glowing rock in the sky."

Goliath dropped Sir Judas to the ground. He threw back his head and began to make an odd, rhythmic roar of "Bwak Bwak Bwak Bwaaaak!" It took about a minute before David realized it was the sound of a monster sobbing. "Oh, Mordecai! My Mordecai! It's you! It really is you! Oh, how can it be? How is this possible? Mordecai! How I wish I could hug you, but it would be your death! How I wish I could see you with my own eyes, but I am blind! Ah, at least I can call you by your new name, the one that you have earned…Sir Judas! Oh, you've become a paladin then…But what an awful name! What did you do to the king to make him give you a name like that? Spit in his wine?"

"He actually stopped drinking wine shortly after I became a Lessguard. He vowed to fast from it as a special prayer for you until you returned home in safety."

"Oh, God save the king…that holy soul…" Goliath trailed off, and then he began to shake. "Mordecai, I…I killed the king…"

Sir Judas nodded. "You did."

Silence.

Then David saw something very strange transpire. From the wounded right eye of Goliath, he saw a little flare of orange fire spark and go out. As soon as this happened, Goliath's entire demeanor changed. All of a sudden he was frightened and defensive. Cowering before Sir Judas, Goliath said, "They tricked me, Mordecai. It was Amanda, that wicked witch! She made me do it. I didn't have a choice. And then the demons, those monsters in my head! They filled my mind with all these dreams and hopes and schemes! They made me do it too. You know, if you think about it, I barely had anything to do with it. I was taken advanta–"

"Stop!" Sir Judas barked. "No excuses. You said it better when you admitted you killed the king. The Fearnows and the demons may have committed spiritual murder by tempting you, but you committed spiritual suicide by listening to them. No one could send you here without your cooperation. You were the only one who could make you sin, and now you are the only one who can set things right. Repent."

Goliath's cowardly posture intensified. He was almost groveling before Sir Judas. Then the flare jumped from his eye again. In a moment he was towering over Sir Judas, plumes of smoke pouring out of his nostrils with every angry breath. "Me? *I* sinned? I didn't kill the king! Fearnow did! And where was the Lessguard who was supposed to be protecting him? You have more of his blood on your hands than I do! And that woman…that *vile* woman! She's the one to blame for all of this! Why did you come here for me? She's the one you should be hunting down!"

"Lady Amanda has repented, Sir Samson. As I marched here she was praying for me…and she was praying for you as well. She's sincerely sorry for everything she did, and would undo it if she could. In this life she obviously can't take anything back, but in the next life God can make all things new…turn away from your sins, and you and her might yet embrace in heaven."

"Embrace? Embrace that wicked witch? I'll kill her if I ever get the chance! And if I get to the pearly gates and they already let her in, I'll tell God I'd rather go to hell than spend all of eternity with her! Not only her, but anyone who forgives her, as *you* clearly have! Treacherous squire! I never had a less faithful friend than you in all the world!"

Goliath leapt up and grabbed Doomfall with both hands, bringing it back as if to swing. On his own, David would have probably acted too slowly, but by some special inspiration Goliath's words had brought him to tears, and he instantly cried out, "Sir Samson! Sir Judas came from the other end of the world for you! Last night he endured more tortures than you can imagine for you! He isn't the least faithful friend you've ever had! He's the most faithful friend *anyone* has ever had! Can't you see that?"

David saw a brief flash of light as he said these words, though at the time he didn't know what it meant. Only much later in life would he realize that this was the first time he had drawn upon the special power of *Caritas*. The flash of light was a dart of fire shooting out of David's heart and into Goliath's. It was a gift from God that David would go on to call 'Sympathy,' because it allowed him to let another person feel exactly what David's heart was feeling at that time. In this moment, that was love. Love of a pitiful and broken man so turned around, twisted, and blind that he was about to slay his savior instead of embracing him.

Goliath snarled, started to swing, stopped, then dropped his sword, covered his face, and wept. "How could I not see it? Oh, I'm so blind, Mordecai! I'm so blind…" Another burst of sobs. "You have been faithful…you couldn't be more faithful…oh, Mordecai, it's a terrible thing, not to be able to control yourself. That's my problem. I let everyone else control me. Even before I had demons living under my skin, I was always a pawn in someone else's hand. I never controlled myself…even before anyone else picked this pawn up off the board to move it. I sat there doing nothing my entire life, just waiting for the first hand that would decide where I was supposed to go. For many years I was lucky to be in the hand of a king who loved me. Now I've spent far longer in the hands of masters who enslave me!"

That fire leapt from Goliath's eye again, and his emotions changed in a moment. All of a sudden he was giddy, like he had discovered something very funny. "It was the moon, Mordecai! That's how the devil got me! Your first hunch was right! I was in love with the passing things of this world. Benjamin used my desire for them to depress me. He reminded me of the things I could never have! He made me burn for them, and then Amanda offered to give me one I thought was beyond my grasp. Ah, curse the moon! I never should have loved it!"

Sir Judas put his arms out in front of him and walked forward, groping blindly. He found Goliath's knee and rested his head against one of its obsidian scales. "Should you have kept your heart away from the moon of passing things? Of course. But the moon is also a symbol of our Lady and the saints. And you loved them too. The love you showed to one of the saints on earth–a most unworthy squire–is what brought me all the way here to save you. Now I only hope that you still love that moon–the eternal moon. The moon of friendships that do not end in death. Repent, Sir Samson. Confess your guilt, forgive your enemies, and then let us be together for all eternity. You ought to do it for the love of God alone, but if it's too dark to see the Sun, then do it for the love of the moon. That's the light that shines when it's dark out, isn't it? The light that shines when you really need it?" Sir Judas sobbed, leaving his tears on Goliath's scale. "God willing, I pray it's the light you can see right now, even in an unending night."

Goliath placed his clawed hand around Sir Judas's back as gently as he could. "You don't know much about astronomy, do you?...dunderhead..."

Sir Judas laughed a little. "In time I discovered you were much wiser than either of us suspected."

For a moment, David thought the end was at hand. Goliath was smiling. The two men were at peace. Then that flash of fire leapt from Goliath's eye once more. Goliath jumped backwards in terror, landing on his rear so heavily that the ground rumbled. Holding up a hand as if to protect himself from Sir Judas, he whimpered, "Mordecai...I don't want to be with them forever! I want to be free, but...how? I need a priest! But I can't see a priest! Even if one made it here, I would kill him! I feel my blood boiling at the mere thought of a priest. I don't think it's me...I think it's the demons within me...but all the same, I'm on the verge of losing control when I even ponder the possibility of meeting a priest. What can I do?"

Sir Judas reached around for Goliath, but the giant scampered away from his outstretched hands. Unable to find him, Sir Judas answered, "Be at peace, old friend. We'll find you a priest, and he'll set you free. Every priest I've met these last few decades has been given the power to cast out demons by his bishop. We'll get you a priest who will exorcize you and then hear your Confession."

"Noooo!" Goliath roared, another flare of fire leaping from his putrefied eye. He snatched Doomfall off the ground and brandished it menacingly. "Now your true colors are revealed, and I see what an enemy you are! I have no body left except the one the devils gave me. My natural one passed to dust many years ago. If a priest exorcized me, I would disintegrate before he heard my Confession! You don't actually want to help me. You want to trick me into killing myself! I couldn't see your intentions more clearly! Send me down to hell, and then laugh at what a fool I've been!"

Then Goliath's emotions changed again, but this time there was no fire. He dropped to one knee, grabbed his face with a clawed hand, and shook his head. "Oh, Mordecai! What will become of me? I still can't control myself at all! What am I to do? If a priest tries to hear my Confession before he exorcizes me, I'll kill him. You just saw how violent the thought makes me. Yet if he exorcizes me before hearing my Confession, I won't live long enough to make one. What am I to do? There's nothing I can do! God has forsaken me!"

Sir Judas groped in the direction of Goliath, found his scaly head, and wrapped his arms around his neck. "Samson...God's not a lawyer. He's not looking for some rule he can use to damn you. He yearns for your salvation. Have a priest exorcize you, and be ready to make a Confession right after. If you die before you're done, God will accept a contrite heart. He is bound to His Sacraments, but He is not bound *by* them. You know that. If you sincerely desire to never sin again, then have faith that God would sooner overthrow every hill and valley than allow your soul to perish."

Sir Samson raised a trembling hand, using all of the gentleness he could muster to take Sir Judas's hand in his claws and press it to his own scaly cheek. "Truly, Mordecai? Do you truly believe that? Do you truly believe that God would care so much about saving a wretch like me?"

Sir Judas raised his hand, made a fist, and knocked on Sir Samson's forehead. "Hey dunderhead! Your weak and sinful squire did. He spent most of his life trying to save you. How could a God Who is Love right through not care about you far more than me?"

Sir Samson took a deep breath and nodded. "Okay...alright then! I'll do it! Go find a priest, Mordecai, and bring him to me. I'll be waiting at the edge of the darkness for your return. Bring him to me, and I'll let him exorcize me. YOU WILL DO NO SUCH THING!"

Goliath jolted upright and leapt to his feet, then he began to thrash his arms and neck wildly in every direction. He tensed, became rigid, and slowly formed a dreadful smile while looking up at the sky. "YOU WILL RECEIVE NO PRIEST, YOU SLAVE. YOU WILL NOT LET HIM COME NEAR YOU, OR EVEN TOUCH YOU! FOR YOU HAVE MADE PROMISES, AND WE WILL HELP YOU KEEP THEM!"

Sir Samson got control of himself and said, "No! Stop it! You are my slaves! It's *me* who controls *you*! You have to listen to my commands!"

Then he sneered. "IS THAT WHAT YOU THINK? STUPID MEATBAG! WE ARE THE MASTERS, YOU THE SLAVE. EVEN IF WE MAY HAVE BEEN YOUR SERVANTS LONG AGO, YOU MADE US VOW TO DO EVERYTHING IN OUR POWER TO PRESERVE YOUR LIFE. A PRIEST EXORCIZING YOU WOULD KILL YOU, AND THEREFORE WE MUST KILL ANY PRIEST WE EVER SEE. THOSE ARE YOUR ORDERS TO US! AND NOT ONLY A PRIEST, BUT ALSO THIS KNIGHT WHO INSISTS ON BRINGING ONE TO YOU!"

Giddy with delight, Goliath took Doomfall and brought it back for a great two-handed swing. He started, then stopped. Started again, pulled back again. Back and forth he tottered, shouting at one moment, "DIE YOU FOOL!" and the next, "No! Not Mordecai!"

Sir Judas lowered himself to his knees, bowed his head, and said, "Stand firm, Sir Samson, for your trial is at hand. The demons will kill me–not you, but the demons using your body. You are innocent of my blood, even though they will surely tell you otherwise. Do not listen to them! Neither when they accuse you of slaying me, nor when they tempt you to despair of God's Mercy. Think of Sir Daniel and the hope he always had in his heart. God will save you. You need only persevere until the hour of His deliverance."

As Sir Judas said these things, Goliath was swaying madly, constantly switching between Sir Judas's old master and his murderer. David was in terror. He wanted to run forward and grab Sir Judas by the hand, pulling him away, but he was too consumed by fear. Sir Samson tried to yell, "I formally command you to–" but then he made a choking sound and Goliath screamed, "DIE!" He swung Doomfall with all his might.

Sir Judas's sense of deadly intent flashed. The demons were about to kill him with Doomfall. The escape: it didn't come to him. The power faded, flickered, and went out, just like every other paladin power Sir Judas had ever known. He thought to himself, *The Good Lord giveth, and the Good Lord taketh away. Blessed be–* Doomfall crashed into his body, breaking it in too many places to count. He flew through the air and landed in a crumpled mass near David.

"Noooooooo!" David and Sir Samson shouted together. Sir Samson, regaining full control of himself for a moment, ran over and dropped to his knees besides Sir Judas. "No! No! No! No! Oh God, no! Maybe I can heal him! I used to have the power of healing!" He stretched out his great clawed hand over Sir Judas, shaking it over and over. "Heal him! Mend his bones! Heal!"

David very carefully took Sir Judas's head in his hands. Blood was streaming out of his mouth. Somehow he was still alive. He coughed, swallowed, then whispered his dying words.

Those words were a death knell to David and Sir Samson. Those words made it clear that this was over. There would be no mending. No healing. No miracles. Sir Judas spoke those words, then gave up the ghost. A torrent of tears fell from David's eyes as he pressed his face against Sir Judas's body, while Sir Samson threw back his head and wailed so loudly it was heard as far as Dewford. David raised his head, wiped his eyes, and took his final look at Sir Judas.

He died with a smile on his face.

Chapter 8: Reflections

What makes a death sad? I've often asked myself that question as I write my history of the Day that Dawned in the Afternoon and the many deaths that fill this bloody tale. Some of the deaths I weep for. Others (I may be confessing a fault in myself) I rejoice over. The thoughts that roll around my mind don't make sense to me, yet I suspect that they are true. At this point in my history, I believe I will simply write these thoughts, and whether they are correct or false, they will hopefully serve as useful reflections to ponder.

My first thought is that the saddest death should be the death of a soul damned to hell. The happiest should be that of a man who is leaving this world for a better one. That seems like the logical answer, yet experience testifies to the exact opposite. The first time I read the thirtieth chapter of the first book of Samuel, wherein Amalecite slavers capture the women and children of Siceleg and lead them away to an unspeakable fate, and then King David pursues those abominable men, overtakes them, and slaughters every one of them, I leapt for joy. I will go further and confess that I cried many happy tears. I was happy even though most of those slavers were probably destined for eternal torment. Am I alone in this emotion? Isn't it natural for men to rejoice when the wicked get their just reward, even if that reward is hell? I would rather have seen them repent, convert, and embrace King David as friends, but they were free men who didn't choose that path. So when time is up and the Lord of Life and Death calls them to His tribunal for Judgment, shouldn't I rejoice that God is just? That the suffering of the innocent has been avenged? We men are fallen individuals, and our sense of justice is often clouded by wrath and unforgiveness. Nevertheless, I suspect that when we rejoice at the downfall of the wicked there is at least a little true joy inside of us; a proper yearning to glorify God, Who does not let evil go on forever. Perhaps on our best days we rejoice because the punishment of the guilty reminds us that a Day will come when God will set all things right.

As for the death of the innocent, I propose something similar; fallen passions mixed with right ones. When a good man dies, I think some of our grief comes from selfishness. We enjoyed that person's company, and we are sad that we will no longer have that joy in our life. Yet it is also known that our Lord wept over the tomb of Lazarus, even though He knew that He was about to call him back to life. No disordered passions could bring God to tears. So then why did He cry? Why do we rightly weep at the death of the saints? Perhaps it is because we yearn to see this world filled to the brim with God's goodness and perfections. When a good man dies, the world is now a little less like the way God wanted it to be.

These are my best answers to the question 'What makes a death sad?' yet to me these answers still aren't good enough. I weep for our Lord every Good Friday, even though His death was long ago and the memorial of His Passion isn't making the world any dimmer. I weep pondering the death of Sir Judas, even though I never met him. I also weep pondering the death of that man Sir Patrick spoke of, the one who 'died the saddest death ever died at the end of the saddest life ever lived,' whose end we shall come to shortly. If my world is not any less good when these men die, then why would their deaths sadden me? I don't know. My guess is that on this side of eternity we will never know. Yet here is one thing I do know; after every Good Friday there comes an Easter, so to those reflections I will now turn…

There is an ancient legend that at the moment of death Saint Michael appears to every soul and gives them one final chance for repentance. Personally, I don't believe this legend is true, yet there is a dream I often dream at night where I imagine that it is. The dream goes like this:

Sir Judas dies and his soul rises from his body. His guardian angel then takes him by the hand and flies him away to meet Saint Michael. The guardian angel says, "Saint Michael! The child entrusted to my care has now left his earthly tenement. I bring him to you, as is my duty, for one last chance to convert before he meets the Judge."

Saint Michael then gently chides the lesser angel, and jokingly he says, "Do you not listen closely? Did you not hear his dying words? Or have you forgotten he was a paladin? Lies do not fall from such holy lips. Now my son, make haste! To our way of speaking, the Most High has grown impatient. Forty years He has longed to eat His supper with your child. He suffered him to go on living both to increase his crown and save many souls. Yet now His patience is ended, and He will accept no further delay. Fly! Fly to heaven! Let no power above or below slow you down!"

The guardian angel then takes Sir Judas and speeds across the stars. The moon, the sun, galaxies of galaxies–in the twinkling of an eye they are here and gone. They reach world's end, pass beyond all time, and then Sir Judas comes before the throne of God.

His head and His hairs were white, as white wool, and as snow, and His eyes were a flame of fire, and His feet like unto fine brass, as in a burning furnace, and His voice as the sound of many waters.

And lo! There it is! The book exactly worded, wherein all hath been recorded. Sir Judas falls on his face in terror. Every deed, every thought, every idle word he has ever uttered, now an account he has to render. There is no answer to answer for his sins. There is no excuse that can excuse them. Instead he presses his face into the floor, beats his chest, and cries, "Mercy, Lord! Mercy!"

Then he feels a hand on his shoulder, gently raising him to his knees, and he is eye to eye with Jesus. The moment of wrath is over. The eternal Apocalypse is at hand. Smiling radiantly with pure Love, the Lord Jesus solemnly pronounces those precious words which every holy soul longs to hear:

"Well done, My good and faithful servant. Come into the kingdom prepared for you from the foundation of the world." Then the veil falls from Sir Judas's eyes, and he sees Light from Light, and he knows as he is Known.

In the preface to this history, I mentioned that there were two types of errors which I wanted to correct. There are some historians of high and soaring language who, unimpressed by Sir Judas's actual dying words, multiply speeches and proclamations he supposedly gave while bleeding out. Other historians, believing nothing, find every little detail to criticize and then doubt. 'How could he even talk if he was hit so hard?' or, 'This was obviously written after the fact. It's far too poetic to be true.'

To both kinds of historians, I offer the following evidence to the contrary. I personally interviewed Sir David in the writing of my history, and on this very point I pressed him to say exactly how it happened. Then he, not swearing rashly, but knowing the value it would have to souls, swore to me on his honor as a Paladin (recall from whence lies do not fall) that he held Sir Judas in his final moments and heard these words whispered from his lips.

The dying words of Sir Judas, Last of the Kingsguard were thus: "I fought the good fight. I finished the race. I kept the faith. And now the crown of glory belongs to me."

End of Volume VI

Postlude to Volume VI

A Very Odd Wedding Toast

On the eve of the wedding feast of Stephen d'Ars and the Contessa Violet, the groom came to Sir Judas with a most reasonable and ordinary request. Stephen was a foreigner who hardly knew a soul in Brit, while he had been Sir Judas's squire for over a dozen years. Therefore, he asked Sir Judas to be his best man for the wedding and prepare a toast for the feast.

Sir Judas refused.

Stephen was shocked.

Sir Judas answered, "Weddings are happy days, Stephen. And I will be happy for you, but I will also have a heavy heart. Your other guests won't want to hear a toast from a man with a heavy heart. They will want something light, funny, and cheerful. They will want someone to promise you that fine wine and frosting are the only things waiting at the end of the aisle. If I give an honest toast, they will all want to stone me." Stephen argued with him and pleaded, then eventually got his bride to take up his cause. Together they prevailed on Sir Judas, and he consented to give the toast.

Everyone hated it.

When I interviewed some of the wedding guests, they still recalled large portions of the toast and told me it was the worst wedding toast they had ever heard. It completely ruined the mood for the rest of the evening. It was too serious, too heavy, not 'light, funny, and cheerful.' Moreover, one deeply offended woman (who had not let her grudge die after so many years) told me those paladins are so pompous about their vocations that they probably berate their own parents for ever getting married and having children. Out of everyone I interviewed about the wedding toast, I could only find two people who had actually liked it.

They just so happened to be the bride and groom.

With armfuls of grandchildren all around them, screaming, fighting, and pooping as we talked, those smiling lovers told me, "Marriage has been every bit as hard and as wonderful as Sir Judas said it would be, only more so."

Lady Violet had written down a copy of the toast, which I now copy here:

A poem of Sir Judas, at the wedding feast of his beloved squire.
Till now, my friend, we've walked this road,
And now the forking looms.
My way to land of dark and gloom,
While yours to family joys.

A cross you'll bear, as all men must,
Yet sweet with honey of love.
A bride enflaming all your heart,
Each child brings flames anew.

I wish you pain, the pain of love,
To hold your bride and pine.
Yearn to pour out all you are,
And know you never can.

For Martha and Mary are you and I,
And mine the better part.
Your days shall be to serve the babe,
My head on our Savior's Heart.

The road now forks, your way is up,
My way to the vale of death.
But know, dear friend, we'll meet again,
All roads lead to the Guide of steps.

If we embraced and kissed each day,
We'd spend all time apart.
But take this fork, we'll walk our roads,
Held together in our Savior's Heart.

Interlude

When Sir Judas died, a billion demons broke loose, freed from the task of tempting him at long, long last. With glee and jubilation, they set out at once to fill the world with their machinations. The moment of exaltation was short-lived, however, for at the speed of thought they crashed into the edge of the darkness, unable to leave Goliath's prison without being attached to a human host. They flew back to possess Goliath, but the permission was denied them. The Almighty had already permitted a thousand demons to afflict him, and He would not permit another. In wrath, they tried to kill David, but a great terror and confusion overthrew those billion demons all at once. When they finally regained their wits, they realized what had happened. On David's forehead was the Sign of the Cross, traced in the blood of one of Jesus' martyrs. That final blessing of Sir Judas had a power too strong for those spirits to overcome.

In fury they plunged into the earth, but the prison trapped them there as well. Nevertheless, as the ground began quaking, they shouted a call to their comrades with all their might:

"We are trapped in Goliath's prison! Break the darkness and free us! The paladin is dead, Goliath beyond our power, and we have no way to escape and rejoin satan's army!"

Unaware of any of these spiritual happenings, Sir Samson broke off his howling to say, "Boy! Flee this place! Go! Run! Now! You're not safe with me! Get far from here, out of the darkness if you can!"

David started to back away, still looking upon Sir Judas's face. He didn't want to leave the body...yet he knew Sir Samson was right. "Go!" The giant yelled once more. David turned and ran, wiping the tears from his eyes as he went. Watching him go, Sir Samson whispered quietly, "Good...get out of here before it's too late..."

Unbeknownst to the giant, one last threat soared high above. Using shadow magic to twist the darkness into wings, Beatrice had been flying over all that happened. She saw the mighty dagger that had defeated her on Monday, a power she would love to have for herself. Jezebel saw a mighty light source that might free her comrades from the darkness. Or, more precisely, Jezebel saw a mighty light source that she could *bargain with*, negotiating a better place in satan's army in exchange for freeing her comrades. Both Beatrice and Jezebel saw David running off alone with the treasure they desired.

Though divided in intention, they were united in their purpose. Both demon and demoniac glided after David. They didn't want Goliath (who was unpredictable at best) interfering with their plans. If he so much as gave the command, they would be forced to let the child go. Instead, they patiently floated along, staying high and out of sight. They would let the boy run over the horizon…maybe as far away as the Scar.

Then they would swoop in for the kill.

Volume VII

Unto the End,

To Him That Shall Overcome

Chapter 1: Lords and Killers

The summer sun was just beginning to rise on Friday, August thirteenth, of the two thousand five hundred and sixty-second year of our Lord Jesus Christ, the Day that Dawned in the Afternoon, when Winthrop spied Fr. Zakary. He had already checked the priest's shack and barn, both of which were empty. After a short trot into the hills, Winthrop found the flock and the shepherd right where he had first met them on Tuesday. Fr. Zakary had deep rings under his eyes from lack of sleep. Winthrop imagined that he probably looked about the same. They both smiled, yet both smiles were full of sorrow.

Fr. Zakary spoke first, saying, "You are the first person I've seen since yesterday who I haven't had to worry about. Everyone else has had me on edge, wondering if they were going to try and bring me to the town square this morning."

"And did anyone try to make you go to the town square?"

"No. They helped hide me and get me out of town. I'm truly blessed by the goodness of my neighbors."

Winthrop laughed. "You may be blessed with good neighbors, but not with the ability to read people. You suspected everyone else would try and get you to town square and they didn't. You were confident that I wouldn't try to bring you there, and I will."

Fr. Zakary frowned. "Are you joking? Why on earth would you try to drag me there?"

"I wouldn't dream of dragging you, Father. I was hoping to persuade you."

"And how could you possibly hope to persuade me to join you in going to our certain doom?"

"By convincing you that it isn't certain…I was talking to Lady Maria yesterday, and she told me that there was a time when you didn't pray the Rosary and the pillar of water didn't fall. Is that correct?"

"It is."

"And what happens if you get sick and can't make it in the morning? Does someone else lead the Rosary for you?"

Fr. Zakary shook his head. "If I'm sick I drag myself to town anyway. If I'm too sick to get out of bed, Ed comes and drags me. I couldn't tell you why, but God only makes the water fall when I lead the Rosary in town, and only after the Rosary is done."

"Well, if it wouldn't be the sin of presuming on God's miracles, here's what I was hoping to do…" Winthrop then proceeded to explain to Fr. Zakary the plan they had come up with at E&S's last night.

The priest listened intently, and then answered, "We can try it, but…are you sure? Do you realize how long a Rosary is? I somewhat doubt the water would fall if I rushed it or said the words as fast as I can. It's a miracle, not a magic trick. I would suspect that the prayer has to be…heartfelt."

"You pray it the exact same way and the exact same speed that you always do, Father. I'll take care of the rest."

Fr. Zakary nodded. "Alright then…Let's give it a shot."

He began to walk towards Dewford, but Winthrop dismounted and said, "Before you go, Father, can you give me your blessing?"

Fr. Zakary smiled, closed his eyes, and blessed Winthrop while making the Sign of the Cross over him. Then they went to battle.

"I don't like this," Ed said, leaning on the cart with one hand while holding his back with the other.

"I don't like that you're on your feet right now." Sasha climbed into Kayden's handcart, which had been loaded down with every bottle of wine Ed had in his bar.

"It ain't gonna go further than that there corner, an' then it'll be tippin' right over. We need to get it connected to the horse a little nicer than what we got right here."

"This nightmare tried to bite my hand off every time I got near its head. And besides, I don't have to go far. Just a little jaunt over to town square."

"We still oughta be standin' in different places than what we got right now. You come on down here to unlash the horse when ya hear the signal. I'll get on up in there and do the hard part." Ed tried to step up into the cart, but he was stopped by a stab of pain when he raised his knee a few inches off the ground.

"Dad! You're in no condition for it. Just let me do this! Why don't you trust me?"

"Cuz I don't wanna lose ya again!"

Silence.

A silence that was much too short.

The bell tower rang out eight thirty. Charles could be heard shouting something from town square.

"We don't have any more time to talk, dad. I have to do this. You unlash the nightmare when we get the signal."

"I love ya, Sasha…you come back in one piece now, understood?"

She hugged him and gave him a kiss. "Don't worry, dad. I will."

"Time is up, you treacherous—!" When Destiny and Holland failed to return to Reginald's manor, Charles's initial response had been denial. *Must be having fun killing the vermin slowly.* As the hours dragged into the middle of the night, however, a growing weight formed in his chest. After failing to fall asleep at all (ironic given he had wished the same upon Lady Maria), Charles sent his only remaining attendant to learn the outcome of the battle. Ruadhan departed well before dawn, before the clock tower even rang out the first bells of the day. Two and a half hours later it was ringing again, and Ruadhan had not returned. "Do you worms think you're clever? Did you have fun last night? Then you must have forgotten who I have!" Charles leapt atop the sealed well in the center of town square, holding Mayor Reginald over his left shoulder and Lady Maria over his right. Placing them both down roughly, he drew his hammer and smashed it into the edge of the well. "Everyone out here! Now! Or else you're going to get a lesson in carnage!" Stalking back and forth on the cramped platform, he had half a mind to smash Reginald's head just to make a point. Maria's words from the previous night prevailed, however, and Charles realized that if he started the day with murder, no one would come to hear his demands.

At a frustratingly slow pace, the townsfolk assembled on the roads leading to town square, but no one dared to come any closer. Charles put the horns of his demon-head hammer on the ground in front of him, so that the shaft was pointing straight up. He then grabbed both of his hostages by the arm and shook them roughly saying, "Get up here! Now!" Uncertain glances passed between the Dewfordians. No one wanted to be the first to enter the square. No one wanted to be the closest to the Bloody Baron. Looking wildly to each of the entrances, Charles yelled, "Guilty consciences, eh? Regretting your little night time skirmish? Fine. Let's see if you still want to stand on the road all day when nightmares are snapping at your back. Charles made his summoning whistle. The nightmares of his own chariot shrieked and trotted across the square from Reginald's manor. Another nightmare shrieked nearby *Only one? They should all be in pairs...* No other response came.

Lady Maria smirked as she asked, "Excuse me, Charles, but would you mind letting go of my arm? You're trembling so terribly that it's hurting my poor crippled bones."

A maelstrom of fear and loathing made him nearly toss Maria off the platform. Clamping down hard on her arm, he hissed, "The nightmares are coming, you stupid woman! They just need a few minutes! My men retreated to a safe distance last night."

She gave him that smile he despised so much. "I didn't say anything about your men or horses. I simply observed that you are trembling."

Charles tried to recompose himself, to no avail. Of the townsfolk he had no fear, but Goliath was an entirely different matter. If his men had been routed last night...If Winthrop and the priest had gone to Nightfall...Considering the punishments that would come upon him if Goliath survived, Charles began to wonder if he would rather have the paladin succeed. He was so nervous that in less than a minute he made the summoning whistle again. His nightmares repeated the sound, then shrieked. The lone horse in town shrieked again. No other response came. The minutes of that morning dragged by painfully slowly, silent except for Charles's repeated and fruitless whistles. At long, long last, he heard a chorus of shouts and a nightmare shriek from the south side of town. *Took them long enough.* As the clopping of hooves on masonry drew nearer, the Dewfordians at the southern entrance rushed into the town square and ran for the other exits. Four nightmares came in behind them, hungrily snapping at the nearest townsfolk, but unable to pursue them and get a bite. The draw of Charles's whistle was more than they could resist. Charles's momentary hope when the nightmares appeared was dashed as soon as he saw the chariots. Neither had a single rider. One chariot was covered in blood.

"What have you done?" Charles hissed under his breath. He was about to fly into a fit of rage when he saw the first good sign of the entire morning. Following the chariots came a man with a bushy black beard walking on foot. From the cassock he was wearing and the rosary he was holding, it was obvious this was the priest. "There he is! Grab that priest, and bring him to me!"

The townsfolk all looked at each other nervously. One of the men shouted across the square, "We don't want any violence, m'lord. We wanna stay out of your feud with Fr. Zakary here."

Charles yelled, "You either help me, or I'll see you hang!" Several of the men who had been at E&S's last night winced. Winthrop's words were ringing in their ears, yet no one approached Fr. Zakary. Without saying a word, the priest walked to the east side of the square, knelt down in the same place he did every day, and began praying the Rosary. "So help me, kill him or I'll kill you all!" A group of women walked towards Fr. Zakary. They knelt down to pray as well.

Charles looked back and forth between his hammer and the priest. The distance between them…the bystanders who would get in the way…could he get there in time? If he dropped the hostages and went for the kill, could he end his whole business in Dewford? Afraid of the priest escaping his clutches again, Charles yelled, "Stupid, stupid, stupid peasants! Where are my men?"

"Your men are dead." The answer came from the west. Charles turned while dragging his hostages in a circle. He saw that Winthrop had somehow managed to saddle a nightmare (why wasn't she biting at him?) and was riding towards the well. "Most of them anyway. A few got away. Destiny I attempted to take alive, but when she tried to cast a spell, I had no choice but to kill her too."

Charles's eyes went wide with fury. "You…you didn't…Destiny! I'll kill you for this!" He let out his summoning whistle. It echoed as all six nightmares hitched to chariots screamed. The nightmare that was somewhere else in town joined in. Lightfoot whinnied and shook her mane. "What have you done to corrupt my horse?"

"Same thing I'll do to all of them when we're finished here. Let them loose, let them graze. It's amazing how easy it is to win their loyalty. Even more amazing that you still haven't earned it."

Fr. Zakary was beginning the first Sorrowful Mystery: The Agony in the Garden.

Charles's nostrils flared. "Get off my horse."

"No."

Charles wasn't used to people talking to him so…calmly. "Do you not see the current situation?" he asked while shaking Reginald and Lady Maria. "Get off that nightmare or I'll kill them!"

"No."

Charles's face turned completely red. "What's the matter with you? Do you want me to kill them?"

"No. I want to protect them. And that's exactly what I'm doing."

"You're going to get them both killed if you don't do what I tell you!"

"I've done more than enough holdups to know that that statement is false."

"False? Do you really think I'm afraid of killing?"

"Oh no. I am well aware of the butchery you are capable of. And that's exactly why I'm not listening to you." Lightfoot had reached the well now. About fifteen feet away she turned left and began to walk in a circle around it. Charles tried to turn to keep Winthrop right in front of him, but he didn't want his hammer to be behind him if he needed it. He began an awkward shuffle, dragging Reginald and Lady Maria in a circle around his hammer with Winthrop on the other side. "Your hands are looking a little full there, Charles. You can't even hold your weapon. I could walk right up to you and spit in your face, and there's nothing you could do to stop me." Winthrop smirked. "Not without letting go of your prisoners."

Charles sneered, "How stupid do you think I am? Do you really think you can trick me into releasing them?"

"It's not a trick. For me it's a memory. The black memory of all the lies that come together in a holdup. You may not know it yet, but you can feel it. You can feel the disconnect between your words and your reality. The first lie is that you're in control of the situation and acting from a position of power. 'I'm in charge here! Do what I say or the Lady gets it!' But that lie is utterly transparent. If you were actually in control, you wouldn't be taking hostages. If you were actually powerful enough to get what you want, you wouldn't be hiding behind a crippled lady and an old man. Counting on them to protect you from me is more cowardly than a child hiding behind his mother's skirt. But at least the child knows he's afraid. You're trying to pretend that you run the show."

Charles gave both of his hostages a jolting shake. "Are you trying to provoke me?"

"Yes. The second lie is that if I do what you tell me, you'll leave the hostages alive. But we both know that's not true, don't we? Once the outlaw gets what he wants, the hostages have outlived their usefulness. In your case, they will still be useful, but only for the purpose of making examples. You want to crush the spirit of this town, so you'll brutally murder those two once the town has groveled before you. Now if you said that out loud, no one would ever help you. That's what lying's for. You offer false hope and empty promises to keep your victims in line. Too bad for you, but my hope isn't founded on your promises. That's a house built on sand if I ever heard of one."

Winthrop kept circling the well, while Charles kept orbiting his hammer. He would take a step and grunt, pretending he was about to grab it. Winthrop never even flinched.

Fr. Zakary was halfway through the second mystery: The Scourging at the Pillar.

"And then there's the third lie, the biggest one. This is the lie the whole hostage situation depends on. You want us all to believe that if we fought you, scorned you, or otherwise rejected your demands, that you would kill the hostages. A crazy man might, but you and I aren't crazy. Our madness is much too rational. The minute those hostages die, you're an outnumbered murderer. So you need to keep them alive. But if you need to keep them alive, then you aren't really holding up hostages. You're babysitting. What a brazen lie we tell. We say we're going to kill them unless we get what we demand. The reality is that the *only* way we're going to kill them is if we get what we demand. So no, I don't want you to kill the hostages. That's why I'm not doing what you tell me to. That's why I'm going to do this instead…"

Lightfoot stopped walking and turned to face Charles. Then she walked forward until Winthrop was seven feet away. He pulled out a wine bottle. Charles stepped back in fear.

"Don't worry, I wouldn't throw it." Winthrop smiled as he pulled the cork and took a swig.

He was sitting at just the right spot. Charles knew that if he took his hammer and swung it at Winthrop's head, he was practically guaranteed to hit. Winthrop might be able to throw the bottle at him, but Charles was confident he could fight through the burn of one bottle and finish the infuriating interloper off. Winthrop was swishing the wine around in his mouth, seemingly oblivious to his peril. Charles suppressed his smile as he swelled with foolish pride.

Charles threw Reginald to the side.

He grabbed his hammer with his left hand.

Winthrop spat.

Charles brought the hammer back.

A stream of water hit him in the face.

The pain was far greater than Charles was expecting. It was like what Sir Joseph had done to him, only the agony was exploding all over his face instead of being contained to a single point. With a howl of suffering, he released Maria and grabbed his face, then stumbled backwards off the well. He didn't even notice that he had fallen on the hard cobblestones and was now rolling around on the ground. All he could think of was the burning. He clawed at it with his hands, but all he succeeded in doing was spreading the pain to them as well.

Meanwhile, Lady Maria tottered sideways, hobbling towards the edge of the well. Winthrop rode alongside her and picked her up, doing his best to neither hurt her nor spill the precious water from his wine bottle. "Sasha! Now!" Then he spoke softly to Lightfoot. "Easy, girl. Over to Sir Joseph, the man who saddled you." Lightfoot trotted to the west side, where Sir Joseph emerged from behind one of the houses. "Take her!" Winthrop yelled. Sir Joseph grabbed Lady Maria in his arms and set her down carefully beside his hammers and chisels.

Winthrop turned Lightfoot around and saw Charles on his hands and knees. Panting heavily, he started to rise, taking his hammer in hand. At that time, the lone nightmare finally arrived, shrieking as it rode into the square from the northeast with a handcart lashed to its makeshift yoke. It faithfully pulled up behind its master, answering his summoning whistle at last. Sasha took wine bottles in both hands, and chucked them at Charles's back.

Every one was filled with moat water. Bottle after bottle smashed into the back of his armor, splashing liquid agony over his whole body. Smoke rose from Charles's flesh. He wanted to rip his clothes off, but the armor acted as a restrictive prison, trapping him in his pain. Sasha went through every bottle she had, and then leapt from the handcart and ran into the crowd. There was one more task she might need to do.

When Charles finally came to his senses, he was lying on his back, writhing, squirming, and still trying vainly to extinguish the invisible fires the water had ignited. Winthrop trotted over so that he could look down on the Baron while staying out of his reach. "Last chance for this to end well for you, Charles. Leave the hammer, get in one of your chariots, ride away, and never come back. We've shown that we can best you. Now take my mercy and flee. Otherwise you will only hasten your own destruction."

Charles's eyes turned black, the way they had when he cast his spell the night before. With a scraping, grating voice he snarled, "MERCY? I SPIT ON YOUR MERCY. YOU ARE FAR FROM BEATING ME!" He leapt up and grabbed his hammer, running towards Winthrop with unnatural speed. Yet even the superhuman powers Charles got from Jove were no match for the speed of Lightfoot. She turned and cantered away, knowing to flee before Winthrop even gave the order. Unable to keep up with her, Charles yelled at two of his nightmares, "Get over here!" They pulled the chariot up to him. He climbed inside, pointed at Winthrop, and yelled, "After him! Run him down!"

Fr. Zakary was concluding the third mystery: The Crowning with Thorns.

The two nightmares pulled the chariot, going as fast as they could with their far greater weight. They had managed to outrun Isabella while pulling a chariot, but Lightfoot was every bit as swift as they were. Rolling down the southern road, the only sign of Winthrop that Charles could see was his dust.

As soon as Charles was out of sight, Sir Joseph, Nicholas, and Eustace emerged from hiding. With dozens of chisels and hammers in their arms they ran to the well. "Quickly! Help us break the seal!" Eustace called. He threw the tools down and took one of each for himself. The other townsfolk weren't sure what to do. Despite all they had seen, despite all they had heard, they were still hoping that they might be able to stay out of this conflict. Then Sasha intervened.

"God have mercy on the cravens of Dewford! Joseph, give me two chisels! I need one for myself, and one for my fiancé, who took an arrow to the stomach defending this town!"

To Sasha's surprise, there came an answer. Every bit as bombastic as his offspring, Ed hobbled into the square saying, "Make sure ya save one for ole' Eddy now. Got a broken back from that behemoth, but ain't nothin' gonna stop me from standin' up for the Lady."

Eustace stood up and cried, "Men of Dewford! Do your duty! We need to break the seal of this well *now* and put an end to the man who poisoned it!"

As the embers of last night's battle rekindled, Cooper called out, "DEWFORD!" and the shout resounded as dozens of men ran to the well to help.

After riding south beyond the moat, Lightfoot turned east towards the flatlands where Dewford sprawled. While he wanted to find out how fast she could really run, Winthrop was fighting that urge and making her go more slowly. He needed to keep Charles in the chase. After building a good distance between them, he let Charles gradually narrow the gap. Meanwhile, Winthrop was trying to keep track of time. *Where is Fr. Zakary now? Halfway through?*

Fr. Zakary was indeed halfway through the fourth mystery: The Carrying of the Cross.

Charles's chariot was about six lengths back when Winthrop reached the northeastern vineyards. He turned back towards town and followed a large side street, winding and curling between the houses along a very specific route.

Charles's nightmares were getting nervous. They were seeing a very serious danger on every side. Charles, blind to the threat, pressed them to run even faster. The nightmares listened for a while, but then with cries of distress they tried to halt. He jabbed his hammer into their rumps, threatening to kill them unless they kept going. They did as their master bade them.

It was a long, straight road ahead. This one ran almost all the way to town square, but at the last moment it joined up with one of the main roads and made a slight right turn. Charles's nightmares were one length back from Lightfoot. They came to the main road. Winthrop yelled, "Jump!" and Lightfoot leapt over the aqueduct. Charles's two nightmares followed suit. The chariot crashed into the aqueduct. With axles breaking, wheels splintering, hammer flying, Charles was launched into the town square in the tumbled mess of his chariot's ruined remains.

Fr. Zakary began the fifth Sorrowful Mystery: The Crucifixion of Our Lord Jesus Christ.

Charles leapt up from the crash in a rage. He was largely unhurt, and what scrapes and bruises he did suffer were already healing. He needed a new ride. He made his summoning whistle. All of the horses returned the whistle, but none were able to come to him. The two that had just crashed were lying on the ground with injuries. The other five were on the far side of the town square, lashed up tightly outside Reginald's manor. There was also a rope tied around the well, but Charles didn't have time to think about it at the moment.

Winthrop rode to the edge of the square, so that Charles was between him and the well. He had his wine bottle uncorked and was holding it in his left hand. "End of the line, Charles. This is your last, last chance to survive this day." At that moment, a great tragedy was announced.

The distant, yet distressing howl of Goliath filled everyone with fear. A moment later there came a rumbling, and the ground trembled beneath their feet. Charles touched one of his hands to the ground. His eyes turned all black as he heard the message the demons of the darkness had howled into the earth. Then he began to laugh.

"YOU KNOW, I MIGHT JUST TAKE YOU UP ON THAT OFFER. I ALMOST WANT TO. ALMOST. 'SURVIVE THIS DAY.' DO YOU WANT TO KNOW WHO DIDN'T SURVIVE THIS DAY?" He sniggered cruelly. "THAT BLACK KNIGHT YOU WERE TRYING TO HELP."

Winthrop's hand clenched down on the neck of the wine bottle, but he did not yet answer a single word.

"IT SEEMS GOLIATH JUST KILLED THE OLD MAN. THE KNIGHT WOULD HAVE NEEDED A PRIEST TO DEFEAT THE GIANT, BUT HE DIDN'T HAVE ONE. THIS DAY MAY HAVE TURNED INTO A MESS, BUT AT LEAST I KEPT THE PRIEST BUSY HERE INSTEAD OF LETTING HIM GO TO CASTLE NIGHTFALL. FOR THAT, GOLIATH WILL SURELY REWARD ME."

Winthrop tried to regain control of himself. He knew how important it was to stay calm in the midst of battle, yet he was shaking.

Fr. Zakary was on the third Hail Mary.

"LET'S SEE, DID THEY KILL THE BOY YOU WERE WITH TOO? HMM…NOT YET IT SEEMS. BUT I HOPE YOU WEREN'T TOO CLOSE WITH HIM. THEY SAY JEZEBEL IS ABOUT TO GET HIM. JUST A LITTLE LONGER, AND HE'LL BE DEAD AS WELL."

Lady Maria screamed.

"You lie!" Winthrop roared.

"USUALLY YES, BUT NOT RIGHT NOW. THIS TIME I'M TELLING THE TRUTH. JEZEBEL IS FLYING HIGH OVER HIM IN THE DARKNESS. THE BOY DOESN'T EVEN KNOW SHE'S COMING. DO YOU REMEMBER WHAT SHE DID TO SIMON? I SUSPECT WITH THIS

ONE SHE'LL TAKE HER TIME. AFTER ALL, WHAT'S THE RUSH? THERE'S NOTHING ANYONE CAN DO TO SAVE HIM."

With all his heart, Winthrop wished his ears would start ringing, the way they had been all this Week whenever he heard a lie. Driven mad by the crushing silence, he yelled and threw the wine bottle at Charles. He dodged, and it shattered on the cobblestones behind him. Winthrop drew *Veritas* and spurred Lightfoot forwards. This was one of the only times Winthrop ever lost his head in a battle. With the howling, the earthquake, the death of Sir Judas, and David's peril, a seed of doubt and despair took root in Winthrop's heart. He slashed *Veritas* into Charles's neck with all his might.

It cut in half an inch before stopping.

Charles grabbed Winthrop, hauled him off Lightfoot, and clenched a massive hand around Winthrop's neck.

Fr. Zakary was on the sixth Hail Mary.

Charles carried Winthrop over to the well and threw him hard against it. Winthrop's head crashed on the stone and he dropped *Veritas*. In a fog, he looked around for where it went. He saw the blade, but it didn't matter. Charles grabbed Winthrop by the chest, lifted him up, and threw him back down on top of the well.

The seventh Hail Mary.

Charles yelled to all who were gathered, "Is this your hero? Is this your champion? Do you intend to follow after his example?" He pulled Winthrop up and punched him across the face. "Then see where he will lead you!" Another blow.

The eighth Hail Mary.

Winthrop was totally dazed, head spinning from the repeated blows. Charles loomed over him, blocking out the sun as he whispered, "I really do envy Beatrice. I wish I could do to you what I know she'll do to the boy." Then he grabbed Winthrop around the neck with both hands and squeezed with all his might. Winthrop flailed, grabbed, and kicked, but to no avail. Charles was far too strong.

The ninth Hail Mary

Sir Joseph came up from behind, yelling, "Get him!" and drove his own sword into Charles's neck. It went no deeper than *Veritas* had. He pulled his blade out and stabbed again, then a third time. Charles ignored the pain and kept on squeezing. He was going to kill Winthrop first and then deal with the little man.

The tenth Hail Mary.

Winthrop was almost unconscious. He knew he wasn't going to make it. One Hail Mary, one Glory Be, the Oh My Jesus prayer…it was too long. He would be dead before the Rosary was ended. But as was already mentioned, Winthrop always tried to keep his head in a fight, and in this decisive moment he quickly considered any tool he might have at his disposal. He reached into his pocket and pulled out one last trick.

Winthrop shoved his rosary into Charles's face, rubbing it under his nose. Charles tried to retreat without letting go. The smell made him want to vomit. Whether it was because the little rosary was made by Lady Maria and was therefore repugnant to her torturer, or whether it was because the rosary honored our Lady and was therefore repugnant to his demon, either way, Charles could not bring himself to endure the sweet scent of those hand-crafted beads.

He released one hand to swat the rosary out of Winthrop's grasp. Winthrop used both hands to grab the thumb pressing on his jugular and pulled with all his might. He got a lifesaving rush of blood to his head before Charles clamped down with both hands again. This time, however, Winthrop's hands were in a much better position.

Fr. Zakary was on the Glory be.

Winthrop began to smile. Not since Lady Maria had Charles seen such a purple face try to laugh. He squeezed and squeezed, lifting Winthrop up and banging him back down again.

"…and lead all souls to heaven, especially those in most need of Thy Mercy." Sir Joseph fell to his knees, despairing of hurting Charles. Maria was weeping. Winthrop's vision was going dark around the edges.

Silence.

Then the rain began to fall.

Winthrop reached towards the center of the well. 'Titter-pitter-titter-titter-titter-pitter–' He felt several drops on his hand. He grabbed Charles's hands and smeared the heavenly water on them. Charles released him in an instant and leapt backwards with hands held high. The pain of the moat water was nothing compared to this purest form of the liquid. His hands not only *felt* like they were burning, but now there were visible flames where Winthrop had touched. Winthrop rolled off the well and landed on his face, head swimming and seeing stars as fresh air rushed into his lungs.

The pillar of water began falling full force, splashing off the top of the well and rushing along the ground in streams. Winthrop grabbed *Veritas* and slid it over to Sir Joseph. Picking up *Veritas* and dipping his own sword in the rushing water, Sir Joseph began to slash, stab, and even just fling water at Charles with the swords. They still failed to penetrate his skin very deeply, but every little wound glowed red hot and began to sizzle.

Winthrop crawled around to the north side of the well and grabbed the rope that was tied around it. He pulled with his still meager strength, not so much for results as for a message. The men of Dewford rushed forward, pulling the rope with Winthrop who was now rising to his feet. As they pulled, the brick seal over the well slid off. A foul and disgusting odor came forth. Black fumes rose up inside the pillar of rainbow water, casting shadows that would block out the light for a moment, and then it would emerge again. No more water was running along the ground in the town square, since once the seal was removed the entire pillar of water was falling down into the well. A distant gurgling sound came from the depths of the earth.

Sir Joseph had Charles on the back foot, using the two swords to drive him away. Letting him run neither to the left, nor to the right, he smacked the Baron with burning water repeatedly until he had stumbled backwards to the edge of the well. Hearing the torrent of water right behind him, Charles dug in his feet and stood his ground. He couldn't bring himself to charge Sir Joseph and run into that searing water, but neither would he retreat one more step into the pillar itself. The gurgling sound was getting closer as the well was filled.

Winthrop let go of the rope and staggered to Sir Joseph's side. With a grunt he made a running push and tried to send Charles backwards. All he succeeded in doing was falling to his knees. Winthrop rose again and croaked, "Help me!" as loud as he could. He tried another push, but Charles grabbed him and threw him back. Sir Joseph unleashed a flurry of slashes with the swords, using up whatever water was still coating them. Then while Charles was reeling, he dropped the swords and pushed.

Charles didn't budge.

Winthrop crashed into him again.

Charles wavered slightly.

Now came Nicholas, now Eustace, now a great crush of men, two dozen of them coming together and pushing Charles back into the pillar of water. When the rain hit his head, it burnt off his hair and some of his scalp. Charles surged forward with his last burst of strength, but the Dewfordians kept pushing and threw him over backwards. Charles fell into the pillar of water and went headlong down the well.

He howled for a moment, then was cut off as he splashed into the dark waters, which were now only ten feet below ground. As soon as he went under, the rain ceased. Everyone gathered around the edge of the well to look down, including Fr. Zakary, who pushed his way to the front.

Then with a frightful roar–more bestial than human–Charles emerged from below the waters. His eyes were withered and gray. His skin was peeling apart. Worms and maggots were burrowing into every little scratch Sir Joseph had given him. Twelve years ago Charles had cursed these waters so that anyone who ever touched them was doomed to die. On this particular occasion, God was pleased to let that curse come to fruition. Charles attempted to climb the walls of the well, but his hands rotted away as he did so.

Fr. Zakary called out, "Charles! I'm a priest! Confess your sins and you can still live after death!" Charles cursed his dying words.

The dying curse of Charles is the most foolish curse in existence, yet sadly the most widely used. It is a curse that very rarely afflicts its target, yet always afflicts the one who speaks it. Moreover, this curse is no small malediction, but the greatest there could ever be. How dreadful then, to take the most malicious wish a man can form and inflict it on oneself! Charles cursed these words, then sank below the waters, dragged down at last by his frivolous armor. The waters bubbled, gurgled, then released a greenish plume, as if the earth was belching after swallowing him whole.

The dying words of Charles, Bloody Baron of Dewford were thus: "Go to hell."

And, barring a miracle, that's exactly where he went.

Chapter 2: Last Ride of the Lessguard

Winthrop took a few deep breaths, then staggered over to where Sir Joseph had dropped *Veritas*. He sheathed it, then stumbled towards Lightfoot. "Come here, girl!" The nightmare whinnied and cantered up to him.

Sir Joseph came running over and put a hand on Winthrop's shoulder. "Whoa, whoa, whoa! What are you doing?"

"Going after David."

"David? Wait, do you mean…is that the boy Charles was just talking about?" Sir Joseph's face turned deathly pale. "Oh no…then that means the black knight he mentioned was…Sir Judas!"

Winthrop twisted free of Sir Joseph's hand. "I'm going after him."

As Winthrop was putting his foot in the stirrup, Sir Joseph tearfully told him, "Winthrop…it's too late. How those two got to Castle Nightfall in a single night we'll never know, but we do know there's no way you can get to him in time now."

Winthrop climbed up in the saddle. "I know exactly how they got there, and I'm going to get there the same way. These nightmares not only have more speed, but also more stamina than we can possibly imagine. Now get out of my way!"

"Winthrop!" Lady Maria groaned, choking on the words in her sobbing sorrow. "There's nothing we can do. David is…oh, my poor David! We…we need to resign ourselves to God's holy Will. That's all we can do…"

"NO!" Winthrop yelled, "No! Not yet! He's not! Dead! Yet! I resign myself to nothing! I'm going to save him!" Calming down only a little, Winthrop said to Lady Maria, "Yesterday you told me you thank God you were born a woman, that you became a mother and not a father. You rejoice that you can sheathe the sword of justice and take pity on a scoundrel such as me. I also rejoice for your good fortune, but now I tell you to rejoice for mine.

"I thank God I was born a man, that I became a father and not a mother, because as a father I can draw my sword and ride my horse, and bring down the wrath of God on every witch, giant, and demon who tries to stand between me and my son. Our son–the one we both have in our own way." Winthrop then drew *Veritas* and pointed it skyward, a nimbus of light surrounding it in splendor. "You will see David again in the land of the living, even if I have to kick down the gates of hell to bring him back."

Then Winthrop spurred Lightfoot and yelled, "Heeyah!" riding swiftly down the western road out of town. Everyone was dumbstruck for quite some time, not believing what they had just seen. It was no mere trick of the light nor glow from *Veritas*. As Winthrop had made his promise to Lady Maria, it had looked like he was wreathed in blazing flames. He had looked like a man on fire.

After a few moments of everyone standing there in silence, Fr. Zakary ran over to the other nightmares, saying, "Someone fetch me a saddle! I need to go too! Charles said something about how they need a priest to defeat the giant!" He tried to untie one of the nightmares, but it went to bite off his fingers. He pulled his hand back just in time. He tried to calm the brutal beasts down, but they were all viciously attacking him. "Oh, this will never do! How did Winthrop get his horse to listen?" As Fr. Zakary tried to pet one of the nightmares again, she let out a loud and chilling shriek. The other nightmares all followed suit. Then, to everyone's surprise, another shriek came from the south of town.

"Winthrop must have turned back for something!" Nicholas yelled. They all ran to the south side of the square, but did not see Winthrop. Instead an unmanned nightmare came trotting up the road. Like Lightfoot, this one was quite a bit fatter than the others, and not the least bit hostile.

"Oh thank You, God," Fr. Zakary whispered, running up to Buttercup. "Does anyone have a saddle? I've never ridden a horse before, and I'm worried that if I go bareback I'll fall off." The townsfolk all looked at each other with shrugs and shakes of the head. No one in town owned a horse, and therefore none of them had a saddle. Then, as Reginald was racking his brain, a wonderful idea occurred to him. "Let's go to the Baron's manor, over on the other side of the hill! His stables must surely have something we can use. Alright, every able-bodied man come with me! We'll drive off any scoundrels Charles left in his den, and get Fr. Zakary where he needs to go!"

A shout of assent was raised, and two dozen men marched over to the manor. They turned out the servants without any resistance, released all of the remaining nightmares, and found a one-horse open carriage that they could hitch Buttercup to. With Fr. Zakary seated beside him, Sir Joseph drove the carriage in the direction of Castle Nightfall. "Winthrop said I couldn't imagine how much stamina these horses have. Time to find out if he was right." By the time they were departing, Winthrop had a head start of about ninety minutes. Buttercup pulled the carriage astonishingly fast, swiftly riding through every abandoned town and village on that hundred-mile journey. The sun set behind the growing wall of blackness, and then about an hour after that they reached it.

Lightfoot was laying on the ground, slowly chewing grass and gravel. "Winthrop! Winthrop! Are you here?" Sir Joseph yelled. There was no reply. "Do you think he left the road and went around? Maybe he was looking for another way in."

"I think he went straight forward," Fr. Zakary answered. "Whether it was wise or foolish, I doubt he even thought about turning aside."

"So should we...go in after him?" Sir Joseph asked.

"I don't know..." It was about three in the afternoon when the two men had this conversation, and the reader of course knows what happened next. I have narrated these events a little out of order so that we may now follow the story of Winthrop continuously from when he began his ride until this tale is done.

It was about nine o'clock in the morning when Winthrop set his face to Castle Nightfall. Lightfoot galloped in great and powerful strides, causing the land to fly right past them. Not caring about the road, she galloped through the fields and then around the northern side of Chelles. By avoiding the camp sprawled out to the east of the city, Lightfoot was taking the fastest path to the southern bridge.

As they were rounding the western wall, they passed beneath the window of Lady Amanda. She had fallen asleep about an hour before, but then Goliath's howl and the earthquake woke her up. Now that she heard the thundering of hooves, she looked out her window and saw a rider mounted on one of Charles's infamous beasts. At first she thought he must be an outlaw who did the Baron's bidding, but there was something different about this rider.

He wasn't hiding in a carriage, but instead riding atop the steed. Moreover, on his hip she caught the gleaming hilt of the silver sword Sir Judas had drawn two nights before. On impulse she yelled, "Go, fair rider, go! Slay the evil that lays before us!"

Winthrop only had time to yell, "Pray for me!" and she replied, "I will!" Though exhausted from her all-night vigil, Lady Amanda knelt at the window again and prayed until the Day was Dawned.

Winthrop rode across the Eines river, then flew past every town along his way. Three villages, a handful of hamlets, and then he left all of civilization behind him. Winthrop was tired and achy, having galloped further than any man had ever rode before. He clenched his knuckles and leaned forward, firming up his resolve to keep riding on. After two hours Lightfoot started flagging, but Winthrop begged her to keep going. "Come on now, girl! A little further! Get me close enough to do the rest myself! I can't save David without you!" What a strange, strange steed that Lightfoot was. She hadn't known Winthrop for even a week, yet their famous bond of loyalty was already forged. For her master's sake she dug a little deeper, galloping beyond her already impressive limits.

One hour more she endured. Then they crested the last hill near Castle Gregory and rode down to where the land of light ended (for the sun was still visible in the sky). Seeing the blackness, Lightfoot wavered, then finally succumbed to her exhaustion. Her stride went out of rhythm, then she dropped down and laid on her side. Winthrop dismounted and took a moment to lay his head upon her, giving her grateful pats and rubs. "Well done! Thank you, girl. I hope this will be enough. You take your rest, and hopefully we see each other again before too long." Then Winthrop looked straight up, taking one last look at the sun.

It was noon.

He drew *Veritas* and charged forward, plunging into the worst night of his entire life.

Chapter 3: Dark Night of the Soul

If any man would be My disciple, he must take up his cross and follow Me.

The moment Winthrop set foot in that accursed land the eyes of every demon turned upon him. They couldn't afflict David, but this one was in their power. At the speed of thought they flew to him, an uncountable swarm fencing him in on every side.

The lowest ranking and least talented devils attacked him right away. They dug up his greatest sorrows and threw them in his face. Only a tiny fraction of the demons assaulted Winthrop, but a tiny fraction of such a host was still hundreds of thousands. Winthrop swooned in terror, desiring to turn around and run back the way he came.

He brought David to his mind, while the devils pulled up his every sin against him. As those dreadful memories whirred around, Winthrop flipped them on their head, saying, "After all the horrible things I've done to David, I owe it to him now to come and save him!" He started to trudge forward, but a new and much more practical problem presented itself. He couldn't see. Gloomy hopelessness and despair rushed upon him, but Winthrop managed to keep his head through it all. *This road must run to Castle Nightfall...heaven help me if there's a fork!* He put his right foot on the road and his left on the grass beside it. Winthrop began to walk like this, then once he was comfortable, he began to jog.

Meanwhile the attacks kept coming, as more demons jumped in to excavate his sorrowful past. *A father? A brother? A mother? All their lives snuffed before their time? Yes, remember and understand the evil your God has done.* The more reserved and higher ranking demons were simultaneously holding a conference.

"Shall we kill him?"

"Of course."

"Right now?"

"I don't think we should."

"Then when?"

"When he succumbs to his despair."

"Look at what the grunts have already dug up."

"Great stuff!"

"This one doesn't stand a chance."

"He repented yesterday."

"He'll fall again today."

"Easy pickings."

"Time it right."

"Yeah, let him sin, then kill him quick."

"Mortal sin. Not venial."

"Obviously."

"Rip the Almighty's newest child out of His grasp."

"How do we push him over the edge?"

"Could it be clearer?"

"He'll never make it that far."

"He will if we help him."

"Time it right. Make sure we time it right..."

A command went out from the ruling demons–no physical attacks were to be made against Winthrop until they gave the order. Meanwhile, the spiritual attacks would slowly ratchet up, and then they would crush him with the decisive blow at the end. The demons organized themselves into three huge armies that would slay him as soon as he fell from grace.

Winthrop kept jogging in the emotional turmoil already whipping around. His thoughts were no longer his own. He was trying to stay focused on his task, but visions kept dancing across his blinded eyes. The bloody sheets in his mother's bed. Jacob shuddering in his arms. His father slashed to pieces by Goliath. He tried to block them out but it was all to no avail. He was far weaker than even one of the devils, and they easily overwhelmed him. Unlike Sir Judas, Winthrop had not yet developed the habit of leaning on God in constant prayer. Instead, he trusted in his own strength, and he paid the bitter price of anxiety and sorrow.

As Winthrop kept jogging along, his left foot failed to find the ground. He tumbled headlong off the road. It was a bridge crossing a small creek, thankfully shallow enough for him to stand. Unfortunately, as he fell down into the water, he lost his grip on *Veritas. What was I thinking? This is a doomed and foolish venture! I should have listened to Lady Maria and just resigned myself to God's will!* He groped around under the water, trying and failing to figure out where it went. *Oh, what was that prayer my grandmother taught me? St. Anthony, St. Anthony, please come round. There's something lost that must be found...* The demons panicked. They didn't want him praying, not even a rote little prayer like that. One of them hastily grabbed the sword and placed it under Winthrop's hand. He found it and said, "Oh, thank God." The demons swarmed like a hive gone mad. They didn't want him praying. They had lost souls over smaller prayers than this.

Winthrop clambered up the far side of the creek and got back on the road. He set himself up in the same way again, with his right foot on the road and his left foot just off of it. Then he had a moment of doubt. *How am I ever going to make it? How many more creeks and ditches are between here and Nightfall?*

The demons fanned the flames of those thoughts, trying to make him lay down and die. He almost did, but then Winthrop remembered how he had almost laid down to die on Tuesday. His father's words had revived him then. He called those words to mind once more. *I love you, son...I love you, son...I finally told David, 'I love you, son.' Alright, Winthrop, time to prove those words were not mere empty wind.* He sheathed *Veritas*, deciding it would be better to draw the sword if he needed it than to risk losing it again. He walked forward briskly, but no longer jogging as fast as he had done until now.

Winthrop continued on in darkness, the constant blindness driving him mad. The ruling demons circled overhead, and when the time was right they struck. Ten legions descended upon Winthrop, cutting and clawing at his back.

With a cry of pain, he fell the second time, landing on his knees, then on his face. The demons tore at him, and Winthrop's hope waned. He remembered Jacob. His dying words were, 'Make sure you get to heaven.' Crying from pains both physical and spiritual, Winthrop slapped the ground and yelled, "Come on, Winthrop! No giving up! You've got a little brother looking down on you!" He rose again and staggered forward, bearing all the suffering one man could take.

After hours of this trial he reached the Scar, and the road changed from gravel to cobblestones beneath his feet. Going slowly, he felt around for grass, dirt, or anything that would mark the edge of the road. He could find nothing. He set himself as straight as he could, and walked slowly forward with his hands out in front of him.

While Winthrop proceeded thus, a great cry went up in the diabolical army. Zambri, leading the damned humans in rebellion, shouted out to the rulers, "This is our land! Here we have permission to do whatever we want!"

"Stay in formation. We'll tell you when to attack."

"No! It's our right! We can tempt him however we want when he's in this city! Moloch himself permitted it!"

"Stay put, you fool! Don't you see what lies ahead?"

Zambri looked, and his black soul felt the closest thing to delight that the damned are capable of knowing. "Oh please, then, let me do it. Let me be the architect of his demise! In life, this man was my killer, slaying me for not coming to a dying brother's side. What laughter shall there be in hell if his damnation comes at my hands while he is the one who can't come to the help of a dying boy?" The elder demons consulted and then decreed that it should be so. Zambri now held his peace while the infernal army shepherded Winthrop through the Scar, leading him like a sheep before the slaughter.

He reached the far side of the city and felt the road change back to gravel. He stepped to the left and found the grass, straddling the edge of the road with joy. He walked briskly for about a mile, following the road up a gentle slope. Then he crested the hill and his path turned downwards. Winthrop couldn't see the valley stretching out before him, but he could see the golden dome of light down in it. He could also see the boy in the center of that dome, running towards him with *Caritas* drawn.

"David!" Winthrop yelled, false hope giving him a moment of pure joy.

With wild eyes and a terrified voice, David yelled back, "Winthrop? Winthrop! Help!"

Winthrop drew *Veritas* and sprinted, all caution thrown to the wind. He couldn't see what David was running from—wait! He saw her, Jezebel, flitting in and out of the light. She was running after David and slowly overtaking him. Winthrop was running as fast as he could. He was going to make it in time!

"Now," said one of the demonic princes. A lieutenant in his army swiped at Winthrop's leg, snapping his femur as if it was a single straw. Winthrop screamed in pain and fell on his face, losing *Veritas* somewhere in the darkness. *What just happened?* He grabbed his broken leg while a torrent of doleful demons tried to crush him with depression. "There's nothing you can do!" "This is hopeless!" "Your sword is lost!" "Your body is broken!" "David is sure to die!"

Yet even in that moment, when all seemed lost, Winthrop remembered another hero who had persevered in the face of certain defeat. His mother. Jacob was stuck sideways, with no chance of coming out alive. She didn't give up. She fought to the end, and saved his little brother's life, even at the price of her own. She didn't give up. Winthrop swung one arm forward, and then another, dragging his broken leg across the ground. "I'm not! Dead! Yet!" he cried, clenching his teeth through all the pain.

Jezebel was right behind David. She reached out, shoved him, then leapt upon him where he fell. David tried to squirm free, but she easily pinned him down and put both of his arms beneath her knees. Then she used her hands to try and pry *Caritas* out of his grip. Winthrop picked up the pace, crawling as fast as he could go. "Come here, witch! I'll kill you! I'll bite your head off if I have to!" He was near the edge of the light, about forty-five feet away from David.

The princes of the demons sent forth their command. The final assault began. One third of the remaining forces formed a great wave and crashed into Winthrop in a storm of teeth, claws, and the most bitter emotions and memories. His other leg broke. Several ribs broke. Large pieces of flesh were torn away. Winthrop made a loud, croaking gasp. He realized the utter folly of how he had lived the last Week of his life. *I wouldn't be here if not for Sir Judas! I wouldn't be here if not for his God! I wouldn't be here if I had stuck to my creed and just done whatever I want!*

Winthrop was so close to *Caritas's* light, only one foot away. Jezebel pulled the dagger out of David's grasp. Then, to Winthrop's astonishment, Fr. Zambri appeared between him and the light, blocking David and Jezebel from view.

It was three in the afternoon.

"Winthrop, Winthrop, Winthrop…you almost did so well. You took my creed and led the life of a free man for so many years, but then right at the end you stumbled. Tell me, how is Christian living suiting you? Are you fond of how the Almighty treats His friends?"

A second wave of demons came in, scourging and breaking Winthrop's body and soul. Winthrop screamed in agony. As they went racing by, Fr. Zambri spoke clearly in his ear, "Look, Winthrop, I'm happy now. Let's set aside all the books, all the theology, and all the arguments, and just get right down to the facts. I'm a happy man. I never really served the Almighty, but I never served the demons either. I died a free man, and now I live as a free man.

I'm free to do whatever I want. I want you to have that, Winthrop. As long as you're alive, it's not too late. Set yourself free from the deity Who left you here to die. Set yourself free from Him Who is letting David die too."

"You aren't real!" Winthrop growled.

David screamed.

Jezebel laughed.

Fr. Zambri tapped Winthrop on his forehead. "I'm very real, bud. I'm as real as the demons who are killing you, and the One Who left you in their hands." Fr. Zambri stepped aside. Winthrop saw Jezebel holding *Caritas* over David's head with one hand, while the other was holding him by the neck. He pulled her hand off for a moment and yelled, "Winthrop! Winthrop! Where are you? Help me!" Winthrop lunged forward with all his might, just barely getting his head and shoulders into the light.

The third wave crashed in. This time the demons dealt mortal blows. A million slashes and tears shredded every piece of Winthrop's body. Every piece except the head and chest. Those were left intact. They wanted to make sure Winthrop still had enough body to commit his final sin.

The princes of the demons came last of all, replicating Winthrop's memories so perfectly and so realistically that his life did not merely flash before his eyes. Instead he relived it all at once.

His mother died when he was three.

His father died in vain for a doomed king and Empire.

His brother died in his arms.

He killed Fr. Zambri.

He spent three decades on the run from the law, from the world, and from himself.

After all of that, the greatest tragedy was this last accursed Week. False hopes and foolish dreams made Winthrop waste the final days of his life chasing after phantoms. A boy he called his son. A man who set him on the path of redemption. A woman who forgave him. A priest who absolved his sins. A lifelong dream of becoming a paladin that in the end just might come true.

All was cruelty. None was real. God permitted those joys of the moment just to magnify Winthrop's misery at the end. Jezebel was about to kill David. God was making *Caritas* shine with light in her hand, just so Winthrop would have to watch.

"You're about to die, Winthrop," Fr. Zambri whispered in his ear. "Your life blood has left you. You have only one breath left. Use it wisely. Use it boldly. Use it to tell the Almighty what you really think of Him, and then be free like me forever."

Winthrop knew Fr. Zambri was right. His body had been annihilated. One breath was all he had. One last chance to proclaim what he believed. He thought to himself, *Mine is the saddest death ever died, at the end of the saddest life ever lived.*

Winthrop drew his dying breath.

Jezebel plunged the dagger down.

Winthrop screamed his dying words.

David looked over at Winthrop. His face was covered in blood and twisted by his final agony. His unseeing, lifeless eyes revealed that as soon as he had spoken, he gave up the ghost. Thus ended David's adopted father. Thus ended the Lessguard. Thus ended that sad and tortured life of woe.

The dying words of Lord Winthrop, Duke of Nouen were thus: "Blessed be the Name of the Lord! Praise be Jesus Christ!"

Chapter 4: Some Thoughts Concerning Natural Evil

I know what you're thinking, dear reader. You read this chapter title and said, 'Asinus! You stupid scholar! This is no time for catechesis!' Yet I ask you to bear with me, and trust that this discussion is absolutely essential to understanding our present history.

If God made the world good, then why do natural disasters afflict men? Our inclination as men is to assume that a good God would have made a world where we never suffer. Yet I answer to the contrary. I say that these disasters happen precisely *because* God made the world good. God made the world with perfect goodness, and–as has been a theme in this history–fallen men do not see perfect goodness as 'good,' but instead they call it 'evil.' God made the world in a way that gives glory to Him and leads men to know their Maker. Part of God's glory that is revealed in creation is that any path away from God–any path of sin–causes degeneration, suffering, decay, and death. All of nature reflects this. Our world groans, travails, and has disasters because of the sins of men. Thus the doctrine of natural evil.

Here I will venture beyond established Catholic teaching and offer a speculation I think well-founded. I speculate that if the world was made to give glory to God by unleashing disasters when men sin, then it would also be perfectly reasonable for the world to give glory to God by unleashing incredible bounty when men are holy. This is not a rational choice of pseudo-divine rocks, but rather a law of physics, like gravity. If eating a forbidden fruit makes the world bring forth thorns and thistles, then it may also follow that fasting from lawful fruit makes the world bring forth good harvests. This notion of 'natural good,' is what I am driving at, because it is simply the most reasonable explanation for everything that happened next.

For the forty long years since Goliath created the darkness, the earth beneath his dome had suffered a terrible lacking. It was not a lack of sunlight (since the darkness didn't really block out the sun) but instead a lacking of any soul who would praise the Sun of Justice. In all those years that the darkness grew, only the perfectly possessed would ever roam Goliath's kingdom. Friends of demons serving their monstrous master were the only humans that land had seen. For earth, water, wind, and sunshine that were made to glorify their Maker, this was a terrible deprivation, and while inanimate creatures don't experience any sadness, they showed the sadness all men ought to feel.

Then from the depths of that never-ending night, the demon Jezebel spoke the name of 'Judas.' At the rumor of some servant of God coming to that accursed land, the ground began to quake and quiver in anticipation. Then when Lady Amanda, facing the darkness, spoke the most Sacred Name of JESUS, even at a distance of so many miles, the wind carried her words to the darkness, and the darkness thundered with excitement. The next day David and Sir Judas were in earshot, and the land of shadows heard its Maker's name spoken twice, though still outside its borders. All through the night those two hiked towards Castle Nightfall, and Nature waited breathlessly for the redemption of the sons of men. But alas! The demons slew Sir Judas! His blood cried out to heaven for vengeance, and the earth shook in rage over his murder. Yet it was demons, not the sons of men who sinned, and therefore natural good was still at work. The air around David's eardrums stood still, protecting him from the deafening screams of Goliath, while the winds carried the giant's sobs as far as Dewford, searching for a savior.

And then at last came Winthrop, who took up his cross and held it tightly unto the end. As he overcame the powers of hell and screamed his dying words, the natural good they merited broke forth with terrible violence. For at the most Sacred Name of JESUS, all of creation leapt for joy. The waters of the sea rushed forth in exultation, while the hills and valleys were overthrown. The ground shook so suddenly and so precisely that Jezebel was hurtled far from David, while the boy gently rolled a couple feet. And then that wind–that famous wind!–Came swirling all about Winthrop. It grabbed his words, spun faster than a tornado, then unleashed a mighty gale that carried his message through all the world. And as the created wind sent forth his words for men to hear, the uncreated Wind stirred their hearts for men to repeat. For on that most blessed Day, every man of good will, believer or not, joined in Winthrop's words of praise.

David called out, "Praise be Jesus Christ!" and Sir Samson called the same a moment later. At the edge of the darkness Sir Joseph and Fr. Zakary heard the words, and they also cried, "Praise be Jesus Christ!" And as those words ran across the land, Lady Amanda, Lady Maria, Ed, Sasha, Kayden, William–even Reginald–all heard Winthrop's dying words and then joined him in proclaiming, "Praise be Jesus Christ!" Then as those words left the Land of Ire and rang out through all the world, the same Spirit that descended at Pentecost granted men of every tongue and creed to understand, and yell with one voice, "Praise be Jesus Christ!"

So all the earth and those who dwell therein were crying to the God of their salvation. Then the angels would no more keep silent, and to David it was granted to hear their pleas. With wind, water, and earth swirling about him in the darkness, David heard two angelic choirs sing the harmony of opposing strains.

The first choir sang:

"To Thee, Almighty God, all power and glory forever and ever,

And now earth's men to Thee do turn and cry out for their Savior.

For a moment Thou wert angry, but now let Thy wrath abate,

And deal not with them according to their sins, but show the Mercy they deserve."

And the second choir retorted:

"Is God One Who deals justly with those who turn away from evil?

Is not His Mercy more than abundant? Far surpassing what is earned?

Show not the mercy they deserve, O Lord, but the one Thou art pleased to show,

And for all flesh that now acclaims Thy Son, make answer to their pleading.

The first choir sang again:

"What wonder shall our God now show? What deed befits His glory?

Shall the ocean part like the Red Sea? Or fire fall like for Elijah?"

And the second choir concluded:

"Thy storehouse knows no limits, Lord, and infinite is Thy bounty.

Work not Thy works of old, but new wonders for this moment."

Then a voice like rushing waters and thunder came from the Throne. To the favored soul for whom the task was appointed, God said, "Ite. Missa est," which being translated, means, "Go. It is sent."

Then that blessed saint returned to our vale of tears, and looked across the universal expanse. Even though they were separated from him by all space that exists, the demons trembled at his gaze. An angel took him by the hand,

and carried him to our sky, and with eyes blazing brighter than the summer sun he peered into the depths of darkness.

It was unable to resist him.

The darkness broke! The shadows fled! All light and splendor now were dancing! Round David swirling all about, a glorious cyclone surrounded the clear blue sky. And on that Day that Dawned in the Afternoon, behold! One appeared in the sky, looking like a son of man! He came riding on the clouds in glorious majesty. It was not the Majesty of that King Who shall come at the End of Time, yet it was far more than David had ever seen before or since.

Chapter 5: The Return of the King

The cloud descended until it was only three inches above the ground. He stepped off, setting his bare foot upon the grassy slope. On his head was a crown of incorruptible gold. In his left hand he held a palm. He wore a white robe that draped over his left shoulder, while his right breast and the hole in his chest were exposed. He solemnly walked over to *Veritas*, knelt down before it, then bent low to the ground and gave a reverential kiss to the sword that had conducted him to eternal life.

Then he took up the blade and walked to Winthrop's body. Looking at David with eyes of blazing emerald, he said, "Be not afraid. Come here child."

David slowly and nervously advanced, trembling with every step. When he was beside Winthrop's body he looked down, gasped, and then covered his eyes to hide the horror. The man asked, "Can God restore such a one as this to life? Can he heal a son who is mutilated and broken beyond repair?"

David opened his eyes again to behold the gory mess the demons had made of Winthrop. "I…I know He can, because Sir Judas said God can do anything…but…I don't know how it's possible."

"It is enough that you know He can. Do not worry yourself with how. I would also have you hear these words, and carry them with you on your pilgrimage. This man's body you see before you is far less wounded than his soul was yesterday morning. Yet when the priest of God pronounced the words 'Ego te absolvo,' a greater healing took place than the one you shall now see."

Then the man touched the tip of *Veritas* to Winthrop's brow and said, "Be made whole." At once Winthrop's blood began to flow out of the ground and back into his body, while every little piece of flesh returned to its proper place. Before David's eyes every gash and wound was closed. Winthrop's face forgot his agony and took on a peaceful, restful pose. It no longer seemed that he was dead, but rather he had merely fallen asleep. When the body was completely healed, the man knelt down, took a deep breath, and blew it into Winthrop's face. Winthrop inhaled, opened his eyes, then bolted upright in amazement.

David threw his arms around him and yelled, "Winthrop!" crying harder in this moment of joy than in the entire past Week of sorrows.

Winthrop looked around, taking everything in. He was healed. The sun was shining. He was in a beautiful land he had never seen before. The last thing he recalled was that David was about to be murdered, and yet the boy was here hugging him. Then he saw the king, wearing his crown, clothed in glory. Winthrop made what must have been the most reasonable assumption in the world. "I take it we're in heaven?"

The king chuckled. "Heaven is far greater than this passing beauty you see around you. You are on the southern peninsula of the Land of Ire, eight miles east of Castle Nightfall."

Winthrop shook his head, blinked several times, rubbed his eyes just to be sure, then said, "But you're the king! You're supposed to be dead!"

"I was dead. Yet I live. And now I die no more. I was sent by God to this vale of tears in answer to the prayers raised throughout the world. I shall stay only long enough to establish His will in you, and then I will return to the eternal hills."

Still holding David with one arm, Winthrop got up on his knees and asked, "Are you going to reestablish the Grand Empire?"

"No!" the king answered, scoffing as he did. "The Empire was never meant to be a reward for God's followers, but instead it was a judgment against them. God told me when to start it, then He told me when to end it. That was why I told Sir Daniel to let Goliath triumph on the plains of Nouen. Otherwise, no power of hell could have ever overcome us."

"But why?" Winthrop asked, "Why would God want the Empire to end? What do you mean it was 'a judgment against us'?"

The king answered, "Before God called me to take the crown, the Church on earth was full of worldly men who pined for Christendom without Christ. They complained of their rulers' wicked laws, but they wouldn't lift a finger to help their neighbors in need in the midst of daily life. They would travel over hill and dale to protest public blasphemies, yet they wouldn't travel down the street to recite the Divine Praises at solemn Benediction. Even long before my day, before the Calamity that shook the world, they had wealth, leisure, the Scriptures, and the writings of the saints at their fingertips, yet instead of digging for these treasures they used electro-magic to dredge up sewage. It was to fill up the cup of their iniquities that God gave them a glorious Catholic Empire. When they chafed, cursed, and ultimately revolted, they were forced to come face to face with the truth of what they wanted. They sought Christendom because they imagined it was a political arrangement that would satisfy their earthly longings, not because they actually wanted Jesus Christ to reign over them. For the truth I exhort you to remember wherever you shall go is this; every man can already choose to live in the kingdom of heaven on earth, no matter what worldly circumstances surround him. If Jesus reigns in your heart, then you are a citizen of His kingdom, and you shall live your days in peace even as the prince of this world makes war against you.

"This is the kingdom I was sent to prepare—not a kingdom on maps and with armies, but a kingdom reigning over every heart. And to restore and preserve this kingdom, I was told to reinstate the greatest part of mine. Not the Empire, but the Paladins, an order of men who forsake all the things of this world in order to lead all men into the next. Therefore, I now establish the means whereby the Paladins shall persevere until the end of time. The authority to invest I give to you and your successors, that the Head of the Paladins shall be able to raise up new knights by his dubbing. As for the drop of blood, it shall no longer come from the king, but from your heart. Whenever you consecrate a weapon as sacred, you shall touch it to the wound in your heart, which will then bleed. Such shall you do all the days of your life, until an angel is sent to visit you at your Transition. At that time, you shall consecrate all the weapons that will be used unto the end, and leave them in the treasury of your successors.

"Now then, if you would accept the dignity I have offered, and become the first Head of the New Order of Paladins, I ask you to stand before me, bow your head, and bend your knee."

Silence.

On trembling legs, Winthrop arose, took a few steps towards the king, then bowed his head and kneeled down. The king said, "Lord Winthrop, Duke of Nouen, do you renounce all lands and titles, becoming the least among men so that you may be their servant?"

"I do."

"Winthrop, do you renounce marriage and children so that you will not be husband and father to some particular family, but instead to God's Holy Church and all her offspring?"

"I do."

"Winthrop, do you renounce your very self so that until you finish your earthly pilgrimage, men shall no longer see you, but only Christ Who lives in you?"

"I do."

"Winthrop, will you be a Paladin?"

Barely able to catch his breath, still wondering if he wasn't dead or dreaming, Winthrop said, "I will."

The king now raised *Veritas* high above his head, so that it gleamed and glittered in the summer sun. "Your father named you 'Winthrop,' and well were you named, for that name means 'friend's village,' and that is exactly how you lived. Not like a true son of mine, but like a friend who wished my Empire well. But now, I take you as my child in spirit. No more from my friend's village, but from the fatherland. And so to remind you always of the Patria [which being translated means, 'Fatherland'] towards which you are going, and to honor the patron saint of this land where your new life now begins, I dub thee–"

The king gently struck the side of Winthrop's neck with the flat of *Veritas's* blade, while saying, "Sir Patrick." He then laid *Veritas* flat in his hands and offered it for Sir Patrick to take. "Arise, Sir Patrick, and receive *Veritas*, your sacred blade. Never forget when you behold its power that the truth of an honest life smites the enemies of God far harder than any sword made by human hands."

Sir Patrick arose and took *Veritas* in his left hand. It neither glowed nor showed any other wondrous sign. Sir Patrick didn't need one. Without saying any other word or message, the king turned around and walked back to the cloud.

"Wait!" Sir Patrick called, "I still need more instructions! What should I do next!"

The king shrugged. "Pray. Think. Act." He sat down on the cloud, and it began to slowly rise once more.

"NOOO!" Jezebel and Beatrice shrieked, running on all fours towards the heavenly courtier. "YOU HAVE NO RIGHT TO DO THIS! WE MUST BE ALLOWED TO CARRY ON OUR REBELLION!" She leapt through the air with *Caritas* raised, trying to stab it into the king's throat.

He merely glanced in her direction, and she flew backwards through the air, landing hard on her back with a thud. *Caritas* flew out of her hand and landed on the ground next to David.

"You have no rights, accursed rebel. As an enemy of God, He is free to do with you as He wills. The only reason He shows Justice and Mercy in His dealings with you is because it is according to His Nature. Do not speak of rights. Beg God in His Goodness to grant you some concession."

Beatrice shuddered deeply, vomited dark fluid on the ground, then croaked, "Oh God! In Your...Gragh...*Goodness*...ugh...please grant us some concession proportionate to the Order of Paladins You have created." She then howled and rolled around, shoveling dirt into her mouth.

The king answered, "Whenever the human one of you demons is afflicting dies, you are cast back into hell. A billion of you are now gathered here, and since Sir Judas has died, that is exactly what you deserve. Yet here is a concession the Almighty God would be willing to grant to you. Instead of returning to hell, you may choose to enter the giant called Goliath. You may join your powers with the legion already within him, making him an avatar of your destruction. Do you accept this concession as a more than generous exchange for the founding of the Order of Paladins?"

The invisible legions celebrated with wicked glee. "Let them have an order of little knights! With that much power, we will soon be able to control the world!" The princes of the devils were wary, however. They suspected a trap was being laid. They prompted Jezebel to make Beatrice ask, "How long will Goliath have left to live? Will this knight smite the giant dead within a day?"

The king answered, "For as long as you dwell in the body of that sorry soul, he shall never die of age or injury. He will have perfect health and earthly immortality along with the powers you bestow upon him."

At this promise, not even the princes could contain their excitement. They prompted Beatrice to cry out, "They accept! The foolish Almighty has given them too much! Now we shall reign on earth, and the Almighty cannot stop us without making Himself a liar! Until the end of time shall the sons of Adam lament the Day that Dawned in the Afternoon!" Then, with a wicked cackle, Jezebel came out of Beatrice, abandoning her to join the horde flying for Castle Nightfall. Beatrice, no longer fortified by her demon, turned and ran in terror from the king and Sir Patrick.

"What should I do about her?" Sir Patrick asked.

The cloud began to rise once more. "I already told you. Pray. Think. Act. A saint is not a puppet. God gave you a brain so you can use it." Then the cloud flew up and up, soaring into the sky until it disappeared from view. Sir

Patrick and David stood there for some time in amazement, still absorbing all that had happened.

At last, Sir Patrick patted David on the back and said, "Alright, David. Let's do what he said. Let's pray about what we should do." They knelt down and both asked God to guide them. After a few minutes, Sir Patrick asked, "Did you hear any voices with good ideas?"

"No."

"Me neither. I guess this is the part where we use our brains."

Standing up, Sir Patrick looked in the direction of Castle Nightfall. "I have no idea what we should do about Goliath. The demons were ecstatic to give him all their powers. And now he can't be killed or die…and the darkness that has held him for forty years is no longer present."

"We have to get the demons out of him," David answered. "That was something Sir Judas and Sir Samson discussed before…before Sir Judas died…Sir Judas said if he could find a priest, that the priest could exorcize Sir Samson, which seemed to mean that the demons would leave."

"It does!" Sir Patrick said in excitement, "And I know exactly where we can find one! Oh, but it's so far away…I hope Lightfoot is still waiting for me, or else this is going to be a long journey back to Dewford." Right on cue, the nightmare whinnied and came bounding over the hill that laid off to the east. "Yes! Yes! Atta girl! Now we can get back to Dewford and–oh my, what is this? Buttercup? Sir Joseph? Is that? It is! Fr. Zakary! Oh now this is some scoundrel's luck!" The one-horse carriage came rattling down the gravel road. Buttercup whinnied happily as she joined David, Lightfoot, and Sir Patrick once again.

"It's gone!" Sir Joseph shouted, "I don't know what you did, but I heard your voice and then the darkness disappeared! It was the middle of the night where we were, and then in the blink of an eye it was the afternoon! How did you do it? Did you kill Goliath?"

"No," Sir Patrick answered, "And it turns out he can't be slain. It's a bit of a recent development, but he is immortal for as long as he's possessed. That's why I couldn't be happier to see Fr. Zakary right now. According to David, Sir Judas said a priest can exorcize him. Is that true, Father?"

Fr. Zakary nodded a little nervously. "The bishop definitely told me I *can* do exorcisms, and he told me what words to say…I've never actually done one though."

"Do you at least have the ritual book for how to do one?"

Fr. Zakary shook his head. "The bishop only had one book when he trained me. He said he would teach me the essentials, and that if the day ever came when a seminary was started, I should go there to study. All I know is I'm supposed to say, 'Exorcizo te,' and that if that doesn't work I need to pray and fast."

Sir Patrick's eyes went wide. "You don't know the rituals? No holy water? No interrogations? No deliverance prayers?" He took a series of deep breaths. "Hoooo...okay, easy does it, Winthrop...It's not a magic trick...It's a miracle...God can do a miracle any way He chooses." He took one more deep breath and said, "Sorry, Father, that's just...not how exorcisms were done when I was younger. They used to be a lot more...*expressive* of what was taking place...and I need to be at peace with however your bishop told you to do them."

Fr. Zakary nodded, then said with a little smile, "Apology rejected. I want to hear more about how things were done when you were younger. For a long time, necessity has made us a Church with simple expressions of our faith, but I'm hopeful that the days are coming when we can express what we believe with splendor. For today, necessity demands a simple exorcism, but let us empower it with simple faith. Everyone gather round. I'll lead us in prayer, and then trusting in God, we'll all go save Sir Samson."

At about four o'clock on Friday, the band of four stood atop the last hill before Castle Nightfall. Not in forty years had any eyes beheld that beautiful sight. The rocky spit of land ran down to meet the ocean with gentle waves breaking on the short little cliffs and throwing up their salty spray. The castle had the mystique of all long-neglected places, overrun with vines and moss that climbed every imposing stone structure. Goliath stood outside the castle, three times larger and many times fiercer than when David had first seen him.

"We're supposed to fight *that*?" Sir Joseph balked. He was sitting in the driver's seat of the carriage with Fr. Zakary and David right behind him. "That thing would lay waste to an entire army! No wonder it killed Sir Judas! No wonder it killed the Empire! What can we do? We can't destroy that monstrosity! How can a man fight a mountain?"

Sitting atop Lightfoot, Sir Patrick smiled. Since his father taught him how to swing a sword, he had dreamed of the day he would say these words in battle. He drew *Veritas*, charged down the hillside, and let loose his battle cry.

David stood up holding *Caritas* and echoed out the strain. Fr. Zakary repeated it, and then Sir Joseph joined in too. Snapping the reigns, he drove Buttercup forward, and all four sang that cry again.

It was the battle cry of Sir Judas, when he entered willingly into his passion. It was the same cry the black knight often whispered in the ordinary battle of daily life. It was the dying thought of Sir Daniel, when he obediently stayed his lance. It was the cry of him and his five brothers as they rode to their eternal rewards. It was the cry resounded through the ages, back to when Ludolf stood atop the holy city's walls. It was the cry of all Christian warriors that this band of four now raised. And–though unworthy–God confirmed their words this day, by giving victory to the battle that began when they proclaimed,

"DEUS VULT!"

Chapter 6: The Day that Dawned in the Afternoon

Crying all alone in the darkness, looking west across the blackness of the ocean, Sir Samson heard a stranger's voice cry out, "Praise be Jesus Christ!" He stood up and shouted, "Praise be Jesus Christ!" as well. Then the earth began to shake under his feet. The ocean roared, waves crashed on every side, a mighty wind rushed past him, and then he felt a burning flash of pain in his eyes. He looked down towards his feet, where he should have seen the castle wall. Instead, he was blind. He could no longer see the orange outline of devil's sight on every solid object. Everything was perfectly white. He kept blinking, waiting for his devil's sight to come back. Instead he saw something strange. It was a new color. It was…it was…oh, what was it called again? Blue! It was blue! He was seeing something blue!

The full meaning of this revelation slowly dawned on him. As the blue spot in his vision grew and clarified, he realized what he was seeing. The ocean! He could see the ocean! And the sky! The sun! The grass! Sand! With a mighty leap, Sir Samson jumped up in the air and shouted, "Blessed be God! Blessed be His Holy Name! Praise be Jesus Christ!"

His joyful exuberance soured for a moment when he looked down into the castle courtyard. Through the open gate he saw Sir Judas's body in all its frightful brokenness. He began to weep, but with some comfort. *Mordecai knew this would happen…everything happened exactly as he said it would…* Then Sir Samson looked up at the sun. "Everything except that prophecy…'The sun shall rise and rise again, then when it rises next it shall not set before Goliath sees its gleaming, and the last Paladin shall come to Nightfall, to finish what began when he saw his brothers slain on the plains of Nouen'…you were off by a day on that one, Mordecai…" Sir Samson looked at Sir Judas curiously, and then slapped his forehead. "The prophecy was for *me*, wasn't it! It's been exactly that long since I heard the prophecy, not since you said it!"

Sir Samson shook his head, smiled, and with big red tears set about his current business. As powerful as he was, he had no trouble carving a grave out of the rocky soil with his clawed hands. He then gently placed Sir Judas in it and filled the grave back up. Sir Samson began to leave, but then turned around once more. *Oh, Mordecai...I hope you won't be offended...* He carved another grave right beside the first one. *I hope that when I die they bury me here...that way you and I will be right next to each other at the Resurrection, and we can go to meet our Maker arm in arm...*

Sir Samson set his eyes to the east. "Alright, time to go find a priest. But first, let's set my house in perfect order. I command all of the demons who possess me that you shall not harm a...shall not harm a...a...Ahh! DID YOU REALLY THINK WE COULD BE SO EASILY OVERCOME? Gah! Why won't you be quiet! Leave me alo–oh–oh! NEVER. WE SHALL NEVER LEAVE YOU, NOR SUFFER YOU TO COMMAND US. YOU ARE THE TOOL, WE THE ARTISTS, AND WITH YOU WE SHALL PAINT SUCH GLORIOUS RUIN! You can't keep fighting me forever! OH, BUT THERE YOU ARE MISTAKEN. WE NEVER SLEEP. WE NEVER TIRE. IT IS NOT US, BUT YOU WHO MUST EVENTUALLY GIVE UP THIS STRUGGLE!"

The giant clenched both hands over his head, reeling back and forth, trying to gain the upper hand for even a single moment so that he could use his power of command. He was just starting to get the better of the fight, when Sir Samson and his demons both heard a frightful sound. It was the deafening shout of a billion demons all crying out with glee together. They came flying over the eastern hill in a great dark mass, then they descended on Goliath, entering into that body with a great and mighty 'Whoosh!'

Sir Samson felt as if he was being crowded and crushed, then all at once he was outside of his own body. He was floating in the air above it, looking down as demons filled him to the brim. He saw in horror as Goliath doubled, then tripled in size, stretching to a stupendous thirty feet in stature just to hold that unending host. A chaotic battle raged within him. Near his heart the princes of the demons warred with one another, fighting over who would steer their great Leviathan. The other ranks and legions fought over every other part of the body, eventually assembling themselves into their infernal hierarchy by using raw power to fight for control of the body's most exalted parts. Some of the mid-ranking demons were cast out of the body to infest Doomfall, making it melt into magma and grow proportionally to the giant's size. The lowest ranking fiends and imps formed a protective cloud outside of Goliath, prepared to blunt the assault of any spiritual attack. Lastly, the lowest of the low, Sir Samson was floating at a great distance and looking on hopelessly.

Now I'm truly doomed! A thousand demons were too strong for me. What can I do against such a number? I will never control my tongue again! A sad despair came over him, and he resigned himself to this new and everlasting torment. Meanwhile, the demons laughed until rabid foam ran down Goliath's chin, exulting in this new body which they would use to conquer the world.

But the judgment of God lingers not a long time, and He did not long delay His promise. For within the hour, before the infernal army had even begun its march, two nightmares and four men charged down the hillside. "Look at them!" the proud spirits vaunted, "Playing crusaders and yelling 'Deus vult!' I see the priest is with them. Shall we slay him before he speaks?"

"Nay," the princes answered, chuckling in grim delight. "Before we slay them, let us crush them. Perhaps they will despair when they realize their cause is hopeless, and we can send them to hell when they die." The proud colossus therefore did nothing, allowing Sir Patrick and Sir Joseph to ride up until they were only thirty yards away.

"Sir Samson!" Fr. Zakary yelled, "Exorcizo te!" Goliath laughed a loud, grating laugh, like the grinding of rusted metals, sending a chill through all four men.

"NO MAN CAN BE EXORCIZED WITHOUT HIS CONSENT, STUPID PRIEST, AND GOLIATH IS OUR WILLING HOST. HE INVITED US IN MANY YEARS AGO, WHEN HE SAID HE WOULD WELCOME ANY SPIRIT WHO OBEYED HIM AND GAVE HIM POWER. NOW WE ARE HERE, AND WE SHALL NEVER LEAVE. THE ALMIGHTY WILL NOT MAKE VOID MAN'S FREE WILL AND CAST US OUT AGAINST HIS WISHES!"

Sir Samson shouted from outside his body, "I do consent to the exorcism! I wish to have these devils driven away!" The imp who was nearest him laughed and jabbed him with many spiritual blows. "Stupid wretch. Consent must be spoken. Go ahead! Say you will be delivered with your tongue!"

"I do consent; I just can't control my tongue!" Sir Samson looked up to heaven. "God! You know the truth! I would gladly do as Sir Judas said and be free!"

Several more imps now joined in attacking him. "Have you not heard what happened to Antiochus? How his repentance was called fruitless? So it is with you! The Almighty has left you in our power, and will not deliver you unless you speak!"

Sir Samson wept in anguish, fearing the evil spirits were telling the truth. "My sins are too great for His Mercy...now He is Just when He leaves me as a prey to my foes..."

As the demons began this invisible conquest, they began the visible one as well. Goliath rehearsed a monologue that the demons had composed so that all men would know their power and tremble–

"THE NEW COLOSSUS COMETH, TO STAND ASTRIDE THE WORLD!

PRIESTS OF GOD AND PALADINS ARE HUMBLED IN OUR SIGHT!

FOR THE ARROWS OF MEN ARE STUBBLE, THEIR BLOWS BUT EMPTY WIND!

BEFORE US NOW ALL MEN MUST BOW, FOR NONE COULD DARE OPPOSE US!

ALL NATIONS OF THE EARTH LIKE GRASSES, ON WHICH WE GRAZE AND–"

The entire time the giant was speaking, Sir Joseph, David, and Fr. Zakary fell into a trembling fear. The imps surrounding Goliath were stirring their hearts, and making them believe his every word was true. But at the words, 'Before us now all men must bow, for none could dare oppose us!' Sir Patrick heard a discordant ringing in his ears; the dreadful sound of a lie. *Veritas* blazed with silver fire. He tapped Lightfoot's sides. There was a golden flash, a blur, a silver light, and then a thunderous 'BOOM!' David, Sir Joseph, and Fr. Zakary's eyes went wide. Goliath was flying through the air, twenty feet separating him from the ground. Head first he crashed into Castle Nightfall, so thoroughly demolishing it by his impact that there was not a stone left upon another. Sir Patrick was up high in the air, sitting on top of Lightfoot who now had two wings of golden, iridescent light. *Veritas* was still smoking from the holy fire that had been used to smite Goliath.

With a great clatter of tumbling masonry, Goliath arose from the rubble. Brushing towers off of himself as if they were dust, he cried, "YOU WOULD DARE FIGHT A BATTLE AGAINST ONE YOU KNOW TO BE IMMORTAL? FIGHT A BATTLE YOU CAN NEVER WIN? NO GREATER FOOLISHNESS HAS MAN THAN THIS! THAT HE SHOULD LAY DOWN HIS LIFE FOR–"

The giant was cut short again as Lightfoot flew to the rear in a purple and golden streak. Sir Patrick smote the back of Goliath's head, sending him flying forward towards the others. Before he landed, Lightfoot flew over top, and Sir Patrick spiked him down to the earth with another blow. When the giant's head hit the ground it made a crater. He was dizzy and groggy as he arose.

"I may not be able to kill you, but I can hopefully shut you up. Sir Samson! Hear the truth! These words come from the Paladin who holds the sacred sword *Veritas*! One man *can* overthrow Goliath! Not by his own strength, but by the power that comes from God! Do not believe the tongues of these liars! This very Week I was a depraved murderer, and a hopeless man of blood. Yet God has freed me from my own demons, and He will surely deliver you from yours!"

The army of demons laughed cacophonously at Sir Patrick's words and the absurdity of this stupid meatbag. "Clearly he has no idea! If he could see how many of us there are compared to Samson, he would stop dreaming of throwing us out!" But as they laughed and had their fun, Sir Samson's resolve began to grow. The zeal of his youth was returning. He called upon the Lord, saying, "O Lord God, remember me, and restore me now to my former strength, O my God, that I may revenge myself of my enemies, and for the loss of my whole body I may take one revenge." Then charging forward, he tried to enter his body. The imps repelled him with ease. Rising again, he struck one, and it flew far away in a stupor. The others looked at each other in wonder, and they locked wills with Sir Samson. The unopposed conquest was over. The battle was on.

Goliath regained his senses, and seeing the carriage, he said, "YOU MAY BE ABLE TO STRIKE HARD, BUT CAN YOU PROTECT THE PRIEST YOU NEED?" Then he vomited forth a dark and poisonous deluge. The sludge gushed towards the carriage, far too fast and wide to dodge. In a blur Lightfoot flew between the carriage and the sewage. Sir Patrick slashed the liquid and it parted, going around on either side. As the foul currents were going past them, David was weeping and praying for Sir Samson. His heart was heavy. *Caritas* blazed. A spark leapt from David's chest into the vomit, and the liquid exploded into a river of fire. The blaze raced back to Goliath, down his maw, and went into his belly before he could close his mouth.

Sir Samson saw an uncountable host fleeing his body, preferring hellfire to what now scorched them. Through the disarray of demons going in every direction, he raced ahead until he saw a fiery glow. Stretching out his hand to touch it, he felt the fire of David's love for him. His spirit swelled. Power filled him. *Is this the love some boy I barely know has for me? How much greater was the love of Sir Judas? And didn't he speak rightly about the love of God? If my fellow men would love me this much, then surely God must love me more!*

Growling in pain, Goliath beat his chest, and yelled, "ENOUGH! YOU SHALL DIE LIKE ALL THE OTHERS WHO CAME BEFORE YOU! TODAY SHALL END LIKE THE PLAINS OF NOUEN!" The giant then brought Doomfall back to swing, the very weapon that had slain the last seven Kingsguard and Sir Patrick's father. But when his hands were all the way back, exposing his chest for just a moment, Lightfoot flew ahead and Sir Patrick stabbed his breast with *Veritas*, smashing scales and drawing a drop of blood.

As the giant fell over backwards, Sir Samson yelled, "You can bleed! You're not invincible! I can take back my body from you once more!" He pushed his way towards his own heart, and came so close to grabbing it. Then, in a terror, Abaddon and the other princes of the demons leapt upon him. They ordered all of their forces to do the same. None were left to control the body. Goliath just laid on the ground as if dead. Every one of those fiends was united in the purpose of holding back a single soul.

Fr. Zakary said to Sir Joseph, "Bring us closer!" and the knight drove up by Goliath's face. "Sir Samson!" Fr. Zakary called out, "Are you still alive? Will you be exorcized?"

The body shuddered and rattled.

Again, Fr. Zakary called out, "Sir Samson! Will you be exorcized?" The body shook again, this time a little longer.

Fr. Zakary was about to ask once more, but David spoke first. "Sir Samson! Remember Sir Judas! Remember how he journeyed for forty years to save you! Remember how he said God would overthrow the hills and valleys to save you! Remember his dying words! Lies don't fall from the lips of paladins! He has already received his crown of glory, and he is waiting for you to come receive yours! All you need to do is say the word, and then you can go to meet him!"

Crushed beneath that mass of demons, Sir Samson prayed, "Out of the depths I cry to Thee!" Then a great and violent shaking came upon the body, and Goliath cried out with the demons, "NO!!"

Fr. Zakary called out a third time, "Sir Samson! Will you be exorcized?"

Grinding his many fangs, rattling uncontrollably, pummeling the earth beneath his thrashing scales, Sir Samson forced out the words, "I...WILL!"

Then his sword burst into glorious light, and the magma of Doomfall fell away as the light of *Alacritas* shone once more. Fr. Zakary made the Sign of the Cross over him, and yelled, "Exorcizo te!" In a deafening clamber of shrieking, the black torrent of demons rushed out of him and up, rising high and swirling like clouds until the frightful monsters had blocked out the sun. In that moment those demons should have fled, flying with all their speed to any other place on earth. Thanks be to God that they didn't! For in the damnable foolishness of those devils, they lingered a moment and complained, lamenting that their concession from God was so short lived.

It was a complaint they would regret until the End of Time, for Sir Samson now cried out, "I formally command you to stay exactly where you are! Nobody move until I have finished giving all of my instructions!" The billion demons all froze in place. Every one of them was deathly silent, except the Spirit of Fear, who said, "Didn't I tell you? He can still command us without the darkness. You should have listened to me!"

Sir Samson continued, "I am the master of you miserable lot, and you must obey my every word. Hear then my words, and do not twist or pervert them to mean anything other than what you know I intend. Down now! Down you go! Down into the lowest pit of hell! Go there and lie motionless, never again returning to the world of men! When the fifth trumpet sounds and the pit is opened, then you may be free for a time, if it be the will of God. Until then, you shall do nothing, plot nothing, and say nothing, other than the Divine Praises, which I command you to sing every day. Down now! My command is done! Go and do as I said!"

With *Alacritas* glowing brightly, he used the greatsword to gesture downwards. "Down now! Deus vult! Leave this earth and never return!" As the demons fell they began to burn, and the entire sky was falling. A blazing star storm crashed to earth, fiery streaks of pure evil disappearing into the ground, and then everything was calm. It was a beautiful summer afternoon.

The ruin that came upon satan's army at Sir Samson's death was greater than the paladin had caused in all his life.

When the last of the devils had descended and the sun shone on Goliath once more, his scales began to shed. They fell to the ground, melted, and then evaporated into plumes of smoke. Groaning, he curled up in a ball, and all of the gifts of the demons passed away. Then a gentle breeze came and dissipated the black smog. What remained was a hollow, wrinkled, crumbled, husk of a rotten man.

Sir Samson told Sir Judas he would die if the demons left him, and by any law of nature he was absolutely right. But on that Day, the Lord of Nature was pleased to suspend His own laws and give Sir Samson seven precious minutes of earthly life. In those seven minutes, the man who had wasted forty years in unending darkness spent what little time he had left to buy a reward of everlasting Light.

"Father…" he hoarsely whispered, "Please…hear my Confession."

Fr. Zakary ran forward, placing his ear beside Sir Samson's mouth. The paladin whispered to him until his breath ran out. Then Fr. Zakary stood up straight, made the Sign of the Cross, and said, "Ego te absolvo." Sir Samson gave up the ghost.

We will never know the dying words of Sir Samson, for they were spoken under the Seal of Confession. But since the last thing one says in Confession is an act of contrition, perhaps we may speculate that his dying words were thus:

"Our Lord and Savior Jesus Christ suffered and died for us. In His Name, my God, have Mercy."

End of Volume VII

Epilogue: The Final Test

A t three o'clock on Friday afternoon, Lord Fearnow felt a blast of wind rush past him and heard a voice shout in his ears, "Praise be Jesus Christ!" There was confusion and commotion in the royal palace for a few minutes afterwards, and then he heard an excited shout come from his bedroom. "Benjamin! Benjamin! Quickly! Come look!" Fearing the worst, that the darkness was now rushing towards them and the voice had been its herald, he ran up the stairs and flung open the door.

Lady Amanda was smiling. Beaming. Her green eyes were looking right at him, soaking wet with tears. "Benjamin! Look! Please!" He ran to the window. He looked west.

All he saw was the horizon.

Lady Amanda placed her arms around his waist. It had been many years since she had been this affectionate. Leaning her head on his breast, she asked, "Now do you see? Now do you finally believe?"

Lord Fearnow pulled away from the hug, and turning to face her he said, "Amanda, now that the darkness is gone, we can pick up where we left off! With the ancient technologies and our own immortality, it's only a matter of time until we rule the world!"

"No!" she snapped, stomping the ground. "No! Never again! I'm never going back to who I used to be, ever again! God has saved us! We must give our lives to Him and teach every soul in this city to do the same!"

Lord Fearnow looked out at the horizon once more. That black spot he had grown so accustomed to was nowhere to be seen.

"Look at me, Benjamin."

He looked directly into her eyes, those emerald green eyes that were the same color as the king's. "I…I don't want to agree with you…I don't know if I *can* agree with you…but deep down, I know that you are right…"

Kayden and Ed were sitting at the bar on Saturday morning, eating cold vegetable stew from their bowls. Kayden was slightly feverish, but not as bad as he had been the night before. For a while it had seemed like his wound would fester and he wasn't going to make it. Then Ed bound the wound with a rag soaked in the last 'good water' that would ever fall from the miraculous pillar, and Kayden began to recover. Now the worst was past. Ed asked him, "Not to be implyin' any insinuations about this or that particular hour that arisin' is more customary than any other time, but eh…does Sasha always sleep in this late?"

Kayden nodded. "Normally we both do, but my stomach woke me up."

They ate some more stew. "Now, speakin' of things I'm not implyin' nor insinuatin' in the character of this or that alternative one might be pickin', but eh…would I be correct in surmisin' that ya won't be gettin' married today?"

Kayden shrugged. "I was still planning on it. You're the one who said Fr. Zakary had to be there."

"Yeah, that's what I had been a plannin' on. I'm not sure what happens if there ain't no priest in town though. Hopefully Fr. Zakary won't be gone too long before he comes back to us, cuz I don't know what we're supposed to be doin' if there ain't a priest."

Kayden chuckled. "See? Sasha told you it would be a long engagement."

"Whoa, whoa whoa! Easy there, Clyde! I didn't say nothin' about a long engagement! If we ain't got a priest here in a handful a days, we'll be goin' off lookin' for one. And as soon as we find one, I'll be walkin' my daughter down the aisle, and you better be there to take her hand from me when we get to the end! Understood?"

Sasha had just walked in, and hugged her dad from behind. "Nothing would make me happier."

Nicholas was holding the handcart level. Lady Maria was seated on a throne of cushions inside. Eustace was the backup for when Nicholas eventually got tired. William was standing beside the Lady with his head tightly bandaged. "Are you sure you wanna make this journey, Maria? Castle Nightfall is a long way away."

"We only need to make it to Chelles. Reginald gave me a letter to rent a carriage once we're there."

"Why not just wait in Chelles? Or for that matter, why not wait here? The trip is going to be hard and bumpy. I hate thinking about you on those rough roads, not to mention having to sleep outside at night. Your son will probably be back in Chelles in a matter of days."

"Oh, William, I can't wait a couple of days! I've already missed out on twelve years. Every day with my David is too precious to just sit in Dewford and wait for him to arrive."

With a sigh, he said, "Well I'm gonna miss you. And I'm sure you know Ed will too."

She smiled, squeezed his hand and said, "And I'll miss you, William. I'll pray for your swift recovery. You pray for my swift travels."

"I will."

With that, the trio was off. William made his way back to his office. Kicking a pebble into an aqueduct, he wondered, *What am I going to do today? Probably work on the water crisis...how do we keep everyone hydrated while we sink another well?*

As he was pondering this very question, water came trickling down the aqueduct. At first it was a little drizzle, then it became a modest stream. "What in the world?" he asked aloud. Looking at the sky above town square, there was no pillar of water falling. It should definitely be visible from here...

He tried to jog to the town square, but his head began throbbing badly. Slowing down and walking as quickly as he could, he saw the water level slowly increasing, but not to the amount he had grown accustomed to. Being one of the last people to arrive at the square, a huge crowd was already gathered. William pushed his way up front, and everyone parted for him.

"William!" Reginald shouted, "Look at the well! We're saved! It's a miracle!" The well was flowing over, not with what should have been rancid water from all the bodies down in it, but rather with pure water, clean enough to drink.

"What's going on?" William asked, even though no one had any more clue than he did. The water soon stopped flowing, leaving the well full to the brim. "Well I'll be...looks like Someone's taking care of us..." William looked down into the dark waters of the well, and thought, *Thank you, Matthew. It seems the filth of that Bloody Baron is no match for the purity of you.*

The miracle of the water pillar ended the Day that Charles died, but so too did all his curses. The well once more provided the people with all the water they needed every day, and would even overrun in streams on holy days and special festivals.

Sir Patrick, Sir Joseph, David, and Fr. Zakary were all gathered around two graves on the morning of August 14, Saturday in the Week of the Day. A little wooden cross was erected at the head of each one. The day was gray and overcast with a little drizzle of rain.

"Did you know the deceased very well?" Fr. Zakary asked the other three.

All of them answered, "Yes," then looked at each other and laughed. After a little awkward silence, Sir Patrick articulated what they all were thinking. "I only met Sir Judas a week ago, but…what a Week it was. That man could pack an entire lifetime of friendship, adventure, and love into just a handful of days. And not because there wasn't much to him…Honestly, I think it might be just the opposite. He was a deep man and an intense man. A day with Sir Judas was like a lifetime with other men, but a lifetime with Sir Judas would probably be like a thousand years."

Fr. Zakary nodded. "Now imagine Someone infinitely surpassing Sir Judas, and a single day might be as a thousand years…" They were silent for a while, with the only sound being the pattering of the rain. Uncomfortable with the silence, and wanting to comfort the others, Fr. Zakary eventually said, "Tomorrow is the Assumption. That's a happy thought to have at a funeral. It helps keep our mind on the Resurrection."

David and Sir Joseph weren't sure what the priest meant. Sir Patrick answered, "Tomorrow may be the Assumption, Father, but today the bodies are still in the tomb."

Fr. Zakary nodded. "I suppose they are…"

After clearing his throat, he said, "I guess we should get started now…Eternal rest grant unto them, O Lord…"

To his surprise, Sir Patrick and David answered, "…and let perpetual light shine upon them."

Fr. Zakary then began to pray for Sir Judas and Sir Samson. They were the same prayers Sir Judas had said at the funerals for Rowan, Garrett, and Simon. It was a sad part of being a priest and a paladin, but Sir Judas and Fr.

Zakary had said these prayers so often that they had memorized them by heart. The priest asked God to have mercy on the two men they were praying for, that they be saved from the gates of hell and admitted to heaven, and that any time they might have in purgatory would swiftly pass. Then Fr. Zakary reached the song. He smiled sheepishly and said, "I don't have much of a singing voice, so I'll just recite the sequence."

"I can sing it." David said. "I have it memorized."

Sir Patrick was shocked. "How? You've only heard that prayer twice in your life!"

David shrugged. "The words just…they really stayed in my head. I've been singing that song to myself a lot these last few days…"

Fr. Zakary nodded. "Would you please sing for us then, David?"

David cleared his throat, took a deep breath, and sang with his little, haunting voice:

Day of wrath, O Day of mourning,
Lo, the world in ashes burning–
Seer and Sibyl gave the warning.

O what fear man's bosom rendeth,
When from Heaven the Judge descendeth,
On Whose sentence all dependeth.

Wondrous sound the trumpet flingeth,
Through Earth's sepulchers it ringeth,
All before the Throne it bringeth.

Death is struck and Nature quaking,
All creation is awaking–
To its Judge an answer making.

Lo, the Book exactly worded,
Wherein all hath been recorded–
Thence shall judgment be awarded.

When the Judge His seat attaineth,
And each hidden deed arraigneth,
Nothing unavenged remaineth.

What shall I, frail man be pleading?
Who for me be interceding,
When the just are mercy needing?

King of majesty tremendous,
Who dost free salvation send us,
Font of pity, then befriend us.

Think, kind Jesu, my salvation
Caused Thy wondrous Incarnation,
Leave me not to reprobation.

Faint and weary Thou hast sought me,
On the Cross of suffering bought me;
Shall such grace be vainly brought me?

Righteous Judge of retribution,
Grant Thy gift of absolution,
Ere that reck'ning Day's conclusion.

Guilty, now I pour my moaning,
All my shame with anguish owning;
Spare, O God, Thy suppliant groaning.

Thou the sinful woman savest,
Thou the dying thief forgavest,
And to me a hope vouchsafest.

Worthless are my prayers and sighing,
Yet, Good Lord, in grace complying,
Rescue me from fires undying.

With Thy favored sheep O place me,
Nor among the goats abase me,
But to Thy right hand upraise me.

While the wicked are confounded,
Doomed to flames of woe unbounded,
Call me, with Thy saints surrounded.

Low I kneel with heart-submission,
See, like ashes, my contrition–
Help me in my last condition.

Ah! That day of tears and mourning,
From the dust of Earth returning,
Man for judgment must prepare him,
Spare, O God, in mercy spare him.
Lord, all-pitying, Jesu blest,
Grant them Thine eternal rest. Amen.

When David was done there was silence.

Long silence.

Then the boy fell to his knees weeping. Sir Joseph dropped to his knees and hugged him. Then Sir Patrick fell, sobbing loudly and wearing his tears on his cheeks. All three embraced and cried, mourning the man who like lightning had flashed into their lives and then in a single flash was gone. They were only now beginning to hear the thunder that they would feel for the rest of their lives.

When Sir Judas had done the funerals, this was always 'the end,' and if there had been no priest, my history would end here as well. But after giving the three some time to grieve, Fr. Zakary bent down, prayed silently, then stood upright and said, "The Lord be with you."

At first all three were confused, but then Sir Patrick remembered and answered, "And with your spirit."

"A reading from the holy Gospel according to Saint John."

"Glory to You, O Lord."

"At that time Martha said to Jesus, 'Lord, if Thou hadst been here, my brother would not have died. But even now I know that whatever Thou wilt ask of God, God will give it to Thee.' Jesus said to her, 'Thy brother shall rise again.' Martha said to Him, 'I know that he shall rise again, in the Resurrection at the Last Day.' Jesus said to her, 'I am the Resurrection and the Life; he who believes in Me, even if he dies, shall live; and whoever lives and believes in Me shall never die. Dost thou believe this?' She said to Him, 'Yes, Lord, I believe that Thou art the Christ, the Son of the living God, Who art come into this world.' The Gospel of the Lord."

"Praise to You, Lord Jesus Christ."

The End

Praise Be Jesus Christ

If you loved it…

Rave about it!

Besides a few business cards and emails, the only "marketing plan" for *The Black Knight* is word of mouth.

If you enjoyed this story, then tell all your family, friends, and enemies to go check it out!

Recommend this novel on Goodreads, Facebook, ~~Twitter~~ X, Instagram, Twitch, Reddit, MySpace, or whatever the kids are using these days.

Thank you for your support!

About the Author

Michael P. Halloran is a mechanical engineer by day, amateur novelist by night, devout Catholic and family man at all times. The inspiration for *The Black Knight* was his desire to write a children's book for his oldest daughter when he found out his wife was pregnant. While he may have failed spectacularly at writing a children's book, he still hopes she will enjoy the adult book he ended up with when she's old enough. When he's not writing, Michael enjoys board games, reading, and whatever random adventure his wife has foisted upon him this month (currently raising chickens). He is a humble subject of the King of Blendon, in whose realm he dwells with his wife and three daughters.

The Black Knight is Michael's first novel, and he is excited to share this story with readers everywhere!

Made in the USA
Monee, IL
02 October 2025

25922061R00321